Anonymous

The Hamilton Manuscripts

Anonymous

The Hamilton Manuscripts

ISBN/EAN: 9783337389253

Printed in Europe, USA, Canada, Australia, Japan

Cover: Foto ©Andreas Hilbeck / pixelio.de

More available books at **www.hansebooks.com**

THE HAMILTON MANUSCRIPTS:

CONTAINING SOME ACCOUNT OF *Wm. O'Donnatan.*

THE SETTLEMENT OF THE TERRITORIES OF THE UPPER CLANDEBOYE, GREAT ARDES, AND DUFFERIN, IN THE COUNTY OF DOWN,

BY SIR JAMES HAMILTON, Knight,

(Afterwards created Viscount Claneboye,)

IN THE REIGNS OF JAMES I. AND CHARLES I.; WITH MEMOIRS OF HIM, AND OF HIS SON AND GRANDSON, JAMES,
AND HENRY, THE FIRST AND SECOND EARLS OF CLANBRASSIL (OF THE FIRST CREATION);
AND OF THEIR FAMILIES, CONNEXIONS, AND DESCENDANTS.

PRINTED FROM THE ORIGINAL MSS., AND EDITED BY

T. K. LOWRY, ESQ., LL.D.,

ONE OF HER MAJESTY'S COUNSEL.

WITH APPENDIXES, CONTAINING COPIES OF GRANTS FROM THE CROWN, INQUISITIONS OF OFFICE, DEEDS,
WILLS, AND OTHER ORIGINAL DOCUMENTS RELATING TO THE FOREGOING TERRITORIES.

INTRODUCTION.

"THE following MSS. are without name or date, but contain internal evidence of having been written
" by a member of the Hamilton Family, about the latter end of the 17th century, and certainly prior to
" the year 1703, in which the death of one of the family occurred, who is mentioned in them as being
" alive at the time they were written. They were, therefore, composed almost contemporaneously
" with the celebrated *Montgomery MSS.* (written between the years 1698 and 1704), and with
" which the narrative contained in them is intimately connected. The originals are in the possession
" of the family of the late well-known Archibald Hamilton Rowan, Esq., of Killyleagh Castle,
" County of Down, who entrusted them to their present Editor, in the year 1834, for publication
" at some future time, with a request that he would illustrate them with any observations he might
" consider necessary. The mass of valuable facts and documents which the Editor has since collected
" for this purpose, and which, in the few leisure intervals of a busy professional life, he has been able
" to connect with the MS., in the form of Notes, will best prove the manner in which he has fulfilled
" the trust. We have great satisfaction in being made the medium of first communicating these
" curious papers to the public in the pages of our Journal."—*Ed. Ulst. Journ. of Archæology.*

Such was the notice with which the first three chapters of the following Manuscripts, which
appeared in the third and fifth volumes of the *Ulster Journal of Archæology*, were introduced by its
Editor; and now that, in consequence of the discontinuance of that valuable periodical, the printing of the entire of the MSS. in one volume has been rendered necessary, it seems only proper
that some further account should be given of the circumstances under which their publication was
undertaken by their present Editor, which he considers cannot be better done than by publishing

the following letter written to him on the subject by the late Mr. Hamilton Rowan, shortly before his death :—

"Rathcoffey, 14th February, 1834.

"MY DEAR LOWRY—The enclosed Manuscripts contain several historical anecdotes respecting my "family from the period of their settling in this country ; together with some memorials of my own "life, down to my return from America, when I retired from public life, which were drawn up by "me during my leisure moments for the entertainment of my family and friends, with no intention "of publication at the time, as you are already aware : but as I find that several writers have, per- "haps unintentionally, mistaken some facts which are fully explained in them, and drawn therefrom "unfavourable conclusions, I think it would not be doing myself justice to withhold them altogether "from the public. I have, therefore, been induced to request you to accept them, and undertake "the publication of them at some future time, which I leave entirely to yourself, illustrating them "with any observations you may think are necessary, which, I have no doubt, from my knowledge "of your character, will be done impartially and fairly as I could wish, and I know you would not "undertake it on any other conditions.—I am your obliged and sincere friend,

"ARCHIBALD HAMILTON ROWAN.

"T. K. Lowry, Esq."

Notwithstanding Mr. Rowan's having so requested the present Editor to undertake the publi- cation of both the Hamilton MSS. and the memorials of his own life, at a future time, which he left altogether to himself, his daughter, Miss Rowan, was so anxious that the memoirs of her father should be published immediately after his death, that the present Editor, not being then able to undertake it, handed them over to Miss Rowan for the purpose of being edited by the late Rev. Dr. Drummond, who, in his introduction to the work, thus correctly states the circumstances under which he undertook it :—

"Mr. Rowan, when his life was drawing near to its close, committed the MSS. to the care of "his young friend, Thomas Kennedy Lowry, Esq., Barrister-at-Law, accompanied with a letter "[copied above]. That Mr. Lowry, had he undertaken the task, would have executed it in a

" manner as creditable to himself as accordant with Mr. Rowan's wishes, no one who has the pleasure
" of that gentleman's acquaintance will question. It appeared, however, from his correspondence
" with Miss Rowan on the subject, after Mr. Rowan's death, that it might be a considerable time
" before his professional duties would permit his making any great progress with the work ; and Miss
" Rowan having informed him that the Rev. Dr. Drummond, one of her father's most respected
" friends, had expressed so much interest on the subject, that she was sure that, with Mr. Lowry's
" approval, he would undertake the publication immediately, Mr. Lowry at once consented, at
" the same time stating as his reason, that he conceived the trust reposed in him by Mr. Rowan [as
" to the memoir of his life] would be much more effectually and better executed in the hands of
" Dr. Drummond, than if he had himself attempted it. The Manuscripts [of it] were accord-
" ingly placed in the hands of the present Editor, who, though he cannot accept Mr. Lowry's
" compliment as his due, feels truly grateful for the courtesy and promptitude with which that
" gentleman communicated with him on the subject, and hopes that the task has been performed
" so impartially and fairly as to meet Mr. Lowry's approval."

Whilst bearing a willing testimony to the impartiality, fairness, and ability with which Dr.
Drummond's Memoir of Mr. Rowan was executed, the present Editor thinks it right to add, that
he has not abandoned the intention, should another edition be called for, of giving to the public,
from the copy of it which he retained, what may be more strictly called the Autobiography of
Hamilton Rowan, than the Memoir of him published as such by Dr. Drummond, under Miss
Rowan's directions.

The Hamilton MSS., which form the subject of the present volume, being a work of an entirely different character from the Autobiography of Mr. Rowan, and necessarily requiring a great
deal of time for their proper annotation, the Editor has held over their publication until it suited
his entire convenience. The result of his labours is now given to the public, with what success it
is not for him to anticipate. The MSS. themselves were in some places very much obliterated ;
but the Editor preferred printing them in their imperfect condition, rather than attempting to re-
store them. As above stated by the Editor of the *Ulster Journal of Archæology*, the narrative contained in them, which breaks off in the year 1689, is intimately connected with that of the Mont-

gomery MSS., and would appear to have been written almost at the same time with them, by a member of the Hamilton family. Who that person was, does not distinctly appear ; but, as stated in the note, at p. 145 of the work, the Editor has come to the conclusion, from the internal evidence contained in the MSS. themselves, that it was Mr. William Hamilton, of Edinburgh, a nephew of the first Lord Claneboye, and known in the family as " Secretary Hamilton,"* who was their author. He died about the year 1712, at Killileagh Castle, where he had settled some years before, having come to this country at the request of his eldest brother, " James of Neilsbrook," to assist him in the litigation then pending for the division of the Clanbrassil estates, in consideration of which he made over to him and his brother Gawen a moiety of his share of them. In an introductory memoir to the *Caldwell Papers*, printed at Glasgow in 1854, and referred to at p. 3, *post*, it is stated that the same William Hamilton had consigned or bequeathed to his relatives in Scotland, the Mures of Glanderstone, several bundles of letters and miscellaneous papers, which once formed part of his collection, and were then in the Caldwell repositories, from which that volume had been printed. But the MSS. printed in this volume appear to have remained among the family papers at Killileagh Castle from his death, and so to have come into the possession of his grand-nephew, the late Mr. Rowan, by whom they were intrusted for publication to the present Editor, who, after having had them copied for the printer, has restored the original MSS. to Mr. Rowan's representatives for safe custody.

BALLYTRIM-HOUSE, KILLILEAGH,
    11th February, 1867.

---

* Among the letters referred to at p. 145, *post*, there is one from Ja: Ferguson, dated at Edinburgh, 19th May, 1692, and addressed " For Master William Hamilton, Secretary Department for the Kingdom of Scotland, Whitehall."

THE HAMILTON MANUSCRIPTS.

9th Judges, 19th v.—If ye then have dealt truly and sincerely with Jerubbaal and with his house this day, then rejoice ye in Abimelech, and let him also rejoice in you :—20th v.—But if not, &c.—

CHAP. I.

OF THE REV. HANS HAMILTON, OF DUNLOP.[a]

*	*	*	*	*
that in	*	*	*	*
should be received	*	*	*	*
as deserving (so far as	*	*	*	*
public notice and observation	*	*	*	*
This Gent. was born eldest son to a Gentleman[b]	*		*	*
descended of the Duke Hamilton's family	*		*	*

by his lands Raploch, now of 400 years standing or thereabouts. This Hans, being found a very hopeful youth, of good parts and disposition, was bred at Schools and Colleges so far as was then usual, yet of no other design, but to give him the accomplishments becoming his station and natural endowments. But as it fell out that he was drawn to appear for the Queen Regent[c] in arms, in his youth, and by ill advice, he contracted the displeasure of the reforming party,[d] and thereby, through the malice of the friends of his father's second wife,[e] was deprived of the estate whereunto he was born the righteous heir,[f] and so exposed to what other way of livelihood God would provide for him.

---

[a] In Ayrshire, Scotland.

[b] Archibald Hamilton, of Raploch, in Lanarkshire, who married, first, Marion, daughter of Ogilvy of that Ilk, widow of Weir of Blackwood, and of Dunbar of Blantyre.

[c] Mary of Guise, mother of Mary Queen of Scots.

[d] The Duke of Chatelherault, who had been obliged to resign the office of Regent in favour of the Queen-mother, in a conference with the Lords of the Congregation, agreed to join them in resisting the violent and arbitrary measures of the Queen-Regent against all those who professed the Reformed faith, which she had hitherto favoured, to which she was instigated by her brothers of the House of Guise. The Duke embarked most heartily in favour of the Con-

gregation, and continued to employ all his power and influence in support of its measures ; and the Earl of Arran (his eldest son) distinguished himself in various encounters with the troops of the Regent in 1559.—*See Robertson's Hist of Scotland*, Vol. I., p. 192.

[e] Margaret, daughter of John Hamilton, of Newton, by whom he had two daughters, Margaret, married to Sir James Somerville, of Cambusnethan, and Elizabeth, married to Robert Baillie, of Park.

[f] By his uncle, Gawin Hamilton, commendator of Kilwinning, who had a precept of *clare constat*, from James Duke of Chatelherault, for infefting him in the lands of Raploch, of date 3rd March, 1559. Having been bred to

A

In this case, as he had made very commendable progress in humane literature, he was advised to betake himself to the study of Divinity, wherein his progress and good behaviour were so observable and commendable, that he was ordained Minister of Dunlop, in Cunningham, where he lived very usefully and commendable in the whole remainder of his time.　　*　　　　　　　　　*

　*　　　　　　　*　　　　　　　　*　　　　　　　　*　　　　　　　　*

　　*　　　　　　　*　　　　　　　　*　　　　　　　　*　　　　　　　　*

and died within　　*　　　　　　　　*　　　　　　　　*　　　　　　　　*

love betwixt them　　*　　　　　　　　*　　　　　　　　*　　　　　　　　*

their neighbours and with　　　　　　　*　　　　　　　　*　　　　　　　　*

them.—2. That they bred all their sons to creditable employments, and married their daughter creditably to one William Moor, of Glanderstown.—3. That they were much courted to entertain and breed the most considerable gentlemen and noblemen's sons (by the help of good schoolmasters, whereof he had still one of good reputation), which they did to the great obligation of parents and youths committed to them.—4. He was a very painful, profitable, and wise Minister, friend, and neighbour, in the esteem of all good men in his time.—5. In his homely way of speaking, he called his six sons (in allusion to the country expression) his plough; and, on the account of the death of his third son (whereof hereafter), he used often, with grief, to say that his plough was broken. Ten days before he died (being then in good health, though considerably aged), he called for five or six of the discreetest of his parishioners to him, and desired them to accompany him to the church, where he told them, " I (sayd he) shall die within few days, and thought fit to acquaint you that I design to be buried in this (pointing to the place) spot of ground, and put it upon you to see it so done." On his return to his house, he called at a carpenter's house, and enjoined him *

　*　　　　　　　*　　　　　　　*　　　　　　　*　　　　　　　*　　　　　　　*

by him　　　　　*　　　　　　　*　　　　　　　*　　　　　　　*　　　　　　　*

---

the Church, he was made Dean of the Metropolitan Church of Glasgow in 1550, which office he soon after exchanged with Henry Sinclair, commendator of Kilwinning, for the commendancy of that Abbacy. He was the intimate friend and, along with the Archbishop of St. Andrew's, the confidential adviser of the Duke of Chatelherault. He obtained a breviate from the Pope, appointing him coadjutor and successor to Archbishop Hamilton in the archiepiscopal see of St. Andrew's. On the establishment of the reformed religion in Scotland, he followed the example of many Churchmen of that period, and took to wife Margaret, second daughter of John Hamilton, of Broomhill, by whom he had issue, after the marriage, one daughter, Jean, married to Robert Dalziel of that Ilk, ancestors of the Earls of Carnwath; though before that she had a son to him, Gavin, who afterwards became his successor in the lands of Raploch, under a charter of vendition, dated 13th May, 1560, granted by the commendator in favour of the above Margaret, in life rent, and to Gavin Hamilton, her son, in fee, which charter was confirmed on the day following by James Duke of Chatelherault. Gavin, commendator of Kilwinning, was slain in a skirmish between the Queen's troops and the forces of the Regent Lennox, 28th June, 1571.—See *Anderson's Memoirs of the House of Hamilton*, pp. 364-5 and 472.

his eldest son   *   *   *   *   *

to be erected, whi   *   *   *   *   •

much out of repair) and a school   *   *   *   *

back of it of considerable value ,

ᵉ This passage in the MSS., which is greately obliterated by time, evidently refers to a massive stone Chapel or Mausoleum, and within it a handsome marble monument, to the memory of his parents, whose sculptured figures are there represented kneeling face to face on a sarcophagus, which his eldest son caused to be erected in the Parish Church of Dunlop, in the year 1641, an etching of which is given in the 5th vol. of the *Ulster Archæological Journal*, p. 22. The following is a copy of the inscription on the monument:—

"Here lye the bodies of Hanis Hamilton, sonne of Archibald Hamilton, of Raploch, Servant to King James the Fift, and of Janet Denham, his wife, daughter of James Denham, laird of West-Shielde. They lived married together 45 years, during which time the said Hanis served the cure of this Church. They were much beloved of all who know them, and especially of the Parishioners. They had six sonnes—James, Archibald, Gawin, John, William, and Patrick, and one daughter Jean, married to William Mure, of Glanderstown."

On a stone of the floor of the Chapel is this inscription:—

" Heir lyes the bodye of Hanis Hamiltoune, Vicar of Dunlope, quha deceist ye 30 of Maii, 1608, ye age 72 yeirs ; and of Janet Denham his spous."

Over the door of the Chapel is the date 1641 ; also on the School house attached, with this inscription:—

" This School was erected and endowed by James Viscount Clandboyes, in love to his Parish, in which his father Hans Hamilton was Pastor 45 yeirs, in King James the Sixt his raigne,

"I V C."

These cyphers, which are also visible on the door of the Chapel, stand for "James Viscount Claneboye."

In an introductory memoir in the *Caldwell Papers*, printed at Glasgow, in 1854, from which the foregoing statement is extracted, it is added, that " The friendly connection between the Glanderstone family and the Irish Hamiltons was maintained down to the commencement of the ensuing century, both by correspondence and marriage. In the Caldwell repositories are several bundles of letters and miscellaneous papers, which once formed part of the collection of " Secretary Hamilton," and appear to have been consigned or bequeathed by him to his Glanderstone relatives. Such portion of them as seemed to possess interest have been printed in the volume. During several generations it was customary for the heads of various

families connected with the venerable Vicar of Dunlop, or his spouse, the Hamiltons of Clanboyes and Killileagh, the Denhams of West Shields, and the Mures of Glanderstone, to subscribe each a small sum from time to time for the repairs of their ancestors' tomb. But, from the following letters in the correspondence of the Laird of Caldwell and Glanderstone, it would appear that funds were no longer procured from Irish sources ; and the care of the monument has now devolved exclusively on the Caldwell family. It is still in good preservation, and was put in thorough repair a few years ago :"—

" Wo. Cusine—The uncertaintie of ane sure hand made me delay the sending of the enclosed until the bearer, ane old serveant of my sister Mure's, came in my way. It was written at Carmichael, where you was kindly remembered, and your health drunk by that kind lord, Mr. Carstairs, the Principal of Glasgow, with diverse other friends, who long for your hasteing over. It will be your interest. What is written by my lord Halcrnig I know is to that effecte, and will have more influence with you than I can ; although none would be better satisfied to see you fixed in some post suitable to your meritte than yrs most sincerely,

" to serve you,

" Wm. Mure.

" Glanderstoun, June 5, 1699."

" See iff you can procure anything from Westshields, towards the repairing of our tomb, that if ye make any stay here ye shall be witness to the agreement for it. Take no less than a guinea, which was what he promised me.

" For

" Mr William Hamilton,

" att Lieutenant Gavin Hamilton's,

" att Lisrene, in Ireland.

" Glanderstoun, Nov. 2, 1704."

" Dr. Cos.—Having sent over my nephew Willm. to transact and end my Lord Halcraig's affair and mine with Lady Tullymore, I must recommend him to your best advice in what occurs in that affair. I have likewise sent with him Claneboy's note I spoke to you of, to give you the first offer of it. There is nothing yet done in the repairing of ye burial place at Dunlop, your directions being wanted about it, in respect you did not name what you allowed for yrself, as weel from whom it should be had. Besides, it's hard you should solely be at the expenses, while Westshields and your relations in Ireland are equally related. What you can procure send with the bearer, with what you order yourself to be given to the minister of the place, who will see the thing applyed, together with a line to Westahields for his proportion, wherein also I shall concur, and shall not be wanting in what comes to my share. If it be longer neglected, it will be so spiled that it will be in vain to do any

CHAP. II.

OF THE AFORESAID SIX BROTHERS, THEIR   *   *   AND OUTWARD ESTATE.

THE names of the above-mentioned six sons, in the order of their birth, are James, Archibald, Gawin, John, William, and Patrick. James gave very early indications of his great aptitude for, and disposition after, learning, and so passed his time in schools until he had received all the usual parts of learning taught in that Kingdom, and was within a little afterwards looked upon as one of the greatest scholars and hopeful wits in his time, insomuch that he was noticed by King James and his grave Council as one fit to negociate among the Gentry and Nobility of Ireland for promoting the knowledge and right of King James's interest and title to the Crown of England, after Queen Elizabeth's death; and, on this account, was advised to write a book of his said interest, which was done to very good effect, and   *   *   *   of all persons concerned in the three Kingdoms. Therefore, he was called to keep a public Latin school at Dublin,[a] being instructed in the meanwhile and creditably supplied for conversing with the Nobility and Gentry of Ireland for the King's service above mentioned, and he was very serviceable and acceptable therein.*   *
to   *   *   *   *   *
gu   *   *   *   *   *
perfect   *   *   *   *   *
account   *   *   *   *   *
philosophy *   *   *   *   *
Elizabeth, *   *   *   *   *
in that country for teaching philosoph   *   *   *
parts of academical learning. James Usher[b]   *   entered with him the first scholar, and both continued that station 'till the said James Usher finished his course, and passed all the degrees

---

thing in it. My service to Captn. Stevensono and all my Cos. with you. Quherein I can be capable to serve you, command me. Your most obliged Cos. and humble Servt.

"WIL. MURE.

"For
"Mr. William Hamilton,
"of Killileagh, Esq.,
"Ireland."

The following lines were also engraved on their tomb in the Churchyard of Dunlop:—

"The dust of two lyes in this artful frame,
Whose birth them honoured from an honoured name;
A painful pastor, and his spotless wife,
Whose devout statues emblem here their life.

Bless'd with the height of favours from above,
Blood, grace, ablest memorial, all men's love,
A fruitful offspring, on whom the Lord hath fix'd
Fortunes, with virtue and with honour mix'd.
Then live, these dead above in endless joyes,
Here in their said noble blood oboyes;
In whom (grant see, O Heaven) their honoured name
May never die but in the death of fame."

Scot's Magazine, Vol. vii., p. 902.

[a] In Great Ship Street.

[b] Born 4th January, 1580-1; was made Bishop of Meath in 1621, and Archbishop of Armagh in 1624; he died in March, 1655-6.

usual in that or any other college, with great approbation of both masters and scholars, which the said James (afterwards Lord Primate of Ireland) acknowledged with all gratitude, in an epistle dedicatory, which he prefixes to one of his learned books, which he dedicates to the said (at that time) Lord James Claneboy.[*]

Therefore, on the aforesaid design, he is stationed at London, to negotiate privately with Queen Elizabeth, her Court, Council, and other Nobility and Gentry,[f] until at last he becomes the welcome

---

[*] A strange combination of circumstances supplied Dublin at this time with two schoolmasters of very superior attainments. James VI. of Scotland, doubtful of succeeding quietly to the throne of England on the death of Elizabeth, sent to Dublin, in the year 1587, two clever emissaries, James Fullerton and James Hamilton, to keep up a correspondence with the Protestant nobility and gentry in the neighbourhood; and they, to conceal more effectually the object of their mission, opened a school, in which Fullerton acted as the master, and Hamilton as the usher. Although the office of schoolmaster was assumed merely for the purpose of concealment, yet both these individuals seem to have been eminently qualified to discharge its duties. It is most probable that Fullerton was an early pupil of the learned Andrew Melville, who had brought from the Continent to the University of Glasgow a knowledge of the learned languages rarely possessed at that period, and who devoted himself to the instruction of those committed to his care. Dr. M'Crie has suggested the possibility that both Hamilton and Fullerton were class-fellows of Melville, at St. Andrew's, because there appears in the list of admissions for the year 1588, the names of James Fullerton and James Hamilton; but this seems absolutely impossible, for, as none of his class-fellows could be younger than Melville (who was admitted at twelve years of age), Hamilton must have been ninety-seven years of age at the time of his death in 1643; and yet, only two years before, he received a commission from the Lords Justices and Council to raise the Scots in the North of Ireland, and put them under arms, in order to resist the violent progress of the rebellion. It seems, then, nearly certain, that the James Fullerton who came to Ireland was not the class-fellow, but the pupil, of Andrew Melville, laureated at Glasgow in 1581. Hamilton may also have been under the same tutor at St. Andrew's; for, in 1585, James Hamilton was made Master of Arts, and at that time Melville had been for some years Principal of New College. To the school in Dublin, opened under such extraordinary circumstances, James Ussher was sent, when eight years of age, and he continued there for five years, exciting the admiration of his instructors by his diligence and quickness.

The pupil was not insensible to the value of the instruction he received from his masters; for Dr. Parr states, that "whenever he recounted the providences of God towards himself, he would usually say that he took this for one remarkable instance of it, that he had the opportunity and advantage of his education from those men who came thither by chance, and yet proved so happily useful to himself and others."—*Elrington's Life of Archbishop Ussher*, p. 2. On the College being opened, Fullerton and Hamilton were appointed Fellows, in addition to the three persons named in the Charter; and James Ussher was admitted as a student under the tuition of his former master, James Hamilton, being then thirteen years of age.—*Ib.* p. 5. Parr, in his life of the Archbishop, says that Hamilton was appointed Senior Fellow, but this is a mistake, for the distinction of Senior and Junior Fellow appears to have been first made in 1614.—*Ib.* p. 6.

Birch, in his "Life of Henry Prince of Wales," gives this account of Fullerton:—"There was a Scots Gentleman of great learning and parts, sent out of Ireland to be chief governor for the Duke (Charles I.). This gentleman, whose name was Sir James Fullerton, who had been first usher of the Free School in [Ship Street,] Dublin, while another Scotsman, Mr. James Hamilton, afterwards knighted, and at last created Viscount Claneboye in Ireland, was master of it. The first foundations of their fortunes being laid at Dublin, in the latter end of Queen Elizabeth's reign, by conveying the letters of some great lords of England, who worshipped the rising sun, to King James, and his letters back to them, that way being chosen as more safe than the direct Northern road."

[f] The following most interesting letter which was written whilst he was so stationed inLond on, to James Fullerton (mentioned in the preceding note), who was then in Edinburgh, gives a more minute account of the Earl of Essex's rebellion than is to be found in any English History. The statements in it differ materially from those made by Camden; but, as it would seem from its contents that Mr. Hamilton accompanied Essex to the city, and continued with him till the last of the proclamations which he mentions, this gives a high degree of authority to the state-

B

informer and messenger from the Queen's Council of England, that the said Queen, being dead, by

---

ments in the letter, which strongly corroborate the account of the same transaction given in a life of the Earl, lately published by the Honourable W. B. Devereux:—

"Having written these other letters this morning, and purposing to have sent them by sea with Jacob Baron's man, who came to receave a part of th' annuitie for the Erle of Marr, the strangenes of an admirable occurrent hath moved me to alter my purpose and send these and all by post. This it is, Sr.—Yesternight late a warrant came from court (by Sr Walter Raughley and the Lord Cobham, as is saide to the Erl of Essex, with this purport (as is yet surmisedd), that he should com to the court, to wch he answered that then it was no tyme, and that next morning he would. Others say that it was to carry him to the Tower; but, well, Sr., he stood suspitious of the malice of those that brought the said warrant, fearing lest they might put hand on him, and so refused. Now, this morning ther was sent to him the L. Keeper, Ld. Cheef Justice, L. Trer., and Sr, William Knolles, to Essex House, after ten (as is seid), for ther speeches they are not knowen, but that it should be for the former matter. [Of this there is no great certinty; but the Erl coming out of Essex House, cried ' I am for the Queen! God save the Queen! I stand for my lif; this I do that I be not murdered in my house, as Raughley and Cobham would have done to me upon my bed the last night ;' and this he and his people did deliver still in all the streets. The Lord Keeper and the rest were sent to him as I do write, and they cam by cotches to Essex House, but returned by water, presentlie, upon their return to the Court. Essex was proclaimed traitor at the Court, &c., and so burst out of his house to London, &c.,] Those prticulars alreadie set down, although they be in most mens mouths, and that I have them from men of special knowledg, yet I will not aver them absolutelie in every point, till hereafter, that I shal be able to resolve you, but they are alledged for the grounds of the things that taus ensued, web you shal receave for certain and upon my word. Upon the web departure of yonder people and Counsellors from the said Erl, the Erl presentlie cam from Essex-House to London about a quarter of an hour after eleven, and cam in at Lodgate, and so to Cheapsyde (the L. Mayor, Sheriffs, and all the people being at a rimont), accompanyed with the Erls of Southampton, Bedford, Rutland, and Lords Mounteagle, and (as some y Ritch and Sands besyds, with a great number of knights and gentlemen, amounting to som 2 or 3 hundred; and, at I coming into London, both at Lodgate and in Cheapsyd, he and they that wer with him did publicklie deliver, that r y Lord was escaped a norther web was to have been don by Sr Walter Raughley and the Ld Cobham, web the people, that greatlie indeed did affect him, hearing did rejoice. And so he went alongs (with som 3 hundred with him, all of them with rapiers in their hands, holding them up, and with proteies) towards Sheriff Smithe's in Fanshaws Street. Now, Sr. whether ther was a resolution to have then apprehended him, or what it was, I do so imagine that at the court they had a conceat of som uproar and sedition upon this apprehension ; and, therfor about some nyne of the clock, or soon after, watchwords were given from the court that

the constables and watches should all be in arms and ready, and should look to ther wards and gates ; whereupon the gates wer shut about som ten a clock ; but upon his coming to Lodgate it was set open, and so receaved in, and so went alonge in forme, as I have said, to Sheriff Smithe's. Presentlie, warning was given to the Lord Mayor and Sheriffs, who left the serment at Paules, and cam away neer half an hour, before the end. The Erl went to Sheriff Smithe ; stayed a great part of the dinner ther, but did eat nothing, his people staying below at the Sheriff's dore, and so he stayed ther till one a clock. In this meanwhile, it was from the court appointed that he should be proclaimed traitor, and all they traitors that stood with him ; and because som wer stammering to doe it (it is said that Mr. Secretarie did first undertake it, and said he would, if non els would) ; and so Mr. Secretarie, with a herald, first proclaimed him at court, and then cam from Whithall to Charingcrosse, and did proclaim him traitor about xi a clock (so as I do conjecture that the Erl had knowledge that he was proclaimed er he left his house.) Then the Lord Borleigh did proclaim him, after the same manner, traitor in Fleet Street ; and at Essex House in the Strand, with herald and sound of trumpet, and then at Lodgate he was proclaimed. After this, the Lord Burghley, who is Lord-president of York, and now at this tyme Lord Lieutenant of London, cam to Cheapsyd,and ther proclaimed him traitor, and those traitors that should tak his part. All this was don befor the Erl cam back frome Sheriff Smithe's ; and som say, that as the Erl cam to the lower end of Cheapsyd next to the Exchange, they who proclaimed him wer in the upper end and in sight one of another. But, Sr, the Erl went on with the L. Mayor and Sheriffs up Cheapsyd after he was thus proclaimed, praying for the Queen's safetie, and wishing that he might die a dog's death if ever he meant harme ether to her Matie or the Comonwell, and protesting that he was ther only to save his lif from his privat adversaries, who (as it is reported he should say) sought his lif this last night, and wer the men that had sold the Queen and kingdome to the Spaniards. And thus he came up towards Paules with the Lord Mayor, Sheriffs, and many others accompanying him, even after he was proclaimed ; and in the upper end of Cheapsyd, they say, he and my Lord Burghley met, where the Lord Burghley called him traitor, and the Erl answered that he lied in his throat, but non offered to lay hands on him. A whole hour he stayed on a horse web some one had lent him (for he and his people came out a foot), and some speechis he used to the people, and so he went with some 4 or 5 hundered people towards Lodgate, web with all other gates of the citie was fast shut up, that non could have entries into the citie for fear his followers should increase ; but Lodgate being the passage to Fleet Street, and so to the Court, portcullies was let fall. The Erlo's people thus coming through Paules Church-yard, when they cam to the west end of Paules over against the Bishop of London's, the Bishop had given chardg ther to the constables, &c., to stop his passing downe to Lodgate, because he was now proclaimed traitor, and therfor should not be permitted to go to the Court, which was the thing that the Erl designed. And ther his people wer, by such as wer sent to keep the streets ther,

her latter will and testament, and consent of the said Council, he, the said **King James**, was pro-

---

commanded to stand, but they chardging the officers and constables, &c., and dischardging some pistolles upon them, the said officers did then eucounter with them, and dischardged some shot of cullever and musket, by wᶜʰ my Lord of Essex's page was slane hard by his Lord; Sʳ. Christopher Blunt shot in the throut and dead as is thought, or verie neer; Sʳ. Gh. Travest killed, and the Erl himself shot through the hat twice ; yet, if the gates and portcullies had not been made fast, they had burst through. But seeing that passag damed up, the Erl cam back through Watling Street (for Paules and Paules church-yard were all shut up), and so all alongst that street till he came to Bow-lane (the Mayor and Sheriffs with him still, and many others, that wer all of them amased at this strange event.) Then he turned downe Bowe Lane by Mr. Freland's house, and went to Queen Hyve, where he took boats and some fortie with him, and so these went with him to Essex House by water, wher now he is enclosed. Bedford did shrinck from him upon the proclamation, and so did many moar ; and they that did follow him were forced to leave him at the water syd, for ther was not means to cary them. Now, Sʳ, ther were some 3 proclamations in Cheapsyd, of which the last was that her Maᵗⁱᵉ did pardon all those that did forsack him and not stick to him. Now he, Southampton, Rutland, Mounteagle, and the other two Lords (if they were with him), ar all enclosed in Essex House ; for presentlie, after he was thus gon, a round cheque came to the Lord Mayor and Sheriffs for not apprehending of him, and so they to shewe their diligence sent many companyes to surround Essex House. All the street, on the foresyds towards the Church is full of armed men, foot and pyk and horsemen, of which the Lᵈ * is said to be the leader, being, as I wrote, released some six days ago. That syd that is to the water is lykwise cumpassed about ; the water gate is broken downe, so they are entered into the garden and into the banqueting-house. Some shotts have been made out of Essex House, and wounded some, and, as they saye, killed some others ; one man's thigh is burst, a horse killed, &c. The L. Burghley himself cam to the gate and knocked, but some within bid him be gon, or they protested they would knock him about the head with bullets. This much this Sonday till eight a clock at night that the watch was set. About six a clock some pece of ordnaue wer brought from the Tower to beat his house, and about ten he yealded himself and his people, and so is caryed this Sonday at night in shewe to the Court to Whithall, but as most men think to the Tower, or if not, he and his will be ther shortlie, or then they will loose their heads very presentlie, wᶜʰ I look for every hour. For this matter is desperat, and they are but dead men in my conceat. I pray you, if you look to hear any thing from me, yeald me the posts ; for you have as great reason to look for advertisments now as ever you had these hundreth years, in wᶜʰ tyme the lyke hath not been seen. I have been at chardges of other posts that ar com downe, and few are com that I have not given lardglie to, wᶜʰ I pray you consider of how I can do it.——The Lord God preserve his Maᵗⁱᵉ, and his Queen, and their children.—I. H.—London, this 8 Februarie, 1600.

"It is expected that they will be behended to-day at Westminster ; for the adversarie doth follow the rage of the age.

"To Mr. Fullerton in all haste."

This letter, though addressed to Mr. Fullerton, was evidently intended for the perusal of James VI., by whom, on his accession to the English throne, he was afterwards knighted. The original letter is now in the possession of the Hamilton family.

The following letter written, in cipher as to the names, from Edinburgh on the day before the foregoing letter from Hamilton to Fullerton, by George Nicholson to Sir Robert Cecil, then principal Secretary of State to Queen Elizabeth, (the original of which is in the State Paper Office,) shows that Hamilton was then in London, and in communication with Cecil on the subject of King James's succession to the English throne :—

"It may please your honor,—I received your Honor's last letter of the 29th of the last, understanding Her Majesty's gracious bounty towards me of £20 in reversion, for which I yield most humble thanks, praying God to preserve her long over us, with happy and comfortable days, to our joy which depend thereon. The King hath ever of late been so very exceedingly occupied with writing anent my Lord of Marr's dispatch, as I have had little speech with the King; only this day I told him your Honor had advertised me that Pory Oglevy was taken, and that your Honor had directed me to learn his pleasure how he would have Her Majesty dealt with for his stay or release, showing that because he was his subject, Her Majesty had that regard as to know his mind therein. He replied, it was long since he was taken, that he would have him tried and hanged and done with as Soggy was ; that if he got him he would try him as he did Sir Walter Lindsay, and, unless he cleared himself, hang him ; that he heard his letters should be (were) taken with him ; that, if it were so, he would have him hanged for counterfeiting them ; concluding he cared not what he did with him, and so without more left me. So as I had no more speech but to these effects with him, yet because Pory Oglevy is of many friends, and that I have this but by word, and that the King's Ambassador have direction and the King's pleasure in this, to the same effect, I remit the more certainly of the King's mind therein to their reports.

"My Lord of Marr, and my Lord of Kinloss, hold journey, and that with diligence, about Thursday next. On Monday, Mr. David Fowlis is to be sent afore by post to prepare all things for them. So far as now, I hear they have no employment anent our parliament matters (I mean the suggestious here of the same), nor the matter of succession, but only upon advertisment out of England, that such slanders and reports do come hither of him, that he should be (is) a dealer with Romish, Spanish, and Papists' courses, &c., as unless he someway free himself thereof, Her Majesty and the people of England may be further possessed therewith than were good for him, and that therefore he had need to remove in time these suspicions, lest they be harder to remove, and prove dangerous to the King hereafter ; the King sends them to clear his part in all things with plainness for Her Majesty's contentment, if they can, and to assure Her

claimed King of Great Britain, France, and Ireland, at several public places in London, to his, no doubt, great satisfaction.

Majesty of the King's honest mind to run her course in all things may content her, and withal to offer her sundry good offices, and to give Her Majesty surety of the same in the King's name, and to undertake it themselves to see it performed, and to remove all suspicions and to settle the two Princes in kindness without jealousy hereafter. This, I hear, their negociation is for, and for no other dealing; but I can give no certainty what is or will be, for they no way acquaint me with anything, no, not with their going; what they mean by it I know not, neither do I care, so long as I please where I owe my duty. The conjectures and conceits of this ambassage are exceedingly strange and many, yea, with councillors and wise men; and the wisest are at gaze to see what may follow it, the reason is it is so secret, the Council being no way acquainted with the errands or grounds of. The Secretary no Secretary in this, but only the King. Sir Thomas Erskine goes not, but stays here to be watchful with Sir George Hume, that nothing grow in the Earl's absence to his prejudice. And, to make the matter more sure, my Lord of Kinloss was sent to the Queen (Anne) to inform her of this negociation, and to satisfy her towards my L. And this day the Earl returns by Dunfermling to take his leave of the Queen, whither the King goes this day also and returns on Monday. My Lord of Marr hath gotten the King's licence for Mr Robt. Bruce to return and remain where he please in England; yet with condition that he behave himself as the King's subject in strait words. All these things and others are done to win the Earl a love and grace. Mr. Robt. Bruce, I judge, shall meet him at London, or soon after be with him. The Earl goes on his own horse and charges, in hope of the King's consideration of it some way again to him. As this sudden employment is wondered at, so it is exceedingly grudged at, as I see not but his absence will breed him danger some one way or other, for all the surety given him by the King and the plat laid for his surety. But this matter I leave to the sequel.

"For the convention it holds—what will be the end, I know not, but shall advertise as I know it. For me, I rest in their old manner of suspicion, and as much as they can hindered from intelligence; yet within few days I hope to know more. I have delivered *Monbray* his letter, acquainted him with what your Honor directed me, from whom shortly your Honor will hear. *Sir Ro. Kerr's* employment is dashed now.

"*Beltress* is not here. *Aston* is very diligent, but under great suspicion, watched here and to be watched *in England.* He knows it; he is *your Honor's,* and will so show *your Honor.*

"Mr. James Hamilton is in great hatred, some say for, *your Honor.* Mr. James Fullarton is presently out of taste, yet not charged with anything, as they do and intend to do Mr. James Hamilton. Sir Thomas Erskine hath wrought this. Mr. Aston goes with my Lord of Marr. The King hath commanded him.

"Sir Thomas Erskine was on Tuesday night on the borders, I cannot say where; but I doubt not but your

Honor knows who sent the first advertisment of that time from thence of this employment, and what letters were sent from hence, as I have reason to judge, yet know not, and by the same will perceive, if such be, how I am avoided in this matter, and not yet by them acquainted with that the world now knows here. It must needs be either many letters have been written by the King, or great curiosity (care) in them he writes, for he hath plied it this week. (He has been writing the whole week past.) And thus, with mine humble duty and service, I pray God preserve your Honor. At Edinburgh, the 7th of February, 1600.

"Your Honor's humble, at commandment,

"GEORGE NICHOLSON.

"Mr. Hamilton knows what Fullarton knows and will show it *your Honor.*

"*Nicholson* grieves to see *Sir Thomas Erskine* work *Mr. Hamilton* disgrace, by charging him with over much familiarity with *your Honor,* and with £100 per annum, &c.

"It may please your Honor to cause give the enclosed to Mr. Hamilton. Mr. David Fowlis carries the King's discharge, and returns Mr. Hamilton thence. Their actions are still mutable, and slippery hold have any they that build on them here."

Superscribed—" To the Right Hon.ble Sir Robert Cecil, Knight, Principal Secretary to Her Majesty. *Endorsed—* " Mr. Nicholson to my Mr.," in the same hand the ciphers are deciphered in.

The original of the following letter from James Hamilton to Sir Robert Cecil, but without date, is to be also found in the State Paper Office :—

"MAY IT PLEASE YOUR HONOR,—The things referred to me by the D. (? Duke's) letter are these—that I should declare his earnest affections to perform all good offices tending to the advancement of Her Majesty's service, according to his master's will declared in that behalf to Her Majesty, and Her Highness's great favours lately shown to him, binding him thereunto, in respect of which, both he is emboldened to offer and to crave every thing that may give *esperance* to further Her Majesty's service, increase the amity, and to enable himself by credit to go forward in this so dutiful resolution.

"Next, that according to his promise to Her Highness, he hath taken order for barring of all means that might proceed from the Western ports to the aid of the rebel, and also for procuring of our intercourse between the said ports and the garrisons of Loughfoyle and Knockfergus, for the better supplying of the said garrisons with victuals, &c., which shall be continued with all readiness to enterprise whatsoever further service agreeing with his ability and allegiance.

"But, it being a thing greatly lamented by such as keep this correspondency, that these Northern parts of Ireland not affording any commodities fit for their country, they are forced to take the payment of their

After this, he waits upon King James for several years at Whitehall, and receives from him Knighthood as a mark of his favour, and is found a man of great wisdom, learning, and in great request with his Majesty, as being very faithful to, and very active for him in, his interest, and so highly honoured of all great men in Court and City.[f]

---

victuals and merchandise in base money, of which notwithstanding, they cannot have the exchange unless it be by direction from hence. His desire therefore is, that for the continuance of the said traffic to the behoof of the garrisons, he may have a letter in the behalf of his people, signifying Her Majesty's pleasure to the Treasurer of Ireland and his ministers, that, according to Her Majesty's proclamation, they may have letters of exchange, both for such base money as doth now lie upon their hands, and for such as from time to time they shall receive for their victuals and merchandize.

"Further, that in the late intended employment of the Scots, offer was secretly made to him to withdraw some from the rebel for the furtherance of that service, which offer he hath entertained, the rather for that there is hope to procure them upon the assurance of reward, to do some service at their withdrawing, which may be instead of a pledge for their future faithfulness. *Espérance* is also given by persons of credit, that some of them in whose behalf this offer is made (by reason of their grievances, grudges, and desire of great rewards), are very fit to be dealt withal for attempting somewhat against the head of the rebellion, which if they will not be brought to undertake—yet the first service being well prosecuted, will be of very good consequences for the advancing of Her Highness's service. Upon the signification of Her Majesty's pleasure, he will do what he can to bring them to the best issue, or any other means of that nature, that may occur to hurt or annoy the rebel.

"Lastly, that whereas Her Majesty was pleased out of her gracious favour to promise him all such means from her, as might best serve for the increase of his credit with his master, and his enabling to the performance of all good offices for the maintenance of the amity. And that upon those Her Majesty's gracious promises, he hath been encouraged to give hope to his master, that none should be able to procure better and more means tending to the establishing of the peace, than he shall. His humble desire to Her Highness is, that, as in the time of the Earl of Marr's employment, Her Majesty upon good considerations was pleased to increase the annuity, so now she would be pleased (his master having greater and more means of charges) to let him know in secrecy, if by his mediation also (when some good opportunity shall draw him hither), a proportionable increase might be granted again to the King, giving a meeting to his so kind offers for concurrence against the rebel, and being a good means to increase and confirm their so great and growing friendship. And that Her Majesty will think none fitter to be the means of so good an office than himself, he is humbly bold to be persuaded, both in respect to her princely promises, and for that (as he trusteth) none shall be found of better means, more honorably minded,

and of readier and more purest good will to procure the strengthening of the amity for the best services of both the princes. And Her Highness being the King, whom next to his master he does most honour, and is most desirous to serve, he hopes she will not afford to any that shall come after him greater means of credit than he shall now have hopes to obtain at her hand.

"And that he doth crave your means to Her Majesty in his behalf, it is in respect of the place which you hold near unto her, and that the chief of his desires is the increasing and settling of the amity between the two Sovereigns, and deriving from the same the greatest kindness, that may issue to both their contentments, for effecting of which whatsoever concurrence in this or the like particular your honor shall give, he doth stand assured it shall be very acceptable to Her Highness, courteously and kindly thought of by his master, and which shall remove that imputation that hath been conceived of your alienation from this their amity. The special advancement also of Her Majesty's affairs (according to his power and allegiance), being in this one of his principal aims, he is encouraged to crave this correspondency of you, to whom he knoweth the same is and hath ever been most tender and precious.

"Your Honor's most humble,
"JAMES HAMILTON."

Indorsed—Memorial, Mr. Hamilton.

[f] It would appear, from the following statement in the Montgomery MSS., that Hugh Montgomery, the sixth Laird of Braidstane, in Scotland, whose fortunes were afterwards so closely connected with those of Sir James Hamilton, recommended himself to King James in a similar manner:—

"Appearing at the Court in Edinburgh he was respected as a well accomplished gentleman, being introduced to kiss King James the Sixth's hand, by divers noblemen, on whose recommendation he was received into favour (and especial notice taken of him), which encreased more and more by reason of a correspondence he had with his brother George (then Dean of Norwich in the Church of England), whereby he received and gave frequent intelligence to His Majesty of the Nobility and State Ministers in Queen Elizabeth's Court and Council, and of the country gentlemen as they were well or ill-affected to His Majesty's succession." Again, at pp. 19 and 20:—"And now halcyon days shined throughout all Scotland, all animosities being compressed by His Majesty (who in a few months afterwards) having certain intelligence of Queen Elizabeth's sickness and extreme bodily weakness, and not long thence of her death, which was on the 24th of March (according to the English computation), An. Dom. 1602, James the Sixth being proclaimed King in London and Westminster, by the Lord Mayor, with the Lords of the Privy

At this time it fell out that Ireland had many lands and estates forfeited in a late rebellion,[b] and now to be disposed of by his Majesty; and his Majesty, designing to gratify his Scotch Nobility and Gentry, and by them to carry on the planting of Ireland, was very disposed to grant, and accordingly

did *   *   *   *   *

Sir J *   *   *   *   *

Scotland *   *   *   *   *

to Ireland *   *   *   *   *

with a great   *   *   *   *

himself *   *   *   *

him yearly *   * thousand pounds sterling in *   *

with duties valuable to more than 12 hundred   a year; he is chosen one of his Majesty's Honorable Privy Council for that Kingdom, and created Lord Viscount Claneboy;[i] so continues at great favour at Court, and power and splendour in this Kingdom.

In this time his second brother, Archibald, is educated in learning; then bred a Writer to the Signet in Edinburgh; afterwards settles Commissary at Limerick; becomes a man of great judgment and integrity, and purchases a good estate, and lives in great plenty and good esteem for wis-

---

Council, and by them solemnly invited to take progress and receive the Crown with the Kingdoms of England, &c., into his gracious protection. Accordingly, His Majesty (as soon as convenience would allow) went to Westminster, attended by divers noblemen and many gentlemen, being by greater numbers conveyed to the border, where he was received by English Lords, Esquires, and Gentry, in great splendour. Amongst the Scottish Lairds (which is a title equivalent to Esquires) who attended His Majesty to Westminster, he of Braidstane was not the least considerable; but made a figure more lookt on than some of the Lords' sons, and as valuable in account as the best of his own degree and estate in that journey."—*Mont. MSS.*, pp. 8, 9.

[b] Of the celebrated Shane O'Neill, in consequence of which an Act was passed in the Irish Parliament, in the 11th year of the reign of Queen Elizabeth, Chap. 1, sess. 3, entitled, *An Act for the attainder of Shane O'Neile, and the extinguishment of the name of O'Neile, and the entitling of the Queen's Majestie, her heires and successors, to the Country of Tyrone, and to other Countries and Territories in Ulster.* The extensive grants in Ireland made to Sir James Hamilton by King James, as a reward for his services, will be hereafter referred to; but as the most extensive one, and that respecting which these MSS. are principally conversant, consisted of the territories of the Upper Clandeboye and Great Ardes, in the County of Down, formerly the property of Con O'Neill, in which Sir James Hamilton alone was named as a trus-

tee for himself and Con O'Neill, and also for Sir Hugh Montgomery; and as no account of that transaction is given in these MSS., it has been thought proper to give in an Appendix to this Chapter the entire version of it as found in the Montgomery MSS., especially as the latter are now out of print.

[i] The date of the Patent is the 4th of May, 1622, in the 20th year of James the First. A copy of the *constat* in Latin is given in the first volume of the Irish Lords Journals, p. 93, but as it contains only the granting part and not the recital of the grounds on which it was conferred, and as they throw considerable light, not only on Sir James Hamilton's personal history, but on the then state of the country, a translation of a copy of it, which has been obtained from the Irish Rolls Office, is here inserted:—

"The King and so forth: To all Archbishops, Dukes, Marquises, Earls, Viscounts, Bishops, Barons, Provosts, Freemen, and all our officers, ministers, and subjects whatsoever to whom these present letters shall come, greeting. Know ye, that We, considering the great fidelity and labour our trusty servant, Sir James Hamilton, Knt., of Bangor, in the County of Down in our Kingdom of Ireland, has practised and done to the most serene Queen Elizabeth of Happy Memory, and not only in our affairs and business, but also in our more private Councils of our Kingdom of Ireland, and in the public assemblies of the same Kingdom, and that by his great labour and expence there has been brought a plantation of British subjects of

dom, wealth, and piety, in that Kingdom generally during his whole life; married first to   *
*   *   *   by whom he had two daughters.ᵏ

The third son, Gawin, after due improvements in humanity at home, is bred a merchant in Glasgow; becomes a great and successful proficient therein; purchases, possesses, and manages some lands in Scotland, at the foot of Clide, in   *   , and some lands in Ireland, at Hollywood, near Belfast; obtains a lease of the great Bann, near Colrain, and provides himself with three merchant ships, and carries the product of the aforesaid lands and fishings and other commodities of this country abroad, and brings home to Scotland, especially to Glasgow, and   *   , viz., the Northern sea-ports and Dublin, wines and other effects from the places to which he had carried his other effects, and so becomes very wealthy and great in his station and way of living.

our Kingdom of England into Ireland, and to those other parts of Ulster, particularly Claneboy and 'the Ards,' (the antient Retreat of the Rebells,) and erected roofed Fortresses, and improved them with buildings such as are in Villages and Towns, restraining the Rebells, or for the sake of the better preservation of life, restoration and bringing back of religion, the increase of the Republick, and the advantage of those in power, and he has procured the tranquility of the Province of Ulster, of our special grace, certain knowledge, and mere motion, We have erected, preferred, and created the aforesaid Sir James Hamilton to be Viscount Claneboye in our County of Down, in our Kingdom of Ireland, and him the said James Viscount Claneboye aforesaid, by the tenor of these presents, we do erect, prefer, and create, and have given, granted, and preferred, and by these presents do give, grant, and prefer to the said James the name, state, degree, dignity, title, and honor of Viscount Claneboye aforesaid. To have and to hold the same name, state, stile, degree, dignity, title, and honor of Viscount Claneboye aforesaid, with all and singular pre-eminences and and other honors to such name, state, stile, dignity, degree, title, and honor of Viscount Claneboye appertaining or belonging to the aforesaid James Hamilton, and the heirs male of his body lawfully begotten, and to be begotten, for ever: Willing, and by these presents granting for us, our heir and successors, that the aforesaid James, and his heirs male aforesaid, may successively bear and have, and every of them may have and bear the name, state, degree, stile, dignity, title, and honor of Viscount Claneboye aforesaid, and be successively called and known, and each of them be called and known, by the name of Viscount Claneboye aforesaid, and that the same James and his heirs male aforesaid successively shall be held in all things Viscount Claneboye, and as a Viscount of our said Kingdom of Ireland shall be held and reputed, and every of them be held and reputed, and they may have, hold, and possess, and every of them may have, hold, and possess, a seat, voice, and place in Parliament, and in the publick meetings and Councils of us, our heirs and successors, within our Kingdom of Ireland, amongst other Viscounts, and before all Barons of our said Kingdom of Ireland, as Viscount Claneboye; and also the said James and

his heirs male aforesaid may enjoy and use, and each of them may enjoy and use, by the name of Viscount Claneboye, all and singular such rights, privileges, pre-eminences, and immunities to the degree of Viscount of our said Kingdom of Ireland truly and of right appertaining, which other Viscounts of our said Kingdom of Ireland before this time more decently, honorably, and quietly used and enjoyed, or at present use and enjoy. And, because by the encrease of the state and high dignity, the expence and high charges are necessarily increased, and that the said James, and his heirs male aforesaid, may and can, and each of them may and can, the better more decently and more honourably maintain and support the said degree of Viscount Claneboye, and the charges imposed on the said James and his heirs male aforesaid, therefore, of our more abundant grace, We have given and granted, and by these presents for us, our heirs and successors, We do give and grant to the aforesaid James, and his aforesaid heirs male for ever, the fee or annual rent of thirteen pounds six shillings and eightpence, current money of Ireland, by the year: To have, levy, and receive annually the said fee or annual rent of £13 6s. 8d. to the said James, and his aforesaid heirs male aforesaid, out of the issues, rents, and profits great and small, customs and subsidies granted or due to us, or hereafter to us, our heirs and successors to be granted or due, coming, increasing, or emerging within the Port of our City of Dublin, to be paid by the hands of the collector of us, our heirs and successors, of the customs and subsidies of us, our heirs and successors, there for the time being, at the Feasts of Saint Michael the Archangel and Easter, by equal portions. We will also and so forth. Without fine in the Hanaper and so forth: Altho' express mention and so forth. For Witness whereof and so forth.—Witness the King at Westminster, the fourth day of May.

" By Writt of Privy Seal."

ᵏ Her sirname was Simpson, and one of their daughters, Jane, was the wife of Archibald Edmonstone, of Braidenisland, in the County of Antrim, Esq. He was married a second time to Rachel Carmichael, by whom he had twenty-two children, who will be mentioned in the next chapter.

The fourth son, John, after due education at schools at home, is invited and brought over by his eldest brother in Ireland; and he is by him employed in agenting of his law affairs for a time, and thereafter, by his industry, purchases a considerable estate, partly at Monellan (now Hamilton's Bawn), in the County of Armagh, and partly at Coronary, in the County of Cavan, of a considerable value, on which he lived very plentifully and creditably.

The fifth son, William,[1] having his younger education as his forementioned brother, was called into Ireland by his eldest brother, by whom he was educated into the management of his country affairs, of letting his lands, receiving his rents, and proved therein very effectual and active, to the very good acceptance both of my Lord and his tenants, and also purchased for himself a very competent estate in several places in the County of Down, partly of my Lord, and partly of other places adjacent to his estate, wherein he lived plentifully, and in very good respect with all.

The sixth brother, Patrick, had his younger education at home in learning, wherein he became very hopeful, and was put to college for further improvement and * * He followed the study of Divinity, wherein his proficiency was so great that he was called to, and settled in, the ministry at Enderwick, in East Lothian in Scotland, where he lived all his lifetime, painfully and acceptable to all concerned, in a very staggering time.

---

[1] This William Hamilton was nominated the first Provost of the Borough of Killileagh, in the charter of incorporation which was granted to it in the tenth year of the reign of James I. The following laconic letter, under the date of 9th July, 1619, addressed to his brother William, has been found among the family papers:—

"WILLIAM,—I have written lately to you by Patrick Shawe, but in good trueth not so much as I thinke. I will write no more than that if there be not a greater care had, things will fall out that you and I both will be sorry for it; it being strange that of about fourteene hundredth pounds ster., and more, all payable before or at this May day, besides sundry casualties not accounted, I have not hitherto receaved one penny. Mr. Ormsby hath called to me eagerly for his money here, and hath told me that Harry Corragh is not only likely to fall into decay, and to be disabled from paying of any thing, but doth also seeke to lay reproches upon me of a bad bargaine, by reason of your not keeping of condicions. What your condicions were, by my truth I do not know, but they seem not to be the same to me at Dublin as you wrot to me of at Clanchie; for you wrot to me that the barrell of oats was sold to him for   , and I understood at Dublin, that the same was to be but , I bearing the fraight and all chardges; so as in effect the same came not but to half a crowne the barrell. Get your money from him the best you may, for it is like otherwise you will have ill getting it, and then my graine is

brought to a faire markett. You had don well and wisely if at Dublin you had taken his absolut bond for the money with an acknowledgment that he had receaved the grain, according to the condicions. I have written this inclosed to my Lo. Chancellor, albeit if you had made your bargain more wisely, I should not have neede to be troubled. I am to pay alsoe some money to Mr. Hogg, wch he did expect to be paid here; he is now at Dublin himself; it will be more easy to pay him there some fortie or fifty pounds, which I do wish to be done ere he com away. The rest I leave to my former letters.—Farewell. I have warned Mr. Ormsby to expect his money from you there, with some respect to his forbearance, notwithstanding wch he thinks himself hardly used.

"Your brother,

"JAMES HAMILTONE.

"9 July, 1619.

"If you find that you cannot be otherwise paid, then you may deliver this letter to my Lord Chancellor, wch I would not otherwise doe if you can receave satisfaction.

"To William Hamilton, Esq."

The Lord Chancellor referred to was Sir Adam Loftus, Knight, afterwards Viscount Loftus, of Ely, who was appointed Lord Chancellor of Ireland, by patent dated 13th May, 1619, but was removed, and Sir Richard Bolton, Knight, appointed in his place, by writt of Privy Seal, dated 6th December, 1639.

APPENDIX TO CHAPTER II.

[Extracts from the Montgomery MSS. referred to at page 10, *ante*, note g].

" When the said Laird[a] had lodged himself in Westminster, he met at Court with [the said] George[b] (his then only living brother), who had with longing expectations waited for those happy days. They enjoyed one the other's most loving companies, and meditated of bettering and advancing their peculiar stations. Foreseeing that Ireland must be the stage to act upon, it being unsettled, and many forfeited lands thereon altogether wasted, they concluded to push for fortunes in that kingdom, as the Laird had formerly done; and so, settling a correspondence between them, the said George resided much at Court, and the Laird returned to his Lady and their children in Braidstane, and imploying some friends who traded into the next adjacent coasts of Ulster, he by them (from time to time) was informed of the state of that country, whereof he made his benefit (though with great cost and pains, as hereafter shall be related), giving frequent intimation of occurrences to his said brother, which were repeated to the King. After the King was some months in his palace at Whitehall, even in the first year of his reign, the affairs of Ireland came to be considered, and an office of inquest by jurors was held before some judges, whereby the forfeited temporal lands, and Abbey lands, and impropriations, and others of that sort, were found to have been vested in the Queen, and to be now lawfully descended to the King[c]; but the rebellion and commotions raised by O'Doherty and his associates in the County of Donegal retarded (till next year) the further procedures to settlement.

" In the mean while the said Laird, in the said first year of the King's reign, pitched upon the following way (which

a Hugh Montgomery (who, as stated at p. 10, *ante*, had attended his Majesty King James VI. on his accession to the English throne) was the eldest son of Adam the fifth Laird of Braidstane, in Scotland, and was born about 1560. In 1622, he was created Viscount Montgomery, of the Great Ards. " His patent purposes to be granted ' on account of the many and great deserts, and the assistance strennously afforded by our dear and faithful Hugh Montgomery, of Braidstane, in our kingdom of Scotland, knight, in pacifying of Clandeboye, after rebellion, in the tumults of the peasants of Ulster; also, in pacifying of Ardes, in our kingdom of Ireland, a colony of Scots being brought in the beginning of our reign over from Great Britain into Clandeboye and Ardes. towards the increase of the reformed religion, and towards the obedience of the peasants towards us.' In 1626 he had a licence from King Charles I. to import arms for the use of his tenants, and to pass into Scotland to carry over materials to build a church at Port Montgomery (now Portpatrick), which he had purchased, together with Dunsky Castle and the estate, from Sir Robert Adair of Kinhilt, besides getting Newtown-Ards

made a Borough to return two Members to Parliament, with many other privileges. He rebuilt the mansion-house there, repaired the old Castle, and the Church, and also the Churches at Greyabbey and Comber, and built a large Church in Donaghadee, and another in Portpatrick, and repaired the Church in Kilmore Parish, and furnished all these six houses of God with large Bibles of the new translation, and Common Prayer Books of 1603, being a firm professed friend to the Established Protestant religion. He also built that very useful work, the quay and harbour of Donaghadee, and erected a great school in Newtownards, which he endowed. He departed this life at his house there, after a long and useful life, on the 25th of May, 1636, in the seventy-sixth year of his age, universally revered and loved, obeyed by the Irish, and much esteemed by Con O'Neill and his followers, but especially by his own tenants and planters, who deeply lamented his loss, as their great protector and patron."—*Mrs. Reilly's Genealogical History of the family of Montgomery, pp.* 41-2.

b Then Dean of Norwich, and Chaplain to the King, and afterwards Bishop of Meath, to which See he was promoted in 1610, and died in 1620.

he thought most fair and feazable) to get an estate in lands, even with free consent of the forfeiting owner of them, and it was thus, viz.:—The said Laird (in a short time after his return from the English Court) had got full information from his [said] trading friends of Con O'Neil's case and imprisonment in Carrickfergus towne, on account of a quarrell made by his servants with some soldiers in Belfast, done before the Queen died, which happened in manner next following, to witt :—The said servants being sent with runletts to bring wine from Belfast [aforesaid], unto the said Con, their master and Great Tcirne, as they called him, then in a grand debauch at Castlereagh, with his brothers, his friends, and followers ; they, returning (without wine) to him, battered and bled, complained, that the soldiers had taken the wine, with the casks, from them by force. Con inquiring (of them) into the matter, they confessed their number twice exceeded the soldiers, who indeed had abused them, they being very drunk. On this report of the said servants, Con was vehemently moved to anger ; reproached them bitterly ; and, in rage, swore by his father, and all his noble ancestors' souls, that none of them should ever serve him or his family (for he was married and had issue) if they went not back forthwith, and did not revenge the affront done to him and themselves by those few Boildagh Sasonagh soldiers (as he termed them). The said servants (as yet more than half drunk', avowed to execute that revenge, and hastened away instantly ; arming themselves in the best way they could, in that short time, and engaged the same soldiers (from words to blows), assaulting them with their weapons ; and in the scuffle (for it was no orderly fight), one of the soldiers happened to receive a wound, of which he died that night, and some other slashes were given ; but the Teagues were beaten off and chased, some sore wounded and others killed ; only the best runners got away scott free. The pursuit was not far, because the soldiers feared a second assault from the hill of Castlereagh, where the said Con, with his two brothers, friends, and followers (for want of more dorgh) stood beholders of the chase. Then in a week next after this fray, an office of inquest was held on Con, and those of his said friends and followers, and also on the servants, and on all that were suspected to be procurers, advisers, or actors therein, and all of whom the Provost Marshall could seize (were taken), by which office the said Con, with some of his friends, were found guilty of levying war against the Queen. This mischief happened a few months before her death ; and the whole matter being well known to the said Laird, and his brothers, and his friends, soon after the King's accession to the English Crown, early application was made to his Majesty for a grant of half the said Con's lands, the rest to Con himself, which was readily promised, but could not, till the second of his reign, by any means be performed, by reason of the obstacles at the settlement of Ireland aforesaid.

"But I must a little go retrograde, to make my report of their affairs better understood. The Laird having met with his brother, and returned from London (as before mentioned), came home (his second son being then about the third year of his age), and industriously minded the affairs in Ireland ; and, by his said brother, gave frequent intimations to the King, or his Secretary for Scotland, of all occurrences he could learne, especially out of Ulster (which had never been fully made subject to England) ; which services of the Laird, and the King's promise, were by his brother renewed in the King's memory, as occasion served to that purpose. And the effects answered his pains and expectations, which was in this manner, viz.—The Queen being dead, the King filling her (late) throne, O'Doherty soon subdued, and the Chief-Governors in this kingdom of Ireland foreseeing alterations in places, and the King's former connivance of supplies, and his secret favors to the O'Neils and McDonnells, in counties of Down and Antrim (being now well known), as to make them his friends, and a future party for facilitating his peaceable entry and possession in those northern parts of the country (if needful), it so came to pass that the said Con had liberty to walk at his pleasure (in the day time) in the streets of Carrickfergus, and to entertain his friends and tenants in any victualling house within the towne, having only a single sentinel to keep him in custody, and every night delivered him to the Marshall. And thus Con's confinement (which lasted several months after the Queen's death) was the easier, and supportable enough, in regard that his estate was not seized by the escheators, and that his words (at his grand debauch aforesaid) were reputed very pardonable, seeing greater offences would be remitted by his Majesty's gracious declaration of amnesty, which was from time to time expected, but delayed on the obstacles aforesaid.

"In the mean time, the Laird used the same sort of contrivance for Con's escape as he had heretofore done for his own ; and thus it was, viz.:—The Laird had formerly employed, for intelligence as aforesaid, one Thomas Montgomery, of Blackstown, a fee farmer (in Scotland, they call such gentlemen feuers), he was a cadet of the family of Braidstane, but of a remote sanguinity to the Laird, whose actions are now related. This Thomas had personally divers times traded with grain and other things to Carrickfergus, and was well trusted therein; and had a small bark, of which he was owner and constant commander; which Thomas being a discreet, sensible gentleman, and having a fair prospect given him of raising his fortune in Ireland, was now employed and furnished with instructions and letters to the said Con, who, on a second speedy application in the affair, consented to the terms proposed by the Laird, and to go to him at Braidstane, provided the said Thomas would bring his escape so about as if constrained, by force and fears of death, to go with him. These resolutions being with full secrecy concerted, Thomas aforesaid (as the Laird had formerly advised) having made love to the Town Marshall's daughter, called Annas Dobbin (whom I have often seen and spoken with, for she lived in Newtown till Anno 1664), and had gained her's and parent's consents to be wedded together. This took umbrages of suspicion away, and so, by contrivance with his espoused, an opportunity, one night, was given to the said Thomas and his barque's crew to take on board the said Con, as it were by force, he making no noise for fear of being stabbed, as was reported next day through the town.

"The escape being thus made, and the bark, before next sunset, arriving safe at the Larggs, in Scotland, on notice thereof our valourous and well-bred Laird kept his state, staying at home, and sent his brother-in-law, Patrick Montgomery (of whom at large hereafter, for he was also instrumental in the escape), and other friends, with a number of his tenants, and some servants, all well mounted and armed, as was usual in those days, to salute the said Con, to congratulate his happy escape, and to attend him to Braidstane, where he was joyfully and courteously received by the Laird and his Lady, with their nearest friends. He was kindly entertained and treated with a due defference to his birth and quality, and observed with great respect by the Laird's children and servants, they being taught so to behave themselves. In this place the said Con entered into indenture of articles of agreement, the tenor whereof was, that the said Laird should entertain and subsist him, the said Con, in quality of an Esq., and also his followers in their moderate and ordinary expenses; should procure his pardon for all his and their crimes and transgressions against the law (which indeed were not very heinous or erroneous), and should get the inquest to be vacated, and the one-half of his estate (whereof Castlereagh and circumjacent lands to be a part), to be granted to himself by letters patent from the King; to obtain for him that he might be admitted to kiss his Majesty's hand, and to have a general reception into favour; all this to be at the proper expenses, costs, and charges of the said Laird, who agreed and covenanted to the performance of the premises on his part. In consideration whereof, the said Con did agree, covenant, grant, and assign, by the said indenture, the other one-half of all his land estate, to be and enure to the only use and behoof of the said Laird, his heirs and assigns, at which time the said Con, also signing and registering, but no scaling of deeds being usual in Scotland, he promised by an instrument in writing to convey part of his own moiety unto the said Patrick and Thomas, as a requital of their pains for him, which he afterwards performed, the said Laird signing as consenting to the said instrument, the said agreements being fully endorsed and registered (as I was told) in the town council book of the Royal Burgh of Air or Irwine. The original of that indenture to the Laird, I had and shewed to many worshipful persons, but it was burnt with the house of Rosemount, the 16th of February, 1695.

"Upon the said agreement the said Laird and Con went to Westminster, where the said George had been many months Chaplain and Ordinary to his Majesty, and was provided with a living in London, in commendam, with above £200 per annum, and the Laird was there assumed to be an Esq. of the King's body, and soon after this was knighted, and therefore I must call him in the following pages by the name of Sir Hugh Montgomery, who made speedy application to the King (already prepared), on which the said Con was graciously received at Court, and kissed the King's hand, and Sir Hugh's petition, on both their behalfs, was granted, and orders given, under the Privy Signet, that his Majesty's pleasure therein should be confirmed by letters patent, under the Great Seal of Ireland, at such rents as therein expressed, and under conditions that the lands should be planted with British Protestants, and that no grant of fee farm should be made to any persons of meer Irish extraction; but in regard these letters took no effect, as in the next paragraph appears, I shall make no further mention thereof, but will proceed to what afterwards happened to the said Sir Hugh and Con.

" Now these affairs, as also Con's escape and journey with Sir Hugh, and their errand, took time and wind at Court, notwithstanding theirs (and the said George's) endeavours to conceal them from the prying courtiers (the busiest bodies in all the world in other men's matters which may profit themselves), so that in the interim one Sir James Fullerton, a great favourite, who loved ready money, and to live in Court, more than in waste wildernesses in Ulster, and afterwards had got a patent clandestinely passed for some of Con's lands, made suggestions to the King that the lands granted to Sir Hugh and Con were vast territories, too large for two men of their degree, and might serve for three Lord's estates, and that his Majesty, who was already said to be overhastily liberal, had been over-reached as to the quantity and value of the lands, and therefore begged his Majesty that Mr. James Hamilton, who had furnished himself for some years last past with intelligence from Dublin, very important to his Majesty, might be admitted to a third share of that which was intended to be granted to Sir Hugh and Con. Whereupon, a stop was put to the passing of the said letters patent, which overturned all the progress (a work of some months) that Sir Hugh had made to obtain the said orders for himself and Con. But the King sending first for Sir Hugh, told him (respecting the reasons aforesaid) for what loss he might receive in not getting the full half of Con's estate by that defalcation, he would compensate him out of the Abbey lands and impropriations, which in a few months he was to grant in fee, they being already granted in lease for twenty-one years; and that he would also abstract out of Con's half, the whole great Ardes for his and Mr. James Hamilton's behoof, and throw it into their two shares; that the sea coasts might be possessed by Scottish men who would be traders, as proper for his Majestic's future advantage, the residue, to be laid off about Castlereagh (which Con had desired) being too great a favour for such an Irishman.

" All this being privately told by the King, was willingly submitted to by the said Sir Hugh, and soon after this he and Con were called before the King, who declared to them both his pleasure concerning the partitions as aforesaid, to which they submitted. On notice of which procedure Mr. James Hamilton was called over by the said Sir James Fullerton, and came to Westminster, and having kissed the King's hand, was admitted the King's servant (but not in a great while knighted; therefore, hereafter I shall make mention of him as Sir James Hamilton, in its due place); all which contrivance brought money to Sir James Fullerton, for whose sake and request it was the readilyer done by the King. Sir Hugh and Mr. Hamilton met, and adjusted the whole affair between themselves. Whereupon letters of warrant to the Deputy, dated 16th April, 3rd Jacob. 1605, were granted to pass all the promises, by letters patent, under the Great Seal of Ireland, accordingly, in which the said Sir James Fullerton obtained further of the King, that the letter to the Deputy should require him that the patent should be passed in Mr. James Hamilton's name alone, yielding one hundred pounds per annum to the King; and in the said letter was inserted that the said lands were in trust for the said Mr. Hamilton himself, and for Sir Hugh Montgomery, and for Con O'Neill, to the like purport already expressed.

" Then the said Con, Sir Hugh Montgomery, and Mr. Hamilton entered into tripartite indentures, dated ulto. of the said April, whereby *(inter alia)* it was agreed that unto Con and his followers their moderate ordinary expenses from the 1st of August preceding the date now last mentioned, being already paid them, should be continued them, till patents were got out for their pardons, and also deeds from Mr. Hamilton for Con's holding the estate which the King had condescended to grant him. Soon after this Mr. Hamilton went to Dublin to mind his business, and to ply *telis extremis* for the furtherance of it.

" All this being done, and Sir Hugh having no more business (at present) at Whitehall, he resolved with convenient speed to go through Scotland into Ireland, to follow his affairs, which he did so soon as he had renewed his friendship with the English and Scottish Secrecarys, and laid down further methods, with his said brother, of intercourse between themselves for their mutual benefit; and the said Con, well minding Sir J. Fullerton's interposition for Mr. Hamilton (whereby he was a great loser), and that the patent for his lands was to be passed in Mr. Hamilton's own name, and only a bare trust expressed for his (Con's) use, in the letters of warrant aforesaid, he thought it necessary that Sir Hugh and he should look to their hitts. They therefore took leave at Court; (and being thoro' ready) they went to Edinborough and Braidstane, and after a short necessary stay for recruits of money, they passed into Ireland, taking with them the warrant for Con, his indemnity, pardon, and profit.

"Mr. Hamilton having gone to Dublin, as aforesaid, then (viz.) on the 4th July, 1605, (being two months and four days posterior to the said tripartite indenture), a second office was taken, whereby all the towns, lands, manors, abbeys, impropriations, and such hereditaments in Upper Clanneboys and Ardes, were found to be in the King ; it bearing a reference (as to spiritual possessions) for more certainty, unto the office taken concerning them, primo Jac. Ao. 1603 ; and also it was shuffled into it, that Killulta was usually held to lye in the County of Down ; this office being returned and inrolled in September then next following, it was (by inspection thereof) found to vary from the jurors' briefs and notes, and from many particulars in the office taken 1st Jac., and the matter of Killulta was amiss.

"About this time, the inquisition found against Con and his followers for the feats at Belfast aforesaid, being vacated and taken off the file in the King's Bench Court, and the pardon for himself and all his followers, for all their other crimes and trespasses against law being passed under the Great Seal, and the deed of the 6th Nov., 1605, from Mr. Hamilton of Con's lands, being made to himself, Con then returned in triumph over his enemies (who thought to have had his life and estate), and was met by his friends, tenants, and followers, the most of them on foot, the better sort had gerrans, some had pannels for saddles (we call them back bughams) and the greater part of the riders without them ; and but very few spurs in the troop, yet instead thereof they might have thorn prickles in their brogue heels (as is usual), and perhaps not one of the concourse had a hat ; but the gentry (for sure) had their done wosle barrads, the rest might have sorry scull caps, otherwise (in reverence and of necessity) went cheerfully pacing or trotting bare-headed. Con being so come in state (in Dublin equipage) to Castlereagh, where no doubt his vassals (tagg-ragg and bob-tail) gave to their Teirne More, Squire Con, all the honour and homage they could bestow, presenting him with store of beeves, colpaghs, sheep, hens, bonny blabber, rusan butter (such as it was) ; as for cheese, I heard nothing of it (which to this day is very seldom made by the Irish), and there was some greddan meal strowans, with snush and bolean, as much as they could get to regale him ; where I will leave him and them to congratulate each other's inter-view, till other occasions to write of him offer themselves, and he gave them not many months after this time. But good countrymen (Erinagh or Gelagh), Irish or English, if you believe not this treat as aforesaid, neither do I, because I could not see it, nor was I certainly informed ; many histories have stories in them, for writers make Kings' and Gentlemen's speeches, which, perhaps, they never uttered ; however, the worst on my part in this is, that it is a joke, and such I hope you will allow it, and also the Pope's own country Italian proverb, used in the holy city, and the mother (Church) Rome itself, viz. :—*Si non e vero e ben trovato*—if it be not truth, it is well invented for mirth's sake, and so I intended it, for it is not unlikely.

"But before I recount the after actions I mean to treat of, I must mention two transactions more between him and Sir Hugh, viz :—On 14th March, the same 3d Jac. according to English supputation, Ano 1605, but by the Scottish account 1606 (for they have January for the first month of their year, as the almanacs begin the calender),[a] Con, specifying very honorable and valuable considerations him thereunto moving, makes and grants a deed of feoffment of all his lands unto Sir Hugh Montgomery (then returned from Braidstane to prepare habitations for his family), John M'Dowel, of Garthland, Esq., and Colonel David Boyd, appointed to take and give livery of seizin to Sir Hugh, which was executed accordingly the 5th September following, within the six months limited by the statutes in such cases made and provided, the other was added from Con conveying by sale unto Sir Hugh Montgomery, the woods growing on four townlands therein named—this sale was dated the 22d August, 4th Jac°. 1606. Patrick Mont-

---

[a] An English Act of Parliament was passed in 1751, entitled, "An Act for regulating the commencement of the Year, and for correcting the Kalendar now in use," the preamble of which recites that, according to the legal supputation in England, the year began on the 25th of March ; that this practice had produced various incon-veniences, not only from its differing from the usage of neighbouring nations, but also from the legal computation in Scotland, and from the common usage throughout the whole Kingdom ; that the Julian kalendar, then in use, had been discovered to be erroneous, by means whereof the vernal or spring equinox, which at the time of the General Council of Nice, A.D. 325, happened on the 21st of March, now fell on the 9th or 10th of that month ; that this error was still increasing ; that a method of correcting the kalendar had been received and established, and was generally practised by almost all other nations of Europe ; and that it would be of general convenience to merchants, and others corresponding with foreign nations, if the like correction were received and established in his Majesty's dominions.

E

gomery and John Cashan being Con's attorneys, took and gave livery of seizin; accordingly this much encouraged the plantation which began in May this year. Likewise, the said Mr. Hamilton (as he had done to Con) by deed dated next day after that conveyance to Con, viz., on the 7th November, 1605, grants to Sir Hugh Montgomery divers temporal and spiritual (as they call them) lands in Clanneboys and Great Ardes; thus part of the trust and covenants in the tripartite indenture was performed to him. So Sir Hugh returned from Dublin, and (as hereafter shall be said) taking possession, he went forthwith to Braidstane, and engaged planters to dwell thereon.

"Now, on the whole matter of Sir Hugh Montgomery's transactions with and for Con O'Neil, the benefits done to him will appear very considerable, as the bringing them to pass was very costly and difficult, as followeth, viz. :—Con (by the said transporting and mediation for him) had escaped the eminent danger of losing both his life and estate; because, by the said inquest against him, his said words (and perhaps his commands, too) were proved fully enough; or they might have been entered therein, and also managed (in future) so dexterously by the covetors of benefit arising out of the forfeitures, as to make him guilty of levying war against the Queen, which (by law in Ireland) is treason.[d] Moreover, Con's title was bad, because *imprimis* by Act of Parliament in Ireland, 11th Elizabeth, Shane O'Neil, who had engaged all Ulster in rebellion, being killed by Alex. Oge M'Connell (so the statute surnames the M'Donnell), the whole sept of O'Neil were all attainted of treason, and the whole country of Clanneboys, and the hereditaments belonging to them, or any of their kinsmen and adherents (besides Shane's patrimony in Tireowen) now vested in the Queen's actual possession, and did lawfully descend to King James, and was his right as wearing the Crown. And

---

[d] The Act of 10th Henry VII., c. 13, *Ir.*, entitled " *An Act that no person stir any Irishry to make war*," is probably that alluded to in the text, and enacts " That whatsoever person or persons fro' this day forward, cause assemble, or insurrection conspiracies, or in any wise procure or stirre Irishry or Englishry to make warre against our Sovereign Lord the King's authority—that is to say, his Lieutenant, or Deputy, or Justice, or else, if any manner person procure or stir the Irishry to make warre upon the Englishry, be deemed traytor atteycnt of High Treason, in likewise such as assemble an insurrection had been levied against the King's own person."

[e] The Editor of these MSS. thinks it right to observe that this argument of the author of the Montgomery MSS., which has been followed by every subsequent writer on the subject, founded on the allegation of Con O'Neill's bad title, is not borne out by the Act of Parliament above referred to (11th Eliz., sess. 3, chap. 1), which is one of the most extraordinary on the Irish Statute Book; because, although the statute, after stating at great length the several treasons committed by Shane O'Neill, proceeds to attaint him for them, and to extinguish and extirpate the name of O'Neill, and enacts, " That all the lords, captains, and people of Ulster, shall be from henceforth severed, exempted, and cut off from all rule and authority of O'Neyle, and shall onely depend upon your Imperiall Crowne of England, and yeeld to the same their subjection, obedience, and services for ever," yet the 4th section contains the following remarkable provision :—" And where diverse of the lords and captains of Ulster, as the sept of the Neyles, which possessoth the country of Clanneboy, O'Cahan, MacGwylin, the inhabitants of the Glynnes, which hath been sometimes the Baron Misset's lands, and of late usurped by the Scots, whereof James MacConyll did call himselfe lord and conqueror, MacGynnes, O'Hanlon, Hugh MacNeile Moore; the four septes of the MacMahounnes, MacKyvan, and MacCan, hath been at the commaundement of the said traytour Shane

O'Neyle, in this sharp and trayterous warre by him levied against your Majestie, your Majestie's crown and dignitie; for whose offences, be it enacted, &c., That your Majestie, your heyres and successors, shall have, hold, possesse, and enjoy, as in right of your Imperiall Crown of England, the countrey of Tyrone, the countrey of Claneboy, the countrey of Kryue, called O'Cahan's countrey, the countrey of Rowte, called Mac Gwylin's country, the countrey and lordship of the Glynnes, usurped by the Scots, the countrey of Iveagh, called MacGynnes' countrey, the countrey of Orry, called O'Hanlon's countrey, the countrey of the Fnes, called Hugh MacNeyle More's country, the countries of Ferny, Ireel, Loghty, and Dartalry, called MacMahon's countries, the countries of the Troo, called MacKynan's, and the countrey of Clancanny, called Mackan's country, and all the honours, manours, castles, lands, tenements, and other hereditaments whatsoever they be, belonging or appertaining to any of the persons aforesaid, or to their kinsmen or adherents, in any of the countries and territories before specified; and that all and singular the premisses, with their appurtenances, shall be, by authoritie aforesaid, forthwith invested with the reall and actuall possession of your Majestie, your heyres and successors, for ever. And now, most gracious and our redoubted Sovereign Lady, albeit that the said lords and captains be not able to justifie themselves in the eye of the law, for the undutifull adhering to the said traytour O'Neyle, in the execution of his false and trayterous attempts against your Majestie, your crowne, and dignitie; yet, having regard to his great tyranny which he used over them, and the mistrust of your Majestie's earnest following the warre, to deliver them from his tyrannical bondage, as you have most graciously and honourably done, wee must think, that rather fear, than any good devotion, moved the most part of them, to stand so long of his side, which is partly verified in that many of them came unto your Majestie's said Deputie, long before the death of the said traytour, and that after his decease, Tirrelagh Leinagh, whom the countrey had elected to be

Con's title being but a claim by tanistry, whereby a man at full years is to be chosen and preferred to the estate (during his life) before a boy, and an uncle before a nephew-heir under age, whose grandfather survived the father ; and so

O'Neyle, and all the rest of the said Lords and captains, came, by their owne voluntarie accord, into the presence of your Majestie's said Deputie, being then in Ulster, and there, with signs and tokens of great repentance, did humbly submit themselves, their lives, and lands, into your Majestie's hands, craving your mercy and favour, with solemne oathes, and humble submissions in writing, never to swerve from that their professed loyaltie and fidelitie to your Imperiall Crown of England. And, therefore, we your Majestie's ancient, obedient, true, and faithful subjects of this your realm of Ireland, with these your strayed and new-reconciled people, fleeing now under the wings of your grace and mercy, as their onely refuge, most humbly and lowly make our humble petition unto your most excellent Majestie, that it would please the same to behold with your pitifull eyes the long endured miserie of your said strayed people, and rather with easie remission, than with due correction, to looke into their offences past, and not onely to extend unto them your gracious pardon of their lives, but also to have such mercifull consideration of them, as each according to his degree and good hope and desert may receive of your most bounteous liberalitie such portions of their sayd several countries to live on by English tenure and profitable reservations, as to your Majestie shall seem good and convenient ; in the distribution whereof your Highnesse said Deputie is best able to inform your Majestie, as one which by great search and travayle doth knowe the quantity of the said countreys, the nature of the soyles, the quality of the people, the diversities of their lynages, and which of them hath best deserved your Majestie's favor to be extended in this behalf." And it would appear, from the following documents, that, in pursuance of the foregoing provision in the statute of Elizabeth, Con M'Neale Oge, the then captain of Claneboy, was not only allowed to remain in peaceable possession of his lands from the date of the foregoing Act, passed in 1569, but that he became a dutiful subject of her Majesty, by whom he was knighted; and that, in 1586, he surrendered his manor and lordship of Castlereagh, for the purpose of being re-granted to him to be held of her Majesty, her heirs and successors; and that, in 1587, it was re-granted to him accordingly, in consideration of his faithful services and allegiance :—

"24th March, 1586—28th Elizabeth.—To all to whom these presents shall come, Con M'Neal Oge, Knight, sendeth greeting: Know ye that I, the aforesaid knight, for divers good and reasonable causes me thereunto specially moving, and for the better government of the County of Downe, in the Province of Ulster, of my free will, have given, granted, surrendered, and confirmed to the most illustrious Princess and Lady, Elizabeth, Queen of England, France, and Ireland, and Defender of the Faith, &c., my whole manor or lordship of Castlereaghe, in the County of Downe, and all and singular other manors, lordships, castles, messuages, lands, tenements, rents, reversions, towns, townlands, or hamlets, mills, waters, water-courses, meadows, pastures, feeding of pasture, trees, woods, underwood, houses, edifices, granges, dovecotes, fisheries, annuities, weirs, pools, advowsons, pat-

ronage of churches, chapels, and courts of every kind, courts leet, views of frank-pledge, and all the rights, possessions, lands, and temporal hereditaments whatsoever, of whatever kind, nature, or species, that may be, or by whatsoever names they are commonly known, with all and singular the rights, members, and appurtenances to the aforesaid manor or lordship of Castlereagh and the other premises aforesaid, belonging, or in any manner appertaining, situate, lying, and being in the aforesaid County of Downe, or elsewhere within this Kingdom of Ireland, and also the rents, issues, and profits of all and singular the aforesaid premises above expressed and specified, To Have, Hold, and enjoy the aforesaid lordship or manor of Castlereagh, and all and singular near the aforesaid lordships, manors, territories, tenements, and other hereditaments whatsoever above mentioned, with all and singular their rights, members, and appurtenances to the aforesaid Lady our Queen, and her successors for ever, to the use of the said Lady the Queen, her heirs and successors. In testimony whereof I have hereunto affixed my seal, this 24th day of March, in the 29th year of the reign of our aforesaid Lady, Queen Elizabeth, A.D. 1586.

"SIR CON, X his marke.
(Seal.)

"MEMORANDUM—That the aforesaid Knight, on the day and year aforesaid, made and delivered this his surrender to the use of the said Lady the Queen, in presence of us whose names follow, at the Chancery, Dublin.

"ROG. WILBRAHAM.
"RO. LEGGE."

"30th March, 1587—29th Elizabeth—By the Lord Deputy Perrott.—Letters Patent enrolled in the Chancery of Ireland.—To all to whom these presents shall come, greeting: Whereas our beloved subject Con M'Neale Oge, of Castlereagh, in the County of Downe, Knight, of his own free will, in writing, under his seal, sealed, bearing date the 24th day of March, in the 29th year of our reign, in this Chancery of Ireland, of record, and enrolled, gave, granted, and confirmed to us, our heirs and successors, his manor or lordship of Castlereaghe, in the aforesaid County of Downe, and all and singular other lordships, manors, castles, messuages, lands, tenements, rents, reversions, towns, townlands, or hamlets, services, mills, water-courses, meadows, pastures, feedings, trees, woods, underwoods, houses, edifices, granges, dove-cotes, fisheries, waters, weirs, pools, annuities, advowsons, patronage of churches, chapels, and courts of every kind, courts leet, views of frank-pledge, and all privileges to the same belonging, and all the rights, possessions, customs, privileges, liberties, and temporal hereditaments whatsoever, of whatever kind, nature, or species they may be, and by whatever names they are commonly used or known, with all the rights, members, and appurtenances to the said lordship or manor of Castlereagh and other the premises aforesaid belonging, or in any way appertaining, situate, lying, and being in our said County of Downe, or elsewhere within our Kingdom of Ireland, *to the intent that we, by our Letters Patent, should re-grant all and singular the premises to the said Con Oge O'Neile, Knight, and his heirs*, To Hold of

many times they preferred persons, and their descendants intruded by strong hands, and extruded the true lineal heir. And Con's immediate predecessors, Brian Fortagh O'Neil, &c., Con's reputed grandfather, and father, were intruders

---

ns, our heirs and successors, *in capite*, as by the said Letters Patent will more fully appear, Know Ye that We as well in consideration of the grant and surrender aforesaid as in consideration of the faithful services and allegiance of the said Con M'Neale Oge, Knight, and his heirs, to us, our heirs and successors, from time to time offered and done, of our special grace, certain knowledge, and more motion, and with the advice and consent of our well-beloved and faithful counsellor, Sir John Perrott, Knight, our Deputy and Governor-General of this Kingdom of Ireland, according to the form and effect of certain letters under our hand and seal, dated from our manor of Greenwich the 20th day of January in the 27th year of our reign, to the said Deputy and Governor-General directed, and enrolled in the Chancery of Ireland, We do give and grant, and by these presents, for us our heirs and successors, have given and granted to the aforesaid Con M'Neale Oge, Knight, during his life, and after his decease to his reputed son Hugh O'Neale, and after his decease to the heirs male of the body of the said Hugh lawfully begotten, and for want of such issue male of the body of the said Hugh, lawfully begotten, or to be begotten, then with remainder to the heirs male of the body of the aforesaid Con M'Neale Oge, Knight, lawfully begotten, or to be begotten, the aforesaid manor or lordship of Castlereagh, in our aforesaid County of Downe, and all houses, edifices, lands, tenements, rents, reversions, services, liberties, and hereditaments whatsoever belonging, or in any manner appertaining, with all and singular other the lordships, manors, castles, messuages, lands, tenements, rents, reversions, towns, townlands, or hamlets, and all other and singular the premises to the same belonging and appertaining, with all and singular the rights, members, liberties, and appurtenances to us, in form aforesaid surrendered, excepting and reserving always to us, our heirs and successors, all manors, houses, castles, edifices, lands, tenements, rents, services, liberties, and hereditaments of every kind, being part, parcel, or member, or appurtenant to any abbey, priory, chantry, monastery, or religious house, which devolved upon us or our progenitors, whether enacted by Act of Parliament or coming by any other means whatsoever, To Have, hold, and enjoy all the aforesaid manors, lordships, messuages, lands, tenements, and other hereditaments, with all and singular their rights, members, liberties, and appurtenances above specified in the form aforesaid, except as before excepted, from the day of the date aforesaid, to the said Con M'Neale Oge, Knight, during his life, and after his decease then with remainder to the aforesaid Hugh O'Neale, his reputed son, and the heirs male of the body of the said Hugh, lawfully begotten or to be begotten, and for want of such issue then with remainder to the heirs male of the body of the aforesaid Con M'Neale Oge, Knight, lawfully begotten and to be begotten, To Hold of us, our heirs, and successors, *in capite* by knight's service—viz., by service of one knight's fee when the scutage happens, and rendering and paying to us, our heirs and successors, annually, during the estate interest and remainder aforesaid, between the festival of Michael the Archangel and All Saints then next following, 250 cows or oxen, called beefs, at the Newrye, into the hand of the Vice-Treasurer, or of the

Receiver-General of this our Kingdom of Ireland, or into the hand of some other, and so from time to time imposed by legitimate power or authority ; And, further, that the aforesaid Con M'Neale Oge, Knight, and Hugh O'Neale, his reputed son, and the heirs male of their bodies, shall serve, answer, and attend in and upon our Deputy, or other the Governor or Governors of our Kingdom of Ireland, or upon the Governor or Governors of our Province of Ulster, in the Northern parts of our Kingdom of Ireland, for the time being, at all hostings, risings-out, and journeys, with sixty kernes or footmen, and twelve horsemen, armed in warlike manner, and victualled for forty days, for our service in any place where they shall be assigned or appointed to serve against the rebels, or enemies of us, our heirs and successors, in form aforesaid within this our Kingdom of Ireland. Provided always, that upon any necessity requiring it the aforesaid Con O'Neale Oge, Knight, and Hugh O'Neale, his son, and their heirs aforesaid, shall from time to time find, and keep, and with victuals sustain and maintain, for the service of us, our heirs and successors, 60 knights called soldiers, during which time of sustentation of 60 soldiers the aforesaid rent of 250 cows or oxen, called beefs, shall altogether cease, and from the aforesaid Con M'Neale Oge, Knight, and Hugh, his son, and their heirs aforesaid, shall not be demanded nor required. And, further, of our special grace, with the advice and consent aforesaid, we will, and by these presents do grant for us, our heirs and successors, that the aforesaid Con M'Neale Oge, Knight, and his son Hugh O'Neale, and his heirs aforesaid, may have and enjoy one moiety, or half of all the goods and chattels of felons within the aforesaid premises, or the liberties or jurisdictions within the same, attainted or convicted, and a moiety of all and singular waifs and estrays within the premises aforesaid at any time accruing or happening, the other half to us, our heirs, and successors from time to time, always reserved for the use of us, our heirs, and successors, for ever, at the receipt of our Exchequer in Ireland. And, further, for the considerations aforesaid, we will, and for us, our heirs and successors, do give, and by these presents grant to the aforesaid Con M'Neale Oge, Knight, and Hugh O'Neale, and their heirs in form aforesaid, that the aforesaid Con and Hugh, and their heirs aforesaid, may be henceforth free, quiet, and exonerated from all and singular compositions before this time made or imposed, excepting and reserving only our prerogative over our subjects in the Northern parts aforesaid, and all rents and other agreements and provisions specified above in these Letters Patent: Provided always, that if the aforesaid Con M'Neale Oge, Knight, or the aforesaid Hugh O'Neale, or any of the heirs male of the body of either of them begotten or to be begotten, shall alienate, sell, or dispose of any of the premises above granted, except for the term of their life, or twenty-one years in possession, then these Letters Patent shall be void and of no effect in law, and thereupon it shall be lawful for us, our heirs, and successors into the premises, and every part thereof, to re-enter, and the same to have again in our former estate anything herein contained notwithstanding; And we will, and by these presents, for us, our heirs and successors, do grant unto the aforesaid Con

as himself also was) into the Queen's right and possession, in those troublesome times especially, whilst Hugh O'Neil, whom the Queen restored to his predecessor's possessions, and to the title of Earl of Tircowen (*alias* Tireogen in Irish speech), rebelled and ravaged over all Ulster, and most other parts in Ireland, until the latter end of the year of the Queen's reign, of whose death he had not heard till he had submitted himself prisoner to the Lord Deputy Chichester, in Mellefont. The said Brian Neil and Con so intruding into Clanneboys and the Great Ardes, in those days of general confusion, and (for peace sake) winked at, they continued their profession, and at sometimes more avowedly (by reason of the fewness and weakness of the English Garrisons) did take up rents, cuttings, duties, and cesses; coshering also upon their underlings, being therein assisted by their kindred and followers, whom they kept in pay, as soldiers, to be ready on all occasions (when required) to serve him.

"This being the pickle wherein Con was soused, and his best claim but an unquiet possession, usurpation and intrusion against the laws of the kingdom, neither his ancestors nor himself being released from that attainder aforesaid, nor he anywise set *rectus in curia* for joining with Hugh O'Neil, it must needs follow, by all reasonable consequences, that Sir Hugh Montgomery had done many mighty acts for the rescue and welfare of Con himself, his friends, and followers, as hath been fully proved were done for him and them; the very undertaking and prospect of which welfare could not but be very strongly obliging on Con O'Neil, kindly and with hearty thanks to accept of and to agree to the articles signed to Sir Hugh Montgomery at Braidstane, aforesaid.

"We have in the foregoing narrative a few of the many generous acts of the sixth Laird of Braidstane; let me trace him on the back scent, as well as I can for want of papers, and of the original articles of Braidstane between him and Con alone, and of the consequencial proceedings thereupon interrupted by Sir James Fullerton, 2d Jac., till we find the time about which he was knighted, pursuant to which I observe, *Imprimis*, by the letters patent (passed 5th November, 3d Jacobi, A°. 1605) to Mr. James Hamilton, who therein is named James Hamilton, Esq., and called by the King his servant. Our sixth Laird is styled Sir Hugh Montgomery, Knight, in which patent the letters to the said Deputy Chichester for passing it (dated 16th April foregoing), that Nov. is *in terminis* recited. Item, in a deed 1st October, that same year 1605, it appears that James Hamilton, Esq., servant to the King† (as aforesaid) pursuant to the first trust grants unto our said Laird (by the name of Sir Hugh Montgomery, knight, one of the Esqrs. of his Majesty's body,) the abbey lands of Movilla, &c., which is a prior date by a month and five days to the patent last named. This was so early done because abbey lands were first passed to James Hamilton, Esq., by patent, dated 20th July the said year, 1605, Sir Hugh Montgomery not being then come to Dublin, but in September yᵉ next month following, the said 20th July, notwithstanding all the expedition he and Con had made through Scotland, that they might look to their hits aforesaid.

M'Neale Oge, Knight, and Hugh O'Neale, and their heirs male aforesaid, that these our Letters Patent shall be firm, valid, good, and sufficient, and in law effectual, as regards us, our heirs and successors, as well in all our courts as elsewhere, without any other confirmations, licenses, or tolerations to be obtained from us, our heirs or successors, by the aforesaid Con or Hugh, or their heirs aforesaid, and notwithstanding bad naming or bad reciting, or non-reciting of the aforesaid Manor and other the premises, and notwithstanding any other defects in the right reciting or naming any of the premises above expressed or specified; And that without express mention, &c. In witness of which, &c. Examined by me,

"Robt. Legge, Deputy Remembrancer of the Queen.
"Rogᵃ. Wilbraham."

† The author of the Montgomery MSS. here repeats the expression, "Servant to the King as aforesaid," not as the description of Mr. Hamilton given in the deed to which he is referring, but manifestly as his own construction of the description of him given in the patent of 5th Nov., 1605, as to which he observes that "*Mr.* James Hamilton is therein named James Hamilton, *Esquire*, and

called by the King his servant," whilst "our 6th Laird is stiled Sir Hugh Montgomery, Knight." But it appears from the authorised translations of the patent of 1605, that the author of the Montgomery MSS. fell into a mistake in translating the description in the patent of "*servientem ad regem*" into "Servant to the King," instead of "King's Serjeant," a description which, it appears from Lodge, Mr. Hamilton was then entitled to: "After King James was settled upon the English throne, he made him his Serjeant-at-law; called him into his Privy Council, and liberally rewarded him."—3. *Lodge's Irish Peerage*, p. 1. Even, however, if the translation of "servant" by the author of the Montgomery MSS. were correct, it could not bear the construction of menial servant, nor could it have been used in any other sense than as the highest offices in the State are to this day said to be filled by "Her Majesty's servants;" or, as Sir Francis Bacon, in his constitutional argument, when Attorney-General, in a case *de rege inconsulto*, speaks of His Majesty's Counsel :—"For the King's Counsel, we are the King's poor servants, but yet we shall be able so to carry the King's business as it shall not die in our hands."—*Collectanea Juridica*, p. 126.

F

" Item, I observed by the tripartite indenture, dated ult⁰. April, 1605, aforesaid, that James Hamilton, Esq., was to bear equal share in the expenses of Con and his followers from the 1st of August preceding that indenture. This August was A⁰. 1604, which was 2d Jacobi, and was many months after Con was brought to Whitehall by our Laird, in all which time and till the said letters to the Deputy, dated the 16th April, 1605, our said Laird and his brother George, the Dean, had solicited Con's pardon, and the grant for half of his estate, the other moiety to the Laird himself, and obtained the King's letters of warrant to the Lord Deputy to pass letters patent conformably to the said articles of Braidstane. But this affair taking time, and wind, at Court, was interrupted by Sir James Fullerton, as you have already heard; and that therefore the said Con and Hugh Montgomery, of London, Esq., and James Hamilton, of London, Esq., adjusted affairs between themselves, so that it seems our Laird was knighted in April, 1605, or not long afterwards, but of Knights Bachelor no record is kept, so that for want thereof I must desist my enquiry.

" Item, we have heard also how that after the said overthrow given to the Laird and Con by Sir James Fullerton's procurement, a letter of warrant to the Lord Deputy, Arthur Lord Chichester, dated the 16th April, 1605, aforesaid, was granted to pass Con's estate, and some abbey lands, by patent, to James Hamilton, Esq., in his sole name, in trust for himself, our Laird, and Con, and that yᵉ last day of yᵉ said April yᵉ tripartite indenture was made between the said three persons.

" Now, to facilitate the performance thereof, Mr. Hamilton returned soon to Dublin with an order for an inquisition on the lands of the said Con, and on yᵉ abbey lands, which was held the 4th July, 1605, and being returned enrolled in Sept. next following, and wherein was a reference (for more certainty) unto the office taken 1st Jac. A⁰. 1603, and from which and the jurors' breefs the last above said inquisition did much vary, as hath been before now related. However, Mr. Hamilton, yᵉ 20th of yᵉ said July, passed letters patent in his own name, of the premises; and Sir Hugh Montgomery being arrived in Ireland, with Con, they went to Dublin as aforesaid, where, pursuant to the former said agreements, he did, 1st October next following (as is said), grant the lands of Movilla, Newton, and Grey Abbey, &c., to Sir H. Montgomery; then, on the 5th Nov., 1605, passed a more ample patent of Con's estate, and of all the abbey lands therein; and, pursuant to agreement with the said Con, Mr. Hamilton grants him his lands in and about Castlereagh, yᵉ very next day after the date of the said ample patent last above mentioned. So Con's whole affair being done for him, and he releasing Sir Hugh Montgomery and Mr Hamilton of all contracts and expenses relating thereunto, soon returned to Castlereagh, where I left him treated by his friends and followers as before herein briefly related. In this dispatch is seen Sir Hugh Montgomery's kindness to Con and himself.

" Observe further, as aforesaid, that the said Mr. Hamilton, on the 7th day of the said November, 1605, again grants to Sir Hugh Montgomery the lands of Newton, Grey Abbey, &c. This was done the next day after Mr. Hamilton had given the deed to Con. No doubt this dispatch pleased every of the three parties for their respective private reasons: Con being contented to the full for aught I find to the contrary, and Sir Hugh with whatever he go (de bene esse) in part for the presents, that they both might more closely follow the plantations they were bound to make, and therefore Sir Hugh also, after a small stay, returned from Dublin, and on the 15th January of the same year, 1605, livery of seizin of Con's lands was taken by Sir Cuthbert Montgomery, and given to Sir Hugh in trust for Con's use, and much about the same time livery of seizin was given to Sir Hugh, pursuant to the said deed, dated 7th of November aforesaid, Jo. Shaw and Patrick Montgomery, Esqrs., being appointed attornies by Mr. Hamilton to take and deliver the same accordingly.

" These few last rehearsals, being the sum of the chief transactions between Mr. Hamilton, trustee aforesaid, and Sir Hugh Montgomery and Con before, A⁰, 1616, I thought it necessary to be recapitulated before I proceed to other matters done between them after the 2d of August, 1606, on which day the said Con had sold to Sir Hugh Montgomery the woods of four town-lands as aforesaid, and then I will (as well as I can) give the narration of Sir Hugh promoting and advancing his plantation after the last-mentioned August. But first I must intimate two things, of which I shall not write hereafter: The first is that Mr. Hamilton and Sir Hugh were obliged in ten years time, from November, 1605, to furnish British inhabitants (English and Scotch Protestants) to plant one-third of Con's lands granted to himself. The second thing was that Mr. Hamilton passed another patent in February, 1605, which is posterior as you now see to that of the 5th November the same year, according to English account or supputation current in Ireland, by virtue of which patent in November now mentioned, it was that Mr. Hamilton gave the deeds aforesaid

·of the 6th and 7th of the same month, unto Con and Sir Hugh as is (herein) before-remarked.".—*Montgomery MSS., pp.* 25 to 45.

"I begin again with Sir H. Montgomery and Con O'Neill's further dealings together. The last I mentioned was Con's conveyance to Sir Hugh, dated 22d August, 4 Jacobi, of the woods growing on the four townlands. I find also, that, in pursuance of articles of the 24th December, 3d Jacobi, and of a former treat and covenant, and Sir Hugh's part to be performed, mentioned in Con's deed of feoffment, dated the 14th May, 3J Jacobi, (for Con made then such a deed poll, which was accepted, because of mutual confidence between them.) I say, pursuant to the premises, Sir Hugh made a deed of feoffment, dated 15th May, 1610, purporting a gift in taile to Con and his heirs male of all his own lands, excepting ten towns. And the same day Con releases to Sir Hugh all the articles and covenants he had on Sir Hugh; and releases also thereby, the said excepted ten towns, and this done in consideration of £35 paid in hand, and of £1000 sterling (formerly given, at several times, to yᵉ said Con), and now remitted by the said Sir Hugh.

"And so here I leave off to write of Con, but will relate some troubles which came upon Sir Hugh, but not so grievous as those which were occasioned by that killing dart, Sir James Fullerton, when he procured the letters to yᵉ Lord Deputy, with that clause, that yᵉ patent for Con's estate should pass in James Hamilton's name alone; but Sir Hugh's courage and conduct (at long run) cured in part that great hurt.

"The first succeeding troubles and costly toils which I read of after this last spoken of transaction with Con, which Sir Hugh met with, sprang from the petitions and claims of Sir Thomas Smith, against him and Sir James Hamilton; they began in April, 1610, and the 6th April, 1611, Sir Thomas gets an order of reference to the Commissioners for Irish affairs (of whom Sir James Hamilton was one) to make report of his case (for he claimed by grant from Queen Elizabeth, and the Commissioner judged it fitt to be left to law in Ireland). What he did pursuant to his report I know not, but on the 30th September, 1612, inquisition is taken, whereby Sir Thomas his title is found void and null, for breach and non-performance of articles and covenants to the Queen.—See Grand Office, folios 10 and 11.

"But it seems this was not all the trouble put upon Sir Hugh, for I find (folio 40 of Grand Office) he gave unto the Lord Deputy, Sir John, the King's letter, dated 20th July, 14th Regis, inhibiting any lands to be passed to any person whatsoever away from Sir Hugh Montgomery, to which he had claim by deed from James Hamilton or Con, and this *caveat* with a list of the lands he entered in the Secretary's office in Dublin.

"Between this [1613] and the year 1618, divers debates, controversys, and suits, were moved by Sir Hugh against Sir James Hamilton, which were seemingly taken away by an award made by the Right Honourable James Hamilton, Earle of Abercorn, to which both partys stood; in conformity to which award, and the King's letter relating thereunto, at least to the chief parts thereof, Sir James Hamilton conveys several lands to Sir Hugh Montgomery, and both of them in the deed are stiled Privy Counsellor; which deed bears date 23d May, 1618, George *Medensis*, and William Alexander, &c. subscribing witnesses. I presume this might be done at London, for much about this time Sir Hugh and his Lady lived there, and made up the match between their eldest son and Jean, the eldest daughter of Sir William Alexander, Secretary for Scotland, whom I take to be one of the witnesses in that great concern, by reason, the match aforesaid was about this time or some months afterwards completed.

"The produce of this marriage, which lived to come to age, was two sons and a daughter, which only survived that comely pair. The eldest left behind him two sons, now alive. One of which hath also two males living and life-like. And of the 1st Viscount's second and third sons, there are in good health two old Gentlemen, past their grand climacterick; and the eldest of them hath his son married above 11 years ago; of whose loins there are three male children, unsnatched away by death, and he may have more very probably. The other old Gentleman is father to two proper young Gentlemen, one lately married, and the other able to ly at that wedding-lock above four years past.

"Yet, for all our expectations, I neither can (nor will) divine how long these three families may last, seeing that neither the said Earle of Abercorn, nor heirs of his body (that I can learn) hath any children, only his brother's (the Lord of Strabane) offspring enjoy the title, either from his said father, or by a new creation of one of the two late Kings, the Stowards; and seeing, likewise, the 1st Viscount Clanneboy left but one son, who left two, who are both dead, without leaving any issue behind them, the more is the pity, for many reasons too well known, as by the records in Dublin doth appear. This consideration, on the duration of families, is to prevent overmuch care to raise posterity to grandeur.

"The said Sir Hugh had (no doubt) further troubles between the said year 1618 and 1623, because, at his chief instance and request, and for his greater security, the King granted a commission and order, directed unto Henry Lord Viscount Faulkland, Lord Deputy of Ireland, for holding an inquisition concerning the lands, spiritual and temporal, therein mentioned, which began to be held before Sir John Blennerhassett, Lord Chief Baron, at Downpatrick, the 13th October, 1623. This inquest is often cited, and is commonly called the Grand Office. Again, Sir Hugh (that he might be the more complete by sufferings) is assaulted by Sir William Smith, who strove to hinder the passing of the King's patent to him; on notice whereof, Sir Hugh writes a large well-penned letter (which I have) with instructions to his son James how to manage that affair. This is dated 23d February, 1623, about four months after the Grand Office was found. I have the original, every word written by himself. I should greatly admire at the exactness thereof, both in point of fact and law, but that so ingenious a person, and so long bred (by costly experience) to the law (as for 20 years before this Sir Hugh was used), could not want knowledge to direct his son to pass that ford which himself had wridden through.

"But to continue the troublesomeness of Sir Thomas Smith :—King James died Aº 1624, and on the 11th April, 1625, the Duke of Buckingham writes to the Judges to make report to him, in William Smith's and Sir James Hamilton's case, that he might inform the King thereof, which they did in the same manner as the Commissioners for Irish Affairs before had done (in Aº 1611) viz. :—That Smith should be left to the law in Ireland, and herein the said James Montgomery was agent, for I have a letter dated from Bangor, 4th November, 1625, to him, signed "J. Clanneboy" (who was then possessed of Killileagh), advising him to consult Sir James Fullerton, &c., in the business against Smith, for James Monotgmery was then going to Court about it, his father, some months or days before that time, being created Lord Viscount, for his patent was prior to the said Clanneboys, and so henceforth I must stile him the first Lord Viscount Montgomery.

"The 30th April, 1626, Sir William Smith, in a new petition, complains against the Viscount Montgomery, and prays orders to stop the letters patent to him for any lands; and obtained warrants of Council, dated May and June next following, requiring the said Lord Viscount to appear before some English Lords authorised to report their cases that both his Lordship and Smith might be heard; which orders were served on James Montgomery, as agent to his father; but the said agent being then Gentleman Usher of the Privy Chamber in Ordinary to King Charles, Hamilton petitioned his Majesty, setting forth that Sir Thomas and Sir William Smith's cases (both in the late King's time and in the beginning of his Majesty's reign) were adjudged to be left to the law in Ireland ;ˢ and that no stop was put to the passing the respective patents, in behalf of the Lord Chichester, the Lord Claneboys, or Foulk Conway. Thereupon, A.D. 1626, 2 Car., said Lord Montgomery's patent for his lands, conform to Abercorn's award, was ordered by the King to be passed, under the broad seal of Ireland, which bears date ————

"Moreover, to the Lord Montgomery further trouble arose. For I find there was a decree in Chancery the 12th December, 1626, touching underwoods and timber; whereby the Lord Montgomery was to have those growing it, Slutevils and Castlereagh, as should be awarded or recovered from Francis Hill, Esq. So the reader may observe, than from the date of the tripartite indenture, ulto. April, 3d Jac. Aº. 1605, till December, 1633, there arose many difficulties between Sir James Hamilton and Sir Hugh Montgomery (Viscount 1623), occasioned by that ominous and fatal interposition of Sir James Fullerton aforesaid, and chiefly by the clause he procured to be inserted in the letter of warrant, dated April, 3d Jac. Ano. 1605, whereby Mr. Hamilton was nominated as the only person in whose name alone the letters patent for Con's estate and the abbey lands in Upper Claneboy, and the great Ardes were to be remembered.

ˢ It will be seen by extracts from a rare and curious Life of Sir Thomas Smith, printed at the end of this Appendix, that his descendants continued to press their claim to the Great Ardes down to the reign of Charles II. when a similar order was made upon it.

" Yet, in all my reach of papers and enquiry of knowing more, I cannot find or hear what became of Sir James Fullerton, or of his posterity, or whether he died childless, there being none of that sirname (that I can learn) in Scotland, above the degree of a gentleman, only I read in Bishop Ussher's life, that he lies in St. Erasmus' Chapel, where that Primate was buried.[h]

" There arose also difficulties (after December, 1633) between the first and second Viscount Mont'gomerys, plaintiff, and the Lord Claneboys, defendant, concerning the articles of agreement made 17th December, 1633, not being fully performed to the Lord Montgomery *(ut dicitur)*, which ended not till the rebellion in Ireland began 1641, verifying the Latin adage, *Inter Arma Silent Leges.*—So I find that many are the troubles of the righteous, but the Lord delivereth them out of them all.

" All which differences sirceasing that last-named year, and so were sedated, or buried, or forgotten, that they were never stirred up again, I shall therefore leave no memory of the Montgomerys' losses therein by mentioning them either by word or writing, because of the love and kind deference now among us all Montgomerys and the Hamiltons of that family."—*Ibid. pp.* 56 to 64.

[Extracts from "The Life of the Learned Sir Thomas Smith, Knight, Doctor of the Civil Law, Principal Secretary of State to King Edward the Sixth, and Queen Elizabeth," published in London, An. 1698, referred to at p. 24, *ante*, note g.]

" Anno 1572.—This year Sir *Thomas* procured a colony, to be sent unto a land of his in Ireland, called The Ardes. It was a rich and pleasant country, on the Eastern coast of Ulster, of considerable extent, lying well for trade by sea ; bordering upon a country where *Sorleboy* contained himself with his party. He was an Hebridian Scot (the Hebrides bordering upon this province), a long time detained prisoner by *Shon O'Neal*, the chief Prince of Ulster. This country was called Clandeboy, where these Scots lived; but they were beaten out once by this *Shan*, who called himself Earl of *Tir Oen*, and had killed two of the brethren of *Mac Conel*, of which family was *Sorleboy*, whom he

---

h In Dr. Elrington's Life of Archbishop Ussher, the following statement occurs, in the description of the Archbishop's funeral, p. 279 :—" The body was deposited in St. Erasmus' Chapel, next to the tomb of Sir James Fullerton, his early instructor ;" and a lately-published " Panorama of London," containing the description of Westminster Abbey, under the head of " Chapel of St. Paul," has the following passage :—" On an ancient table-monument are the effigies of Sir James Fullerton and his lady." On reference, also, to the Patent Rolls of Ireland, the following grants to him of lands and franchises are thus recorded :—1. Jac. I. xiv. 9.—Grant from the King to James Fullerton, Gent., of lands in the Counties of Westmeath, Tipperary, Waterford, and Sligo. 1. Jac. I. xv. 11.—Same to same. Grant of lands in Donegal. 1. Jac. I. xvi. 11.—

Same to same. Grant of lands, &c., in the City of Dublin, and in the Counties of Westmeath, Roscommon, Kerry, Dublin, Kilkenny, Kildare, Antrim, Queen's, and Cork; and in 2 Jac. I. a grant from the King to Sir James Fullerton, to hold a weekly Saturday market and two fairs at Sligo, with a Court of pye poudre and the usual tolls. He is named, also, as Sir James Fullerton, M.M.G., one of the Commissioners of the Court of Wards and Liveries, in the years 1606 and 1609, with the then Lord Deputy, Sir Arthur Chichester, and others. And, in the year 1616, he was nominated by Sir James Hamilton, with his wife and his faithful friend, the then Earl of Abercorn, as one of the executors of his will, which bears date on the 10th of December in that year, and will be hereafter referred to.

then had taken prisoner, but afterwards in an extremity gave him his liberty. This *Shan* was afterwards, in a revenge, slain by *Sarleboy* and his party.

"Sir *Thomas*, in the year 1571, had procured a patent from her Majesty for these *Ardes*, the substance whereof was, that Sir *Thomas* was to be Lieutenant-General there for War, and for the distribution of lands, orders, and laws in the matters thereunto pertaining. In a word, to obtain and govern the country to be won, following instructions and orders to him to be directed from the Queen and her Council. And this for the first seven years. Afterwards, the Government of the country to return to such officers as the customs and laws of England did appoint, except the Queen should think him worthy to be appointed the Governour thereof, as being a frontier country. The right to remain only in him, as to the inheritance, the authority to muster and call together his soldiers throughout the same country, and to dispose of them upon the frontiers as he should see cause for the better defence of the country.

"In this patent, his base and only son, *Thomas Smith*, was joined with him And, under his conduct, Sir Thomas this year sent thither the colony beforesaid, having this good design therein, that those half-barbarous people might be taught some civility. And his hope was, that the place might be easily defended by garrisons placed in a strait neck of land, by which it was joined to the rest of the island. And there was a reward of land to every footman and horseman. But this extensive project took not its desired effect, for the hopeful gentleman and his son had not been long there, but he was unhappily and treacherously slain. It was pity it had no better issue. For Sir *Thomas* a great while had set his thoughts upon it, undertaking to people that north part of the island with natives of this nation.

"But for his more regular and convenient doing of it, and continuance thereof, he invented divers rules and orders. The orders were of two kinds:—1st. For the management of the wars against the rebels, and the preserving the colony continually from the dangers of them.—2nd. For the civil government.

"To preserve their home manners, laws, and customs, that they degenerated not into the rudeness and barbarity of that country, he divided his discourse into three parts. First, to speak of wars, and therein of military officers to be used there. Secondly, concerning laws for the politick government of the country to be possest, for the preservation of it. Thirdly, in what orders to proceed in this journey, from the beginning to the end, which Sir *Thomas* called *a noble enterprize, and a Godly voyage*.

"His son being now with his colony upon the place, proceeded commendably in order to the reduction of it. He was in a good forwardness of reducing *Sarleboy* to obedience, for they had much converse together, and came at length to articles of agreement, the main of which was that he should be made a denizen of *England* by the Queen, and hold his land of her and him, and the same privilege should the rest of his *Scots* enjoy, paying to the Queen a yearly rent in acknowledgment, and he to become homager to her by oath, and so to be a faithful subject, or else lose his right. Mr. *Smith* also began a new fort in this country.[1] He laboured also to unite the *English* and *Scots* that were there, who did not, it seems, very well agree, that their strength being united, they might be the more able to withstand the wild *Irish*. And this the *Scots* were for promoting, as, considering that if the *English* and they should strive together, when the one had weakened the other, the wild Irish, like the Puthawk (it was Sir *Thomas*' own similitude), might drive them out, or carry away both.

"Besides the pains Sir *Thomas* had already taken for the settlement of the *Ardes*, he drew up this year instructions to be sent from the Queen to his son, containing directions upon what terms *Sarleboy* and his followers should hold their lands from her Majesty and him. Likewise he drew up a draught for explaining certain words doubtful in the indentures between the Queen and him, and his son; as about his son's soldiers, if they should marry in that country, as it was likely they would, the Secretary entreated the Lord Treasurer to steal a little leisure to look these writings over, and correct them, so that he might make them ready for the Queen's signing; and this, he hoped, when once dispatched, might be as good to his son as five hundred *Irish* soldiers.

---

[1] Called Newcastle, standing boldly over the sea on a neck of land, three miles east of Portaferry.—*Harris's History of County Down*, p. 67.

"At Mr. *Smith's* first coming hither, he found some few that claimed themselves descended of *English* blood, namely, the family of the *Smiths*, and the *Savages*, and two surnames more. And these presently joyned with the *English*, and combined with them against the wild *Irish*. But all the rest were mere *Irish*, or *Irish Scots*, and natural haters of the *English*.

" The Queen had a force of men in those parts for necessary defence. and for the keeping of *Knockfergus*, a very important place for curbing the *Irish*. But to retrench her charge in *Ireland*, she was minded now to discharge them as she had done some already, expecting that *Smith* would secure those quarters, nor would she grant any foot or horse to him. Sir *Thomas*, therefore, in February, interceded with her by the means of the Lord Treasurer, that at least for that year she would suffer those bands to be there, to countenance and support the new begun aid and Fort, and not to leave it so naked as it had been, it seems, all that winter, by losing those bands that were heretofore the defence of *Knockfergus*, and the bar of the North. And he told the Lord Treasurer upon this occasion that it was certain, if his son had not retrieved a band of the Lord of *Harvey's* at his own charge, *Knockfergus* had been in great danger, or else lost.

" But while these matters thus fairly and hopefully went on, Mr. *Smith* was intercepted and slain by a wild Irishman ; yet Sir *Thomas* did not wholly desist, but carried on the colony, and procured more force to pass over there, for in *March, anno exeunte* (his son being but newly, if yet, dead), there were *Harrington*, *Clark*, and some others, adventurers on this design, that gave certain sums of money for lands there to be assured to them. In the beginning of March, 1572, the ships, captains, and soldiers were ready to be wafted over, unhappily some persons concerned had started some new matter in regard to the bargain, which put a stop to their departure, and one *Edward Higgins*, the chief of the gentlemen and captains that were going over, and forward in this generous expedition, was hindered for want of the money agreed upon. Hence it came to pass that the captains lay at great charges, when their ships, mariners, and soldiers were ready, and they did nothing but dispend their money. This troubled Sir *Thomas* not a little, as appears by a letter he wrote to one Mrs. *Penne*, a gentlewoman that had an influence upon some of these persons that made the stop, to whom, therefore, Sir *Thomas* applied himself, praying her to call upon them to consider at what charge the captains did lie, and to do what she could in any wise to help them away, whereby she should do the Queen's Majesty good service, and him and them great pleasure. It being a matter, said he, in which, indeed, for the goodness of it, I take much to heart. This was writ from *Greenwich* the 6th of March.

" This case the Secretary continued. For a year or two after I find him drawing out other passports and licenses for transportation of victuals for certain that went to the *Ardes*, and expressing himself then to a friend that it stood him upon, both in profit and honesty. not to let the present month pass, which was *May, An.* 1574. And so, during his life, Sir *Thomas* laboured in the civilizing and settlement of this his colony. But upon his death it seems to have been neglected for some time. And tho' the family and heirs of Sir *Thomas*, who are extant to this day, have often claimed their interest in this land, which their ancestors did so dearly purchase and well deserve, yet they enjoy not a foot of it at present.

" For as I have been informed by some of that worshipful family, Sir *William Smith*, nephew and heir to one Sir *Thomas Smith*, was merely tricked out of it by the knavery of a *Scot*, one *Hamilton* (who was once a schoolmaster, though afterwards made a person of honour), with whom the said Sir *William* was acquainted. Upon the first coming in of King *James* 1st, he minded to get these lands confirmed to him by that King, which had cost Sir *Thomas* (besides the death of his only son) £10,000, being to go into Spain with the *English* Ambassador, left this *Hamilton* to solicit this his cause at Court, and get it despatched. But Sir *William* being gone, *Hamilton* discovered the matter to some others of the *Scotch* nobility, and he and some of them begged it of the King for themselves, pretending that it was too much for any one subject to enjoy. And this *Hamilton* did craftily, thinking that if he should have begged it all for himself he might, perhaps, have failed of success, being so great a thing, but that he might well enjoy a part, especially with the concurrence and interest of some of the powerful men about the King, when they begged for themselves. And never after could Sir *William Smith* nor any of his posterity recover it. For the premises had been so long possest by others, that neither Sir *Thomas Smith*, who had suffered much for his unshaken loyalty to King *Charles* 1st, had success in his petition preferred to King *Charles* 2d upon his return, nor yet Sir *Edward Smith*, still surviving, in his, upon the late revolution. He that is minded to know more at large how this case stood, may in the *appendix* find the petition of the present Sir *Thomas Smith* exemplified, as it was humanely communicated to me by his son, together with the King's order thereupon.—*Life of Sir Thomas Smith, pp.* 176 *to* 183.

---

* The following is a copy of the memorial, as given in the appendix to Sir Thomas Smith's life:—

" To THE KING'S MOST EXCELLENT MAJESTY.—The humble petition of Thomas Smith, Esquire, uncle and heir of Edward Smith, Esquire, deceased, son and heir of Sir William Smith the younger ; and heir of Sir William Smith the elder ; who was nephew and heir of Sir Thomas Smith, Knight, deceased, sheweth :—

" That the said Sir Thomas Smith, the Petitioner's ancestor, had the honour to serve as Secretary of State to your Majesty's most noble Progenitor, Queen Elizabeth, of happy memory, and served her in that employment many years. And in the 13th year of her reign, the said late Queen did make a grant of Letters Patent under the great seal, to the said Sir Thomas Smith and Thomas his then son and heir apparent, of divers Manors, Castles, and Lands thereto belonging, in the County of Downe, in the realm of Ireland, which were then possest by divers persons, who were in actual rebellion against Her Highness, with command that the said Sir Thomas Smith should enter upon the parts infested by the said rebels, and by power of arms obtain the same from them.

" And the said Sir Thomas Smith did at his great charge raise an army, and entered those parts and gained them unto their due obedience. In which said service the said Thomas his son was slain. And then the said Sir Thomas Smith assigned the said Sir William Smith, his nephew, to take the charge of prosecution of that war, and came over to England to attend the further service of Her Majesty, and to solicit Her Majesty that the lands might be surveyed, and the rents ascertained, and his grant and title perfected. And her Majesty taking notice of such the great service of the said Sir Thomas Smith was pleased several times graciously to declare that her royal intentions to the said Sir Thomas should be made good. But, by reason of the many great troubles falling out in her time, the same was not done during all the time of her Reign. And afterwards the said Sir William Smith, the elder was commanded by the said Queen upon service into Spain. And upon his departure out of England, he desired Sir James Hamilton, Knight, to prosecute his grant on the said Sir William's behalf, and procure the same for him, and the said Sir James Hamilton, in the time of your noble grandfather, King James, upon some undue pretences, contrary to the trust in him reposed by the said Sir William Smith, obtained the said lands to be granted to himself upon pretences of a valuable consideration paid, which in truth was

never paid. But, in truth, according to the intention of the late Queen, the said lands are the right of your Petitioner.

" That Sir William Smith died about 40 years since, and Sir Willim, his son and heir, since died, and left his son and heir an infant of two years old ; and until he came at age nothing could be done, and the troublesome times happening since his death, the petitioner and his ancestors have sit down by the loss ; yet your petitioner hopeth that the long discontinuance shall not be a bar to his just right :

" But humbly prayeth your Majesty to cause an examination of the premises to be made, and certified to your Majesty ; and then the petitioner hopes that when the truth of the fact shall appear, your Majesty will be graciously pleased to do therein for the petitioner's relief what shall be agreeable to justice, and your petitioner shall, &c.

" At the Court of Whitehal, 14th Nov., 1660.

" His Majesty is pleased to refer this petition to the Right Honourable Sir Maurice Eustace, Lord Chancellor of Ireland, who, having examined and considered the contents and allegations of this petition, is to certific his Majesty how he findeth the same, and what his Lordship conceiveth to be just and fit for his Majesty to do therein, and then his Majesty will declare his further pleasure.

"EDW. NICHOLAS."

" Sir Maurice Eustace, his certificate :—

" IT MAY PLEASE YOUR EXCELLENT MAJESTY,—I have, according to your Majesty's gracious reference, considered the petition of Thomas Smith, Esquire, And, considering that the petitioner doth ground his title upon a patent made 13th Elizabeth to his ancestors, and that the said title has been very much controverted, and the possession gone for a long time against the petitioner, and some descents cast, I humbly conceive that it is neither fit nor convenient for your Majesty to determine this cause upon a paper petition. But your Majesty, in regard your Courts of Justice in Ireland will be soon open, may be pleased to have all parties pretending interest in the said lands to your Majesty's Courts of Justice in that your Kingdom, to be proceeded in as they shall be advised by their counsel. And the rather, for that the Earl of Clanbrazil, who is interested in the said lands by descent from his father, is a minor, and under years, and cannot be concluded by any order which can be made against him during his minority, all which is humbly submitted to you Majesty's judgment.

" MAURICE EUSTACE, Canc."

CHAP. III..

OF THE MARRIAGES, DEATH, PROGENY,　　*　*　　CHARACTER, WITH OBSERVATIONS.

The Lord Claneboy had three ladies,*　　*　*　*　*　*　*　*

*　The last, lady Jane Phillips, proved a very excellent lady for solid piety and virtue ; bore to him one son called James, afterwards Earl of Clanbrassill. My lord lived to a great age, viz., 84, or thereabouts, in great prosperity and honour, through God's blessing upon his wisdom and industry. Of him are these remarkables :—1st. His two first ladies proved but little comfortable to him, and his putting away of his second lady was not with general satisfaction to his friends and contemporaries. 2nd. He had much ado to keep himself　*　in King James's time, and was once at the point of ruin as to the King's esteem;[b] and, in Wentworth's time, he had much ado to keep himself from　*　and ruin. He made great use (as some of his best friends conceived) of a public gout and gravel, that

---

* The first was Penelope Cooke. The second was Ursula, sixth daughter of Edward, first Lord Brabazon of Ardee, and sister of William, first Earl of Meath, from whom he was divorced, and who died in 1625. The third (mentioned in the text as Lady Jane Phillips) was Jane, daughter of Sir John Phillips, Bart., of Picton Castle, in Pembrokeshire, who survived him, and was mother of his only son, James Hamilton. The two latter only are mentioned in Lodge.

[b] The following document, in Sir James Hamilton's handwriting, which has been found among the family papers, and is endorsed thus, "The directions of the Lord Deputie to me, Sir J. H.," has no doubt reference to the above passages in the text:—
"12 Octob., 1618.—The patents past to Sr James Hamilton upon Thomas Ireland's letter:—
1.—Patent dat. 20 July, anno 3, Jacobi Regis, of the manor of Moygare and other lands, &c.
2.—Patent dat. 14 Febr., anno 3, Jacobi Regis, of lands in the countie of Antrim, &c.
3.—Patent dat. 13 Martis, anno 3, Jacobi Regis, of rents of assize in Trym and others.
4.—Patent dat. 17 Martis, anno 3, Jacobi Regis, of the Castle of Moybore, in Westmeath, and other lands, &c.
5.—Patent dat. 13 May, anno 6, Jacobi Regis, of certaine lands in the countie of Wexford and others, &c.

"The patents past upon John Wakeman's letter:—
A patent, dat. ulto. Febr. anno primo Jacobi Regis.
A patent dat. 2 Martis, anno 3, Jacobi Regis, of the fishing of the Ban, &c.
A patent dat. 11 Aprilis, anno 4, Jacobi Regis, of the Customes.
A patent past to Sr James Hamilton and Sr James Carroll, Knights, assignees to John Wakeman, dat. 23 Febr: anno 6, Jacobi Regis, of St. Marie Abay.

A patent dat. 5 Novembris, anno 3, Jacobi Regis, of Con O'Neil's lands by special letter.
The last patent past of the Customes aforesaid upon another letter, the date whereof, viz., of which patent, is about the 9 Jacobi Regis, which you may see in the enrolment of the Chancery.

"His Majesty's pleasure is, that you, Sir James Hamilton, Knight, shall exhibit to the Lor: Deputie the principall of the Letters Patent aforesaid.
"His Majesty's further pleasure is, that you, Sir James Hamilton, Knight, shall also exhibit to the said Lord Deputie all such other writtes as concern the premises."

"13th October, 1618.
"May it please your Lp.—Being yesterday commanded by you to writ verbatim what is above written, and to receive the same as a direction to myself without your hands thereunto, and your Lp. &c., also intimating unto me verbally the secrett carriage thereof, I have entered into due consideration of the premisses, and do ingennouslie professe that I understand not the extent of the severall words following, viz.:—
"First—' The principall of the Letters Patents aforesaid.' —Whether your Lp. &c., mean any one principall or chief Letters Patents of all the rest, and which that is; or whether you mean all the originall Letters Patents particularlie above mentioned, or what els ?
"Secondly—' All such other writtes as concern the premisses.'—Whether your Lp. &c., mean his Majesty's letters or warrants for the passing of that and principall or chief Letters Patents, or the warrants and letters for the passing of all those Letters Patents, or any conveyances thereout deryved, or counterpt, thereof, or els all my evidences whatsoever, or what els ?
"Thirdly—Whether by the word exhibit your Lp. mean that I should deliver unto you the Lord Deputie the said Letters Patents, or other my evidences to be perused in myn own presence, and so to be delivered back again to me,

H

he might hide himself in his house-gown. 3d. He had several tedious and chargeable law-suits with his neighbour, my Lord of Ards, about   *   of land and other trifles, wherein pride and in-

---

or what els to yon mean by the word exhibit? In these particulars I humbly crave your Lp's explanation in writing, that I may be the better enabled to make your Lp a dutiful answer as becometh me, these being matters wᶜʰ do concern my estate, and I am confident it will stand with his Maᵗʸ pleasure that I should recrave plain and clear direction in that which I have commanded me in his name, which I do as much revere as any subject living can do.
"J. H."

In 1622, an information at suit of the crown, in the name of Sir Wm. Ryves, Knight, his Majesty's then Attorney General, was filed on the Revenue side of the Exchequer against Viscount Claneboy, charging him with having usurped all the liberties and franchises, granted to him by his several patents, within the Great Ards, Upper Clandeboy, and Dufferin; but it appears, by the record of that information on the Communia Roll of the Exchequer, that Viscount Claneboy, on pleading his patent, obtained judgment against the Crown. It also appears by the following extract from the Communia Roll of Easter Term, 1639, that during Strafford's Viceroyalty a fresh information was filed at suit of the Crown in the Exchequer, against Viscount Claneboy, and that he again obtained judgment against the Crown for his claim to Bangor as a sea-port, which was one of the franchises mentioned in the information of 1622, and for which he then had judgment; but the Crown obtained judgment for the Court of Admiralty at Groom-port, alleged by the quo warranto to be claimed by Viscount Claneboy, but which by his plea he disclaim'd :—

" County of Down.—Sir Richard Osbaldeston, the Attorney General, informs the Court that James Viscount Claneboy for the space of divers years past has used, and still us s, and claims to have, use, and enjoy without warrant or Royal Grant the office of Admiralty, of all things to the Admiralty pertaining, in and within the manor of Groomesports, in the county aforesaid, and the liberties, precincts and creeks of the same; also the power of holding a Court of Admiralty there, and to do, determine, and execute all things in the same which to a Court of Admiralty pertains; and that neither the Admiral of the said Lord the King, his heirs or succeʳˢ of England, or their Lieutenant, nor any other Deputy or minister should in any manner intermeddle, or either of them intermeddle, in the manor aforesaid, or the liberties, precincts, or creeks of the same either by land or by water, for any execution of office there; and that he may have, hold, receive, seize, and enjoy, and may be well and able to have, hold, receive, seize, and enjoy for ever, to his proper use and behoof, all and singular profits, fines, issues, forfeitures, perquisites, commodities, and emoluments, from and out of the aforesaid Court, or by reason of the execution of the office of Admiralty aforesaid, in whatsoever manner, arising, growing, or emerging, without account or any other thing therefor, to the said Lord the King, his heirs or successors, to be rendered or paid. The aforesaid James Visᵗ. Claneboy claims also, that there may be a Sea Port in, and upon, and near, the sea, nigh to, and at the town of, Bangor, in the county aforesaid; and that the aforesaid Port my be named, called, and deemed, the Port of the town of Bangor; and that the creeks of Gillegroomes and Holliwood may be and be accounted members of the same Port of Bangor, aforesaid; and that it may be a port for the plying, arrival, and stationing of ships and boats, and for the loading and (unloading) of all and all manner of goods, merchandize, and wares whatsoever, as well to be imported as exported, with all and singular the rights, members, jurisdictions, free customs, and priviliges, to a Port belonging, due, or to be due; and, that the aforesaid Port, roadsteads, and creeks, aforesaid, should belong to the aforesaid James Visct. Claneboy, his heirs and assigns; and, that he, the aforesaid Viscount, his heirs and assigns, from time to time, may have, enjoy, and take to his and their proper use and behoof, all and singular plankage, anchorage, wharfage, cranage, fees, and profits, due or payable of and for all or any ships, skiffs, boats and barges, in the aforesaid port or roadstead, or creeks aforesaid, or either of them, plying, anchored, laden, or to be unladen, upon the wharfs, banks, or soil, of the aforesaid James Viscount Claneboy, his heirs or assigns, without account, or any other thing therefor, to the said Lord the King, his heirs or succeʳˢ, to be rendered, paid, or made; all the which liberties, franchizes, and privileges the aforesᵈ. James Visᵗ. Claneboy, for the whole time aforesaid, upon the said Lord, the now King, has usurped. &c. The Defendant being summoned, appears by his attorney, Anthony Dopping, and pleads Letters Patent, under the great seal of England, bearing date at Westminster, Co. Middlesex, the 14th of March, 19th of James the 1st., produced in Court, whereby the King granted to the Defendᵗ. the town of Bangor, in the county of Down, for ever; and the King by the same letters patent, willed, ordained, and constituted, that thenceforth for ever, there might, and should be, a Sea Port in, and upon, and near the sea, nigh to and at the aforesaid town of Bangor, and that the aforesᵈ. Port should and might be, named, called, and deemed, the Port of the town of Bangor; and that the roads or creeks of Gillegroomes and Holliwood, in the county of Down, aforesaid, might and should be accounted members of the same Port of Bangor, aforesaid; and the aforesaid Lord the late King, made, erected, created, and established the aforesᵈ. Port of Bangor, with the members aforesaid, one Sea Port aforesaid, by his said letters patent; and that it might be a port for the plying, arrival, and stationing of ships and boats, and for the loading, and unloading of all manner of goods merchandize and wares whatsoever, as well to be imported as exported, in time thenceforward, into any the ports of the said kingdom of Ireland, by the laws and statutes of the Kingdom aforesaid; with all and singular the rights, members, jurisdictions

cendiaries occasion great expense of money and peace ; and one (in some respects) worse than all, with his brother William's widow, yet outlived them. 4th. He made a great use of the services of his brethren and nephews as they came upon the stages, as also of some other very fine gentlemen he kept about him for business (wherein he was most exact and laborious), but reserved the bulk of rewards to his latter will (which proved too late for them), and thereby obliged them to dependance on him all his life; but it was believed he intended liberal rewards for all, especially his brethren and their families, but his will[c] was either not finished, or suppressed after his death, I shall not say by whom, only it fell so out, that as he outlived all his brethren, so his nephews were all abroad at the wars, and inferior servants ruled that part. 5th. As he was very learned, wise, laborious, noble (especially to strangers and scholars), so there is great ground to judge he was truly pious, as he was certainly well principled. It is true he countenanced the Episcopal course, yea, outwardly, the persecutions of that time that were against the godly (called then puritans) by the Black Oath,[d] &c.; yet, 1. His

---

free customs, and privileges to a Port belonging, due and to be due ; and the aforesaid late King, by the said letters patent, gave and granted the Port aforesaid, with the members aforesaid, and the aforesd. roads and creeks aforesaid, to the aforesaid James Hamilton, Knt., Visct. Claneboy, by the name of Sir James Hamilton, Knt, his heirs and assigns, for ever ; and the aforesaid James, the late King, by his aforesaid letters patent gave and granted that the aforesaid James Hamilton, Visct, of Claneboy, by the name of Sir James Hamilton, Knight, his heirs and assigns, might, and might be able to have, enjoy, and receive, all and singular plankage, anchorage wharfage, cranage, and the fees and profits, due or payable of and for all or any ships, skiffs, boats, and barges, in the aforesaid Port, or roads, or creeks aforesaid, or either of them, plying, anchoring, laden, or to be laden, upon the wharfs, banks, or soil [wharfus, ripas, aut solum,] of the aforesaid James Hamilton, Visct. Claneboy, by the name aforesaid, his heirs or assigns, without account or any other thing therefor, to the said late King, his heirs or successors in any manner to be rendered paid or made, saving to the said late King, his heirs or successors, the impositions of wine and of other merchandize, and the subsidies and customs for the same, due and accustomed : And by this warrant the Defendant has used and still uses, the liberties, privileges, and franchises, in the plea mentioned ; but as to having and exercising the office of Admiralty, and of determining, doing, and executing, all things to an Admiralty Court pertaining, within the manor of Groomesport, and taking the issues and profits of an Admiralty Court, as supposed by the information, he disclaims the same. Absque hoc, &c. The Attorney General prays judgment for the said Court of Admiralty, and having viewed the Letters Patent in defts' plea pleaded, confesses the plea to be true, and says he will no further prosecute ; and judgment is given for the Crown, quoad the Court of Admiralty, &c., at Groomesporte, and for the defendant as to the remainder of the privileges."

c A copy of this remarkable document will be found in the Appendix to this chapter.

d Dr. Reid, in the first volume of his History of the Presbyterian Church in Ireland, pp. 242 to 248, gives the following account of the origin and imposition of this obnoxious oath :—

"Wentworth, in pursuance of his precautionary plans for preventing the Scots in Ulster from joining in the Covenant, or opposing, in any way, the designs of the king, had recourse to an expedient more illegal in its character, and more oppressive in its effects, than any which he had yet adopted. This was the imposition, on all the Northern Scots, of an oath, styled, from the dismal calamities which it occasioned, THE BLACK OATH, in which they were compelled to swear never to oppose any of the king's commands, and to abjure all covenants and oaths, contrary to the tenor of this unconditional engagement. The first idea of this measure originated with Charles. In the month of January, 1638, he suggested it to Wentworth as likely to furnish an additional security to his cause in Ulster, against the apprehended machinations of the Scottish Covenanters. The deputy approved of the plan, and thus wrote to Charles for instructions :—'In case any Scottish refuse to take the oath of abjuration, what is your pleasure we should do with them ? Shall we, lege talionis, here, as there, imprison the parties delinquent, and seize their lands and holdings to your Majesty for the use of the public ?' Shortly after, he summoned several of the Scottish noblemen, clergy, and gentry, on whose cordial co-operation he could rely, to meet him in Dublin on business, as he alleged, of especial importance to his Majesty's service. When assembled in the latter end of April, in the apartments of the Lord Viscount Ards, Wentworth opened to them his design. He apprised them of the disorders which had occurred in Scotland; of the surmises entertained of the Scots in

younger education seasoned him well; 2. He was observedly a great studier of the Scripture and

---

Ulster favouring these seditious proceedings; and of the propriety of their vindicating themselves from such injurious suspicions. He concluded by reminding them how much more acceptable and becoming it would be for them to enter into a voluntary declaration of their fidelity and obedience to the king, than delay the tender of their loyalty, till extorted from them by the increasing dangers of the State. This suggestion of the deputy was hailed with acclamations by the bishops who were present. It was not opposed by the noblemen and other gentlemen, who appear to have been very passive instruments in the hands of Wentworth and the prelates. The Bishop of Raphoe immediately framed a petition to the deputy and council, in the name of the Ulster Scots, praying to be permitted, by oath or otherwise, to vindicate themselves from approving the proceedings of their countrymen in Scotland. This petition was in due form presented to the Council. It was signed by Hamilton, Lord Claneboy, and Montgomery, Lord of Ards; by the Bishops of Clogher, Raphoe, and Down; by the Archdeacons of Armagh and Down; by ten knights, and by twenty-four individuals, the majority of whom were clergymen. The form of the intended oath was submitted by the council to the consideration of the petitioners. Objections were made, by some of the laymen present, to the unconditional manner in which they were required to swear never to oppose, nor even to 'protest against any of his Royal commands.' They entreated that the qualifying phrase of 'just commands,' or 'commands according to law,' might be inserted,' but Wentworth would admit of no alteration, and they silently, though reluctantly, acquiesced. As a rebuke to their scrupulosity, the Bishop of Raphoe lamented that that part of the oath which appeared so obnoxious had not been rendered more strong and explicit; and, in a spirit of affected disappointment at the moderation with which the doctrine of passive obedience and non-resistance was expressed therein, he exclaimed, 'that the oath was so mean, he would not come from his house to take it.' The following is a copy of this celebrated oath, as set forth in the proclamation :—' I,——do faithfully swear, profess, and promise, that I will honour and obey my sovereign lord King Charles, and will bear faith and true allegiance unto him, and defend and maintain his Royal power and authority, and that I will not bear arms, or do any rebellious or hostile act against him, or protest against any of his Royal commands, but submit myself in all due obedience thereunto; and that I will not enter into any covenant, oath, or bond of mutual defence and assistance against all sorts of persons whatsoever, or into any covenant, oath, or bond of mutual defence and assistance against any persons whatsoever by force, without his Majesty's sovereign and regal authority. And I do renounce and abjure all covenants, oaths, and bands whatsoever, contrary to what I have herein sworn, professed, and promised. So help me God, in Christ Jesus.' By a proclamation from the deputy and council, dated the twenty-first of May, 1639, and containing a copy of the petition, all the Scottish residents in Ulster above the age of sixteen years, were required to take this oath, 'upon the holy

evangelists, and that upon pain of his Majesty's high displeasure, and the uttermost and most severe punishments which may be inflicted, according to the laws of this realm, on contemners of sovereign authority.' The commissioners were directed to proceed in the most summary manner. The ministers and churchwardens were required to make a return of all the Scots resident in their respective parishes. The oath was publicly read by the commissioners, and then taken by the people on their knees; but from the persons called on to swear, the privilege of a deliberate perusal of it for themselves was studiously withheld. It was imposed equally on women as on men. The only exception made, was in favour of those Scots who professed to be Roman Catholics; these alone were not required to take the oath. The names of those who scrupled to swear were immediately forwarded to Dublin, whence the deputy dispatched his officers to execute his pleasure on the recusants. Contrary to his expectations, great numbers refused to take the oath in the unqualified form in which it was proposed. None of them had the least hesitation to swear in the terms of the former part, expressive of bearing true and faithful allegiance to his Majesty. But they conscientiously and firmly refused to take the latter part, by which they would have been bound to yield an unconditional obedience to all his Royal commands, whether civil or religious—just or unjust—constitutional or unconstitutional. On these individuals the highest penalties of the law, short of death, were unsparingly inflicted, frequently under circumstances of extreme cruelty. Thus, pregnant women were forced to travel considerable distances to the places appointed by the commissioners. If they hesitated to attend, and still more, if they scrupled to swear, they were treated in a barbarous manner; so that crowds of defenceless females fled to the woods, and concealed themselves in caves, to escape their merciless persecutors. Respectable persons, untainted with crime, were bound together with chains, and immured in dungeons. Several were dragged to Dublin, and fined in exorbitant sums; while multitudes fled to Scotland, leaving their houses and properties to certain ruin; and so many of the labouring population abandoned the country, that it was scarcely possible to carry forward the necessary work of the harvest."

The following letters, addressed to Wentworth by Lord Claneboy on this subject, are published in the second volume of Strafford's Letters, pp. 382 to 385:—

"THE LORD VISCOUNT CLANEBOYE TO THE LORD DEPUTY.

"My much observed Lord,

"May it please your Lordship to know, that the master of the ordnance, when he had his meeting at Bangor, with the lord Montgomery, lord Chichester, and myself, for taking order according to your lordship's directions, for such as refused to take the oath, he had then the view of the books which were given up to us by the preachers and churchwardens of the parishes in the Claneboyes and Ards, of such of the Scots as were to take the oath. And we are hopeful that he both saw by our

progress upon the said books, and hath showed to your lordship the willingness of the people, and our diligence in the work, although by the greatness thereof and paucity of the commissioners, who are to be at least thrice at every swearing, sundry of the parishes were then remaining uncalled, of which the people, as we are able to come at them, are since come in, and have taken their oaths, except the gleanings everywhere of sick or absent persons, who are remitted and directed upon their recovery or return home, to come to Killileagh, where the oath is to be given to them of the territory of Dufferin, and of the adjoining parishes, which is to be the last sitting for this service, and is to make the perclose of our books, and what we may say upon the whole matter. For which purpose I am come to Killileagh, where, contrary to my expectation, I find the people much altered in my absence from what I left them, and to be made apprehend much unlawfulness in the oath, and much danger of soul to take it. Insomuch, that upon notice of my coming hither, many are fled out of the country, and especially servants, that their masters are doubtful to find sufficient to reap their corn; for whose apprehension, as they may be found, I have sent out warrants. It is conceived, that some aspersions, lyingly cast upon the oath, and a suggestion that it is greatly disliked in Scotland (for which I can find no author to lay hold on, albeit this might have operated with them in part), hath been the cause of this averseness. But, indeed, I do apprehend, that the chief, if not the only cause, is proceeded from Mr. John Pole, the preacher at Killileagh, the old blind man that was once with your lordship; who, instead of obviating such aspersions, and satisfying the people in their doubts, hath very presumptuously and perversely, both in his common conferences, and in his public sermons upon the Sabbath-day to the people in the church, taxed the oath to be without any ground, to be unnecessary, uncertain, doubtful, and in the branches of it, unlawful, and contrary to all former oaths. I have herein taken the examinations of sundry persons of respect, which, tested with their own hands, I herewith send to your lordship, that by them, he may be presented to your lordship in his own words. I lay not my hand upon any clergyman, especially a preacher, without direction, otherwise I had sent him myself. I altered also, upon this rub, for a short time, the day of calling the people to the oath, that there might be opportunity to settle the minds of the people to their true duty. Wherein I doubt not but your lordship shall find the faithful endeavours of him, who, leaving all to your lordship's wisdom, is ever your lordship's most humble, and most obliged servant,
                                    " J. CLANEBOYE.

" Killileagh, Aug, 23, 1639."

" THE LORD VISCOUNT CLANEBOYE TO THE LORD DEPUTY.

" My much honoured Lord,

" Your lordship's noble favours to me at all times, and especially by your last letters of the 27th of August, do bind me to a continual loving and honouring of your lordship, and expression of the same, as any your lordship's service shall require; which I hereby profess. If Mr. Bole, who is now carried up by a pursuivant, shall deny any of the

things charged against him, which is too usual with him, boldly to speak, and more boldly to deny it, witnesses who have, under their hands, tested the same, are of credit, and and, if required, shall repair thither, and upon their oaths, make it good in his hearing. Since my last to your lordship, I made intimation to the people of the parishes hereabout, who especially were possessed with a prejudice of the oath, that if any were doubtful of any thing contained in it, they should freely repair to me, and that I would satisfy them to the full, before they should be put to take it. Very many came in, of whom some had been misled by foul reproaches cast upon it, others by misconstructions of it, and some by their apprehended doubts of what might be required of them hereafter, if they should take it. But, in a short debating, they had all contentment, and were sorry of their shunning. Amongst the rest, Mr. Bole came to me, hearing that his speeches had been revealed to me, and made profession of his bounden duty to his majesty, and of his respect to the oath. But I told him I was sorry to hear of his much miscarriage against both, of which he desired to hear the particulars. I said he would hear of them soon enough in another place, and willed him to remember himself what he had said. And not long thereafter, upon that day which we had appointed for the people to come in for taking the oath, I sent to him, and required him to be there; for that was the form, that the minister and churchwardens, and chief men of the parish, were made leaders to the people in taking the oath. I did likewise direct the provost of the town to be with him. But he desired that (in respect it fell out, that the same day was the day of the week, upon which he ordinarly used to have weekly an exhortation to the people), he might be heard in his sermon first, and to declare himself concerning the oath in hand, wherein he hoped to give satisfaction to us and the people, which we thought not amiss to afford him, to see how he would amend himself. His text he took out of the sixth chapter of the Prophet Daniel, the 6, 7, 8, 9, and 10th verses. Your lordship will see how pertinent that text was to such a purpose; and he indeed accordingly handled it so, as none, I think, could tell what he was seeking, or in what or how he gave any satisfaction to the people for the matter of the oath. Much he taxed the princes of Persia for abusing the king, and destroying the soul, by leading him upon a false decree to destroy Daniel; and, by the way, come admonitions he gave us, the commissioners, to take heed that we did nothing that might give us cause of grief hereafter. But for the oath nothing expressly, but that some had reported to him, that he had made the oath doubtful and unlawful, wherein he said they had done him wrong, and that therefore they should see him then take it in the pulpit himself. And, without more, he swore and protested generally his loyalty and fidelity to his majesty, and concluded with an exhortation to me, to explain the oath to the people before they took it; and so ended with the usual form. Thereupon I called him and the people unto me, and told them, that according to Mr. Bole's desires I was ready, if they would show me their doubts, to explain the oath for the same, and to give them satisfaction. But, for that I believed the doubts were made by Mr. Bole himself, I would first address me

I

out of Scotland, and planted all the parishes of his estate (which were six)* with such ;' communicated with them ; maintained them liberally; received even their public reproofs submissively, and

to him, who was best able to move them, and to discern of the answer I should give to them. In effect, there was nothing propounded but their misconstructions, fears, and surmises, of what hereafter might be drawn upon them by the power of the oath; and, having heard him and the people, in all they could say, I gave them so full satisfaction, that they all confessed the oath was rightful to be taken. Whereupon I willed Mr. Bole, the provost of the town of Killileagh, and the churchwardens and some of the aldermen, to kneel down and I would give it them. Mr. Bole told me, that he had taken it already. I asked him where? He said he had taken it in my hearing in the pulpit. I told him that shuffling would not serve his turn; he should take it in the express words of the prescribed oath, following me as others did. And after two or three bouts, in the hearing of the people, I required him either to kneel with the rest, and to take it in the ordinary form, or, if he refused, he should instantly hear me in another sort; and then indeed he did kneel and take it with the rest. I pray your lordship to excuse this prolix narration, which is drawn on to show your lordship that he hath taken the oath, and by what degrees he was brought to it. And since, as I hear, he did persuade the people to it, why nevertheless come nothing so cheerfully in, as they did in other parts. But nothing shall be undone of my part to forward and finish the business, and to pray for the increase of all happiness to your lordship, which is the affectionate desire of your lordship's most humble and most obliged servant.   " J. CLANEBOYE.
"Killileagh, Sept. 2, 1639."

Dr. Reid also copies this letter, and observes, in a note to p. 253 of the first volume of his Presbyterian History :— " One cannot read this letter without feeling deeply for the hardships to which this aged and venerable minister was exposed. How cruel to dragoon the old and blind man into the swearing of this obnoxious oath! And yet how adroitly he endeavoured to evade it himself, and indirectly to warn his people against its ensnaring obligations ! What became of him, when dragged up to Dublin, I have no means of ascertaining." The following documents, found among the family papers, though not a satisfactory answer to Dr. Reid's inquiry, throw some additional light on Mr. Bole's history, and are therefore considered worthy of being given at length :—

" To the Right Honble Anne, Countess of Clanbrassill.
" According to your honour's directions, we have taken the examination of Mistris Montgomery and Widow Campbell, witnesses brought before us by Jean Bole upon oath : —The examination of Mistris Montgomery, who deposeth upon oath that she remembers that Mr. John Bole was possessed of some lands lying near to the old church, and that she heard the old Lord Claneboy tell his Lady Jane Claneboy that he had given Mr. John Bole, in satisfaction for the said lands, six aikers of land lying near the bridge, his own and his daughter, Jean Bole's, lifetime, and no

further sayeth.—The examination of Widow Campbell, who deposeth upon oath that she had in keeping from Jean Bole a lease made from the old Lord Claneboy to the sd Jean Bole of the six aikers of land lying near to the new bridge for her lifetime, and that she was to hold the said land during the said time, paying only one peppercorn by year, if demanded ; and further sweareth that the said lease was lost, with several other goods of her own, at the siedge of the Castle of Killileagh. This 18th February, 1674. Alexr. Read.—A. D. Williamson."

Certificate of Anne, Countess of Clanbrassill.

" My son having some years since sett a lease to his groom, Will. Brown, of the 6 aikers of land (near to the bridge of the town of Killileagh) which belongs to Jane Bole, widow to William Murdoch, the said unworthy fellow, William Brown, being desirous to gett into the present possession of the said parcell, did last winter most falsly inform Sir Robt. Maxwell that the said widow had no right to that 6 aikers of land, whereupon the said Knight sett a lease of it to Will. Brown; but the widow, Jane Bole, being thereby very much wronged petitioned Sir Robert and me to permitt her wittnesses to be examined upon oath, that her right to that 6 aikers might be cleared; hereupon I directed Alexr. Read, the present Provost of the town of Killileagh, and Captain Williamson, to examine Widow Montgomery of Rathcunningham, and Widow Campbell, and received from them these lines last 18 Feby hereabove written in this paper, this annexed certificate also signed the 25th of last Feby. by Mr. McWhid, and this certificate, signed by Mr. Phillips the 26th of last Feby., were also then brought to me ; and when the groom saw that the widow's right was so fully asserted, he quitted his claim, and threw off the lease given him by Sir Robt. Maxwell. The reason of my asserting these truths is, lest my son or any other person should, after my decease, molest Jane Boal (Widow Murdoch) by disposing of that 6 aikers of land which is her proper right during her life, and to certify that I will never consent that it shall be taken from her. As witness my hand, this 18th of June, 1675.—Anne, Clanbrassill."

Mr. McWhidd's Certificate.

" These are humbly to certifie whom it may concern. That about the year of our Lord 1632, I being reador to Mr. John Boile, the Reverend Minister of Killileagh, do very well remember that the Rt. Honble. James, Lord Viscount Claneboys, for several good causes, especially his religious Lady Jean being god-mother) to Jean Boile, daughter to the said Mr. John Boile, he did very nobly give a gratuity of about six aikers of land to the use and profit of the said Jean Boile during her life, and confirmed a lease of the same for him and his, paying a peppercorn yearly upon demand ; which lease, among his books and other papers, I had the charge of for the space of seven years together in his house, where I waited on him, being his servant. The truth whereof, as it is well known to the old inhabitants, so the contents of what is above specified I shall be willing to make out on oath, and some more persons if need require. The said six aikers lye as we leave the bridge on the right hand, the

had secret friendly correspondence with the ministers and others that were persecuted for conscience sake; yea, some hid in his house when his warrants and constables were abroad looking for them.

Glebland adjoining it on the one side, and the Logh on the other. Witness my hand, February 25th, 1674. Alex. M. Whidd. vicar of Drumballironie, in the Diocess of Dromore. Being present when this Certificate was signed by Mr. McWhidd, — Will. Waring, Paul Waring, Will. McWhidd."

Mr. Philipp's Certificate.

"I, Hugh Philipps, of Caradorne, in the County of Down, at the request of Jean Boill, daughter to Mr. John Boill, Minister of Killileagh, deceased, do certifie that I was my Lord's receiver of the rents several years before the wars, and at a certain time did demand the rent of six aikers of land belonging to Mr. John Boill, lying near to the bridge of Killileagh, whereupon there was one lease produced to me which I did read, given under hand and seal of the old Lord Viscount Claneboy, made to the said Jean Boill for her lifetime, paying therefore if demanded one peppercorn by year; so that in all the time of my being receiver I never had or demanded any rent for these lands. And further, I do certifie, that I heard my Lord tell my Lady Claneboy that he hoped Mr. John Boill would preach or speak no more of Naboth's vineyard, for he had given to him during his own and his daughter Jean Boill's lifetime the above specified six aikers of land in lieu of some other lands formerly possessed by Mr John Boill lying near to the old church. This I do certifie, which I will depose upon oath, if need be. In witness whereof I have hereunto set my hand this 26th day of Feby., 1674.—Hugh Philips. Witness present at the signing hereof, Alexr. Reid, Ro. Hamilton."

Letter from Mr. McWhidd to Jane Boal, alias Mordoch.

"Mistress Jane,—I have received your letter, being heartily sorry that among so many obliged witnesses your business should need any dispute. I have sent you my certificate to help that I heard and saw your father possessed of above 40 years ago, and I marvell much that such a noble person does not add rather than diminish from such a small gift. He is misinformed, I conceive. However, if my appearance at any time may be steadable, I shall not disappoint your warning. Mr. Phillips is a discreet gentleman, and lived with my lord near that time. I am persuaded none that knew your father but will wish you well, and especially for your mother's sake. Peruse this certificat, and take advice from surest friends, and the God that commands to judge the fatherless, and plead for the widow, assist you and help you in need. So wisheth your well-wisher and friend to his power—Alex.: McWhidd."

. Viz., Killileagh, Bangor, Killinchy, Craigavad and Holywood, Talpeston or Ballybalbert, and Dundonald:—

1. *Killileagh.*—JOHN BOLE, M.A., is returned in the Ulster Visitation Book for 1622, as minister of the parish of Killileagh, and is described as "resident—church ruinous." This church was never repaired, but a new church was built in 1640, by Viscount Claneboy; which, having become dilapidated, was re-built in 1812, at an expense of £2,000, by James, Baron Dufferin and Claneboy, to whom

a monument is erected in it with the following inscription :—

"IN THE FAMILY VAULT ADJOINING THIS CHURCH ARE DEPOSITED THE REMAINS OF JAMES STEVENSON BLACKWOOD, BARON DUFFERIN AND CLANEBOYE, SECOND SON OF SIR JOHN BLACKWOOD, BART., AND OF DORCAS, BARONESS DUFFERIN AND CLANEBOYE. HIS NAME WILL BE LONG REMEMBERED AS A ZEALOUS SUPPORTER OF THE CHRISTIAN RELIGION, ESPECIALLY IN THE CHURCH ESTABLISHED IN THIS COUNTRY, TO WHICH HE HAS LEFT A MEMORIAL OF HIS ATTACHMENT BY THE RESTORATION OF THIS SACRED EDIFICE. EVER LOYAL TO HIS KING, A FIRM YET TEMPERATE ADVOCATE OF THE LAWS AND LIBERTIES OF HIS COUNTRY, HIS ENERGY AND HIS EXERTIONS WERE NEVER-FAILING IN THEIR DEFENCE. A BENEVOLENT AND ZEALOUS FRIEND, A KIND, CONSIDERATE, AND INDULGENT LANDLORD, UNOSTENTATIOUS IN HIS GENEROSITY, AS IN THE EXERCISE OF EVERY OTHER VIRTUE, HE BELIEVED IN HIS REDEMPTION THROUGH THE INCARNATION OF OUR LORD JESUS CHRIST, AND PROVED BY HIS PATIENCE THE UNWAVERING SINCERITY OF HIS FAITH, FULFILLING THE DUTIES OF SON, OF HUSBAND, AND OF BROTHER, WITH UNABATED AFFECTION; ABOUNDING IN CHRISTIAN CHARITY TO ALL; FORGIVING AS HE HOPED TO BE FORGIVEN; HE POSSESSED THE LOVE, THE GRATEFUL ATTACHMENT, THE DEVOTED RESPECT OF ALL WHO KNEW HIM; AND LONG AND DEEPLY WILL HIS LOSS CONTINUE TO BE DEPLORED WITHIN THE CIRCLE THAT IMMEDIATELY SURROUNDED HIM. HE WAS BORN AT KILLYLEAGH, IV. SEPTEMBER, 1755. HIS LONG AND USEFUL LIFE WAS CLOSED AT BALLYLEIDY, ON THE 8TH OF AUGUST, 1836, IN MERCIFUL COMPOSURE BOTH OF MIND AND BODY. IN THE YEAR 1793 HE RAISED THE 3RD. REGIMENT OF LIGHT DRAGOONS; HE WAS COLONEL OF THE ROYAL NORTH DOWN MILITIA, AND AN AIDE-DE-CAMP FOR THE MILITIA OF IRELAND, TO KING WILLIAM THE FOURTH."

The following is a list of the Rev. John Bole's successors in the Episcopal Church of Killileagh to the present time :—

THOMAS MURRAY, who was brutally massacred in the Irish Rebellion of 1641. It appears from a petition presented by his widow to the General Assembly of the Church of Scotland, at St. Andrew's, in 1642, that he was actually crucified on a tree; her two sons killed, and cut to pieces before her eyes; her own body frightfully cut, and maimed in sundry parts; her tongue half cut out; and that she was kept in prison and inhumanly used by the rebels; from whom at last, by God's merciful providence, she escaped, —all which was testified under the hands of the best nobles and councillors of the kingdom, and humbly praying them to extend their charity to her, which was granted.—*MSS. Records of General Assembly.*

WILLIAM RICHARDSON, ordained in 1649; deposed by Bishop Jeremy Taylor for nonconformity in 1661.

ROBERT MAXWELL, died 1686. He is described as of

4. In managing of his estate he was careful and wary in giving inheritances or leases above three lives, and went that length but with very few ; he was very saving of his oak woods (whereof he had great store) expecting greater advantages by them in after time, and deliberately (for a time),

---

Killileagh, County Down, clerke, in a deed dated 30th June, 1674, whereby, in consideration of £900, Henry Earl of Clanbrassill, and Alice, his wife, conveyed to him in fee-farm the townlands of Granshogh and Groomsport, with certain houses and tenements in Bangor, and the lower grist mill of Ballymaconnell, and the mill lands belonging to it; the townland of Ballygrany, 120 acres of Ballow juxta Bangor, 88 acres of Ballymagee, 10 acres called the Quarries Acres, and 10 other acres in the same townland, part of Ballyhome, 168 acres of Ballymagee, &c.

JAMES CLEWLOW, presented in 1686.

PATRICK HAMILTON, presented in 1735.

ROWLEY HALL purchased the living, and, after presenting himself to it in 1749, sold it to Trinity College, who have since presented to it—

JOHN FOSTER, in 1770,

WILLIAM DAY, in 1789,

WILLIAM STACK, in 1794,

WILLIAM MAGEE, D.D., in 1812,

PETER CARLETON, in 1813, and

EDWARD HINCKS, D.D., in 1825. •

The following is a list of the Presbyterian Ministers of Killileagh after the deposition of William Richardson for nonconformity, in 1661, to the present time:—

WILLIAM RICHARDSON, died in 1670.

ALEXANDER FERGUSON, translated from Sorbie, in Scotland, in 1670, and died in 1684.

PATRICK PEACOCK, appointed in 1684.

JAMES BRICE, in 1689.

GILBERT KENNEDY, ordained in Lisburn, 1732; translated to Killileagh, 1733; removed to Belfast, 1744; died 1773.

WILLIAM DUNNE, appointed in 1745; removed to Dublin 1765.

JOSEPH LITTLE, ordained in 1768; died 1813.

WILLIAM D. H. M'EWEN, ordained in Dublin 1808; removed to Killileagh in 1813, and to Belfast in 1817, where he died in 1828.

HENRY COOKE, D.D., ordained in Duncan, 1808; removed to Donegore in 1811 ; to Killileagh in 1818 ; and to Belfast in 1829.

ANDREW BREAKEY, ordained in Keady, 1819; removed to Killileagh in 1831.

2. *Bangor.*—JOHN GIBSON, M.A., is returned in the Visitation Book for 1622 as minister of the Parish of Bangor, and is described as " Dean—resident, and serveth the cure,

and maintained by a stipend from Sir James Hamilton—church repaired." In the south wall of the Church of Bangor is a stone erected to his memory, with the following inscription : —" HEAR LYES BELOUE ANE LEARNED AND REVEREND FATHER IN GODES CHURCH, MESTER JOHN GIBSON, SENCE REFORMACIONE FROM POPARY THE FIRST DEANE OF DOVNE, SEND BY HIS MAIESTIE INTO THIS KINGDOM AND RECEVED BY MY LORD CLANEBOY TO BE PREACHER AT BANGOR. AT HIS ENTRY HAD XL COMMUNICANTS, AND AT HIS DEPARTOUR THIS LYF, 23 OF IVNII, 1623, LEFT 1,200, BEING OF AGE 63 YEARS. SO CHRIST WAS HIS ADVANTAGE BOTHE IN LYFE AND DEATH."

ROBERT BLAIR, his successor, had been a professor in the college of Glasgow, but being much opposed by Dr. Cameron (who had been appointed principal with the view of bringing the college to approve of prelacy), had resigned his situation, and, being invited over by Lord Claneboy, came to Ireland in May, 1623. He thus narrates the circumstances of his settlement at Bangor :—

" When I landed in Ireland, some men parting from their cups, and all things smelling of a root called rampions, my prejudice was confirmed against that land. But next day travelling towards Bangor, I met unexpectedly with so sweet a peace and so great a joy as I behoved to look thereon as my welcome hither ; and, retiring to a private place, about a mile above Craigfergus, I prostrated myself upon the grass to rejoice in the Lord, who proved the same to me in Ireland which he had been in Scotland. Nevertheless, my aversion to a settlement there continued strong ; and, when my noble patron renewed his invitation and offer, I was very careful to inform him both of what accusations had been laid against me of disaffection to the civil powers, and that I could not submit to the use of the English liturgy nor episcopal government, to see if either of these would prevail with him to pass from his invitation. But, having been informed by a minister present of my altercations with Dr. Cameron, he said, ' I know all that business ;' and, for the other point, he added, that he was confident of procuring a free entry for me, which he quickly effectuated. So, all my devices to obstruct a settlement there did evanish and took no effect, the counsel of the Lord standing fast in all generations; yea, his wisdom overruled all this, both to procure me a free and safe entry to the holy ministry; and that, when after some years I met with trials for my nonconformity, neither patron nor prelate could say that I had broken any condition to them. Having been invited to preach by the patron, and by Mr. Gibson, the sick incumbent, I yielded to their invitation, and preached there three Sabbath days. After that, several of the aged and most respectful persons in the congregation came to me by order of the whole, and informed me that they were edified by the doctrine delivered by me;

and till it was too late, admitted of ten thousand pounds debt to continue upon his estate (as he expressed himself to some) to acquaint his son with the trouble of debt, that he might avoid it, and find a need of living frugally and regularly.

intreated me not to leave them; and promised, if the patron's offer of maintenance was not large enough, they would willingly add to the same. This promise I slighted, being too careless of competent and comfortable provision, for I had no thoughts of any greater family than a boy or two to serve me. But, on the former part of that speech importing the congregation's call, I laid great weight; and it did contribute more to the removing of my unwillingness to settle there than anything else. Likewise the dying man did several ways encourage me. He professed great sorrow for his having been a Dean. He condemned episcopacy more strongly than ever I durst do; he charged me in the name of Christ, and as I expected his blessing on my ministry, not to leave that good way wherein I had begun to walk; and then, drawing my head towards his bosom with both his arms, he laid his hands on my head and blessed me. Within a few days after he died, and my admission was accomplished as quickly as might be, in the following way:—The Viscount Claneboy, my noble patron, did, on my request, inform the Bishop Echlin how opposite I was to episcopacy and their liturgy, and had the influence to procure my admission on easy and honourable terms. Yet, lest his lordship had not been plain enough, I declared my opinion fully to the bishop at our first meeting, and found him yielding beyond my expectation. The bishop said to me, 'I hear good of you, and will impose no conditions on you; I am old, and can teach you ceremonies, and you can teach me substance, only I must ordain you, else neither I nor you can answer the law nor brook the land.' I answered him, that his sole ordination did utterly contradict my principles; but he replied, both wittily and submissively, 'Whatever you account of episcopacy, yet I know you account a presbytery to have divine warrant; will you not receive ordination from Mr. Cunningham and the adjacent brethren, and let me come in among them in no other relation than a presbyter?' This I could not refuse, and so the matter was performed, on the 10th of July, 1623." Blair thus describes his ministerial labours at Bangor:—"My charge was very great, consisting of about six miles in length, and containing above 1,200 persons come to age, besides children who stood greatly in need of instruction. This being the case, I preached twice every week besides the Lord's day, on all which occasions I found little difficulty either as to matter or method. But, finding still that this fell short of reaching the design of a Gospel-ministry, and that the most part continued vastly ignorant, I saw the necessity of trying a more plain and familiar way of instructing them; and, therefore, besides my public preaching, I spent as much time every week, as my bodily strength could hold out with, in exhorting and catechising them. Not long after I fell upon this method, the Lord visited me with a fever; on which, some, who hated my painfulness in the ministry, said, scoffingly, that they knew I could not hold out as I began. But in a little space it pleased the Lord to raise me up again, and he enabled me to continue that method

the whole time I was there. The knowledge of God increasing among that people, and the ordinance of prayer being precious in their eyes, the work of the Lord did prosper in the place; and in this we were much encouraged both by the assistance of holy Mr. Cunningham, and by the good example of his little parish of Holywood. For, knowing that diversity of gifts is entertaining to the hearers, he and I did frequently preach for one and other. And we also agreed to celebrate the sacrament of the Lord's Supper four times in each of our congregations annually, so that those in both parishes who were thriving in religion, did communicate together on all occasions." "The first time," says Blair, "I dispensed the Sacrament of the Lord's Supper, the solemnity was like to have been disorderly on this account. My noble patron and his lady would communicate kneeling; and, even after reasoning, his lordship continued obstinate; so that I parted from him with sorrow, and resolved to delay that work until another time. But, his lordship remembering that his pew joined to the upper end of the table, and was so enclosed that only one's head could be discovered in it, he promised not to kneel on condition he received the elements within his own pew. For peace sake, I rashly yielded to this offer, but was so much discomposed by it next day, that when I came to the public, I was for half an hour so much deserted of God that I was in great mercy pitied and helped me. For, preaching upon the words of the institution, 1 Cor. xi chap., and handling these words, 'This cup is the New Testament in my blood,' as soon as I begun to discourse of that New Testament or Covenant, I found light and life flowing in upon my soul, enlarging it, and opening my mouth to speak with comfort and courage: and, with this assistance, I went to the table and administered the Sacrament. The action being ended, my patron, and especially his lady, professed their great satisfaction with that day's service, and proved my most tender and real friends ever after."

Blair thus describes his introduction to Archbishop Ussher, and his conversations with him on several of the topics which were then agitating the religious world:—

"In March, 1627, my noble patron having had a great esteem of Primate Ussher, would have me to accompany him to a meeting of the nobility and gentry of Ulster with the Primate. Accordingly I went, and had a kind invitation to be at his table, while I was in town. But, having once met with the English liturgy there, I left my excuse with my patron, that I expected another thing than formal liturgies in the family of so learned and pious a man. The Primate excused himself, by reason of the great confidence that was there, and had the good nature to entreat me to come to Tredaff [Drogheda], where his ordinary residence was, and where he would be more at leisure to be better acquainted with me. I complied with the Primate's invitation, and found him very affable and ready to impart his mind. He desired to know what was my judgment con-

5. As to the education of his son, he was much concerned to make the best of one eye, yet was most fond of him.   He choosed for him a very learned, discreet, and religious master, one Mr. James Trail

---

cerning the nature of justifying and saving faith. I told him, in general, that I hold the accepting of Jesus Christ, as he is freely offered in the Gospel, to be saving faith. With this he was well satisfied, and by a large discourse confirmed and further cleared the same, by the similitude of a marriage, where it is not the sending or receiving of gifts, but the accepting the person that constitutes the marriage. From this he passed on to try my mind concerning ceremonies, wherein we were not so far from agreeing as I feared. For, when I had freely opened my grievances, he admitted that all these things ought to have been removed, but the constitution and laws of the place and time would not permit that to be done. He added that he was afraid our strong disaffection to these would mar our ministry; that he had himself been importuned to stretch forth his hand against us; and that, though he would not for the world do that, he feared instruments might be found who would do it; and he added, that it would break his heart if our successful ministry in the North were interrupted. Our conference ending, he dismissed me very kindly, though I gave him no high titles; and, when trouble came upon us, he proved our very good friend."—*Blair's Life*, p 64.

The following notice of a conference which he had with one of the Judges of Assize, before whom, when on the Northern circuit, he had the opportunity of preaching at Downpatrick, is also taken from his life :—

" After sermon on the Lord's Day, one of the Judges, wanting to confer with me, sent for me to his lodgings ; where, after professing his satisfaction with what I had delivered, especially in my last sermon, ' for therein,' said he, ' you opened a point which I never heard before, viz., the covenant of redemption made with Christ the Mediator, as head of the elect,' he entreated me to go over the heads of that sermon with him ; and, opening his Bible, he read over and considered the proofs cited ; and was so well satisfied, that he protested, if his calling did not tie him to Dublin, he would gladly come to the North, and settle under such a ministry."—*Ib.* pp. 69, 70.

Blair was suspended in September, 1631 ; a second time in 1633; and finally deposed, by Bishop Echlin, for nonconformity, in Nov., 1634.—*See Reid's Presb. Hist.*, pp. 134, 183.

JAMES HAMILTON, who succeeded Blair, was the incumbent in 1670, and afterwards became Rector of Knockbreda and Dundonald. He is styled as " of Ballygraffen" in his will.

ROBERT HAMILTON succeeded him about the year 1698, and continued to be the incumbent certainly till 1721, in which year his name appears at the Annual Visitation.

JAMES CLEWLOW's name appears in the Annual Visitation list for 1730, and continues till 1748. The name of

PETER WINDER, or WYNDER, is given as his successor at

the Annual Visitation held in 1752, and again in the year 1770. His successor was

JAMES HAMILTON CLEWLOW, whose name appears on the list at the Annual Visitation held 31st July, 1771, and, for the last time, in the year 1801.

The Annual Visitation List of 1802 declares the living vacant, but it appears, by the Parish Vestry Book of Bangor, that

PIERCE MEADE presided at a vestry held 3d October, 1802.

GEORGE M'DOWELL JOHNSTON presided at a vestry held 7th April, 1803, and

STEPHEN DICKSON at a vestry held 5th May, 1804, for the first time, and, for the last time, on 26th April, 1819.

HENRY WARD presided at vestry, for the first time, on 3d April, 1820, and, for the last time, on 1st March, 1823, when he became Rector of Killinchy.

ROBERT LLOYD presided at vestry on 29th April, 1824.

GEORGE ARMSTRONG presided at vestries held on 5th April, 1825, and 19th Sept., 1826.

HENRY GEORGE JOHNSON presided, for the first time, at a vestry held on 17th April, 1827, and, for the last time, at one held on 9th April, 1849 ; and

RICHARD BINNEY, D.D., the present incumbent, presided, for the first time, at vestry on 22d April, 1850.

The living is an impropriate curacy, and the reputed patrons are Viscount Bangor and the Earl of Carrick.--*Erck.* 28.

The following is a list of the Presbyterian ministers of Bangor :—

ROBERT BLAIR, after his deposition for nonconformity in Nov., 1634, continued to discharge in private the duties of the ministry until Sept., 1636, on the 9th of which month he sailed from Lochfergus (Carrickfergus, or Belfast Lough), intending to go to New England ; but, meeting with heavy gales of wind at sea, the ship was driven back, and Blair, in 1637, went and dwelt at the " Strowe" (or Strand), near Belfast, and was, early in the following year, (1638,) chosen colleague to Mr. Wm. Annan, of Ayr. —*See 1st Reid's Presb. Hist.*, pp. 137, 144.

Bangor appears to have had no settled minister from the year 1636 till 1646. In 1642, the Presbyterians of a large portion of the County of Antrim, and of the northern parts of the County of Down, agreed to petition the General Assembly of the Church of Scotland for a supply of ministers ; and the Parish of Bangor, at a meeting held on the last Wednesday in July, in that year, made special application for the restoration of Mr. Blair, by a petition signed by 63

and directed that he should be managed according to his genius, and not much thwarted or over driven in ye prosecution of learning and other improvements, saying he would not lose the substance

heads of families. Mr. Blair was sent by the General Assembly to visit them, and accordingly spent some three months in the latter part of that year in Bangor and its neighbourhood.

GILBERT RAMSAY was ordained to the charge of Bangor in 1646, having been recommended to the people by their former minister, Robert Blair. Mr. Ramsay's meeting-house was demolished in 1669 by order of Alice Countess of Clanbrassill, and he died in August, 1670.

ARCHIBALD HAMILTON succeeded Mr. Ramsay at Bangor, in the year 1670. On 14th March, 1689, he was one of the nine Presbyterian ministers who waited on the General Council at Hillsborough, for the purpose of offering certain suggestions in relation to the defence of the country. In 1689, Mr. Hamilton removed to Wigton on account of the troubles, but his connexion with Bangor did not wholly cease upon his removal; for, in 1691, he is described as minister of the Irish congregation in Bangor, and also of the Scottish Parish of Wigton. He died at Wigton, 29th June, 1695, aged 75 years.

Mr. HAMILTON, a grandson of the foregoing Archibald Hamilton, whose Christian name is also supposed to have been Archibald, succeeded his grandfather for a short time at Bangor.

WILLIAM BIGGAR, from Scotland, was installed 1st March, 1704. He resigned the charge in March, 1728, and returned to Scotland. Mr. Cochrane, of Kilraughts, was called to Bangor in 1731, but his translation was not sanctioned by the Synod, and Mr. Biggar's successor was

JAMES MACKAY, who was ordained 15th Nov., 1732, and continued minister till 1747; but, in 1748,

Mr. COCHRANE having received a second call, he was installed on 6th Dec., 1748, his annual stipend being £60, and 20 bolls of oats yearly.

JAMES HULL, previously of Cookstown, was installed 4th January, 1763, as assistant and successor of Mr. Cochrane, who died 2nd June, 1765.

DAVID TAGGART was ordained 21st May, 1793, as assistant and successor to Mr. Hull, who died 30th March, 1794, and Mr. Taggart was drowned at Bangor Quay on the 17th March, 1808.

HUGH WOODS was ordained 15th Nov., 1808, and is still living, aged 86.

JOSEPH CRAWFORD M'CULLAGH, of Tipperary, was installed as assistant and successor to Mr. Woods, on 24th Feb., 1857.

The Editor of these MSS. is indebted to his friend, R. S. Nicholson, Esq., of Ballow, for the foregoing lists of

the successors of Blair, in the Parish of Bangor, both Episcopalian and Presbyterian, to the present time. The lists of Bole's successors in Killileagh parish were kindly supplied to him by the Rev. Mr. Breakey, the Presbyterian minister, and were submitted to the Rev. Dr. Hincks, the Episcopal clergyman of that parish, for his revision. But he regrets that he has been unable to obtain similar lists for the other parishes.

3. *Killinchy.*—Occasionally called Killinchenemaghery, the "island church of the plain," to distinguish it from Killinchinckille, the "island church of the wood," which is now called "Killinchy in the Woods," and is a townland in Killyleagh parish.—*Reeves' Eccl. Ant.,* p. 10. The parish church stands in the old churchyard, " seated on a high hill, and therefore by some called in jest the *Visible Church.*"—*Harris's Co. Down.* p. 76. This parish is a Rectory, and the present reputed patrons are Viscount Bangor and the Earl of Carrick.—*Erck's Irish Eccl. Reg.,* p. 28. Killinchy is not mentioned in the Ulster Visitation Book for 1622, but JOHN LIVINGSTON, A.M., thus narrates the circumstance of his removal from Scotland to it in 1630:—

" Being in Irvine, Mr. Robert Cunningham, minister at Holywood, in Ireland, and some while before that, Mr G. Dunbar, minister of Larne in Ireland, propounded to me, seeing there was no appearance I could enter into the ministry in Scotland, whether or not I would be content to go to Ireland? I answered them both, if I got clear call and a free entry I would not refuse. About August 1630, I got letters from the Viscount Clanniboy, to come to Ireland, in reference to a call to Killinchy; whither I went, and got a unanimous call from the parish. And because it was needful that I should be ordained to the ministry, and the bishop of Down, in whose diocese Killinchy was, being a corrupt timorous man, and would require some engagement, therefore, my Lord Clanniboy sent some with me, and wrote to Mr Andrew Knox, bishop of Rapho; who, when I came, and had delivered the letters from my Lord Clanniboy, and from the Earl of Wigton, and some others, that I had for that purpose brought out of Scotland, told me he knew my errand; that I came to him because I had scruples against episcopacy and ceremonies, according as Mr Josias Welsh and some others had done before; and that he thought his old age was prolonged for little other purposes but to do such offices; that, if I scrupled to call him ' my lord,' he cared not much for it; all he would desire of me, because they got there but few sermons, was, that I would preach at Ramallen the first Sabbath, and that he would send for Mr. Wm. Cunningham and two or three other neighbouring ministers to be present, who, after sermon, would give me imposition of hands; but, altho' they performed the work, he behoved to be present; and, altho' he durst not answer it to the State, he gave me the

for gaining of accidents, and would rather have no scholar than no son. He judged it most convenient to send him (with the aforesaid Mr. Trail) to travel some years for his improvement, which

book of ordination, and desired that anything I scrupled at I should draw a line over it on the margin, and that Mr. Cunningham should not read it. But I found that it had been so marked by some others before, that I needed not mark anything; so the Lord was pleased to carry that business far beyond anything that I had thought, or almost ever desired."—*Livingston's Life.*

When in Ireland, he thus narrates the ordinary proceedings of himself and his brethren in the ministry:—

"Not only had we public worship free of any inventions of men, but we had also a tolerable discipline ; for after I had been some while among them, by the advice of heads of families, some ablest for that charge were chosen elders, to oversee the manners of the rest, and some deacons, to gather and distribute the collections. We met every week, and such as fell into notorious public scandals we desired to come before us. We needed not to have the communion oftener"—(than twice a year in each parish)—"for there were nine or ten parishes within the bounds of twenty miles, or little more, wherein there were godly and able ministers that kept a society together, and every one of these had the communion twice a year at different times, and had two or three of the neighbouring ministers to help thereat, and most part of the religious people used to resort to the communions of the rest of the parishes. Most of all the ministers used ordinarily to meet the first Friday of every month at Antrim, where was a great and good congregation, and that day was spent in fasting, and prayer, and public preaching. Commonly two preached every forenoon, and two in the afternoon. We used to come together the Thursday's night before, and stayed the Friday's night after, and consulted about such things as concerned the carrying on of the work of God : and these meetings, among ourselves, were sometimes as profitable as either Presbyteries or Synods."—*Ibid.*

Livingston was silenced for nonconformity by Bishop Echlin, on the 4th of May, 1632, and then retired for a time to Scotland ; but Strafford, the then Lord Deputy, having, in the month of May, 1634, written to Bishop Echlin, to withdraw for six months his sentence of suspension, Livingston was thereupon restored to the exercise of his ministry in Killinchy, from which however he was finally passed by Bishop Leslie, in November, 1635, and formally excommunicated by Melvin, the minister of Downpatrick. In September, 1636, he sailed for New England, with 140 other emigrants, who for the sake of enjoying liberty of conscience, intended settling with him, in the then uncultivated wilds of America ; but after a stormy voyage of between three and four hundred leagues from Ireland, the ship in which they sailed sprung a leak, and they were obliged to return to Loch Fergus from which they had sailed, on the 3rd of November in that year. He then continued for some time to discharge in private the duties of the ministry, residing chiefly at the house of his mother-in-

law, Mrs. Stevenson, at the iron furnace at Malone, near Belfast, twelve miles from Killinchy, where he preached almost every Sabbath ; but, a warrant having been issued against him, he retired to Irvine in Scotland, where he remained till July, 1638, when he was admitted minister at Stranraer. Whilst he was settled there, great numbers usually went over from Ireland, at the stated celebration of the Communion ; and, on one occasion, 500 persons, principally from the County of Down, visited Stranraer, to receive that ordinance from his hands. From Stranraer he was removed in 1648, to Ancrum in Teviotdale.

On his banishment from Scotland, at the Restoration, he wrote a farewell letter to his parishioners, in which, after giving them many important counsels, he adds:—

"I recommend to you, above all books, except the blessed Word of God, the Confession of Faith and Larger Catechism."

This eminent servant of God, after numerous trials and vicissitudes, died at Rotterdam, in Holland, in 1672, and on his death-bed he made this solemn declaration :—

"I die in the faith that the truths of God, which he hath helped the Church of Scotland to own, shall be owned by by him as truths, so long as sun and moon endure."

4. *Craigavad and Holywood.*—ROBERT CUNNINGHAM, M.A., is returned in the Ulster Visitation Book for 1622, (MSS. Trin. Coll. Dub.) as minister of the parish of Craigavad and Holywood, and is described as "resident at Hollywood—serveth these cures, and maintained by a stipend from Sir James Hamilton—church repaired in part." Dr. Reid, at p. 101, of the first volume of his Presbyterian History, states, that he had been chaplain to the Earl of Buccleugh's regiment in Holland ; but, removing to Ireland on the return of the troops to Scotland, he was, on the 9th of Nov., 1615, admitted to the ministry by Bishop Echlin.

The following description of these parishes is taken from Dr. Reeves' Ecclesiastical Antiquities of Down and Connor :—" *Cragger*, now Craigavad, 'the rock of the boat,' a townland in the north part of Holywood parish, and bordering on Belfast Lough. At the Dissolution, this church, with the tithes of five adjacent townlands, was appropriate to the Abbey of Bangor. The foundations of the Church, measuring about 48 feet by 18 feet, still remain in a rocky field, which lies between Craigavad House and the Lough ; and beside them stands a solitary tombstone, sacred to the memory of James M'Gee, who died in 1714."—*Haliwode*, now Holywood Parish. The ancient church, which is a building of great age, measuring 78 by 24 feet, was used till lately, for divine worship. Instead of the English name, the form *Sanctus Boscus* is sometimes met with.

he did the length of Rome, very safely and successfully, and returned with great improvements in such things whereunto his genius allowed or agreed unto.'

A.D. 1210, July 29, King John halted 'apud Sanctum Boscum,' when on his way from Carrickfergus to Downpatrick.—Rot. de Prestito, 12 Johan, Tur. Lond. A.D. 1217, Jordanus de Saukeville was confirmed by Henry III. in the possession of his lands ' de Sancto Bosco.'—Hardy's Rot. Claus., vol. 1, p. 304 b. At the Dissolution, a small religious house of the Third Order of St. Francis existed here; it was dependent on the Franciscan Abbey of Bangor, and was endowed with five townlands.—Monast. Hib., p. 121. Lord Dungannon is the reputed patron of the impropriate curacy of Holywood.—Erck's Ir. Ec. Reg., p. 28.

5. Talpestown or Ballyhalbert.—GEORGE PORTER, M.A., is returned in the Visitation Book for 1622, as minister of the parish of Talpestown, or Talbotstown; and is described as " curate and resident—maintained by a stipend from Sir James Hamilton—The Prebend of Talpeston is vacant, Pat. Hamilton being deprived by the Lord Primate for non-residence—church repaired." Harris, in his History of County Down, at p. 8, being unaware of the identity of Talbotstown and Ballyhalbert, states that the tithes and lands of Talbotstown were then entirely lost, although, in the same page, he mentions that the vicarages of Bally-walter, Ballyhalbert, and Innishargy were united by statute 2 Anne; and Dr. Reid, in the first vol. of his Presbyterian History, p. 432, remarks of Talpeston or Talbotstown, " I have not been able to ascertain the locality of this parish." Dr. Reeves, however, with his usual accuracy, at p. 20, of his Ecclesiastical Antiquities of Down, identifies Ballyhalbert with Talpeston, and states that the ancient name was derived from the family of Talbot, which settled in the counties of Down and Antrim soon after the invasion. The primate is the reputed patron of this vicarage.—Erck, p. 28.

6. Dundonald.—JOHN LEATHEM, M.A., is returned in the Ulster Visitation Book for 1622, as minister of this parish, and is thus described: " Resident—serveth the cure, and maintained by a stipend from Sir James Hamilton—church ruined." This parish derives its name from a large earthen fort which stands beside the church. In the modern parish of Dundonald have merged the ancient chapelries of Castlebeg and Ballyoran.—Reeves' Eccl. Antiq., p. 11. Lord Dungannon is the reputed patron of the Rectory of Dundonald.—Erck, p. 28.

Dr. Reid, at p. 123 of the first volume of his Presbyterian History, says :—" The support of some of these ministers was derived from the tithes of the parishes in which they laboured ; while others received a fixed endowment,

paid, as in Scotland, by the patron, in lieu of the tithe which was received directly by himself; and to this endowment was occasionally added a stipend from the people. Blair relates, that, at his settlement, the people of Bangor promised, if the patron's offer of maintenance were not large enough, they would willingly add to the same. His predecessor, Gibson, had been maintained solely by a fixed endowment paid by Sir James Hamilton, the landlord and patron of the parish ; and, Cunningham, of Holywood, was supported in a similar manner. On the other hand, Livingston's support was derived entirely from the people ; though he states he ' never had of stipend in Killinchy above £4 sterling by year.' "

f Whilst on this tour, Lord Claneboy received the following letter from Mr. Traill :—

" Paris, October, 1633.

" Right Honourable and my own Honourable Lord and Master,—Your lordship's first and last of the 20th September came to my hands two hours ago, as we were going to supper, directed to Mons. Rugier, the King's agent here. They were to me matter of joy, because of the continuance of your lordship's health, as they satisfied the master's longing, of which your lordship may easily judge, knowing his dutifulness and affection, which no son can have more, and none such but he that has such a father. The consideration of the season made us hasten from London, reserving much to our return (God willing) and our passage by sea; our journey has been forwarded hitherto without risk or impediment. The best towns between this and our landing lay directly in our way—Boulogne and Montruil, strong garrison towns, and Abbeville. As for Calais, which we desired to see, it was so far out of our way, as to see it we must have gone direct back again, and we were loath to begin our journey by a retrogradation. Amiens was a little aside, but so infected with the plague, that we shunned it of purpose. While we are here this winter, as the holidays fall out, we intend some excursions to the places hereabouts ; and whatever may benefit the master by sight shall not be neglected :—and thus far your lordship's letter has led me. By former letters from this place (for I have written every week, and some weeks twice) your lordship, I hope, knows our arrival here ; how we are lodged ; that the master is entered into his exercises of riding, and dancing, and fencing ; and how he spends his time otherwise.

" In the morning about seven o'clock he goes to the academy, and after two hours or more abode there, he is either busied reading French or Latin ; then, a little after dinner, the dancing master comes to him ; then the fencing master ; then one for the French tongue, with whom he spends an hour before supper either in reading or translating French for the perfecting of his pronunciation and understanding of that language, of which, when he is in some measure master, some time may be had for the elements of logic and mathematics. Thus yr. lordship has

L

6. He lived till he settled all his affairs peaceably. His son was married creditably and comfortably and had some issue; and he had many and very hopefull nephews and some nieces, of all which he took a loving care and oversight. He lived to see the war of Ireland, and by his wisdom and power of his tenants, and the interest he had at Court, was very successful for the preservation of Ulster from the power of the enemy, as he was very charitable to distress'd people that came in great numbers from the upper countrys. He was of a robust, healthfull body, and managed to the best advantage; died without sickness unexpectedly ere he finished his will (which he was about) or settlement he then intended, at least ere it was published,[e] though I am very creditably, I may say certainly, informed, he published a Deed of Settlement of his estate as to the succession thereof, many years before he died. He was very honourably intombed in the place he had prepared for himself in the church of Bangor,[b] in which his whole family is now laid by him.

---

an account of all his time, save that which is morning and evening, first and last, his duties of piety, and the time of diet and sleep, of which praised be God, his health gives very good account.

"My lord, that which I would have him chiefly direct his endeavours to, is his riding and fencing for exercise, and most of all his knowledge of men and business, without which there cannot be confidence or discretion in a man's carriage. As his judgment ripens, sight and conversation will give him more assurance. As to the nerfs and sinews of our domestic affairs, they shall be dispensed as frugally as we can, if you approve of our design to begin the circuit of France about the end of March, or 1st of April, and to rest in Geneva the last months of the summer till the 1st of October. For that journey and time of abode in Geneva, we shall have need of no less than £350 sterling, which should be made over to us, as here we might receive a part of the money, and for another part bills to Bordeaux, and for the rest bills to Geneva; and from which place, if your lordship will have the master step into Italy, new bills must be had for such sums as that journey for at least six months will require. But at that distance a letter of credit will supply us better than bills of exchange. If you so please, the letter may be so contrived that the money be not delivered, but unto the master himself with me. And, moreover, for our journey to Italy another pass must be had, because that which we had in London has an exclusive clause, as your L^dship may have seen by the copy which I sent you from London, barring us from all countries and persons, not in amity and league with our sovereign—this chiefly at Rome.—The master would be glad it might fall out that James Stevenson, or some other of these parts, were at Bordeaux, at the time when we shall be there, or, at least that we knew the time of their coming. Our time there, if it please God, may be about the end of April, or beginning of May rather. The master is very desirous that your lordship and my lady shall drink wine of his tasting; to send it by a ship to London to Mr. Archibald, and from him to Ireland, would be double trouble and charge, and not so sure.

"JAMES TRAILL."

Lord Claneboye also received from his son the following letter while on this tour :—

"22nd April, 1635.

"Right Honourable and most dear father,—I did write unto your lordship when I was at Rome, and have seen all the things that are to be observed; but because the air was not good to stay there in summer, therefore am I come to Florence in good health, thanks be to God. I do purpose to live here quietly for a while, and write to your lordship as often as occasion will permit; also I will seek out here for an honest Italian boy, as your lordship hath commanded ; so I rest, craving your blessing, and praying God to keep your lordship in good health.—Your most obedient sonne, "JAMES HAMILTON."

He also wrote to his mother as follows :—

"Right hon. and most dear mother,—This is the 3d letter I have written to your ladyship since I came to town. I am glad to hear of your ladyship by my father's letter, wherein I hear that your ladyship did write unto me, but I have not received it yet. I hope the blessings which your ladyship hath sent in my father's letter shall not be in vain, because they are sent from so loving a mother. So I rest, praying God to keep your ladyship in good health, and leave your blessing to your most obedient sonne, "JAMES HAMILTON."

[e] A copy of it is given in the Appendix to this chapter.

[b] The present church of Bangor was built within the old Abbey about the year 1616, by Sir James Hamilton, and was not finished till the year 1623; both which particulars appear from dates on a stone in the south walks, and on an old oak pulpit now lying in a corner of the church. The steeple of it, through which the entrance is into the church, is supported by an arch of nine strings of beads, not centring in a point, as many others do, but springing at equal distances round the arch from side to side; and an inscription thereon declares it was raised in 1693, at which time the church was well repaired by James Hamilton, Esq., and afterwards beautified by his widow, Sophia Mor-

The second brother, Archibald, married first to[1] *   *   then Rachel Carmichael, daughter to one named by his lands   *   who was of great account in his time, whose eldest son was Lord Carmichael,[k] and whose family still flourishes in Scotland.   She proved a very virtuous woman, and good mother to his numerous family, and lived in widowhood all her life thereafter, and died of a great age ; she bore twenty-two children   *   sons and   *   *   daughters, whereof six sons came to be men, viz., John, James,[l] Archibald, Gawin,[m] William, and Robert, and his daughter Janet lived to a good age—of those more particularly afterward.   This gentleman was really eminent for wisdom, piety, dexterity in his calling, and that, by God's blessing upon his honest endeavours, he purchas'd a good estate, partly in Scotland,[n] and partly in Ireland ; lived to a great age, and died much lamented.

The third brother, Gawin (as has been said),[o] was bred unto and followed merchandise with great industry and success.   He married Helen Dunlop, of a family then and now in good account in the same parish, whereof Hans was   *   and had by her two sons, Archibald, and James, and two daughters, Jane and Helen—of whom afterwards.   He died by water near Colrain, using some means in a cog boat for guiding out his three ships over the Bar of Colrain.   There were two shipmen with him, whereof one died with him in the overturning of the boat, and the other was saved by swimming.   He died under thirty years of age, and was creditably buried in the church of Colrain, with great lamentation, partly on account of the accident, and partly that he was a very obliging and thriving gentleman, and likely to have been very beneficial to all that place.

---

daunt, sister to the late Earl of Peterborough.   It is, indeed, handsomely adorned, the chancel, with a neat and well-carved altar-piece, is supported with Corinthian pillars fluted ; the rails about the Communion Table and the pulpit carved, the seats regularly laid out, and the whole executed with oak timber.—*Harris's County Down*, p. 61. The following is a copy of an inscription on a monument in Bangor Church :—" Sacred to the memory of James Hamilton, of Bangor, Esq., descended from the family of the Lords of Claneboy ; and Sophia Mordaunt, his consort, daughter to John Lord Viscount Mordaunt, and granddaughter to the Earl of Peterborough, and to the Earl of Monmouth.   This monument (as an act of filial piety) was erected pursuant to the will of Anne, their eldest daughter (relict of Michael Ward, Esq., late a Justice of the King's Bench in Ireland), who departed this life in Dublin, on the 17th day of May, 1760."   On the present site stood the ancient church of Beanchuir, or Banchor, the foundation of of which is thus recorded by the Four Masters, at the year 552 :—" Ecclesia Benchorensis fundata per Comgallum Benchorensem."—*Rer. Hib. Script.*, vol. 3, p. 157.   Dr. Reeves, at p. 18 of his Ecclesiastical Antiquities of Down and Connor, states, that, though Bangor is placed by the taxation in the rural deanery of Blaethwyc, it has been from the earliest period regarded as belonging to the civil territory of the Ards.   Thus, the Book of Armagh relates that " Comgallus constituit magnum monasterium quod vocatur Bennchor in regione, quæ dicitur Altitudo Ultorum."—*Fleming, Collectan*, p. 305, col. 2.

[i] See note to page 11, *ante*.

[k] Sir James Carmichael, Bart., of Hyndford, representative of that ancient family, was created a peer of Scotland, as Baron Carmichael, with remainder, failing his direct descendants, to his male heirs whatever, 27th Dec., 1647.   He died in 1672, and was succeeded by his grandson, John, second Lord Carmichael, who was created Earl of Hyndford on 25th June, 1701.—*Burke's Ex. Peerages*, p.721.

[l] Of Neilsbrook, in the County of Antrim, the ancestor of the present Right Hon. Frederick Temple, Baron Dufferin and Claneboye, in the peerage of Ireland, and Baron Claneboye, in the peerage of Great Britain.

[m] Of Killileagh Castle, in the county of Down, ancestor of the present Gawen Rowan Hamilton, Esq.

[n] At Halcraig, in Lanarkshire.

[o] At page 11, *ante*.

The fourth brother, John,[p] married Sarah Brabson,[q] of a creditable family, and had children by her which came to age, Hans, James, and Francis, sons, and Mary and Helen, daughters—of whom more in due time. He was a prudent person, and painfull man; lived to a good age, and died,[r] much la-

---

[p] Of Hamiltons-Bawn, in the County of Armagh, and Coronary, in the County of Cavan.

[q] Daughter of Sir Anthony Brabazon, of Ballinasloe, in the County of Roscommon, Knight, Governor of Connaught.

[r] On the 4th of December, 1639. At page 11, *ante*, it is stated that he was employed by his eldest brother, Sir James Hamilton, "in agenting of his law affairs for a time." The following letter, which was written by him whilst he was so employed, has been found among the family papers:—

"Sir,—I have receaved your letters which you sent me by Anthonye, and according to your direction I cam to Dublin with the best speed that I could, but as yet cannot make any agreement for St. Mary Abay, for that no parcells of it is past: neither had they fully condissendit what parcells to pass by reason of some differances of the opinion of Mr. Delahyd and Mr. Recorder, and of Sr Francis Anneslye, and Sr James Carroll's business, in other affayres that could not attend it. Notheless they have now resolved by God's grace to pass the grant, and to dispose of it befor Sr Francis com for England, if they can conveniently do it, but howsoever to pass it, for which purpose I mynd to attend here till that be effected, but since my coming we could not meet with one that would buy the whole and pass it, nor yet your half of it, but syndry would buy particular parcells when it is past. As for Plarye, Mr. Croe did enter his suit as you wrote, but proceeded no further, he being content himself to forbear it, and the state of that matter being made known to the Judges, and that you were absent to whom the right did belong, who also had the writings and evidences that might clear that matter with yourself, they thought fitt that it should be deferred till your coming, which both Justice Sibthorpe and the rest of your friends have thought was the best course, and I could not see any disadvantage to you in it, and therefore let it rest so, but yet had regard that he should not proceed any further—and now since the receipt of your letters we have had som conference with Mr. Croe, concerning the purches, but as yet he is not com neer to the least that you demand by more nor a fourth part, and withall doth seek syndry clauses of warrandyse of any thing don by Sr Francis and his ladye, which we will not meddle with; but he hath promised to-morrow to give us his absolut answer, thereupon we shall follow that course that we shall think shall be best for your benefit, and advertise you with the best speed that we may; for, if we do not agree with him, we shall trye what we can do with others.—As for Anthonye, befor my coming from Clanchie, I brought all your tennants befor him, showing both to him and them what was due by every of them, which they promised to pay him with all the haste that they could, praying to forbear them for some short time that they might sell some of their commo-

dities at som faires which were near, and then they would pay him; so he is collecting of it with the best speed that he may to bring it to Mr. Croe, which I hope he shall do very shortlie; but in truth money is very scarce in this country. I hear also that Patrick Shawe is come to Bangor to receave the rents due there. My cousin Bayley hath sent the letter herewith enclosed to Mrs. Bayley. He hath been very desirous to com over before this tym, but hath not got his land passed as yet, altho now he hath taken a course of it, as also the money was very scarce here, so that he could not com in that sort that he thought was fiting; but now he hath made himself ready to come over before the end of this month, God willing, and doth intreat you to cause delyver this letter to her, and of yourself to excuse his stay here, which he could not help. I have sent the houshold furniture that my lady left here to Bangor, according as she did direct. Your accompt that you wrote for, concerning Mr. Wakeman, shall come over with Anthonye, and so also I hope shall the discharge that you desyred from Sr Arthur Savage, who hath promised it, but will not meddle with anything concerning St. Mary Abbay. I have spoken with Sr James Carroll concerning Mr. Wakeman, and the money that is due to him, and he sayeth that, for his part of that money, he disbursed it at the direction of the Earl of Devonshyre, and of Mr. Earth and Mr. Wakeman, as may appear by their letters and other writts, which I have now in your custody, by which you might caus them to allow it if you would; for if he were there with these writts he might do it. And he doth also alledge, that at the purchase of that grant he did disburse the money in great, and did receive it again in such small parcells, as it came never together to a sum to do him good, and with all, that you kept for your own use the chief and principal parcells wherein was most benefit, and that he got those that were meanest, or at least rate to be had for, and that therefor you should regard him; so that, howsever it be, we can not get him to send over any money, or to relieve you of that debt; but you must take the best course that you can there for it, and we shall do what we may here, and advertise you more fully by the next. So, my ductye remembred to yourself and my ladye, with my loyal nevoy, praying God to bless and preserve you all, I rest your loving brother, to be commandit, "JOHN HAMILTON.

"Dublin, 10th May, 1621."

"Sara hath sent to Coronary for the lynen clothes and yearne that my lady desyred, and I hope it shall be here shortly.

"To the Honourable and my very loving brother Sr James Hamilton, Knyght, one of his Matis privie counsell in Ireland."

This letter is thus endorsed in Sir James Hamilton's handwriting—"10th May, 1621.—John Hamilton, for his proceedings upon St Marie Abay, and the Abay of Plarie, business in Dublin, after my letters recd by him from Antonie:—Also concerning Mr. Wakeman."

mented and beloved of all that knew him; was laid in a vault at the church of Mullaghbrack, in y* County of Armagh, which he had prepared for himself and family.

The fifth brother, William,' married   *   Melvill, daughter to Sir John Melville, in Isle-a-Kail, and had children by her, James, John, Hans, and William, Ursula, and   *   *   He was a prudent, industrious, and pious man, very usefull in the country, and to my Lord Claneboy ; he died of middle age; had but little satisfaction in his wife, but was very patient towards her ; was creditably buried, and with great lamentation, at Hollywood, having left his wife and children a very competent estate, as was formerly noticed.

The sixth brother, Patrick, married one   *   Glenn, daughter of a gent. of the neighbourhood where he was Minister, viz., Enderwick, a very frugal wife, but not altogether so prudent as his station and disposition required; and he had children by her, James, Alexander, Archd., and Elizabeth. He lived in very good esteem and usefullness in his Ministry, and among the gentry in that whole country, and left his family competently provided; died of middle age, and was buried with great regret at the church where he was Minister.

The things observable of them are—1. That they were all men of very good, both natural and acquired, parts; of good persons ; tempers religiously disposed; and of great respect with all that were acquainted with them.—2. They abounded in natural affection toward each other and their families, and so became very usefull and comfortable in the raising and supporting of one another while living, and carefull of their families who were dead; especially, my Lord Claneboy acted the part of a parent to all his nephews and nieces whilst he lived, though they were much disappointed in the expectation he himself had raised in them at or after his death, thro' some accidents partly hinted at, and others not to be too scrutinously digged up to posterity.—3. My Lord had great credit, comfort, and strength, by his nephews, in the war that broke out in 1641,' whilst they proved

---

* Of Newcastle, in the Ards, County Down, the ancestor of the present Viscount Bangor, in the peerage of Ireland.
† This Rebellion broke out on the 23rd of October, 1641, and, in November, the Lords Justices sent commissions to Lords Viscounts Claneboye, and of the Ards, for raising Scots in the northern parts, and putting them into arms. —Temple's Irish Rebellion, p. 53.—The Lords Justices sent commissions by sea to Ulster, the communication by land being interrupted by the rebels, empowering Captain Arthur Chichester, and Sir Arthur Tyringham to take the command of all the forces in the County of Antrim, and urging the Lords Chichester, Claneboy, and Ardes, with several knights and gentlemen, to use their best efforts for the suppression of the rebellion.—1 Carte, 187. These des-

patches were followed by others from the King, at Edinburgh, received on the 7th Nov., assuring the Northern Protestants of speedy and efficient support. Shortly after, he forwarded commissions, dated the 16th of the same month, to the Lord of Ards, and Sir James Montgomery, in the County of Down, authorising each of them to raise a regiment of 1,000 foot, and a troop of horse. These forces, however, were in great want of arms. The Lords Justices had sent 400 muskets, with a due proportion of ammunition to the Lords Claneboy, and Ards (Temple, 91) but this supply was insufficient, as Lord Claneboy soon after sent to Scotland to purchase an additional quantity of arms. This application was made January 21, 1642, by Richard Tweedie, servitor to the Lord Claneboy, (MSS.

M

very industrious, and remarkably courageous in that war, which became very advantageous to his

---

Gen. Reg. House, Edinb.) ; and the following is a copy of the Bond entered into on the occasion. :—

"At Edinburghe the twentie sexte of Januar, M.D.C. fourtie twa yieres. In presence of y⁰ Lordis and utheris comissioneris appoyntit for the comoun burdingis of this kingdome, comperied Mr. James Baird, advocat pro⁰ for Williame Muire, of Glanderstoun, and Robert Twedie, servitor to y⁰ Viscount of Clandeboyes, in Ireland, and gave in the Bond underwritten, desiring y⁰ same to be insert and registrat in y⁰ said comissioneris yair buikes, to have the strenth of ane decreit with lettres and executioun to be decreit y⁰upon in maner y⁰in contained. The whilk desire the saidis comissioneris thought ressonable, and thairfor hes ordained and ordaines : The said Bond to be insert and registrat in yair sadis buikis, decernes y⁰ same to have y⁰ strenth of y⁰ decreit, and ordaines lettres and executiouns to be direct y⁰upon in manner specifiet y⁰intill wrof the tenor followis :—Be it kend to all men be yir p⁰ⁿᵗ. lettres, We Williame Mure, of Glanderstoun, and Robert Twedie, servitor to y⁰ Viscount of Clandeboyes, in Ireland ; Forsamekle as by order and warrand from y⁰ comissioneris we have r⁰savit from Colonell Alexauder Hamiltoun, generall of y⁰ artailziarey furth of y⁰ comoun magazine of y⁰ said kingdome, the number of four hundreth muskets, with yair bandeleires at ten punds y⁰ piece, to be payit at Witsunday next : Thairfor we be yir pntis Bonds and obleis us our aires, ⁰xrs, and successors conjunctlie and severally to mak thankfull payment of y⁰ forsaid sowme of ten pundis as y⁰ liquidat pryce agried per us for ilk ane of y⁰ saidis four hundreth musketts, with yair bandeleirs, extending in all to four thowsand pundis Scotis money ; To y⁰ saidis comissioneris for y⁰ comoun burdeongs, and to yare re⁰ce⁰vⁱris in yair names, or any utheris haveing yair warrand for yat effect ; and yat within the burghe of Edinburghe betwixt y⁰ dait heirof and y⁰ * * * and * * * of Witsunday next, but langer delay ; Togither with y⁰ sⁱwme of four hundreth punds of liquidat expenses in caise of faillzie, Togither with y⁰ wrent and profeit of y⁰ said priacipall sowme conforme to y⁰ act of parliament soe lang as y⁰ sⁱmyn shall remayine unpayit after y⁰ terme of payment above written. Provydeing, yat if betwixt the last day of Marche next we came really deliver back again to y⁰ said magazine at Ed⁰, or Leith the saidis four hundreth muskets with yair bandeleirs in als gude caise as we have now r⁰savit the same : In yat caise we and our forsaids to be frie of y⁰ payment of y⁰ pryces y⁰of abovewritten, and of yis present Bond, and of all yat may follow y⁰upon. And for the mair securitie we are content and consent thir pnts be insert and registrat in y⁰ saidis comissioneris yair buiks to y⁰ strenth of ane decreit. That lettres and execution of horneing on ten dayes and nyts necess⁰. may pas heirupon informe as effeires. And constitutes Mr. James Baird advocat our procurator, for remitting decrate. In witness y⁰of we have subscryvit thir presents with our hands, written be William Merschell, servitor, and Robert Hepburne advocat clerk to y⁰ said comissioneris an Edinburghe y⁰ twentie sixt day of Januar, M.D.C. fourtie twa years. Befor their witness, Gavin Blair, of Halylie, Captaine Robert Blare, his sone, and y⁰ said Williame Merschell, and his subt. W⁰. Muire, Robert Twedie—Gavin Blair, witness, R⁰.

Blair, witness, W. Merschell, witness.—Extractum de libris actorum dict. comissionariorum per me, R⁰. Hepburne."

The following letter from Lord Claneboye to his brother-in-law, William Mure of Glanderstone, has reference to these arms, and also to the erection of the Chapel mentioned in the note to page 3, *ante* :—

"GOOD BROTHER,—I have sent you by this gentleman, M⁰. Hogg, a Bond for yo⁰ hundred and thirty-two pound, and a Note for some money whiche you layd out about the Chappell. I have sent you alsoe a counterbond for your security for the Mosquetes all w⁰ʰⁱᵉ are pütted, and w⁰ʰ you will receive from him. I have written alsoe to my Lord Chancellor, that, in regard of our troubles heere w⁰ʰ disable us for soe speedy paym⁰ᵗ as the Bond imports, I may have a longer time upon consideration for the forbearance. I heard, by Tweedie, that some foolish lying reporte of my death put you and my sister and yo⁰ family in great anguish. Though, I thank God, I be readie for death at all times, yet I do not love to have my friends put in greife with lying reports, w⁰ʰ some well affected to us are ready to broach without any ground. I heare Rob⁰. Ross was a speciall venter of it there, as a thing certaine, and certainly received from his man and his sonne heere, who hath been upon some practices to draw in S⁰ James Montgomerie upon my lands with his Regiment, and to trouble the rest of the people, and hath been very slow to pay me my rent w⁰ʰ is very needful in this time, that were not slow to give to others gratis. I desired a curtesie at Robert Rosse, w⁰ʰ I well deserved, and w⁰ʰ he to avoid raised up the lye. He might have refused it in a fairer fashion. It is like enough his sonnes will have cause to repent their ill carriage to me ; for himselfe, I will say nothing, but that I merited better at his hands. I shall not need to write anything of our estate heere, knowing that this bearer and your sonne's letters will ease me in all that. To which for the present I must refer you. Yo⁰ sonne James is a Captaine of my Regem⁰ᵗ, and, in truth, deservedly, both for valor and understanding. He hath chosen all his officers of his owne name. My Regm⁰ᵗ is like to be drawne out into the ffeilde shortly, and will require collors for the several captains, w⁰ʰ must be as other collors are, of red and white. I pray you send me ffortie ells of Taffata sarsenet, such as will not run and scatter in the threads for thinness, nor will not fret by stiffness. Four ells of it should be altogither white ; and the other six and thirty, the one halfe of it white, and the other halfe red. Let it be handsomly wrapt up and delivered to Rob⁰. Tweedie's boy to bring unto me, unless you find a surer carryer, or that Rob⁰. Tweedie's brother-in-lawe send over a man. The barque with the armes touched upon the shore, and by contrary winds was driven back againe. I pray God send her safe hither ; we wonderfully want her. Further I will not trouble you with at this present, but only to entreat my sister she will not be troubled with any foolish lyes she shall heare of my death, or of any disaster unto us ; for I thank God I never better brooked my health, and God hath been pleased to favour us with much successe against the Rebell. God Almightie have all you and us in keeping.—Yo⁰ verie loving Brother, "J. CLANEBOYS.

" Killileagh, 12 Aprill, 1642."

state and credit, having not only the common enemy, but also some encroaching and invidious neighbours to do with.

The following curious particulars, respecting Belfast and its vicinity during this rebellion, are extracted from an extremely rare tract, entitled.—" *A true relation of several Acts, Passages, done, undertaken, &c., by Captain Robert Lawson, now one of the Sheriffs of the City and County of Londonderry, upon and since the first beginning of the great and general Rebellion, in Ireland, &c.* Printed at London, 1643 :"—

"About the 16th of October, 1641, before any notice of an insurrection, having occasion to take a journey from Londonderry to Dublin, and to travel by way of Belfast, to the iron-works, within two miles thereof, wherein he had some stock and interest, he took his journey from thence to go to Dublin, upon the 21st of October following ; but, on arriving at Newry, and receiving information that the rebellion had broken out, he returned to Killyleagh, to the Lord Hamilton's, and came in the night by Comber, through the Lord of Arde's county, about by Little Belfast, and came to Great Belfast, and up to the iron-works, near thereunto, about three of the clock in the morning, where his wife was then resident; and, having sent several messengers before, to enquire after him, they were taken and robbed. But Captain Lawson, not having rested there above two hours, arose, calling the horsemen with him ; and, in the morning, being Monday, went down back again to Great Belfast, where they found most of the inhabitants fled and flying, and carrying away their goods to Carrickfergus, and the old Lord Chichester shipped aboard in a ship. So Captain Lawson went throughout the town, and blamed them for offering to leave the town, and intreated for some arms, either by buying or lending, but could not prevail. At last he found at Master Lesquire's house seven muskets and eight halberts ready in the street to be shipped to Carrickfergus; which arms he took, and bought a drum, and, beating the same through the town, raised about twenty men, who came with him again up to the Iron-works, having Mr. Forbus and some number joined with Captain Lawson, where, also, in all, he gathered in all about 160 horse and foot, who, about two of the clock, upon the same Monday in the afternoon, being the 21st of October, the second day after the rebellion, marched into Lisnagarvi, and there entered the town about four of the o'clock of same day ; all the people with the troop there engarisoned, having left the town to the enemy's mercy the Sunday before, and they quartered all that night in the house the Bishop of Down lived in, and put many candles in the market-house, and sentries out in every quarter of the town, making show of six or seven lighted matches for every piece to astonish the enemy, who came to the sentries that night, intending to have burned the town ; but our show and carriage was more than our force, the enemy being strong and many in number, by which means they were affrighted and beat off that night ; and the next morning, being Tuesday, the enemy appeared above the town's end, and drove before them about 400 cows ; whereupon, Captain Lawson, with 45

horses, issued forth, leaving the rest to guard the town, and it pleased God, by their good labour and industry, they took the prey of cows and some prisoners, and killing others of the enemy ; and got seventeen of their mantles. After sending the prey into the town, they adventured three miles farther, and brought in before night as many more cows, and kept them within the bawn wall of the Bishop's house, and all the next night secured the town also, Sir Conn Magennis threatening he would burn the town that night. But it pleased God they were prevented and beaten off, and the town kept in safety ; and often issued forth amongst the enemy, to prevent their gathering to a great head, until at length, upon the next day, being Wednesday, the troop and townsmen came in again to the town ; hearing and understanding what service Captain Lawson and his small company of men had done there, in securing the same, the preservation whereof, under God, was a means of the safety not only of Lisnagarvi and Belfast, but of most of those parts thereabout, being the first that opposed the enemy in in those parts. At night came the Lord Arde's forces, and the Lord Hamilton, Sir Arthur Tiringham, Captain Chichester, Sir Thomas Lucas, and Sir James Montgomery, and Mr. Arthur Hill, with their forces, who gave Captain Lawson and his men great thanks for their good care and service in the town, and offered him a commission, which he was very unwilling to accept of, in regard of his calling, being a merchant, but which he at length accepted. So there being come up to Lisnagarvi, about 1,500 horse and foot, himself, his men, and company, had their orders by their commission, and quarters about the iron-works, in the barony of Belfast, and then left with the army about 400 cows, and only brought with him from thence about 60 cows for his own company."—*Lawson's " True Relation,"* &c.

" On the 23d of October, 1641, and within a few days after, the Irish rebels made slaughter of all men, women, and children which they could lay hands on, within the County of Antrim, that were Protestants, burning their houses and corn; and such as escaped their fury took sanctuary in the towns of Carrickfergus, Belfast, Lisnagarvey, Antrim and Larne, and the two houses of Templepatrick and Edindoughearrick ; all the said towns and houses lying near the one to the other. The rebels had the command of all the rest of the country, and within musket-shot of the towns, and up to the very walls of the two houses, until the middle of June, 1642."—*State of County Antrim in 1641-2, Rawdon Papers,* pp. 91-2.

" While the Protestants in the County of Antrim were thus occupied in providing for their security, their brethren in the County of Down were not inactive. The Lords Claneboy and Ards,—the former resident at his castle in Killileagh, which the rebels had attempted to surprise, but without success, and the latter at Newtownards,—stood upon the defensive, and effectually checked the progress of the insurrection in the adjoining districts."—1 *Reid's Pres. Hist.,* 319.

APPENDIX TO CHAPTER III.

[Copy of Sir James Hamilton's Will, referred to at page 42, *ante.*]

16 *December*, 1616.—In the name of the Lord Jesus, I, S^r. James Hamiltone, of Bangor, in the Countie of Down, in Ireland, Knight, being of perfect memorie at the making hereof, doe commit my soul to the Lord Jesus, the Redeemer thereof, and my body (if it can be convenieutlie don) to be buried in the new-built chapell at the church of Bangor, aforesaid.

Imprimis—I do appoint my wif, Jean Hamilton, *alias* Phillips, and my faithfull friends, the Right Noble Lord James and now Erle of Abercorn, and S^r. James Fullerton, Knight, to be my executors of this my last will and testament.

Item.—I doe leave and give the breeding and keeping of my son, James Hamilton, unto his mother, the said Jean, during the tyme of his tender aige, and so long as he shall not be fitt to be sent abroad to schooling. But so soon as convenieutlie, and without danger of his health, he may be sent abroad, I do appoint him to be disposed of to his learning and breeding, in such sort, place, and fashion as the said Jean, the said Erle, and the said Sir James Fullerton, or the survivor of them, shall think fitt, with a speciall regard that he be under the tuition and goverance of a dyscreet, learned, and honest man, during the time of his schooling ; and that he be bred to all pietie and virtue, and be chieflie in the keeping of the said Jean, so long as he shall remain unmarried. But with this provysion, that, if the said Jean shall marie, and that the said Erle and the said Sir James Fullerton shall fynd that husband whom she shall have married not to be carefull of the childe's breeding, as aforesaid, or to use him wrongfullie, or to take any disposing or interest in him without their direction or advyse first had, or the direction or advyse of the survivor of them, and of the mother, or that ther be cause of fear that he will seduse or drawe the childe to any hurt of his estate, or to any unfitting match, or to any match at all, without the assent or privitie of the said Erl, or the said S^r. James, or the survivor of them, then it is my pleasure that the said Erle and the said S^r. James, or the survivor of them, shall take the childe, my said sone James Hamilton, and dispose of him for his learning and breeding, as they, or the survivor of them, shall fynd best for the child's good.—And the Lord that hath been ever my God, be the like God to him and his.

And whereas I have made a feoffment of my lands in the Countie of Down, in trust to sundrie persons to the use of me, my heirs, and assigns, dissoluble at my pleasure, upon the payment of twelve pence stg., to any person whatsoever, to the use of the said feotfes, as by the said feoffment, inrolled in the Chancery of Ireland, may appear, which feoffment is chiefly to this extent, that I might be enabled to pay my debts, and that my yearly profitts and rents of my lands in money and provisions of corn, beeves, muttons, and such lyk, at the lowest rate now in certain about two thousand pounds stg. a year, besydes all casualties of mills, fynes, forfitures, amerciaments, herriots, releeves, and besydes many of my lands which are not yet lett, and besydes other lands which are lett for very few yeares, and which comeing into my hands may be lett for far greater rates, with the benefitt also of the tenant ; and besydes all my demesnes at Bangor, and Killileagh, and Ringhadie ; and besydes the lands now got from Con, and to be had from S^r. Hugh Montgomery, I do therefore appoint, that the rentall books, which I have, be viewed, and that my brother, William Hamiltone, and my officers, or such others as my executors shall find best able, give up a rentall book of my rents as now they ar (for that they are encreased since the making of the rentall book which I had for this year, 1616, and do daylie increase) to my said executors; and that they, my executors, with my said rents and profitts, deducting and allowing to my wif and child child fouer hundreth pounds yearly for ther mantenance, dureing the tyme that the debts ar a paying, (together with the houses, demesnes, and stock of Bangor, Ringhadie, and Killeleagh) do pay all my debts, of which I have, so neir as I can remember, left herewith a doquet or catalog, and if they shall fynd any other justlie due, that they be lykewise honestly paid, and every man trulie satisfied and conscionable. And, my debts being payed, I do give to the said Erle and S^r. James, equally betwecn them, one thousand pounds of the two years' rent which shall next ensue after the payment of my said debts. And if the said Erle and the said S^r. James shall think fitt to take up so much money as to pay the most urgent of my debts, and such as they see greatest need of, that money so taken up by them may rest unsatisfied for the principall, until the other debts be paid out of the yearly growing rents, and that then that money be also payed and satisfied to them of whom the said Erle or the said S^r. James have so taken it up, together with the consideration, if any have not been payed, or omitted to be payed, in any of the yeares from the taking up of it. Then, my debts being so payed, I do give to the said Erle and S^r. James Fullerton, equally between them, besydes the above mentioned £1,000, fouer hundreth pounds more, making to every of them seven hundreth pounds in all, in respect of my love to them, and of their chardge and paines for payment of my debts and preservation of my estate to my child, and furtherance, and help, and oversight, of my wife and child. And this fourteen hundreth pounds to be taken so much as can conveniently (allowance being made to my wif and child of fouer hundreth pounds as aforesaid yearly) be had out of the first two or three yeares' rent that shall next ensue after the payment of my debts, and what shall remain unsatisfied in those two or three years to be taken out of the next year thereafter. And, for all the remaine of the rents and profitts that shall grow due over and above the satisfaction of such debts and sumes of money, and as shall come and arise out of my lands and other things yearlie, I leave and appoint it to be disposed in this forme, until my said sone, James Hamiltone, the sone of Jean Philips aforesaid, be of twenty yeares of age, if it please God that he live so long; that my wif Jean Hamiltone, *alias* Philips, have yearlie four hundreth pounds stg., during her natural liff; and, so long as she shall romane unmarried, that she shall have the use and keeping of all my houses, and of the demeanes of them, viz., of Bangor, Ringhadie, and of Killileagh, and also the taking up and receaving of all the rents, profitts, and casualties of my lands and other things; but, so as every yeare, once, it be made apparent to my other two executors, or to two of my brothers, how much it is that she hath taken up over and above the said fouer hundreth pounds; and that the same be made apparent to my other two executors, or to two of my brothers, Archibald, John, and William Hamiltones, and that the same be disposed a convenient part to the mantenance and breeding of my said sone. And, if it please God that my said wif be now conceaved with any child or children, one third part yearly thereof, during the said tyme, until my said sone be of twentie years of age as aforesaid, (from the tyme of the payment of my debts and of the sumes of money devised by me hereby, to the Erle of Abercorn and S^r. James Fullerton) to be put apart of the said whole profitts and rents for the said child that she shall be conceaved with, or for more children if she shall fall out to be conceaved with more, until the sum of two thousand pounds sterling a piece be made up for every of them, and put upon good assurance for their behoof, or three thousand pounds if there be but one child which she shall be conceaved with; the same to be paid to them, and every of them, being sones, when they shall be sixteen years of age, or put to their best behoof, by the advise of their mother and of my executors, or brothers aforesaid; and, being a daughter or daughters, to be payed as aforesaid, £2,000 to every daughter, or £3,000 if there be but one daughter, to be payed to them respectivelie within ten days next after their marriage, to any such man as by the advise and consent of their mother, and of my executors or said brothers, or any one of them, with the mother, if there be so many alive, they shall marry unto, not being of the children or posteritie of Sir Hugh Montgomery, of Newton, knight.[a] And if they shall marry with any of the posteritie of Sir Hugh Mont-

---

[a] In the foregoing MSS., at page 30, it is stated that "he had several tedious and chargeable law-suits with his neighbour, my Lord of Ards, about * of land and other trifles, wherein pride and incendiaries occasion great expense of money and peace," which might in some measure have accounted for the bitter feeling here expressed towards Sir Hugh Montgomery; but as the particulars of these differences, and of their subsequent reconciliation, are so minutely given in the Montgomery MSS., the entire passage has been extracted at pp. 23 to 25, *ante*; and, in

N

gomery, or without the consent and good liking of their mother, then I do appoint their portions to revert to their brother, my son, or my next heir, and they to receave such portion as he shall think meet. And I do desyre my wif, as also my said sone, or sones and daughters, if my wif fall out to be now with child of any sone or daughter, that, upon my blessing, they, nor none of them, match nor marie not with any sone nor daughter of the house or posteritie of Sir Hugh Montgomerie, now of Newton, knight. And for the remaine of the revenues or profitts of my leiving, which shall be over and above my wife's said portione during her widowhood, and the maintenance of my sone, and such portion as is now set downe for my other children, if any I have, or in case I have no other children but my said son, I do appoint all the said remaine to be put by my wif during her widowhood, or my son's nonage, to his best bene-fitt, and purchase of lands and good breeding, by the advyse of my executors, or of my brothers, or two of them ; and to give to every of my nephews—I mean to Gawen's three sons, Archibald, James, and Dick, or Richard, viz., to Archibald, so much as with a portion out of my part of the tithes, will mak him up twentie pounds a year ; and to James, his brother, so much more ; and to Richard so long as he is in the Grammar School, ten pounds a year, and during his tyme of being in the colledge twentie marks a year ; also, to William, his son James, £10 a year during his being in the Grammar School, and, during his being in the colledge, twenty marks a year ; and Robin Wallace, £10 a year, until he leave and passe his course in the colledge ; and to Patrick, my brother's son, James, £20 a year ; all these last sumes to be taken out of my part of the tithes, or out of the two partes of the tithes called the parsonag ; and to be continued unto them until they shall be provyded of some meanes of living ; and if the tythes shal fall short by any casualitie, means, or occasion, then that there some payment be holpen out of my temporalities, if it can not be had out of the tithes. And if my said wif shall marie again, then I do appoint the taking up of all the rents and profitts to be by some of my brothers whom my said wife and executors shall choose during the tyme thereafter, untill my sone shall be twenty yeares of aig, to be accountable to my wif and executors for the same, until my sone be of aig ; and, from thenceforth, I do appoint to my said wif, during her naturall liff, fouer hundreth pounds a year, yearly ; and further, if she shall match with the advyse and good liking of my brothers, or executors, or most part of them, I ap-point to her during her lif, the choise of Ringhadie, or Killeleagh house and demesnes.

Item —for the Tithes or Spiritualities, I appoint that the vicarag, or third part be sovered off from the parsonag or two parts, and that the vicar have the same third part for his maintenance to serve the cure at the severall parishes of Ballehalbert, Bangor, Holiwood, Dundonnell, and Killeleagh ; and if every of the severall vicars shall not by that vicarag have £20 stg. yearlie, besydes ten or twelve acres of gleb land, I do appoint that, out of my two partes or par-sonag, they be severally made up £20 by the year, besydes the said twelve acres of gleb land, to every church or vicar ; provyded, that such of the severall vicars as shall not take this £20 stg. and 12 acres of gleb land in full satis-faction of his stipend, surceasing all other claims and demands, then he to be left to take the benefitt of his own third part, and not to have any part of the parsonag nor g'eb land, which now for their help I do allow out of my own leiving to them. And, for such profitts as shall be made of my two partes or parsonag, I do appoint the schoolmasters to be mantayned as now I have appointed them—one at Ballehalbert (and at Whitchurch or Ennishargie, at the choyce of my wif, a schoolmaster), one at Bangor, one at Holliwood, one at the foord of Belfast,[b] one at Dundonnell,

---

addition to this, at p. 109, of the Mont. MSS., the Lord Clanoboy is named as being in the procession, at the fune-ral of the first Viscount Montgomery, in 1636 ; and, from the following passage at p. 113, it appears that he was one of the chief mourners :—" Then walked the Viscount Clane-boy and the Earl of Eglinton together ; the Lord Alexander and the Lord Montgomery together, John McDowal, of Garthland, and the Baron of Howth's son. — St-Lawrence, Esq.; and Sir William Stewart, Knight Bart., and Privy Counsellor, in one rank. All these, as chief mourners, who were attended by some of their own servants, ap-pointed to wait upon them, and be near their persons."

[b] Although the situation of the ford of Belfast has of

late been the subject of controversy, especially in the long litigated ejectment, at suit of the Marquis of Donegall, against Lord Templemore, it is plain that, in the year 1616, it was as well known as any of the other places named in the above clause of Sir James Hamilton's will. The old bridge of Belfast, commonly called the " Long Bridge," had not then been built ; and Harris, in his History of County Down, says :—" The foundation of it was laid about the year 1682, and it was not completely finished until the Revolution ; soon after which, in spring, 1692, seven of the arches fell in, the bridge having been weakened by Duke Schomberg's drawing his heavy cannon over it some time before, as well as by a ship driving against it. But it was

and one at Killeleagh, and fyve pounds a year to be given to every of them, out of the said parsonag tithes, besydes such monies as they shall have from the scholers for their teaching ; and, for that I give this specially for a regard of learning, and of the poorer sort, therefore a regard to be had of them that their stipends be easie. And for the

soon after repaired by a new charge on the two counties, and continued ever since in tolerable good order, till of late, having received considerable damage from winter storms and floods ; and, if proper care be not in time taken, it may probably suffer more. Before it was built, the nearest bridge travellers had to pass from one county to the other was Shaw's Bridge, upwards of three miles south of Belfast, which was formerly small, but now [1744] consists of six arches. Yet a communication was maintained here over the Lagan by a ferry, where this bridge now stands ; which ferry probably gave name to the town.— *Beal* signifies a mouth, and *Farshady*, a ferry, i.e., *Belfast*, or the mouth of the ferry."—*Harris*, 129. Dr. Reeves, however, proves that Harris was inaccurate in this definition ; that its proper meaning was the mouth of the ford ; and, that the word *Fearsad* is of frequent occurrence in Irish writings, in the sense of the crossing of a river at its mouth, or near an estuary. He says :—" The name of Belfast, or Bealfarst, as it is found in some old documents, is compounded of the two words *Bel*, a mouth, and *Feirste*, or *Feirsde*, the plural of *Fearsat*, or *Fearsad*, which, according to O'Brien and O'Reilly, signifies ' a pool of water remaining on the strand at low tide ;' and, in a secondary sense, seems to correspond to the Latin *Vadum*, and the Saxon *Ford*. Saint George's Church, in Belfast, occupies the site of an earlier religious edifice, which is represented in an old map of the town, preserved in the Library of Lambeth. Near this was one of the fords by which the Lagan was commonly crossed, which, being the lowest down on the river, and therefore the most convenient for the inhabitants of either side of Belfast Lough, was called ' par excellence,' *the* Ford. William de Burgo, Earl of Ulster, who was assassinated at this spot, June 6th, 1333, held, at the time of his death, 'apud *le Ford*, manerium in quo est unum castrum prostratum per guerram Johannis de Logan.'—(Inquis. P. M. 7 Ed. III., 39, Tur. Lond.) Another ford lay higher up on the river, at Stranmillis."—*Reeves' Ec. An.*, p. 7, note q. Again, in his description of the parish of Shankhill, Dr. Reeves says :—" Belfast is called *Beal-Feirste*, by the Four Masters, at the years 1476, 1489, 1503, 1512, 1537, and 1552, where it is mentioned in connexion with its castle. Among the English settlers it was called *Belferside*, or *Bealfarst*. This name had reference, as has been already observed, to the *fearsat*, or *ford*, by which the Lagan was usually crossed at this place. The old map of Belfast, preserved in the MS. collection of Lambeth Library, as well as the plan of the town, constructed about the year 1660, represents an extensive ford, reaching in the direction of the present Corn Market, and communicating with the enclosure of the castle."—*Reeves*, p. 183. In p. 249 of the 3d vol. of the *Ulster Archæological Journal* will be found a copy of the plan referred to, which was originally published in a translation of Rapin's England, but has been subsequently copied into Benn's History of Belfast, published in 1823. Dr. O'Donovan, the distinguished Irish scholar, has given it as his opinion that "Belfast" is derived from two Irish words signifying

" mouth of the ford ;" he says that *Fersad* means a bank of sea sand, or gravel, washed down by some river and met by the tide, forming what is called a " bar ;" that he knows of several *Fersads* in Ireland, as *Fersad-more*, at the mouth of the River Swilly, in Donegal ; *Fersad*, on the river Sligo, near its mouth ; the *Fersad* on the Ballysodare river, in the county Sligo ; and *Fersad Tresi*, at Rathferan Bay, barony of Tyrawley, county Mayo. All these *Fersads* are natural gravel and sea sand banks, and are still well known to the people, and are crossed habitually. The country people still use the phrase—" to get the *Fersad*," meaning to get to the bank at that state of the tide which will enable them to cross. The *Fersad* at Belfast was a natural ford, not an artificial one, and was opposite the castle, which was evidently built to command it : it was always usual to have a castle at a ford to command and watch it. The following early notices of the Ford and Castle of Belfast are strongly confirmatory of Dr. O'Donovan's opinion :— In the year 667, this ford is thus mentioned, in the Annals of Ulster, as the scene of an encounter between the inhabitants of the district on either side :—" The battle of the Ford, between the Ulidians and Picts, where fell Catusach, son of Lurgein." In 1262 the following entry is made on the Pipe Roll of 46 Henry III. of record in the Exchequer Office, Dublin :—" Richard of Exeter accounts for £254 7s 6d, for many debts, &c.; £30 granted by the King's son, Edward, to him for the custody of the Castle Craefergus ; £20 for the custody of the Castle of Antrim ; £ for the Castle Del Rath ; £10, which Edward, the King's son, granted to him for the custody of *the Castle of the Ford* ; and £10 for the custody of Greencastle." " The name appears in the Taxation in the Latin form *Vadum* ; and again, in 1333, as a place where the castle of the Earl of Ulster stood, and where William de Burgo was assassinated."—*Reeves*, p. 184. " A.D. 1503, The Earl of Kildare, having gone to England, returned triumphantly, and brought his son with him who had been imprisoned there by the King of England ; and the same earl marched with a force of the English and Irish of Leinster into Moylenny (in Antrim), and to Carrickfergus, demolished the Castle of Belfast, and appointed the son of Santalach (probably Sainthill) constable of Carrickfergus."—*Annals of the Four Masters, translated by Connellan*, p. 349.—" A.D. 1512, Gerald, Earl of Kildare, Lord Justice of Ireland, marched with a force into Trian Congail (in Down and Antrim) ; took the Castle of Belfast ; demolished the Castle of Mac Eoin (Mac John) of Glinns (in Antrim) ; plundered the Glinns and a great portion of the country, and carried with him, as prisoner, the son of Niall, son of Con (O'Neill)."—*Ibid.*, p. 370.— A letter from the Earl of Kildare to Henry VIII., dated in 1523, contains the following passage :—" For the which rescowes I brake a castell of his, called Belfast, and burned 24 myle of his countrie, and took and burned two other piles that Scotts kept there."—*State Papers of Hen. VIII.*, vol. 2, p. 100. Lord Chancellor Cusack thus writes to the Duke of Northumberland, on the 8th of May, 1552 :—" The same Hughe (McNeile Oge) hath two castles ; one called

remaine of all the parsonag tithes, I do appoint, as formerly I have set down, for the maintenance of my nephewes, Archibald, and James, the sons of Gawen, twentie pounds a peece a year; to the aforesaid Richard, as above is set down for him; and also to James my brother, William his son, as is above sett down for him; and the lyk to Patrick his sone, as is above sett downe for him; and to Robin Wallace, £10 a year for six years to come;

Belfast, an oulde castle standing upon a *fourde* that leadeth from Arde to Clanneboye, which being well repayred, being now broken, would be a good defence betwixt the woods and Knockfergus; the other called Castleriongbe, &c."—*Harl. MSS., Brit. Mus.*, No. 35, fol. 188 v.—194 v. *Holinpshed's Chronicle* states, that, "in 1545, the Earl of Ormond marched with his soldiers from Carrickfergus to Belfast, which is an arm of the sea about a quarter of a mile broad and little less, and there waded over on foot." Sir Henry Sidney, writing in 1575, states "the Clandeboy to be utterly disinhabited;" and adds, "at the passage of the water at Belfast, by reason of the tide's extraordinary return, our horses swam, and the footmen waded very deep." Father Edmund McCana, in his Irish Itinerary, supposed by Dr. Reeves to have been written shortly after 1643, in describing Lower Clandeboy, says:—"The lake of the Calf, or *Loch Laodh*, in Irish, flows between and bounds either Clandeboy, the bend of which, when the tide is out, may be crossed on foot by a ford which is called *Beall-fearst*. Beside it formerly stood the castle of the lords of those territories, in the naval, as it were, and central point of the two regions. Previously to the present war, that old castle was repaired by Lord Chichester, an Englishman, who made it his own residence. The town which is built there is no mean one, accessible to the inhabitants of either district, as well as of Scotland. From the ford of which I have just spoken it takes the name of *Beall-fearst*, where the river empties itself, which is called the river of the Laggan, or of the Valley, yielding a plentiful supply of salmon, and dividing in its course the two regions of Clandeboy, on the north and south."—*Ulster Arch. Journal*, vol. 2, pp. 57-8. The following interesting note on the Ford of Belfast was written (May 31, 1847), by the late Mr. Berwick, author of *Historical Collections relative to the Town of Belfast:*—"As it is styled the ford of *Belfast*, it must have been at or very near the town, and not a mile or two up the river. In fixing the position of it, we must take the river *at low water*, for it could not have been fordable at high water. The low-water mark is, in all probability, the same now as it was in 1805, or nearly the same, and is now marked by the line of quays and embankments to the Lagan Bridge. It has not varied in my recollection (say, since 1797); the slob, as I observed before the Queen's Quay was formed, seemed much more elevated than 50 years before, but the line of the low-water has never appeared to me to vary. On account of the depth of water at low tide, the river could not have been fordable opposite the town, or nearer, I should think, than the 'Gooseberry Corner.' A fordable place, however, may have existed at the site of the old 'Long Bridge.' It might have been shallow there, and 'Ann Street' might seem to have been the thoroughfare leading to it. To this objection I reply, that if a ford had existed at the end of Ann Street, public-houses, &c., must have been built there for the convenience of passengers. But, on the contrary, even in the Lambeth Map, which was surveyed for before the castle was destroyed in 1708,

not a house or building of any kind is marked; and Ann Street at that time seems not to have extended, if I recollect owll, farther than Forest Lane. In truth, Ann Street would seem not to have been completed to the Bridge until the reign of Queen Ann, for from her it most probably takes its name, and so Prince's Street from her husband, the Prince of Denmark, and Marlborough Street from the Duke. The town, therefore, did not extend even to the Long Bridge, till Hanover Quay was founded, after 1714. If a ford had existed at the end of Ann Street or Waring Street, so important a point would have been strongly defended by a *fort*; but no fort exists in any ancient map. By placing the ford at the spot now known as the Police Office, or near it, we have the authority of the map (supposed, and very probably too, to be) of the date of 1660; for it has a double line indicating a connexion between this spot and the opposite shore. The river in that map is represented at *high-water*, which then came up to near the east side of Joy Street: ' *the very end of the Lough* (says a traveller in 1685) touching upon Lord Chichester's garden and back-side.' (See my *Hist. Col.*, p. 11.) Consequently, no bank or sea-wall which is represented in the map of 1791 (and which I well recollect), could then have existed. It must have been a much later erection, since the Long Bridge was built, and for the purpose of keeping the sea from flooding the grounds to the West of it, up to the town-wall and the back of the gardens. This long bank, therefore, is of no material consequence in the present question. It may be objected, that if there was no fort to protect the landing-place at the end of Ann Street, so neither do we find any at the point which I have taken, namely, the site of the present Police Office; but it is easy to show, from a comparison of the present map of the town with that of 1660, when its ramparts were perfect, that one of the *demi-bastions* stood upon, or near, the site of the present Theatre, which commanded the landing-place of the ford, at or near the Police Office, and the street leading to it from Corn Market. At this demi-bastion the rampart seems to have terminated. The nearest bastion to it was situated at or near Mr. McDowell's house in Upper Arthur Street, which was, of course, connected with the other bastion by the curtain of the rampart, lined with cannon. The line of the *sea-bank*, marked in the map of 1791, pointed to that part of the county Down far above the Lagan Foundry—too remote and improbable a place for a ford; but the lines marking the supposed ford in the map of 1660 point to, or near to, the Lagan Foundry, which is a very short distance from the Gooseberry Corner, from which proceeded the *only* road to Donaghadee, &c., prior to the formation of the 'New Road' (as it is sometimes still called) passing through Ballymacarrett. This conjecture is clearly confirmed by the testimony of an old acquaintance of mine, aged about seventy, who frequently heard his mother relating the dangers which were experienced by her ancestors in crossing the river at or

and something to be given to every of my nephewes and neices at the discretion of my wif, wherein I wish some respect to be had of my brother Gawen's second daughter. Now, all the rest of the parsonag tithes I leave it whollie, whatsoever may be made of the said parsonag tithes belonging to me, to be employed to good-

---

near the Gooseberry Corner, prior to the building of the Long Bridge—the plunging of the horses, &c."—*Berwick MS.*

In reference to the schoolmaster above directed to be maintained at the Ford of Belfast, an old woman named Jenny Boyd, who had resided all her life near "Watson's Corner," in Ballymacarrett, in the year 1848 informed Mr. Cranston, Lord Templemore's agent, that she recollected a very old School-house, situated a little above Watson's Corner, on the old paved road, which was kept by a man called Hand; that there were large stones outside the school-house on which the children used to sit; and that the school-house was taken down upwards of fifty years ago, when a Mr. Telfair got a lease of the ground on which it was built. And, in a book of survey of lands belonging to the Right Honourable the Lord Viscount Clandeboye, by Thomas Raven, in 1625-6, there is a map of the townland of Ballymacarrett, upon which a building is marked corresponding exactly with the situation of, and which, from its appearance, there can be little doubt is, the original school-house referred to in Lord Clandeboye's will.

The following passages in the judgment of the Court of Queen's Bench, delivered by Mr. Justice Crampton in the case of *Donegall* v. *Templemore*, in 1848, which is reported in the 12th vol. of the *Irish Law Reports*, p. 191, have reference to the old Ford of Belfast:—" The controversy between the parties was as to the point where the river Lagan terminated and the sea began. The plaintiff contended that the river Lagan, and of course its bed and soil, extended down the Channel into the Lough of Belfast as far as Garmoyle, three or four miles below the Long Bridge, and where the water at high tides is six miles broad. The defendant contended that the river (to which the plaintiff must be deemed to be entitled) terminated at a ford some short distance higher up the stream than the Long Bridge was. That the terms, 'River,' and 'Channel' have in modern times been applied to the flowing water as far as Garmoyle was confessed, and, indeed, clearly proved. But the defendant contended that in 1605 and 1620, when the two rival patents were granted [to Sir James Hamilton and Sir Arthur Chichester], the term 'River' was applied only to so much of the flowing water as was above the Long Bridge; that in 1605 the river was supposed to terminate, and the sea to begin, at *the old ford*, called the 'Ford or Passage of Belfast.' To establish this point, the defendant relied upon the patent of 1605, and on some parol evidence, to which I shall advert presently. The patent of 1605 describes the boundaries of Clandeboye and Ardes (in the first of which territories the townland of Ballymacarrett is situate) with great precision, making on one side the Bay of Knockfergus (now the Lough of Belfast), and the river Lagan to be its noted boundary; and the river Lagan is made the boundary from the passage or ford of Belfast up the river for eight miles, until the Lagan joins another river called Garryeloth. It is plain, therefore, that, in 1605, the ford or passage of Belfast was a well-known place, and that, at that ford, what was then called the river Lagan terminated, and the lough or the bay began. No doubt in the lapse of time, since 1605, many changes may have been made in the river, and in its course and banks; but, if we could now find that ford or passage, we should at once arrive at the decision of this case. Where is that passage now, or rather place?—for the ford or passage of Belfast has altogether disappeared; wherever it was, the bridge superseded it: what it was in 1605, we may well assume it to have been in 1620. Now, the plaintiff says the river and its bed and soil run all along to Garmoyle. The defendant says it [the ford] was above the Long Bridge, near the place called Watson's Corner. We must assume there was a passage or ford over the Lagan when these patents were granted. Where was it? An old map might have thrown light on the subject, but there was none in evidence. If we compare the evidence of the plaintiff as to this point with the evidence of the defendant, we must say that both are slight; but, can we say that that on the plaintiff's part preponderates, so as to make this a verdict against evidence, or even against the weight of evidence? The plaintiff's evidence consists of the opinion of seafaring men,—that the river Lagan, or the channel of that river, goes down as far as Garmoyle. But, can it be believed that the ford of Belfast was there? It is not even pretended that it was, and we must assume that the terminus in 1620 was at that ford of Belfast. *   * But still the inquiry is, what was held to be the *terminus* of the river in 1605 and 1620? Where was *the* ford or passage of Belfast? The defendant's evidence consisted of parol evidence, showing that there is a place near Belfast called Gooseberry Corner, at which three leading roads met; that these joined with one road leading directly to the river above the Long Bridge, to a place called Watson's Corner, and that there the road terminated, and that a line over the river from that point led directly to the Castle of Belfast. This ford, wherever it was, must have been in use before the building of the bridge, and there seems to have been no entrance from the Down side of the river into Belfast, from the roads thus meeting at Watson's Corner, except by a passage somewhere over or through the river. There was also evidence of pavement running across part of the river near Watson's Corner. This evidence was slight; but it is impossible to say that there is not at the least as much evidence that the ford of Belfast was above the Long Bridge as there was that it was below it. I should rather say that the evidence for the defendant on that point was the stronger. This, then, was a jury question; there was evidence for the jury on both sides, and they have on this, the fourth trial, found for the defendant. How can we, on the ground of the verdict being against evidence, find for the plaintiff?"

The judgment of the Court of Queen's Bench was accordingly given in favour of Lord Templemore; but, Lord Donegall being dissatisfied with it, brought a new ejectment in the Court of Exchequer, in which, after several trials, judgment was also given for Lord Templemore, which was confirmed by the Exchequer Chamber on a writ of error having been brought into it by Lord Donegall, and the judgment of that court will be found reported in the 10th vol. of the *Irish Common Law Reports.* Upon the trial of

o

lie and religious uses, for the service of God, manteyning of churches, breeding of scholers and preachers, and for the poor, and charitable works; and, the lik use to be made of those pensions as they shall fall, which I have hereby appointed for my nephewes and others; and I do appoint my sone and heires to take knowledg hereof, and of a wryting under my hand, concerning the religious imployment of my tithes, wherein the tenent of the land is not to be neglected, but used with favour in the payment of them. And, for my wif and executors, to the end that this may be the better don, I think fitt that for a tyme they appoint certane collectors (wher the vicareges are endowed) of my two parts, leaving the vicar to his third part; and wher the wholl tithes are myne own, as in Bangor, and such places, that the collectors do justlie take up all, and, the vicar or server of the cure being payed, the rest be disposed of as I have here sett downe.

I do appoint that my mother have the profitts of the towne of Portavoe during her lyf, yearly, sent to her in season, at two tymes in the year; and that John, my brother, be the receaver of it from my wif, and sender of it to her, and that if she do owe any debts at her death, the same be payed out of my rents or goods; and, for other kyndnesses, I leave her to Jean, and to her grandchild, to send to her what Jean shall think that she wanteth.[e]

And, whereas I have made and perfected some deeds to some of my tenents in the Ards, and received the counterparts of them, I will that those deeds be truelie kept, as my deed to John Maxwell; but, whereas I made up other draughtes or formes of deeds, and signed and sealed them at Dublin, for sundrie other of my tenents of the Ards, as for William Wallace, Edward Maxwell, Michael Craig, and others; but for that the heads or minutes of our agreement, was not then at Dublin, and that I was then going to sea, and therefore willing to leave some sorte of securitie to be perfected

---

this ejectment in the Court of Exchequer, the following conclusive evidence was given as to the site of the old ford or passage of Belfast:—

"JOHN FRAZER, C.E., who, being sworn, deposed, that he recollects the old Long Bridge of Belfast, and, when it was taken down, saw people there repeatedly crossing the stream between the two bridges (that is between the Long Bridge and Coates's Bridge), but not just so high up as Watson's Corner, nearer the Long Bridge, and on the County Down side; he himself waded across the river opposite May's Dock; when the tide was coming in, it took him up to the thigh, and he found the ground firm in the bed of the river; that Watson's Corner is at the edge of the water at high-water mark; that several very old paved roads come down from different parts of the County Down (which he has marked on the map produced and given in evidence), and meet at a point called Gooseberry Corner, and from thence a single old paved road leads direct to Watson's Corner, which is paved to the edge of the water, and takes a slight turn to the right down the stream, across which parties ford to the Antrim side must have forded before the bridge was built, and it is still fordable here; that he was Surveyor for the County of Down when the new bridge was building, and that the same was built partly under his superintendence; that he made borings in the bed of the stream for the purpose of ascertaining the best site for the new bridge; that the borings were made from the old Long Bridge as far down as opposite High Street; that the bed of the river sea-ward of the old bridge was all soft sleech; that he never attempted to ford the river below the bridge, because from the borings taken he knew it would be impossible; that the Counties of Antrim and Down wished to have the new bridge built opposite High Street, if possible, but, from the soft nature of the soil below the bridge, this plan was abandoned as impracticable; that above the bridge the men employed came upon a solid foundation."

"FRANCIS RITCHIE, who, being also sworn, deposed that he was the contractor who built the present Queen's Bridge; it was on the exact site of the old Long Bridge; that he also built Coates's or the Lagan Bridge; that, about the year 1842, he was employed by the late Mr Alexander Montgomery to build a quay wall a little above the Long Bridge, and opposite May's Dock; when building said wall, he came upon an artificial kind of causeway, made of very large stones, and about 25 feet broad at the top; that about the same time witness was building a quay wall at May's Dock, exactly opposite the place where he found the causeway, or passage, on the Down side; and, when building said wall, he discovered another causeway exactly similar to the one found on the Down side, and also 25 feet broad at the top; that both said constructions ran as if across the river to meet each other; and, when the Long Bridge was removed for the purpose of building the Queen's Bridge, the water above the bridge was lowered considerably, and exposed to view at low water a large mass of stones in the river, and that he took away several lighter loads of them; that, previous to building the Queen's Bridge, he had borings made above and below the Old Long Bridge, as far sea-ward as Ritchie's Dock; that a bed of soft sleech commenced 20 or 30 yards above the bridge, and continued down the channel all the way he made the borings. About 20 or 30 yards above the bridge, which is still fordable all the way, and whilst building the new bridge, saw great numbers of persons crossing at low water to avoid the toll bridge, which was then erected below the Bridge; recollects before the road was made from Watson's Corner to the Long Bridge, and its site being covered by the tide at low water; but does not recollect the making of any of the old paved roads leading to Watson's Corner and ending there. They were in existence long before he was born."—*Report of Trial in Donegall v. Templemore.*

[e] His mother was at this date a widow, his father, the Rev. Hans Hamilton, having died on the 30th of May, 1608.

to these tenents, and did therefore then deliver them all to my then steward, Francis Maynard, to be by him all of them delivered to my brother, William Hamiltone, by him to be examined severally, and being found agreeing with our minutes and counterparts, being made up from the tenents respectively to me, then to be delivered by my said brother William to every of them so respectively as deeds, of which deeds and writings the said William to receave a counterpart from the tenents respectively for me, and so to be my deeds and not otherwise; now, in respect the said Francis Maynard, either out of want, indigence, or out of some other collateral respect, hath underhand sold several of those engrossed wrytings (contrarie to the direction given to him before sundrie persones at the deliverie of them to him, and contrarie to a letter of attorney, or a power sent by him the said Maynard from me to the said William under my hand), to several of the persones to whome they were to have been delivered in maner as aforesaid by my brother, and that neither examination hath been used by my brother, nor counterpart by him thereof receaved for me, nor deliverie made as was directed, and that therefor the same or no deeds, and the tenents only deceaved thereby, I do therefor also appoint, that if they who have so bought such supposed deeds shall give up the same cheerfully and readilie, and do also confesse their oversight in underhand buying of them so indirectly, then I do appoint that they shall have new deeds according to the minuts and agreements between us duly perfected, they satisfying all arreares of rent and other ducties due heretofore out of the lands thereby entended to them; or, if they shall refuse so to do, and stand to take benefitt by the supposed deeds which they have so cantelouslie bought, I doe appoint, in respect the writings are not perfected, and that they have no estate in the land, that the lands which they seek of myn by those deeds be entered upon and disposed of as lands yet to be lett, and that all my tithes and the vicar's third part of tithes be taken of them, and all other advantages, profitts, and perquisits that is fallen due to me by any wayes. And, for all other minutes which any of my tenents have under my hand intending an agreement for lives or years, my will is that the same be perfected to them respectively, honestlie, and justlie, according to the purport of the minut which they have under my hand; and, for such of my tenents as have no note or minuts off me, specially such as are of the poorer sort, and have long dwelt under me, I will that they be favourablie agreed withall, in such sort as I have agreed with other tenents of their qualitie. But, when I have given license to some men to dwell upon my land during pleasure, paying little or no rent for townes or lands of good value, such as are old James Odornan, Manus O'Hammell, and such, my will is, that they, careing themselves well, honestlie, and truly, shall be permitted to dwell still so long as my wif and sone shall find them duetifull servants to them; but, upon either of their deathes or ill caring, that that land be taken in and disposed for the best advantag to Scottishmen or other such tenents. Owen Omulerove his towne is requisit for seafaring men and fishers at Gilgroomes port [d] and may be lett at a very good rate, but then the poor man should be elswher provyded for with favour; the lyk is also of Towl Og Ogilmore for his part of Ballesallagh, who is to be lykwise provyded for, and may be better in some other place, and these townes with far greater advantag, and far better service to his Majestie, lett to Scottishmen. Thomas Kelso hath had during pleasure, from year to year, without any minut, a great towne of me for sundrie years past, and two quarters of land, besydes the two quarters which my brother William hath. He hath hitherto payed me only four pounds. I would make no agreement with him, because I was still of purpose to tak it in, or a great part of it, to the plaines of Belfast. A great part of it may well be taken in, and can not be wanting from that town. The rest may either be lett to him for a reasonable rent and services of his facultie, with condition to forfeit it if he does not perform the same faithfully, or otherwyse he may be elswher provyded of some parcell of land and that land be lett for a very great rent. [e] I do wish him to be more regarded for his wive and children's sake, who

---

[d] Now Groomsport. See, at p. 30, *ante*, reference to a patent of 19 Jac. 1, which Sir James Hamilton had obtained, making Bangor a sea-port, and the roads or crecks of Gillegroomes and Holywood, members of the port of Bangor.

[e] By lease dated 15th Oct, 1644, from the Right Honble. James second Viscount Claneboy, to William Kelsoe, merchant and burgess of Ayre, in the realm of Scotland, after reciting, that, by agreement bearing date the 3rd of April,

1624, the late Viscount Claneboye, deceased, had granted to Richard and Harry Whiteshead a lease of the Townland of Ballymacarrott, as it then was possest for twentie-one years, from All-Hallow-tide then next ensuing, the said Viscount Claneboye thereby demised unto the said William Kelsoe, his executors and assigns, the said towne of Ballymacarrett, with the appurtenances thereunto belonging (excepting and reserving thereout unto the said Viscount, his heirs and assigns, all

are honest and poor and my kinsfolk, than for his self being given to too much forgetting of his duetie to himself and me. And that all other lands be accordinglie disposed of for the uses aforesaid and for my sone's best benefitt. And whereas I have given a minut to my brother Archibald of two townclands, Ballcerot and Balloscalle, it is my pleasure that he have an estate made to him of those lands according to the said minut; and I do hereby confirm the tenor and purport of that note to him according to the true meaning of the same. And lykewise I do appoint to my brother John the

---

and all manner of royalties, tithes, heryots, fines, amerciaments, woods, underwoods, suits, services, customs, anchorages, fishings, and fishery places, with the parcel of land already set off for the ferry, and held and enjoyed with the same, being by estimation six acres, lordes-fishes, and tithe-fishes, mills, mill-steads, mill-draughts, mill-ponds, waters, and water-courses, with two acres of land to the same, deducting therefor proportionably of the rent as was answered out of the whole premises, with full liberty of ingress, egress, and regress, into and from the premises, at all times and upon all occasions whatsoever). To hold the said Townland of Ballymacarrett (except as before excepted) unto the said William Kelsoe, his executors, and administrators, and assigns, for 21 years, to begin from All-saints, 1650, at the yearly rent or sum of £32, with six days' work of a man and horse. Upon this lease the following memorandum is endorsed :—"That before the signing, sealing, and delivery hereof, it is covenanted, concluded, and agreed, by and between the within-mentioned persons to these presents, that if it shall see fall out that Richard Pierson (who hath a lease of the said townland for seven years, to end at All-saints, 1650), his executors administrators, or assignes, shall quit the lease of the said land, and shall leave the same before the expiration thereof, that then the within specified 21 years thereof to the said William Kelsoe, his executors, administrators, and assigns, shall be and begin, from and immediately after the next tearme day, either of May or All-saints, that he, the said Richard Pierson, shall see give up the said land to the said Lord Viscount, his heirs and assigns, or remove themselves therefrom. Signed, sealed and delivered, in the presence of Hans Hamilton, Alexander Sloane, Isaiah Forest, Alexander Smith."—A further lease, dated 16th Sept., 1669, from the Right Honble. Henry Earl of Clanbrassill to John Kelso, of Ballymacarrett, gent, witnessed that the said Earl, for and in consideration of the yearly rents duties, and services thereinafter expressed and reserved, and especially for, and in consideration of, the sum of £500 sterling, current and lawful money of und in England, thereby set, and to farm let, unto the said John Kelso, the Townland of Ballymacarrett, lying and being within the Barony of Castlereagh and County of Down, aforesaid, with the appurtenances. (Excepting and always reserving out of the said demised premises, unto the said Earl, his heirs or assigns, the mill of Oyn O'Cork, with six acres of land to the said mill). To Hold the above townland, with liberty of the ferry-boat, with all the benefit and profit that could be had thereby, or that should grow due out of the same, together with all the houses, meares, and marshes, of the said townland, as it was then meared and bounded, with their and every of their appurtenances, for and during the full term, time, and space of three score and one years, to be and begin from the 1st of Nov. then next: Yielding and paying therefore, unto the said Earl, his heirs and assigns, £12 sterling, yearly, during the first two

years, to begin from the 1st of Nov. then next, and also paying yearly thereafter, during the said Earl detaining the said sum of £300 sterling in his or their hands, £25 yearly, at May and All-saints; and when the said £300 should be repaid in one entire sum unto the said John Kelso, his heirs, executors, administrators, or assigns, then paying thereafter the sum of £55 yearly, at the terms formerly mentioned; and the said John Kelso did, thereby, amongst other things, covenant to do suit and service to the Courts Leet and Courts Baron of the said Earl, his heirs or assigns, to be held for the Manor of Hollywood, and to be ruled by the Steward of the said Courts for the time being. Upon this lease there is also endorsed the following memorandum :—

"Before the signing and sealing of the within demise, I, the within-named Henry, Earl of Clanbrassil, do, for me, my heirs and assigns, during the years within mentioned, convey and make over to him, the said John Kelso, his executors and assigns, all the fishing that of right doth belong to me, and that formerly the tenants of Ballymacarrett were possessed of.—Signed, sealed, and delivered, in presence of John Swadlin, and William Richardson."

A Fee-farm Grant of this date (24th July, 1672), from the Right Honourable Henry, Earl of Clanbrassill, to Thomas Pottinger, of Belfast, in the County of Antrim, merchant, witnessed that the said Earl, in consideration of £360, sold, and confirmed, unto the said Thomas Pottinger, his heirs and assigns, for ever, the Townland of Ballymacarrett, alias Ballinacrett, in the Parish of Knock, in the Barony of Castlereagh and County of Down, and then in the tenure and occupation of John Kelso and Captain James McGill, their undertenants and cottyers, together with all and singular the castles, &c.; loughs, ponds, fishings, marshes, and waye of water, ferrie and ferry boats, and all and singular other profits, commodities, emoluments, immunities, rents, reversions, remainders, appendances, rights, members, advantages, and appurtenances whatsoever, to the said townland, incident, belonging, or in any waye appertaining, by what name or names soever the same be called or known, by or belonging to, or to the same usually had, occupied, enjoyed, or reputed, accepted, used, and known as part and parcel thereof; and also the corne mill called by the name of Owen Corke Mill, situate neere or upon the premises; together with the lands belonging to the said corne mill then, in the possession of John Wilson, and his undertenants and cottyers; that was to say, six acres of land, part of Ballymacarrett, aforesaid, and six acres of land, part of Ballyhackamore, together with the nett profits of toll or mulcture thereunto belonging, issuing and payable out of the townes and lands of Ballymacarrett, Ballyhuckamore, Knocke, Ballyloghan, Strandtown, Ballymather, and Ballynaser; and also the fynes payable thereout by the tenants inhabiting the said townlands, for not grinding their corne and grayne at the said mill, according to the covenants therein exprest, and all other lyke estate in the townes of Balle-Robert and Balle-Davie, and that William have such lands as I appointed to him according to the notes and minuts which I gave to him. The lyke to William Moore, my brother, for the note which he hath. And, for that my brother Archibald is in debt, I do appoint that when my debts and such sumes of money as I have appointed to be paid by my executors are payed, that Archibald have at once, with the gratuities which my executors are to have, as is above sett down, a help towards the payment of his debts, which I do leave to the love of my wif, not being under two hundreth pounds. And if it fall out that all that be too heavie to be payed at once, that it be payed at times as my state may bear within two years. And I do ordane my wif and child to love and use well my brothers, and all honest and faithful servants, specially such as have been honest to me, and chiefly those of my name, and to deall well and kindlie with them, and to be advysed by them as occasion shall afoord, and as they fynd them true and trustie. And I do lykwise ordain my brothers faithful·y to aid my wif and child, and to counsell and assist them, and all my servants and kinsfolks under me to do the lyk. And I pray for the encrease of all love and concord between them, and the blessings of God to dwell and settle for ever upon them and their generation.

I leave Olive, Lettice, and Margaret Peuicook to Joan; the first two to have one hundred pounds a peece, to be payed as she may convenientlie, and Margaret to have twentie marks sterling a year well payed.

Towards the payment of my debts there is to be receaved the rents due at Alhallowtyd last, and fyve hundreth pounds out of the lease of the plaine which I b ught of Mr. Hope latelie, and of which I do wishe the overplus that shall be made over and above the said fyve hundreth pounds to be devyded between Patrick Shaen, who is to have two-thirds, and Owen and Anthonie M'Gohagan one third.

Item—I do give my moveable goods between my son and my wif, if my said wif be not now conceaved with any other children; and if she shall be found to be conceaved with any other child, I do leave all my said moveable goods between her and the children or child that she is conceaved with.

I have made over the lease to John Kenedy, my servant, which I had from Mr. John Whyt, of the lands of Duffrin, and all that estate for years, which I did in trust for that I was to take the feefarme of the said Duffrin from the said

incident profits and dutyes to the said mill belonginge: Yielding and paying yearly and every year, to the said Earl, his heirs and assigns, yearly for ever, the full sum of £30 sterling. By an endorsement on the foregoing deed, reciting the lease and mortgage to John Kelso, of 16th September, 1669, and further reciting that the whole interest of Kelso, to the lands, and to the said £300, was since legally come to James Magill, of Ballynesterragh, Esq., and that the same was then wholly and absolutely in him; and further reciting that the said Earl, by his deed bearing date the 4th day of July, 1672, did make over the reversion of the said lands, and the power of redeeming the same, to Pottinger. It was thereby witnessed that the said James Magill had received from the said Thomas Pottinger the said sum of £3 0, according to the said deed of lease; and the said James Magill did thereby release, acquit, and discharge the said Thomas Pottinger, his heirs, executors, administrators, and assigns, of the said sum of £300, and every part thereof."

The Townland of Ballymacarrett continued in possession of the Pottinger family till the year 1779, when they sold it to arry Yelverton, Esq., then Recorder of Carrickfergus (afterwards Chief Baron of the Irish Exchequer, and raised to the peerage by the title of Viscount Avonmore), for a sum of £18,113 5s, which agreement was afterwards carried into formal execution by a deed of 1st July, 1781, whereby Eldred Pottinger, and Anne, his wife, conveyed to him, "All the town and lands of Ballymacarrett, and the mill and mill lauds of Owen Cork, otherwise Owen O'Cork, together with all the tithes, both great and small, coming, growing, arising, and renewing for ever in and out of the

same, and all dwelling-houses, &c., woods, underwoods, mills, mill-dams, and mill-ponds, waters, water-courses, strands, shores, fishings, fisheries, fishing-places, wrecks, waifs, estrays, deodands, forfeitures, easements, profits, advantages, emoluments, and hereditaments whatsoever, to the said lands and premises, and every part or parcel thereof belonging, or in anywise appertaining." By a deed of conveyance, dated 1st July, 1787, Lord Chief Baron Yelverton conveyed the townland of Ballymacarrett and Owen O'Corke mill, in consideration of £25,000, to Arthur, Earl of Donegall, who, by his will, dated 7th August, 1795, devised them to his second son, Lord Spencer Chichester. whose grandson, the Right Honble. Henry Spencer, Baron Templemore, is the present owner. His rental out of Ballymacarrett amounts to upwards of £1,000 per annum, and is daily increasing; but that represents only a small portion of the present value of the townland, which with, the buildings upon it, was valued in the poor-law rate-books of 1855 at £18,891 10s, which must be considered as a wonderful realisation of the estimate formed of its value in the above will of Sir James Hamilton, dated upwards of 240 years before, that the townland, which only then produced him £4 a year, would eventually be let at a great rent; and the still more extraordinary prophecy contained in it, "that a great part of it might well be taken into the plains of Belfast, and cannot be wanting to that town," is at present on the eve of complete fulfilment, by the embankments of the Harbour Commissioners, and the formation of the People's Park, out of the residue of the unreclaimed slob-lands of Ballymacarrett.

P

John Whyt in myn own name, and the trust appeareth that I have still used and enjoyed the said lands as before, and have the deed in myn own custodie, an I John Kenedy, my said servant, for anything that I know, knoweth not thereof.* All this estate of lease, and use and right thereunto of the Duffrin, and all my lands and interest to any lands in the kingdome of Ireland, and all right, use, possession, title, and interest after the expiration of my naturall lif, and

---

* The Barony of Dufferin was not included in the original grant to Sir James Hamilton by James the First, but was purchased by him from White, and was included in the confirmation patent which was obtained by him of his estates in the reign of Charles the First. The following is a translation of an old inquisition respecting the title of the Whites to this barony:—

"Ardwhin, 4th July, 1605—PATRICK WHITE, late of Flemington, in the county of Meath, Knight, Second Baron of the Exchequer in this kingdom of Ireland, born of the English nation and race, was seised as of fee and of ancient inheritance of the manors and castles of Renescaddle and Killalngh, with their appurtenances; also of all manors, castles, towns, and lands in the territory or precinct called the Duffren, otherwise Duffrens, in the County of Downe, in the Province of Ulster, which territory comprises in itself the towns, lands, &c., following:—viz., Ballinemona, Ballibholliken, Ballimallagh, Corbally, the castles and towns of Ballyrasianwilliam, Ballinecabry, the castles and towns of Killaleigh, Tallogh mormartio, Ballyrathconevan, Ballymacorbal, the castles and towns of Rindofirin, otherwise Moylerton, Ballyomeran, Ballynearcau, the castles and towns of Rathgormin, Ballikitinegan, Carrick-rouske, Ballinchey, Ballow, Ballinncoshoo, Ballemackirelly, Ballcogullone, Ballibregah, Ballillegan, Ballylishduffe, Ballinoy, Ballicley, otherwise Clegh, Bally-drommore, Ballicoskrigan, Castlegalvy, Lissonagh, Ballitough, otherwise Toy, Balligavan, Balliroyan; the castles and towns of Casclaunecgayse, Ballilegan, Ballimullin, Baliholliard, Ardagone, Ballyboynemery, otherwise Tollymery, Ballitarim, Ballrcogh, Ballicooly, Rathkirin, Ballicounety, otherwise Clonay, Ballicargah, Tullyconyah, otherwise Knoise, Ballakillchanan, and Ballisherman, and also of divers islands in Loughconu, viz, the islands of Ranchedy, and Rannys, Polle-ile, Read-ile, Contagh-ile, Much-ile, otherwise Ilanduare; Dunsbagh-ile, Innishmae [ ] Inish-lowran, and Ilaud-darragh; and also of certain advows ms and churches. viz, the Rectory of Killinchinemaglory, Reuechaddy, Killawreys, and Killaleagh, with all and singular their rights, members, and appurtenances—The aforesaid Patrick White, Knight, being so seised of all the premises, by deed bearing date 21 September, in the 2d year of the reign of the late Queen Elizabeth, appointed Rowland White, his second son, his attorney, &c.—The same Rowland White, by deed bearing date 13th October, in the aforesaid year, granted all the premises in the Duffren, otherwise Duffrens, to JOHN BAKER, of the City of Dublin, for the term of 21 years.—Afterwards the same John Baker, by deed bearing date 31 January, in the year aforesaid, granted to the said Rowland White, all his executors and assigns, all his interest and term of years in the premises.—Afterwards, Patrick White, late of Flemington, in the county of Meath, son and heir of Nicholas White, son and heir of the said Patrick White, by deed bearing date 29th May, in the 5th year of the same reign, de-

mised to the aforesaid ROWLAND WHITE, all his right, claim, and interest, which he had in the premises aforesaid.—The same Rowland White, being so seised of the premises, died at the City of Dublin, 10th August, in the 14th year of the late Queen Elizabeth—John White, of Killaleagh, aforesaid, his son and heir, was then of the age of 23 years, and unmarried. The premises are held as of the manor of Carrickfergus by fealty.—*Inquisitions of Ulster, Record Com.*, vol. 2.

In July, 1610, John White, and his son, Nicholas, assigned these lands, castles, and advowsons to Sir James Hamilton, subject to the rent of £40, and the Crown rent of 6s 8d; and, by an inquisition, taken at Killileagh, 14th January 1644, after Lord Clancboy's death, he was found to have died seised, *inter alia*, of the advowson, donation, right of patronage, and free disposal of the aforesaid rectories, vicarages, chapels, and churches of Killileagh, Kilnadreas, Reuechady, and Killinchinemaghery. As to *Killandreus*, Dr. Reeves says:—"In the townland of Toy and Kirkland is a burial-ground, which contains the ruins of a church that measures 56½ by 17½ feet. The masonry is of a very ancient character, and the walls are in some places 5½ feet thick. The spot is locally called *Killaraey*, or *Killandrews*, and gives name to the Prebend of St. Andrew's, in the Cathedral of Down, being the first name on the list of its corps. ' *Killinidreus*, an union,' is noticed by the Terrier between Ringhaddy and Killyleagh. Though annexed by the charter to the Prebend of St. Andrews, and thus made collative by the Bishop, it was afterwards severed from it, and incorporated with Killyleagh, inasmuch as the advowson was not at the disposal of the Crown in 1609.'—*Ecc. Ant. Down and Connor*, p. 187. And, as to "*Reuechady*, now Ringhaddy, a portion of Killinchy Parish, lying in Strangford Lough. It was originally an island, but having been from time immemorial connected to the mainland by a causeway, it presents on the map the appearance of an elongated neck of land, running northwards into the Lough. Hence, probably, the name 'The Long Point.' On it remain the walls of the church, measuring 45 by 24 feet."—*Ib.*, p. 10. At page 54, *ante*, it is stated in the MSS. that Lord Clancboy planted all the parishes of his estate, which were six, with pious ministers out of Scotland; but, in the foregoing will, he only enumerates five, omitting Killinchy, to which he afterwards presented John Livingston in 1630. At the date of this will however, in 1616, it is probable that the two modern parishes of Killileagh and Killinchy were joined together, and that the church of Killileagh served for both, for the following reasons:—1. The church of Killwynchie, or Killinchy, only, is returned in the Taxation of 1306-7; for it is plain that the church of Kilmeyleyt, returned in it, does not refer to Killileagh, but to Loughinisland, as suggested by Dr. Reeves—*Ec. Au.*, p. 48. 2. There are no remains of any ancient church at Killinchy; but near the Castle of Killileagh stood an ancient church called Killowen, of which the east gable still remains. 3. Although Sir James Hamilton purchased the advowson of this Church, as also

after my debts payed and such things satisfied as I have appointed to be satisfied by these presents, and to be don and performed to his mother, and to all others as is hereby expressed ; I say all my lands, tenements, and hereditaments whatsoever I do leave to com and be to my said sone, James Hamiltone, the son of the said Jean Hamiltone, *alias* Phillips, after the expiration of my naturall lif, and after my debts payed and other things by me hereby directed to be don, accomplished, and fulfilled, to be to the said James Hamiltone, the sone of Jean Hamiltone, *als.* Phillips, afd., and of myself, and to his heires of his body, for ever (if it shall please God that I depart out of this mortal lif before I do return to him and his said mother). And if it shall please God that my said sone, James Hamiltone, shall depart this lif without heires of his body, then the said lands and hereditaments, and all right, use, interest, and title to them to be to such sone or daughter, sones or daughters successively and lineally, as the said Jean Hamiltone, *als.* Philips is, or may now be, conceaved with, if any such she be conceaved with, and to their heires successively and respectively for ever. And if it shall please God to determine the heires of my body, then the said lands and hereditaments to be to the heires male of Archibald, he paying £1,000 stg. to every of my brothers, John Hamiltone and William Hamiltone, and £1,000 to my brother Gawen's children, Archibald and James, between them ; and three hundreth pounds to Patrick, my brother ; and so much to my sister Jean, her children, and performing such things as ar in this my will ordayned to be performed ; and those above-mentioned sumes, to be payed to my said brothers, and brother's children, by the said Archibald, within six years after his entrie to said lands ; and he also leaving to my brother John my castle and lands of Clanchie. And if it shall please God to determine and cut off the heires males of my brother Archibald, then I do appoint and ordane my said lands and hereditaments to be equally divyded in three parts ; the first part to be between the two children of Gawen—viz., Archibald and James, and the heires males of their bodies ; the second part to be to my brother John, and the heires males of his body ; the third to my brother William, and the heires males of his body ; and all these three parts to repay within six yeares to the said Archibald's daughters and heires of his body, after that the said Archibald, James, John, and William shall have receaved the said lands, the sum to be payed by them, the said Archibald and James, the sones of Gawen, and by my brothers, John and William, to the daughters of the said Archibald, my brother, and their heires respectively, according to the proportion of their partes. And faiiing of the heires males of the bodyes of all these, the said Archibald, James, John, and William, (whose partes I appoint to fall to the survivor for want of heires males), then to the heires males of the body of my brother Patrick, and, failing of such heires males, then to my right heires for ever.

There is also one hundreth pounds to be payed to Alice Penicook, during her lif, which I do appoint to be well and truely payd to her if she cary herself without troubling of my said wif and sone, otherwise not ; and I leave something to be given to James Penicook to relieve his wants.

In witness of this my last will I have signed the same, and put thereunto my seall the said 16 day of December, 1616.†

All other things I do
leave to the discretion of }
my executors aforesaid.

JAMES HAMILTONE. (Seal.)

---

of Ringhaddy, Killandreas, and Killileagh from the White family, in 1610, yet John Christian, who had been presented by the crown, in 1609, to the Prebend of St. Andrews, held all these livings till 1616, as did Andrew Moneypenny, who succeeded him in that year, and Arthur Moneypenny, in the year 1620. 4. Bishop Echlin, in 1622, returned the Church as Killinscoah, *alias* Killileagh; and, even after Lord Claneboy had asserted his right by presenting Livingston to Killinchy in 1630, it appears from the following entry in the Regal Visitation Book for 1633, that John Bole, who was also appointed by the crown, is returned as Rector for all these livings:—" Dunensis Diocess—*St. Andrews*, in Rosse —valet £100, Johannes Bole, Rector. *Killenstree*—Idem Johannes Bole, Rector. *Kilscalan et Ringhady*—Idem

Johannes Bole, Rector. *Killileagh*—Idem Johannes Bole, Rector." There were also merged in the modern parish of Killinchy, the old parishes of Ringhaddy, Balligowan, and Drumcreagh, the cemetery of which latter is called Killkeeran, lying in the townland of Drumreagh. Mr. J. W. Hanna, in his " Gossipings about the parish of Inch," states, " that Drumcreagh Parish contained the townlands of Drumreagh, Raffrey, Killinchy-in-the-Woods, Ravarrn, Ballycloghan, Levally-gowan, (now Ballygowan,) Levallyaghin-darragh, (now Aughnadaragh,) Barnamaghery, (which contains Killyban, the Church of St. Fergus, first Bishop of Down,) and Creorybeg, all of which were in North Claneboy."

† This remarkable document, which is all in Sir James Hamilton's own handwriting, although formally signed

and sealed by him in 1616, as his will, does not appear to have been ever witnessed or published as such, although he lived for twenty-seven years after its date; and he therefore died legally intestate, as stated by Lodge; but this document is still a most valuable one for its local and historical statements and allusions. It appears to have remained undiscovered among the family papers until the year 1832, when it was found by the late A. H. Rowan, Esq., and the present editor, when making a search among them, at Rathcoffey, County Kildare. From a passage in the last paragraph, wherein he says, "If it shall please God that I depart out of this mortal life before I return to him (his son) and his said mother," it would seem to have been drawn up in his absence from home. The particular occasion it is, of course, impossible now to ascertain; but it is not improbable that it was upon his being sent to England, in 1616, as one of the deputies from the Irish House of Commons with such acts and propositions as the House desired to be transmitted to England for approval. The following are the circumstances under which he was so selected:—"On the 18th of May, 1613, the first Parliament held in Ireland during an interval of twenty-seven years, and which Lord Clare, on his motion for the Union, described as the first assembly which Ireland ever had that could be called a Parliament, was opened with great pomp by Sir Arthur Chichester, the then Lord Deputy. Sir James Hamilton and Sir Hugh Montgomery were returned as the members to the House of Commons for the County of Down. Since last a House of Commons had been assembled in Dublin, seventeen new counties had been formed, and forty boroughs incorporated; and, in fabricating these boroughs, so little had either law or honesty been consulted, that most of them consisted of only a few scattered houses, built by the undertakers in Ulster. Against this mockery of legislation several of the Lords of the Pale spiritedly remonstrated, complaining that they, the ancient nobility and gentry of the Pale, 'were set at nought and disgraced by men lately raised to place and power; that the new boroughs had been incorporated with the most shameful partiality, and that their representatives were attorneys' clerks and servants.' These lords concluded by manfully demanding that all laws which had for their object to force consciences should be repealed. Their bold appeal, however, proved unavailing. The Lord Deputy continued to furnish new boroughs, according as they were wanted; and many of them were not incorporated until the writs for summoning a Parliament had already issued. Notwithstanding these active exertions on the part of the Government, so nearly balanced were the two parties, or so uncertain still their relative strength, that the Catholics counted sanguinely on a majority; nor was it until the meeting of Parliament that, to their great mortification, they found they had miscalculated their numbers. Of the 232 members returned, 125 were absent, 125 were Protestants, and 101 formed a recusant, or Catholic party. The Upper House consisted of 16 temporal barons, 25 Protestant prelates, 5 viscounts, and 4 earls; and of these a considerable majority were friends of the Administration. The first trial of the strength of the parties was on the election of the Speaker—the competitors for this office being Sir John Davies, the Irish Attorney-General, and Sir John Everard, a respectable recusant, who had been a Justice of the King's Bench. Before they proceeded to the election, a question was raised by Everard's party, whether those returned for boroughs illegally constituted

had not thereby forfeited their right of electing The altercation on this point was becoming angry and disorderly, when Sir Oliver St. John, Master of the Ordnance, remarked that controversies of this description were best decided by votes, and that the affirmative party usually went out of the House, while the negative kept their seats. He therefore called upon those who voted for Sir John Davies to attend him to the lobby, and was followed thither by all his party. Meanwhile, the recusants, whether believing or merely presuming that they were the majority, proceeded to elect Sir John Everard; and, having hurried through the accustomed forms, placed him triumphantly in the Speaker's chair. They were then rejoined by the Government members, when another and still less dignified scene took place. Exclaiming against this outrage, they declared Davies to be duly elected, and after in vain endeavouring to force the sturdy recusant from the chair, seated their Speaker in his lap. The restless spirit which these events kept constantly alive, was regarded with the more apprehension, from the scanty means now left to the government of preserving the public peace; the whole military force of the kingdom having been lately reduced to the trifling amount of 1700 foot and 200 horse. Finding it impossible to make any progress with an assembly so constituted, the lord-deputy prorogued the Parliament, and shortly after a deputation from the the Irish Catholics proceeded to London, to lay their petition at the foot of the throne. The reception given at first to the Irish delegates had been harsh and insulting. The English council had tried to intimidate them, and two of their number, Talbot and Luttrell, were committed prisoners, one to the Tower and the other to the Fleet. By the king the delegates were rated in his own peculiar fashion. The letter which the lords of the Pale had addressed to him,—'a few men,' as he contemptuously styled them, 'who threatened him with rebellion,'—he declared to be 'rash and insolent;' and, with respect to those returns to Parliament of which they had complained, 'nothing faulty,' he said, 'was to be found in the government, unless they would have the kingdom of Ireland like the kingdom of heaven.' To the complaint made of the numerous boroughs constituted by him, the royal reply was, 'What is it to you, whether I make many or few boroughs? my counsel may consider the fitness, if I require it. But, what if I had made forty noblemen, and four hundred boroughs? the more, the merrier; the fewer, the better cheer.' Finally, he dismissed the Irish delegates with a severe reprimand, telling them that their proceedings had been 'rude, disorderly, and inexcusable, and worthy of severe punishment, which, however, by reason of their submission, he would forbear,—but not remit, until he should see their dutiful carriage in his Parliament.' Meanwhile a commission of inquiry was granted; the complaints made by the recusants were promptly attended to, and, among other important admissions, it was conceded, that members for boroughs incorporated after the writs were issued had no right to sit during the session."—*Moore's Ireland, 4th vol., p. 163 to 167.*

This commission was directed to Lord Chichester, Sir Humphrey Winche, Sir Charles Cornwallis, Sir Roger Wilbraham, and George Calvert, to inquire, on oath, whether there were not writs sent into all counties for the elections, and returns to be made as well of knights of shires as of citizens and burgesses, for the cities and ancient boroughs within the same shires; and whether there were not burgesses chosen and returned for all ancient boroughs that had a right to send members to Parliament, and whether there were any omitted ; and if there were, the cause and reason, and on whom was the fault ? To which the commissioners certified, that on the 12th Nov.. in the City of Dublin, they made diligent inquiry, as well by depositions of witnesses, search of records, certificates from the archbishops, as by other good ways and means, and made the following return concerning matters of Parliament :—"In the county of Down, May-Day was the county court for the election, which the Sheriff held at Newry, at which day the Sheriff, proceeding to the election, moved the freeholders to choose Sir Richard Wingfield and Sir James Hamilton, being recommended to him by the Lord Deputy; but the natives named Sir Arthur Magennisse, and Rowland Savage, whereupon all the British freeholders, being 131, cried 'Hamilton and Montgomery,' omitting Wingfield ; and the Irish, to the number of 101, cried 'Magennisse and Savage.' Exception being presently taken to divers of the British for want of freeholds, 14 were examined on oath by the Sheriff, and deposed they were freeholders; whereupon, the Sheriff returned Hamilton and Montgomery, to which some of the Irish made objections, which were found partly untrue, and partly frivolous."— *Pat. Rolls.* 16 *Jac.* 1. IV., 9.

No debates in the Irish Parliament were published at this date ; but the following extracts from the Journals of the Irish House of Commons, present not only an outline of several debates in which Sir James Hamilton took part, but the substance and the arguments of the various speakers, and in some measure even their style of speaking :—

"*Die Sabbati*, 22 *Aprilis*, 1615.—The House being all met and set this day, by eight of the clock in the morning, with intent and purpose to read the act of subsidy ; before it began to be read,

"Mr. SUTTON moved the House, that in regard it tended to the king's private profit, it might be deferred till other acts that tended to the common good of the weale publick were first read ; alledging, that the old saying would else be verified :—*Little said soon amended*; *a subsidy granted, the Parliament ended.* But, it was answered by

"Sir JAMES HAMILTON, that it concerned not the king's private profit ; but, as his Majesty is head, so his subjects are the members of that head, and that it concerned every of their own good ; and, therefore, desired that his Majesty's bill might have the pre-eminence as to begin first, and then those that concerned the commonwealth ; so, that thereby they may proceed hand in hand.

"So thereupon the said act, entituled 'An act for the grant of one entire subsidy by the temporality,' received the first reading."

"24 *Aprilis*, 1615.—This day an act, entituled an 'Act for the granting of one entire subsidy by the temporality,' was the second time read.

"1. Mr. FRANCIS BLUNDELL spake first for the bill of subsidy : *Verbum sapienti sat est.* By granting it you shall obtain 1, Glory ; 2, Gain ; and it will be the only means to make this a flourishing kingdom, and you a happy people.

"2. Mr. FERNHAM—Divers reasons why it should be granted : 49 Edward III., the king, being sick, put the government of his land into John of Gaunt's hands, and called a Parliament, and laid great taxes on the commonwealth ; but they ought not to lay extraordinary taxes upon their subjects. Motives :—1. The great expense of his Majesty since his entrance to the crown is to be considered.

2. Bounty and justice, the two principal virtues that belong to a king ; the necessity of Princes stoppeth the passages of all noble designs ; 1,900,060 odd pounds it cost Queen Elizabeth, from the defeating of the marshal in the North till her death.

"3. Mr. TREASURER—The motives to induce the granting of a subsidy two :—1. Either on the behalf of the king to supply his Majesty's necessities, which are either ordinary, or extraordinary ; as the marriage of Lady Elizabeth with the Palsgrave, *reipublicæ causa.* 2. In our own behalfs. It cost Queen Elizabeth £400,000 from the Earl of Essex's time till the Lord Mount-joye's Kingsale's charges came to near £500,000. The subsidy, being granted, will be but like a vapour drawn up into a cloud, which doth but disperse and fall amongst us again.

"4. Sir CHRISTOPHER NUGENT—*Dignum et justum.* He findeth every one ready with alacrity to give it, whereunto he is willing ; but, for the manner of levying it, he desireth to have it committed.

"5. Mr. Justice SHTHONP—A thing not only in duty to be granted to so good a king, but fortified with many precedents:—as, 21 *Hen.* VII., 13s 4d to be taken off every plow land ; the like for ten years, 3 & 4 *Phillipi et Maria*; the like in the 11° Eliz. In the days of Augustus Cæsar, &c., an edict was sent out, that all the world under his government should be taxed ; every child to his father, every citizen to his mayor, &c., are willing to give their aid ; then, how much more every good subject to so religious a prince !

"6. Sir JAMES HAMILTON rejoiceth to see King James triumphing and rejoicing in the hearts of all his subjects ; many look in men's faces, that knoweth not what is in their purses ; therefore, some such as dwell in every shire to be appointed to be petitioners to the Lord Deputy, for the nominating commissioners for the levying the subsidy ; but not to have the bill committed.

"7. Mr. WADDING—For the expounding of each that must pay, who must be worth £3, to be petitioners to the Lord Deputy for explaining it, whether English or Irish money be intended ; and, in respect that the second payment cometh so near the first, that some further respite of time might be given for that.

"8. Sir JOHN EVERARD—That the first gentleman prevented him in priority, yet he hath as many wings to show his affection as any other ; neither glory nor profit moveth him—that were merchandise. The king and the subject be relatives ; if good be done to the king, the subject is the better ; that nourishment which is given to the head, the concoction after is in the body; so, the subsidy being granted the king, the subject will be the better for it. Yet, 1, the the composition ; 2, the infliction of the statute for recusancy ; 3, death of cattle disableth them ; therefore, he desireth some of the honorable gentlemen to be intercessors to the Lord Deputy for the mitigation of these three inconveniences ; and, that each county, as they have chosen knights of the shire, so to choose collectors ; and thinketh the bill fit to be engrossed.

"9. Mr. LUTTEREL—1, The glory of God ; 2, The weal publick ; 3, The benefit of the king, are to be respected. Subsidies are, in England, conditionally granted; alledging that the people were poor, and that the King sometimes of England had aliened those lands of the crown that would have satisfied his debts ; alledging that in the time of wars in this kingdom, the gentlemen of the said realm spent as much as the Queen ; instance of a gentleman of ten hundred pounds per annum, who spent in those wars three thousand pounds. The bill therefore to be committed, that his Majesty may be notified if any inconvenience happen therein of the composition.

"10. Captain GRIFFITH—To have it engrossed.

"11. Sir ADAM LOFTUS, senior—Finding no inconvenience in it, to have it engrossed.

"12. Mr. MOORE—The occurrence is so free that no body will contradict it. His motion one, that those places where money is not to be spared, there cattle, corn, &c., might be taken, especially where his Majesty's garrisons are, unto whom part of the subsidy is to be distributed.

"13. Mr. VERDAN—As we ought to give, so we must look to the performance ; therefore, to have it committed.

"14. Mr. DALLWAY—To have it engrossed.

"15. Sir ROBERT DIGBY explained the manner of levying it, which the commissioners are to have a care in assessing the same.

"16. Mr. TREASURER again explained his former speech, alledging that in England he is cessed at forty pounds land, which is eight pounds to the king.

"So put the question.

"All that would have it to be engrossed, say yea.

"All that would have it committed, to say no.

"The greater number was yeas ; so, agreed to be engrossed.

"1 *Maii*, 1615.—Mr. GEO. BAGNALL, upon the beginning of the reading of the bill of Scots, desired that the bill of the natives might have the precedency in reading.

"Sir JAMES HAMILTON condescended that the Bill for the natives should have the precedency, and that in old time Ireland was called *Scotia major*, and Scotland *Scotia minor;* therefore, amity be betwixt both.

"Sir OLIVER LAMBERT, and Sir ADAM LOFTUS—To have it transmitted, and both to be put in one act, and that the natives of this kingdom might be capable of offices here.

"Mr. TREASURER—That is a mark of distinction there to be taken away.

"Mr. Dr. REEVES—The acts to be suspended, and both transmitted in one.

"Sir JOHN EVERARD—To have an act for restitution to their ancient liberties, but not to capitulate or indente ; and, because the imputation will lie upon the Irish, therefore his motion that they both pass, and that the house be an humble suitor, that a new act be desired, with addition.

"Mr. Justice SIBTHORP—That both English, Irish, and Scots, living under one God and one king, should be equally capable of preferment.

"Mr. ANNESLEY—The bills are not denied ; therefore, he desired that the blemish should be taken away; therefore, both to be read and committed, and the house to be an humble suitor to the king for the repeal of any statute that shall disable any native to be capable of any office in this realm."

"2 *Maii*, 1615.—This day the act of his Majesty's gracious general and free pardon was the first time read, after it came from the lords, being read once before.

"Mr. LEYESTER, and Sir JOHN EVERARD moved that part of Sherlock's money be bestowed upon one Parker, in prison in Exeter ; but others to bestow it here.

"Sir CHRISTOPHER PLUNKETT would have the general pardon committed, to see whether it were general indeed.

"Sir JOHN EVERARD—To accept of his Majesty's pardon.

"Mr. TALBOTT—To have it committed, that suit might be made that it might extend to the next sessions.

"Mr. Dr. REEVES—Never *to* refuse God and the King's pardon.

"Sir JAMES HAMILTON—Not to question his Majesty's bounty.

"Mr. CROOKE—To accept of his Majesty's liberal and free grace, and not to defer it till the next sessions, lest that in the meantime any one be hanged, which by this pardon might be saved ; and, if it go into England, it is a question whether it shall ever return, or whether we shall have another sessions.

"Therefore, being put to the question, whether to be again read or committed, the whole voice was yeas. to have it read ; so, it was again read, and being put to the question, it passed, with a general consent, the whole house."

"8 *Maii*, 1615.—The bill for repeal of divers statutes, concerning the natives of this kingdom, was the third time read.

"Sir ADAM LOFTUS, junior, Sir EDWARD FISHER, and Mr. BAGNAL, against the bill.

"Mr. TALBOTT with the bill ; to take it in part till God send more.

"Sir JAMES HAMILTON—Petitioners are no choosers, and the countenance of a prince is that which promiseth more gifts of a prince, ever accompanied with love ; better to follow the course of the giver, and not of the petitioner.

"Sir JOHN EVERARD—No man would think him a wise man, that, being restrained to the castle of Dublin, or tower of London, and might have the liberty to walk on the walls, would refuse it ; and, so, if one should owe a merchant a thousand pounds, and if he should remit five hundred pounds, would refuse it; so he conceiveth by the scope of this act—beggars must not be choosers; and, because we cannot have our desire, it savoureth of pride and obstinacy to oppose this bill ; therefore, to the question; which being put to the question, the yeas were far greater; so it passed."

"12 *Maii*, 1615.—Mr. BLUNDELL moved that Mr. Treasurer, Sir James Hamilton, Sir John Everard, Sir Robert Digby, and Mr. Bolton, might be appointed to go into England.

"Whereupon, it was ordered, that the grand committee shall consider what persons, members of this house, shall be thought fit to be presented to the Lord Deputy, with desire to be recommended by his Lordship to go over after this session into England to his Majesty, with such acts and propositions as the House shall desire to be transmitted into England, to be propounded the next sessions, and to consider of all fitting circumstances of the persons that shall be appointed to go."

"15 *Maii*, 1615.—Upon question had, touching the persons, members of this House of Commons, that were to be sent, into England from the said House by special election, Sir Thomas Ridgway, Vice-Treasurer, and Sir James Hamilton, knights, both of his Majesty's privy councell here, and Sir John Everard, knight, and Richard Bolton, Esq., were named and chosen by the knights, citizens, and burgesses of the Commons House of Parliament, to be recommended first to the Lord Deputy, with humble desire that his lordship would be pleased to recommend them, with the affairs of the commonwealth given in charge, whereof his lordship shall think fit to give allowance and approbation to his sacred Majesty, and the lords of his most honourable privy councell in England."

On 16th May, 1615, Parliament was prorogued till the 24th of October following, when it was dissolved, and no new Parliament met until the 14th of July, 1634. Sir James Hamilton, and Sir Hugh Montgomery, appear in the records as the members entitled to serve in this Parliament for the County of Down, although they had in the meantime been raised to the Irish peerage by Patent, with the titles of Viscount Claneboye, and Viscount Montgomery.

The Parliament which met on the 14th of July, 1631, continued its sittings until the 18th of April, 1635, when it was prorogued, and a new one called, which met on the 10th of March, 1639. The following account of the election of members for the County of Down to this Parliament is given in the Montgomery MSS:—

"The other thing memorable of Sir James Montgomery (before the grand Irish rebellion) is his concerting with our two Viscounts [Montgomery, and Claneboye] how only such as they thought best should be elected knights of the shire, to serve in the Parliament, anno 1640. Their lordships, both in affection and prudence, pitched on their brothers, the said Sir James, and John Hamilton, Esq. Those gentlemen were (as is required by the writt) Idonii, fit persons, and fully qualified to sit in Parliament. Each of them had been for twenty-three years conversant and employed in business of the county (of which they had exact tallys and keys), and of the respective familys therein, and those two lords' plantations did now surmount all wastes; so that these gentlemen's good conduct could not fail to have the farr major number of votes in the election, although the Trevors, Hills, M'Gennisses, O'Neills, Bagnalls, and other interests were combined against them—divers sham freeholders being made to encrease the number of choosers, which the dexterity and dilligence of those gentlemen discovered before ye face of the county, to the utter shame of the servants and agents who had practised the cheat, to sett up other pretenders who stood to be knights for the shire. It was contended much in the fields; and there you might have seen the county divided into four parties, each having him mounted on men's shoulders whom they would have their representative; and, as neither of them would yield ye plurality to ye other, the Sheriff would not determine ye controversy on view, but, like a skilfull gardner, brought all the swarms into one, and so the poll (carefully attended, and ye truth of each man's freehold searched into) ended the difficulty by the reckoning made of them, which gave it by a great many votes to Montgomery and Hamilton, many of the Lord Cromwell's tenants appearing to their sides, the rest of them being newters or absent. I was told (as I remember) by persons acting at that election, that Sir James Montgomery had many more voices for him than Mr. Hamilton; for, not a few joyned him out of the other partys, which were all generally for him to be as one

chosen; so that his business lay most to strengthen the Hamiltons, who brought a third part more voters of their own people than Sir James could conduce of his brother Montgomerys; but all the Savages, with their interest, the Fitzsymonds, the Echlins; also, Mr. Ward's, and most of Kildare's and Cromwell's tenents, were for him and his colleague partys. Our two Viscounts who, though present) behaved as spectators only. This election was evident proof what their lordships could atchieve by their own Scottish interest; and so their regard was the greater with the Governors and Parliament."—Mont. MSS., p. 124.

John Hamilton, of Coronary, County Cavan, and Monella, or Hamilton's Bawn, County Armagh, Esq., the third brother of the first Viscount Claneboye, who is above mentioned to have been so elected with Sir James Montgomery, died at Killileagh, County Down, on the 4th, and was buried at Mullabrack, County Armagh, on the 10th of December, 1639, (o.s.). He, consequently, never sat for the County of Down in Parliament, which did not meet till the 27th of Feby, 1639 (o.s.), following, whence it appears, by the Journals of the Irish House of Commons, that Sir Edward Trevor of Rose Trevor, and Sir James Montgomery of Rosemount, knights, were returned as the sitting members. The following list of members for the County of Down in the Irish Parliament. from 1585 till the Union, has been extracted from the Liber Munerum Publicorum Hiberniæ, and the Journals of the Irish House of Commons:—

1585, April—Sir NICHOLAS BAGNALL, Knight, The Newry.
Sir HUGH MAGENNIS, Knight, Rathfriland.
1613, May 18—Sir JAMES HAMILTON, Knight, Bangor, and Killileagh.
Sir HUGH MONTGOMERY, Knight, Newtown.
1634, July 14—Sir HUGH MONTGOMERY, Knight, Newtown.
Sir JAMES HAMILTON, Knight, Bangor, and Killileagh.
1634, Oct. 22—VERE ESSEX CROMWELL, Esq.*
1639, Mar. 16—Sir EDWARD TREVOR, Knight. Rose Trevor.
Sir JAMES MONTGOMERY, Knight, Rosemount.
1661, May 8—MARCUS TREVOR, Esq., Rose Trevor.
ARTHUR HILL, Esq., Hillsborough.
1662, Oct. 22—VERE ESSEX CROMWELL Esq, vice Trevor, created Viscount Dungannon.
1665, Nov. 16—MARCUS TREVOR, Esq., Rose Trevor, vice Hill, deceased.
1692, Sept. 27—Sir ARTHUR RAWDON, Bart., Moira.
JAMES HAMILTON, Esq., Tullymore.†

---

* Afterwards Earl of Ardglass; married Catherine, only daughter of James Hamilton, of Bangor, and Margaret Kynaster, who was then the widow of General Richard Price, and mother of General Nicholas Price. By her second husband, she became mother of an only daughter, Lady Elizabeth Cromwell, who married Edward Southwell, Secretary for Ireland in the time of Queen Anne, and was great-grandmother of Edward Southwell, the late Lord De Clifford, who died in 1832.—Mrs. Reilly's Memoirs.

† James Hamilton, of Tullymore, the eldest son of William, nephew of the first Viscount Claneboye, married Anne, youngest daughter of John, first Viscount Mordaunt. He was an active and steady asserter of the liberties of his country, and a chief promoter of a general rising of the Protestants of Ireland, in 1689, to shake off the tyranny of King James's government,

and was empowered by the gentlemen of Ulster to fix on a proper person in Dublin to carry their address to the Prince of Orange on his arrival there. His endeavours to defend his religion and his country did not rest here; for he and his first cousin, James Hamilton, of Bangor, raised each a regiment of foot, for which they were attainted by King James's Parliament, and had their estates sequestered. He was member for Downpatrick Borough, and for the County of Down, as above stated, in 1692. He was also Governor of the County, and embodied the Militia, with which he maintained peace at home, while he supplied King William with provisions and stores on his march to victory at the Boyne. He was sent to England, in July, 1693, to prosecute the Lords Justices of King James, and was one of the Commissioners for forfeited estates in Ireland in 1699. He died in London in 1701.—Ibid.

1695, Nov. 8—NICHOLAS PRICE, Esq., St. Field, vice Rawdon, deceased.*
1704, Sept 21—NICHOLAS PRICE, Esq., St. Field.
JOHN MAGILL, Esq., Gill Hall.
1713, Nov. 7—NICHOLAS PRICE. Esq., St. Field.
MICHAEL WARD, Esq., Castle Ward.†
1715, Oct. 29—TREVOR HILL, Esq., Hillsborough.
MICHAEL WARD, Esq., Castleward.
1717, Sept. 10—Sir JOHN RAWDON, Bart., Moyragh, vice Hill, created Viscount Hillsborough.
1723, Mar. 12—ROBERT HAWKINS MAGILL, Esq., Gill-Hall, vice Rawdon, deceased.
1727, Sept. 25—ROBERT HAWKINS MAGILL, Esq., Gill-Hall.
Hon. ARTHUR HILL (TREVOR), Belvoir.
1745, Oct. 31—BERNARD WARD, Esq., Castleward, vice Magill, deceased.‡
1761, Apr. 29—Hon. ARTHUR TREVOR, Belvoir.
BERNARD WARD, Esq., Castle Ward.

1766, Mar. 14—Hon. H. SEYMOUR CONWAY, vice Trevor, created Viscount Dungannon.
1768, July 15—BERNARD WARD, Esq., Castle Ward.
ROGER HALL, Esq., Narrow Water.§
1776, June 11—Right Hon. ARTHUR HILL, Viscount Kilwarlin.
ROBERT STEWART, Esq.
1783, Oct. 14—Right Hon. ARTHUR HILL, Viscount Kilwarlin.
Hon. EDWARD WARD.‖
1790, July—Right Hon. A. HILL, Earl of Hillsborough.¶
Hon. ROBERT STEWART.
1794, Jan. 22—FRANCIS SAVAGE, of Ardkeen, Esq., vice Right Hon. Arthur Hill, created Marquis of Downshire.
1798, Jan. 9—Right Hon. ROBERT STEWART, Viscount Castlereagh.
FRANCIS SAVAGE, Esq.

---

* Afterwards General Nicholas Price, who was son of General Richard Price, by Catherine, only daughter of James Hamilton, of Bangor, and great-grandfather of the late Nicholas Price, Esq., Saintfield, which property his mother purchased from her nephew, young James of Bangor. He was also great-grandfather of the late Cromwell Price, of Hollymount, who left his property to his nephew, Francis Savage, the son of his only sister, Anne Price, who had married Charles Savage, of Ardkeen. This Francis left the Ardkeen estate to his only child, Mary Anne Savage, and she was the last of his name who held that property, which had been in possession of that branch of the Savages ever since the reign of Henry II. She was the first wife of the late Colonel Forde, of Seaforde (uncle to the present Colonel Forde, M.P. for County Down), and died in 1826.—Mrs. Reilly's Memoirs.
† Michael Ward, the second son of Bernard Ward, of Castleward, who, in 1690, when Sheriff of the County of Down, was killed in a duel by Jocelyn Hamilton, brother of James Hamilton, of Tollymore, who was mortally wounded at the same time. The dispute arose in the Grand Jury-room, and they immediately went out and fought close to the Abbey of Downpatrick. Michael Ward, by the death of his elder brother Nicholas, became possessed of Castleward, and was afterwards a Justice of the King's Bench. He was an excellent and clever man. He is mentioned in Harris's History of the County Down, as the first person who introduced marl as a manure. He was also a great promoter of the linen trade. He was, when a handsome young barrister, married to Anne Catherine Hamilton, the eldest daughter of Mrs. Hamilton of Bangor, at the age of eighteen, not much to his mother's satisfaction. Mrs. Ward died in 1760, having survived her husband but a short time, as he died on the 17th of May preceding.—Ibid.
‡ Bernard Ward, the only son of Judge Ward, succeeded him at Castleward, and was member for the County of Down, from 1745 till 1770, when he was made a Peer by George III., under the title of Baron Castleward and Viscount Bangor. He built the present house at Castleward. His wife was Lady Anne Bligh, the eldest daughter of John, first Earl of Darnley, and the widow of Robert Hawkins Magill, of Gill Hall, in the County of Down, to whom she was not more than four or five years married, when he died at Seaforde, during a great hunting party, at which most of the gentlemen of the County were assembled. As he had been member for the County of Down for twenty years, he recommended to the gentlemen to choose Bernard Ward as his successor. Mr. Ward not only succeeded him in his seat for the County, but married his widow, also, in about three years after. Lord and Lady Bangor had a very large family, but her ladyship fancied during the last fifteen years of her life, to withdraw herself from them all, and to live at Bath, where she died in 1789, having survived Lord Bangor eight years. He died in 1751, leaving three sons surviving him.

§ This Roger Hall was married on 10th September, 1740, to Catherine, only daughter of Rowland Savage, Esq., of Portaferry, and was grandfather of the late Roger Hall, Esq., of Narrow-water Castle.
‖ Second son of Bernard Ward, first Viscount Bangor, and father of Edward, third Viscount. He died in 1812.
¶ The following account of this election is taken from a series of most interesting "Reminiscences of the Last Century," by the late Aynsworth Pilson, Esq., which appeared from time to time in the Downpatrick Recorder Newspaper:—"In the latter part of the century, a Whig Club was formed in the county of Down, which comprised many of the leading gentlemen of the county. Some of its most distinguished members were—Robert, Lord Londonderry; Robert, Viscount Castlereagh; Edward, Baron de Clifford; Sir John Blackwood, Bart.; Hon. Edward Ward; Hon. Robert Ward; Gawn Hamilton, Esq.; Francis Needham, Esq.; Matthew Forde, sen., Esq.; Matthew Forde, jun., Esq.; William Sharman, Esq.; Arthur Johnston, Esq.; John Crawford, Esq.; Nicholas Price, Esq.; Simon Isaac, Esq.; Eldred Pottinger, Esq., &c. This club signalised itself in 1790, by an active and energetic support in favour of the Hon. Edward Ward, and the Hon. Robert Stewart, in the great contest for the representation of the county, against Arthur, Earl of Hillsborough; which contest began on the 1st of May, 1790, and was maintained for three months, Mr. Stewart being under age at the commencement of the poll, but he gained his majority before its termination. Mr. Ward retired before its conclusion, soon after which Lord Hillsborough and the Hon. Mr. Stewart were declared duly elected by Colonel M'Leroth, the then High-sheriff and returning officer. Ribbons, flags, and other insignia of party were profusely displayed. The colours of Ward and Stewart were buff and blue, and the party called the 'Junction.' The colour assumed by Lord Hillsborough was orange. Ribbons worn on the breast and the motto 'Ward and Stewart' impressed on silver foil, and the like by the party of Lord Hillsborough inscribed in the same manner with 'Hillsborough,' together with cockades of their respective colours, were generally displayed. The Whig Club held its meetings, from time to time, and having assumed a political character, some of the principles of which were reform in the parliamentary representation, the exclusion of place-men and pensioners from the House of Commons, and the non-interference of Peers in parliamentary elections. These, with some other points, formed the elementary principles of the club. Mr. Gawn Hamilton took a prominent part in its deliberations, and occasionally presided at its meetings. Mr. Hamilton's refined manners and courteous disposition, together with his advanced years, claimed for him that deference which was so justly accorded to him. He was chiefly attached to field sports,—kept a fine stud, with other requirements of rural occupation and amusements. He was greatly beloved by his tenantry and neighbours; and many sons of the yeomanry were called after his name."

CHAP. IV.

Of the Children of the Six Brethren, their Marriages, Children, and other Remarkables.

1. My Lord Claneboy being dead, his only son, James,[a] came upon the estate, having, before his father's death, married one Honble. Lady Anne Carey, daughter to the Earl of Monmouth,[b] in England, who had borne to him a son, nam'd James, before his father's death, as afterwards a daughter, nam'd Jane, and two sons, Henry and Hans. This lady, as she was naturally very

---

[a] Second Viscount Claneboye, was created (by Privy Seal at Oxford, 4th March, 1646, and by Patent at Dublin, 7th June, 1647) Earl of Clanbrassil, in the County of Armagh.—See copy of his Patent given in the *Irish Lords' Journals*, p. 93.

[b] This was Henry Carey, the second Earl, and eldest son of Robert, the first Earl of Monmouth, who, upon the death of Elizabeth, on the morning of the 24th of March, 1603, rode to Edinburgh from London in three days and two nights, and arrived there before midnight on the 26th of March, four days before the message from the Privy Council, and was the first person to announce to King James his accession to the throne of England, producing and presenting to his Majesty "the sapphire ring," which his sister, Lady Scroope, had thrown out of the window to him, as he stole out of Richmond Palace, the gates being shut, by order of the Privy Council, on the Queen's death, to prevent their own announcement of that event being anticipated. This sapphire ring was sent by Sir James Fullerton to Lady Scroope, with positive orders to return it to King James, by a special messenger, as soon as the Queen actually expired. Lady Scroope had no opportunity of delivering it to her brother Robert whilst he was in the Palace of Richmond; but, waiting at the window till she saw him at the outside of the gate, she threw it out to him, and he well knew to what purpose he received it. The second Earl of Monmouth was brought up with the Duke of York, afterwards Charles I; and was a great sufferer by the civil wars. He had two sons—Lionel, who was killed at Marston Moor, and Henry, who also died before him; and eight daughters, of whom the eldest, Lady Ann Carey, married James, Earl of Clanbrassil, in 1635. At his death, in 1661, the title became extinct, and he was buried at Rickmansworth, in Hertfordshire, where a monument was erected to his memory.

The following letter, which has been found among the family papers, would appear to be written by her father, the Earl of Monmouth, to the Countess of Clanbrassil,

his daughter, about two years before the Earl of Clanbrassil's death. She survived him, and afterwards married Sir Robert Maxwell, of Waringstown, in the County of Down, Bart., and died in 1688:—

"December, the 6th, 1657.

"My deare Nan,—I writ to you in my last that your mother had beene to wayte upon my Lady Fleetewood in relation to your business, and y^t missing of her y^b, she resolved to visit her some 3 days after; but shee was brought to bed, I think, ye next day after, so it was not civill for my wife to make her first visit of compliments till yesterday, wch she then did; and, that being over, ye next (w^ch, God willing, shall be very shortly) shall be in your concernment. God give a blissing to it, I beseech Him. I can promise no great good y^win to myself, considering how the cavallyers are of late much more severely persecuted than y^ey have beene yet. One day's edickt comes forth for ye payment of ye 10th part of y^err reall estate yearly, and ye 15th part of y^err personall estate towards ye raising of a new Militia; an oy^er day's edickt silenceth all our late King's ministers, not suffering y^em ey^er to preach, marry, nor baptise; not to teach scoole, nor so much as to be chapleyns in any privat men's houses—and y^is reaches to all y^t were ministers in our late King's tyme. Y^e next news w^ch (as y^ey say) we are to heare is, y^t all such as have served ye King in y^ese late wars, and have not £100 per annum land, or £1,500 personall estate, shall bee sent to Jamico; and y^is, tho it be not yet come forth, is so true as S^r. Edward Sidnahm brought a copy of ye ordinance, as I am informed, 3 days agoe to Salsbury House. But ye best is, y^t though our orthodox ministers' mouths bee stopt, ye Jews' mouths, y^ough not y^eyre eyes, are to be opened, whoe, as I heare, are to have two sinagoges allowde y^em in London, whereof Paul's to be one. Well, my hart, God's will must be done, and wee must submit unto it. But, as for your businesse, assure your selfe all shall be done in it y^t may bee, and y^en, when we shall have done our dutyes, we must leave the event to God; whoe y^t Hee may please to blis you and all yours, and comfort all afflicted Christians, is ye prayer of your ever loving father,

"MONMOUTH.

"For the Countesse of Clanbrassill at Killileagh."

["Let y^is letter be left wth Mr. William Dixon, at his house, in Skinner's Row, at Dublin."]

handsome, and witty, so, by education and industry, became a woman extraordinary in knowledge, virtue, and piety My Lord was, of necessity, engaged in the war against the Irish, and was therein very laborious, with a very good measure of both dexterity and courage, being effectually assisted by many of his kinsmen and tenants, and much straitened in his estate, whilst a great part of it was wasted by the war, and the remainder under great burthens, not only by maintaining and quartering of the army then on foot, but also supporting many of the Protestants that fled from the upper country.[c] In the year 1648, he judg'd it his duty to join himself and his

---

Lady Fleetwood, mentioned in the foregoing letter, was wife of Charles Fleetwood, who had married—first, Frances, the daughter of Thos. Smith, of Winston, Norfolk, by whom he had three children ; but this lady being dead, he was fixed upon by Cromwell, from political motives, to marry Bridget, his eldest daughter, the widow of Ireton. Soon after he became his son-in-law, the Protector nominated him Commander-in-Chief of the forces in Ireland, when he was also invested with commissionership for the civil department, and afterwards became Lord Deputy.

[c] The following passages are extracted from the *Montg. MSS.*, as not only giving a more detailed account of the part which Earl James took in the war then going on in Ulster with the Parliamentary arms, but as containing a very comical personal anecdote related of him in connexion with it :—

"And now our Visc.[t] [Montgomery], and the Earl of Clanbrassil, Sir J[ames] M[ontgomery], Sir Geo. Moore, and the rest of the Scotish nation, being apprehensive (especially the officers under their command were) of being served by Monck in the same way as he had done to the Scottish army, and that the King's party in Ulster would be shortly wholly ruined ; therefore, his Lop, a principal actor, and Sir J. M. (as one chief contriver), and the persons afores[d], made up a friendship with the Presbitarian ministers, who stirred up the commonality against the Sectarians (for so they called their late dear brethren,), and by their advice the Solemn League and Covenant was renewed, and, by universal desire of all sorts, his Lop. was chosen Gen[l] of all the forces in Ulster, and his Majesty Charles the 2nd. was proclaimed King, in Newtown. * Now, our L[d] Visc.[t] (Gen[l] of Ulster), making a numerous party, and declaring for the King, rendezvouzed an army, and expelled Monck, who retired to Dundonald with his adherents, and they made friendship with Owen Roe O'Neil, afores[d] ; S[r] Chas. Coote (President of Connaught) being with a strong garrison at that time in Londonderry, holding the same, and Connaught for the Parliament : as these affairs took up many months, and the K. was then at Breda, treating with Com[rs] from Scotland, and being advertised of his Lop's actions for him, and praying his authority to proceed therein, his Majesty sent him his Com[n] to be Gen. of all the forces in Ulster who owned his right to the Crown, with divers powers therein, &c. * But I must return to some remarkable passages after the said surprise of Carrickfergus :—Col. Monck, returning from Colerain, which was surrendered to him the same Sept., 1648, he sent Major Gen[l]. Robert Mouro, prisoner to the Parliament, w[h] committed him to the Tower of London. Col[o] Monck thus done, called a general council of war, of all the Br[h] Colo[s], L[t] Colo[s], and Majors, to meet at Lisnagarvy, his head-quarters, in Oct[r], 1648, to satisfy them of his doings, and to consult with them of the future safety, and proceedings ; but, in truth, with the design of sending over more officers prisoners the same way. Our Visc[t] (by advice of his uncle, (S[r] J. M.) and also the Earl of Clanbrassil, (by the like advice of his friends), stayed at home, upon their guard against the like surprise, and wrote their several excuses, sending some field officers, (well cautioned and instructed) to represent, &c., for their respective regim[ts], S[r] J. M. went out also to find out what intrigues he could learn, telling his L[d] and nephew, he feared much of his being snap'd, and undoubtedly believed his Lop. the chiefest person aimed at, to be ensnared by his appearance (should he be at that court-martial), and it was better himself should venture his liberty and life, than his Lop, and the King's cause should suffer by any circumvention ag[t] his Lop's person ; and, as it was guessed, so it happened, for the court being sat, and the two lords' letters of excuse read, S[r] J. M. speaking to the same purpose, was, by order of Col[o] Monck, made prisoner ; but he giving Col[o] Conway, and others, bondsmen for his appearance before the Committee of Parliament, sitting in Darby-house, in London, he had leave to return home and settle his own and nephew Savage of Portaferry's affairs, and to prepare for his journey. About the same time S[r] Robert Stewart, who kept the fort of Culmore, w[h] commanded the passage by water to Derry, was trepanned into a visit and christening of his friend's child, in the town of Derry, and Col[o] Audley Mervin was also insidiously taken, and both of them sent by sea, prisoners to England. So the mask fell of Monck's face, and our Visc[t]. with the Earl of Clanbrazil, were upon their guard still, and the Lagan forces headed by S[r] Alex. Stewart, Bart. (who sided with the Covenanters), was also upon his guard, having a strong party out of S[r] Robert Stewart's and Col[o] Mervin's reg[ts] joining him ; for it now plainly appeared, that Col[o] Monck would not rest at his breaking the Scotch reg[ts] who were born in Scotland, but, (if he cou'd) he w[d] also discard all the Br[h] officers and soldiers of the Scotish race, tho' born and bred in Ireland, which, therefore, made them cleave together the more (especially having renewed the Covenant), both there and here. There had long ago been great animosities between the families of Ards and Claneboys, by reason of the law-forces (so many as would adhere to him) with the Duke of Ormond, in the pacification made with the Irish, and in opposition to the Parliament's army, then in Ireland; in which course the Duke and he, with all their adherents, were suddenly suppressed by the Parliament's army,[d] and he was

suits which the first had against the latter; and the occasion of them (tho' partly removed before A°. 1639) was not fully taken away as yet; but a cessation began, A° 1641, when Daniel O'Neil gave the s⁴ disturbance against them both, and then those animosities were laid in a deep sleep by the Irish rebellion, and the deaths of our 2d Viscount [Montgomery] and of the first Lord Claneboys; for, *inter arma silent leges*. The hardships also w^h our third Viscount [Montgomery] and the first Earle of Clanbrassill were now like to undergo from Monk, and which they actually and jointly suffered from the usurpers, who aimed at the total destruction of both their families, had totally mortified and buryed those differences between those interwoven neighbours, and had made them good friends, as they were fellow-sufferers in one cause; so, that the last two named lords often met on divers affairs, both publicly and privately, eat and drank together, without jealousy or grudging to one another. It happened, in the time when consultation and strict union was most needful against Monck, that the Earle of Clanbrazil stayed with our Viscount all night in Newtown-House; the Earl had taken medicine on^b against ficabitings, but (as the story goes) was abused, or rather affronted, by a spirit (they called them 'Brooneys' in Scotland, and there was one of them, in the appearance of an hairy man, which haunted Dunskey Castle, a little before our first Viscount [Montgomery] bot it and Portpatrick lands from Sr Robert Adair, Knt.); which spirit was not seen in any shape, or to make a noise or play tricks, during any of our lords' times. But it pleased his devilship (that night, very artificially,) to tear off the Earle of Clanbrazil's Holland shirt from his body, without disturbing his rest; only left on his Lo^p the wristbands of his sleeves, and the collar of the shirt's neck, as they were tyed with ribband when he went to bed. The Earle awaking, found himself robbed of his shirt, and lay as close as an hare in her form, till Mr. Haus (afterwards Sr Hans Hamilton), thinking his Lo^p had lain and slept long enough to digest his *hesternum crapulum*, knocked at the door, and his Lo^p calling him, he went in, and his Lo^p showing him his condition, prayed one of his shirts to relieve him in that extremity, bidding him shut the door after him, and to discharge servants to come at him 'til after his return; and, having put on the shirt w^h he was to bring him, his Lo^p said, 'Cozen Hans, I w^d rather £100 than my brothers Mont^s. of Ardes shou^d hear of this adventure, and therefore conceal it;' which was done till his Lo^p was three miles off. But the further mishap was, that Mr Hamilton had no shirt clean but an Holland half shirt, that being then in fashion to be worn above the night shirts, w^h did not reach his Lo^p's navel; but, having got on his breeches and doublit, with Mr. Hamilton's help (for his Lo^p was excessively fat), his servants were let in and dressed him; and his Lo^p having called for the chamberpot (now called in taverns a looking-glass, for reasons I know), his Lo^p found his shirt admirably wrapt up and stuffed therein; but his servants were enjoyned silence,

and his Lo^p came to the parlour, where his brother, the L^d of Ardes (as he called him) attended his Lo^p. They took a morning draught and dined; after which his Lo^p went to Carnaseure, near Comer, the habitation of one of his capt^s. and cousin, called, also, Hans Hamilton, and, telling him his misadventure, had a long shirt, which he put on, and so went to his Countess at Killileagh. All I shall remark on this event is, that I presume to think that his Lo^p would not, for the hundred pounds he spoke of, have stayed another night (tho' he was heartily entreated); for he understood not 'Brooney's' manner of fighting, tho' himself had learned in France to fence with a *cû cû et le pour pout bas*; as (himself did often say) he was taught and did in his travels."—*Monty. MSS.*, pp. 209 to 213

[d] If the meaning of the foregoing passage he, that Ormond (then a Marquis, and not a Duke, as stated in the MS.,) was personally present at the battle in which the Earl of Clanbrassil was defeated, it will be seen from the following authorities that the writer was mistaken in this, although Ormond sent him a reinforcement under the command of Daniel O'Neill and Colonel Mark Trevor, but it arrived too late (see 2 *Carte's Letters*, 418):—

Monro, having burned Antrim, and Lisburn, had joined Lords Clanbrassil and Montgomery in the County of Down; and, in expectation of a reinforcement from Ormond, they were preparing to attack Venables at Belfast, with the view of relieving the garrison at Carrickfergus, before its final surrender into his hands. Coote and Venables, apprised of their plans, met them on "the plains of Lisnegarvey," at a place called Lisnestrain, not far from Lisburn. On the 6th of December, 1649, the engagement took place, when the Royalists, led on by Lords Clanbrassil and Montgomery, and their horse by Sir George Munro, were defeated, and totally dispersed. Many inferior officers, and nearly a thousand men were slain: and their baggage, arms, and ammunition were taken. Monro fled to Charlemont, and thence to Enniskillen, and the Lords Clanbrassil and Montgomery with difficulty escaped, and joined Ormond in the South.—1 *Reid*, 224. The particulars of this decisive engagement are only to be found in a small pamphlet entitled, "Two letters from William Basil, Esq., Attorney-General of Ireland; one to the Right Hon. John Bradshaw, Lord President of the Council of State, the other to the Right Honourable William Lenthal. Esq., Speaker of the Parliament of England, of a great victory obtained by the Parliament's forces in the North of Ireland, on the plains of Lisnegarvey, &c., with a relation of the taking of Drumcree (in Armagh), and of the surrender of Carrickfergus upon articles,"—printed at London, 1649. At the end of the first letter, which is dated from Dublin, December 12, 1649, is the following postscript, giving a summary of the whole affair:—"This night Col. Chidley Coote is come to town, with letters from his brother, the Lord President. The substance of his brother's letters, necessitated, for his life and estate, to undergo the fine of £9,000 Stg. to the Commonwealth of England;ᵃ by reason of all which he was necessitated to contract a great deal of debt upon his

---

and his own relation, is briefly thus:—The Scotch Lords and George Munro fell into the Claneboys with 4,000 men; and on the 5th of this instant the enemy drew out their army, and would have fought, but our party, wanting some horse, forbade to engage. The next day the enemy drew off, and our army, following them, sent out a forlorn hope of 200 men, the horse commanded by Captain Dunbar, of Sir Theophilus Jones his regiment, and the foot by Major Gore, of the Lord President's regiment; the 200 men fell upon the rear of the enemy, and, before the army could come up, with the loss of one corporal and two private soldiers, routed the whole army, of whom were slain in their place a thousand men. The President writes:—And a party of horse, commanded the nearest way to the Black-water, to stay that pass, slew 400 there, where George Munro saved himself by swimming."

In "Whitelocke's Memorials of the English Affairs from Charles I. to the Restoration," the following account is given of the affair:—

"*Decr.* 25, 1649.—Christmas Day, the House sat, and letters came from Chester, that, from the North of Ireland, they understood that about 4,000 horse and foot of the enemy, who came to relieve Carrickfergus, were routed by Sir Charles Coot and Colonel Venables; that the Irish were commanded by Monroe, the Lord of the Ardes, and the Earl of Claneboy; that 1,000 of them were killed, and 500 horse taken, and but 200 of the Parliament's forces did fight; that Claneboy was slain, or sunk in a bog, being corpulent, and Colonel Montgomery, and Colonel Hamilton, taken prisoners. Other letters of the defeating of the Lord of Ardes, Claneboy, and Monroe, by Sir Charles Coot and Colonel Venables; that they took all their arms, ammunition, bag, and baggage, killed Colonel Henderson, and 1,400 more, Colonel Hamilton, and most of the foot officers; that the horseman lost their horses, and betook themselves to bogs; that the English lost but one corporal and three soldiers."

"*Decr.* 26.—Other letters confirming the victory of, against the Lord of Ardes and the rest, and that it was done by only 200, who were sent out as a forlorn, and fell upon the rear of the enemy, who fell into disorder, and were wholly routed by these 200 only."

"*Decr.* 31.—That the slaughter in the North was greater than at first reported; that the Earl of Claneboy was not slain, but rendered himself prisoner to mercy.—*Whitelocke's Mem.*, p. 435.

The following brief account of it is also given in the *Montg. MSS.*, p. 217:—

"Our third Viscount [Montgomery], with his few loyal followers and adherents, and the Earle of Clanbrasil, with his men (all that were preaching-proof); their Lopᵗˢ kept their forces together, and being personally present (as they were *afterwards* with Ormond), and by their example encouraging their soldiers, were routed at Lisnestrain (as it was sᵈ, by Sir Geo. Munro's mismanagement near Lisne-garvey aforesᵈ,) by Sⁱ Chaˢ. Coote and a party of O. C.'s

army; Clanbrasill, with some flying horse, and his castle of Killileagh still standing out, he resorted to Ormond."—See also "A letter from the Attorney of Ireland concerning the taking of the towne of Wexford by storme, on the 11th of October last, with some other intelligence from the North and South of Ireland," printed at London, 26 October, 1649, in which it is said, "We are now possessed of all the North, saving Knockfergus, Colraine, and Killileagh."

Killileagh Castle was not taken by the Republicans till the month of December following, when it was partly demolished, but it was afterwards substantially repaired, in 1666, by Henry, second Earl of Clanbrassil, when the second round tower was added to the front of it, which was not in existence when the sketch of it was made in the Clandeboye map of 1625-6 (which will be found copied into the third volume of the *Ulster Archæological Journal*, p. 144); and it was, with the exception of the two round towers, completely rebuilt in 1850, by its then proprietor, the late Archibald Rowan Hamilton, Esq., as shewn at p. 149 of the same volume.

ᵃ "Our third Viscount [Montgomery] stayed with the Marquis [of Ormond], and was included among the Protesᵗˢ (as the Earl of Clanbrassil also was) with whom O. C. made capitulations for their coming home, and peaceably living there without deserting the realm or acting agsᵗ the Parliamt, and for being admᵈ to their estates upon composition money to be pᵈ by them as the Parlᵗ should think fit; wʰ done, O. C. went to Engᵈ, in winter, 1649, leaving Ireton to attend the blockade of Limerick, to wʰ the Irish had retired for their last refuge to obtain conditions of peace. The Marquis of Ormond went to wait on the K. (Chˢ the 2d)."—*Mont. MSS.*, p, 218, 9.

A declaration, or proclamation, was published by "the Commissioners for the settling and securing the Province of Ulster," dated at Carrickfergus the 23d of May, 1653, specifying the conditions on which it was proposed to transplant the leading Presbyterians in the Counties of Down and Antrim to certain districts in Leinster and Munster, which was accompanied with a list of 260 persons (including Lord Claneboye), who, by their known attachment to monarchical and Presbyterian principles, and by their station or influence, were most obnoxious to the reigning faction, who were required, within a specified time, and under certain penalties, to embrace the terms so offered. A copy of these proposals of the commissioners for effecting this extensive revolution in the population and property of a great part of Ulster is printed in the second volume of *Reid's Presbyterian History*, p. 272; and

estate, and so lived with his family in a much lower   *   than his father had done in his time. His son James, a very hopefull youth for parts, temper, piety, and other good improve-

in the *Appendix* to the same vol. p. 493. Immediately after the publication of this proclamation, preliminary steps were taken during the summer towards effecting the proposed transplantation.

"But matters in England being in a'continual unsettledness through Cromwell's driving on his design for his own advancement to the supreme government, and the opposition of many in the army, wholly against the government being settled on any single person, this motion of the Governors here in Ireland had no bottom to rest upon, and, therefore, their project of transplanting the Scotch into Tipperary, did evanish within a little time ; and the ministers and people in this country began to have a quiet calm for all the former storms which they had endured." —*Adair's Narrative, by Dr. Killen,* p. 203.

The Earl of Clanbrassil was included among the Protestants with whom the Protector capitulated to live peaceably at home, and to regain their estates upon a composition settled by Parliament. After his estate had been sequestered, and for six years and a half the profits arising from it had been received by Cromwell, he compounded for the fine mentioned in the MS., of which he paid about the half. The following debates in Cromwell's Parliament in reference to the Lords of Ardes' and Glainboise's [Claneboye's] estates, are extracted from *Burton's Parliamentary Diary:*—

"*Wednesday, Dec. 3, 1656.*—An Act for settling Henry Whalley and Erasmus Smith in certain lands fallen to them by lots upon the adventures in Ireland : acres, Irish measure, 11,750, formerly of the Lords of Ardes, and Glainboise. They pretend that one may compound, per the Lord Protector's ordinance ; and, that the other has articles of war (viz., Lord of Ardes). It was desired, that these lots, being cast in first, might, notwithstanding these claims, be settled upon them.

"Sir JOHN REYNOLDS, and Colonel MARKHAM, would have some expedient found upon committing of the Bill, to satisfy Judge Advocate Whalley some other way ; for Lord Glainboise has compounded for these lands, according to the ordinance of his highness. You ought to be tender likewise in the articles which Lord Ardes pretends to ; and hope you will use mercy rather than rigour.

"Mr. —— SCOTCH—Lord Glainboise hath been faithful to you, though he had the hap to be a little wrong, for which he was sequestered ; and, having compounded, if it be reversed, who is secured ?

"Mr. ROBINSON—These adventurers ought to be specially respected ; for they were the first that trusted you, as that gentleman told you. If you be not steady, who will trust you ? I would rather violate the other claims, than those which were so much grounded upon trust and confidence in your cause when, it was but in its infancy. I speak it not for Judge Advocate Whalley, nor for Mr. Smith. I know them not ; but I speak for the justice and credit of your old cause. I would not have that trust violated, of all trusts whatsoever. The good old interest ought to be borne up.

"Lord LAMBERT—Lord Glainboise did compound, and was to pay £10,000, which was as much, if not more, than the estate were worth if it were to be sold. Lord Ardes, by the articles, was to enjoy his estate till the Parliament took further notice. Now the Parliament has taken further notice by the declaration whereby time was given for such persons, with their estates, to be gone. All parties have been heard, too, and again, in this last case, both before the Committee of Articles (who thought they had power to hear, but not to determine), and before his highness, and his council, who thought they had not power to do it. So they were transferred into Ireland, to be relieved according to the orders and ordinances of Parliament. I would have this committed, and if you find a clear right in these Lords, or either of them, to their estates, it may be provided some other way for the adventurers ; for, it may be other men's cases as well as theirs. But, I would have you specially tender in performing your trusts and credits. I know that Judge Advocate Whalley and Mr. Smith have taken a great deal of pains in the business.

"The MASTER of the ROLLS—If this adventure be taken from them which they have assigned them by lot, they can never resort again ; so, by this means they lose the whole. I care not, so it be not totally lost. It was your first faith, and it may be well called an adventure ; for Ireland was almost all lost when they adventured. 'The King made himself merry,' said Luke Robinson, 'by saying of those adventurers, that you carved the lion's skin before he was dead.' I desire that it may be committed for the relief of the adventurers.

"Major WARING—I am against the committing of this Bill, for there are other trusts and faiths to be performed, and other members concerned. I desire that you would not take one and leave another, but consider all together ; there are faiths of greater concernment unsatisfied.

"Sir WILLIAM STRICKLAND, and Major-General KELSEY —These adventurers should be satisfied out of the composition monies ; for you ought to take care of them that out of mere confidence trusted you, and to respect the justice of the Parliament and the army too.

"Major MORGAN—Lord Ardes' articles have been twice affirmed. Lord Glainboise hath done you more service than his dis-service. I would have them repaired, but rather that their estates might be assigned them in some other part of the nation ; for, in the North, the Scotch keep up an interest distinct in garb and all formalities, and are able to raise an army of 40,000 fighting men at any time, which they may easily convey over into the Highlands upon any occasion ; and you have not so much interest in them as you have in the inhabitants of the Scotch nation. I would have the adventurers have the land fallen to them by lot, and the other claimers provided for elsewhere.

"Resolved—That this Bill be committed in the Duchy Chamber to-morrow.

"Mr. BAMFIELD, and Mr. ROBINSON—All that serve for Ireland should be on this Committee.

"Sir GILBERT PICKERING, and Mr. HIGHLAND—Against any such distinction of members. It is an ill precedent,

ments, died at 15 years of age, and his daughter in her infancy.[f] His   *   especially by the death of his   *   brought him low in his disposition of mind comparatively with himself in former times: he became corpulent, scorbutic, hydropic, and so decayed gradually, 'till at length he died in June, 1659.[g] He was naturally mild, loving, and just; by his education humane,

and looks not like an union. Desire that they may all be named, and name as many as you will, but let them not be exclusively added.

"Mr. ASHE, the elder—As they sit in Parliament, they are not Irishmen, but mere Englishmen.

"Resolved—That all that serve for Ireland be of the Committee."

"*Wednesday, December 24, 1656.*—Sir WILLIAM STRICKLAND reported the amendments from the Committee, to whom the bill was referred for settling upon Judge Advocate Whalley and Mr. Erasmus Smith lands in Ireland, fallen to them by lot as adventurers there. Lord Ardes' and Lord Glanboise's lands were fallen by lot to the said adventurers; but the Committee reported that other lands are set out in lieu of those lands.

"Major-General DISBROWE, and Lord LAMBERT, proposed that they be set out by any three or more of his highness's council, whereof the Lord Deputy to be one.

"Mr. ROBINSON—The amendments are quite otherwise than the Bill. It is a matter of great concernment. Here are 9,000 acres, English measure, settled upon them; for Irish measures are double; and you leave it to them to make their election. Surely they will not chuse the worst. If you give such large exhibitions, I doubt you will find some fall short—they that come last. Other public debts are to be satisfied out of Irish lands. I would have these gentlemen performed with to a penny, but I would have no more given them than is their contracts; I like not those general terms—'All other advantages.' I desire it should either be recommitted, or put in more particular terms. Here are 5,000 Irish acres.

"Sir WILLIAM STRICKLAND—I hope it is put into the hands of such persons as will be very faithful to you in seeing that no more be let out than is due.

"Colonel JONES—By the orders of the House, the member concerned ought to withdraw. You must be careful in the measure, for you may be much mistaken in that, for Irish acres are double ours.

"Mr. ATTORNEY-GENERAL—Unless the member be accused of some crime he need not withdraw. In such cases the member stands up in his seat, makes his defence, and then is to withdraw.

"Major-General BRIDGES—There is no such difference in the measure, as is represented to you.

"Major-General GOFFE—Put all the amendment to the question to settle in the gross.

"Resolved—That the lands be set out by three or more of the council, whereof the Lord Deputy and Chief Governor of Ireland to be one. Amendment upon amendment.

"Captain SCOTTEN—Seeing you have left out the house of Portumna, I desire that you would assign them a house in Galloway.

"Mr. SPEAKER—Pressed that a house should be assigned them.

"Resolved—To agree with the Committee in all these amendments.

"Resolved that this Bill be engrossed."

The following extracts from the *English* Commons Journals, contain the only references to the same transaction:—

"*Wednesday, the 3rd of December, 1656.*—A Bill for settling Henry Whalley, and Erasmus Smith in their lands in Ireland, fallen to them by lot as adventurers, was this day read the second time, when the question, committed to Sir John Reynolds, Colonel Markham, Mr. Trayle, Mr. Robinson, Lord Lambert, Master of the Rolls, Major Waring, Captain Blackwell, Colonel Rous, Mr. Lucy, Lord Chief Justice Glyn, Mr. Trevor, Mr. Lyster, Mr. John Ash, Mr. Disbrow, Major-General Kelsey, Sir. Wm. Strickland, Major Morgan, Alderman Foote, Alderman Drury, Mr. Bisse, Sir Thomas Honeywood, Mr. Downing Dr. Clergis, Colonel Chadwick, Colonel Weldare, Colonel Crompton, Colonel Beamont, Major-General Goff, Sir Theophilus Jones, and all that serve for Ireland, are to meet to-morrow in the afternoon at two of the clock, in the Duchy Chamber.

"*Wednesday, 24th December, 1656.*—Sir WILLIAM STRICKLAND reports amendments to the Bill for settling Henry Whalley and Erasmus Smith in lands fallen to them by lot in Ireland, which were twice read, and, upon the question, assented unto.

"Mr. DOWNING tenders an additional clause to the said Bill, which was read the first and second time.

"Resolved—That the blank in this clause be filled up with the word 'four.'

"And the said clause so amended was, upon the question, assented unto.

"Ordered—That the Bill so amended, be ingrossed."

[f] James, his eldest son, was born 7th September, 1642; died 8th May, 1658; and was buried at Rickmansworth, in Hertfordshire. The following is a copy of the inscription on his monument in Rickmansworth Church:—"Here lyeth the body of James Hambledon, Lord Claneboy, eldest son to James Earl of Clanbrassil; born September 7, 1642; deceased May 8, 1658." Jane, his only daughter, also died before him, and was buried beside her brother in Rickmansworth Church. Henry, his second son, survived him, and became second Earl of Clanbrassil; and Hans, his third son, who also survived him, married, and died without issue.

[g] On the 20th of June, and was buried with great splendour at Bangor, beside his father, on the 29th of July, 1659. The procession was made from a pavilion in the fields.—See a copy of his will in the appendix to this chapter.

judicious, and complyant with his circumstances, beyond what would have been expected of one so highly educated, and in expectation of so great a fortune. His education and conversation inclined him to be Episcopal; but he was therein very moderate, and paid a great respect to all good persons, and was in his practice Presbyterian, and died (in the sense of all good people about him) very Christianly, and ordered the affairs of his family with great discretion and respect to the former transactions, whereof afterwards he testified, both living and dying, great respect to his kinsmen, though it fell out, after his father's death, that all his servants were strangers, and his relations inconversant in his affairs, greatly to his prejudice, and not a little to theirs.

2. Of HALCRAIG's[h] family, the eldest son, John, in his youth was neglected in his education, and, falling in friendship with persons above his quality and estate, spent too liberally; upon which, on a time, some of his near relations (too likely for their own ends) persuaded and concurred with him to sell his father's purchase in Scotland,[i] and come to Ireland with the remainder of his money, where he married a gentlewoman named West, daughter to a gent. of good estate in Isle-a-Kail, by whom he had two daughters, Jane[k] and Rachel;[l] and, being employed in the war in Ireland, was a captain of horse; after some years died unfortunate by water. His natural parts were not contemptible, but not improved to the best advantage; he was plentifully just, kind, and courageous, and left a very competent estate in Ireland with his family.

James, the 2nd brother, was bred in his youth to merchandize in Scotland; but, disliking that

---

[h] Archibald Hamilton, of Halcraig, or Harrage, in the County of Lanark, Esq., eldest brother of James, first Visct. Claneboy.—See appendix to this chapter.

[i] The following letter from Lord Claneboye to his cousin, Gawin Hamilton, of Raplock, would shew that he was surety for some of those debts which his nephew, John, of Halcraig, had contracted in Scotland, and on account of which he was obliged to sell his father's purchase there:—

"NOBLE COSEN,—I am sorry to hear the bad successe w[ch] you have had for the sale of Halcraig. I could do no more than for my part to performe what I undertook, w[ch] I have done and more, and w[ch] I wold never have done one jott of, if I had not conceaved assured hopes of the performance of all the parts w[ch] was then confidently assumed unto me, whereof, except what I did myself, I hear not of anything that is done for him, w[ch] I can but regret, and mine own mishapp, that paretaken on the moneys w[ch] I paid for him, and yet owe them and pay consideration for them, and he notwithstanding never a whitt the better. It is told me that he hath made over the absolute estate of Halcraig to yourself and Sheiles, w[ch] if it be so, I am confident that you and he, in your loves to that man, and respects to your owne reputacons, will give a proof how tender you are of his standing: I will speak to James, of Ballewalter, as you desire; but, believe it, he is of himself carefull and painfull, and the moneye come not in here so readily and so soon as there; besides John's rents are fetched, as you know, from the Countie of Cavan, w[ch] is ill provyded in money: I shall also speak to John to the effect w[ch] you desire. I shall have a care of the Black Laird's money to send it, seeing it is desired to be brought in. Sheiles doth write to me to buy Arch[d]'s. lands here. I am not for buying of any land at all, when you and other friends stand ingadged for my debts there, w[ch] in credit and conscience is to be my first purchase to redeeme you out of. And, good Cosen, if theis advises and conclusions, w[ch] by you all were laid downe here, hold not, I am putt out of all further advise for matters in that kingdome, to the affairs of w[ch] God knoweth I am a meer stranger. This is more than I have written to any wth mine owne hand this long time, being much payned with a megrim. Comend me to your lady, whom, wth Arch[d]. and the rest, I comend to God's favours, being your affectionate Cosen to serve you.   "J. CLANEBOYE.
"27 Aprill, 1632."

This letter, which has been found among the family papers, is endorsed thus in Lord Claneboye's handwriting —"Copy of my answer to Raploch, concerning Halcraig, &c."

[k] Who married William Hogg, Esq.

[l] Who married John Stevenson, Esq.,

employment, came to Ireland, and was very kindly entertained by his uncle, my Lord Claneboy, who had a great esteem of him; kept him much about himself for a time, and then made him a captain of foot, wherein he behaved very vigilantly and courageously in all the time of the war of Ireland; and thereafter married Agnes Kennedy, daughter to Sir   Kennedy, of Colane, in Carick, by whom he had two daughters which came to age,[m] besides some others which died young. He lived upwards of sixty years, and died at his own house; [n] was creditably buried, and much lamented.` He was naturally judicious, and sagacious; was diligent in prosecuting his affairs; and, in the whole course of his time, very sober, and pious, though unfortunate in falling upon some affairs that occasioned great trouble and expense to him by lawsuits; nevertheless, left a competent estate with his wife and children, which survived him.

Archibald, the 3rd brother, being on the road of improvement by learning, was withdrawn into y[e] war of Ireland, in which he soon appeared to be extraordinary for strength, courage, and conduct; in a short time he was advanced to be captain of horse, and was always valued much above his station. He joined with my Lord in the Association, from the singular respect he bore to him and others. In a skirmish at Dromore, one of his thigh bones was broken by a shot; he was taken prisoner, and carried to Lisnagarvy, where he soon after died of his wounds, being very honourably treated and buried by his enemies, who honoured him highly as a very gallant gentleman. His natural parts were very great; in a short time he gave proof of great solidity in judgment, courage, strength, and dexterity; plentifull of natural affection to all his relations; was a great honorer of all worthy and religious persons, and was himself really such. He regretted much the last step of his actions, joining in the Association, as being therein a slave to that which is counted honor, but a rebel to his conscience, and the public good of the nation. At his death he evidenced great magnanimity, patience, and true Christian submission, with faith in God, through Jesus Christ. He was greatly lamented by all good people, especially his near relations, and greatly honoured of all that knew or heard of him.

Gawin,[o] the 4th, and William,[p] the 5th, brothers, being yet alive, I shall only now say of them, as their education guided them to be of different employments, the first in the way of soldiery, the last in the practical part of the law, especially in and of Scotland, it will be generally allowed that they deserve a creditable esteem of all wise and honest men. All I shall now say of them is, they have shown great integrity to their profess'd principles, both by doing and suffering, without tergiver-

---

m Rose, wife of William Fairlie Esq.; and Anne, wife of Hans Stevenson, Esq.

n At Neilsbrook, in the County of Antrim.

o See page 43 *ante.* He married Anne, daughter of Archibald Hamilton, Esq., County Armagh, in 1683, and died in October, 1703.

p William Hamilton, Esq., of Killileagh. He died unmarried and without issue. His will is dated 1716.

sation, or complying with contrary courses, tho' sometimes under great temptations, to the great destruction of profits and honours they might have had. As it hath fallen out, in the course of their time, and way of their business, that they have been conversant in affairs with all ranks of persons, from the highest to the lowest, and many in all ranks, for these many years by *
and in matters of great moment, I never heard they gave cause of offence or complaint to any at any time, but that they were generally and deservedly in good esteem with all, as well for their integrity as abilities, which are certainly not contemptible. Let him and other witness testify what shall fall out hereafter.

Robert, the 6th brother (now dead), had a disadvantage of being confined into attendance upon his aged mother and her affairs, and so fell under education much below his parts and spirit. Tho' thus obscured and injured, he was chosen and fit (and after trial so found) for managing the late Earl Henry's estate and country affairs, to the great satisfaction of all he was concerned with. He married a near kinswoman of the late Countess Clanbrassill, * Meredith, daughter to Sir * Meredith, who, as she was well descended and educated, proved a very discreet and pious woman.[q] He died without issue, leaving behind him a very good name for wisdom and piety; was looked upon, by all that knew him, as eminent for natural parts, good morality, and true friendship, if education and opportunity had given him advantages for greater improvements.

3. Of GAWIN's[r] family, was first, Archibald, who, soon after his father's death, was taken by my Lord Claneboy under his particular inspection; and, being found of very good parts and disposition for learning, was kept at schools and colleges until he had imbibed all the ordinary parts of learning, and found to have made a very good proficiency in all. His inclinations were found to be to the study of the Ministry; but, after some tryals made, upon more mature deliberation, he was bred to the law, at the Inns of Court, where he made very great proficiency. After a while, my Lord Claneboy, now become aged and less capable to stir abroad, employed him in attendance upon his affairs at Court in England, and some lawsuits he had then * , wherein for a time he proved very successful and acceptable to my Lord, and in very good esteem with persons of the best stamp and quality in and about the City of London. At this time, he married a gentlewoman that fell through domestic society into his acquaintance, unequal to his then visible station, and what was expected of him, but concealed it as much as he could, especially from his friends, least perhaps my Lord should come to know of it, and be displeased with it. By her he had two sons, who soon died. This being noised abroad, came at last to my Lord's ears, and was highly offensive to him, insomuch that he withdrew his countenance and employment from him,

---

[q] She died 25th December, 1636. [r] Gawin Hamilton, third son of the Vicar of Dunlop.—See pages 11, and 43, *ante*.

T

and so left him under hard circumstances, which being known, he soon was lowered in his esteem and acceptance at the Court and elsewhere; and, after some time, he came to Ireland, and was again employ'd by Earl James about his family, with small encouragements from himself, and no great respect from his other friends and acquaintances in the country. He died, in the year '62, not much lamented, yet with regret of his more ingenuous and candid friends, that his latter end should have been so dissonant and unsuitable to his beginnings. He was of very excellent natural parts, and good temper, but vitiate with too much Court air, and overladen with the contempt and poverty he fell under by his own indiscreet management, tho' it was whispered by some, that my Lord dealt severely with him, and upon design (having opportunity), lest he should bring my Lord to an account of his intermission with that part of his father's estate that was in Ireland, which indeed was never enquired into, nor could be, considering the great interval of time, and that this man could only call him to question.

The other* brother was James, whose youthfull education was committed and faithfully performed by his uncle Arch[d]. of Halcraig, in Scotland, 'till he had passed through all the parts of learning usually taught in schools and colleges in that kingdom, with great approbation. Soon after, my Lord Claneboy commanded his attendance upon him, with design to apply him to the care of his secular affairs, the which he underwent for a time with all diligence, patience, fidelity, and acceptance with my Lord, and all the tenants of the estate, the rents whereof he received and disposed by my Lord's directions, tho' still his disposition and private diligences moved toward the Ministry, which he so carefully concealed, and prudently, that my Lord and his good Lady were never 'ware of it till they saw and heard him preach in the pulpit in Bangor. My Lady was pleased to compliment him thus:—"James, I think your gown and pulpit become you very well; I will bestow the gown, and my Lord (if he will be advised by me) shall bestow the pulpit,"—both which were soon performed by his settlement in the parish of Ballywalter. My Lord seemed angry, and chid him that he concealed his purpose so much from him, and so made him guilty of giving him so great diversion, who otherwise was disposed to nourish his pious purpose.[‘] He mar-

---

* Another brother, Richard, is mentioned in Lord Claneboy's will at p. 50, *ante*, to whom he left £10 a year so long as he was in the Grammar School, and, during his being in College, twenty marks a year; but, as he is not mentioned in the MS., it is probable that he did not attain his majority.

[‘] See note at p. 36, *ante*, as to Blair's settlement at Bangor, as minister. Shortly after, he was the means of inducing the above-named James Hamilton, to join the ministry, who is described in *Adair's Narrative*, p. 12, as—

"An honest and godly young man, being a daily hearer of Mr. Robert Blair, showed much tenderness and ability. He being then chamberlain to the Lord Claneboy, his uncle, Mr. Blair, and Mr. Cunningham, (the then minister of Hollywood,) put him to private essays of his gifts, and, being satisfied therewith, Mr. Blair invited him to preach publicly at Bangor, in his uncle's hearing, he knowing nothing till he saw him in the pulpit, (they fearing my lord would be loath to part with so faithful a servant). But, when my lord heard him in public, he put great respect upon him the same day, and, shortly after, entered him unto a charge at Ballywalter, where he was painful, successful, and constant, notwithstanding he had many

ried a gentlewoman, Eliz^{th.} Watson, daughter to Mr. David Watson, Minister of Killeavy, near Newry, who was placed with the noble Lady Claneboy for her improvement's sake. He had by her 15 children, tho' none came to maturity, but one son (Arch^{d.})," and three daughters, Jane, Mary, and Eliz^{th.} He was continued in that station ten years, until, by the rigiditys of my Lord Wentworth, and the then Bishop of Derry (Bramhall), new terms of Church Communion, to be sworn to, were imposed upon the whole Church of Ireland, whereunto he could not submit, and upon the account whereof he sustained a public dispute with the then Bishop of Down, Henry Lesly, before several noblemen, many gentlemen, and the whole clergy of the diocese, with many others from both town and country.' To this dispute came B^{p.} Bramhall, whose courage was evidently supercilious and

---

temptations to follow promotion, but was graciously preserved from these baits, and made a successful instrument in the work of Christ in these parts."

Blair thus describes him :—

"Being satisfied with his gifts, I invited him to preach in my pulpit, in his uncle's hearing, who, till then, knew nothing of this matter ; for, Mr. Hamilton, having been his uncle's chamberlain, and chief manager of his affairs, we were afraid the Viscount would not part with so faithful a servant. But he, having once heard his nephew, did put more respect on him than ever before. Shortly thereafter (about the year 1625), Mr. Hamilton was ordained (by Bishop Echlin) to the holy ministry at Ballywalter, where he was both diligent and successful, and notwithstanding he had many temptations to espouse episcopacy, and might easily have obtained promotion in that way, yet the Lord did graciously preserve him from being ensnared with those baits, and made him very instrumental in promoting His work."—*Blair's Life.*

Livingston, also describes him as "a learned and diligent man," and adds, that "his gift of preaching was rather doctrinal than exhortatory."—*Livingstone's Life.*

ᵘ This Archibald was long a leading minister in the Presbyterian Church in Ireland. He was ordained at Benburb, about the year 1668 ; thence he was removed to Armagh, in 1673 ; and finally, in 1693, to Killinchy, where he died in 1699.—2 *Reid,* 49.

ᵛ Henry Leslie, the new Bishop of Down and Connor, held his Primary Visitation at Lisburn, in the month of July (1636), and, agreeably to the orders of the late convocation, he required from his clergy their subscription of the canons. On this occasion, five of the ministers refused to comply, and assigned their reasons. These were Mr. Brice, of Broadisland, Mr. Ridge, of Antrim, Mr. Cunningham, of Holywood, Mr. Colvert, of Oldstone, and Mr. Hamilton, of Ballywalter. The Bishop, impressed with the importance of retaining these men in the Church, of which they were among the most zealous and influential ministers, held on this occasion a private conference with them, in the hope of inducing them to

relinquish their scruples, and promise conformity to the canons. This attempt, however, proving ineffectual, he was urged by Bishop Bramhall, to proceed forthwith to their deposition. He accordingly summoned his clergy to meet him in the church at Belfast, on the tenth of August. The Bishop opened the business of this memorable Visitation by preaching from the ominous text—"But if he neglect to hear the church, let him be unto thee as an heathen man and a publican."—Matt. xviii. 17. See the first vol. of *Reid's Presbyterian History,* pp. 188 to 193, where the substance of the sermon is given ; and the author adds,—

"This characteristic discourse being ended, the five nonconforming ministers were called forward. The Bishop complained, that the result of his former confidential conference with them having been misrepresented, and the victory in point of argument attributed to them, he would not again converse with them in private ; but he now proposed to debate the matter openly in the church on the following day, when he would defend all that was required by the canons. This offer was at once accepted by the brethren ; and, Mr. Hamilton, who had been a member of the convocation, was appointed by them to conduct the conference in their name. Accordingly, on Thursday, the eleventh of August, this singular and interesting discussion commenced, in the presence of a large assemblage of the nobility, gentry, and clergy, of the diocese. It was conducted according to the forms of syllogistic reasoning ; and displays great readiness and acuteness on the part of Hamilton, and more moderation on that of the Bishop than could have been anticipated from his sermon. Bramhall was present to encourage his brother prelate ; and he occasionally mingled in the discussion, but in a very arrogant and disorderly manner. As it too often happens in public debates, the controversy merged into the discussion of some of the less important points of difference. It, therefore, by no means affords a favourable view of the grounds on which the ministers refused the required conformity. The debate was maintained with good temper, and great spirit, for several hours. But Bramhall, resenting the liberty afforded the ministers, suddenly interrupted the

imperious. The Bp. himself, who disputed, behaved moderately, ingeniously, and discreetly; the opinion of the matter and discourse was various, according to the several inclinations and dispositions or interests of the hearers—the common product of all such public reasoning. The conclusion was, that he, with many other Ministers of his persuasion, were deposed from their several offices and benefices, and thereafter severally pursued and sought to be apprehended by pursuivants, but none of them were taken. Under these circumstances, he, with his family, was necessitated to go to Scotland, where he was disposed of to a great congregation and maintainance, at the town of Drime-frice, in Niddsdail, where he continued Minister other ten years. In this time, being appointed by the General Assembly of Scotland, to make a visit to the Northern parts of Ireland, for three months, he was taken prisoner by a party belonging to Sir Alex. M'Donnell, of the West-highlands of Scotland, and kept prisoner in a Castle there, Migreor Migirne, under extraordinary wants and necessities for a year, before he could be relieved, and then was, by the General Assembly of Scotland, transported unto Edinborough, where he continued fifteen years.*

---

conference, and Leslie adjourned the meeting, first to the afternoon, and then to the following; morning. In the meantime, Leslie was prevailed upon by the Bishop of Derry, not to resume the discussion, but to proceed in a summary way to pass sentence on the ministers. Accordingly, when the meeting was assembled on the morning of Friday [12th August, 1636], the brethren found themselves deprived of any further opportunity of stating their objections; and, as they continued, with unshrinking firmness, to refuse all subscription to the canons, the Bishop proceeded to pronounce the sentence of their deposition."—See a narrative of the occurrences of this eventful day, in *Reid's Presbyterian History*, vol. i., p. 194, and of the public discussion at Belfast, between Leslie and Hamilton, in the *Appendix* to the same vol., pp. 434 to 454.

* Of the remaining ministers who had yet to visit Ulster, agreeably to the Act of Assembly, the Rev. James Hamilton, then minister of Dumfries, but formerly minister of Ballywalter, was selected by the civil and ecclesiastical authorities in Edinburgh to be the bearer of the Covenant. With him were associated in this work three others of the ministers formerly appointed, viz., the Rev. Hugh Henderson, minister of Dalry, in Ayrshire, the Rev. William Adair, minister of Ayr, and the Rev. John Weir, minister of Dalserf, in Lanarkshire. The appointment of Hamilton to superintend the administration of the Covenant in Ulster, was, on the 26th of March, 1644, notified in a letter from the Committee of Estates to the officers of the Scottish army. The bearer of this letter was Major Borthwick, of Lord Lindsay's regiment. In it they thus expressed themselves:—

"As our cause is one that has common friends and enemies, so we must, with God's assistance, stand and fall together; and, for our firmer union, the Commissioners of the Assemblie, and we, have sent Master James Hamilton (a faithful minister in this kingdom, and whose integritie is well known in Ireland) with the Covenant to be sworne by the officers and souldiours of our army, and all such others of the British as shall be willing to enter into this Covenant, which is alreadie universallie receavit in this kingdome, and by the Houses of Parliament and their armies, and is ordained to be taken by all sorts of persons in England. Concerning the fittest time of swearing this Covenant, we remit it to your discretion, and the messenger sent with it; but the sooner yee doe it, we think it so much the better, which will confirme the confidence this kingdom has in you, and will be a character to difference between the well and disaffected. In the meane tyme, we trust that you, and such of the British forces as love religion and the safetie of thir kingdoms, will stand the best way you may upone your guarde against the invasione of the rebells."

Hamilton and his colleagues lost no time in entering upon their mission. They reached Carrickfergus in the end of March, and immediately commenced the arduous work entrusted to them. An authentic record of their proceedings at this memorable crisis has been fortunately preserved, and is published in the second volume of *Reid's Presbyterian History*, pp. 27 to 42.

See also a minute account of the administration of this Covenant in Ulster, on this occasion, at Belfast, Comber, Newton, and Bangor, County Down; also, at Broadisland, Islandmagee, and other places in County Antrim; and at Derry, Raphoe, Ramelton, and Enniskillen, in the seventh chapter of *Adair's Narrative*, which concludes thus:—

"From this the Ministers returned to the congregations of Antrim and Down, where the covenant had been before

In this time he was appointed by the General Assembly one of his Majesty's chaplains, and in this attendance was taken prisoner (as many of the nobility, army, gentry, and ministry) at Eliot, in Angus, by a party sent by General Monk immediately after his taking of Dundee; thence, he, with several others, as aforesaid, were sent to the Tower of London, where he was kept two years by Oliver Cromwell, and thence dismissed by him for no other reason, apology, or address, but that he found himself under great obloquy by all good people in Scotland and England, and that he found himself so settled in Scotland that there was little hazard of the raising any armed power there to his prejudice.

In this time (towards the close) all the other Presbyterian Ministers, who adhered to their principles throughout the whole kingdom, were expulsed from their places of abode, and discharged all

administered, partly confirming the people, who had entered into it already, and partly administering it to some who had not taken it before, among whom was the Lord of Ards. Thereafter they did administer the communion in Newtownards, Hollywood, and Ballywalter, in which three places Mr. Adair, Mr. Weir, and Mr. Hamilton (who all this time had staid in these parts) did divide themselves for this work. Mr. M'Cleland being then come to the country on commission, did also join in celebrating the communion, and those who were ministers in the country and army concurred. After all this, the holy, wise providence of God so ordered it, that these worthy men immediately met with sad troubles, lest they should be exalted above measure upon this great work wherein God had assisted them so signally. Mr. Adair fell into a long and dangerous fever, and relapsed again at Newtownards, and thereafter in Stranraer, as he was going home. But Mr. Hamilton, and Mr. Weir, met with a sorer trouble. The occasion of which was, that at that time my Lord Argyle, being Chief-Justice of the Isles, had one Col-Kittoch in custody, who had been guilty of many enormous things. He had a son named the same way, who was prompted by Satan's instigation to meet the vessel wherein Mr. Hamilton and Mr. Weir were going to Scotland, and did take them prisoners to the Highlands, thinking thereby to get his father loosed by the Lord Argyle. But, upon some weighty considerations, it could not be granted, whereupon these godly ministers were kept in great restraint and sad straits, without any accommodation or refreshment to their bodies, till Mr. Weir died; and Mr. Hamilton, with much ado, and great hazard of his life, was got delivered, and lived long after that, useful to the Church at Dumfries, and Edinburgh."—*Adair's Narrative*, p. 117 to 118.

Dr. Reid, at p. 46 of his *Presbyterian History*, vol. ii., states, that the trials to which those two ministers (Hamilton, and Weir) were now exposed originated out of the following circumstances:—

"The Earl of Antrim did not continue long in prison. Though strictly guarded in the castle of Carrickfergus, he once more succeeded in effecting his escape. He had been committed to the custody of Captain James Wallace,

a truly Christian officer, to whom frequent references will be subsequently made in these pages. With him was associated, as his lieutenant, another officer, named Gordon, who, by the following stratagem, facilitated the escape of Antrim:—' This Lieutenant Gordon craftily conveyed up unespied, in his breeches, certain tows [ropes], by the which the earl escaped, and was freely away, to Wallace's great grief; and the lieutenant followed, and fled also. His escape was wrought in October, whereat Major Munro lough not a word.' Antrim made his way directly to O'Neil, at Charlemont; thence he proceeded to Kilkenny to confer with the confederates; and afterwards to the king at Oxford, where he arrived in the end of the year. Here he completed his arrangements for carrying into effect the enterprise which had been partially disclosed in the papers found on him, when taken prisoner in May; and the object of which was to assist Montrose to excite a commotion in the North of Scotland, in favour of the declining cause of Charles. For this purpose, Antrim, on whom the king now conferred the dignity of a marquis, agreed to supply Montrose with two thousand native Irish, chiefly those who were then in arms in Flanders, and who, ' from the affinity of language, manners, and origin, were expected to be well-qualified to co-operate with Highlanders.' The first draught of this stipulated number, under the command of Alaster Macdonnel, the noted Colkittagh, and protected by a frigate, were on their way to Argyleshire, when, unfortunately, on the third of July, they fell in with the vessel in which the Rev. Messrs. Hamilton and Weir, with many other passengers, were returning to Scotland. They were immediately taken prisoners by Colkittagh. The ministers, with a few of the more respectable passengers, were removed on board the frigate, where they were detained until he had effected a landing on the island of Ardnamurchan, which the following extract from a contemporary annallist shows he soon accomplished:—' This mighty Montrose, having gotten the king's patent to go upon the Covenanting rebels in Scotland with fire and sword, and either bring them under subjection and obedience, or otherwise destroy them all, their lives, lands, and goods, gives order to this Alaster M'Donald to ship his soldiers, and land them in Ardnamurchan, an island belonging to Argyle, and destroy his country, and promised

exercises of their ministry, whereupon he withdrew from Edinburgh, and lived privately at Innerisk; yet it so fell out, that, on the account of having the better assistance of phisicians for his health, he repaired for a time into Edinborough, where he died the 10th of March, 1666.

I shall not insist on his character, only as it is evident he was, in providence, from his infancy to his grave, exposed to many afflictions and temptations, so he was helped to carry with great steadfastness, wisdom, and patience—yea, cheerfulness. He was naturally of an excellent temperament, both of body and mind; always industrious, and facetious in all the several provinces or scenes of his life; he was delightful to his friends and acquaintances—yea, beloved of his enemies. Much

---

to meet him in Scotland. M'Donald takes the sea, and, the eighth of July, lands in the foresaid isle of Ardnamurchan, plunders the haill goods and gear; kills the inhabitants, and burns the haill country; takes in a strong castle, and mans the samen with all provision necessary.'"

To this castle called Meagrie, or Mingarie Castle, situated on the eastern coast of the island, he removed his prisoners, and committed them to close and rigorous confinement. Here they suffered incredible hardships; until, at length, Mr. Weir, worn out with long confinement, fell sick, and, being destitute of every necessary accommodation, his strength rapidly declined; and, after lingering a few weeks, he died. The following interesting notices of their capture and imprisonment, and of the character and death of Mr. Weir, were written at the time by his fellow-sufferer, Mr. Hamilton:—

"All that knew Mr. Weir from a child of ten or thereby, might have discerned in him a perpetual preparation for death by his grave and holy behaviour. But when our Lord saw his time of departure approach, he set himself apart in a marvellous manner to make himself ready for eternity. For, first, according to the appointment of the General Assembly held at Edinburgh, 1643, he went to Ireland, and spent three months in painful preaching of the Gospel, viz:—all April, May, and June, 1644. Almost every day he laboured in spreading the Covenant of God, with Mr. William Adair, Minister at Ayr, who together persuaded the people to embrace the said Covenant in Carrickfergus, Antrim, Coleraine, Derry, Raphoe, and Enniskillen, and in all the country churches which lay about there, the Lord working mightily with them. In the time of his travell in Ireland, he helped to give the communion at Derry, with Mr. William Adair; at Newton, in the county of Down (June 23), with Mr. John M'Cleland; and at Killyleagh (June 30), with Mr. James Hamilton. In those two places he gave the communion upon the last two Sabbaths of his being in Ireland, God seeing it meet to make him take a double meal, because the journey was great before him, and he was to go in the strength of that food to the mountain of the Lord. Upon the second day of July, which was the last day wherein he was in Ireland, he preached at Donaghadee, on *Hebrews*, 12th chap., and three first verses, the matter of which did much refresh

him in all his sufferings afterward. Upon the same second of July, as he was returning from Ireland with his wife, Master James Hamilton, minister at Dumfries, Master David Watson, father-in-law to the said Master James, with Master Thomas Johnson, preacher, and many other passengers, were taken prisoners at sea by a Wexford frigate, called 'The Harp,' wherein was Alaster Macdonell, general major to Antrim's forces, coming along with three ships more full of soldiers, to invade Scotland. The said Alaster determined to keep the said prisoners till he could get his father, Coll-Macgillespic, *alias* Colkittagh, and his two sons, brethren to said Alaster, relieved for them. Wherefore he took seven of the said prisoners aboard in the frigate, leaving the rest in the prize whence these seven were taken, viz:—Mr. David Watson, Mr. John Weir and his wife, Mr. James Hamilton, William Hamilton, of Glasgow, William Irving, of Dumfries, and Archibald Bruce, a dweller beside Hamilton. These seven were kept prisoners in the said frigate till the fifteenth day of July, at night. They got not liberty jointly to exercise worship together; but every one did as he best might, apart ; only they had now and then conferences of what they read, for their Bibles were spared to them by the good providence of God. And, also, when the frigate was pursuing any bark or boat, the said prisoners, being all closed under decks and alone, took opportunity to pray together. Upon the said 15th of July, the said prisoners were carried from the said frigate to Castle Meagrie, and were all put in one chamber together. Every day twice, the said Mr. Weir and Mr. James Hamilton, did both of them expound a psalm or a part of a psalm, the one praying before, and the other after the said exposition. This they did in the hearing of those other fellow-prisoners, which were above-named, so long as they were together, which was till the twenty-third of September, in which time they had proceeded in expounding to the eighty-first psalm."—*MSS. Bib., Jurid. Edin., Rob.* iii., 6, 1, No. 24.

During their confinement, their sufferings were much increased by an unsuccessful attempt of the Marquis of Argyle, to obtain possession of the place :—

"He sent a party to beleagure the castle, thinking to liberate the prisoners with strong hand, but that attempt failed him; for, after that he had, for seven weeks together, beleagured it, his captain was forced to give over and leave the castle and prisoners in it, who, during the time of this

might be say'd of his boldness for truth, and tenaciousness in everything of moment; tho' he was naturally, and in his own things, amongst the mildest and   *   sort of men, he was rich in all parts of learning which might contribute for the usefulness and ornament of his ministry; he was intelligent, yea, judicious in all civil and state affairs ; he was great in esteem with the greatest and wisest ; as he was highly valued by the meanest sort of his acquaintances, so he was denied to the favours of great men and popular [assemblies.] His ambition was to be spotless and usefull ; his covetings, to have acceptance with God, the love of his friends, and peace in his own conscience ; he lived always frugally ; bestowed what at any time he had gathered upon his children (who were all married long before his death); was very open-handed to the poor ; and died even with the world.

4. Of JOHN's* family was first Hans. In his youth he was bred at   *   Schools ; went to the college of Glasgow, in Scotland ; was much disposed for learning, and very capable of it, but by his father's death, and the urgency of his affairs, was soon called back again to Ireland, where

---

siege, suffered incredible hunger and thirst, having nothing to drink but the rain-water that fell from Heaven on the bartisans of the castle, which they were forced, because of the thick mud, to seethe through their teeth, they winking all the while, for they could not look upon the green glut that was with it; and their meat was for most part unground rye, which they were sometimes forced to grind betwixt two slate stones for their extreme hunger! Much misery they suffered all the time of their captivity; but all was nothing, in respect of these seven weeks during which the castle was beleagured."

Though Macdonell had successfully repulsed this attempt of Argyle, yet finding the maintenance of eight prisoners too heavy a burden, he took steps to rid himself of a part of them. On the third of September, he liberated Mrs. Weir, she being then near her confinement ; and, on the twenty-third, the three merchants, Messrs.W. Hamilton, Irving, and Bruce, "were relieved on bond and caution for paying their ransom, and Master Thomas Jordan was also relieved because he had no charge in Scotland, though he had been a minister in Ireland. The three ministers—to wit, Masters J. Hamilton, Watson, and Weir—are kept close, and Alaster gave strict orders, that upon no condition any of them should be let free ; for he resolved that they should liberate his father, old Colkittagh, and his two brethren, Archibald, and Angus, that were then prisoners, taken by Argyle, but the Marquis, carrying a great indignation against all the clan, specially against old Coll, would not liberate them." Their captivity therefore assumed a very hopeless aspect. No prospect of relief appeared, and their spirits began to despond ; but the consoling truths of that Gospel, which they had so faithfully preached sustained them, and "though their flesh, and their heart failed, God was the strength of their heart, and their portion for ever." It was at this period that Mr. Weir became indisposed. On the second of October, he first complained of sickness, and, on the sixteenth, he died, "with great peace and joy," in the thirty-fourth year of his age. Mr. Hamilton, and his father-in-law, Mr. Watson, were left alone, and spent a gloomy winter in that secluded, and cheerless castle. Mr. Watson sunk under his sufferings, and died in the month of March following; but Mr. Hamilton was graciously preserved, until, after many efforts on the part both of the General Assembly, and the Scottish Parliament, to procure the release of this esteemed Minister, he was at length, by an exchange of prisoners, liberated, on the second of May, 1645, after an imprisonment of ten months. While in Ireland, prior to this afflicting captivity, Hamilton's labours were, in a great measure, confined to the County of Down. His former parish at Ballywalter was a special object of his ministerial care. Towards the close of his stay in Ulster, he presided as Moderator, in a meeting of the Presbytery at Bangor, on the 25th of May, 1664, when a third petition from the Presbyterians of the province, to the General Assembly about to meet at Edinburgh, was submitted to the Court for their approbation and sanction, which will be found, at p. 53, of the second volume of *Reid's Presbyterian History.*

x John Hamilton, of Monilla, in the Co. of Armagh, fourth son of the Vicar of Dunlop.—See pages 11, and 44, ante.

he attended his affairs carefully and discreetly till the war of Ireland broke out, at which time duty and necessity obliged him to give his assistance therein, by my Lord Claneboy's advice. His years and parts early promoted him to be a captain of horse; as in progress of time he became Lieut.-Colonel, he joined, with the Earl of Clanbrassill, in Ormond's Association. That war being ended, he married Magdalen Trevor, daughter to Sir Edward Trevor,[f] and had by her some children, whereof only his daughter Sarah came to maturity. His business then being to improve and plant his estate, lying mostly in the upper country; and, by reason of his very good natural and acquired parts, and justice to the King's interest and family, after King Charles II. his restoration, was knighted and made Bart., and afterwards one of his Majesty's Privy Council in Ireland, and was very much intrusted by the Government in the oversight of the upper country;[g] died of a good age, in great esteem, and generally much bewailed; lyes in the tomb with his father, mother, lady, and daughter. He was guilty of great errors—whereof afterwards. His natural parts and improvements were both very considerable; his deportment, in his younger years, very commendable; but, his estate being much burthen'd, his disposition to live high and aim to purchase great things, occasioned many to think (as a gent. of his neighbourhood and great acquaintance once say'd) that "Sir Hans Hamilton was never so honest as Hans Hamilton by half." He was unfortunate in that his daughter married*   *   * contrary to his disposition, and the measures he had proposed to himself. He fell at last in great variance with his nearest friends, and affliction by the death of his lady and daughter; went to Dublin, with design, as it is believed, to do something that was great for his family against his friends, but failed of it, and died in the enterprise, but did not perform it.

The second son, James,[b] was, partly through necessity of the times, and partly his own inclination, drawn to the service of the war, tho' the heat of it was now much over. He served in the station of a cornet, and acquit himself very commendably in it. After, he married Jane Baily, daughter to Bishop Baily, of Clunfert, by whom he had Henry,[c] Hans,[d] and Margaret.[e] He was of very good natural parts and disposition, and not contemptible in his acquirements; yet the liberty

[f] And sister of Marcus Trevor, first Viscount Dungannon.

[g] At Hamilton's Bawn, County Armagh.

[a] She married Sir Robert Hamilton, Bart., of Mount-hamilton, and left an only child, Sir Hans Hamilton, who became heir to his grandfather, John, of Monilla, and married Jane Sheffington, eldest daughter to the Viscount Massereene. They had an only daughter, Anne Hamilton, who married James Campbell, of London, who took the name of Hamilton, in order to possess her estate, and was well-known in the family as "Campbell-Hamilton." He died in London, in 1749, at the age of 80.

[b] Of Bailieborough, County Cavan.

[c] Also of Bailieborough; married Miss Blackwell, by whom he had issue, and was killed at Limerick.

[d] A Brigadier-General; died without issue.

[e] Married a gentleman named Cuppaidge.

of his younger education, and way of living with the Bishop, (having married his only child) enured him to greater liberty and good fellowship (as some call it) than was profitable for his estate and family, or advantageous to his health. He was overtaken in middle age by the fever, and died.

Francis,[f] the third son, is yet living, and hath evidenced himself a stout soldier and a very serviceable brother, but not equal (in the opinion of some not injudicious) in distributing his kindness among his friends, as having exceeded towards some, and been defective (to say no worse) towards others.

5. Of WILLIAM's [g] family. His first son, James, of good natural parts, bred a soldier, advanced to be a captain, and judged very worthy of it, died young, being killed at Blackwater fight, and lies in the Church of Benburb, where there is a decent tomb erected over him. [h] He married   *   *   *   *   had two children, James[i] and Catherine,[k] and left his estate much the same as he found it.

John, the second son, was much under the same circumstances. He was a captain, and left no issue behind him.[l]

The third son, Hans,[m] under the same education and necessities, was advanced to be a captain of foot, and very active in his station. After the war was over, he married Mary Kennedy, daughter to Mr. Kennedy, of Killern, by whom he had three children that came to maturity—viz., James, [n]

---

[f] Of Tullybrick, County Armagh, married Elizabeth Echlin, sister of Henry Echlin.

[g] William Hamilton, of Newcastle, *alias* Bangor, in the County of Down, the fifth son of the Vicar of Dunlop.—See pages 11 and 45, *ante*.

[h] The following extract from "Annals of Charlemont," as to the Battle of Benburb, refers to him :—

"Among the slain was also Captain James Hamilton, of Newcastle, *alias* Bangor, in the County of Down. According to tradition, he was killed making his escape at Tullyrean (now Tullylearn), lying between Benburb and Blackwatertown. His body, as well as that of Lord Blaney, was honorably interred in Benburb Church, the succeeding day, by order of Owen Roe. Subsequently Lord Blaney's was exhumed, and removed to Castleblaney; but Captain Hamilton's still remains in its original cemetery, alongside the pulpit of the church, where the following inscription is sculptured on a handsome tablet with foliated scrolls, surmounted by the Hamilton arms, in an antique urn-like shield :—

"HERE LYETH THE BODY OF
CAPTAIN JAMES HAMILTON,
LATE OF NEWCASTLE, IN THE COUNTY OF DOWN,
SON AND HEIR OF WILLIAM HAMILTON,
OF NEWCASTLE, IN THE SAID COUNTY, ESQ.,
BROTHER TO THE RT. HONBLE. THE LORD VISCOUNT CLANEBOY.
THE SAID JAMES WAS SLAIN IN HIS MAJESTY'S SERVICE
AGAINST THE IRISH REBELS, NEAR BENBURB,
THE FIFTH DAY OF JUNE, 166.
Vivit Post Funera Virtus."

[i] James Hamilton, his only son, always styled " of Bangor," married the Honourable Sophia Mordaunt, third daughter of John, Viscount Mordaunt, and was father of Mrs. Ward and Lady Ikerrin, his co-heiresses, his only son, James, having died a minor—all already mentioned. He was member for the County of Down in 1692; died in 1707, and was buried in the church of Bangor.—*Mrs. Reilly's Memoirs.*

[k] Catherine Hamilton, the only daughter of James Hamilton and Margaret Kynaston, first married Gen. Richard Price, and was mother of Gen. Nicholas Price, who was great-grandfather to the late Nicholas Price, Esq., of Saintfield.—*Ibid.* See note * to page 64, *ante*.

[l] He was member of the Irish Parliament, in 1639, for the Borough of Bangor, together with his elder brother, James.—*Ibid.*

[m] Hans Hamilton, of Carnsaure, in the County of Down, was a captain in the army, under his cousin James, first Earl of Clanbrassil. He married Mary, sister of David Kennedy, of Killarne.

[n] James Hamilton, who married Christian Hamilton, his first cousin. Their only child and heiress, Margaret, married John Cuffe, first Lord Desart, who died in 1749.

Jane, and Ursula. He became a very industrious and usefull man, both to his family and country; lived well, and died* much lamented; was creditably buried at Hollywood, leaving his children very young.

The fourth son, William, of the same education, was made captain, and behaved very well in that station; after the war he married.ᴾ That which is most considerable in him is, that, tho' he was the youngest brother of the family, and so had least patrimony, and had three wives, with whom he had but very small portions, yet he still lived plentifully both at home and abroad, and, to boot, purchased a very plentifull estate, which he left almost equal betwixt his two sons, Jamesᵠ and Jocelin.ʳ He was a man of great understanding in country affairs, and no less industry and regularity; was a great artist in courting his superiors, keeping even with his equals, and keeping his inferiors at a due distance. He was a great honorer of the clergy of his own profession, and very civil to those of other professions, and, upon all occasions, avoided to be instrumental in persecution of such as were of different persuasions from himself. He died of sixty years of age, leaving his family very plentifull in all things, and his name under various characters—tho' I believe few men of his best acquaintance will contradict what I have say'd of him. Perhaps more may be say'd of him in the subsequent.

6. Of the sixth family,ˢ the eldest son was James. He was bred in the University learning; a man of good parts and temper; marriedᵗ * * * but had no children by her; was Parson of Dundonald, and Hollywood first; lived of a good age; died at Dundonald, where he

---

* 28th December, 1655. (ᴀ err: p. 165, note)

ᴾ His first wife was daughter of Henry Usher; and his second, was daughter of Brian MacHugh Aghorley Magennis, who was mother of his two sons, James, and Jocelyn, and of two daughters, viz., Eleanor, married to Mr. Mathews, and Christian, who was married to her first cousin, James Hamilton, of Carnysure.

ᵠ James Hamilton, of Tullymore.—See note + to page 63, ante.

ʳ This Jocelyn Hamilton, was killed in 1690, in a duel which he fought with Bernard Ward, then Sheriff for the County of Down. The dispute arose in the grand jury room, and they immediately went out and fought close to the Abbey of Down, when they were both killed in the duel. A letter relating to it is still extant, in the possession of the Earl of Roden, at Tullymore Park, of which the following is a copy:—

"Downpatrick, October   , 1690.

DEAR BROTHER—I came here upon that unfortunate affair between the Sheriff and poor Jocelin; they were both buried yesterday. Jocelin was basely kil'd by a pistol wᵇ the Sheriff carried unknown to yᵉ brother, and shot him with it, tho' he called out it was not fair; and, having recᵈ the shot, made so home a thrust that he run the sword almost to the hilt thro' the Sheriff: for further particulars, I wave until meeting. The main cause of my writing is to inform you that severall have designs upon the Sheriffship, upon wᵗ designs uncertain, but no doubt they have an eye upon the chattells of the Ducliers. I therefore desire you would consider of it, and make it your interest to have some honest man put in, that will neither do you nor the country any prejudice by their griping and covetesness. I am just going home, and will add no further but that his will and papers are safe.—I am, your humble servant,

"JAMES HAMILTON."

Addressed thus—"For James Hamilton, of Tullymore, Esquire, now neare Belfast."—See note to page 64, ante.

ˢ Patrick Hamilton's. He was sixth son of the Vicar of Dunlop.—See pages 11 and 45, ante.

ᵗ His wife's name was Echlin.

had been Parson for several years before his death; he was a peaceable man, very civil to all, and affectionate to his relations, especially to his brother Alexander's family.

The second brother, Alexander,[u] thro' his inclination, and the necessity of his country, was bred to be a soldier; was shortly made a captain of foot, in which station he was very usefull and of good account. He married one Mary [Reeding,] a gentlewoman in this country, by whom he had one son, Patrick,[v] and two daughters,[w] who lived to maturity. He died young, and was very well beloved, though a little passionate in his temper.

The third brother, Archibald, being bred at schools and colleges, and in very good account for parts and piety, was settled in the ministry, first at   , in Galloway, in Scotland, thereafter transported to a more eminent place, to wit, Wiggtown. Afterwards (through the calamity of the times) came to Bangor Parish, in the County of Down. He married Jane Hamilton, daughter to Mr. James Hamilton, second son of Gawn Hamilton above-mentioned, by whom he had many children; those that came to maturity were John, Archibald, Henry, and Mary.   *   *

As to   *   *   being yet alive, I need say little of him, but suppose it will be generally allowed by all who are acquainted with him, as he hath been steadfast and laborious in his ministry, so he hath acted the part of a discreet friend, and prudent and frugal parent.

---

[u] Of Granshaw, County Down. His will bears date, 2nd April, 1696, and was proved 18th November, 1700.

[v] Also of Granshaw. He married Letitia Norris, and had issue by her, two sons, James, who died unmarried, and the Rev. Patrick Hamilton, Rector of Killileagh, and three daughters, Barbara, Eliza, and Lettice.

[w] Mary, wife of William Stewart; and Elizabeth, wife of Captain Philip Wilkinson.

APPENDIX TO CHAPTER IV.

[Copy Will of James, Second Viscount Claneboye, and First Earl of Clanbrassil, referred to at page 71, *ante.*]

In the name of God, amen.—The Last Will and Testament of me, James, Lord Viscount Claneboy, and Earl of Clanbrassill, being sound and perfect in memory and mind, though sick in body.—Written the 18th day of June, in the year of our Lord God, One Thousand Six Hundred Fifty and Nine.

Imprimis—I recommend my soul into the hands of Almighty God, and my most gracious Redeemer, who hath sanctified me with the Heavenly Graces of His Holy Spirit; and my body to be decently interred, with funeral rites, in my father's sepulchre, at Bangor.

2d. I leave my wife, the Countess of Clanbrassill, the one-third of my whole estate, and the other two parts to go to pay my debts, and the education of my children.

3d. In case my mother departs this life before my wife, it is my will, and I do hereby appoint, that she have a third out of that estate which my mother hath for her third, and the other two parts to be employed as aforesaid.

4th. That the lands of the parishes of Dundonell, and Holliwood, with all to them appertaining, and so much more next to them adjoining, as will make, five hundred pounds by the year, be the portion of my son, Hans Hamilton, my second son now living, after his coming to age, and until my debts are paid ; and, after they are satisfied, I appoint him to have the first part out of my whole estate, being in five parts to be equally divided, which I *will* to descend upon him and his heirs male, lawfully begotten of his body, and, failing of such, then to revert unto my eldest son, Henry, Lord Claneboy, he paying the portions of the said Hans's daughters, lawfully begotten, proportionally to the estate, if any such he have.

5th. It is also my will, that my wife have her residence in the Castle of Killyleagh; and, that all patents, deeds, writings, evidences, books, and papers, concerning my estate, be carefully kept for the use and behalf of my children and posterity ; and that she, with the advice of my mother and friends hereafter mentioned, have a regard to the preservation of my well affected tenants throughout all the lands, lordships, and manors belonging unto me.

6th. It is my will and earnest desire, that my wife, my mother, and children, with a competent number of useful servants, keep house together, without breaking up, or severing the family.

7th. It is my further will and pleasure, for the better management and improvement of my estate for the future, that my mother, Arthur Annesly, Esq., Lieut.-Col. Traille, Lieut.-Col. Hans Hamilton, my cousin, Mr. Archibald Hamilton, Captain Collin Maxwell, Captain John Bailie, and Alexander Sloane, be aiding and assisting to my executors in setting, letting, leasing out, and bettering the rents of such lands as are to be set, the leases whereof are already determined, or may run out before my eldest son come to age, for the time and space of one and twenty years at the utmost; any two or three of the said parties to be still privy and consenting to the making or perfecting any such leases, whereof my mother during her life to be always one.

8th. That the aforesaid persons be always carefull to see well into the right manageing of the whole estate to the best advantage, and the present breeding of my children in the most commendable way.

9th. That my tenants, whether fee-farmers, lease-holders, or tenants for life, be used with all the favour that may be, as the occurrences of the time will permit, they behaving themselves as becometh.

10th. Let the use, interest, and forbearance of my debts be yearly answered for the sums I do owe, until the principal and original debts can be cut down and paid by degrees.

11th. It is also my will, and I do hereby authorise my executors, or any one of them, with the advice aforesaid, to sell the tithes of the Rectories of Rathmullen, Clonuff, Allmancy, Grongatter, B. Galgat, B. Gurgogan, with all other tithes not accruing out of or upon my own lands, for the payment of my foreign debts, provided the same be sold at the best advantage.

12th. That the Ministers in the several parishes within my lands be paid their stipends and salaries, according to the agreements and payments made unto their predecessors and them in my father's lifetime, or as they have under my own hand in writing since the year 1650; and that the schoolmasters in the several parishes have the like allowance continued unto them, as they enjoyed in my father's time.

13th. That my servants' wages, due till May day last, may be satisfied, and such only retained as can be most serviceable, and the rest discharged after the celebration of my funeral is past.

14th. If it do happen that my sons decease, without issue and heirs of their bodies lawfully begotten, before my debts be satisfied, I do then appoint that my debts be first paid, and that then thereafter there be twenty pounds a-year given to the school at Bangor, twenty pounds a-year to the school of Killyleagh, ten pounds a-year to the school of Holliwood, ten pounds a-year to the school of Ballywalter, and ten pounds a-year to the school of Tonoghnieve, and the remainder of my estate to be divided into five equal portions amongst the eldest sons or issue male of my five uncles, as the lands can be laid out in most equal and just divisions.

15th. I do authorise and appoint my executors, with the consent aforesaid, for the speedier payment of my debts, as they think fit, to sell so much of my lands as shall amount to £500 a-year or under, but no more.

16th. And, as for the schools of Bangor and Killileagh, I do appoint £20 a-year for the present, to begin from the first of November next ensuing the date hereof, to be duly paid for the masters, enabling of them to educate poor scholars.

17. Lastly, I do appoint my son and heir-apparent, Henry, Lord Clancboy, and my beloved spouse, Anne, Countess of Clanbrassill, to be my sole executors of this my last will and testament; and I leave my said son and his brother, my second son, Hans Hamilton, to the education and instruction of my mother and my wife during their minority, earnestly praying that they may be brought up in the true Protestant religion, and after the best form and manner of civil nurture used in any of the three nations, beseeching God to give them a full measure of his saving knowledge, and of all the requisite graces of his sanctifying Spirit: And this I publish, manifest, and declare to be my last will and testament, as witness my hand and seal the day and year above written.

Signed, Scaled, and delivered to the Countess, by his Lordship,
to the behalf of herself and her children, in presence of

WILLIAM RICHARDSON,	GILBERT HOW,	
ST. JOHN WEBB,	THOMAS BRADLIE.	CLANBRASSILL.
EDMOND KINGSTON,		

[Memoir of the Family of Halcraig, extracted from " Anderson's Memoirs of the House of Hamilton," referred to at page 71, *ante.*]

"HALCRAIG, *Parish of Carluke, Lanarkshire.*

"I. ARCHIBALD HAMILTON, the 2nd son of Hans Hamilton, Vicar of Dunlop, and brother of the first Viscount
W

Claneboy, was the first of this family. He was Sheriff-depute of Lanarkshire, from 1625 and upwards. He married Rachel Carmichael, by whom he had issue :—

"1. *John*, his heir.

"2. *James*, of Neilsbrook, County Antrim.

"3. *Gavin*, of Killileagh, from whom Hamilton Rowan, Esq., of Dublin, is descended.

"4. *Patrick*, who was a great preacher and nonconformist during the persecution on account of religion under Charles the First.

"5. *William*, also a preacher and nonconformist, who being thrown into prison, in 1679, died therein shortly after.

"1. *Jean*, married to Archibald Edmondstone, of Duntreath, and had issue.

"II. JOHN HAMILTON, of Halcraig, who was severely fined, in 1662 and 1634, for nonconformity and refusing the test, by the Earl of Middleton. He married Jean, second daughter of William Mure of Glanderstown, by whom he had issue.

"III. Sir JOHN HAMILTON, of Halcraig, who was severely persecuted and fined for nonconformity during the reign of James the Second. After the Revolution he was made one of the Lords of Session ; and, about the same period, was knighted by William the Third. He had a charter of the lands and barony of Shawfield, dated 1st May, 1699. He made a tailzie of his estate, in 1705, to himself in liferent, and his son John in fee; which failing, to his heirs female, the eldest always succeeding without division. He married, in 1668, Ursilla, daughter of William Ralston, of that Ilk, by whom he had issue :—

"1. *John*, his heir.

"1. *Isabella*, married to Sir William Gordon, of Dalfolly and Invergordon, and had issue. Sir John had issue other daughters.

"IV. JOHN HAMILTON, of Halcraig, who, dying without issue, in September, 1706, was succeeded by his eldest sister, Lady Gordon, who possessed the estate until her death in 1740. It was afterwards enjoyed by her husband, Sir William, till he died in 1742.

"Mr. Charles Gordon, Advocate, the second son, who took the name of Hamilton Gordon, got the estate from his father, and raised an action against his brother, Sir John Gordon, to denude ; but it was found that Sir John could not take the estate without bearing the name and arms of Hamilton.

"In 1753, 23d February, Mr. Charles Hamilton Gordon, of Halcraig, had a charter under the Great Seal of the lands of Wester St. Martins, in the County of Cromarty."—*Anderson's Memoirs*, p. 302.ª

ª However accurate Mr. Anderson's elaborate work, from which the foregoing memoir is copied, may be as to the other branches of the House of Hamilton, of which it contains such ample records, it is singularly inaccurate as to those branches connected with the family to which the above MSS. relate. The Editor of them has already, at pages 1 and 2 *ante*, had occasion to correct a grave mistake made in Mr. Anderson's work, as to the Vicar of Dunlop, the head of the Clanbrassil branch, in his memoirs of it and the Raploch branches; for which purpose, however, it was only necessary to refer to the MS. itself. But, in the preceding article on the Halcraig branch, so many mistakes have been made, that it becomes absolutely necessary to point them out in detail : And, 1st—The fact of Archibald of Halcraig's first marriage to a lady named Simpson, by whom he had two daughters (as stated in the MS., at p. 11, *ante*,) is altogether omitted. 2nd—The above statement, that he had only five sons and one daughter by his second wife, is also incorrect, as it appears by the MS. (at p. 43, *ante*,) that he had twenty-two children by his second wife, Rachel Carmichael. 3rd—The names of only five of his sons are given in the memoir, and one of them incorrectly, as he had no son named Patrick; and Archibald, and Robert, who (as the MS. states at p. 43, *ante*) came to be men, are altogether omitted in the memoir. 4th—After correctly stating that John was Archibald's eldest son and heir, instead of going on to state that he had no issue except two daughters, as mentioned in the MS. (at p. 11, *ante*,) and that he had sold the Halcraig estate in his lifetime, the foregoing memoir actually traces its direct descent from him, 1st, to Sir John Hamilton, of Halcraig, as his son by Jean, second daughter of William Mure, of Glanderstown ; and, 2ndly, to John Hamilton, of Halcraig, as his grandson, though he had neither a son nor grandson, and was never married to Jean Mure. That the Sir John Hamilton who succeeded him in Halcraig, as the purchaser of the estate, was a relative, there can be no doubt; but in what degree the Editor of these MSS. has been unable to discover. James, of Neilsbrook, the second son of Archibald, of Halcraig, in consequence of his eldest brother John's death, without male issue, succeeded to a fifth share of the Clancboye estates, which James Earl of Clanbrassil, by his will (at p. 85, *ante*) devised to the eldest sons, or issue male, of his five uncles, in the event of his own sons dying without issue, which happened on the death of Earl Henry.

CHAP. V.

OF EARL HENRY, HIS MARRIAGE, CARRIAGE, DEATH, AND CHARACTER.

This young nobleman, being committed to the care of his mother, Countess Ann Clanbrassill, was for a time bred to literature at home, and, as he was fit for it, afterwards sent to Oxford, in England; and, with respect to his affairs, was called home to Ireland before he attained to ripe age, giving a great hope to all who were concerned in him that he should be a very considerable man in his post. The matter of his marriage was of great concernment to all his friends and relations. It was judged very necessary, in order to his affairs, that he should settle in some family by which he might have good friends and a good portion, which, as it was his interest, seemed also to be greatly his own design; but it fell out soon otherwise, he being decoyed by one of his own servants, whom he and his mother trusted too much. He was soon drawn to court a daughter of the Earl of Drogheda's,[a] viz., Lady Alice Moor, by whom, as he could expect no portion, and but few friends, so he was very much drawn to idleness and low companionship. In a short time the marriage was accomplished, to the great grief of his mother, and trouble of all his relations. She was indeed a very handsome, witty, and well-bred lady; but soon appeared very high in her housekeeping and apparel, and giving too much opportunity and access to noblemen and gentlemen reputed vitious, to frequent her house and company, the pretence being to pay respects to my Lord in his quality (who was deservedly reputed learned, intelligent, and humane,) at least   *

    *   to gratify her own vitious inclinations she   *   *   in her prodigality and dis-

---

[a] Henry Moore, third Viscount of Drogheda, upon his father's death, was recommended by the Earl of Ormond to succeed him in his employments; whereupon, the king, by warrant, dated at Oxford, 18th October, and by commission, at Dublin, 13th January, 1643, gave him his troop of horse, and the government of the Counties of Meath and Louth, the Barony of Slane, and the Town of Dundalk, with all the forces within the same. On 11th January in that year, he was chosen one of the Commissioners, to receive the propositions of the Irish confederate recusants; and, in 1645, repairing to the Court in England, the king (he being under age) favoured him with a special livery of his estate. In 1647, upon the surrender of the Government to the English Parliament, he had the command of a regiment given him, with which, in 1649, he helped to reduce the Kingdom, after which his estate was sequestered by the Parliament; but, upon his petition, 8th April, 1653, he was permitted to enjoy one full third part thereof, and to receive the issues and profits till further order, paying contribution and other country charges; and, for his services and affections to the king and his country, was advanced to the dignity of Earl of Drogheda, by patent, dated 14th June, 1661. His Lordship married Alice, fifth daughter of William, Lord Spencer, of Wormlayton, by the Lady Penelope Wriothesley, his wife, daughter to Henry, Earl of Southampton; and deceasing, 11th January, 1675, had issue three sons and three daughters, the second of whom, Lady Alice, first married, in May, 1667, to Henry Hamilton, Earl of Clanbrassill, who died in January, 1675; and, secondly, in 1676, to John, Lord Bargany, of Scotland, by neither of whom she [left] issue, and died, in Roscommon House, Dublin, 26th December, 1677.—See Lodge's Peerage of Ireland, vol. i. p. 326.

position to be much abroad, partly in the country, much to the City of Dublin, and afterwards to the Court of England.[b] Her prodigality and disposition aforesaid, necessitated my Lord (whose great desert was in rendering himself obsequious and indulgent to her inclinations and prodigality) to contract a great deal of debt upon his estate, formerly under great burthens, and nothing bettered by her portion; so as, at last, he was induced to sell off a very considerable part of his estate among his own tenants, and some others. In this time, it fell out, that my Lady bare a son, named James, who soon died; after which she fell upon a design (before my Lord or she were eight-and-twenty years of age) to persuade my Lord (his brother Hans, and son James, being now dead,) to settle his heritable estate upon herself and her heirs, or to her disposal after his death, and with a clause, that an estate of £500 per annum should be settled upon one of his name and family. That which stood in the way of it was, 1st, that my Lord and she, being both young, might yet have children; 2nd, that it was uncertain whether my Lord might not survive her; 3rd, that my Lord having many kinsmen of near relation of his own family, it seemed unjust to put the estate wholly out of his own family; 4th, and particularly, his father, Earl James Clanbrassill, by his last will and testament, duly perfected and published, had made a full and distinct settlement of the whole estate, and all its concerns, in case his sons should die without issue (yet extant and inforce upon him); 5thly, he was plainly advertised by my Lady Ann Clanbrassill, his mother, that it was more than probable, that, in this design, there must be another of taking away his life, in which case his Lady might follow her pleasures in the ruining of that estate; and with this plain advertisement:—"Son," say'd she, "expect that within three months after you perfect such deeds, you must lodge with your grandfather and father, in the tomb of Bangor." In this affair my Lord shewed a great deal of anxiety and trouble of mind, but at last was prevailed with (as Sampson in the like case) to perfect a deed, and will,[c] according to the aforesaid contents; and, within three months after, under very suspicious circumstances, he died suddenly; was embowelled within five hours after, and privately (I say not secretly) buried in Christ's Church, in Dublin, and soon after, his corpse was lifted, and sent to be privately intombed in Bangor. This nobleman was very much lamented for the misfortunes of his life and death, being a man of great fame, very good temper,

---

[b] No mention of her visit to Charles the Second's Court is made in either Pepy's or Evelyn's Diaries; but the following sentence, in a letter from Lord Conway to Sir George Rawdon, dated 20th June, 1671, which is printed in the Rawdon Papers and Letters, evidently refers to her, though Mr. Berwick, the Editor, in a note, says "if her name is Clanbrassil," that he never heard of her as one of Charles's mistresses:—

"This relation I had from Lord Winser on Friday last, at the funeral, where my Lord Brook was also, and many others; nor is he sparing to publish it in all places, and I hear his reception at Winsor is not like to be much better, unless my Lady Clanbra. alter the case; for she thinks to trip up Nell Gwin's heels, and you cannot imagine how highly my Lord Arran and many others do value themselves upon the account of managing Lady Clanbrn. in this matter."—*Rawd. Let.*, 251.

[c] See copy of the will in the appendix to this chapter.

honored not only by his birth, but, with respect to his eminent parts, to be of the King's Privy Council for the Kingdom of Ireland. He wanted not sense of his misfortunes by his Lady, but strength to restrain them; and so, unwarily, admitted to his own ruin, and made way for the great injustice and affliction his friends sustained after his death, whereof (and some other things not mentioned in his life) hereafter.

APPENDIX TO CHAPTER V.

[Copy Will of Henry, Second Earl of Clanbrassil, referred to at page 88, *ante.*]

March 27, 1674.—In the name of God, amen, I, Henry, Earl of Clanbrassil, considering the confusions and troubles that may after my death arise, if it should please God to call for me out of this life before I should settle my estate, for the preventing whereof, being now in perfect health and memory, praised be God, I do hereby, revoking all former Wills and Testaments, make this my last Will, written with my own hand, and sealed with my own seal, in these words following, viz. :—

First—Commending my soul to my gracious and merciful God, who gave it, believing through the righteous merits, mediation, and sufferings of Jesus Christ, my only Redeemer and Saviour, and, by virtue of His precious blood, to have the same saved, I direct my body to be interred with my father in the sepulchre of Bangor.

Item—It is my will and pleasure to leave unto my dear and beloved wife, the Countess of Clanbrassil, her heirs and assigns, for ever, all my estate in the kingdom of Ireland, with all and singular the castles, lordships, manors, honours, and chiefries, royalties, freedoms, immunities, franchises, and privileges thereunto belonging, of what nature soever, in as large and ample manner as I or any of my predecessors held the same by letters patents under the great seal of Ireland.

Item—I leave unto her all my goods and chattels of what nature soever, and I do hereby appoint her to make due payment out of the same of all my just due debts, and out of my real estate, which, by this my last Will and Testament, I do bequeath unto her.

Item—It is also my pleasure, that all deeds and leases made by me to any tenants be duly kept, and construction made upon them, to the best, and according to the true intent and meaning of them.

Item—I appoint my said dear and loving wife, at or before her death, to leave £500 per annum to some one of my own name and relation, as she shall see fit.

Item—I leave the poor of Bangor £10.

And, lastly, I appoint my dear wife, Alice, Countess of Clanbrassil, sole executor of this my last Will and Testament: All which upon serious consideration I have done, as witness my hand and seal, the day and year first above written.

Witness present,

ST. JOHN WEBB,
SARAH TRAIL,
EDMUND KELLY.

CLANBRAZILL.

Vera Copia.—Exd., J. COGHILL, Regr.

x

C H A P .   V I .

OF THE LADY ALICE, AND HER PROVISION FOR A LAW-SUIT.

I enter upon this part of the history very unwillingly, and could choose to pass it with silence (as I have done many things), but that the main part of the subsequent history doth necessarily require it; for in this is the fountain out of which the following calamity did arise.

In this narrative I must go back to tell you—1st, that upon Earl James's marriage with Countess Ann Clanbrassill, my Lord Clanbrassill settled a considerable jointure upon her, (as there was one formerly settled on the Lady Jane Claneboy,) to the yearly value of at least £1,500, in which was the Castle of Killileagh, with other very good conveniences, upon which the said Lady lived all her son's time and many years afterwards.—2nd. The Earl James, a little before his death, had made and perfected a will, wherein, 1, he ordained his eldest son Henry, the heir of his whole estate; 2, he settled £500 a year on his son Hans, of the lands about Hollywood; 3, that in case both his sons should die without issue, his estate should be (after the payment of his debts) divided in five equal shares, and so to be settled upon the heirs male of his five uncle's sons, and he appointed his Lady and his son his executors.

Of this last, it is to be considered—1st. That the will being perfected, it was delivered, immediately by my Lord's direction, to be kept by her for the uses therein mentioned, and so proved in common form before the Prerogative Court in Dublin.—2ndly. That it fell out at the writing thereof, which was done by Archibald, eldest son to Gawin,[a] being then aged, that after it was entirely written, folded, and endorsed, he had occasion to correct some little thing in it, and being called in haste to carry it to my Lord, he designed to dry what was newly written, but instead of the sand box, (unwarily) he lifted the ink box, and dropped some ink upon it, yet cleaned and dried it as well as he could, and so brought and read it to my Lord, and presented it to be signed by him, which my Lord being ready to do, observed the blot, refused to sign it, and directed to write it over again, saying it was not fit a paper containing things of such moment should be blotted, which was accordingly done, and then signed and sealed by him, and so delivered to his Lady, at which time it was advised that the first written paper should be kept with the second at least for a wrapper, and for the safety of the other, which was accordingly done by the Lady.—3rd. The will being thus lodged, there was no more use for it, until about eight years thereafter, that the second brother Hans required to have his estate settled upon him according to his father's will. This being urged by his

---

[a] See page 73, ante.

mother, and other friends, on the account that my Lord could not supply him with what was needful for the time (his Lady could and would not spare it), there was a commission brought from
Dublin to examine the witnesses to the will about the perfecting of it. Some of them were cor-
rupted by the young lady, and offered to swear that my Lord was not *compos mentis* when he
signed it; others, and of greater credit, offered to swear that he was sound in his memory and
judgment. My Lord, or rather his Lady and counsellor, perceived that the design of making void
the will would not then be carried, and proposed to settle an estate upon Hans, to as good a value
in other lands, but   *   *   *   in the lands mentioned by the will, these being the nearest
to   *   place of abode, which was agreed unto; and, accordingly, deeds were drawn and perfected, with this narrative, " that there being an estate provided for Hans by his father's will, of
such date, &c., it was now agreed, and accordingly perfected, betwixt my Lord and his brother,
&c." This affair being thus transacted, my Lord demanded the will and keeping of it from his
mother, as being now only of his concern, My Lady Clanbrassill unwarily yielded to it, which
being done, my Lord gave it to his servant Swadlin (then chief favourite), and bid him put it up
amongst his other papers, which being done, his Lady Alice suddenly withdrew to her chamber,
and sent one to direct Mr. Swadlin to come to her. He came instantly, with all the papers they had
then use for in his hands; then bid him shut fast the door; then, said she, " Swadlin, give me that
troublesome will." He, looking only at the endorsement, gave her the copy of the will; she, likewise so satisfied and in a hurry, tore it all to pieces, and threw it into the fire, where it was
quickly consumed. " Now," say'd she, " it shall trouble us no more;" then went suddenly and
very cheerfully to my Lord and the rest of the company, leaving Mr. Swadlin to put up his papers,
without discerning the mistake.

For some years my Lord and Lady took their pleasure in great housekeeping and company, none
like it any where for plenty and jollity, and great store of company, of all sorts of gentry and
nobility. After some time, my Lord and Lady became pinched for want of money, and became
inquisitive how their lands were set, and got information that Swadlin had ruined their affairs by
taking bribes from the tenants, and so lessening my Lady's rents, and thereupon quarrell with him,
and find him without defence, and very guilty of betraying them for his own profit, which was a
sad truth, but their faults who trusted to him alone.

Mr. Swadlin is in a great perplexity and contempt, and sets about making off, and to sort his papers and his Lord's, for his own ends, and then finds, among my Lord's papers, that was perfected
by Earl James for his will and testament, yet is so enraged with my Lord and Lady, that he will
not so much as acquaint them with it. The contention heightens, and my Lord is persuaded to put
a padlock upon Mr. Swadlin's closet door, where all the papers were, and so dismisses Swadlin from

his service, with as much disgrace as he could, and choses one J'. Hamilton, (a son of one Ja'. Hamilton, say'd to be a natural son of Gawen's, but not currently believed, no mention being of it before his death) named, of Ballygilbert, and puts him upon the papers, and to receive his rents. He soon finds the will, and conceals it from my Lord and Lady, out of love to the friends of the family concerned therein ; yea, lets them know of it, but soon after he sickened and died. My Lord then admitts one of his cousins, William (fourth son to my Lord's brother, William),* to come upon all the papers in James's custody, on the acc'. or pretence, that there had been many affairs transacted betwixt them wherein they had been mutually bound for one another, and that he would make up James his accompts betwixt my Lord and the tenants, &c. The friends of the family (concerned in the will) enquire of him if the will was in his hands; he acknowledged it was so ; they then charged him for the preservation of it, and to be countable for it, when they should need to require it.

I * * * that (since the troublesome will was burned, and especially that my Lord's brother and son were dead) there has been a great deal of business and courtship carried on about this great little court. Some (very few) courted my Lord and Lady out of friendship ; others my Lord for my Lady's sake ; others my Lady for my Lord's sake, and to bring my Lord to their measures ; others their servants for finding out, and fra ning good bargains for money ; and one (more cunning than the rest) left his son (then a lusty stripling of about twenty years of age) to court the Lady, whilst he came now and then to prepare for and frame a lusty bargain (I pretend not to know of what extent), and for some weighty consideration, having the benefit of the patents of the Duffran (the far or greatest part of my Lady's jointure) either for pledge or direction, and having prepared papers or deeds for my Lord's signing, had my Lady's faithfull promise to assist in it, and resolved to make up either by cadjoling or cudgeling (for one heat must do all), prepare their attack upon my Lord, having got him alone. He proving more than ordinary intractable, they go to high words, threaten my Lord uncivilly. My Lady took this ill, and seemed to withdraw from the measures agreed unto ; they deal rudely with her, and a great noise heard in the room. Some inferior servants came up and found all in tumult; my Lord directs one of them by a whisper to call for one of his kinsmen then in the house; he being come, found my Lord and Lady all agast and in great agony ; the tumultuous words that were among them ; so discovered the matter, which was also formerly under suspicion; took upon him to talk boldly, and in severe language, which quelled the fray. The father and son withdrew, and next morning very early go home, without good morrow of my Lord and Lady, and carry the deeds of the Duffran * * with them, (as the other

---

* See page 82, *ante*.

unperfected) with little contentment, and less credit. This made a great noise; my Lord's principal kinsmen are sent for and come; my Lady tells how uncivilly (perhaps brutally) my Lord and she were dealt with; a course is taken to command back the deeds; and it was found necessary that the young man should take him to his travels abroad for some years till the noise of this courtship and enterprise should fall under oblivion, which he did. When this is over, there falls anew great care and solicitude how to get money—*i.e.*, how to secure bargains, and the only remedy is, that my Lord shall pass a fine and suffer a recovery, and that the troublesome will be extinguished. For this end great pains and charges are undergone to corrupt the surviving witnesses, and make them swear my Lord, Earl James, was not *compos mentis* when it was pretended to be perfected by him; all which being sufficiently prepared, it is resolved that my Lord and Lady (then in Dublin) shall come down in great pomp, and bring a commission from my Lord Chancellor (with all the privity they could); and, by virtue of the aforesaid commission, to examine the prepared witnesses, and so have the will found null, for that Earl James was not *compos mentis* when it was perfected. Meantime, immediately before his intended journey, my Lord became unwell (as has been say'd), unexpectedly, at Dublin.

<hr>

OF THE LAW-SUIT BETWIXT THE FRIENDS CONCERNED IN THE WILL, AND THE LADY ALICE CLANBRASSILL; OF HER MARRIAGE, AND DEATH.

Upon my Lord's death, as this Lady lost no time to prepare herself for a law-suit, so it fell out that James of Newcastle was with Sir Hans Hamilton, at Hamilton's Bawn, and they agreed to send by messengers letters to the other three cousins concerned,* desiring them to give them a meeting on an appointed time, that they might consult on what was now proper for them, my Lord being now dead without issue, which was done accordingly. In this meeting, Sir Hans laid open the affair, and proposed the question, if we should jointly agree to set on foot, and support, and pursue a law suit with Countess Alice, for getting the will proved and made effectual? It was say'd she was provided with a will made by Earl Henry, settling the whole estate upon her, and her heirs, &c., and a deed perfected to the same purpose afterwards. However, they unanimously resolved they would join in a suit ag' her title, and for evincing of their own title, at the equal

<hr>

* James Hamilton, of Neilsbrook, Archibald Hamilton, and Patrick Hamilton.

Y

charge of the five, and so to adhere firmly to one another, &c., until the suit should be finished, and then divide their shares equally, according to Earl James's will;—that Sir Hans, and James of Newcastle, should follow and manage this law-suit from time to time till it were finished;—that, for the first assay, James of Newcastle, should immediately repair to Dublin to provide lawyers, and by them obtain judgment of the title and estate conveyed to them by the said will, and use what other diligence should be advised;—that he should correspond with Sir Hans by post, and receive his advice, and for this end be supplied with money for the lawyers, and have 10s per diem allowed to him for his personal charges;—and that the five should meet together once before every new term for consulting, and getting accounts of what was done, and agreeing upon the sums to be provided for each term. At this time, Sir Hans was very encouraging as to his judgment, and promised his very effectual assistance, and that, before the suit should fail for want of money, he would sell the best part of his estate, and so say'd all the rest proportionably, and that so long as any of them had it, none of the rest should want money for this end. There were no witnesses by them, but, being very near kinsmen, and besides of long acquaintances and great friendship, they were very forward, free, and cleverly in this conjunction and design as was possible for men or friends to be. It was considered that the Lady was very well provided with lawyers against friends, &c., and that in her deeds she had made use of the ablest lawyers then upon the stage, but hoped that her wicked contrivances would not be blessed, yea, such a case not countenanced by men of conscience or honor. Sir Hans further say'd, that the deed which the Lady had would make void the will, and that he was very creditably informed that there was a rasure in the deed which would make it void.

In a short time we got very good constructions from lawyers of the will, and we doubt nothing the proving of it. The method of proceeding must be—first, that, by an order from the Chancery Court, Earl James's will be produced and settled in Court (which was soon obtained), but the Lady is not put to deposite her Lord's will, or deeds; next, that there be commissions granted for the examination of witnesses which were to be produced for proving of the several wills and deed, and the first struggle was, whether the father's or the son's should have the preference, and it was carried for the Lady; so a commission was granted for the examination of the Lady's witnesses. When the day appointed came, one of the commissioners on my Lady's side was was absent, and the commissioners on the friends' side were kept back, so this diligence was lost. The next commissioners were to examine for the friends, and it was judged fit that this work should be done by some officers of the Court; in this the Lady had her choice, and the friends the next * or best worst. When they were to come down, my Lady's examinator pretended indisposition by the gout; the other came down, and the friends were advised to proceed with one examinator, which they did, at a vast charge (for the honor of the cause), in Downpatrick, but the Court rejected all this diligence, and denied the benefit of the testimony. In this time it must be allowed that noble widow was much and highly courted by many great persons, and tho' some say'd she was not ill to court, yet having many offers, must make her choice, and this proved to be my Lord Bargany, of Scotland,[b] who in her first Lord's time had made acquaintance with her, and, as some say'd, intimately, and who appeared to her very generous, witty, but, especially, well furnished with money, for which she had now great use. In their first step, he secured to her a jointure of £600 per annum, out of an estate in Scotland which he had sold privately, immediately before he came to Ireland, and she secured his life rent in the estate she possessed, which she had clandestinely settled on her brother, Mr. Henry Moore; and what money she borrowed from him was to be repaid   *   by deeds of inheritance out of her estate!

After some time, another commission is granted to have examinators of the Court, one for each suit; and my Lady and her Lord resolved to come down to Down in great splendour, with many of her city and country friends about her, to attend this affair, especially to manage such as were prepared aright; but it fell out, in the week before the fixed time for their down coming, that their

<hr>

[b] The following Memoir of Lord Bargeny, County of Ayr, in Scotland, is extracted from "Anderson's Memoirs of the House of Hamilton:"—

"Sir John Hamilton, only son of Sir John Hamilton, of Lettrick (natural son of John, first Marquis of Hamilton), by Jean Campbell, his wife, who obtained a legitimation under the Great Seal, 22d December, 1600, and acquired considerable estate, had the designation of Cairiden in the lifetime of his father, to whom he was served heir, 23d April, 1642. He had previously been created a peer of Scotland, by the title of Lord Bargeny, in 1639, with limitation to the heirs-male of his body. He accompanied the Duke of Hamilton in his unfortunate expedition into England, in 1648. His attachment to the royal cause was so conspicuous, that Cromwell excepted him out of his act of grace and pardon, 12th April, 1654; and he died April, 1658.

"His Lordship married Lady Jean Douglas, second daughter of William, first Marquis of Douglas, and had issue:—

"1. John, second Lord Bargeny.

"2. Hon. Major William Hamilton, married, April, 1662, to Mary, daughter of Sir Patrick Hay, of Pitfour, relict of George Butter, of Clashberry.

"1. Hon. Margaret Hamilton, married first to John Kennedy, of Culzean, who died 1665; second, to Sir David Ogilvy, of Clova, and had issue by both.

"2. Hon. Anne Hamilton, married to Sir Patrick Houston, of Houston, in the County of Renfrew, Bart., and died 1678, her death being occasioned by a party of soldiers coming to that place during her husband's absence in London, and threatening her at such a rate, that she

ordered the portcullis to be let down to keep them out of the house; but two of her sons being without, she was so terrified at their menaces against her boys, that she fell into a fever, which soon carried her off.

"3. Hon. Grisel Hamilton, who, by attending on her sister, Lady Houstoun, fell into the same distemper, and died 1678.

"4. Hon. Marjory Hamilton, married to William Baillie, of Lamington, and had a son, William, who died in his seventeenth year.

"5. Hon. Catherine Hamilton, married (December, 1676) to William Cunningham, of Enterkine, in Ayrshire, and had issue, and died 11th January, 1740.

"John, second Lord Bargeny, was served heir to his father, 17th October, 1662. Being obnoxious to the ministry of King Charles II., he was imprisoned in Blackness Castle, in November, 1679, and from thence removed to Edinburgh, where, on the 24th of February, 1680, he was indicted for high treason, for having compassed the life of the Duke of Lauderdale, and others of the nobility; having encouraged rebellion against the King, and entertained rebels in his house, and openly declaimed against episcopacy and the curates. This indictment was not brought to trial, for want of evidence. The King, on the 11th May, 1680, issued a letter to his Privy Council in Scotland, bearing that he had received a petition from Lord Bargeny, representing his father's loyalty and sufferings, asserting his innocence of the crimes he was indicted upon, and attesting God thereupon; and he was released, on finding security in 50,000 merks, to stand trial. After he was at liberty, he discovered, by diligent investigation, that Cunninghame of Montgrenan, and his servant, two of the prisoners taken at Bothwell-bridge, were suborned by Sir

house took fire very suddenly and fiercely, so as with much ado some of the servants escaped with their lives, but almost all things in it were consumed with fire. I myself heard my Lord give this account of it; 1st, say'd he, "I never could find out yet how it took fire;" 2nd, "All in it were instantly and irrecoverably consumed;" 3d, "No other adjoining house received any harm by the fire, tho' some families lost much by putting out of their household goods for fear of it."

When the time came, and all concerned, with their friends and witnesses, the examinators proceed not very hastily, and both sides lived very high in their provisions, and, with their attendants, and making visits to one another, very complimentally, and chargeably, so as sometimes they lost themselves (*videlicit*, their senses) in the complm^ts, for a whole month together ; but the most lamentable tragedy was of the persons sworn, and their testimonies, and the considerations upon which they did so swear, not fit to be expressed without some urgent necessity, tho' it may be told, that my Lord and Lady left their quarters without a farewell, and their charge was not refunded for several months thereafter, and with a great deal of trouble, to the honest innkeeper. After this, the great debate at the Court of Chancery was, how the validity of the testimonies *pro* or *con* should be judged; at last the Chancellor committed this work to a jury of gentlemen in the King's County, to be by them tried and judged against a limited day, and the verdict to be—"A will, or no will?" The

---

Charles Maitland, of Hatton, and Sir John Dalrymple, to give false evidence against him. Their depositions, which also affected the Duke of Hamilton, were prepared beforehand, and they were promised a share of the confiscated estates ; but, as soon as ever the trial approached, their conscience revolted against the crime. Bargeny's evidence was ready to be produced before Parliament, 28th July, 1681. Perjury and subornation, charged, in open Parliament, against a judge and an officer of state, demanded public investigation, condign punishment, or the most ample retribution. But the Duke of York interposed to prevent inquiry. Lord Bargeny entered heartily into the Revolution, raised a regiment of 600 foot for the public service, 1689, and died 25th May, 1693, at 10 p.m., as his son's *retour* bears.

"His lordship married, first, Lady Margaret Cuninghame, second daughter of William, ninth Earl of Glencairn, Lord High-Chancellor of Scotland, and had issue:—

"1. John, Master of Bargeny, who died before his father. He married, 19th June, 1658, Jean, daughter of Sir Robert Sinclair, of Longformacus, Bart., and had one daughter, Johanna, heiress of Bargeny.

"2. William, third Lord Bargeny.

"1. Daughter, Hon. Nicholas Hamilton, married, 24th April, 1690, to Sir Alexander Hope, of Kerse, Bart., and had a son, Sir Alexander Hope, of Kerse, born 3d January, 1697.

"Lord Bargeny married, second, in 1676, Lady Alice Moore, eldest daughter of Henry, first Earl of Drogheda, widow of Henry, second Earl of Clanbrazil, to whom she was married, 1667, and who died without issue, 12th January, 1675. She had no children to Lord Bargeny, and died at Roscommon-house, Dublin, 12th December, 1677. He survived her, and died in 1693, succeeded by his son,

"WILLIAM, third Lord Bargeny, who died in 1712, leaving a son (by his second wife, Margaret, daughter of Robert Dundas, of Arniston, a Lord of Session),

"JAMES, fourth Lord Bargeny, who died in 1736, unmarried and without issue.

"On the title of Bargeny, the Lords of Session observe, in their returns to the House of Peers, 1743, that 'the Patent has not been met with in the records. By the proceedings in a case which lately depended before the Court of Session, and which was brought by appeal before your Lordships, touching the succession to the estate of Bargeny, it appears that there are no heirs-male existing of the body of John, Lord Bargeny, who, in 1688, made the settlement of his estate on which the question depended; and no person has at any election, since the death of the last lord, claimed a vote in right of that peerage ; but, as they cannot discover from the records the limitation of that dignity, they cannot take upon them to say whether it is extinct or not.' A competition arose for the estate between—1st, the children of Johanna, Lady Dalrymple, only daughter of John, Master of Bargeny; 2d, the children of Mrs. Buchan, of Cairnbulgh, daughter of the third Lord; and 3d, Sir Alexander Hope, of Kerse, son of Nicholas, daughter of the second Lord. It was ultimately decided in the House of Lords in favour of the first."—*Anderson's Memoirs*, pp. 216 to 219.

Lady now knew what she had to do, and bestirred herself accordingly, and to good purpose, as one of her greatest agents and intimates told me expressly, so as she had the whole gentlemen of the jury engaged for her, and to do her work in the time of this debate. As she, in her opinion, fortified herself by marrying my Lord Bargany, by whom she might be supplied of money; obliged her own friends by settlemᵗ of the estate upon her brothers,—her servants, and agents in the country, by great gifts,—and her counsellors and agents with exorbitant fees, she endeavoured to divide the friends of my Lord's family by some kind proposals. She offered to James of Neilsbrook, £500 per annum of inheritance, and as much money as would pay all his debts, on condition he would forbear to join with the other cousins in their bill and stand by her title, and to another £2,000 in ready money; but, finding them generously resolved to stand by one another, and pursue their bill for the will, and the whole estate, she contented herself in the confidence she had of overthrowing the will, and outswearing the friends of the family, some of them being aged, and others of no great estates or skil[^l] for law debates, even tho' Earl James's will should be found good; yet fell under some uneasy accidents, for my Lord Bargany straitened her so very much for money, that she could neither live to her mind, nor gratify her friends, nor defray small debts; 2, the loss of apparel and household stuff was very great (about £4,000), and she could not get herself recruited to that splendour she designed; 3, she fell under a general obloquy and contempt (which was much heightened by some of her greatest friends), and was severely   *   by the great wits of the time; 4, being thus disappointed, and also under great distemper of body, she fell under a high fever, and rage, and distraction, by it; resented her own folly and too great kindness to her own friends, that made her take unjust courses to defraud her good Lord Clanbrassill's friends of their right; called for the box wherein chief papers were, that she might destroy the deed she procured from her Lord Henry, and those she had made on behalf of her brothers and others, that she might destroy them, (but her mother, the Countess of Drogheda, being with her, would not permit this box to be brought); again and again regretted the infamy and misery she had brought herself to, and the sad state of her soul thereby, and so died, my Lord Bargany being in Scotland;* her own friends neglecting her (tho' they kept her papers and what else she had), her servants took course to have her corpse sent to Bangor privately, and so buried, without any the least solemnity. This fell out about a month before the time appointed for the jury of the King's County, their determination or judgment of the proof of the will.

---

* Although Lord Bargeny was in Dublin with the Countess at the time their house was burned there, it does not appear that he ever resided with her at either of the family seats in Down, though in the list of Justices or Commissioners of the Peace for the County of Down, in the reign of Charles II., his name appears among them as having been appointed on the 12th of July, 1677.

OF THE JOINT PROCEEDINGS OF THE FRIENDS OF THE FAMILY, IN ORDER TO THE WILL AND THE ESTATE, AFTER COUNTESS ALICE'S DEATH.

As hitherto, the friends of the family had proceeded according to their first measure by Sir Hans and James of Newcastle's management, in trust for their relations and for themselves; so they now call their other three cousins to consult of what measures should be taken with respect to this exigency of my Lady's death, and they agree to have a meeting at Bangor (the place of Earl Henry's residence, and in the middle of his estate), and to call to them all the chief tenants of the estate whereof Earl Henry died and left his Lady possessed, and endeavour to persuade them to turn tenants to themselves, that so being in possession of the estate, they might have the stronger plea against such as should pretend any right to the estate by virtue of the Countess Alice, her deeds, and so put them to a necessity of parting with their pretended right to them upon easy terms, perhaps easier, at least safer, than a law-suit might prove; and here it was advised and resolved, that each of the friends should provide themselves with so much money as their affairs might require; and here were kind offers of assisting, and being bound for one another, &c. Accordingly, the day of meeting was agreed on, and letters of warning from the five sent to them for keeping of such a meeting with them upon affairs to be intimated. At the time appointed, the tenants met punctually—the tenants, or at least chief of them, came generally; here some time was spent to inform them of the injuries the friends had sustained by the Lady, Countess Alice, her   *   practices; of the undoubted and honest right they had by Earl James's will; that their title was also rational and natural; and that by and of them they might expect all kind and fair dealing, &c.; to all which they agreed very heartily, and were willing to proceed in what methods the friends thought best. At this time some took leases from the five, and possession was peaceably given by my Lady Alice's servants and tenants, of the house and demesne of Bangor, to the five cousins; one of them was sent to Ringhaddy, with commission from the other four, to take possession of it in their names, which was also peaceably given and taken. This conversation continued a fortnight or thereabouts, and the tenants were entertained with meat and good liquors plentifully at the charge of the five. It was now agreed again, that Sir Hans and James should continue to manage the law-suit; and that money should be given them for two terms charges, viz, £40 a piece (which was accordingly soon done); and, that they should meet again, after the two terms, to get account of what was done, either of law or agreements, and consult what might be then pertinent, and state their acct^s, &c. It was also now agreed, that Mr. David Kennedy, a great friend to all the kinsmen, and brother-in-law to one of them, who was employed from the very first time, and accordingly did attend and assist in all the former terms and meetings, should attend and assist them at the next term.

All things seemed here to proceed very unanimously and lovingly, only Sir Hans and James were not willing to press the tenants to making attornment and giving of possession, lest some few or one might refuse, and that rumours and clamours would rise to our greater prejudice; but they had no ground to doubt of the ten[ts], their justice, yea, kindness to us, so far as we should need the same, for that we were assured of the chief and leading tenants, and that this was done by their advice and on their assurance.

This was for the time sufficient to plain dealing gent[n] that distrusted nothing of such near relations under so honest a cause; but here was the cockatrice's egg laid, which soon after produced incredible mischiefs; for, at this time, one Captain John Baily, with a few chief tenants, had a private cabal, in a secret unsuspected place, with Sir Hans, and James of Newcastle, and advised them to stop the attornment of the tenants to the five, and their title, and that these two should procure a title, either from my Lord Bargany or from the Moors, for themselves two, and so shake off the other three, and that, in this case, they would bring all the tenants to attorn to these two, and their title. This was soon agreed to, and put under a promise of mutual fidelity and proportionable kindness, and then under secrecy, which was sealed in a glass of wine and a kiss that went about. As it may be thought strange how this could grow to such a perfection in one night, and become so pleasant to two gent[n] in such circumstances as they were then under, so it is scarce credible what firm rooting it took, and what growth it had, and fruit it bare, but the proverb is, "A wool buyer knows always a wool seller." Their former education and practices made the advisers ready with such counsel, and the advised to take hold of it, and practice it effectually, as the following discourse will shew. But here give me leave to digress from my chief scope into the character and account of this captain general of this machination, because he must be often mentioned hereafter, as he had also a great hand in many things past in Earl Henry and Countess Alice their time :—He was born of very mean but virtuous parents, who, in their thriving condition, bred him at schools so far that he was * years in the university, but applied himself to * He spent on this account some time under the Marquis of Argyle, in the West Highlands of Scotland, against the McDonalds and the Marquis of Mountrose his party then in Scotland, as * to E James Clanbrassill, under K * and P * against the Irish in that party; swore to the Solemn League and Covenant; then joined with the Duke of Hamilton in the cessation with the Irish. When that party was beat, he joined with Cromwell's party; was made by them a justice of the peace, and took the test then called positive or negative; kept the Anabaptist meetings, and withdrew from Presbyterians; thereafter (when King Charles the Second returned to his Government) betook himself to the Episcopal way, yet so as at sometimes he professed to be Presbyterian, and heard, yea, communicated with them in the time of Countess Ann Clanbrassill's widowhood; was her great assistant in managing the estate, being entrusted thereunto by Earl James his will; and for it, in Earl Henry's time, he gave his full endeavours and utmost assistance to suppress it, and get the whole estate in his power; and a great contriver with his Lady, and assistant to her for destroying of the will; then turned to Sir Hans, and James of Newcastle, against the other three cousins; but still, rationally,—*i.e.*, for his own profit and gain; and, indeed, he gained well after Earl James's death (at which time he was judged not to be well worth £100 in all), for ere he died he procured *(viis et modis)* upwards of £400 per annum. He had two sons, and two daughters that became marriageable, and cast off one son and one daughter without portions, and died with this character, that he was a well-bred, fair-fashioned, subtle, selfish man—a time-server, a flatterer, a proteus, a self-seeker; in all, his motto might well be, " *non marte sed arte*," or " *viis et modis*,"—a true soldier of fortune, true to himself, and false to all the world.*

But to return to my purpose.—According to our late agreement, Sir Hans, and James of New-

---

* This Captain John Bailie was son of Alexander Bailie, Esq., who was second son of Sir William Baillie, of Lamington, by Marian, daughter of Sir John Seton. They had a numerous issue; and the three eldest sons having maimed a clergyman, who had been taken into their father's house as tutor, for a grievous offence which he had committed in their family, of which injury he died; and the power of the Church at this time being great in Scotland, the three brothers were obliged to fly.—*See "Bailie of Dochfour," Burke's Landed Gentry*, p. 44, 4th Ed. Alexander Bailie, the second son, settled in Ireland, at Innishargie, County Down, in the reign of James I., about the year 1620, and died in 1632. John, his eldest son, who was born in 1623, was connected by marriage with the Raplock branch of the Hamilton family, Gawen Hamilton, of Raplock, having, in 1633, married Janet, daughter of Sir William Baillie, of Lamington (see *Anderson's Memoirs of the House of Hamilton*, p. 363), and was named in the will of James, first Earl of Clanbrassil (see page 84, *ante*), as one of the persons to be aiding and assisting his executors in setting, letting, leasing out, and bettering the rents of such of his lands as were to be set, before his eldest son came of age, so that he was, no doubt, one of his confidential friends; and it must be considered, that the bitter terms in which he is above-mentioned appear from the context to be used by one of the parties who claimed a division of the entire estate, and that he writes, in almost equally severe terms, of at least one of the other claimants who resisted it. His taking part with Lord Bargeny, may

also probably be accounted for by his family connection with him, which is thus stated in *Anderson's Memoirs of the House of Hamilton* :—" The Honble Marjory Hamilton (fourth sister of John, second Lord Bargeny, who married the Countess Alice Clanbrassil, widow of Earl Henry), married William Baillie, of Lamington, and had a son, William, who died in his seventeenth year."—p. 217. Captain John Bailie died in 1687, and was succeeded in Innishargie by his eldest son, James, who was born in 1653, and died in 1710. He was succeeded by his second son, John, who was born in 1697, and died in 1759. John was succeeded by his son, James, who sold Innishargie, and died in 1787. This branch of the Bailie family is now represented by the descendants of Colonel Bailie, a younger brother of James, the last owner of Innishargie. The original name of Innishargie seems to have been " Inyscargi," the island of the rock." The ruins of the Church stand on high ground, surrounded, not by water, but by cultivated fields. It appears, however, that, within the last two centuries human industry has converted the morass into arable land, and the island into a hill; for, in a roll of the reign of James I., mention is made of " an island or lough Inuischargy, and eight townlands about or near the said island."—*Reeves's Eccl. Antiq. of Down*, p. 19. In *Harris's History of County Down*, it is stated, that "about the center of the Ardes stands Inishargy, the mansion-house of John Bailey, Esq., having two fresh water lakes to the North and South of it."—p. 48. These lakes have, however, entirely disappeared since Harris's work was published, in 1744;

castle, repaired to Dublin at Term time, with Mr. Kennedy, instructed and provided as aforesaid; gave in a bill to the Chancery for proving of the will in name of the five kinsmen, against Cornet Henry Moore, now invested with his sister (Lady Alice) her title, and called Hamilton, *alias* Moore, whereupon he was called "*Cornet Alias.*"[b] The Cornet gives in a cross bill, to which the aforesaid Sir Hans and James gave their answer upon oath, affirming that Earl James his will was (as they verily believed) a good will, duly perfected, and carried a title of inheritance for all that Earl James died possessed of to the five, to be equally divided amongst the five ; and that they believed Earl Henry's will to be surreptitious and clandestine, and moreover void by a subsequent deed, whereof they credibly heard and believed that there was a rasure made in it after it was

---

and the mansion-house, which was built immediately adjoining the old Church, is now in a very dilapidated condition. The Church is roofless, and the walls in ruins ; but, on two tombstones lying within them, are the following inscriptions :—

HERE LYETH THE BODY OF ALEXANDER BAILIE, OF INNISHCHARGIE, ESQ., AGED 95 YEARS, WHO DEPARTED THIS LYFE YE 20TH OF AUGUST, 1682, AND HAD TWO SONS, VIZ., JOHN, AND EDWARD, AND ALSO TWO DAUGHTERS, MARGRET, AND JANE.

HERE LYETH YE BODY OF CATHARINE CARY, WIFE TO JOHN BAILIE, OF INNCHARGIE, ESQ., WHO DEPARTED THIS LIFE YE 12TH OF DECEMBER, 1671, AND BARE UNTO HIM SEVEN SONS, VIZ., JAMES, JOHN, ALEXANDER, THOMAS, HENRY, FERDINANDO, AND JANNETO, AND ALSO TWO DAUGHTERS, ANNA, AND JANE.

HERE LYETH THE BODY OF JOHN BAILIE, ESQ., ELDEST SON OF ALEXANDER BAILIE, WHO DEPARTED THIS LYFE THE 4TH MAY, 1697, AGED 64 YEARS.

HERE LYETH THE BODY OF JAMES BAILIE, ESQ., ELDEST SON OF JOHN BAILIE, WHO DEPARTED THIS LIFE THE 9TH OF JULY, 1710, IN THE 57TH YEAR OF HIS AGE, AND HAD FIVE SONS, FRANCIS, JOHN, JAMES, HANS, AND ANNESLEY, AS ALSO 5 DAUGHTERS, JANE, BRAILLIANA, CARY, SOPHIA, ANNE-DEBORAH, ALLICE, ELIZABETH, AND MORDANT.

HERE LIETH THE BODY OF JOHN BAILIE, ESQ., OF INNISHARGIE, WHO DEPARTED THIS LIFE, 6TH AUGUST, 1730, AGED 62 YEARS.

HERE LIETH THE BODY OF JAMES BAILIE, ESQ., OF INNISHARGIE, WHO DEPARTED THIS LIFE, SEPTEMBER 22ND, 1787, AGED 63 YEARS.

Edward Bailie, the second son of Alexander Bailie, of Innishargie, above-mentioned, to whom James, first Viscount Claneboye, in 1636, mortgaged Ringdufferin, otherwise Mylerton (which is situated opposite to Innishargie, on the shore of Strangford Lough), came over and settled there, and from him the present Ringdufferin branch of the family is derived. He married Elizabeth, sole daughter of James Dunbar, to whom Sir James Hamilton had granted Bally-Toy, at an annual rent of £5 ; and, on his father-in-law's death, succeeded to Toy, and obtained a further mortgage

of Ringdufferin from Henry, second Earl of Clanbrassil, in 1668, which his eldest son, Alexander, who succeeded him in Toy, became the absolute purchaser of, in 1674. He was succeeded by his son Edward, who filled the office of High Sheriff of Down, in 1764, and died in the year 1774, at the age of 84. His second son, James, who succeeded him in Ringdufferin, was born in 1735 : he was a magistrate and Deputy Governor of County Down, and, dying in 1810, was succeeded by his eldest son, James, who was born in 1797 ; called to the Irish Bar in 1834 ; was a magistrate, and Deputy Lieutenant of County Down, and died in 1863, leaving an only son, James who succeeded him in the Ringdufferin estate. He took the degree of A.M. in T.C.D. ; was a major in the 87th Royal Irish Fusiliers, and served ten years in the East Indies; but is now settled at Ringdufferin, and is a magistrate of County Down. There is still a portion of the townland of Ballygarvin, in the Parish of Innishargie, attached to the Ringdufferin property.

[b] Henry Moore (afterwards third Earl of Drogheda), assumed the surname of Hamilton, as heir to Henry, Earl of Clanbrazil, who, by his will, dated 27th March, 1674, devised all his real estate to his wife and her heirs ; which she bequeathed to her brother Henry, who, after an expensive law-suit, sold his interest therein, by deeds of lease and release, dated 17th and 18th February, 1769, for £2,400, to Sir Hans Hamilton, Bart., and James Hamilton, of Bangor, Esq. In King Charles the Second's reign he was a cornet of horse. After the Prince of Orange's landing in England, his Lordship was appointed Colonel, and, at the taking of Carrickfergus, 26th August, 1689, commanded a regiment of foot, with which he was at the battle of the Boyne, and at the siege of Limerick, and continued in the command of his regiment until the disbanding of it, in 1698. In July, 1675, he married Mary, second daughter to Sir John Cole, of Newland, near Dublin, Bart., sister to Arthur, Lord Ranelagh, and died 7th June, 1714.—*See Lodge's Peerage of Ireland*, vol. i., pp. 329, 330.

perfected, and words put in it without Earl Henry his knowledge; but, in the meantime (according to the Articles of Bangor), Sir Robert Hamilton (lately become son-in-law to Sir Hans Hamilton), James Sloan, Hugh Hamill (two of Countess Alice's great agents and confidants, converted to Sir Hans, and James of Newcastle, their interest, by the aforesaid articles, and confederates with Captain John Baily), are set on work to agree with Cornet *Alias* for his title and interest in the estate. The last two acted as his friends in persuading the Cornet; the other (or first), as merchant in Sir Hans's name; and at last persuade him to sell and make the agreement for £2,200, which is concluded the very day after Sir Hans, and James of Newcastle, had sworn and given in their answer to the Cornet's bill; but all this is done with the greatest secrecy, and Sir Hans and James of Newcastle, write to their friends in the country, that they are proceeding very successfully against the Cornet. Meantime, they are perfecting writings, and securing in great friendship, and, with consent, obtain the late bill and answer to be got out of the Court. In process of time, the account of the transaction comes abroad, and it is little doubted, but generally believed, that this bargain is for the behoof of the five kinsmen; yea, Sir Hans, being questioned, say'd it was, and should be so, if they were able to provide their proportions of the money (I am sure, and can swear, he said it to be one engaged for against the time of payment). But the Articles of Bangor are yet in force; and the next step is to make agreement, suddenly and with all privacy, with my Lord Bargany's agents, who were empowered by him to sell his interest, viz.—James Ross, of Portavoe, Hugh Hamill, of Ballyatwood, and Hugh Montgomery, of Ballymagown.* This, by the assistance of Captain John Baily, was soon and well done on that same

---

* The following letters from these agents of Lord Bargeny, with a copy of the heads of the agreement which they entered into on his behalf, have been found among the family papers:—

"Donadee, 22 April, 1678.

"RIGHT HONᵇˡᵉ,—The enclosed was the occasion of our meeting here this day, which we have transmitted for your Lᵖ's perusal, and whereby you will have a larger account how affairs at present stand than we can write to you. Since our coming hither, we understand by Mr. Campbell, that by the last boat there came a packet from your Lᵖ, directed only to Mr. Hamill, which occasioned him to send it away to Dublin per post, whereby we know nothing of your Lᵖ's mind therein, but desire that in the future you may direct your letters to Mr. Collinwood, to be by him transmitted to either of us. We are but as yet blind guessers how matters will go, but still retaine good hopes; for, notwithstanding of all Mr. Sloan brags of the invalidity of that paper granted by your Lady to you at Inchargy, Henry Moor hath, since Sloan's going up, written the enclosed to Mr. Rosse, which we take as a *bonum omen*, and do verily believe that if they had found it to be so, they would never have written this letter. Mr. Rosse hath written him a civill and wary answer, a copy whereof is

upon the back of this; and be sure you take no notice of our sending Mr. Moor's or our own letters to you, but only to ourselves, for we resolve in all things to be both free and ingenuous with you; and, therefore, transmit the inclosed back to us. Sloan's brags at Downpatrick did so jumble the Hamiltons, that they did not know what answer to give us, or what proposals to make till they were at Dublin; but we expect to hear speedily from them, whereof your Lᵖ shall have an account, but we pray you will not leave Carrick and Galloway till this and next term be over. Your Lᵖ may perceive, by the enclosed, that money is the tongue of the trump; and, therefore, if you have not in your last writt thereanent, you must by the next think of supplying that defect by a particular order to Mr. Rosse. We can say no more at present, but that you may be assured that wherein we can serve you, we shall be ever ready to approve ourselves to be, my Lord, your Lᵖ's faithfull friends, and humble servants,
"JAMES ROSSE.
"HUGH MONTGOMERY.

"To the Right Honᵇˡᵉ John, Lord Bargany."

"HONORED SIR,—Yours I received, and, if I had not been abroad, would have answered you per last post; and you might also have heard from me sooner, if I had not met

morning in whose evening the other three cousins were advertised to meet Sir Hans, and James

with Mr. Sloan when he came first to this country. I then told him what had passed between you and us at Bangor. He then told me that you did not understand your own affairs to make any such offer, and that if any paper was granted by my Lady Clantrasil to Bargany of a life-rent, it was vague in law. Afterwards, I met with him at our Assizes, in Downpatrick, where he shewed me at a distance a parchment, which he said was a true copy of what my Lady signed, and that it was vague in itself; whereupon I desired him to give me the said parchment, or a copy thereof, and that I and my fellows should immediately go to councill with it; and, that if we found it to be so as he says, that then we would lay down the cudgels as to a life-rent, and come to more easy terms with you; but upon no account would he shew me it in hand, or leave it with me to take councill on it. I then told him I could not understand his reason for so doing, except it were to protract a chargeable suit both to you and my Ld Bargany. I did then believe that all hopes of a composition were at an end, and did thereupon only write to you in civility, according to my promise in Bangor. And now, Sr, if you be the same man as you were at Bangor, in relation to that affaire, we are ready to treat with you; but if you be of Mr. Sloan's opinion, it's to no purpose, except you show us the true copy of that paper granted by my Lady Claubrasill to her Ld Bargany, whereupon we may take counsel; and, if we clearly see and nuderstand it to be vague, then we will treat with you on easier terms; wherefor I pray let me have your mind herein per next, for until I have your answer, I am sure it's needless for me or any else to go up to Dublin on that account. My Ld Burgany is desirous, at least willing, a friendly end he made, but thinks your offer very mean ; for both his Ldp and you be confident of a life-rent, until such time you demonstrate the contrary to us, and then you shall find us to be willing to deal with you upon more rationall terms. I expect to hear from you per next; in the meantime, you may assure yourself that I account all money needlessly spent at law is worse than plays at dice, or cast at the cock, and that a friendly accommodation shall ever be the desire of him who is, &c., "James Ross.
" To Henry Moore, Esq., &c."

" Dublin, 23rd April, 1678.

"Dear Neighor,—I doe admire that I have not heard from you since I came to this place, whether my Ld Bargany hath given any instruction or answer of our letter; and also of what I sent him from this. Since my coming, I have filed a bill agt Mr. Moore, and all the famelly, for discovery, but have deferred the main bill, until they answer that. They have filed a bill agt the Hamiltons, and my Ld, wherein they acknowledge my Ld had such a reservation as we alledge ; but say the same was never perfected, so that you must go to Mr. Read, and gett him again to recollect himselfe, whether there was any power of revocacion in that paper which he saw signed, and give me an acct. I have not as yett come to any proposals with the Hamiltons, nor can we, until we see farther in the matter ; but the maine matter is, that Dr. Topham is taking out his Elegit agt my Ld, for want of his halfe. yeare's rent, and, if he doth, will undoubtedly put my Ld

out of possession, and, besides the giving of it to the enimys, will be our enimy in Court. Here is also Sloane entering up his outlawry, with several others, which if not paid, will undoubtedly stop all my Ld's proceedings ; therefore, my Ld must not faile to send our money to pay Sloane, which is a just debt, and also to pay Dr. Topham's half-yeare's rent, which are things he can never avoyde, and by delay will doe a great dale of evell, whereof I pray write to my Ld, and also to me, of all matters, which, with my service to yr solfe, Madam Hamilton, and my good neighbour, is all from, dear neighbr, your real neighbr, and humble servt, "Hugh Hamill.
" For God's sake write sharply to my Ld.
" To Hugh Montgomery, of Ballymagowne, Esq., neare Belfast—These."

"June ye 25th, 1678.
"Dear Cousin,—My neighbour came hither upon Sunday night, and we have spent yesterday, and this day, takeing advice of councill in my Lord's affair, and find but little ground to depend upon my Ld's life-rent. We have also comond with the Hamiltons, but doe not find that they will, upon any account, deale with us, they being frightened with the great suit the Ld Dunagall hath now against my Ld for the burned house, and Dr. Topham who threatens no less than ruin to us three, and the whole jury that sat upon the enquiry. You nor no man that did not hear what Topham sayes, can imagine what mischeefe he threatens ; besides, the whole creditors are about to outlaw my Ld, and so render him uncapable of any benefit of the law ; and all we can bring the Hamiltons to, for our lives, is, they are contented to pay my Ld what money he really laid out upon the mortgages, if we will save them harmless of Topham. We can say no more at present, but what further in us lyes, shall not be wanting, but we are but in a sad predicament; whatever can be further done you shall know next from your affectionate cousin, and humble servt,,
" Hugh Montgomery.
" Hugh Hamill.
" To James Ross, Esq., att Portivoe, near Belfast—These.'

"Donadee, 8th July, 1678.
" Rt Honble,—We are returned from Dublin, on Friday last late, and this day meet at this place, of purpose to give yor Ldsp an account of our proceedings there, which, in short is—that att, our first meeting with the Hamiltons, they were so mightily puffed up with Mr. Sloane's advice of the invallidity of your Ldsp's life-rent, and insoemuch that Sir Hans Hamilton and James offered att last either to give your Ldsp what really you had laid out on the mortgages, or else to refer all your title, both of the mortgages and of ye life-rents, to ye councill of both sides, to determine with ye debts obligatory upon you since your marriage with my Lady, and which, on consultation with our councill, we durst not venture, as you indeed being lyable to all those debts ; and, therefore, in conclusion, we have thought fit to end thus—viz., they are to give you £2,700, really laid out by you on the mortgages—£300 being abated for the bond in ye Lady Drogheda's hand, and to secure you against that and all ye debts either contracted by my Lady, or by your Ldp on her account on anywise ; and you are to indemnify them of the bond in Baron Henne's hands, and of all your

of Newcastle, at Hamilton's-Bawn, the first meeting being at Macherelin. How my Lord was dealt with by his trustees, I leave to his narrative.

·

other debts, either to Sloane or any other; you are to receive yᵉ May annuity of your £2,700; and they, to secure you of yᵉ payment of your mony by gales, and yᵉ interest as we can agree, your giveing them security of yoʳ sone's conveying the mortgages to them when he comes to age, and towards what charges and expence yoʳ Lᵈᵖ have been at since my Lady's death, and, to make good the former promise which I told your Lᵈᵖ of, they have promised £200 more. The former condicions, and what other circumstances are, time will not now permitt us to give you accᵗ of, yᵉ boat just going; but we are to meet on Thursday next to perfect, when your Lᵈᵖ may be assured of all the faithfull endenvours and dilligence as if it were our own a thousand times, that we may, according to our just inclinations, appear, Rᵗ Honᵇˡᵉ, your Lᵈᵖ's ever real humble servᵗˢ,

"Jᴀ. Ross.
"Huᴳʜ Montgomery.
"Huɢʜ Hamill.
"To the Rᵗ Honᵇˡᵉ Lord Bargany—These."

"Portavoe, yᵉ 16 August, 1676.

"Rᵗ Honᵇˡᵉ,—Wee have this day recᵈ a letter from yoʳ Lᵈᵖ of the 9th instant, from Ballintra, and also another of the 24th July, from Edinburgh, wherein yoʳ Lᵈᵖ desired wee might desist in proceeding further with Sir Hans Hamilton and James Hamilton, wᶜʰ trully did very much surprise us, considering wee had formerly given yoʳ Lᵈᵖ a full accᵗ of our positive agreemᵗ, wᶜʰ then wee informed you was soone after to be drawne into articles; and, allso, having recᵈ, by yoʳˢ of yᵉ 14th July, an accᵗ of yoʳ receipt thereof, which gave noe contradiction, but rather an approbation of yᵉ sᵈ agreemᵗ; whereupon, wee proceeded, according to our then accᵗ, and att Mackerlin entered into articles of yᵉ said agreemᵗ; and, for the true performance and better assurance of yᵉ covenᵗˢ on all sides, we entered into bonds, each to other, of the sum of £5,000, to perfect the same into Deeds att our last Assizes, so farr as was in our power to doe, and yᵗ yoʳ Lᵈᵖ should confirme yᵉ same, according to the covenᵗˢ of the said agreemᵗ, wᶜʰ deeds, at yᵉ sᵈ Assizes, were accordingly perfected and done. But yoʳ Lᵈᵖ's the same day coming to our hands, made us truelly to repent that ever wee had concerned ourselves in soe troublesome and unluckie an affair, considering on how small and uncertain grounds yoʳ Lᵈᵖ gave us such a letter, who, in the sight of God and all just men, have made us soe dilligent and carefull in the preservation of what interest wee could here make for you, without the least advantage to ourselves. And we leave it to all just and indifferent persons who ever understood anything of the merit of yoʳ affairs, whether we have not done thos things wᶜʰ may be answerable before God, and much better to yoʳ advantage than ever otherwise by law you might have expected. And, for the reports of those who wee are certain gave yoʳ Lᵈᵖ yᵉ information you writt of, it is evident, both by that and other particulars, that they gave it rather out of a particular littigious and troublesome humour, for yᵉ vexation of their owne relations not getting part of yᵉ purchase from Henry Moore, than out of either respect or kindness to yoʳ Lᵈᵖ; for, before our agreemᵗ, none ever so much sleighted and undervalued yoʳ

Lᵈᵖ's interest and title as they, tho' now seeme to declare the contrary. And that wᶜʰ, secondly, provoked them against us, was, because in our agreemᵗ we did not make them partners, or desist until they could procure yoʳ Lᵈᵖ's order for it, which if we had done till they had agreed, wee could never have gotten by a thousand pound to what wee have: and it was a thing we durst not venture—the necessity of our affaires by Topham and others urgeing the contrary; besides, having sufficiently found the evill of delays in the beginning of this affaire with Henry Moore, and wᶜʰ, by all appearance, might have been as fatall in this; neither did we ever look upon the words or securitys of those who soe endeavoured * * soe long winded storys, without one farthing money offered, to be worth either yoʳ Lᵈᵖ's delay, or our trouble; but that in conscience, our faithfull service and equity, we were obliged to make the best and surest end for yoʳ Lᵈᵖ's advantage, without respect to any person whatsoever; for truly, wee must acknowledge, had not Sʳ Hans Hamilton's interest in the country been more than we could expect, Doctor Topham's last inquiry had certainly found an estate in you, wᶜʰ, had they done, yoʳ Lᵈᵖ's title here had but signified little. The heads of our agreemᵗ wee have here inclosed, sent you for yoʳ perusall, and desire that by next you will give us an accᵗ whereabouts yoʳ Lᵈᵖ may be waited upon by yᵉ midle of Septemʳ, or thereabouts; for then Mr. James Hamilton, with one of us, intend to write on you for the perfection of what on your part is to be yet done, for till then wee can expect noe further security for yoʳ mony than the covenᵗˢ now agreed on. Mr. Sloane's mony you will finde by the inclosed is ordered as you desired, and all other matters to the best of our endeavours, to give you satisfaction; son, till meeting, shall only conclude, that from being ever concern'd on the like vexatious, troublesome, and hazardous undertakings (good Lord de iver us); and that we are, Rᵗ Honᵇˡᵉ, yoʳ Lᵈᵖ's ever faithfull and humble servᵗˢ,

"Jᴀ. Ross,
"Hu. Montgomery,
"Hu. Hamill.

"To the Right Honᵇˡᵉ Lord Bargany—These."

"The heads of yᵉ agreemᵗ made and concluded between James Ross, Esq., Hugh Montgomery, Esq., and Hugh Hamill, gent., in name and behalf of John, Lᵈ Bargany, of yᵉ one part, and Sʳ Hans Hamilton, Knt., and James Hamilton, Esq., of yᵉ other part, viz.—

"Imprimis—The said James Ross, Hugh Montgomery, and Hugh Hamill, hath firmly granted, sold, assigned, and set over, unto yᵉ sᵈ Sʳ Hans Hamilton and James Hamilton, All that, the sᵈ Lᵈ Bargany, his interest and title in Ireland, of what sort soever, chattels or otherwise, together with yᵉ two mortgages of Bangor and Ballywalter, &c., made to yᵉ said James Ross, with all the arrears of rents, except what is due out of the mortgages, att May last and before, whereof the sᵈ James Ross, Hugh Montgomery, and Hugh Hamill is obleidged in £5,000 bonds, yᵗ yᵉ sᵈ Lᵈ Bargany, and John Hamilton, Esq., Master of Bargany, shall, att or before October next, perfect all such other or further securitys, as by yᵉ councill learned in yᵉ Law of yᵉ said Sʳ

I must now divert a little, and crave pardon—yea, I am sorry for it—to give an account of Sir Robert Hamilton, lately mentioned, because he comes often in our way, and in several capacities,

Hans Hamilton, and Jas. Hamilton, shall be reasonably advised, devised, or required, being att the costs and charges of the s⁴ Sir Ha⁻s and James Hamilton, in consideration whereof, ye s⁴ Sir Hans Hamilton, and James Hami ton, is to enter into a Stat. staple. before the M yor and constables of ye staple of Carrickfergus, of all their lands and tenements. goods and chattels, within the Kingdom of Ireland, as, also, ag̈ainst their bodys, of £6,000, for ye paym⁴ of the sum of £2,900 sterling, with the growing annuity thereupon, att 10 per cent. p⁻ annum, in ye gales following, viz :—£545. on ye first day of Nov. next ensuing the date hereof—£ 25, on the first day of May, 1679 ; £600, on the first of N ber next following ; £575, on the first day of M y, 1 80; £550, the first day of Novr. following ; and £525, the first day of May, 1681. All w⁴ gales or any of them, not being paid at the severall days aforesaid, the said Lord Bargany may extend ye Stat. aforesaid, for ye whole sum of £3,000 aforesaid, ag̈t ye aforesaid lands and tenn ts. &c., also against their bodys.

"*Item*—The s⁴ Sr Hans Hamilton and James Hamilton is obleiged to indemnifie and save harmless ye s⁴ Ld Bargany, of, and from, all the bonds and judgem⁴ granted unto Doctor Jn. Topham, with ye executions thereupon, also from ye house burnt in Angier Street, Dublin; also of one bond and judgm⁴ of 1300 or thereabouts, to Mich Cole, of Dublin ; also one bond of £200 to Allice, Countess of Drogheda; also one bond of £40, or thereabouts, to Cap⁴ William Hamilton ; also one bond on an award for ye payment of £145 to Hugh Nicholson; also from ye wages of all the serv⁴ of the late Henry, Earl of Clanbrasill, and of Allice, Countess of Clanbrasill, late wife of the s⁴ Ld Bargany, and also from all other debts, dues, or demands, shop acc⁴, or other reckonings whatsoever, due or payble by the s⁴ Earl or Countess of Clanbrasill, excepting only such debts as ye s⁴ Lord Bargany made properly his own, and had allowance for.

" The s⁴ Ld Bargany is to save harmless the s⁴ Sir Hans Hamilton and James Hamilton, of all the debts properly due or accountable for by himself, viz., James Rosa, James Sloane's bonds, &c."

" Donadee, ye 16th Sept., 1678.

R⁴ Hon⁴ᴮᴸᴱ.—Y⁻ Ld⁴ᴾˢ of the last August came to our hands the 14th inst. ; and, as to our apprehensions in our last, our great cause of conjecture was meerely from what some of those persons we doubted to ourselves openly declared they had and would endeavour with your Ld⁴ in that affair. nor could we imagine how otherwise y⁻ Lp could be moved to any such thoughts, nor can we yet consider what kind of lawyer that can be, who adviseth so clear a title of Life-rent to y⁻ Lp on that last paper, it being so positively slighted by (we are sure) the best lawyers of this kingdome ; besides. that paper we could never get a sight of, nor advice where we might have it, nor of any person that could swear one word of the contents of it, but severall to the contrary effect, if it had come to tryall; and; as to y⁻ mortgages. it's true they were preferable to Henry Moor's Dred, they being on a valluable consideration, and his a Deed of voluntary gift, which is but fraudulent ag⁴ creditors ; yett, y⁻ Lp must know assuredly, that by law

you were, and must have been, lyable to all the debts contracted by my Lady after marriage, as also all servants' wages ; for that Deed cf Henry Moor only included my Ld Clanbrassill's and her debts, which by the law was resolved to be only such debts as were due before the makeing of that Deed, as also the law makes a man lyable to all his wife's debts ; for, altho' by y⁻ articles of marriage you were denuded of my Lady's estate, yett you were not of her debts, nor could any article with her doe it, which if any lawyer of England advise the contrary, it is to us a wonder (we havi g so fully advised it here with the best), and also a matter of common practise every day As to ye mortgages being drawne in James Rosse's name to avoyde creditors, had we not deferred our answers to the Bill of Dr. Topham against us, y⁻ Ld⁴ knowes wee must have declared that money to have been y⁻ⁿ, and he only in trust; and truelly had not Sr Hans Hamilton's interest prevailed with the jury, as we formerly gave y⁻ Lp an acc⁴, on Randall Brice's evidence, y⁻ owne owning it and discharging of his rent in yr name, it would have unde ubta' y been found in you ; besides, any conveyance or other settlement of an estate made or assigned by the father to the sone, being a minor, is adjudged by our law ag⁴ creditors, *ipso facto*, fraudulent. And lastly, as to the mortgages, you never were legally seized or possessed of Ballywalter, etc.. and so, consequently, must have had a suite for that at comon law, before you could have enjoyed it ; all which Hugh Hamill severally gave y⁻ Lp an account of from Council when he was with you there, and is that, that all lawyers or that understand the law must acknowledge. The £150 bond y⁻ Lp writes of with Baron Henn, that p per whereof Hugh Hamill hath the copy, as also by y⁻ Lp, we really believe it was no part of the mortgages, but on that acct you write of ; therefore, it will and must lie on y⁻ Lp to make it out, or if otherwise, they will expect an allowance for it; but we thought it better to stand to the hazard of makeing that out, than to allow it as part of the mortgages, the one we were forced to doe, and therefore are bound to free them of it, as by our former we gave you an acc⁴, the way of our security we also gave y⁻ Lp an acc⁴ of, which is the only and the best way of security this kingdome affords ; but before it be perfected, some of us must be with you, and then discourse fully with y⁻ Lp of all matters in this affaire. Which, as we formerly have certified you, we hereby again confirm, that what we hitherto have done, we did to the best of our judgments and knowledges, and with the advice of ye best lawyers, to y⁻ Lp's best advantage (lett who will say the contrary). This we doe and will avow before God and man, and with confidence conclude, as we ever have done, R⁴ Honble, y⁻ Lp's most faithfull and humble servants, "JAMES ROSS,

"HUGH MONTGOMERY,

"HUGH HAMILL.

" It will be about the middle of Octob⁻ before Mr. Hamilton can be over; therefor, we pray be not far off, but let us know where y⁻ Lp will be, at or about that time.

" To the R⁴ Hon⁴ᴮᴸᴱ John, Ld Bargany.

" To be sent his Lp from Ballintree, with care and haste.

—These."

2 D

in our subsequent account. As to his descent, or parentage, I can give no certain account, in regard his mother, and grandmother (by her), are under various and dismal characters; yet a good man, and Minister too, owned and gave him his education at the University of St. Andrew's. He was early ambitious of being a R·   *   or Philosophy Professor, and which he purchased, for anything I know, by fair dispute; but, soon after, by ambition to show his great parts, put forth in print (after a reprimand given him by some of his friends and masters of the College, who did see them in writing), philosophical theses, which   *   could defend at the public   *   *   *   of his scholars, which, being taken notice of by the divines and masters of these two Colleges, were found to be very erroneous and blasphemous, such as " *non est naturaliter impossible*   *   *   *   *cum mare,*" and the like. He was advertised to retract these, but would not; whereupon, he was adjudged to deprivation of his office, and his gown (the badge of his profession), for disgrace sake, to be publicly torn over his head, which was accordingly done by public authority, the then Archbishop Sharpe concurring in his authority with this sentence. The disgrace of this put him to abandon his native country, together with fear of further prosecution (least, perhaps, he should have died in his grandmother's bed, and be deprived of a grave and burial), and fly to Holland, and spend some time for diversion and improvements. The next thing we hear of him is, that he comes to England, where, for his improvement in writing, true English, and arithmetic, he serves a brewer, in the quality of clerk to the brewhouse, for some time; thence, creeps into some acquaintance with the Duke of Lauderdale's servants, and, at last, by their kind character, into the Duke's own acquaintance, who (being himself a very learned courtly scholar), finding him to be a sharp philosopher and quick disputant, continues and employs him in some service, particularly being then designed to destroy the liberty of the subject, and put the Government to absolute monarchy; employs him, perhaps concurs with him, to write a book, by way of problem and thesis, to dispute this point in several particulars, such as that it was lawful for the King of England, and his right, to levy taxes from his subjects without the consent of Parliament, and so to make war and peace at his pleasure, and others of this kind; and, for this end, he goes to Holland to print the book, and bring and disperse copies of it in England. With all, he was the fitter for this service that he had nothing to lose, and purchased great friendship and applause at Court, for which he was often in hazard, and forced to walk by moonlight, but the Court generally sheltered him; yet so as it was found convenient to come into Ireland, with assurance of friendship from Lauderdale (especially) and others. His first appearance in Ireland was in the quality of Doctor of the Civil Law, and as a Counseller-at-Law, and so put on another gown; but his practice proved so little, that it could not maintain his gown and man with the green bag; wherefore, he gets friends to move for him that he be entertained as agent for the Scottish nobility and gentry of Ireland, at the Court of England, and this has but little better success; only this, and his reputed learning, especially of the language of Whitehall, promoted him to a great deal of respect with the gentry, insomuch as he assumes the confidence to court Sir Hans Hamilton's only daughter, and with his countenance and allowance for a time, and great acceptance with his daughter and his lady all along. Sir Hans, after some time's acquaintance with him, and hearing reports of him which were unpleasant (such as we have mentioned, and perhaps worse), endeavoured to resist and suppress this   *   but too late; and, importunately, he is drawn and forced to it by his lady and daughters' wishes for it. He, for this, having obtained the honor of knighthood, and a great show of interest at Whitehall, after some fierce resistance, obtains the lady, to the great grief of all her friends, except her mother. And now he dwells with his lady, and has obtained, in one, what he sought for in many years and ways, viz.,— riches, and honour, and a fine lady; yet Sir Hans is shy and unfriendly towards him, and their carriage to one another very variable and unstable. Shortly after, Sir Hans's lady sickened, languished, and died; and, not long after, the young lady died also, leaving one son behind her, so that now Sir Robert must   *   and Sir Hans scrue him to his mind; and Sir Hans must make use of him as his occasions require, yet both doubtful of the issue. And what followed of him the subsequent discourse will give account of, as his life and manner of acting is now no secret. Only (1) it may be well be say'd of him, that he is consonant with himself—for he took early up with arbitrary government, and sticks well by it; he professed the lawfulness of   *

    *   in a single life, and did accordingly; he professed he should never marry a   *   with it; he resolved to marry his son at thirteen years of age, and did it; he declared (and sent the message by his cousin and counsel, Hans Trail,) that he would make no agreement with the friends of the family, but what law would conclude and necessitate him to, and has done it. (2) Whether he hath been more wise or fortunate, and what shall be the end of his course, I can but conjecure,—but time will tell.

CHAP. IX.

OF THE AGREEMENTS AND DISAGREEMENTS OF THE FIVE COUSINS IN SIR HANS HIS LIFETIME;
HIS DEATH AND CHARACTER.

When Sir Hans, and James of Newcastle, had settled themselves in their now   *   and titles thereunto; made their friendship with all Lady Alice, her agents, counsels, clerks, &c.; had got all the papers of the estate into their hands, and the estate into their possession,[a] and so much brass to give them confidence to avow what they had done and designed, then they call for the other three cousins to Hamilton's-Bawn, and make a great shew of kind and learned speeches,

---

[a] The following copy of a rental for the year 1681, of the estate of which Alice, Countess of Clanbrassil, died seized and possessed, which was so purchased by Sir Hans, and James of Newcastle, and according to which, a division of the estate was made between them, has been found among the family papers :—

" A Rentall for the year 1681.

DENOMINATIONS.	TENANTS' NAMES.	YEARLY RENT.		
ALDS.		£	s.	d.
Portavogy and Greenisle	David Boid	14	0	0
Ballyfringe	Robert Allan	14	14	0
Ballyhalbert	James Maxwell	16	19	0
Ballyesbrough	James Maxwell	16	15	0
Rowbane	James Maxwell	18	0	0
Ballyhalbert Mill	John Read	12	8	0
Glasseragh and St. John's Quarter	David Boid	22	14	0
Granshogh	Mrs. Trail	7	4	0
Rowreagh and Ballyfister	James Sloan	12	0	0
Ballygarvan	Three hundred acres—James Sloan	5	0	0
	Sixty acres—Edwd. Baily	0	1	0
Roddins, Dunover, &c.	James Moore	11	6	0
Ballyhamlin Half	John Boid	6	0	0
Inishargie	John Baily, Esq.	10	0	0
Ballyorgin	John Baily, Esq.	12	0	0
Kircubbin and Mill	John Baily, Esq.	6	0	0
Ballylimpt	Hugh Montgomery, Esq.	25	0	0
Ballymagowne	Hugh Montgomery, Esq.	18	0	0
Ballyobikin	Hugh Wallace	10	0	0
Ballyatwood	Hugh Hamill, Esq.	5	4	0
White Church	John Blackwood	8	0	0
Ballyfairis	James Moore	20	0	0
Ganway	Hugh Hamilton	24	0	0
Fisher Quarter	Wm. Hamilton, Esq.	0	0	6
Ballygraffin	Wm. Hamilton, Esq.	13	0	0

DENOMINATIONS.	TENANTS' NAMES.	YEARLY RENT.		
BALLYWALTER TOWN.		£	s.	d.
Water Mill and Wind Mill. The Eight Acre Park. Three Tenements, &c. Ten Acres of land.	James Cringle	20	12	0
	Wm. Stewart	4	0	0
	Wm. Stewart	2	4	0
	Wm. Stewart	2	0	0
	Widow Duggan	0	6	9
	Robert Simpson	1	16	4
	George Byers	0	5	6
	Wm. M'Ciurgh, & Alex. M'Robins, Exis.	1	2	4
	Hugh Montgomery, Esq	1	9	10
	Eneas M'Mullan	1	7	4
	John Johnston	0	11	2
	James Smith	0	10	2
	Widow Browne	0	8	2
	Widow Gregg	0	1	0
	Mr. Beatty's Exrs.	1	10	0
	John Gay	1	1	2
	Widow Scott	4	13	0
	Wm. Byers	0	1	0
	James Hamilton	2	6	6
	John Patterson	2	2	0
	Widow Shearer	0	16	0
	Joseph M'Kittick	5	1	10
	James Mitchell	8	8	0
	Margaret Scott	1	2	0
	Wm. M'Morlan	1	12	0
	Robert Long	2	1	0
	Patrick Orr	2	9	6
	Richard Lockart	0	11	2
	Robt. Campbell	2	5	4
	Robert Warnock	0	5	5
	John M'Narry	0	6	6
	Hugh Hamilton	0	5	0
	James Luthersdale	1	11	10
	Archd. Moore	2	13	10
	James Cringle	6	9	0
	Widow Moore	2	14	8
	Pat. Vance	1	4	0
	John Warnock	2	2	4
	James Aniston	0	8	2
	John Delop	0	18	0

shewing that since their last meeting, they had purchased Cornet Moore's, and my Lord Bargany's titles, by the advice of their lawyers, who assured them that Earl James his will, if it were proven,

DENOMINATIONS.	TENANTS' NAMES.	YEARLY RENT.
BALLYWALTER TOWN, (continued).	Widow Lead -	£0 6 6
	Widow Warnock -	1 4 0
	Thomas M'Cullan -	2 3 4
	Mathew M'Crea -	0 18 0
	Widow Byers -	1 12 8
	Widow Gibson -	2 12 9
	Gilbert Simpson -	1 5 8
	Widow White, during her life, nil.	
	Mr. Archd. Hamilton	2 18 4
	Hugh Hamill, Esq.	10 2 3
	The Rectorial Tithes undisposed of to any, and valued at -	4 14 10

Memorandum, that there is £10 16 8 of the foregoing rents of the manor of Ballywalter, to be held in common between Sir Hans Hamilton and James Hamilton, Esq., their heirs and assigns, during the continuance of my Lord Primate's lease.

DENOMINATIONS.	TENANTS' NAMES.	YEARLY RENT.
HOLLYWOOD LANDS.		
Bally-Robert, - }	David Kennedy	£12 0 0
Ballydavy, &c. }		
Cregivad	David Kennedy -	7 0 0
Ballygreny	David Kennedy -	10 0 0
Dunlady	Mr. Archibald Hamilton	1 0 0
Ballymenaght	John Hamilton -	2 5 0
Carrowreagh. &c. -	Doctor Hugh Kennedy	18 0 0
Ballyknocknegowney &c.	Jas. Ross, Esq. -	22 0 0
Kileene	James Ross, Esq. -	5 0 0
Ballylisnaskeagh -	James Ross, Esq. -	15 0 0
Ballyregan	James Ross, Esq. -	27 8 0
Strantowne, &c.	Wm. Hamilton, Esq.	25 9 0
Ballymaser	Jas. Sloane -	7 10 0
Ballycloghan, &c.	Jas. Hamilton, Esq.	9 6 5
Ballyhackamore	Lient. Gawen Hamilton	5 1 0
BallymcCarret, &c.	Thos. Pottinger	20 0 0
Knock-Collumkill	William Hamilton, Esq.	14 0 0
CHURCH QR. DUNDONELL.		
	Andrew Dixon	£8 4 0
	Niuian Tate	0 5 0
	John Jackson -	0 5 0
	John Dunlap -	1 5 0
	James Lundy -	1 4 0
	Widow Browne, and John M'Neily	1 0 0
	Jane Moore -	0 12 0
	Revd. Jackson M'Gnire, and Mr. Pat. Hamilton	3 0 0
	The Water Mill of Dundonnell, and eightscore of land—William Montgomery	
Ballylisbredan, &c.	John Cumin -	2 0 0
Ballygrany -	Thos. M'Ilrath -	14 0 0
Ballyoran -	William Hamilton, Esq.	10 0 0
Ballyrussely -	Hugh Hamill. Esq.	20 0 0
The Priory House	Mr. George Wallace	5 0 0

DENOMINATIONS.	TENANTS' NAMES.	YEARLY RENT.
HOLLYWOOD TOWN.		
	William Russell -	£2 4 3
	Geo. Mally -	2 1 0
	John M'Dowell -	1 9 0
	Wm. Criswell -	2 16 4
	John Kennedy -	5 9 2
	John Gibbon -	2 8 0
	Gawen Russell -	1 9 0
	Widow Cowey -	3 10 9
	John M'Holl -	0 13 0
	James M'Murray -	0 6 6
	Widow Wardon -	2 2 10
	James Caul -	3 1 6
	James Criswill, sen. -	2 8 10
	John Correy -	0 8 2
	Widow Caul -	0 19 4
	Wm. Fullerton -	2 5 6
	Richd. Coney -	4 17 6
	Widow Lowdan -	0 19 4
	Widow Wilson -	2 1 4
	John Long -	0 6 6
	Geo. Watt, and Geo. Forrest -	2 16 0
	John Robinson -	0 13 0
	Wm. Barclay -	1 1 2
	John Gamble -	1 2 4
	Hugh M'Mullan -	0 8 2
	Samuel Wright -	0 19 4
	Wm. Cowden -	3 11 10
	John Moore -	0 16 4
	Alex Read -	1 14 4
	Widow Cooper -	0 9 8
	Widow Hathhorne, and Wm. Watt. -	1 18 10
	John Robb -	1 13 9
	Widow Dunison -	1 1 8
	Hugh Criswill -	0 19 2
	Widow Wallace -	0 4 1
	James Peticrue -	1 12 8
	James Sim -	1 10 0
	James Chambers -	2 13 0
	John M'Laughlin -	1 3 11
	Archd. Lenox -	1 16 7
	Josias Milton -	0 19 2
	Widow Laughlin -	1 9 8
	John Watt -	19 3 8
	The Tythes, Rectorial and Vicarial, set for per annum. -	11 0 0
	Concealment of lands, valued at -	2 0 0

Memorandum.—That the town of Hollywood is to pay £8 per annum to the College of Dublin, for ever.

DENOMINATIONS.	TENANTS' NAMES.	YEARLY RENT.
Ringhaddy, &c. -	-	56 4 0
Ringdufferin -	Alexr. Baily -	14 0 0
Bredagh, &c. -	Mr. St. John Webb -	5 14 0
Gallwally -	William Beers -	15 0 0

could bring no more to them than Lady Ann her jointure, or some life-rents and freeholds that were not mentioned in the common recovery which Earl Henry made, and whereon a fine was levied;

DENOMINATIONS.	TENANTS' NAMES.	YEARLY RENT.
Tollyard -	Gawen Hamilton -	£8 0 0
Ballyknockan -	Hugh Savage -	22 0 0
Creviheavarick, &c.	John Baily, Esq. -	52 0 0
Ballynegarrick -	Thomas Bradly -	15 0 0
Lisleene -	Wm. Hamilton, Esq.	3 10 0
Tannaghmore -	Gawen Hamilton -	8 0 0
BANGOR LANDS.		
Portavo, &c. -	James Ross, Esq. -	30 0 0
Ballow, *juxta mare*, &c.	James Ross -	15 0 0
Ballymenatragh -	John Hamilton -	27 3 8
Ballymaconnell, &c.	John Swadlin -	2 4 0
Ballymacormick, &c.	John Blackwood -	14 10 0
Ballyleedy -	John Blackwood -	28 0 0
Granshough, &c. -	Mr. Robert Maxwell	41 0 0
Ballyrea -	120 acres—Hugh White	15 10 0
Conlige, half, &c. -	Robert Moore -	9 15 0
Ballow, part, &c. -	William Hogg -	15 0 0
Ballow *juxta* Bangor	Robert M'Creery -	1 0 0
Ballynegee -	60 acres, &c.—Alice M'Mehan	4 14 0
Ballygilbort, &c. -	James Hamilton, Esq.	20 0 0
Ballyvernon, &c. -	Alexr. Hamilton -	16 0 0
Part Killare, &c. -	Wm. Crafford -	17 3 8
Ballyornon, &c. -	Alexr. Hamilton, or Wm. Crafford -	10 16 8
Part Killare, &c, -	John Stevenson -	10 10 0
Ballyskelly -	William Hogg }	16 14 0
Ballygrott -	John Stevenson -	
Ballysallogh, *major* -	Mr. Ramsey's Heirs }	22 10 0
Bryan's Hill, &c, -	Mr. Ramsey's Heirs }	
Part Killare -	Mr. Archd, Hamilton	10 16 8
Twelve acres of Bryan's Burne -	John Stevenson -	2 8 0
BANGOR TOWN.	Patrick M'Mechan -	0 16 0
	Andrew M'Caldon -	0 9 3
	James Blackwood -	0 9 0
	Widow M'Cally -	0 6 9
	Alexr. Parker -	0 9 0
	Finlay Martin -	3 13 0
	Finlay Martin's Widow	0 7 6
	James M'Mechan -	0 10 9
	James M'Mechan -	0 6 9
	Widow Nelson -	0 9 0
	George Kennedy -	0 15 11
	Ninian M'Kelvy -	0 9 0
	James Biglam -	0 18 6
	James Biglam -	1 1 9
	James Biglam -	0 6 9
	James Biglam -	0 8 6
	James Biglam -	0 10 2
	John Stevenson -	1 4 2
	Thos. M'Kelvey -	2 0 10
	Jno. Swaline's Exrs. -	1 10 9
	Wm. Gastle -	0 13 6
	Alex. Ritchy -	0 6 9
	John M'Cardy -	0 18 0

DENOMINATIONS.	TENANTS' NAMES	YEARLY RENT.
BANGOR TOWN, (continued).	Thos. M'Ferran -	£0 9 0
	James Kelly -	0 9 0
	Robert Thompson -	0 13 11
	Jno. M'Mechan, shoemaker	0 13 6
	Widow Lenox -	0 6 0
	John Shaw -	0 9 9
	John Mahaule & mother	1 2 6
	Robert Loggan -	0 6 9
	John Loggan -	0 15 10
	Robert Kindsay -	0 9 0
	Alex. M'Amt -	0 6 9
	Alex Wily -	5 8 0
	Thos. M'Carly -	0 16 6
	James M'Carly -	0 6 9
	Widow Whitla -	1 9 6
	Andrew M'Ferran -	0 10 6
	Ja. Lindsay -	0 6 9
	Robert Sterlin -	0 6 9
	Widow M'Mechan -	1 3 0
	James M'Nily -	0 6 9
	Widow Ritchy -	0 6 9
	Hugh Nicholson -	1 3 0
	William M'll. -	0 13 6
	John Campbell -	0 8 7½
	William Simpson -	0 12 4
	Patrick Hannah -	2 6 9
	Wm. M'Cormick -	1 4 0
	Patrick Cleland -	25 8 0
	William M'Mechan -	3 18 6
	Robert Hamilton -	3 11 0
	Pat M'Dowell -	0 10 1
	Hugh Hamilton -	1 11 1
	Ja. Whitla -	1 9 11
	Widow Cleland -	2 19 0
	Ja. Blackwood -	3 19 4
	Caghtry M'Connell -	0 18 6
	Robert Hamilton, tailor	0 14 3
	John Watson -	0 13 6
	James M'Dowell -	0 6 9
	John Bleakly, senior -	1 5 3
	Wm. Wallace -	1 11 5
	Wm. Gibson -	0 9 6
	James Carmuheall -	0 6 9
	Alex. M'Cattry -	0 13 6
	John Blackwood -	7 3 0
	John Blackwood -	3 1 0
	James Anderson's widow	0 14 3
	Andrew Finlay -	0 6 9
	John Watson -	1 0 3
	James Anderson -	0 6 9
	James Black -	0 6 9
	James Blakely -	0 16 4
	Robert Finlay -	0 16 1½
	Archd. M'Gibbon -	0 7 10½
	John Henderson -	0 12 10
	John Davison -	0 18 6
	Wm. Young -	0 17 0
	John Smith -	1 1 0

that Cornet Moore being resolved to sell his title, and some others resolved and ready to buy it,

DENOMINATIONS.	TENANTS' NAMES.	YEARLY RENT.
BANGOR TOWN, (continued.)	John Patterson -	0 13 6
	Wm. Hollyday -	1 11 10
	Wm. Hollyday, assignee to John Syers -	0 1 0
	Wm. Hollyday, assignee to John Syers -	0 10 0
	Wm. Hamilton -	0 2 9
	Edmond Kelly, or Robt. M'Crery -	1 4 6
	John Luke, Exr. -	6 2 0
	James Aule -	0 6 9
	John Blakely, jun. -	0 6 9
	Andrew Clarke -	5 3 0
	Widow M'Kelvy -	0 13 6
	Alex. Maxwell -	0 13 6
	Widow Purdy -	1 3 0
	Hugh Rea -	2 2 0
	Hugh Moore -	4 6 0
	Jas. Hamilton, John Leslie's Exr. -	0 19 10
	David Montgomery -	2 0 5
	Widow Greer -	0 8 5
	John Cleland, or John Anderson -	3 16 10
	Widow Hamilton -	0 14 4
	John Henderson. John Gibbon's Assign	0 12 6
	Nathaniel Forsythe -	0 14 0
	Mr. Archibald Hamilton	1 0 0
	Thos. Bradly -	1 15 0
	Thos. Bradley, or John Lindsay -	0 17 6
	Andrew Anderson -	1 0 3
	John M'Meehan -	2 4 10
	John M'Meehan -	0 4 6
	John Harris -	1 18 6
	John Petticrew -	0 6 9
	Mr. James Hamilton	0 6 9
	Mr. James Hamilton	0 13 6
	James Dunlap -	2 10 6
	John Dunlap -	0 6 9
	Thos. Orr -	1 6 6
	Wm. Martin -	0 13 6
	Wm. M'Combe -	0 13 6
	John Gilmore -	0 6 9
	Valentine Watson -	0 4 6
	Alexander Dobby -	0 4 6
	John Gilpatrick -	0 4 6
	John Watson -	0 13 6
	James Kennedy -	2 4 6
	Robert Anderson -	0 6 9
	John Gowdy, schoolmaster —	
	Hugh Gervin -	1 8 6
	John M'Kee -	0 6 9
	Thos. Ferguson, Assignee to John Malley -	0 8 6
	Robert Smith -	0 5 0
	Widow Laggan -	0 13 4
	Hugh Wilson -	0 13 6
	Wm. Brown -	1 5 0
	Randulph Price, Esq. -	60 0 0
Drumbo -	James Maxwell -	20 0 0

DENOMINATIONS.	TENANTS' NAMES.	YEARLY RENT.
Drumneligg -	Alexander Hutchison	2 0 0
Tollynastikinagh -	William Gowdy -	28 0 0
Bressagh -	Gawen Hamilton -	30 5 0
Drumgirvin -	Hugh Montgomery, Esq.	8 10 0
Cahard -	William Shaw, Esq. -	5 10 0
Carrowderne -	William Shaw, Esq. -	4 0 0
Ballymt -Raney -	William Shaw, Esq. -	5 0 0
Ballykeele -	Mr. Archd. Hamilton	7 10 0
Carrickuanan -	James Moore -	12 0 0
Raverra -	Wm. Hamilton, Esq.	10 0 0
Tullyhubbert, &c. -	James Moore, -	25 0 0
Ballykeele ;	James Ross, Esq. -	18 0 0
Carricknesure -	Wm. Hamilton, Esq.	3 10 0
Ballynichole, &c. -	Wm. Hamilton, Esq.	10 0 0
Maghericouse -	Wm. Hamilton, Esq.	23 4 0
Ballygowan -	James Moore	10 0 0
Ballyknockan Mill -	Wm Hamilton, Esq.	10 0 0
Munlagh, &c. -	Thos. Hamington -	18 10 0
Drumhirke -	Robert Hamilton -	32 0 0
Cattoggs -	Robert Ross -	40 0 0
Collintragh Mill -	Robert Ross -	14 4 0
Collintragh -	George Browne -	9 10 0
Ballydolloghan -	Wm. Hamilton, Esq.	13 10 0
Grausshogh -	Mr. Patrick Hamilton	9 4 0
MANOR OF BALLYDRINE.		
Tollenekill -	Hugh Ferguson -	21 0 0
Castleaspick -	Robert Cunningham -	2 0 0
Ballydrine -	The several Tenements	29 0 0
Ringneale -	Wi liam Hogg -	39 0 0
Lisbane -	John Syars -	0 12 0
M'Bride's Quarter -	Matthew Marshall -	12 0 0
	John Matthew Marshall	11 0 0
	John Fra. Hewart -	9 0 0
Ballyglighorn, &c. -	James Daziell -	44 0 0
Island M'Kee -	John Blackwood -	4 0 0
ARDS.		
Tythes in the Ards, not included in the foregoing rent-roll, but follow:—		
Portavogie -	David Boyd -	4 0 0
Ballyhalbert -	James Maxwell -	6 0 0
Ballyesbrough -	James Maxwell -	6 0 0
Glasteragh -	David Boyd -	3 6 8
Ballymagowne -	Hugh Montgomery, Esq.	2 10 0
Ballyobikin -	Hugh Wallace -	3 10 0
Grange-Witter -	George Ross -	15 0 0
	Total, - -	£2,156 2 8

" The foregoing rent-roll is a true account of the value of the estate whereof Alice, late Countess of Clanbrassill, died seized and possessed of, or pretended title unto, in the County of Down, from whom Sir Hans Hamilton, deceased, and the defendant, James Hamilton, derived their title, and according to which a division of the said estate was made between the said Sir Hans and James Hamilton, and so given in charge of them to their receiver, Hugh Hamil, Esq., deceased, to receive the rents of the said estate for their use, in the year 1681, amounting in all to the sum of £2,156 2s. 8d., besides the Rectorial Tythes of Rathmullan, which are not included in the foregoing rent-roll, the value whereof I know not. "THOMAS MEAGHER."

they found it convenient to make a bargain with him for themselves, it being a title wholly different and opposite to that of theirs by the will, and which, if it were in other men's hands, they might be troublesome and chargeable to us to debate with them, but that they were willing to give us, without law or any charges, yea, make their purchaser's title a guard and defence to the other, that they might have thereby £30 or £40 yearly, of the life-rents during Lady Ann her life; that, by her consent, the jointure lands might be divided, and they might get some possessions from her which might be much improved, by giving long leases, &c. The other three, finding the air of this conversation much altered from what it ought and wont to be, and having no advice from lawyers in this case, and that they had neither friends, means, nor skill in law, to oppose or contend with the other two ; considering what vast expence they had laid out in the former suit under their management, endeavoured with great calmness to plead as they could, that this seemed not fair dealing; was not according to former communings; would be ill spoken of in the world; would still be a matter of resentment to their families; pressed they might be included in the bargain; told them they had or could got money to defray their charges of what was agreed for ; would be content to give a liberal gratification to Sir Hans for the pains he had been at about it ; made very kind offers upon this account ; that, for credit sake to all, and for peace and love among their successors, they might proceed as they had begun, &c. It was replied, that the bargain was not so great as was judged, considering the many debts now due out of it; that he judged he should be a greater gainer by what was proposed ; but he and his cousin James had engaged themselves to each other, and their fortunes for payment of what was engaged; and that the counting and discounting with so many shares and partners, would be but troublesome and unprofitable ; and so renewed their purpose of giving them all that the will at best could bear, and settle the same in articles, and give bonds for performance. It was further offered and urged by the three friends, that they would agree that some other friends of the family might be consulted, and that by their advice they would consent that so much might be taken from the four as might enable Sir Hans (with his own estate) to take and maintain the honor of the family, (which fell with Earl Henry) provided it might be kept in the family, and be   *   *   on Earl James his will, and the other surreptitious and base title rejected and avoided; but all would not prevail, for Sir Hans told the three plainly, that if they now refused what was offered, they should have nothing by consent, and in these words:—"You have Hobson's choice." The three then seemed to submit, but desired that some other kinsmen, then in the house, might be admitted to hear and help in the discourse, but this could not be admitted; and, instead thereof, the five came out of the room where the former discourse was had, and Sir Hans told them what he had offered, but asked no advice or opinion about it, nor gave any further occasion of discourse or debate about it, but proposed that James of Newcastle, and David Kennedy, should draw the articles, at least minute the heads communed on, that they might be ready for being perfected at the next meeting, which was agreed on to be within three days thereafter.

Thus they then parted, and afterward met by appointment, but no articles nor minute were drawn ; James say'd he could not undertake it, and David Kennedy could not take upon him to do it without his assistance ; but, on both sides, there was a willing delay, both hoping for better terms, and it was agreed they should meet at the next General Assizes, to be held in the County of Down, at the beginning of it, that they might be done by some able counsel at law, and so perfected. It was also then proposed, that we should take account of my cousin, James of Newcastle, his disbursements and receipts relating to the law-suit.

The three postponed cousins went off with a great deal of grumbling and grief that they should be so served, and yet could not find a remedy. The friends (not related in the suit) were offended, for that they were not called to the conference, and blamed the three for their too easy *
* * The three apologized from Sir Hans, and James of Newcastle, their unwillingness, &c., but all were full of trouble, yet found no opportunity for resentment, yea, Sir Robert Hamilton, and Francis Hamilton, their two ladies, and others, appeared very much troubled, yea displeased with the course that Sir Hans, and James of Newcastle, had taken, and were very free in private discourses to declare their thoughts to that purpose. Even Sir Hans, and James of Newcastle, had much ado to keep countenance in this conversation; but the design was formerly laid, and they were now resolved to stick by and carry on the confederacy of Bangor, and it was a fat bit they carved to themselves,—the others paid for the roast. In the first return, at the Assizes of Down, they came particularly as agreed on; but two or three days must pass or Sir Hans, and James of Newcastle, can be got at leisure. At last they meet in haste, and a counsel is brought and commended by the two, as a very able drawer of such writings, one Swift, artist enough, but then known and now famous for making back doors and Welshmen's hosen. Every one gave him a large fee in view, and by consent (within five pence of £5 in all), but what was say'd, or done, or say'd in secret, I pretend not to know. Sir Hans made the narrative, and such as the other four could not con'radict; but there was no time to chat out, for Sir Hans was in great haste, and the counsel had but little time. An hour was also appointed for reading his draught; it was particularly kept; the counsel and paper came ; it was read, but there was no time for considering, amending, or transcribing ; the paper is committed to Pat. Hamilton, (one of the three cousins); and the friends are to meet in some time and place when Sir Hans, and James of Newcastle, should find leisure and conveniency—but no word is here of accounts. A considerable time now goes over without any discourse or advertisement for a meeting and concluding of what was unfinished, yet not without thoughts and designs on either party. At last it falls out, that Sir Hans, James of Newcastle, John Baily, and Pat. Hamilton, are in Dublin. Some discourse falls in betwixt Pat. and the two, about the articles. He is shy and doubtful of doing anything separately from the other two concerned. He consults John Baily, his old friend,

2 D

and intended father-in-law. The captain protests the greatest kindness and concern for him immaginable, for that he had expelled his then only daughter, because she refused to marry Pat. at his advice and earnest desire, and that he had the same kindness for him as if he had married her, seeing that it was both their desires; and, in the next place, advises him to agree with the two on whatsoever terms he could now reach; that certainly it would be a falling market with him and the other two; for that, to his certain knowledge, Sir Hans and James were so invested in titles, and furnished with papers and friends (and what not), that it was in their option whether they should give them sixpence or not. Pat., believing all this to be real and certain, intreats him to set the business on foot with Sir Hans and James, that he might be settled to the best advantage. John Baily sets forward about it (being   *   on both sides), and obtains articles something like, yet far different from, what were at first proposed, and to boot (as a special favour for breaking the ice), and under great privacy and agreement, a rent-charge (with a false bottom) for £50 a-year, during Ann Clanbrassill's life, for or in lieu of the life-rents, and that he abate for ever ten pounds a-year of his share after my Lady's death; and, withall, that he actually renounce all title to the estate purchased from Henry Moore, which he did.

About this time came Mr. William Hamilton, brother to James of Neilsbrook, into the country, and designed to assist his brother for investing of a title made to that family by my Lord Claneboy in a Deed of Settlement, whereof he was informed, by a very faithful witness, that it was perfected by him, and whereby the estate was settled on Halcraig's family, failing heirs of his own body— and that there was such a deed is more than probable. On the account of this deed, and what might be found out about it, the aforesaid James hesitated to proceed with the other four in the proof of the will, and, by consent, gave in a several answer to the Lady's bill from the other four. Being in the country, he courteously visited all his relations, and kindly offered his opinion to some of them that were injured for redress, yet modestly, because he found them leaning to Sir Hans, and James of Newcastle, their conduct and integrity, they being yet ignorant of what politicks the one had learned in the Green Chamber (about the settlement of the '49 arrears), and Court of Claims, and the other had practiced with his cousin, K   Usher, of Balsoon—his intrigues with his cousin, Ann Trail, being not yet discovered, as afterwards they appeared. After some time spent, wherein he could make no progress in his design (all the papers of the estate being in such hands, whose interest forbid them to make such discovery, or were perverted by them), he returned full of grief that he could neither be usefull to his brother and family, nor as yet make his friends sensible of the calamitys they were bringing upon themselves, through the exuberant confidence they put upon Sir Hans, and James of Newcastle—but, soon after, they were sufficiently convinced of and penitent for, their error.

CHAP. X.

OF WHAT ENSUED TILL SIR HANS'S DEATH.

Matters being so far settled for the time, Sir Hans, and James of Newcastle, improve and divide their new purchase, according to the agreement of Bangor, and are, in that estate, the sole land-lords, to the value of £1,800 per annum—(generally) of chief-rents—and have many merry meetings about it. James of Neilsbrook lyes by in discontent with the articles; Archibald and Pat. are promised an account of the disbursements of the life-rents, and that they shall be presently divided, and every one possessed of their share; and so appointments are made from time to time, but still in the County of Down, where the other two have their affairs carrying on, and sometimes to assize time. It's say'd they will settle by advice; but nothing is done but friendly and very chargeable converse, with apologies, new appointments, and fresh promises; for the agreement of Bangor must be now effectually prosecuted, but very prudently, and in these following steps:—1st. An agreement is made with Sir Robert Maxwell for the lease of the Seven Towns,* and

---

* The Seven Towns here mentioned included the entire Manor of Ballydrine, or Ardmillan, the ancient inheritance of the Bishops of Down. By an inquisition taken at Down-patrick, on the 13th of October, 1623, it was, *inter alia,* found—

"That Robert Heamstow, late Lord Bishop of Downe and Conor, was seized of his demesne as of fee, in the right of his Bishoprick of Down, of and in all that teritorie. precinct, scope, or extent of land, comonlie called the Lord-ship or Manor of Ballindrine, *alias* Island Maghee, and of and in the townes and lands following—viz., Ballecaslaneu-picke, Balleliddell, *alias* Balleglegory, Ballellisbane, Balle-martin, *alias* Ballemartinagh, Ballegavegan, and Ballekene-neile, situate, lying, and being in the Upper Clandeboys, in the County of Downe, with all the rights, members and appur-tenances to the same belonging or appertaining: together with the Islands called the Castle Island, Island Reagh, Is-land Rawlie, Island Magneish, in the Countie of Downe, aforesaid; and all and singular, the manors, castles, &c., tithes of corn. &c., as well great as small; and also all offerings, obventions, &c., and the rents and services, emoluments and hereditaments whatsoever, as well spirituall as temporal, to the said Island Maghee, or to any of the premises before recited, or to any part or parcell thereof of any waies belong-ing, apertaining, incident, or apendant, or which had been at any time theretofore accepted, reputed, or knowne, held, occupied, used, or enjoied, as part, member, or parcell of the said Island Maghee, or of any of the premises, or of any part or parcell thereof, being parcell of the lands and possessions belonging to the said Bishop of Downe and Conor: And it was thereby further found, that the afore-said Robert, Bishop of Downe and Conor, being so seized, and in actual possession of all and singular the premises, and every part and parcell thereof, of such an estate as aforesaid, by his deed, indented, duelie perfected, and exe-cuted, by liverie and seizin, and to the jury then shewn in evidence, bearing date the 9th day of Juiy, 1606, for and in consideration of the sume of £100 sterling, in hand paid to him, the said Lord Bishop, before the ensealing tiereof, by Sir Henrie Peirse and Francis Annesley, granted to them by the name of Henrie Peirse and Francis Annesley, of Dublin, gent, all and singular the premises: TO HOLD, with the apurtenances, unto the said Sir Henry Peirse and Francis Annesley, their heirs and assigns, for ever: YIELD-ING AND PAYING yearly for the same, unto the said Robert, Lord Bishop of Downe and Conor, and to his successors, Bishops of Downe, aforesaid, the sum of £6 16s 4d ster-ling, at the feast of St. Michael the Archangel, or within six weekes after the said feast, yearlie: By virtue whereof, the said Sir Henrie Peirse and Sir Francis Annesley were of the said premises seized in their demesne, as of fee: And further found, that the said premises were holden of the King, *in socage in capite,* but by what rent they knew not: And it was thereby further found, that the said Sir Henrie Peirse and Francis Annesley, being by virtue of the said Indenture seized jointly to them and their heirs, John Christian, Archdeacon of the Cathedrall Church of Down, Robert Maxwell, Archdeacon of Conor, and the Clergie of both the [   ], by Deed, sealed with

his obligation and his Lady's to deliver up the Castle of Killileagh and the jointure (after the Lady's death) to Sir Hans and James, and, in the meantime, they get the Library (then at Killileagh) into their possession ; but the Lady is kept ignorant of all till she must be invited to subscribe to the papers, which were many, tedious, and well contrived, and this contrivance to boot, that they are all laid open upon a large table. She, being sensible of the slight already done her, and jealous she might be outwitted by them if she should read them, chooses (which they expected, and were well prepared for,) to decline the reading of them, and to sign them upon their word of honor that there was nothing in them tending in any manner of way to the prejudice of the other three cousins, and their title by her Lord's will. Captain John Baily, being one of the party, is chosen to vouch this, and does it, liberally and confidently, and all the parties say it is so ;

---

their seales, perfected unto Hugh Culme and Anthony Peirse a lease of all the lands and premises before mentioned (the spiritual jurisdiction only reserved to the said Bishop and his successors, of the said Island Maghee, or of any of the premisses before recited) : To Hold to the said Hugh Culme and Anthony Peirse, their executors, administrators, and assigns, for and during the full term and tyme of three score years, immediately ensuing the date of said demise : Yielding and Paying therefore, unto the said Robert, then Lord Bishop of Downe and Conor. and his successors, Bishops of Downe, the yearlie rent of £30 sterling. as therein mentioned : By virtue and form of which Indenture the said Hugh Culme and Anthony Peirse being possessed of all and singular the premises, with their appurtenances. Sir Henrie Peirse, Bart., the said Hugh Culme, and Anthony Peirse, at his request, by Indenture, bearing date the 30th day of December. A.D. 1622, did give, grant, assign, set over, and confirme unto William Hamilton, of Ballymeaghan, in the County of Down, Esq., and John Keneday, of the City of Dublin, Esq., all and singular the premises and every part and parcel thereof, with the appurtenances : To Hold unto the said William Hamilton and John Keneday, their and every of their executors, administrators, and assigns, for and during all the residue of the term of three score years then to come and unexpired, upon confidence and trust to the use and behoof of the said Viscount Clnneboy, by virtue of which Deed they the said William Hamilton and John Keneday were then possessed of all and singular the premises, with the appurtenances accordinglie."

Viscount Clandeboye, being so possessed of this manor, had it surveyed with the rest of his estates; and the townlands and islands of which it consisted, are accordingly included in the Book of Survey so made of them in 1625-6, and continued to be held with the rest of his estates by his son, and grandson, James, and Henry, the first and second Earls of Clanbrassil, and by Countess Alice, the widow of the latter, till her death, as appears by a rent-roll of the estate for 1681, proved by Thomas Meagher (which will be found at p. 108, ante), when a division of the estate was made between Sir Hans Hamilton

and James Hamilton of Newcastle, as the purchasers of Countess Alice's title to it, and then given in charge by them to Hugh Hamill, as their receiver. It appears, however, from a lengthened correspondence on the subject of this and the other estates of Earl James, (which will be referred to in a subsequent note,) that their receiver was not allowed to take the rents uninterruptedly, and that the other claimants of Earl James's estate, under his will, interfered with the tenants of those seven towns, and otherwise asserted their claims to them until the year 1698, when it would appear from one of the letters, dated 4th April, in that year, that some articles were entered into relating to the Seven Towns ; but, as they have not been found among the family papers, the Editor has no means of giving the contents of them, nor of ascertaining in what way the lands were disposed of from that time, until towards the end of the last century, when they appear to have been in possession of the Knox family, as lessees of the Bishop of Down ; and it further appears, that by lease, or renewal of lease, dated 2d May, 1802, the then Bishop of Down demised to Henry Waring Knox, of Waringsford, in the County of Down, Esq., "All that and those the manor, towns, and lands of Ardmillin,—that was to say, the towns and lands of Island Mahie, Ballycaslannaspeck, Ballyliddle, alias Ballygligory, Ballindoun, Ballynanglase, alias Ringneel, Ballylisbane, Ballymartin, alias Ballymartanagh, Ballyhenlinchelly, Ballyavaghan, alias Ballyeastanagh, Ballytulormighanaghan, Island Rowley, and Island Magenis, containing 2,184 acres, be the same more or less, Cunningham measure, together with the Rectorial Tithes of said manor ; also all courts leet, courts baron, customs of fairs and markets, situate, lying, and being in the County of Down, with all and singular the rights, members, and appurtenances unto the said premises belonging or in anywise appertaining : Excepting and always reserving out of said demise unto the said Lord Bishop and his successors, Bishops of Down

whereupon she signs and seals to all the papers.—2. It was, in pursuance of this, contrived, that there should be a settlement of the estate of this jointure by the co-heirs-at-law, Sir Robert Maxwell, his Lady, and the five cousins, upon Robert Finlay (servant to Sir Hans), and Robert M'Creery (servant to James of Newcastle), on trust for Sir Hans, and James of Newcastle, partly for themselves, partly in trust, and for the performance of articles. This is framed and appointed by the general meeting of all, at the assizes time, to be finished; but it fell out, that Sir Hans was then sick and could not attend it, and it could not be managed without him; whereby, as the meeting was useless, so counsel was taken about it by the three. The snare was discovered, and this matter scoffed at, so as it died abortive.—3. It was proposed as reasonable, and the good Lady to promote it, that Gil. How[b] (the only surviving witness who testified of my Lord's being *compos mentis*), should be gratified for his fidelity to us; to this all agreed, and accordingly perfected a

---

and Connor, all mines, minerals, limestone, coals, and all royalties of what nature or kind soever, with full and free liberty for his and their servants and followers to dig, search for, and carry away all such royalties, &c., and also free liberty for them to fish, fowl, and hunt upon said premises: Excepting also out of that demise 40 acres of ground near the wall of the church (plantation measure) for the use of the Vicar and his successors, for which the said Vicar should pay half his proportion of the annual renewal fine paid to the Bishop by the said H. W. Knox: To hold from 1st of May, then inst., for, and during, and until the full end and term of twenty-one years, at the yearly rent of £140. This Henry Waring Knox became greatly embarrassed in his circumstances, and his estates were for many years in the hands of receivers, under the Court of Equity Exchequer in Ireland, to whom the foregoing lease was regularly renewed; but all his interest in the Ardmillan estate was eventually sold under a Decree of that Court, made in a cause of *Scott v. Knox*, and Samuel Murland, Esq., of Castlewellan, became the purchaser of it.

The following extract, from *Erck's Ecclesiastical Annals of Down Diocese*, explains (what is obscure in the inquisition of 1623, above quoted) how a lease for years of Island Maghee was substituted for the grant in fee farm which had been previously made by the Bishop :—

"1604. ISLAND MAGHEE.—Bishop Humston, about this time, leased to fee farm, at a rent of £6 13s 4d, this island, being parcel of the bishoprick : the annual value of which was found, by a visitation made twenty years after, to be £200. The Archbishops of Canterbury and Armagh conceived, in consequence of a reference from His Majesty, that a surrender should be made of the deed of fee farm, and a lease of forty years given at a reserved rent of £30 per annum. (Ware, *in part*, p. 207.)"—*Erck*, 28.

Tullynakill is the denomination of the parish within which the Seven Towns are situate, and the Primate is the

reputed patron.—*Erck*, 29. The parish itself is called "*Ballindrean*, alias *Magheoe*, in the Ul. Vis. (p. 251) ; and the manor, which extends over the parish, is called "*Ballydreene*, alias *Island-Maghie*," in the Ul. Inq. (No. 6, Jac. 1. Down).—*Reeves*, 168.

[b] This Gilbert How was one of the five witnesses to the will of James, first Earl of Clanbrassill, which will be found at p. 85, *ante*; and, on reference to p. 93, *ante*, it appears by the MS. that great pains and charges were undergone by Countess Alice to corrupt the surviving witnesses to this "troublesome" will, and to make them swear that Earl James was not *compos mentis* when it was executed by him, but that she was unable to corrupt this witness; and as a reward for his fidelity to them, the representatives of the five uncles of Earl James, to whom his estates were devised by it, joined by his widow, gratified him with a profitable lease in reversion of some lands included in her jointure, which will be referred to in a subsequent note. Mr. Gilbert How continued for a long time in the service of the Clanbrassil family, and collected the rents of the jointure lands for Ann, Countess of Clanbrassil, as appears by entries for the receipt of them from him, signed by her, in an old memorandum-book kept by him, which is now in the possession of Lord Dufferin. It commences in May, 1657, and comes down to the year 1710; and, in addition to several memoranda of marriages, births, and deaths in his own family, contains the following entries, which are extracted from it as illustrative of the subject of these MSS. :—

"My Lord James and his brother went for England, the 21st of June, 1656."

"My Lord James Claneboy, eldest son to James, Earle of Clanbrassill, dyed the 12th of May, 1658. His father dyed the 20th of June, 1659."

"June the 19th, 1663.—My Lord Henry, Earl of Clan-

profitable lease of some lands in the jointure, to the great joy of the two, whilst the good Lady and the other three were not aware of the design of burying the will, and making the three incapable of proving the will against the two; whilst two other subscribing witnesses had sworn (upon very ponderous and ruinous considerations) that said James was not *compos mentis* at the perfecting of the will, and that, if the three should attempt to prove the will, the third witness could be proved by this grant, or lease, to be bribed.[c]—4. It is pretended and propounded as a great

---

brassill, and his brother Hans, went for England from Portoferrye, being Sunday, att 8 a clocke att night."

" Jany the 25th, 1668.—My Lady Clanbrassill was married to Sr Robert Maxwell; departed this life ye 20th of Jano, 1689; and was buried, the 5th of Febr following, at Bangor."

" My Lord Claneboye was borne the 15th April, 1670; dyed ye 13th of June following. His uncle, Mr. Hans, dyed at Monella, the 27th Septr, 1670."

" Henry, Earle of Clanbrassill, departed this life, at Dublin, the 12th of Jany, 1675-6, being on a Wednesday, at 8 a clocke att night. Alice, Countess of Clanbrassill, departed this life in Decr, '77; was buried, the 13th of Jany following, att Bangor."

" Sir Hans Hamilton died in Dublin, the 11th of Feby, 1681; was buried at Mulabrike Church, the 2d of March following."

" James Hamilton, of Tollemore, died in England, —— May, 1700."

" Patrick Hamilton died in Belfast, the 13th of August, 1700; buried the 15th, at Cumber."

" Captain Gawen Hamilton died the 27th of Octr, 1703, aged 73, or therabouts."

" James Hamilton, Esq., of Bangor, died 18th Jany, 1706."

" Mrs. Rose Fairley died the last of Jany, 1693-4, suddenly. Her husband, Mr. Willm Fairly, May the 11th, '94."

" Hans Traill died in Dublin, May 15th, 1692."

" Captain Bailey died the 11th of May, 1687, at his house in Inishargie. Mrs. Bailey died the 24th of Feby, at her house in Killyleagh, 1691-2."

" Mrs. Bruce died May the 26th, 1706."

" Madam Stevenson died the 2d of Septr, 1706, in the Gate-House."

[c] The profitable lease of lands in the jointure of Ann, Countess of Clanbrassil, here mentioned as having been perfected to Gilbert How, consisted of a lease in reversion of the greater part of the townlands of Ballytrim and Ballygoskin, in the parish of Killileagh. By an Instrument, dated 30th October, 1648, James, Earl of Clanbrassil, had demised to him, by the description of " Gilbert How, servant to the said Earl," All and whole that half of Ballygoskin, in the territorie of the Dufferin, and County of Down, which lies next to John Campbell's half, for thirty-one years, at the yearly rent of 10s. Whilst in possession of this lease, he had also obtained a similar one from the Earl of " All and whole the townland of Ballytrim, except that part thereof possessed by the Weavers," at the yearly

rent of 40s; and it appears by the first entry in this Gilbert How's memorandum-book, referred to in the preceding note, that, " in May, 1657, he came to dwell in Ballytrim." Both these leases were renewed to him on 27th October, 1683, by a memorandum of that date " between Sir Robert Maxwell, of Killileagh, Knight and Baronet, and his then lady, Ann, Countess of Clanbrassil, of the one part, and Gilbert How, of Ballytrim, Gentleman, of the other part," for the natural life of the Countess, who was then in receipt of the rents of Ballygoskin, as part of her jointure lands ; and, it was in the year 1683, and during the existence of this lease, that the lease in reversion mentioned in the text was granted. It was made at the same yearly rent as the original lease, and was for a term of 61 years, to commence and take effect immediately after the death of said Countess, and was executed by Archibald Hamilton, Sir Hans Hamilton, James Hamilton, of Bangor, and Patrick Hamilton, but not by James Hamilton of Neilsbrook, though he was made a party to it. The rents so reserved out of these townlands are included in the rent-roll of the jointure lands for the years 1688, '89, '90, '91, and '92 (which will be found in the appendix to this chapter); and it will be seen, by a memorandum at foot of it, that Gilbert How then claimed these lands in reversion. Though included in the estimate which was made for the purpose of the division of the jointure lands, they were not, however, included in the partition which was subsequently made between the representatives of the five uncles, on the 1st of October, 1696 ; but they seem to have been considered by the owners of the Killileagh proportion as belonging to it, and Mr. Stevenson, one of the joint owners of it, received a moiety of the rents reserved on Mr. How's lease of Ballytrim, from 1711 till 1728, as the receipts for it which are contained in the memorandum-book before referred to shew, the last of which is as follows :—" June ye 17th, 1728.—Received from James How £2 sterling, in full for two years' rent of his holding in Ballytrim, due at All Saints last.—James Stevenson." Whether Mr. Hamilton, the joint owner with Mr. Stevenson of the Killileagh proportion, ever received the other moiety of this rent, or whether either received any portion of the rent reserved out of Ballygoskin by the lease

convenience to all the five, that it were fit to value and divide the jointure in five distinct equal shares, and the good Lady is willing to it; and it is discoursed as very advantageous for enabling

---

in reversion, does not appear; but it is certain, that on the expiration of the term so granted by the reversionary lease of 1668, the then owners of the Killileagh proportion, James Stevenson and Gawen Hamilton, Esqrs., on the 26th of June, 1750, made four several leases, (1) to William Taylor, (2) to William Taylor and Gilbert How, (3) to Gilbert How, jun., and (4) to Alexander Wilson, for terms of twenty-one years, at the yearly rent of 7s per Cunningham acre, of the half of the townland of Ballygoskin, originally demised to Gilbert How. The other half of it, described in that lease as "Campbell's half," afterwards, by grants from the Clanbrassil family, became the property of the Rev. H. Clewlow, and is now vested in Charles Mathews, Esq. On the 26th of June, 1750, Messrs James Stevenson and Archibald Hamilton also made a lease to Gilbert How, sen., of "All and whole the townland of Ballytrim, as then in the possession of the said Gilbert and his undertenants, except that part thereof possessed by the Weavers," at the yearly rent of 6s 6d per Cunningham acre, for a term of twenty-one years. The part of Ballytrim excepted out of this lease as possessed by the Weavers, had, on 21st June, 1734, been demised by James Stevenson, Esq., to Robert Weaver, for a term of twenty-one years, at the yearly rent of 6s per Cunningham acre (amounting altogether to £7 7s 6d) which was regularly paid to Mr. Stevenson alone during its continuance. Messrs. Stevenson and Hamilton having, however, failed in enforcing payment of the rents reserved by the joint leases made by them in 1750, in consequence of the interference with the tenants of Lord Limerick, who had become the purchaser of Archibald and Patrick Hamilton's shares of the Clanbrassil estates, and who, as such, claimed two undivided fifths of these townlands, and not only authorised the tenants to resist the payment of the rents, but to take defence in his name to ejectments which had been brought in the year 1752 for their recovery, by Messrs. Stevenson and Hamilton. The result of which was, that the rents remained altogether uncollected in the hands of the tenants of Ballygoskin, and Ballytrim, originally demised to Gilbert How, until they had acquired a legal title against all the claimants under the will of Earl James by length of possession. The Weavers also set up a claim to hold their portion of Ballytrim in fee simple; but, finding they could not maintain any higher title to it than that of tenants at will, in consequence of their having regularly paid the rent reserved by the lease of 1734, to Mr. Stevenson, and his descendants, Sir John Blackwood, and James, Lord Dufferin, they, unfortunately for themselves, in order to support it, employed a school-

master, named Hans O'Pray, to forge a memorandum of agreement for them, of which the following is a copy :—

"MEM.—That John Blackwood, of Killyleagh, Esq., doth demise to the Weavers of Ballytrim, All that and those, the lands and turf bog in possession of said Weavers, in Ballytrim, and formerly held by them from the late Jas. Stevenson, Esq.: To have and to hold the said demised premises, with their appurtenances, unto the said Weavers, their heirs and assigns, commencing from the first day of November last, for, and during the lives of three persons to be inserted in a lease to be granted to them by the said John Blackwood, and to be renewable for ever, at and under the yearly rent of £7 7s 6d sterling. And the said Weavers shall bind themselves, their heirs, and assigns, in a penalty of £6 sterling, for every acre of said demised premises, to be paid unto the said John Blackwood, his heirs and assigns, if, at any time hereafter, they, or any of them, shall acknowledge any landlord, or pay any sum or sums of money, as rent for said demised premises, to any person or persons except the said John Blackwood, his heirs or assigns: Said lease to be granted and perfected on the above conditions only, when either of the parties shall require the same.

"As witness our hands and seals, this 22nd day of February, 1770 (seventy).

"Present,
"WILL : WILLEY."

"JOHN BLACKWOOD.
"JOHN WEAVER,
"For himself and others.

This instrument was so cleverly executed, and the signatures of the grantor and witnesses to it so well imitated, that it imposed on a number of respectable old witnesses who were brought forward to depose to their genuineness; but the evidence of O'Pray himself (who was produced on the trial which Lord Dufferin was obliged to institute for recovery of the lands), as to the mode in which he committed the forgery, was so conclusive, that the jury at once, without leaving their box, found a verdict condemning the instrument, and Lord Dufferin has since been in exclusive possession of the rents of this portion of Ballytrim. The trial itself was of so unusual and extraordinary a character, that it has been thought worth giving the following report of it, which has been extracted from the Belfast newspapers of the day, as the conclusion of this note :—

"DOWNPATRICK, MARCH 26, 1822.—Trial at Nisi Prius.
(Before the Hon. Baron Smith.)

"Right Hon. James Lord Dufferin and Clneboy, Plaintiff; "Henry Weaver, Robert Heron, and others, Defendants.

"Mr. Robert Gordon opened the pleadings.

"Mr. Blacker, on behalf of the plaintiff, stated, that this was an issue directed by the Court of Chancery to try whether a certain article or instrument, bearing date the 22nd February, 1770, and proporting to have been made between the late Sir John Blackwood, and a person named John Weaver, was or was not a forgery.

each of the five to set long leases, levy fines, build, &c. To this end, three captains are chosen to value all the lands, in order to a dividend ; but Captain Baily must be one ; the other two more

" James Neill, David Cleland, and Gawn Henry, deposed, that they had seen both William Willey and Sir John Blackwood write, and were acquainted with their hand-writing, and that the signatures to the article in question, which bore their respective names, were, to the best of their belief and knowledge, in their respective hand-writings.

" James Richardson bore similar evidence to the hand-writing of William Willey ; and James Craig to that of John Weaver, of Ballytrim, subscribed to said article.

" Thomas Potter, Esq., agent to Lord Dufferin, proved the non-existence of any lease or article to the Weavers, amongst the papers and instruments of Lord Dufferin's family, except one for 21 years, dated in 1734. He stated that Weaver had been served with notice to quit in April, 1813 ; in August, he paid up the May rent, and said nothing of any lease or article ; about the beginning of October, Mr. James Wallace, an attorney, first produced an article to witness, who said it was a forgery ; in October, 1813, Lord Dufferin also saw it, and said it was a forgery ; in April, 1820, a new notice to quit was served on Weaver ; witness now looked at the supposed signature of Sir John Blackwood, with whom he had frequent correspondence, and whom he had seen write, and deposed, that to his belief that signature was not Sir John's handwriting.

" Hans O'Pray was then produced. He swore that he was acquainted with Hans Weaver ; witness was married to his sister ; he knew the Weavers prior to 1797 ; but did not know them much afterwards until 1802 ; he knows the lands of Ballytrim ; the Weavers, prior to 1813, never said that they had any lease of the lands ; Hans Weaver told witness prior to this period, that Lord Dufferin had alleged that they had no title, and had required them to make some bargain for the land, or to that effect ; Hans Weaver told witness in 1813, as he recollected, that they (the Weavers) had taken an opinion of counsel respecting the lands, and he afterwards told witness that he had taken a second opinion, and that the opinions were unfavourable, and he thought it hard that persons who had enjoyed the lands so long should lose them ; Hans Weaver made an application to a person to get a deed or document that would save the property in the hands of the Weavers ; witness said he did not wish to say anything that would criminate any person that was present when the application was made ; an arrangement was made between the person to whom the application was made, and Hans Weaver, how this was to be effected, and that person stated to Weaver that he would try to do it ; witness was present, and the arrangement was accordingly made ; paper that had no watermark was required ; an article made by Sir John Blackwood to a person in Ballyalgan was required to be got ; the article was got ; Hans Weaver sent to the person who agreed to assist him in writing a copy of the Ballyalgan article ; (the copy was here produced to witness ;) witness believed part of the writing on the paper on which the copy was written, was the handwriting of Hans Weaver, but did not know of whose handwriting the remainder was ; witness saw the paper before, viz., in the summer of 1813, after he had had the conversation with Hans Weaver ; there was writing in different coloured inks on the paper ; witness knew *who* wrote them ; (the article in question was then produced to witness ;) witness knew *who* wrote it ; was present when the name ' John Blackwood ' was written ; it was done in the year 1813 ; William Willey's name was written on the same day ; the name ' John Weaver ' was written at the same time ; the words ' for self and others ' were not written at the same time, but witness could not say how long after-wards, it was weeks he believed ; witness knew who wrote the body of the instrument ; it was *the same person* who put the signatures to it ; it bears date 22nd Feb., 1770 ; it was necessary it should bear a date a few years after Mr. James Stevenson's death ; (a receipt was produced to wit-ness ;) witness saw it before ; it was enclosed in the paper or letter which witness proved to be Hans Weaver's hand-writing ; it was necessary to have Mr. Willey's signature ; Sir John Blackwood's was also subscribed to it. The paper upon which the article in question was written, was got from a printer in Belfast ; Hans Weaver was not pre-sent thereat, but witness knew the person ; David Lyons was the printer's name ; old paper that would betray no mark was necessary ; means were taken to prepare ink that would appear old ; witness knew the ink, it could not be purchased, it was made for the purpose ; witness knew that the article was sent to Hans Weaver ; *the person* who made the ink made experiments to try it previously to the article being written ; witness stated *he* knew the paper then produced to him was that upon which the experiments were made ; (several simulated papers or articles, each purporting to have been executed by Sir John Blackwood, were here produced to witness ; they were the same produced to the former witnesses ;) witness stated that he saw them all be-fore ; he knew *the person* who wrote them ; they were all written within a few days back ; it was *the same* person who wrote them that wrote the articles in question. On his cross-examination, witness stated that it was in the year 1813 that the article was made ; *the person* who wrote it suggested all that was requisite for the purpose ; *he* prepar-ed the ink ; it took some time to do so ; the article was prepared in a few days afterwards ; the procuring the paper did not require much time ; *the person* who did all this might be skilful, but he was neither experienced nor prac-tised in forgery ; a person inexperienced who might get ink in every shop would not delay to make ink ; he pre-sumed *the person* who got the paper, manufactured the article and ink ; *that person* was not skilled in forgery ; witness thought the forgery very well executed, but did not think *the person* who did it was experienced in forgery ; no person in court had the same knowledge of the transac-tion *as witness* ; witness repeated that *the person* was not experienced in the art of forgery, though skilled in the re-quisites necessary ; it was likely that Hans Weaver would apply to *a person* who would answer his purpose, but be-lieves he applied to *a person* that never committed forgery ; *the person* who did it was as much committed as Weaver ; Weaver was no fool ; the forgery was committed by *the person* to whom Hans Weaver applied ; the paper on which the forgery was executed, was procured from Mr. Lyons, in Belfast ; witness was present thereon ; Weaver was

(but not both quite) equal.ᵈ—On this account many meetings are appointed, and doubts enquired and answered, till two years expire, ere they can be ready ; and many apologies are made by Captain Baily, who was most defective in meetings—and all are taken well off his hand. At last it is almost perfected, and a lusty　*　is offered of 20,000 acres, besides royalties, castles, mills, tuckmills, towns, woods, &c., and then it is time to set some pretty little engines on foot still in order to the agreement of Bangor, such as—1. Many are set on to ask from the five

not there; witness had not said that he had to go to Belfast, because he lives there ; witness (II O'Pray) was present when the materials of which the ink was composed were mixed ; Hans Weaver and witness alone were present at the first proposal—three persons were present when the forgery was executed; could not state the reason why three persons were entrusted with the secret, but the fact was so ; there was nothing to prevent the *same person* who forged the article to forge or simulate a number of other instruments ; *he* is as capable now as in 1813; thought *the person* could not forge Hans Weaver's handwriting so well as Sir John Blackwood's ; the date was fixed in February ; the 12th would have answered perhaps as well as the 22d ; the receipt enclosed in the paper or letter bears that date ; Hans Weaver was a principal person concerned in the forgery, and the reason why he mentions his name is because he is not in the country and out of the reach of the law ; witness never disclosed it but to a professional man, who could not divulge a secret ; had no particular reason for telling it; but for a particular reason he did not believe it transpired through that channel ; witness does not think that the parties who had a knowledge of the transaction were infamous.

"David Gordon, Esq., was then examined. He swore that he knew Sir John Blackwood long before the year 1786; was well acquainted with him, and with the character of his handwriting ; witness got franks from him and had intercourse with him as his solicitor in 1788 ; continued his solicitor till his death in 1799, and during that period had much intercourse with him, and received several letters from him ; witness did not think the name John Blackwood to the article to be the signature of Sir John.

"David Lyons was next produced. Witness lives in Belfast ; lived there in 1813 ; was a bookseller and printer ; knew Hans O'Pray; recollected his coming frequently to buy school-books ; he was a teacher ; recollected his coming to get some paper ; he inquired for it on one occasion in 1813, as he best recollected ; there was another person with O'Pray, he was a gentleman; O'Pray asked for an old kind of paper, for a leaf or leaves of paper only ; witness shewed him various kinds, none of which seemed to answer; witness shewed him both writing and printing paper ; no reason was assigned why it did not answer ; O'Pray asked witness if he had any large books; witness shewed a number of old books lying in an adjoining room, and, to the best of his recollection, a leaf or leaves were taken out of one of said books, which they took away with them.

"John Woods was the next witness. He stated that he lived in Legagowan ; that he had lands in Ballyalgan, which he held under Lord Dufferin, by an article ; (the witness here identified the instrument by which he held

his lands in Ballyalgan) ; witness knew Hans Weaver; recollected his coming to witness, and asking to see the article, by which he held his lands ; it was executed by Mr. Stevenson; witness shewed it to Weaver; it was about nine years since; witness went in and out of the house during the time Weaver was there, which was about an hour; witness left Weaver in the room ; Weaver had not the article in his hand all the time ; witness's brother-in-law is married to one of the Weavers.

"To a question from a Juror, witness said, that Weaver had time to copy the article when in his house.

"Messrs. William Bleakley and Robert Kennedy, were next produced, and proved that the writing in question was not the handwriting of Mr. William Willey.

"Mr. Lyons was again called, and stated that he had been directed about eight days ago to give some leaves of blank paper to O'Pray, and to write his name previously thereon, which witness did accordingly. The simulated papers having been here produced, witness said they were the same leaves which he had given to O'Pray.

"Both parties having closed, the Judge shortly charged the Jury, who, without retiring, found a verdict for the plaintiff."

d The two other captains referred to in the text as chosen with Captain Baily to value the jointure lands were Captain Mure, and Captain Fairly; and a copy of their estimate, which was made on the 26th of November, 1681, is given in the appendix to this chapter.

The following letter from the five cousins to Sir Robert Maxwell, the second husband of Ann, Countess of Clanbrassill, has been also found among the family papers :—

"1st October, 1680, Bangor.

"Sir—Having resolved to putt our concerns in a way to be deveided, we shall much want the booke off the survey off Differen, to inable the gentⁿ employed in valewing the lands to doe thatt worke withe more ease and certantie. Wee, therfor, desire you will be pleased to send the booke off survey, and the booke off referents to itt, to Capⁿ Baily, and the rest employed ; and itt shall be returned saffe to you, soe soone as they have ended thatt woorke.—Sʳ, yo favor in this, will very much oblige, Sʳ,

"Yoʳ very humble servts.,

"HANS HAMILTON.
"JAMES HAMILTON.
"PAT. HAMILTON.
"ARCH. HAMILTON.
"J. HAMILTON.

"For the Honorᵈ Sʳ Robert Maxwell, Barronett, att Killeleaghe—These."

2 F

gratifications for their kindness and good services, (at least offered,) such as Mr. Richardson, James Sloan, Mrs. Trail, several of Earl Henry's servants, Mr. Ferguson, and Captain Baily; Captain William Fairlie must not be neglected; and David Kennedy must have something from the co-heirs. —2. Three Presbyterian Ministers of the estate must (by the Lady's request) have £5 apiece per annum;" and, by the advice of the two, these must be given them in lands, by long and profitable leases.—3. There is a debt of Earl James's of £100, now become £300, but may be taken off if each of the five will pay or secure £40— that is £200 for all—4. Of so great a matter, it is reasonable to gratify Sir Hans Hamilton with something suitable unto himself, in spite of his great demerits to us, at such a time. It was given out that it was promised to him, but this could not be proved, yea, was briskly denied, and offered to declare the contrary in his face; at least, he would not join in amicable agreement without it. This last must be considered, and, by consent, some are employed to find out what this must be that will please him; a return is made of something (especially mentioned) which would; and, all lovingly, for peace and love sake, it is agreed unto by the other four, and offered to him on the supposition above-mentioned. He thinks not to be so served, yet

---

* A mistake as to this lady, made by Dr. Reid in a note to the 130th page of the Second Volume of his Presbyterian History, in which he states that the Rev. Gilbert Ramsay's Meeting-house, in Bangor, was demolished in 1639, by the order of Lady Clanbrassil, "widow of the second Lord Claneboy, and first Lord Clanbrassil," has been already corrected at p. 39, ante, by stating that it was done not by Ann, the widow of James the first Earl of Clanbrassil, as stated by Dr. Reid, but by Alice, the widow of Henry, second Earl of Clanbrassil; and the following are the grounds for making that correction—1st. The rent-roll of the jointure lands of Countess Ann, the widow of Earl James, who lived at that time with her second husband, Sir Robert Maxwell of Waringstown, in the Castle of Killileagh, is given in the Appendix to this chapter, from which it appears that her jointure issued out of lands immediately surrounding it, principally in the Barony of Dufferin.—2nd. The rent-roll of the estate of which Countess Alice died seised and possessed, is also given at p. 108, ante, by which it appears that the town and lands of Bangor formed part of her estate, and that she alone had control over them at the time the demolition of Mr. Ramsay's Meeting-house took place.—3d. The act itself is quite inconsistent with the character of Countess Ann, but perfectly so with that of Countess Alice as given in these MSS., especially in the 5th, 6th, and 7th chapters; and it is conclusively brought home to the latter, by the following passage in "Adair's Narrative," which has been published by Dr. Killen, since the correction made at p. 39, ante, was in type:—

"Meantime, there fell out a passage in Dublin, at Christ-

mas, 1670, which, though not properly belonging to the History of the North of Ireland, yet, as relating to Presbyterians, is not unworthy to be recorded. There had been, a while before, builded at Dublin, a large stately house with three storeys of galleries, for acting the stage-plays, (in Smock Alley,) at the cost and free-will offering of noblemen and other persons of quality, unto which the bishops contributed largely; though at the time they refused to give countenance or assistance for building a church at Dame Street, where there was great need, through the multiplying of inhabitants in that city; much above what could be contained in the churches formerly built, especially in that place of the city. To this house came a great number of noblemen and ladies, besides other persons, and clergymen, the first day of Christmas, being Monday (26th December). The play acted was one called by them 'The Nonconformist.' And there, among other parts of the play, the poor shadow of a Nonconformist minister is mocked and upbraided, and at last is brought to the stocks, prepared for this purpose, that his legs may be fastened. Those of the greatest quality sat lowest; those next in quality sat the next above; and the common people in the upmost gallery. But, behold, when this shadow is brought to the stocks, as an affront to the Presbyterian ministers, and to teach great persons to deal with like severity toward them, down came the upper gallery on the middle one, where gentlemen and others sat, and that gallery broke, too, and much of it fell down on the lords and ladies. Divers were killed, and many hurt. Among those that were hurt was one of the Lord Lieutenant's sons, and the Lady Clanbrasil, who, the year before, had caused to be pulled down the preaching-house at Bangor. Such providences, so circumstantial in divers respects, will not pass without observation of impartial and prudent persons; for surely they have a language if men would hear."—Adair, p. 304.

will not tell what will please, but declares he will be no longer concerned with us, or them; he will do for himself, and bids others do the like; with some insulting expressions, refuses to perform the articles, or be concerned in proving the will, but—"Let every tub stand on its own bottom"—"Let those that are first weary complain," &c.—and so the five parted, and never met. At this time Captain Baily was in town, but very sick, and Sir Hans must see him often after this (which was much and variously talked of). All the friends being gone of the town, Captain Baily was pleased to tell a friend, that Sir Hans had yet a blast to blow which would push the three cousins off their feet, and he would soon do it. Within a few days, Sir Hans went to Dublin; his occasions were not known but to near friends; and, ere he finished his treaty with William Moore, he died; and Sir Robert Hamilton, who willingly met him there from England and watched him well, concluded the agreement with William Moore; entered himself executor to Sir Hans (though he made no will), and brought him to his burial-place. Upon hearing of this agreement with William Moore—"This," said the wise Captain Baily, "is the blast Sir Hans designed, and went to Dublin to finish."

As to Sir Hans his character, there is too much given of it already in the account of his actions, and we only add, that, as a person of good endowments, so he acquired a great deal of knowledge by reading, but much more by converse and business, wherewith he was extraordinarily exercised in the last twenty years of his age, he being of the King's Privy Council, and Justice of the quorum, and a captain (then) of a foot company; and with many, as tenants and creditors, he was naturally affable, and generous in his conversation, and housekeeping. He was almost equally related to the Irish, English, and Scotch, and had intimacy with some of all, and he spoke readily and truly all these languages in great propriety of speech. What his way was when one of the trustees for managing the arrears due to the Scottish army, and their affairs for 1649, was judged to be much by ill example, and the injuries falling upon friends and comrades at war, were modestly spoken of; and his carriage in the affair of his friends about the estate of Clanbrassill, was imputed much to bad counsel, and not a little to his son-in-law:—at least if he had been just to have performed honestly what Sir Hans agreed and covenanted to do, he had saved much of the honor his name unavoidably sustained, and perhaps will as long as he is named in the world; and this has been often regretted by Sir Hans's friends, that they were sorry they were forced by law-suits to publish his disingenuity, covetousness, and treachery, to the world; and it is certain he was greatly affected in his ill matching of his daughter, and the death of all in a short time, and with universal obloquy, and perhaps too much great contempt for that and several other things which would have been buried with him if his son-in-law had (as it well became him) duly regarded his honor; but, *qui sibi nequam qui b** * .

APPENDIX TO CHAPTER X.

[An estimate of the yearly value of the jointure, made the 28th of November, 1681, by Captain Mure, Captain Bayly, and Captain Fairlie, referred to at p. 121, *ante*.]

DENOMINATIONS.	PROFITABLE.			UNPROFITABLE			TOTAL.			VALUE.		
	A.	R.	P.	A.	R.	P.	A.	R.	P.	£	s.	D.
Killileagh Towne, with Castlewilliam, and a part of Corbely, possest by towne, the tenements and acres ariseth to										176	5	9
Mulloch, and part of Corbelie	285	0	0	37	0	0	322	0	0	38	0	0
Tollechin	302	0	12	16	0	0	318	0	12	30	0	0
Mamoir							191	0	0	33	0	0
Tollemacnolls	115	0	0	15	0	0	130	0	0	15	0	0
Tollevere—												
Possest by Captain Fairlie	300	0	0				300	0	0	34	0	0
Possest by Captain Bayly	60	0	0				60	0	0	10	0	0
Possest by Ja. Huie, and Cleland	43	0	0				43	0	0	8	0	0
The two Corne Mills	10	0	0				10	0	0	40	0	0
And the Tuk Mill	4	0	0				4	0	0	6	0	0
Ardegone	283	0	34	40	3	0	323	3	34	38	0	0
Ballywillono	352	3	32	82	0	0	434	3	32	47	0	0
Ballytrim—												
Possest by Mr. Howe, and that which lieth betwixt the park, and Ned Weyer's part										5	10	0
Cluntoch	500	3	0	111	0	0	611	3	0	50	0	0
Killinchie	723	0	0				723	0	0	56	0	0
Ballyalgin							473	3	0	37	0	0
Darrebouie							493	1	17	50	0	0
Lessna	339	2	21	30	0	0	369	2	21	40	0	0
Bellygascran—												
Possest by Mr. Howe										2	0	0
Possest by John Campbell, and his partners										17	0	0
Clay												
Lisduff	322	2	0				322	2	0	40	0	0
Maymoire												
										£773	15	0
Ballymakarran	163	3	13				163	3	13	£28	0	0
Toy and Kirkland	201	0	0				201	0	0	5	0	0
Ballycrumell	148	0	32				148	0	32	24	0	0
Rafcunningham	162	1	0				162	1	0	24	0	0
Island Taggart	57	0	0				57	0	0	10	0	0
Ballybrega										2	0	0
Ballygigane,	248	2	0	137	0	0	385	2	0			
Carrowgullin	118	0	0				118	0	0	16	0	0
Carureagh,	93	3	0	6	0	0	99	3	0			

DENOMINATIONS.	PROFITABLE.			UNPROFITABLE.			TOTAL.			VALUE.		
	A.	R.	P.	A.	R.	P.	A.	R.	P.	£	s.	D.
Ballymorrin	380	3	0				380	3	0 }	55	0	0
Killinekin	105	2	0				105	2	0 }			
Island Connelie	56	0	0	•						32	0	0
Ballydorn or Tollyhughe	192	0	0				192	0	0	32	0	0
Carroyraskie	211	0	22				211	0	22	20	0	0
Ballowe and the corn mille	313	3	0				313	3	0	45	0	0
Ballymacashin							319	3	0	30	0	0
Ballymacrolie							680	0	0	64	0	0
KILLMORE PARISH—												
Criviekarnonan	369	2	20	182	1	0	551	3	20	36	0	0
Clnntinaglare	533	3	0	149	2	0	683	1	0	45	0	0
Lestouther	304	1	0	73	3	0	378	0	0	32	0	0
The corne mille	6	0	0				6	0	0	18	0	0
Crivicargane	200	0	0	126	0	0	326	0	0	28	0	0
Ballydyan	272	1	0	125	3	0	398	0	0	28	0	0
Killinchy and Lissnp	363	0	0							42	0	0
	further of Globe. }											
										£554	0	0
TONOGHNEVE PARISH—												
Lessoyne	409	0	0	220	1	0	629	1	0	44	0	0
Leggagowine	630	0	0	304	1	0	934	1	0	50	0	0
Bellynecassin or Carsins	452	0	0	208	0	0	740	0	0	50	0	0
The corne mille										18	0	0
Achindarrach, or Drummahay	327	0	0	83	0	0	410	0	0	30	0	0
Druminaconnell	285	2	0	44	3	0	330	1	0	30	0	0
Bellyachergie	110	0	0	7	3	0	117	3	0	13	0	0
Glessdrumand	278	1	0	65	1	0	343	2	0	35	0	0
Lessons	295	0	0	48	0	0	343	0	0	38	0	0
Lessdunnan	278	0	0	30	0	0	316	0	0	30	0	0
Aughlie	457	0	0	32	0	0	439	0	0	36	0	0
Killenuer	297	0	0	110	0	0	407	0	0	34	0	0
Carrignacessanagh	295	0	0	105	0	0	400	0	0	38	0	0
Lessdalgin	179	0	0	169	3	0	348	3	0	30	0	0
Creviologhgare	251	3	0	158	0	0	409	3	0			
										£456	0	0

[Rent-roll of the Jointure Lands of Ann, late Countess of Clanbrassill, referred to at p. 118, *ante*.]

Denominations of Lands.	Old Tenants' Names.	Rents Paid in 1688.	Present Tenants' Names, and Rents to be Paid for 1689, 1690, and 1691.			Rents Payable for 1692.		
KILLILEAGH PARISH. Mullagh.	Jo : Sumers.	£30 0 0	Jo : Sumers, Widow Sumers, and Wm. Hilhouse, to pay for the said three years .. Thos. M'Kee, &c. ..	£11 15	0	£7	10	0
				15	0	7	10	0
Corbally.	Archd. Richy.	4 5 0	Archd. Richy	1	0	1	15	0
Killinchy, and half } Ballywoolin. }	Geo. Maxwell, } James Byers, &c. }	48 0 0	Thos. Nesbitt	0 13	0			
			George Dunn	1 10	0			

2 G

Denominations of Lands.	Old Tenants' Names.	Rents Paid in 1683.	Present Tenants' Names, and Rents to be Paid for 1689, 1690, and 1691.	Rents Payable for 1692.
KILLILEAGH PARISH. *(Continued.)*			Widow M'Ilduffe .. .. — 1 0 0	
			Ja : Gordon .. .. — 0 10 0	
			Wm. Kelton .. .. — 0 6 8	
			Thos. Costbes .. .. — 0 16 0	
			Ja : Blany .. .. .. — 0 13 0	
			Alex. Browne .. .. — 1 12 0	
			Gilbert Brakenrig .. .. — 4 0 0	
			Adam Woods .. .. — 2 10 0	
			Set for 1692, to James Hamilton, of Tollymore, Esq., at	24 0 0
Ballygoskeran, three quarters }	Michael Campbell, &c.	12 0 0	Michael Campbell and Widow Wilson .. .. .. — 5 0 0	4 0 0
		£94 5 0	£46 5 8	£44 15 0
Ardigon	Wm. Alexander	£1 0 0	.. .. — £1 0 0	£0 10 0
	Jo : Hollan	3 0 0	.. .. — 1 0 0	1 10 0
	Jo : Camlin	2 0 0	.. .. — 1 0 0	1 0 0
	Lynton's quartar	10 0 0	Jos. Martin .. .. — 1 0 0	
			Jos. M'Can .. .. — 0 5 0	
			Samuel Lewes .. .. — 0 9 0	4 10 0
			Jos. Corsby .. .. — 0 15 0	
Cluntagh	Ja : Forrest	2 0 0	Refuses to make any agreemt.	
	Beatty's quarter	10 0 0	Waste until '92 ; set to Geo. Ringland, at .. .. —	3 10 0
Toy, in fee farm	Alex. Bailie	5 0 0	.. .. — 15 0 0	5 0 0
Tolemenows	Jno. Wily, sen. }	6 0 0	.. .. — 9 0 0	4 10 0
	Jno. Wily, jun.			
Toleveric, quarter	Ja : Bailie	8 0 0	.. .. — 8 0 0	8 0 0
Mill-hill, and part Toleveric }	Jno. Hui	1 0 0	.. .. — 1 0 0	1 0 0
	Capt. Fairly's qr., and Widow Petticrew's }	34 10 0	.. .. — 34 0 0	17 5 0
	John M'Doran and Widow Woods }	21 0 0	.. .. — 10 0 0	10 0 0
Tolechin	Mr. Trail	20 0 0	.. .. — 20 0 0	10 0 0
Mamore and Millsland	Thomas Tailor	30 0 0	.. .. — 30 0 0	15 0 0
Ballytrim and }	Mr. How	2 10 0	.. .. — 2 10 0	2 10 0
			1 0 0	1 2 0
Ballygoskeran }	Edward Weaver	2 4 0	.. .. —	
Ballygalgan	Mr. Mant	12 0 0	.. .. — 12 0 0	6 0 0
Bally McCromell	Mrs. Richison	3 0 0	.. .. — 3 0 0	1 10 0
Lisna	Mr. Sloane	22 0 0	.. .. — 22 0 0	22 0 0
Derryboy	Geo. Maxwell	20 0 0	.. .. —	14 0 0
Half Ballywoolin	Mrs. Richison	12 0 0	Jno. Seyers .. .. — 1 13 4	0 16 8
			Andrew Woods .. .. — 2 0 0	2 10 0
			George Johnston .. .. — 1 4 6	1 17 6
			Jas. Stevenson .. .. — ..	0 13 4
			Geo. Pollock .. .. —	0 13 4
Rathcunningham	Nathaniel Montgomery	19 0 0	James Irwin .. .. — 1 10 0	
			Widow Montgomery .. — 2 8 0	
			James Irwin and James Spotswood, for '92 .. — ..	9 10 0

Denominations of Lands.	Old Tenants' Names.	Rents Paid in 1688.	Present Tenants' Names, and Rents to be Paid for 1689, 1690, and 1691.	Rents Payable for 1692.
KILLILEAGH PARISH. *(Continued.)* Clay	Captain Williamson	12 0 0	Thos. Wallace, for part of Clay	6 10 0
		£100 0 0		
The House and Demesnes, Mills, &c., of Killileagh KILLILEAGH TOWN.			Offered by Hans Stevenson for '92, and his proposals accepted at	16 3 0
			David Holland ..	1 0 0	0 10 0
			William Brown ..	0 16 8	0 8 4
			Alexander Ferguson ..	0 6 8	0 3 4
			Mr. Sloane ..	0 10 0	0 5 0
			Alex. M'Kee ..	0 11 0	0 7 0
			Andrew Cosby ..	1 0 0	0 10 0
			John Nesbitt ..	3 10 0	1 15 0
			John Bredfoot ..	2 4 0	1 2 0
			John Camlin ..	0 10 0	0 5 0
			David Duffe ..	0 10 0	0 5 0
			Widow and Ja. Heron. ..	2 18 0	1 9 0
			Widow Alexander ..	4 8 0	2 4 0
			Widow Dowy ..	0 10 0	0 5 0
			James Steele, &c. ..	2 5 4	1 2 8
			William Rowan ..	0 10 3	0 5 0
			James M'Connell, &c. ..	1 10 0	0 15 0
			Elizth. Lockert, & Holhouse	0 10 0	0 5 0
			Janet M'Comb ..	0 5 0	0 2 6
			John Espy ..	0 10 0	0 5 0
			Andrew Kernochan ..	0 3 4	0 1 8
			Thos Ferguson ..	0 3 4	0 1 8
			John Shannon ..	0 9 0	0 4 6
			John Ireland ..	0 10 0	0 5 0
			Widow Purdy, or Widow } Williamson }	0 10 0	0 5 0
			Widow Williamson ..	1 10 0	0 15 0
			John Henry ..	0 9 0	0 4 6
			James Steel, jun. ..	0 10 0	0 5 0
			James Worrell ..	1 0 0	0 10 0
			Widow Greer ..	0 10 0	0 5 0
			John Scott ..	0 10 0	0 5 0
			James Irwin ..	1 10 0	0 15 0
			Archibald Wardlaw ..	0 5 0	0 2 6
			William Johnson ..	1 1 3	0 10 7½
			John Severs ..	0 10 0	0 5 0
			David Dggan ..	0 10 0	0 5 0
			James Brown, & M. Carr ..	0 3 4	0 1 8
			Thomas Aiken ..	0 3 4	0 1 8
			A. Cowden ..	0 3 4	0 1 8
			John Jenkin ..	0 3 4	0 1 8
			David Healip ..	0 10 0	0 5 0
			James Lenzy ..	1 12 6	0 16 3
			David Morrow ..	0 15 8	0 7 10
			William Hilhouse ..	0 5 8	0 1 10
			Widow Murray ..	0 10 0	0 5 0

Denominations of Lands.	Old Tenants' Names.	Rents Paid in 1688.	Present Tenants' Names, and Rents to be Paid for 1689, 1690, and 1691.				Rents Payable for 1692.		
KILLILEAGH TOWN. *(Continued.)*			Janet Paradine ..	0	5	0	0	2	6
			John M'Connell ..	0	10	0	0	5	0
			John Fairiss ..	0	10	0	0	5	0
			Hans Finlay ..	1	10	0	0	15	0
			Alex. Spittle ..	0	10	0	0	5	0
			John Finlay ..	1	12	0	0	16	0
			Alex. Read ..	5	4	0	2	12	0
			Robert Paterson ..	1	7	4	0	13	8
			Gawin Paterson ..	0	16	0	0	8	0
			Alex. Gibony ..	0	6	8	0	3	4
			James Dixon ..	0	10	8	0	5	4
			Widow Ritchy ..	0	10	0	0	5	0
			James M'Munce ..	1	0	0	0	10	0
			Thomas Bradin ..	1	2	1	0	11	0½
			John Mathy ..	0	6	8	0	3	4
			Widow Boid ..	0	6	8	0	3	4
			James Lowdon ..	0	6	8	0	3	4
			John Lowdon, jun. ..	0	11	8	0	5	10
			Widow Cleland ..	0	6	8	0	3	4
			John Lockert ..	0	16	8	0	8	4
			John Hamilton or Hilhouse ..	0	10	6	0	5	3
			Robert Irwin ..	0	12	10	0	6	5
			John Lowdon ..	0	6	8	0	3	4
			John Scott ..	0	6	8	0	3	4
			Janet Lyon ..	0	6	8	0	3	4
			Widow Simpson ..	1	18	4	0	19	2
			James Clarke ..	0	7	6	0	3	9
			John Irwin, sen. ..	1	10	0	0	15	0
			John Read ..	4	3	0	2	1	6
			John Clugston ..	0	16	8	0	8	4
			James Morell ..	0	2	8	0	1	4
			Archibald Richy ..	0	6	8	0	3	4
			Wm. Petticrew ..	0	6	8	0	3	4
			Thos. Cooper ..	0	6	8	0	3	4
			David Welsh ..	1	12	0	0	16	0
			Widow Cochran ..	1	5	0	0	12	6
			Robert Hamilton, Merchant	2	0	0	1	0	0
			Wm. Armstrong ..	2	2	6	1	1	3
			Robert Moore ..	2	18	0	1	9	0
			James Browne ..	1	5	0	0	12	6
			Wm. Gowdy ..	0	15	0	0	7	6
	Thos. Bradley claims this in reversion of 10s per annum	..	John Robinson ..	2	10	0	1	5	0
		..	Thos. Bradley ..	5	0	0	2	10	0
			John Ross, &c. ..	1	5	0	0	12	6
			Wm. Holliday ..	2	2	6	1	1	3
			James M'Cullam's Widow..	1	0	0	0	10	0
			James M'Naght ..	0	15	0	0	7	6
			Henry Inch ..	0	10	0	0	5	0
			Philip Mayers ..	0	16	0	0	8	0
			James Stanus, &c. ..	2	3	6	1	1	9
			Thos. Taylor ..	0	6	8	0	3	4
			Robert Hamilton ..	3	14	0	1	17	0
			Wm. Alexander ..	2	5	0	1	2	6
			Widow M'Dowell ..	1	2	0	0	11	0

Denominations of Lands.	Old Tenants' Names.	Rents Paid in 1688.	Present Tenants' Names, and Rents to be Paid for 1689, 1690, and 1691.				Rents Payable for 1692.		
KILLILEAGH TOWN. *(Continued.)*			Widow Campbell	3	14	4	1	17	2
				£51	19	8	£25	19	2
			Captain Williamson	0	4	8	In Arrear
			Captain Williamson	2	18	6	and
			More	0	10	0	made no
			For Castlewilliam	12	0	0	agree-
			More for Lieut. Gann's land	5	1	6	ments.
				£20	14	8	
KILLINCHY PARISH.									
Ballymoran	Alex. Stewart	35 0 0	.. ..	35	0	0	17	10	0
Carrickrusky	Jo : Ross	5 0 0	.. ..	5	0	0	2	10	0
	Widow M'Cullin	4 0 0	.. ..	4	0	0	2	5	0
Bally M'Cosin	The Tenants	24 0 0	Thos. Lowry, &c. ..	3	0	0	3	0	0
			Widow and Jno. Moorhead	6	0	0	3	0	0
			John Patton	4	0	0	3	0	0
			James Thompson, &c. ..	4	0	0	3	0	0
Bally M'Creely	Wm. Hewitt	55 2 6	Wm. Hewitt	3	0	0	3	0	0
			Jas. Hewitt	2	0	0	2	0	0
			Wm. Stewart	3	6	0	3	0	0
			Jas. Oghterson	4	0	0	3	0	0
			Wm. Patterson	0	12	0	5	16	3
			David Aul and Sons ..	4	0	0	2	0	0
			John Patterson, &c. ..	13	0	0	7	15	0
Ballow	Captain Morrow	4 0 0	Henry Carse	2	4	0	2	0	0
			Wm Bole	4	0	0	2	0	0
			Robt. Cudbert	5	13	4	2	16	8
			Wm. Moorhead	4	0	0	2	16	8
			John Throw	0	16	8	0	15	0
			John O'Dair	0	15	0			
			Widow Thompson	0	8	4	0	8	4
Ballydorne	Jas. Savage, Esq.	11 0 0	John Stewart	6	3	4	3	6	8
			Jno. Hamilton, &c. ..	3	15	0	3	6	8
			Alex. M'Teer	2	6	8	2	0	0
			John Hunter	1	18	4	0	19	2
Ballygulin Ballygigon	} Captain Moore	1 0 0	.. ..	3	0	0	1	0	0
Ballybregagh Killinchy		2 0 0	.. ..	6	0	0	2	0	0
	Town's quarter	6 0 0	Waste until '92.				3	0	0
	Ferguson's quarter	6 0 0	Robert Mitchell	0	10	0	3	16	0
	Lynton's quarter	12 0 0	Jno. Hewitt	0	15	0	2	10	0
			Jno. M'Gill	..			1	0	0
			Thos. Bradley	..			1	10	0
Achendarah or Drumabeg	}	21 15 0	Thos. Coulter	..			1	0	10
			Jno. Donnelson	1	0	10	2	1	8
			Jas. Beaty	1	5	0	1	5	0
			Samuel Mossman	2	10	0	2	10	0
			Jno. M'Bride	1	7	6	1	7	6
			Wm. Donnelson	..			1	7	6

2 H

Denominations of Lands.	Old Tenants' Names.	Rents Paid in 1688.	Present Tenants' Names, and Rents to be Paid for 1689, 1690, and 1691.		Rents Payable for 1692.
TONOCUNEIVE PARISH, &c.					
Crevicarnonan	Mrs. Neill, &c.	18 0 0	Richard Graham ..	3 0 0	3 0 0
			Wm. Hamilton ..	1 10 0	1 10 0
			H. Cleland and Sons ..	9 0 0	4 10 0
Creviargan	Wm. Hamilton	2 10 0	.. ..	2 10 0	1 5 0
	David White	20 0 0	.. ..	5 0 0	10 0 0
Carsons, the Mill, and Half Liswine }	Mr. Maxwell	42 0 0	Jas. Sloane ..	1 1 0	
			Thomas Coulter ..	0 17 0	
			Abraham Elliott ..	1 4 0	1 4 4
			Archd. Cooper ..	1 4 0	
			The half town, settled to Cooper for '92, at }	.. ..	6 0 0
			Widow Maxwell ..	4 10 0	4 10 0
			Samuel Brown, &c. ..	4 10 0	4 10 0
			Widow Miller, for the Mill and Land }	13 0 0	10 0 0
Carricknessanagh	Jno. Doblin, &c.	14 0 0	.. ..	14 0 0	7 0 0
	Adam M'Crea	14 0 0	James Dyers, &c. ..	5 10 0	7 0 0
Clontineglar Half Liswine Lagigowne, and Killmore }	Capt. Gawen Hamilton	85 0 0	.. ..	42 10 0	42 10 0
Lessans	Alex. Robb, &c. {	30 0 0	Alex. Robb	3 7 6	1 13 9
		2 10 0	Alex. Robb, for	.. ..	1 3 9
			Jas. Macunson	1 18 9	0 19 4½
			Jas. Rea, the like ..	1 18 9	0 19 4½
			Lodk. Harper	3 17 6	1 18 9
			Andrew M'Calla ..	1 18 9	1 18 9
			Geo. Forman	1 18 9	1 18 9
			Widow Rea	0 19 4½	0 19 4½
			Jas. Rea	.. ..	0 19 4½
			Ja: M'William ..	1 18 9	1 18 9
Drumaconnell	Jas. Blackwood	6 0 0	.. ..	6 0 0	6 0 0
Glasdrunon	Ro: Kyle	16 0 0	.. ..	16 0 0	8 0 0
	R. Ross	16 0 0	.. ..	16 0 0	8 0 0
Listowder	Hu: Fairly	25 0 0	Refuses to make any agreement.		
	The Mill	14 0 0	.. ..		
Ballydian	Mr. Fairly	0 1 0	.. ..	0 3 0	1 0 0
Lisdalgan	Mr. Hutchson	12 0 0	Arthur Hamilton ..	1 10 0	1 10 0
	Andrew Bernet	8 0 0	Robt. Tod ..	3 0 0	4 0 0
			Wm. Johnson ..	2 10 0	1 5 0
			Jno. Thompson ..	3 0 0	1 10 0
			Nath. Forgy ..	0 8 0	1 3 0
Lisdunan	Archd. M'Dowell	24 0 0	.. ..	24 0 0	12 0 0
Oghley	Jas. Baillie	20 0 0	.. ..	20 0 0	20 0 0
Totals of the before-going Rent-Roll,		£101 45 0		£703 0 1½	£613 15 10

WASTE LANDS.—Ballygoskeran, waste 40 acres.—BallyMcCreely, Widow Howitt's holdings, that paid £2 per annum, waste.—Ballow, John Throw, 20 acres waste.—Kelly's holdings in Drum Clay, which paid £2 10s.—Jenkins' and Killin's holdings in Carsons, waste.—Lisdalgan, about 100 acres waste.—Several waste holdings in the town of Killileagh, as Mr. Robert Maxwell's, &c.

A List of Mortgages on the Jointure Lands of the late Countess of Clanbrassill :—

John Hay, on part Ardigon, a mortgage,	..	..	..	..	..	..	£100	0 0
John Finlay's Admor, on a quarter Cluntagh,	..	..	..	..	..	..	100	0 0
John Hay, on part Toleveric, mortgage, ..	..	..	..	..	..	..	40	0 0
Widow Woods, on BallyMcCaran	..	..	..	..	..	..	50	0 0
Mrs. Ritchison, on BallyMcCromell	..	..	..	..	..	..	100	0 0
John Robinson, on Island Tagert,	..	..	..	..	..	..	100	0 0
John Savage, Esq., on Ballydorne, ..	..	..	..	..	..	..	80	0 0
M'Bride's Executors, on Currowreagh,	..	..	..	..	..	..	100	0 0
Thomas Oliver, on a quarter Killinchy, ..	..	..	..	..	..	..	50	0 0
John Blackwood, on Drumaconnell,	..	..	..	..	..	..	100	0 0
Hugh Fairly, on Listowder and Mill,	..	..	..	..	..	..	150	0 0
Mr. Fairly, on Ballydian,	..	..	..	..	..	..	200	0 0
James Forrest, on a quarter Cluntagh, ..	..	..	..	..	..	..	100	0 0
		Total,	..	..	..	..	£1,390	0 0

A List of Lands in Reversion claimed by the undernamed persons of the following Lands :—

James Bailie claims part of Tolleveric in reversion, at the yearly rent of	..	..	..	£8	0 0
Gilbert How, part Ballytrim, and part Ballygoskeran, at	..	..	..	..	2	10 0
James Sloane, Lisna, at	..	..	..	..	..	22	0 0
James Bailie, Oghley, at	..	..	..	..	..	20	0 0
John Blackwood, Drumaconnell, ..	..	..	..	..	..	6	0 0
						£58	10 0

Captain Gawin Hamilton did not claim his reversion of the holdings in Cluntinaglar, but desired a settlement as other tenants.

Persons removed away with rents :—

MULLAGH.—James Sumers, removed to Ballylentin in Lecale, with three years' rent, at £4 10s per annum, ending All Saints, '91, ... £13 10 0

BALLYGOSKERAN.—George Newell, removed to or near Mudock, near the Bann Water, in Mr. Waring's estate, with three years' rent, ending the same time, ... 9 0 0

DERRYBOY.—George Maxwell, removed to the County of Ardmagh, with three years' rent, ended the same time, ... 60 0 0

DRUMCLAY.—Samuel Browne, removed to Liswine, with 4 3 4

Several runaways, that we know not the places of their now residence.

£36 13 4

The house and demesne, &c., of Killileagh possessed by Sir Robert Maxwell until Spring, 1691 ; that Mr. Wm. Fairly entered and had the crop of grazing for that year, and benefitt of the mill, &c. — To have directions in both these particulars how to proceed.

1692.—Mr. Stevenson proposed to pay for the above particulars £76 3s 0d, and his proposal not accepted, but Mr. Fairly continued his possession. — Direction in this.

£30 detained in the Taylor's hands for Mamore rent for building the mill of Killileagh, ..

£16 charged on Toy, held in fee farm by Mr. Bailie, for three years.—Quere, what abatement will be given?

Ballygullin and Ballegagh £1 per annum, charged with the whole; Ballebregagh £2 per annum, with the whole.—Quere, what abatement will be given?

QUERE.—What proposals to be made to the tenants for the year 1693, as to their continuance, and on what terms? for they generally expect to hold as they did the last year, by reason they had no timely notice to remove.

Receipts :—

Of the several sums in the before going rent-roll for the arrears ended at All Saints, '91, received by Robert Kyle, and Simon Isaac, as per the particulars of their receipts may appear, the sum of £477 0 0

Disbursed as followeth :—

	£	s	d
Imprimis.—Chief rent to Mr. Hill,	80	0	0
2..........Paid to Mr. Archibald Hamilton, as per his receipt,	77	0	0
3..........Paid to Mr. Pat. Hamilton and others, on his account,	77	0	0
4..........Paid to Mr. Fairly in cash, and by allowance of rents in his and Captain Hamilton's hands,	89	11	2
5..........Received by Simon Isaac, for account of James Hamilton, Esq., and Hans Hamilton, Esqr's., proportion,	154	4	10½
	£477	16	0½

Arrears to and for All Saints, '91 :—

	£	s	d
MAMORE.—Thomas Tailor,	£30	0	0
OGILEY,	20	0	0
LINNA,	22	0	0
TOY,	15	0	0
James Bailie, Toleverie,	8	0	0
Mr. How,	2	10	0
John Blackwood	6	0	0
Captain Moore's interest,	9	0	0
	£112	10	0
KILLILEAGH TOWN,	60	7	8
	£172	17	8

The remaining £52 1s 0d, remaining due in small sums in the tenants' hands, which will be soon got up.

                                               £650 13 8½

KILLILEAGH, 1st *9ber*, 1692.

HONBLE. SIR,

    In answer to yours of the 27th October last, which came to our hands about ten days since, we herewith send you a Rent-roll of the Jointure-lands of the late Countess of Clanbrassill, as it paid in 1688, by the best information we can find; also an account of the compositions we have made for '90 and '91, and the rents to be paid for the year ended at All Saints, 1692, which you may distinguish by the columns in the Rent-rolls.

    We have also sent you an account of our receipts, and how we have applied the same, and to what persons.

    We have also sent a list of the mortgages, and reversions; and desire to have your directions how we shall proceed in them, and in the collection of the other rents due by Thomas Tailor and others, which we send you the particulars of, and to have your answer and directions as to the other particulars we mentioned, and we shall proceed accordingly.

    We have sent an account of the arrears also, and most of the persons by whom due. For the other small arrears, we shall endeavour soon to get them up, and hope, if we have yours and Mr. Brownlow's answer and instructions how to proceed as to the Leases in Reversion and other particulars, we may soon account for the arrears.

    We are, your Honble.'s most humble servants,

                                   ROBERT KYLE.
                                   SIMON ISAAC.

CHAP. XI.

OF WHAT TREATY PRECEDED THE LAW-SUIT BETWIXT SIR ROBERT HAMILTON, JAMES OF NEWCASTLE, AND THE OTHER THREE, AND MADE THE LAW-SUIT UNAVOIDABLE ON THE PART OF THE THREE.

I must now remind, that Archibald and Patrick were snared under the articles formerly mentioned; but James of Neilsbrook, upon a reference of the differences betwixt Sir Hans and James of Newcastle, stood under an award of arbitrators, who adjudged them to perform according to these articles, and him to be determined thereby; yet Sir Hans never subscribed to the bonds of submission, nor was James of Neilsbrook satisfied with the award, so as there was no further agreement. Meantime, Archibald got nothing, nor could he get so much as accounts stated with them; but, on the contrary, Sir Hans had ordered his agent to possess himself on his account of an estate which Archibald had in the parish of Ballywalter (whereof a part was inheritance, and a part by leasehold), and this was done by distraining the tenants till they got possession, which was performed after his death, for that Sir Robert will not quit it, and Archibald was unwilling (and now not very able) to go to law. Yea, further, whereas Sir Hans was due a debt by bond to Archibald, Sir Robert put him to a suit at law, for clearing the account of byepast annuities which he had received, though Archibald never sued Sir Hans nor him for either principal or annuities, and offered frequently to discount without law, but Sir Robert would do nothing but by law. Patrick had for some few years received £50 by a rent-charge on some lands of the Estate of Clanbrassil, and Sir Robert and James of Newcastle stopt it, and received it for their own uses; so now all the three were in the same circumstances, and very much exhausted of their small estates by the charges of the suit which Sir Hans and James managed to no purpose; and, besides, by frequent and chargeable appointments and meetings of the five, from time to time, and from place to place, upon several pretences, at all which times and places Archibald and Patrick were equal charges with Sir Hans and James, though (besides their own estates and employments) they now possessed £1,800 a-year out of the Estate of Clanbrassill, and had their attendants suitable, it being of the agreement at Bangor, to out-weary and expend them, till they should be glad at last to take any small trifle of money the two should be pleased to give them; for they assured themselves the three would never go to law, having neither skill in it, nor money nor friends for it, yea, were not men of the times. On the other side, Sir Robert Hamilton forces himself into Sir Hans his place, and in this manner Sir Hans, in a late settlement, had committed his estates and affairs to be managed for his grandchild's use, to his own brother, Lieutenant Francis Hamilton, and Major Richardson; and all expected this would have continued, for that it was known Sir Hans his great design was to keep it from Sir Robert his handling; but he found agents to persuade these two to break their trust (for to subvert honest wills and break trusts was now their work, and it was but just that Sir Hans was so served as he had done to others), though formerly none appeared more forward to please Sir Hans and slight Sir Robert than they; but " a living dog is better than a dead lion," and withal he had entered himself as executor to Sir Hans; bought William Moore's title; and had procured of the Court of Chancery to be guardian to Sir Hans's grandchild; and so enters upon his whole estate and affairs. Lieutenant H. came into £600, which law could not have given him; James of Newcastle met with a fit comrade, and got a new title over his head against the three cousins; and Major Richardson was complimented out of his room, and say'd he had no reason to stick by Sir Hans's settlement, when his own brother and cousin (whom he had so much obliged) did forget it. After some time spent in considering how to go about the settlement of the matter, Sir Robert and James of Newcastle are tried by the friends of what course they will take, and they profess liberally a great disposition and desire for an amicable agreement. For this end, a time is appointed, and it is agreed on, that William Hamilton, of Edinburgh, shall be sent for to meet at such a place and such a day.^b At the time appointed, he and others met, and James of Newcastle tells that he did not expect his

---

^a This grandchild afterwards became Sir Hans Hamilton, and married Jane Skeffington, eldest daughter of the second Viscount Massareene. They had an only daughter, Anne Hamilton, who married James Campbell, Esq., of London, who took the name of Hamilton to possess the estate, and was well-known in the family as " *Campbell-Hamilton*." He died in London, in 1749, at the age of 80.—*See Mrs. Reilly's Memoirs*, p. 88.

^b The following letters, which appear to have been written to Mr. William Hamilton about this time, have been found among the family papers:—

" Newtown, 26th March, 1685.

" Sir—I rec^d yo^{rs} of the 25th instant this morning about nine o'clock. I had noe intention of going to Finabrogue on Friday next, until I rec^d yo^{rs}; but if you be all in readiness, I shall never be backward to further so good a work as is intended, and shall not faile to meet you at Killileagh to-morrow by noone, being Fryday. Therefore, be shure you have all persons concern'd to act their part. I know not if Sir Ro: Maxwell be returned from Lisburne yet; but you would doe well to send this night, or early to-morrow morning, to lett him know our intentions of meeting at Killileagh to-morrow; for he is a material verb. I suppose you have acquainted yor cusin, Mr. Patrick Hamilton, likewise. If it were not upon this occasion, I should hardly goe

abroad, having been scarcely well since I saw you. Soe, untill meeting, and ever, I remain, S^r, yor reall friend and servant,
"Ro: COLVILL.

" For his worthy friend, Mr. Wm. Hamilton,
of Edinburgh—These."

[This letter is from Sir Robert Colville, who had purchased the lordship, corporation, and borough of Newtown, and other lands, from the second Earl of Mount Alexander, in Nov., 1675, for £10,640.—See *Lodge*, vol. i. p. 374. He also afterwards, in 1698, purchased from Patrick Hamilton, Esq., of Granshaw, who is mentioned in this letter, one-fifth of the Clanbrassil estate, to which he was entitled under Earl James's will, but soon after disposed of it to James Hamilton, Esq., of Tollymore.—*Mrs. Reilly's Memoirs*, p. 89.]

" Bargeny, 7th September, 1685.

" Sir—I received your's, by Mr. John Hutchesone, upon Thursday last, who told me y^t ane express was sent me by you and my friends a week before, which letters I did not receive till just now. In answer to both yours, I am most willing to travell or doe anything may serve my friends; but the day of the tryall of James Earle of Clanbrassil's will being over, I waite for a second consideration and call; and if then you and they think it necessary, I shall make all the haste the wind will permit; but they and you may consider I have no skill in your law, or making answers to bills, and, for matter of fact or papers, they have that already;

cousin William, and so had involv'd himself in business which he could not now neglect, but he would be able shortly to fix another diet; and thus several fixed times are postponed; and being privately attack'd, he did not stick to say he was not now bound by the articles, for that when he entered into them he had no title to the estate; and now hoped that if they should sue him on that account, the Lord Chancellor would relieve him. After some time thus spent, and that Sir Robert Hamilton had often say'd he would not give the other three cobs apiece for their interest by the articles, for that he held by William Moore's title, and James of Newcastle by him; yea, to this effect he spoke to the friends themselves. Whilst matters stood thus with the three friends, they find it unavoidable that they must go to law, and agree together to assay it, intreating earnestly Mr. William Hamilton's conduct and assistance. He resolves to assay it, yet still as to be ready to hearken to all offers and opportunities for peace. As this goes abroad, and that every body's mouth was full of the discourse of this matter, they offer new conferences, especially one at Dublin, where all must meet. At the time agreed on they meet, but none must be present at any discourse but the parties, and Mr. William Hamilton, who had treated for the three. When the discourse was entered on, Sir Robert, and James of Newcastle, would own no articles but some consideration for friendship's sake, and because they had by an unfortunate conduct laid out money in order to the

---

but if they in the least think my coming will serve them, I will come, and y'fore, I entreat you, after sight, take your horse and goe to S' Robert, and send for Mr. Maxwell and my other freinds, by which I shall be determined soone. My service to Bastoune and all friends. I continue your most affectionate and humble servant, "BARGANY. "For James Ross, of Portavoe, Esquire.—These."

[It does not appear this letter, addressed to Mr. Ross, came among the Hamilton papers; but they were probably handed over to Mr. William Hamilton, at the same time as the correspondence copied at pp. 102, 3, 4, and 5, *ante*, between Lord Bargany and Mr. Ross and his other agents in this country.—ED.]

"Dublin, 27th October, 1685.

"SIR—Yo of the 23d inst. I rec'd yesterday, haveing on Saturday returned an answer to Mr. Fairlie's of the 21st, the perusal whereof will inform you of that day's transactions. You did well in complying with their desire of adjurning to Downpatrick, for the prevention of any pretence of not getting their witnesses examined, that they might offer for procuring further time to examine. And as for the Interogatories, they are never filed with the Register, but only attested by him, and an entry made of the parties' names. My own opinion is, that they, having examined noe witnesses, might alter their Interogatories. If there be no other hindrance of yo serving the *subpœna* to bear judgement than the not closing the commission till 5th Nov., you need not insist upon that, but have those def in the country served; and Sir Robert, being in England, we will have an order of court for serving his cl for him. There is a month's time given for excepting to the answers

to L Bargany and Rosse. I delivered your letter to Mr. Sarg Echiin, who will write to you this night. I believe it would be requisitt that you should be here by the first of Terme, or as soon after as you conveniently can. If any thing occur before yo comeing, the same shall be communicated to you by, S, yo most obed serv,
"CHAR. CRYMBLE.

"Be pleased to acquaint Mr. Fairley, that if their com will meet and joyne in speeding the com in Stewert's cause they may proceed, otherwise they must be summoned again, and have 14 days' notice.
"For Mr. James Irvin, in Killileagh, per Downpatrick, for Mr. Wm. Hamilton, in haste—These."

"Newtown, 6 June, 1687.

"SIR—A Saterday, late at night, I received Mr. Fairly's, with the enclosed. The 2 sealed I sent away early laste morning as directed, and they were delivered to his neice at Comber before 7 o'clock I tynd he hath not seen the open letter I wrote, that he might be with me this morning to have shown it, but is not come, and I will keepe the post as long as not to loose Belfast's. This inclosed is all came alongest writen upon the botom of yours. There are soe many circumstances to be considered, and I have none here to discours with, and of soe great importance, as it is not fitt for me to be positive, capecially being a stranger to many circumstances as might give great clearness; delays have their inconvenience as well as to push forward, and for what I can observe, you are now almost at a lotery; what may seime best may prove worst; and yet you will observe what was granted, and, tho' more than ordinary, how it was taken, and thought not enough, whereby it may be observed wher

proving of the will, and more to this purpose; all of which the three thought was nothing to the purpose, and so resolved to acquaint Sergeant Osborne with this treatment, and ask his advice. Sergeant Osborne being repaired to, had the view of the articles and bonds, and an account of the present treatment (and something of byepasts), and advised of it, and say'd he would discourse the matter with Sir Robert and James; and, as they waited on him thereafter, it fell out that Sir Robert and James came to the Sergeant's. The three and Mr. William Hamilton withdrew, yet overheard loud and vehement discourse on both sides. At last the three were called in to them, and the Sergeant told them that he found Sir Robert and James persuaded and resolved not to own the articles, but stand on their title by William Moore; and that he was sorry for the difference he found among them that were all kinsmen, and lately of one side and in one bottom, for that he could do us no service. There was also the like diligence used with a person of quality, to whom it was supposed that Sir Robert paid a great deference, which proved of no better success—all to prevent a law-suit. But, shortly after, James of Newcastle was pleased to come up to the place where the three and Mr. William Hamilton lodged, and told them, "Gentlemen, I am come to unmask myself, and

the wind bloweth most favorably now, but if any hopes of faire wether, its hardly saife to leave a harbour, and yet for fear of mortality, if you provided soe sure as you offer, if ther wer more possitive rents to force you out, it were well that were done; for if the most materiall were done, and leave one or two least considerable, would it not gain time? It hath bein so formerly with others, and with you in this adventure; and yet, upon the whole, I must return and leave as I have formerly; men must doe the liklyest, and leave the event to God. Being persuaded the Serg⁴ and you will follow those measures you think best. Soe God directe yᵉ and, let the event be what it will, it shall be satisfactory to your's, "ROBERT COLVILL.

"For William Hamilton, of Edinburgh, Esqr., at Dublin.—These."

"Newton, 9 Decembʳ, 1687.

"Sɪʀ—The Dublin post came not to Belfast untill Wednesday morning, and I received not yⁿ until noone, soe I could not write by that day's post; but I imediately sent it to P[atrick] H[amilton], who came here yesterday, and after we had discoursed of sending yʳ letter to the person it was directed to, we concluded better let it alone, and he wrote himself, whereof he promised to give you an account. H. Leslie promised not to faill, and I send againe to him by his father, who left me a Wednesday, soe I thinke he will be here. I shall write to Mr. Knox the night if he be come home, and I hope he will not refuse. If the Comⁿ meet, ther is nothing in yʳ absence to be done but to adjurne. I aprehend yʳ clerk's proceeding with Mr. Rosse may disoblieg, and the rather, because I see they write with P. I advised him to be cautious what he did, and not to appear in it. What yʳ new motion is, I am not curious to know, but I am persuaded it's just;˒soe wish you good success. I must trouble your g⁴in to cause take out a copie of M'Gill's bill against me and others, with a copie of the Register's notᵤs

and rules of court, and send me a close copie, and leave the originals with the Sergeant, to whom I have wrote in this particular. Speak likewise to Mr. Williamson, and desire him to let me know how the outlaruie against them stands, and if bail be given? He should have given me an account of his trust when the cause was removed to Chancery. Learn in what court Johnston hath entered up his judgment against Cunningham, and when; and consult the Sergeant if it will touch reversions. If soe, gard against it, and cause the Sergeant employ some attorney to attend ther motion, that I be not surprized, and you may give Cunningham notice that after he hath received full satisfaction, he need not endevor any such thing, but rather prevent it; for he will at long run come by worst, and it may be by it. A great vessell was driven on Belfast Bridg, and hath done much harm—some say £200 will not make up the damage.—I am, yᵉ, "ROBERT COLVILL.

"To William Hamilton, Esq., of Edinburgh, at Dublin.—These."

Although Mr. William Hamilton was thus sent for and solicited by his three cousins to act for them as their adviser, and in conducting the litigation on their behalf, he had also become personally interested in the result of it, by his eldest brother, James of Neilsbrook, having, in the year 1680, entered into an agreement with him and his brother, Gawen Hamilton, that in consideration of their joining and concurring with him in recovering one-fifth part of the Clanbrassil estate, and advancing a proportionable share of the expenses of doing so, he would grant them an equal moiety of his fifth part when recovered. A copy of this agreement, and of James of Neilsbrook's will, and of a release from his daughters confirming it, will be found in the Appendix to this chapter.

speak barefaced to you, tho' hitherto I was obliged to comply with Sir Robert his methods and discourse. The truth is (say'd he), I purchased a share in William Moore his title for myself, to enable me to perform my share of the articles. If you will pay me for your shares of the purchase-money and charges I have been at, I am content to treat with you on these terms, tho' I cannot bring Sir Robert Hamilton to do as I would." The three and Mr. Wm. thanked him for his freedom, and say'd they would think of what use they could make of his discovery, but at this time no further progress could be made toward agreement. This matter being much noised, especially amongst the friends of the Court, the two offer yet another assay whilst Mr. William Hamilton was in Dublin, making preparations for a law-suit, and it is agreed that on a prefixed day all shall meet at Ballycloughan, the place of James of Newcastle his residence, and that Mr. H, of Bangor, and Doctor H. Kennedy, of Ballycultra, shall be with them. Whereupon Mr. W. Hamilton is sent for, and comes in great haste. At the meeting, great professions of friendship are made; but the communings must not be carried on openly or in the presence of all parties, but the parties keep different rooms; and the two formerly mentioned carry and plead overtures and proposals betwixt the parties, until they seem all to have agreed as things were represented; and for *
*   of all, it is agreed unto, that Sir Robert Hamilton and Mr. William Hamilton shall meet at Dublin on a prefixed day, and present the matter agreed on to counsel, and prepare all things for being perfected by the rest concerned; and that, upon their advertisement, all shall come up to finish the matters and papers so prepared.

At the appointed time (or thereabouts), they met at Dublin; but Sir Robert contracted some indisposition, which kept him in his chamber. Mr. William Hamilton paid him several visits, but proposed nothing of business until Sir Robert urged him to it; their first work was to recapitulate the terms condescended on, and they differ so far as that they can proceed no further in the way of treaty, and so give it up, yet, so as Mr. William Hamilton on the one hand prepared diligences for the suit, suitable to Sir Robert his quality (he being then a member of the Privy Council), but, say'd he would expect to hear further from him ere he would serve his letter missive (having lost a former diligence, by the treaty at B. Cloghan). At last, Sir Robert sent his cousin (and, indeed, all their cousins were concerned in the suit), Mr. Trail, with an express commission (which Mr. Hamilton would not receive till he had provided three or four credible witnesses) to tell him he would treat no more with him, but expected (or desired) that he would enter his suit at law, and make use of his summons or letter missive, which, having taken those gentlemen witnesses, he did on that same day, being the very last day they were in force. But the truth is, Sir Robert had been dangerously unwell, and recovered his litigious humour with his strength; yet his retreat was fair, for he denied what Mr. William alleged was agreed to, and Mr. William could neither prove it, nor oblige him to stand to it if he had.

APPENDIX TO CHAPTER XI.

[Copy Agreement between James Hamilton, of Neilsbrook, and Gawin and William Hamilton, dated 21st October, 1680, referred to at page 136, *ante*.]

THIS INDENTURE, made the 21st day of October, in the year of our Lord One Thousand Six Hundred and Fourscore years, between James Hamilton, of Neilsbrook, in the county of Antrim, Esq., on the one part, and Lieutenant Gawin Hamilton, of Lisowne, in the county of Down, Gentlema n, and Master William Hamilton, of the city of Edinburgh, in the kingdom of Scotland, writer, brother germans to the said Jam es Hamilton, on the other part : Whereas, James, Earl of Clanbrasil, by his latter will and testament, did leave his estat e to the five eldest sons or issue male of his five uncles, if it should happen his two sons to decease without heirs of their body; and, whereas, the said James Hamilton, of Neilsbrook, eldest surviving son to Archibald Hamilton, of Halcraig, the eldest of the said five uncles, did claim and concur with the four eldest sons of the other four uncles, for proving the said will and testament ; and, whereas, the said Gawin Hamilton, and Mr. William Hamilton, brother to the said Jame s Hamilton, did concur with and assist him in the proving of the said will and other suits concerning the same. Now, this Indenture witnesseth, that it is cove- nanted, concluded, and agreed by and between the said parties in manner following :—

Imprimis—That the said James Hamilton, and the said Gawin, and Mr. William Hamilton, his brethren, shall, for preserving the memory of their father's family, join and concur together for recovering the said fifth part, and bear, and advance one proportionable part of the expences to be disbursed thereupon according to their respective proportions after specified of the said fifth part.

Item—The said James Hamilton, for himself, his heirs, executors, and administrators, for the love and affection he hath to his said two brethren, and the other considerations above-mentioned, doth covenant, promise, and grant to and with the said Gawin, and Mr. William Hamilton, his brethren, their heirs, exors., admors., and assigns, that the said James Hamilton, and his aforesaids, shall and will make, do, and execute, or cause and procure to be made, done, and executed, all such gifts, grants, conveyances, and assurances of the law, for granting, assigning, and conveying unto the said Gawin and Mr. William Hamilton, equally betwixt them and their aforesaids, one just equal half or moiety of the said James Hamilton his said fifth part of the said estate of Clanbrasil, and of all lands, money, hereditaments, tenements, freeholds, and other things whatsoever belonging to the said estate, and falling, accruing, pertaining, and belonging to the said James Hamilton, as his fifth part thereof, excepting and reserving to the said James Hamil- ton, and Agnes Kennedy, *alias* Hamilton, his wife, and his heirs, exors., ad.nors., and assigns, the rents and profits of the first part of the freeholds that was in the possession of Earl Henry at the time of his decease, during all the days of Ann, Countess of Clanbrasil, her life-time, by the said latter Will and Testament, or by any other manner of way.

Item—It is further agreed between the said parties, that the said half conveyed or to be conveyed and made over by the said James Hamilton of his said fifth part to the said Gawin and Master William Hamilton, equally betwixt them, and their aforesaids, shall be burthened and affected, and made liable to make payment and satisfaction of the just equal half of all debts, incumbrances, and rewards, to be given to the heirs general, and other persons, and half of all other burdens whatsoever wherewith the said James Hamilton his said fifth part shall be burthened, affected, or made liable to pay, and satisfy, and to relieve the said James Hamilton, and his aforesaids, of the half of the said debts, incum- brances, rewards, and other aforesaids.

In Witness whereof, the parties abovesaid to these present Indentures their hands and seals interchangeably have set, the day and year first above written.

Signed, sealed, and delivered, in presence of
    ARCHIBALD HAMILTON,
    JOHN HAMILTON,
    DA. NICHOLSON.

JA. HAMILTON.   [SEAL.]

WM. HAMILTON, (with my hand.)   [SEAL.]

[Copy Will of Captain James Hamilton, of Neilsbrook, dated 6th September, 1683, referred to at page 136, *ante*.]

In the name of God, amen.—The last Will and Testament of Captain James Hamilton, of Neilsbrook, being sound and perfect in memory and mind, though sick in body, written the 6th day of September, in the year of our Lord, 1683, and the thirty-fifth year of the reign of our Sovereign Lord, Charles the Second, by the grace of God, of England, Scotland, France, and Ireland, King, Defender of the Faith.

Imprimis—I do recommend my soul into the hands of Almighty God, my Creator, hoping to receive full pardon and free remission of all my sins, and to be saved by the precious death and merits of my Blessed Saviour and Redeemer Jesus Christ, and my body to be buried in a decent manner. I do leave to my dear wife, Agnes Kennedy, during all the days of her natural life, all and singular towns, lands, tenements, and interests whatsoever, with the appurtenances, belonging to me in the County of Antrim, and that free of all debts, my said wife maintaining Rose, Ann, and Rachel Hamilton, our three daughters, until such time as they receive portions out of my other estate, left by me to them, competent for their maintenance, with full power to my said wife to provide and dispose of my towns, lands, and interests aforesaid, to such of our said daughters after her own death as she shall think fit.

Item—I do leave to my said three daughters, and their heirs for ever, to be divided amongst them in manner after mentioned, one just equal half or moiety, and also leave and confirm to my two loving brethren, Lieutenant Gawin and Mr. William Hamilton, and their heirs for ever, to be divided equally betwixt them (in consideration of the sum of £ sterling, money advanced by them to me, and applied by me in the suit against Alice, Countess of Clanbrasil, and of the other sums, services, and travel expended and done by them in relation to the same suit), the other just equal half or moiety of my fifth part or share, or of any other share or proportion that was left devised or provided, or otherwise falling, accruing, or belonging to me by the last Will and Testament of James, Earl of Clanbrasil, Lord Claneboye, or by any other manner of way whatsoever, of all and singular the whole manors, towns, lands, tenements, hereditaments, patronage, royalties, advowsons, reversion or reversions, remainder or remainders, goods and chattels, or other estate or estates whatsoever, belonging to the said Earl at the time of his death, with the appurtenances, and of all profits, benefits, and advantages whatsoever, that either may or can accrue out of my share and proportion aforesaid, excepting and reserving to me, my heirs, and assigns, all rents and profits which have or may accrue out of my share and proportion of all freeholds within that part of the estate of Clanbrasil not in possession of Anne, Countess of Clanbrasil, or Sir Robert Maxwell, her husband, and that during the said Countess her natural life only.

Item—I further leave to my said daughters, and their heirs for ever, all my towns, lands, right, title, and interest belonging to me in the County of Monaghan, with my third part or proportion of the two rent charges, which contain £22, granted at first by Art Og M'Mahon to Robert Moore and Christopher Bath, then of Drogheda, Merchants, and assigned by them to Sir Charles Coote, Knight and Baronet, and in the Earl of Munrath, of which he hath given a letter of attorney to Peter Beehan, me the said James Hamilton, and James Duffy, for the use and benefit of the said James Hamilton, Peter Beehan, and John Owens, and is to make over his right to the said Peter Beehan, upon demand to the said Earl or his assigns at any time hereafter, and to the proper use of the said Peter Beehan, James Hamilton, and John Owens, as it shall be equally divided amongst them,—always my said daughters paying my just debts and legacies. I also leave ten shillings a year out of the lands of Tollytollack; ten shillings a year out of the lands of Dawhatty; fourteen shillings and elevenpence out of the lands of Cloufad, which is king's rent paid by me for those lands, with power to distrain for the same, in case of not thankful payment, and that ay and while the said proprietors relieve my said daughters of the said king's rent.

Item—I leave to my said daughters all my right, title, interest, claim, or demand I have, can have, or may claim to an house in Dublin, situate on the Merchants' Quay, and to all past rents since the year of God, 1668, that the trustees received the rents that year, now being received by me ever since, with full power to shew and plead, recover and discharge after receipt. My will is, and I order that my said daughters shall divide the whole estate aforesaid, left to them according to five shares, giving Rose two, and three shares to be equally divided betwixt the other two ;

and if it please God to call any of them before marriage, that then the eldest then living have three shares, and two shares to the youngest.

Item—I ordain my said daughters to satisfy and pay all my just and lawful debts out of the full estate aforesaid left by me to them.

Item—I leave to James, Margaret, Jean, Rachel, and Helen Fairlie, my sister's son and daughters, the third year's rent or profit that my said daughters shall get or recover out of that moiety and half left to them of the estate of Clanbrasil, which year's rent I order my said daughters, whenever they shall receive the same, to pay and deliver unto my said sister's son and daughters above named.

Item—My will is, that if it shall happen my said three daughters to get so much of the whole portion left by me to them as will yield to them £200 sterling per annum of yearly rent, over and above the payment of my debts, that then, at the end of three years after the receipt and possession of their said portions, they shall pay to my dear wife, their mother, £40 per annum during the time she remaineth my widow, which £40 is to be paid proportionally by my said daughters, according to the division aforesaid of the estate and goods left by me to them.

Item—I leave my wife and three daughters my sole executors of this my last Will and Testament, and my two brethren, Lieutenant Gawin and Mr. William Hamilton, and Mr. William Fairley, the elder, and Mr. Thomas Kennedy, of Newtown, and, in case of any of their deceases, the survivors of them, to be overseers, as well in moveables as other things, to my said daughters.

Item—I leave my wife to be manager of my whole estate left to my daughters during the non-divident amongst them, and to take to her assistance my brethren, Lieutenant Gawin, and Mr. William Hamilton, with power to my said wife, with consent of her daughters, to sell off and dispose what lands shall be thought most fit for sale, for the payment of my debts, it always being with the consent of two of the foresaid named overseers, either Lieutenant Gawin, or Mr. William, being always one.

Item—If it shall fall out that any of my daughters marry without the consent of their mother and one of my brethren, or my brother-in-law, Mr. William Fairlie, that then, in that case, it shall be in the power of my wife and brethren, or brother-in-law, to diminish her or their portion who so marries, and to give to her or them so much thereof as they shall think fit, giving the remainder to the other sisters.

Item—My pleasure and will is, that my wife and daughters live together while unmarried; and if any of my said daughters incline to live at any other place, that it be where any two of the overseers shall think fit, and so to be ordered in all things with their mother's consent, with the overseers, always Lieutenant Gawin, or Mr. William, being one.

And this I publish, manifest, and declare to be my last Will and Testament, as witness my hand and seal the day and year above written.

J. HAMILTON.   [SEAL.]

Signed, sealed, and delivered to my dear wife, to the behoof of herself, my daughters, and brethren, and others above named, in presence of

    JOHN WILSON,
    HANS HAMILTON,
    HUGH CAMPBELL.

[Copy Release from Rose and Anne Hamilton to William Hamilton, dated 14th October, 1685, referred to at page 136, *ante*.

THIS INDENTURE, made the fourteenth day of October, in the year of our Lord God One Thousand Six Hundred and Eighty-five, between Rose Hamilton, and Anne Hamilton, both of Neilsbrook, in the county of Antrim, of the one part, and William Hamilton, of the city of Dublin, Esq., of the other part: Whereas, James Hamilton, of Neilsbrook, by his last will in writing, dated the sixth day of September, in the year of our Lord God One Thousand Six Hundred Eighty and Three, and by deeds duly executed in his life time, or one of them, did devise, convey, and settle on Gawin Hamilton, of Lisowin, in the county of Down, and the said William, one moiety, or half of all that portion, or fifth part of James, late Earl of Clanbrassil's estate, which the said James Hamilton had right and title unto, by the last will of the said Earl James, as by the said will and deeds of the said James Hamilton, deceased, may more at large appear.

And, Whereas, the said William hath accepted of an Indenture of Lease, made by Sir Robert Maxwell, Knight and Bart., and the Right Honble. Anne, Countess of Clanbrasil, Archibald Hamilton, of Ardmagh, and Patrick Hamilton, of Grangehaugh, and the said Rose, and Anne, of the Castle, Town, and Manor, of Killileagh and Dufferin, and certain other lands settled in jointure on the said Countess, and lately in her and the said Sir Robert Maxwell, and their under-tenants' possession, to Henry Leslie, of Sheepland, in the county of Down, clerk, and the said William, their executors and administrators, for and during the term and space of sixty-one years, from the first of November last; yielding and paying thereout and therefore, amongst other things, to the said Archibald, Patrick, Rose, and Anne, yearly, during the said term, if the said Countess should so long live, the sum of thirty shillings sterling, and the sum of one thousand and four hundred pounds sterling, yearly, during the residue of the said term, after the death of the said Countess, if she shall happen to die before the expiration thereof, or to that or some such effect, as by said Indenture bearing date the ninth of this instant October, may now at large appear. Now, this Indenture Witnesseth, that the said Rose, and Anne to the intent and purpose, that the said William may not by his acceptance of the said lease be barred, stopped, let, or interrupted, of the full and free enjoyment of the rents, issues, and profits, of such proportion or parts of the said join-ture, as he hath right and title unto by the above-mentioned will and deeds of the said James Hamilton, deceased, and to prevent and avoid any misconceptions or prejudice, that the said William or his estate or title is or may be liable unto by virtue of the said lease, and for and in consideration of the sum of five shillings sterling, to them the said Rose, and Anne, before the delivery of these presents, by the said William satisfied and paid, and for divers other causes and considerations them thereunto moving, have renounced, released, remised, and for ever quit claimed, and confirmed, and by these presents for them, and their heirs, do remise, release, quit claim, and confirm, unto the said William, and his heirs and assigns for ever, one full fourth part of the proportion or fifth part of the said jointure, which the said James Hamilton, deceased, had right unto by the said will of the said Earl James, and also one fourth part of such proportion of the several abovementioned rents, as by equal and just computation is by said lease made payable to Rose and Anne, (that is to say) two shillings and sixpence of the said yearly rent or thirty shillings, and one hundred and sixteen pounds thirteen shillings and four pence per annum of the abovementioned yearly rent of one thousand four hundred pounds, and likewise all the estate, right, title, claim, and demand whatsoever of them the said Rose and Anne, of, in, and to the said fourth part of the said James Hamilton, deceased, his proportion of the said jointure; provided always, and it is hereby declared to be the true intent and meaning of the parties to these presents, that no part of the said several rents is hereby released or intended to be released except only the said several yearly sums of two shillings and sixpence, and one hundred and sixteen pounds thirteen shillings and fourpence; and, notwithstanding these presents it is and shall be lawful for the said Rose and Anne, their heirs and assigns, to take, receive, and enjoy the residue of such proportion of the said rent, as by the said lease is made payable to them, over and above the said yearly sums of two shillings and sixpence, and one hundred and sixteen pounds thirteen shillings and four pence, and to use all legal means for receiving of the said residue reserved to them by the said lease.

In Witness whereof, the parties to these presents have hereunto interchangeably set their hands and seals.

Signed, sealed, and delivered, in the presence of }

WILLIAM FAIRLIE,
DAVID ROBISON.

ROSE HAMILTON. [SEAL.]

ANNE HAMILTON. [SEAL.]

OF THE FIRST PART OF THE SUIT BEFORE CHANCELLOR PORTER, AND WHY IT PASSED IN CHANCELLOR FITTON'S TIME.

Whilst all assays and endeavors for peaceable determining of the differences betwixt the two and the three proved ineffectual, and now the three can have nothing but what they can evince at law, the three give in the bill to the Chancellor for proving the will, and that according thereunto they may have, each of them, the fifth part of the estate whereof Earl James Clanbrassill died seized, settled upon them severally and respectively. Sir Robert, and James of Newcastle, put in their answers upon oath severally, and Sir Robert first answers for Sir Hans's grand-child as his guardian, that the whole estate belonging to him and James of Newcastle, by virtue of a purchase made thereof from Henry Moore, now Earl of Drogheda jointly; then for himself, that the estates belonged to himself, and James of Newcastle, by virtue of a purchase made thereof, from William Moore, brother to the now Earl of Drogheda, but that Sir Hans, and James of Newcastle had agreed with the three upon certain articles, for performance whereof they were always willing; that as to the will made by Earl James they knew nothing of it, nor were concerned in it. James of Newcastle, answers upon oath that Sir Hans and he had purchased a title from Henry Moore, now Earl of Drogheda; that the whole estate belonged to himself, and Hans Hamilton, grand-child to Sir Hans Hamilton, which he believed was a good title; and tho' formerly he believed, and had sworn, that Earl James's will was good and duly perfected, and conveyed a firm title to the five of the whole estate, yet now he believed it was not so; pleaded also that Sir Hans and he had made articles with the three, who had witnesses, and gave in proofs for their title, but the two produced no witnesses. Upon hearing, the Chancellor say'd, whereas, the two as well as the three had sworn in their answers to Countess Alice Clanbrassill, and Henry Earl of Drogheda, their bill, that the will must be received as good, to them all, but, whereas, their answers proposed new matter, viz., of articles whereof the other had nothing in their bill, he directed their bill should be renewed, and the whole matter of difference should be set forth in their bill, and then he would judge of all, the other party saying also for themselves what they could; the which (as they on both sides) were making ready to do, the Chancellor Porter was laid aside from his office,* and ere he had left the

---

* Sir Charles Porter, Knight, who was appointed Lord Chancellor of Ireland on the 16th of April, 1686, was removed, and Sir Alexander Fitton, Knight, appointed in his place on the 12th of February, 1687; but the Great Seal was put in commission on the 1st of August, 1690, and Sir Charles Porter was re-appointed to the office, on the 29th of December, 1690, and continued to hold it till his death in 1696.

city and kingdom, it was moved to him by the three, that he would be pleased to determine the matter, by way of reference, to which all might agree, and settle accordingly. He consented to undertake it; but, the two declined this, having a better prospect in his successor, Sir Thomas Fitton, he being of near kindred to Sir Hans his grand-child, and to James of Newcastle, by their mother, a professed papist, and besides of no great esteem for skill in law, and far less for justice and honor. During his time, all that the three could do was to get (if possible) James of Newcastle, and Sir Robert to answer interrogatories about some known transactions, give account of freehold and other deeds, but it was to no purpose, to expect they should swear to their prejudice; for whatever was of moment, the one knew nothing, and the other remembered nothing of it. In this time it fell out that James of Newcastle   *   in suit of a lady who was kinswoman to the Countess Ann Clanbrassill, which came to visit her before she should be married, and discoursing with her earnestly about it, dissuaded her from it, and by this argument, that he had been very deceitful and injurious to his cousins, and that God would not bless what he had acquired by such unjust ways, and to that effect; nevertheless, she was prevailed with to marry him,[b] but this advice and reason struck heavy upon her; to pacify her on this account, there are new motions proposed for an agreement, and friends are called together, wherein Sir Robert Hamilton impowers James of Tullymore,[c] and James of Newcastle, to determine finally all those differences, and that he would rest satisfied with what they do, or the persons they should agree to as arbitrators, and this under hand and seal. It is also essayed to find out fit persons on both sides, and five persons are nominated on each side, of which two on either side shall have power to determine all, and the adverse party to take out three. With all, it is proposed that James of Newcastle shall acquaint Sir Robert herewith, not of necessity but of good manners, and that they will acquaint the three, and other friends when they shall get Sir Robert's answer; the Lady is convinced of her husband's justice; but they had never the manners to acquaint the three with Sir Robert's answer, or promote what was seemingly agreed on, that not being their design. But now the tumults and stirs[d] in the country are so hot, that all people's

James Hamilton, of Newcastle, and afterwards styled of Bangor, married the Honorable Sophia Mordaunt, third daughter of John, Viscount Mordaunt, by whom he left two daughters, Mrs. Ward, of Bangor, and Lady Ikerron, his co-heiresses, his only son James having died a minor. —*Mrs. Reilly's Memoirs*, p. 90. See a copy of the inscription on their monument in Bangor church, at p. 43, *ante*.

[c] See memoir of him at p. 63, *ante*.

[d] The "tumults and stirs" here referred to are so graphically described in *Reid's History of the Presbyterian Church in Ireland*, which is also the best civil history of

the period which the Editor of these MSS. has met with, that he extracts the entire passage relating to them. Dr. Reid after relating some of the more remarkable incidents of the siege of Derry, which was then going on, proceeds thus :—"In the meantime, the Protestants of Down made a vigorous attempt to preserve their properties from being plundered by the Romanist soldiery. The protections which many of them had received from Tyrconnel and General Hamilton were disregarded by the military ; especially by the regiment of Magennis, of Iveagh, whose companies composed of rude and half-civilized natives from the mountains of Mourne, were stationed in the several towns. Their unminds are other way employed, and Sir Robert, and James of Newcastle, enjoy the estate peaceably and are confident the three cousins will never shake them out of it, tho' still it is uneasy to

authorized and oppressive exactions were, for a time, borne in silence; the people having few arms, and being destitute of a leader. But hearing that Captain Henry Hunter had escaped from Antrim, where he had been confined for nearly three weeks, and had reached Donaghadee with the view of passing over into Scotland, they had recourse to this experienced officer for counsel and assistance. He immediately abandoned his design of leaving the kingdom, placed himself at the head of the Protestants who had arms, and marched towards Newtownards, which the company of Captain Con Magennis were just preparing to plunder. On the fifteenth of April he attacked this party at a place called Kinninghourne, about two miles from the town; and having made prisoners of the greater number, he drove them out of that district. On the same day he dispersed a second party of this obnoxious regiment, stationed at Comber, and rescued that town also from their exactions. Thence, with an increased number of adherents, he proceeded to the Ards, where another large detachment from the same regiment, having crossed over at Strangford, from their head-quarters at Downpatrick, were engaged in plundering the unprotected Protestants of that barony. These he likewise defeated; and compelled them to retreat across the ferry, in such haste, that they left behind them in Portaferry all their plunder, together with several vessels laden with grain, which they had seized not long before. So soon as intelligence of these proceedings reached Carrickfergus, Lieutenant-Colonel Mark Talbot, the Governor, at the head of a small body of a hundred musketeers, marched towards Newtownards; but hearing of the dispersion of the detachment in the Ards, and the increasing number of the Protestants who had risen in arms, he hastily retreated to his quarters. From Portaferry, Hunter returned to Comber, where he received repeated messages from Sir Robert Maxwell, then residing in the castle of Killileagh, urging him to assist in expelling Captain Savage's company, who had been recently quartered upon the inhabitants of that town, and had threatened to take possession of the castle. Hunter accordingly marched during the night to Killileagh, and entered it at daybreak; and, having surprised and disarmed the entire company, he sent the captain and lieutenant prisoners to Portaferry to be shipped to England or the Isle of Man. Magennis, irritated at these repeated discomfitures, and especially at the disgraceful capture of his company under Savage, proceeded with a considerable force from Downpatrick towards Killileagh, with the view of rescuing his officers and men, and checking the further progress of Hunter. But the latter was on the alert, and boldly advanced against him. Both

parties met at the Quoile Bridge, and after a smart skirmish, Magennis was compelled to abandon Downpatrick, and retreat over the strand to Dundrum, leaving the Protestants in possession of that district. Hunter secured a small piece of ordnance, which he placed in Killileagh Castle, and proceeded to Downpatrick, where he liberated all persons confined for political offences. Among the prisoners released from the gaol of Downpatrick, Hunter mentions in particular 'a very aged clergyman, called Mr. Maxwell, of Phenybrogue.' By these unexpected successes the people of Down experienced a seasonable relief from the exactions of the soldiery; the embargo which had been laid on vessels in the sea-port towns of that county was removed, and many persons from the remote parts of the province effected their escape into the sister kingdoms; the garrison in Derry were encouraged by the intelligence of these proceedings; and greater leniency and moderation were thenceforth observed by the Romanist authorities in other places, lest a similar spirit of revolt should be excited. But this triumph of the Protestants was of a short duration. On the twenty-third of April, a few days after their encounter with Magennis, King James arrived at Newry, on his return to Dublin from the camp before Derry. Alarmed at the progress of these insurrectionary movements, he despatched Major-General Buchan with orders to collect a sufficient force from the garrisons at Carrickfergus, Lisburn, and Antrim, and reduce the people of Down to due subjection to his authority. Buchan accordingly placed himself at the head of three troops of horse; and on the thirtieth of April, marched from Lisburn towards Killileagh. He was followed by the greater part of Tyrconnel's, Antrim's and Cormack O'Neill's regiments of foot, under the command of Lieutenant-Colonel Mark Talbot, who overtook the General about five o'clock the same evening. Hunter, apprized of their approach, but not expecting an attack, had collected his followers to the number of two thousand, and had taken up a position between Comber [Lisburn] and Killileagh. Buchan, however, lost no time. On the arrival of the infantry, he immediately attacked the Protestants, and speedily routed these undisciplined volunteers; three hundred were slain in this ' break of Killileagh,' as it was called. Hunter himself was ridden down by the dragoons; but recovering his horse, and finding himself surrounded, he accepted quarter, and delivered up his arms. Being near a deer-park, however, he seized an opportunity to escape, and springing over the wall, fled to the castle of Killileagh, in which he had previously placed a garrison of fifty men. But finding that these had fled, he withdrew to the coast, and succeeded in reaching the Isle of Man in

them to hear how everybody of sense and honesty cry against their treacherous dealing with the cousins, being intrusted by them, and conducting the business at their charge, and with protestations of honesty.*

---

safety. General Buchan, with the horse proceeded to Newtownards, Donaghadee, and Portaferry, driving before him the flying Protestants who had been in arms ; and having left a strong force under Brigadier-General Maxwell, to preserve tranquility throughout that extensive district, he returned to Carrickfergus, and placed his troops in their former quarters.—2. *Reid*, pp. 460 to 463; and see "Case of Captain Henry Hunter," &c. In "Leslie's answer to King," page 155, *et seq.*, he relates these events with a strong bias against both Hunter and the Protestants. He represents Sir Robert Maxwell as sending one John Stuart, an apothecary in Downpatrick, to invite Captain Savage and his company to take up their quarters in Killileagh, to protect the town against Hunter and his rabble, as he calls the Protestants ; and then, as despatching one Gawn Irvine twice to Hunter, urging him to attack Savage, who was betrayed as he alleges by Sir Robert. He palliates the severities of the Romanists, and greatly underrates the losses of the Protestants ; but, at the same time, he deems it of importance to inform us, "that part of Colonel Mark Talbot's wig ¡was shot off his head by a bullet from the Castle of Killileagh, while pursuing the enemy." The account given by Hunter in his "Case" is corroborated by the brief narrative of these proceedings which is given in the " True and impartial Account" above quoted by Dr. Reid. The anonymous author of this important pamphlet states, that after the break of Killileagh, "Lord Duleek's horse chased the Protestants into the sea at Donaghadee ; but one Captain Agnew, riding at anchor, took sixty-eight on board, and conveyed them *gratis* to Scotland." Archbishop King states, that Buchan massacred five or six hundred in cold blood, for several days together, after this engagement; but Hunter, in his petition, is silent altogether as to this ; and Leslie writes, that after the castle was taken, orders were issued granting quarter and prohibiting plunder ; and that the general, in the exasperated state of his soldiers, after a march of sixteen miles, and the evening's engagement, without having partaken of any refreshment, fearing they might injure the inhabitants or their property, encamped them on a hill adjacent to the town. From this they were marched, early the next morning, to Newtownards, bringing with them the captured prisoners, who were there released, on taking an oath not to bear arms again, in opposition to King James. He states, that " Major Callaghan shot one of his men for putting his hand to a Protestant, after order given that they should neither be killed nor plundered." Buchan sent home the foot from

Newtown ; then advanced to Portaferry with some horse, where, having taken one Thomas Hunter prisoner, and settled that district of the Ards, he immediately returned to his quarters. In the townland of Tullymacknows, in Killyleagh parish, a stone has been erected to the memory of two persons, named Cuffey, followers of Hunter, which bears the following rude inscription :—

HERE LYS YE
BODYS OF JOHN
& WILLIAM CUFFIES
WAS KILLED APRIL
YE 30TH 1688 IN DEFENCE
OF THE PROTESTANT
CAUSE.

Mr. J. W. Hanna, in his " *Gossipings about the Parish of Inch*," correctly states that the artist, in engraving the date, made a mistake in cutting 1688 on the stone, for 1689 ; but he is incorrect in stating that this stone was erected on the spot where the "Break of Killileagh" occurred, as it was fought at a distance of nearly a mile from it, and on the old road from Lisburn to Killyleagh, by Ballynahinch, at the point where the wall of Lord Claneboye's deer-park (which is marked on the Claneboye map of 1625-6, but has long since disappeared) joined it, near the foot of Quoilly Hill, and nearly opposite the present residence of Mr. Adam Kenning, whose farm is still called the "Back Park." Mr. Hanna also mentions a fact, which the Editor of these MSS. has not elsewhere met with, viz., that Sir Robert Maxwell had, by Lady Clanbrassil, a son called George, who, during the siege of Derry, served as Lieutenant-Colonel of Sir Clotworthy Skeffington's regiment, in consequence of which, he and his father were both attainted by King James's Parliament.

* The MS. here breaks off abruptly, before the litigation between the representatives of the five uncles of James Earl of Clanbrassil was brought to a conclusion, or any of his estates had been divided among them ; but Mr. William Hamilton, who, upon the internal evidence contained in these MSS., must have been the author of them, and who represented the interests of all the parties in the suit deriving under James of Neilsbrook, has left with the MSS. a mass of letters written to him during the progress of it by Colonel Hans Stevenson, the husband of his niece, Anne Hamilton, who eventually (by the death of her eldest sister Rose, the wife of Captain William Fairlie, without issue, and of her youngest sister Rachel, who died a minor and unmarried,) became the sole heiress and representative of James of

Neilsbrook, who was the eldest surviving son of Archibald of Halcraig, the second brother of James, first Viscount of Claneboye, and the eldest of James Earl of Clanbrassil's uncles. This correspondence the Editor had at first intended printing, as a supplement to the MSS.; but, on further consideration, he does not think it would be of sufficient general interest to justify his doing so, especially as it does not supply the required information, though it extends over a period of ten years—from 1695 to 1705. During its progress, a partition of the jointure lands of Ann Countess of Clanbrassil was made between the representatives of the five uncles, in October, 1696, but the litigation between them as to the division of the remaining lands was still going on at its close; and the following notice, which is appended to it, appears to have been given in despair of its being brought to any successful issue :—

"We, the undernamed subscribers, having a due regard as well for the safety of such persons as have, as of those who intend to purchase any part of the lands whereof either the late, or present, Sir Hans Hamilton were or are possessed of, in the County of Down, as well as for the preservation of our own rights and title thereto as heirs-at-law to the Right Honble. James Lord Claneboy, James Earl of Clanbrasill, his son, Henry Earl of Clanbrasil, his grandson, or as having a right by the settlement of the said James Lord Visct. Claneboy of his whole estate, and by the last will and testament of the said James Earl of Clanbrasill, or otherwise. That we intend by virtue of such our title to call such sales into question for all years and terms bygone and to come, of which all persons concerned are to take notice.

"WILLM. HAMILTON.
"HANS STEVENSON.

" Dated this 11th day of September, 1702."

It is not, at this distance of time, easy, perhaps not possible, to ascertain the exact result of this lengthened litigation; but it appears, that Colonel Hans and Mrs. Stevenson (on behalf of themselves, and of Gawin and William Hamilton), obtained a decree in the Court of Chancery in Ireland against the grandson of Sir Hans Hamilton, James Hamilton of Bangor, and James Hamilton of Tullymore, declaring them to be trustees for them of one-fifth of the estates, which they had purchased from the representatives of Countess Alice. From this decree, however, an appeal was brought to the House of Lords in England; and, in the Appendix to this chapter will be given a copy of the case of the respondents, Hans and Ann Stevenson, printed for the use of the Lords on the hearing of that appeal, which has been found in the Bodleian Library, Oxford. It further appears, by a joint case, stated about the year 1752, on behalf of James Stevenson and Gawin Hamilton, Esqrs., the then owners of the Killileagh Proportion, that this decree was, on the hearing of the appeal, in the year 1701, confirmed in part, and in part reversed ; but that no proceedings had been taken thereon for many years past, by reason of minority, coverture, and otherwise; and, in a letter from Mr. Stevenson to Mr. Hamilton, dated 2nd December, 1752, which has been also found among the papers, he states, " that, although it was the opinion of his counsel that the

suit was a good one at the time, yet it had since branched out into so many different properties, that it would take his lifetime to bring all the parties into Court again; and that, although he believed they were not then barred by time in the suit, if ever it was carried on again, it must be by a man of great application to business, knowledge, and talents that never offered themselves to him, and backed with a good fund." These considerations probably decided them against resuming the prosecution of the suit, which has never since been revived. In a note to the third volume of Lodge's Peerage of Ireland, under the title of "Hamilton, Viscount Limerick," the following statement is given of the parties entitled under Earl James's will, and the mode in which his estates were partitioned; but it will be seen that Lodge does not allude to the fact that the lands so divided were only the jointure lands of his widow, and not the whole of his estates, which had been, greatly reduced by the sales made of a very considerable part of them by Earl Henry among his tenants and others, in consequence of the Countess Alice's extravagance, as stated at p. 88, ante :—

"The representatives of his five uncles were James Hamilton, of Neilsbrook, in the County of Antrim, Esq.; Sir Hans Hamilton, Bart.; James Hamilton, of Bangor, Esq.; the Rev. Archibald Hamilton, of Armagh; and Patrick Hamilton, of Granshaw, Esq. James of Neilsbrook left three daughters, Rose, Anne, and Rachel ; the eldest of whom [Rose, who married Captain William Fairlie] dying without issue, and the youngest of whom [Rachel] dying unmarried, Anne became heir to half of his estate, and married with Hans Stevenson, Esq., her father by will leaving the other half to his brothers, Gawin and William. Sir Hans Hamilton left an only child, Sarah, mother to Sir Hans [the younger], who became entitled to his grandfather's share. Archibald conveyed his share to [James Hamilton, of Tollimore] the Lord Limerick's father. Patrick, in 1693, sold his proportion to Sir Robert Colville, who soon after disposed of it to Lord Limerick's father. So that, the estate being thus divided into several hands, signestrators were appointed, by order of the Court of Chancery, to receive the rents, and pay each their proportion, until the 1st of October, 1696, when Sir Hans, James of Bangor, James of Tullimore, Hans Stevenson and wife, Gawin and William, brothers to James of Neilsbrook, agreed to come to a division, and, in pursuance thereof, made up five lots, each consisting of lands, then set or valued at £300 a-year, and known by the Proportions of Killileagh, Tollychin, Ringhaddy, Tonaghneive, and Lisowine, which upon casting lots thus fell :—Killileagh to Mr. Stevenson and wife, and to Gawin and William Hamilton, as co-heirs of James of Neilsbrook ; Tollychin and Ringhaddy to James of Tullimore, Lord Limerick's father; Tonaghneive to James of Bangor; and Lisowine to Sir Hans ; by the Articles of which partition, it was also covenanted that each party should hold his respective share as a manor distinct by itself."—3. Lodge's Peerage, 260.

A copy of these Articles of Partition, together with the Articles for the subdivision of the Killileagh Proportion into the Castle and Gate-house Proportions, will be found in the Appendix to this Chapter.

APPENDIX TO CHAPTER XII.

[Copy of Agreement for Partition of the Jointure Lands between the Representatives of the Five Uncles of James, Earl of Clanbrassil, referred to at p. 146, *ante*.]

It is agreed, the 1st day of October, 1696, between James Hamilton, of Bangor, Esq., for and on behalf of Hans Hamilton, Esq., grandson and heir of Sir Hans Hamilton, deceased, and as guardian to the said Hans Hamilton, now a minor, of the one part; the said James Hamilton, of Bangor, for and on behalf of himself, of the second part; William Hamilton, of Killileagh, Gawin Hamilton, of Liswine, and Hans Stevenson, of Ballygrot, Esqrs., on behalf of themselves, and of Ann Stevenson, wife of the said Hans Stevenson, and heir of James Hamilton, late of Neilsbrook, Esq., deceased, of the third part; and James Hamilton, of Tullymore, Esq., assignee of Patrick Hamilton, of Granshaw, Gent., and of Archibald Hamilton, heretofore of Armagh, but now of Ballow, Clerk, of the fourth part, for and concerning a partition of certain lands, tenements, and hereditaments, which were heretofore part of the estate of James, late Earl of Clanbrasil, deceased, and hereinafter particularly mentioned and expressed.

Imprimis—It is agreed that the five following Proportions, as hereafter set down, are equal, and that each person or persons who shall have any of the following shares, shall for each share contribute yearly Six Pounds sterling towards payment of a chief rent of Thirty Pounds, payable yearly to Mr. Hill out of part of the following lands, and shall likewise pay one-fifth of all the debts to which the following lands are now liable, being debts of James, Earl of Clanbrasil aforesaid, and hereinafter expressed; and also a fifth part of such charge or purchase-money as shall be necessary either in evicting or compounding for the pretended Leases in reversion of any part of the estate to be divided:—

Killileagh Proportion.	Yearly Value.	Killileagh Proportion.	Yearly Value.	Tollichin Proportion.	Yearly Value.
Castle and Demesnes ..	£110 0 0	King's Rent of 16s per annum, which the territory of Dufferin pays the Crown, and the rest of the Dufferin to be discharged thereof..		Cluntagh	38 0 0
Corn Mill	15 0 0			Ardigon	26 0 0
Maymore and Corduff ..	24 0 0			Half Ballywollen (Mr. Richardson)	20 0 0
Island Taggert ..	10 0 0		100 5 0	Tollyvery (Fairlie) ..	32 0 0
Rathcunningham ..	17 0 0			Mill	14 0 0
Ballymacrummel ..	24 0 0	Total ..	£300 5 0	Derryboy	31 0 0
Killileagh Town and lands (except four acres possessed by James Bailie, Esq., and one house possessed by Jas. Sloane, Esq., and one house possessed by Mrs. Ferguson, together with Castle William), except Seven Pounds per annum subject to the				Clay	30 0 0
				Tollymacknowes ..	12 0 0
		Tollichin Proportion.	Yearly Value.	Tuckmill, and lands to it	4 0 0
				Ballygoskin (part Campbell, Wilson, & Wiley)	12 0 0
		Tollychin	£30 0 0	Toy	5 0 0
		Mullagh	30 0 0	Ballybregagh ..	2 0 0
		Corbally	2 0 0	Out of Castlewilliam ..	7 0 0
				Total ..	£300 0 0

Ringhaddy Proportion.	Yearly Value.			Tonaghaive Proportion.	Yearly Value.			Liswine Proportion.	Yearly Value.		
Ballymacreely ..	£48	0	0	Killinure	22	0	0	To have thirteen acres			
Ballow	27	0	0	Lisdownan	26	0	0	of moss in Tollyveery, ten			
Mill thereof ..	10	0	0	Lessens ..	28	0	0	acres of moss in Mullagh,			
Killinchy in plain ..	35	0	0	Carricknacessanagh ..	30	0	0	twenty acres in Cluntagh,			
Carrickrusky	16	0	0	Glasdrumon	27	0	0	and ten acres in Bally-			
Ballydorn	24	0	0	Carsons	34	0	0	woollen, next adjacent to			
Ballymoran and Killina-				The Mill ..	14	0	0	Killileagh, and as the pro-			
kin	35	0	0	Drummaconnell ..	20	0	0	prietors of the said deno-			
Carrowreagh	12	0	0	Ballyaghargie ..	9	0	0	minations shall set apart.			
Ringhaddy	40	0	0	Aughandarragh ..	20	0	0				
Island Bawn, Tollymore,				Ballymacashen ..	22	0	0	Listowder	£26	0	0
and Ralphgormont ..	23	0	0	Lisdalgan	24	0	0	Mill thereof	13	0	0
Ballymacarran	28	0	0	Half Liswine (John Max-				Criviargan	21	0	0
Tythe of Criviloghgare	2	0	0	well), with a moiety of				Ballydian	25	0	0
				the Rectorial Tithes of				Crivycarnonan	28	0	0
				lands in Tonaghnive	18	0	0	Cluntinaglare	39	0	0
								Liswine (Gawin Hamil-			
								ton's half) ..	18	0	0
								Legagown	42	0	0
								Killinchinikelly ..	40	0	0
								Ballyalgan	29	0	0
								Half Ballywoollen ..	19	0	0
Total ..	£300	0	0	Total ..	£300	0	0	Total ..	£300	0	0

Debts with which the above Lands are charged, being the Five Proportions :—

John Savage, Esq.	..	..	..	..	..	..	..	..	£90	0 0
Widow Wood	..	..	..	..	..	..	..	..	60	0 0
Mrs. Richardson	..	..	..	..	..	..	..	..	100	0 0
John Robinson's Executors	..	..	..	..	..	..	..	..	100	0 0
Fairly of Ballydian	..	..	..	..	..	..	..	..	200	0 0

Whereas the inhabitants of the lands of Killinure, Lisdownan, Lessens, and part of Tonaghnive proportion are to grind their corn at the Mill of Ballyknockan, therefore, and to make up for want of a dwelling in that proportion, one moyety of the Rectorial Tythes of the following lands in Tonaghnive proportion is to belong to that proportion, viz., the moyety of the Rectorial Tythes of the said lands of Killinure, Lisdownan, Lessens, and Tollyglowrie, Carrickna-cessanagh, Glasdrumon, the Carsons, Drummaconnell, Ballyaghargie, Lisdalgan, Liswine, and Legagown ; and the other moyety of the tithes of the aforesaid lands to be settled on Gawin Hamilton, Esq., party to these presents, and his heirs, he surrendering his leases of and in any and all lands now to be divided, and his improvements made thereon.

That the wood now growing on the townland of Killinchy be valued, and the person to whom the land shall fall to pay each other proportion one-fifth of the value thereof.

That twenty-five pounds be equally paid by all the proportions, and therewith a good corn mill built on such ground as shall be allotted for the same, near the present corn mill of Killileagh, for Tollychin proportion ; and that the place thereof, together with a shelling hill, and ground for miller's house and garden, be immediately set off.

That the tuck-mill near Killileagh, which belongs to Tollychin proportion, with the land thereto, be bounded.

That satisfaction be made to Hans Hamilton, Esq., for £45, or thereabouts, disbursed in the year '83, or there-abouts, for repair of Ringhaddy.

That all the parties to this agreement appoint a Seneschal for the Manors within the lands to be divided, but that each proprietor be at liberty to erect his own proportion into a Manor.

In order to settle the articles relating to evicting or compounding for leases in reversion, it is agreed that the numbers of years unexpired of each of those leases be ascertained from Alsaints, 1696, with the yearly profit or benefit of such lease over and above the rent payable out of the leased lands, and a reasonable value in money be put on each of such leases; and that the proprietor of each proportion secure to the person within whose share such leased lands shall lie, one-fifth of such value, in case the said lease is not evicted, and the interest thereof until evicted at £8 per cent., and the principal if the lease cannot be evicted.

That endeavours be used to have, at the common expense of all the said parties, an Act of Parliament confirming the partition that shall be made, and that the management thereof, together with that of settling the debts chargeable on the said estate, and evicting or compounding for the leases in reversion, be put into a proper method, and that, till an Act of Parliament can be obtained, a Decree of Chancery be had at the common expense.

That freehold rents be likewise divided, and that the said William Hamilton, Gawin Hamilton, and Hans Stevenson, have their fifth proportion of them; and that the said James Hamilton, of Bangor, and Hans Hamilton do, out of the lands which shall be in the proportions of each of them, secure to the said James Hamilton, of Tollymore, a full recompense in respect to value, worth, and purchase of his the said James Hamilton of Tollymore's proportion of the said freehold rents, and other rights derived to the said James Hamilton in behalf of Archibald Hamilton and Patrick Hamilton, and William Hogg, or either of them; and the proportion or share of the said James Hamilton, of Tollymore, in the lands of Oghlie, Mr. Bailie's sixty acres in Tullyveery, and four acres near the town of Killileagh, and the lands of Lisnagh, Mrs. Ferguson's house, and Mr. Sloan's house in Killileagh aforesaid.

And it is the mutual agreement of all the said parties to discount with each other for the by-past rents of all the lands and freehold rents aforesaid, and fee-farm rents belonging to the said parties.

Sealed and delivered by the above-named Hans Stevenson, James Hamilton of Bangor, James Hamilton of Tullymore, and Hans Hamilton, in the presence of JOS. CROFTON. JA. REID.	HANS HAMILTON. HANS STEVENSON. JAMES HAMILTON. JAMES HAMILTON.

I, Sir Robert Hamilton, of Mount Hamilton, in the County of Armagh, Knt. and Bart., father and heretofore guardian of the within-named Hans Hamilton, do hereby approve of and consent unto the within agreement, as witness my hand and seal, this 16th day of October, 1696.

ROBERT HAMILTON.

Signed, sealed, and delivered in presence of
    JOS. CROFTON,
    JA. REID.

MEMORANDUM.—Whereas mention is made in the within articles, that a value be put on leases in reversion: It is not thereby intended that such leases in reversion as did belong to Gawin Hamilton, Esq., within mentioned, shall be valued, provision being made for the said Gawin's pretensions on that account, and he being to surrender all such leases.

ROBERT HAMILTON.

Sealed and delivered in the presence of
    JOS. CROFTON.
    JA. REID.

I, the within named Hans Hamilton, being now of the full age of twenty-one years, for me, my heirs and assigns, do approve of, ratify, and confirm the within agreement, made for and in my behalf by the within named James Hamilton, of Bangor, Esq., then my guardian, and do, for me, my heirs and assigns, covenant and agree with the within named Gawin Hamilton, William Hamilton, and Hans Stevenson of Killileagh, Esqrs., to fulfil and perform to them, their heirs and assigns respectively, all and singular the within agreements as fully, to all intents and purposes, as if I

2 N

had been at full age when I signed, sealed, and delivered the within agreement, and as if I had been made directly a party thereunto. In witness whereof, I have hereunto set my hand and seal, this 22d day of February, 1697.

Witness present,   HANS HAMILTON.

    ROBERT HAMILTON,
    PITT HENRY CRAWFORD.

COPY ENDORSEMENT ON THE FOREGOING DEED.

Hans Stevenson and Ann his wife,
        Plaintiffs.

Sir Robt. Hamilton, Knt. and Bart., Hans Hamilton, Esq., James Hamilton of Bangor, Esq., and James Hamilton of Tullymore, Esq.,
        Defendants.

This writing was produced unto James Reid, Gent., on his examination in this cause, on the plaintiff's behalf, by me,
        NATH: BOYSE, Dep. Examiner.

[Copy of Agreement, dated 6th September, 1697, between Gawen and William Hamilton, and Hans and Ann Stevenson, for the division of Killyleagh Proportion into the Castle and Gate-House Proportions, referred to at page 146, *ante*.]

Imprimis—That the Castle be a dwelling-house to one of the said halfs, and the Gate-House, turrets, and stables, a dwelling-house for the other of said halfs, and that the inner court of all belong to the Castle, and the outer court to the Gate-House, and that the entry to the Castle shall be in some part of the inner court from the highway leading from the new work to the town, and the entry to the Gate-House to be as it now is.[a]

2.—That the Castle shall have for an outer court so much ground next to that side of the inner court wall where the entry is to be, as lyeth betwixt the said wall and a stone which is appointed to be the mark betwixt the highway and the said outer court. And the Castle is to have a way to the town alongst the side of the Gate-House court wall, and through the turret upon that side on which the Castle is to have its entry.[b] And the Gate-House is to have for an outer

---

[a] On lots being drawn, the Gate-House Proportion fell to Colonel and Mrs. Stevenson, and the Castle Proportion to Mrs. Stevenson's uncles, William and Gawen Hamilton; and the Gate-House and Castle were respectively occupied by them and their descendants, in accordance with the provisions of the above articles, for nearly two hundred years, the division of the two properties extending down the middle of a gravel-walk in the garden. In 1859, however, the present Lord Dufferin and Clandeboye commenced to rebuild the Gate-House, with the intention of presenting it to his cousin, Archibald Hamilton, to whom the Castle Proportion had in the meantime descended. Unhappily, Mr. Hamilton's premature death prevented the accomplishment of this purpose; but, on the 23rd of Oct., 1862, being the day of Lord Dufferin's marriage with his late friend's daughter, the last stone of the new building was laid, and the keys of the gateway presented by his lordship to Mr. Gawen Hamilton, Mr. Archibald Hamilton's eldest son. As a condition attached to the above gift, the owner of the Castle of Killileagh for the time being, is bound to send a red rose yearly to the Lady of Clandeboye, or in the event of there being no Lady at Clandeboye, a pair of gilt spurs to the Lord Dufferin of the day.

[b] This provision in the second article appears to have been never fully carried into execution until the year 1811, although it had, with other matters mentioned in the Articles of Partition, been the subject of controversy between the then occupiers of the Castle and Gate-House so long before as 1739, as will be seen by the following extract from a charge of Archibald Hamilton, Esq., against James Stevenson, Esq.:—"Mr. Hamilton, by said division, being entitled to a gate or passage through the Turret or Gate-House to and from the Castle and town, Mr. Stevenson has hindered him from such gate or passage; and, therefore, Mr. Hamilton charges 15s. per annum since the year 1696, being forty-three years, for his damage,—£32 5s; and, as to this gate, further claims to have the benefit of it from this time forth for ever, or that Mr. Stevenson may enter into a deed with Mr. Hamilton to pay him a yearly sum for such waiving of his right." In consequence of this claim, a Memorandum of Agreement appears to have been entered into between Messrs. Hamilton and Stevenson on the 28th

court, so much of the ground lying before it as will make a square court, according as the party to whom it shall fall shall order it, but not going further out towards the town than the head of the way leading to the Meeting-House, nor further out towards the way that goes from the back street to the new work, than that side of the turret stairs which is next to the entry to the Gate-House.

3.—That the Castle is to have laid into it that side of the new work that lies next to the quarry meadows, with the dog-house, and also that side of the new work that lies next to the water that comes from the quarry-meadow to the bridge. The Gate-House is to have laid into it all that side of the new work that lies next to the highway leading from the bridge to the town, except so much thereof as is beyond John Harry's house, and is betwixt it and the said water running from the quarry-meadow to the bridge. That that part of the new work falling to the Gate-House shall have fourteen feet in breadth off that side of the new work court lying next to it, and that part of the new work falling to the Castle shall have all the rest of the said court. That the Gate-House is to have belonging to it the byre standing over against the new work betwixt the meadow and the highway leading from the bridge to the town. And the Castle is to have belonging to it the barn and little house at the end of it, and the haggard, and also to have for an enclosure all the ground that shall lie betwixt the Castle courts, the mount gardens, and the quarry-meadow on the one side, and a strait line to be drawn from the corner of the outer court appointed for the new work belonging to it which lies next to the Gate-House side of the new work.

4.—That the north side belonging to the Gate-House is to have belonging to it the logh below the bridge of the town, and the ground lying on the shore from the lower end of said logh, to the lower end of the High Street, and the acre on the back of the churchyard, now possessed by Mr. Bruce, with the whole house possessed by Mr. Clewlow, and all right belonging to Killileagh Proportion of the house possessed by Mr. Bruce, and of the house possessed by Mrs. Ross, and the south side of that proportion belonging to the Castle is to have belonging to it that piece of ground not divided, formerly possessed by John Cochran, lying betwixt Carey-park, possessed by James Erwin, and the house and yards possessed by John Lockhart, Hugh M'Cormick, John Erwine, and John Read, and Robinson's clayholes, and that piece of ground not formerly divided, lying upon the shore beyond Pagan's forth, being about half-an-acre, formerly possessed by George Alexander, and the ground upon the south side of High-street, betwixt the lowest yards on that side of the street and the shore; and the wall going up the hill from the white gate at the back of the garden, to be a common walk, and the grass and trees to be equally divided, but the trees not to be cut; and the pound and school-house to be common.*

of February, 1739, by which it was, amongst other things, agreed between the parties to it, " That the said Archibald Hamilton shall, at all times hereafter, have the absolute right and authority to take possession of the turret, on the 4th day of March next, for the ends and uses mentioned in the Articles of Partition of Killileagh fifth of the joynture." But on this agreement there is the following endorsement, in the late Mr. Rowan's handwriting :—" In the year 1811, Lord Dufferin broke a passage through the turret, at the instance of Archibald Hamilton Rowan." The date above this arch (1666) is, therefore, very far from the real one, but has evidently arisen from an old stone with that date upon it being used in its erection in 1811.

* It will be seen, by the following document, that both the Messrs. Hamilton and Captain Stevenson had, shortly previous to the execution of these Articles of Partition, made provision for the support of a philosophical school at Killileagh, which Dr. Reid, at p. 65, of the third volume of his *Presbyterian History*, states, was established in order to afford facilities for young men to prepare for the Ministry in their native land :—

" We, Captain Gawen Hamilton, William Hamilton, and Captain Hans Stevenson, within the County of Down, out of our good liking for learning, and for the encouragement of the same in this place, and particularly for encouraging the philosophical school now taught at Killileagh, by Mr. John M'Alpin, professor of philosophy ; and in consideration that he is, in the future, to keep and teach the said school, at the town of Killileagh, do hereby oblige ourselves to provide him and his family a convenient dwelling-house, rent free, and four soums' grazing, together with meadow for hay to winter the aforesaid soums ; as also our assistance for bringing home two hundred loads of turf, for firing to his family yearlie ; provided always, that he continue his teaching philosophy in this place, upon the aforesaid encouragement, it being performed unto him.

" In testimony whereof, we hereto put our hands and seals, this 4th day of May, 1697.

" Signed, sealed, and delivered in the presence of
" JAMES BRUCE.
" HANS STEVENSON.

" GAWEN HAMILTON.
" WILLIAM HAMILTON.
" HANS STEVENSON.

Dr. Reid (at p. 69, Vol. iii.) further states, that, in September, 1698, Bishop Walkington forwarded to the Government a petition containing several complaints against the.

5.—That all the gardens and orchards upon the west or north-west side of the gravel walk, shall belong to the Castle and Castle Proportion, and all the gardens and orchards upon the south or south-east side of the said gravel walk, with the ground lying betwixt that side of the garden, and the way to the Meeting-House, shall belong to the Gate-House and Gate-House Proportion, and so much ground to be added to it off that end of the bank lying next to Pomphrey's house, as will make that side of the garden laid to the Gate-House equal in measure with the other side of the garden laid to the Castle, after it is known by measuring the garden how much the Gate-House side thereof is less than the other side.·

6.—That the Burgesses or Freemen to be hereafter elected or turned out, are to be so elected or turned out by consent of each of the said parties; and the equal half of the said Burgesses to be of the inhabitants dwelling within the proportion belonging to the Castle, and the other half of the Burgesses to be of the inhabitants dwelling on the proportion belonging to the Gate-House.ᵈ

Presbyterians of his diocese; and, amongst others, that " they had set up at Killileagh a Philosophical School, in open violation and contempt of the laws;" and (at pp. 72, 3, 4) that the Rev. John M'Bride, Minister of Belfast, having been summoned to Dublin before the Privy Council, and being questioned about the school at Killileagh, told them that no Divinity was taught there; and, as to the Philosophical School there, that it was no more than was done in the reign of Charles II, in whose time there were two such schools; and he added that Mr. M'Alpine had a license for his school from Mr. M'Neill, Chancellor to the Diocese. Again, (at p. 113,) Dr. Reid states "that the High Church party in the North had been long dissatisfied with the establishment and success of the Philosophy School at Killileagh, superintended by the Rev. Mr. M'Alpine; and that they longed to see it forcibly closed, in order to check, if not altogether prevent, further supplies of candidates for the Presbyterian ministry; but that they were unable to effect their purpose by the ordinary course of law; for Mr. M'Alpine had obtained a license from the Chancellor of the Diocese, and had duly taken all the oaths required of teachers; and that they now, therefore, had recourse to the House of Commons, whose temper at this crisis was so congenial with their own, and induced them to adopt the following resolution, which, though general, was intended to apply solely to this particular school:—'1st June, 1705. Resolved, that the erecting and continuing any seminary for the instruction and education of youth in principles contrary to the Established Church and Government, tends to create and perpetuate misunderstanding among Protestants.'" And Dr. Reid adds, "that though the injury intended by this resolution did not reach the seminary of Killileagh, two other resolutions, passed at the same time against Presbyterian ministers, so inflamed the zeal of the High Churchmen of Belfast and its neighbourhood, that an informer was found to swear against Mr. M'Bride before an Episcopalian minister, who was a magistrate, and that a warrant having been taken out for his apprehension, he was compelled in the end of the year [1705] to retire to Scotland, where he was forced to remain above three years."—Reid's Presbyterian Hist., Vol. iii, p. 114.

The Editor has been unable to ascertain anything further respecting the Rev. Mr. M'Alpine, except that, after teaching for about fourteen years, he became the Minister of Ballynahinch, and that the Philosophical School in Killileagh was then closed (ex relatione The Rev. Andrew Breakey); but he has found among the Hamilton Papers the following interesting letter from the Rev. Mr. M'Bride:—

" Dublin, September 7th, 1695.
" SIR,—I was till now big with expectation of seeing you here, but being disappointed, this will inform you that we very much need your assistance, for our affair is like to miscarrie for want of true friends. I fear we shall be drowned with Court holy water, as our act is not like to pass unless the Sacramental Test come along with it, and that is but to put us out of the frying pan into the fire. The way we intend to get it at least brought into the Parliament, is by that committee that is appointed to inquire what profitable laws now in force in England are fit to be enacted here, amongst which the Act for toleration of Protestant Dissenters in England will possibly be thought one. The sole right men are sore run down here, and we are like to suffer by this north wind. Mr. Hans Hamilton is not come to Parliament, so that his Burgeship is vacant. This day six Acts were touched, viz., An Act rescinding King James's Parliament; 2d, One for the additional Excise; 3d, For rescinding the old act de heretico comburendo; 4th, Against foreign education of children; 5th, For disarming Papists; 6th, For the better settling intestates' estates. So that they have made good speed hitherto. If your affairs could allow you to be here, your assistance will be very necessarie, and very refreshing to your affectionate and humble servant,

" J. M'BRIDE.
" To William Hamilton, Esq., in Killileagh."

This William Hamilton (the supposed author of the foregoing MSS.) is mentioned by Dr. Reid, (at p. 109,) as one of the few leading Presbyterian gentlemen who had suffered under the Test Clause, and who presented a petition to the Irish Parliament against it, on the 14th of March, 1705, " on behalf of themselves and the rest of the Protestant Dissenting subjects of Ireland."—Reid, Vol. iii.

ᵈ This Article of the Agreement, as might have been expected, led to more differences among the parties intended to be bound by it than all the others. It was, of course, quite illegal for the owners of the property in the Borough, to which corporate rights had been granted by a Royal Charter, thus to appropriate and attempt to divide among themselves, as individuals, franchises which were granted to, and could only belong to the corporate body thereby created; and, although a mutual bond for £5,000 had been contemporaneously executed by each party to this agreement, for the due performance of all its articles, it could not be enforced for a breach of this one, as to which it was

8.—That the little park lying betwixt the back-park and the highway leading from Mr. How's to the town of Killi-leagh, and the four tenements lying upon the south-east side of the High-street under James Road's garden, and the Island Don O'Neal, are to belong to the Gate-House proportion; and the limestone in Don O'Neal, or in any other place within either of the said proportions, is to be common to all the said parties; and the whole mosses which belong to Killileagh proportion are to be common to all the said parties, together with the Town Common, which is also to be common.

8.—That all the ground lying betwixt the highway leading to the mill, and the water draught now appointed, to be the south-west march of the meadow, and betwixt Spratt's house and the water at the back of the byre shall belong to the Gate-House proportion.*

9.—That all the fir-trees within both the gardens and orchard, except the trees planted for making the walks, are to be cut down by consent of both parties. In witness whereof all the said parties have hereunto interchangeably set their hands and seals, this 6th day of September, in the year of our Lord, 1697.

Signed, sealed, and delivered, in presence of

    JAMES BRUCE,
    HANS STEVENSON.
    JAMES ERWINE.
    GEORGE POLLOCK.

GAWIN HAMILTON.
WM. HAMILTON.
HANS STEVENSON.
ANNE STEVENSON.

---

clearly void. The following letters addressed to Gawen Hamilton. Esq., by two of the Burgesses of Killileagh, in the year 1760, on the occasion of his becoming a candidate for the representation of the Borough, on the death of George II., give, in their own language, an amusing account of what they considered the nature of the trust reposed in them by the persons to whose influence they were indebted for their offices:—

ARTHUR JOHNSTON, ESQ., TO G. HAMILTON, ESQ.

"DEAR SIR.—Yours of the 4th inst. was delivered to me by Mr. Kennedy. I am very sorry it is not in my power, consistent with the trust reposed in me, to comply with your request, as I should at all times, and on all occasions, wish to have it in my power to do what might be agreeable to you. When I was elected a burgess of the borough of Killileagh, *I came in at the instance of, and to serve the interest of,* Mr. Stevenson; and as long as I continue in that office, *I shall think myself in honour bound to do every act he may think consistent with his interest.* If upon the present or any other occasion he shall desire me to vote for you, or *any other person* you recommend in the borough, I shall comply with pleasure; but otherwise I shall not think it belongs to *me* to determine what *he* may think *his* right. I am, with great respect, dear sir, your most humble servant, "ARTHUR JOHNSTON."

EDWARD BAILIE, ESQ., TO G. HAMILTON, ESQ.

"SIR,—I had the favor of yours. I do not at all doubt but that you have given a fair state of your case, although of an old date, which possibly may make the issue doubtful; but you must know, or have heard, that I had the compliment paid me of being burgess thirty or forty years ago, by those of the other side of the question, who confided in me as their friend; and *I am sure you would not desire or expect that I should break the confidence reposed in me, which would be attended by the black crime of ingratitude.* But, *if there was anything I had a right to dispose of,* there would be none readier to pay you the compliment than, sir, your well-wisher, and obedient servant, "December 15, 1760." "EDWARD BAILIE.

The letters of the other burgesses, though not putting their refusal to vote for Mr. Hamilton on the same grounds, were equally decided, and Sir John Blackwood and Bernard Ward, Esq., were returned as the members on that occasion.

* This article was also the subject of difference between the parties, but was amicably settled by the following award:—

"Whereas Captain Hans Stevenson and Mr. Archibald Hamilton, both of Killileagh, did this 18th day of October, 1710, agree to refer a difference betwixt them relating to the eighth article perfected by the said Hans Stevenson and Ann, his wife, and by her two uncles, Gawin and William Hamilton, bearing date the 6th September. 1697, being articles of their several partitions of their interests in and about the town of Killileagh : Now, know all men by these presents, that we, John Haltridge, of Dromore, Esq., and James Hamilton, of Derryboy, Gent., referees appointed by they the said Hans Stevenson and Archibald Hamilton, do award and determine that the march shall run straight from the back side of the byre next to the old pound down to the river. This we do agree upon as our award, as witness our hands and seals, the day and year above.

"Witness present,   "JOHN HALTRIDGE. [SEAL.]
 "JAMES BONER.   "JAMES HAMILTON. [SEAL.]
 "HUGH JOHNSTON.

"We, Archibald Hamilton and Hans Stevenson, do, out of our great sense of the integrity and justice of our good friends, John Haltridge, Esq., and James Hamilton, Gent., freely acquiesce and submit to the within arrangement, and abide and fully submit to the same.

                    "ARCHIBALD HAMILTON.
"19th February, 1710. "HANS STEVENSON.

"I, William Hamilton, of Killileagh, do hereby declare my satisfaction with the within award, and do fully submit to the same, as witness my hand the 19th November, 1710. "WILLIAM HAMILTON."

[Copy Printed Case on Appeal to English House of Lords from Decree of Irish Court of Chancery, in the cause of Hans Stevenson and Ann, his wife, Plaintiffs; Sir Hans Hamilton, and others, Defendants; referred to at page 146, *ante*.]

JAMES HAMILTON and HANS HAMILTON, Esqrs, *Appellants ;* HANS STEVENSON, Esq., and ANN, his wife, *Respondents.*

THE APPELLANTS' CASE.

James, Earl of Clanbrasil, upon the marriage of Countess Ann, his wife, made a settlement of lands, of about £2,000 per annum, on her, for her life, for her jointure; and, afterwards, by will, dated 18th June, 1659, on his death-bed, devised one-third part of his estate to his said wife for her life; and the other two-thirds thereof for the maintenance of his two sons, Henry and Hans, and for payment of his debts; and, if the said two sons should die, without issue, before his debts were paid, then his debts to be first paid, and afterwards the remainder of his said estate to the eldest sons, or issue male, of his five uncles, as it could be laid out in most equal and just divisions; and, presently after, died. Countess Ann entered and enjoyed her jointure, and received the profits of the rest of the estate, as guardian to her sons. Hans, the younger son, died without issue. Earl Henry, the said eldest son and heir of the said Earl James, attained his age of twenty-one years; married, and then levied fines, and suffered recoveries of all the said estate not in jointure to the Countess Ann his mother, except some small parts that were in lease for lives; and, by his will, dated 27th March, 1674, devised all his estates in the Kingdom of Ireland to his wife, Alice Countess of Clanbrasil, her heirs and assigns for ever, and died without issue.

On Earl Henry's death, in January, 1765, Countess Alice entered into all the said Earl's lands not in jointure to the said Countess Ann; and, by virtue of the said Earl Henry's Will, claimed also the reversion in fee of the lands held in jointure by the said Countess Ann; for that the Will of Earl James was not good, the said Earl James being, as she alledged, not of sound mind or memory at the time of making thereof.

In February, 1675, the five eldest sons of the said Earl James's five uncles, mentioned in his Will—viz. Sir Hans Hamilton, James Hamilton of Bangor, Esq , James Hamilton of Neilsbrooke, Esq , Archibald Hamilton, Esq ,and Patrick Hamilton, Esq., agreed that a bill should be brought in the Court of Chancery in Ireland, for proving the said will of the said Earl James; and, accordingly, a bill was filed in their names, against the said Countess Alice, to perpetuate the testimony of their witnesses. Thereupon, Countess Alice, in April, 1676, preferred a bill, to set aside the said will of Earl James; to which the said Sir Hans Hamilton, the appellant James Hamilton, Archibald, and Patrick, put in their joint answers; but James of Neilsbrooke put in his separate answer by himself. In June, 1676, they preferred their cross bill, to prove the said will of Earl James. The said Countess Alice answered and denied the will of Earl James; insisting on it, that the said Earl James was not of sound mind or memory; and many witnesses were examined, on both sides, for and against the validity of the said will, contradictory to each other.

That some time after, James Hamilton of Neilsbrooke, the eldest son of the eldest of the said five uncles, being informed, and pretending he was entitled to the whole estate by prior settlements, made by the Lord Viscount Claneboy, father of the said Earl James (as by his said separate answer, filed in May, 1676, appears), refused to go on any further in the said suite; and, thereupon, Sir Hans, Archibald, and Patrick impowered the appellant, James Hamilton, by Letter of Attorney, dated 19th October, 1676, to prosecute the same on their behalf.

Countess Alice, by Deeds of Lease and Release, dated 23rd and 24th of August, 1676, settled the said estate to the use of herself, and the heirs of her body; and, for want of such heirs, settled £300 per annum thereout, as a rent charge, to Richard Spencer, Esq., her kinsman, and his heirs, and £50 per annum rent charge to James Sloane, Esq., and his heirs; and all the rest of the estate, subject thereunto, to her brother, Henry Moore, Esq., now Earl of Drogheda, in tail-male, with remainders over, subject to her debts, particularly £3,000, which she borrowed from the Lord Barganey, with whom she intermarried, and soon after died without issue, December, 1677.

The said Sir Hans Hamilton, and the appellant James Hamilton, being advised that the remainders limited by Earl James's Will to the said five uncles' sons, were barred by the said fines and recoveries of all the lands whereof the said Earl Henry had the freehold in possession, and a prospect of further suites, and great troubles appearing concerning the validity of the said Earl James's will, or what estate should pass thereby, whether for life only, or in fee, to the said five eldest sons, they the said Sir Hans Hamilton, and the appellant James Hamilton, for valuable considerations, did, in 1678, purchase to them and their heirs, the several estates and interests of the said Henry Moore, now Earl of Drogheda, John Lord of Barganey, Mr. Spencer, and Mr. Sloane, and enjoyed the same; and, for valuable considerations and marriages in their families, for payment of their debts and otherwise, have made several settlements thereof. On the 24th of December, 1678, the said Archibald and Patrick Hamilton, being apprised of the said matters, came to an agreement with the said Sir Hans Hamilton and the said James Hamilton, to accept one-fifth part of the said jointure lands, and of the lands in lease for lives, to be conveyed to each of them and their heirs, by the said Sir Hans Hamilton and the said James Hamilton. But the said James of Neilsbrook still refused to join with the others in their proceedings or agreements as aforesaid, till, after several years' inquiry about the said settlement he alledged to be made by Earl James's father, finding himself mistaken and misinformed therein, he did earnestly solicit the appellant James Hamilton, that if he would undertake for the said Sir Hans Hamilton, who was then absent, as well as for himself, to perform what arbitrators indifferently chosen should award, to refer the matter to arbitration; and, accordingly, on the 5th of May, 1680, they reciprocally entered into bonds of submission of the penalty of £10,000, wherein the said James Hamilton, the appellant, was bound for his own and the said Sir Hans Hamilton's performances. In May, 1680, in pursuance of the said reference and submission, the arbitrators, viz., John Creighton, and Hugh Hamill, Esqrs., deceased, awarded one-fifth part of the said jointure lands, and lands in leases for lives, to be conveyed by said Sir Hans Hamilton and the appellant, James Hamilton, to the said James Hamilton of Neilsbrook, and his heirs, in like manner as they had done to Archibald Hamilton. The said James Hamilton of Neilsbrook acquiesced in the said award, and never controverted the same during his life; but, before any conveyance was made to the said James Hamilton of Neilsbrook pursuant to the said award by the said Sir Hans Hamilton, he died in 1681, leaving three daughters, Rose, Rachel, and Anne

William Hamilton, third brother of the said James Hamilton of Neilsbrook, taking upon him the guardianship of the said daughters, filed a bill against the appellants, and thereby pretended that the said Sir Hans Hamilton, and the appellant, James Hamilton, made the said purchases in trust to all the other uncles' sons, as well as for themselves; and prayed that the said purchases might be decreed to be in trust, particularly as to one-fifth part thereof, to the said three daughters; but therein took no notice of the said award. But the same being set forth and insisted on by the defendants in their answers, and the said cause coming to be heard before the Lord Chancellor Porter in Trinity Term, 1686, he declared that the whole matter was not brought fairly before the Court, and that he might dismiss the said bill; but on prayer of respondent's counsel, they had leave to file a supplemental bill to bring the same, with all its circumstances, before the Court; and, accordingly, did file a supplemental bill, wherein they did take notice of the said award, but alledged the same corruptly obtained, and insisted (as they had done in their original bill) that the said purchases were made in trust for all the said five uncles' sons. To which appellants severally answered, in Michaelmas Term, 1686, and denied any trust to the purchases, or corruption in obtaining the said award, and that they were ready and willing to perform the same.

In January, 1688, Countess Anne died, and two of the said daughters, Rose and Rachel, died without issue, and the respondent, Hans Stevenson, married the said Anne, who revived the said suits, and witnesses were examined on both sides. Depending the said suit, the appellants, in October, 1696, specifically performed the said award, by a partition of the estate made accordingly, to which the respondents were parties, and agreed to and accepted of one-fifth part of the jointure lands, and leasehold lands for lives; and, according to the said partition, and their lot drawn, hold, and enjoy the same; and the appellant Hans Hamilton, being then under age, gave security to perform the same, and accordingly did perform when he came of age. Notwithstanding all which, the respondents afterwards, on 10th February, 1696, brought the said cause to hearing, and the Right Honourable John Methuen, Esq., Lord Chancellor of Ireland, decreed the said will of Earl James to be a good will, and that the respondents should have and recover one-fifth part of all the said purchases, made by the said Sir Hans Hamilton,ᶠ and the appellant, James Hamilton. And, as to the award, his lordship declared he did not think himself so apprized of the matter as to confirm the same, or to declare it to be corrupt, or that he would declare it to be a bar to the plaintiffs' right, but left the parties to take their remedies thereon; and, pursuant to the Lord Chancellor's directions, a bill was brought, in Trinity Term, 1699, against the respondents by the appellants, setting forth the said award, and that the appellants had on their parts specifically performed the same, and that the said respondents had accepted one-fifth part of all the lands so conveyed to them by the appellants, upon an equal partition thereof, and prayed a specific performance of the said award, from the respondents on their parts. To which bill the respondents pleaded the said proceedings and decree in the former causes, which plea the said Lord Chancellor Methuenˢ allowed to be good, notwithstanding the former decree and declaration therein, which left the appellants to their remedy; but, afterwards, on a rehearing, his lordship did, on the 7th of December, 1700, over-rule the said plea, and ordered the same to stand for an answer; and, though the suit is still depending, and many delays used by the respondents therein, the Lord Chancellor did order the appellants forthwith to convey a fifth part of the said purchases to the respondents, and hath since ordered the rents to be sequestered. From which decree and order the appellants have humbly appealed to their lordships, and prayed the same may be reversed as erroneous.

H. POOLEY.

F. SLOANE.

ᶠ It appears by the following extracts from the Journals of the Irish House of Commons, that shortly after the date of this appeal, a great portion of Sir Hans Hamilton's estates had to be sold for payment of his debts :—

"12th Nov., 1703.—Mr. Campbell reported from the committee appointed to examine the matter and allegations in the petition of Sir Hans Hamilton, Baronet, in order to prepare and bring in heads of a Bill for sale of part of his estates for payment of his debts, that they had called before them, and heard the several persons next in remainder in the said estate, and that they are willing that so much of the said estate shall be sold as will pay the petitioner's grandfather's debts; and also such debts as the petitioner hath contracted since he became of age; and that they were come to several resolutions, which he read in his place, and after delivered in at the table,.where the same were again read and agreed to by the House, and are as follows :—RESOLVED—1. That it is the opinion of this Committee that the contents of the said petition are true. 2. That for preserving the petitioner and his estate from utter ruin, so much thereof be sold as will pay the said debts; and, in regard that that part of the petitioner's estate which was in the County of Downe, is limited in remainder after the petitioner's issue to one person, and that part of the petitioner's estate in the Counties of Armagh and Cavan to another person, an equal proportion and share of the said several estates be left unsold. 3. That such part of the said estate as shall remain unsold, continue settled to the same uses, the same is now settled to by said settlement. 4. That there be a saving for the right and title of James Hamilton, son and heir of Henry Hamilton (if any he hath), to part of the manor of Killileagh, being the fifth part of the jointure of Anne, late Countess Dowager of Clanbrazell deceased, that he be not prejudiced by any sale, or this Act. 5. That there be a saving for the right and title of Hans Stevenson, Esq., and Anne, his wife (if any they have), that they be not prejudiced by any sale, or this Act. 6. That provision be made out of the money arising by sale of the said estate, for the debts owing by Sir Hans Hamilton, deceased, to Francis Hamilton. Esq., brother of the said Sir Hans, and for which the said Francis was bound for the said Sir Hans, or on account of the petitioner during his minority; and also such debts as the said Sir Hans, deceased, did owe to James Hamilton, of Bangor, Esq.; and such other debts as the said James Hamilton was bound for, on account of the said Sir Hans, deceased, and such other debts as the said James Hamilton did contract and was bound for on account of the petitioner during his minority, be first paid in equal proportions. 7. That the money raised by a sale of the petitioner's estate, be appointed to be received by persons of integrity, who shall be directed to pay the debts, without permitting any part of the purchase-money to come to the petitioner. 8. That there be a general saving of the rights of all other persons but such only as claim under the settlement of the said Sir Hans Hamilton, deceased, and also of all creditors. 9. That leave be given to bring in heads of a Bill for relief of the petitioner upon the terms aforesaid, according to the prayer of his petition. ORDERED—That Mr. Charles Campbell, and Mr. Connolly, Mr. Attorney-General, and Sir Richard Levinge, do prepare and bring in heads of a Bill on the said resolutions."—Irish Com. Jour., Vol. ii., p. 364.

"19th Nov., 1703.—Mr. Campbell reported from the Committee, that the said heads of a Bill were just and equitable, and for the advantage of the creditors and those in remainders to the said estate, and fit to be passed into a law."—Ib., p. 377.

On 4th March, 1703, "An Act for Sale of part of the estate of Sir Hans Hamilton, Bart., for payment of his grandfather's debts, and for other purposes," received the Royal assent.—Ib.

ˢ John Methuen, Esq., was appointed Lord Chancellor of Ireland, in 1696, on the death of Sir Charles Porter, which office he resigned in 1703, when Sir Richard Cox, who had previously been Chief Justice of the Common Pleas, became his successor.

THE HAMILTON PEDIGREE.

The Rev. Hans Hamilton, Vicar of Dunlop, in Scotland, eldest son of Archibald Hamilton, Esq., of Raploch, in Lanarkshire, descended of the Duke of Hamilton's family. Died 30th May, 1606, aged 72; buried in the Parish Church of Dunlop.—See *Ham. MSS.*, p. 1, *ante.*

Janet = Margaret Denham, daughter of the Laird of Weshiels; also buried at Dunlop with her husband, in the family mausoleum.—*Ham. MSS.*, p. 3, *ante.* *(vide p. 161, err. cml.)*

I.

A

Penelope Cooke, 1st wife.—See *Hamilton MSS.*, p. 29, *ante.* and *Mrs. Reilly's Historical Anecdotes of the Hamilton Family*, p. 34.

= Ursula, daughter of Edward, 1st Lord Brabazon, of Ardee, 2nd wife. She died in 1625, having been previously divorced by her husband, by whom she had no children.—*Ham. MSS.*, p. 29, *ante.*

= Sir James Hamilton, of Killileagh, and Bangor, Co. Down, Knight, Serjeant-at-Law, and Privy Councillor to King James the First; created by Patent, dated at Westminster, 4th May, 1622, Viscount Claneboye; died 1643, aged 84; buried at Bangor, Co. Down.—*Ham. MSS.*, p. 10.

= Jane, daughter of Sir John Phillips, of Picton Castle, in Pembrokeshire, Bart., 3rd wife. She died 4th January, 1661.—See *Funeral Entries in Ulster King of Arms Office*, vol. iv., p. 47.—*Ham. MSS.*, pp. 29, 43, 59, *ante.*

James Hamilton, 2nd Viscount Claneboye, only son; created, by Privy Seal, at Oxford, 4th March, 1646, and by Patent, at Dublin, dated 7th June, 1647, Earl of Clanbrassil in County Armagh. Marriage Articles dated 12th and 13th November, 1655. Will dated 8th June, 1659; proved 5th June, 1661; died 20th June, 1659; buried 29th June following, at Bangor, Co. Down.—*Ham. MSS.*, p. 65.

= Anne, eldest daughter of Henry Carey, Earl of Monmouth; died 20th January, 1680, and buried the 5th of February following, at Bangor.—*Ham. MSS.*, pp. 65, 118, *ante.*

= Sir Robert Maxwell, of Waringstown, Co. Down, Bart. 2nd husband; married 25th Jan., 1668.—*Ham. MSS.*, p. 118, *ante.*

James, Lord Claneboye, born 7th Sept., 1642; died, aged 15, 5th May, 1658, before his father; buried at Rickmansworth, in Hertfordshire.—*Ham. MSS.*, p. 70, *ante.*

Henry, 2nd Earl of Clanbrasil; died without leaving issue, [12th Jan., 1675-6; buried in Christ's Church, Dublin. —*Fun. Ent.*, vol. x., p. 81; and subsequently at Bangor.—*Ham. MSS.*, p. 88.

= Alice, daughter of Henry Moore, 1st Earl of Drogheda, in 1667, who married, secondly, John Lord Bargany, by whom she had no issue; and died 12th December, 1677.—*Ham. MSS.*, p. 96, *ante.*

Hans Hamilton, married, but died without issue, and was buried with his father at Bangor.—*Ham. MSS.* pp. 70, 154.

Jane died an infant, and was buried with her brother James, at Rickmansworth. — *Ham. MSS.*, p. 70.

James, Lord Claneboye, born 15th April, 1670, and died 13th June following.—*Ham. MSS.*, p. 118, *ante.*

a This Pedigree is based on one prepared by Sir William Betham, in the year 1827, but it contained many errors, which the Editor of the foregoing MSS. has been enabled to correct by references to them, and other authentic sources. As evidence of the necessity for, and nature of, these corrections, it will be sufficient here to mention, that, in Sir William Betham's Pedigree, Sir James Hamilton, the head of the family in this country, is stated to have been only twice married; and his second wife, Ursula, daughter of Edward Lord Brabazon, whom he describes as his first wife, is also stated to have been the mother of the second Viscount Claneboye and the rest of his children, although they were all children of his third wife, Jane, daughter of Sir John Phillips.

b Another mistake is committed in Sir William Betham's pedigree as to this lady, which makes her the daughter of Archibald Hamilton of Halcraig by his second wife, Rachel Carmichael, by whom he had a daughter named Janet. The Editor has been enabled to correct this, by reference to the foregoing MSS., and to the valuable Record of Funeral Entries kept in Sir Bernard Burke's Office of Ulster King of Arms, from which the following extract has been obtained :—"Archibald Edmondston, of Braiden-Iland, in the County of Antrim, Esq., eldest son of William Edmondston, of Dontreath, in the parish of Streablin, in the Sheriffdome of Striveling, in the kingdom of Scotland, Esq., eldest son of Sir James Edmondston, of Dontreath aforesaid, Knight, which Archibald married Jane, daughter of Archibald Hamilton, of Halcraige, in the Sheriffdome of Lanirke, in the said Kingdom of Scotland, Esq., second brother to James, Lord Viscount Clandeboy now living, by whom he had issue, William, eldest sonne, deafe and dumme; Archibald, second sonne, upon whom his father conferred his estate, both unmarried as yett; Helen, eldest daughter; Isabell, second daughter, as yett unmarried; and some other children who died young. The said first-mentioned Archibald Edmondston, departed this mortall life at Braiden-Iland aforesaid, the 25th of December, 1636; and was interred in the Parish Church of Templecoran, in the County of Antrim aforesaid, the — of January following. The truth of the premisses is testified by the subscription of James Edmonston, brother to the defunct, who hath returned this certificate into my office to be there recorded. Taken by me, Thomas Preston, Esq., Ulster King of Armes, this 10th of July, 1637."—*Fun. Ent.*, vol. 7, p. 101.

HAMILTON FAMILY.

II.

A ——————————————————————————————— A

| Miss Simpson. 1st wife. By whom he had 2 daughters.— *Ham. MSS.*, p. 11, *ante.* | = | Archibald Hamilton, of Halcraig, in the County of Lanark, Esq., 2nd son of the Vicar of Dunlop. —*Ham. MSS.*, pp. 10, 43, *ante.* | = | Rachel Carnichael, sister to Sir James Carnichael, Bart., of Scotland, created a Peer of Scotland as Baron Carnichael, 2nd wife, by whom he had 22 children.—*Ham. MSS.*, p. 43, *ante.* |

Jane, married to Archibald Edmondstone, of Braidenisland, Co. Antrim.—See *Ham. MSS.*, p. 43, *ante.*[b]

B

| John Hamilton, Esq., of Ballygrott, Co. Down, M.P. for Bangor, in Irish Parliament of 1639. | = | Miss West, daughter of a gentleman of good estate in Isle-a-Kall.—*Ham. MSS.*, p. 71, *ante.* | | James Hamilton, Esq., of Neilsbrook, Co. Antrim. His will dated 6th Sept., 1683; died Oct., 1683.— *Ham. MSS.*, p. 130, *ante.* | = | Agnes, daughter of Sir — Kennedy, of Colane, in Carrick. —*Ham. MSS.*, p. 72, *ante.* | | Archibald Hamilton, a Captain of Horse; shot in the thigh at Dromore, Co Down, and was carried to Lisburn, where he died.—*Ham. MSS.*, p. 72, *ante.* |

| Jane, wife of William Hogg, Esq., of Rathgall, who died s.p. Her husband died 29th September, 1704, aged 59.—*Ham. MSS.*, pp. 118, 155, *ante.* | | Rachel | = | John Stevenson, Esq., of Ballywooly. | | Rose, wife of Wm. Fairlie, Esq.; died, s.p., 31st January, 1693-4. Her husband, Wm. Fairlie, died 6th May, 1694. —*Ham. MSS.*, p. 118, *ante.* | | Rachel, died a minor. | | Colonel Hans Stevenson, of Ballygrott, son of John Stevenson, Esq., of Ballywooly; died 1713. | = | Anne Hamilton, daughter, and eventually sole heiress, of Neilsbrook. |

| Hans. | | James. | | 4 daughters. | | James Stevenson, Esq., only son and heir. | = | Anne, 3rd daughter of Lieut.-Gen. Nicholas Price. |

[Stevenson.]

| Sir John Blackwood, of Ballyleidy, Co. Down, Bart.; born in 1721; died 27th February, 1799. | = | Dorcas, daughter and co-heiress; created Baroness Dufferin and Claneboye, 23rd July, 1800. | | Anne. | | Margaret. |

(L.)

[Blackwood] 2.

| Sir James Stevenson Blackwood, Bart., 2nd Baron Dufferin and Claneboye; born 8th July, 1755; died, s. p., 8th August, 1836. | = | Anne Dorothea, only daughter of 1st Lord Oriel, who died in 1865. | | Mehetabil Hester, 2nd daughter of Robert Temple, Esq.; 1st wife; died 18th Nov., 1839. | = | Hans, 3rd Baron; born Oct., 1758; died 18th Nov., 1839. | = | Elizabeth Finlay, married 8th July, 1801, 2nd wife. |

[Blackwood]

| Price, 4th Baron; born 27th May, 1794; died 21st July, 1841. | = | Helen Selina, eldest daughter of Thomas Sheridan, Esq., and grand-daughter of the Right Honble. R. B. Sheridan; married 4th July, 1825. | | 2 sons. | | 5 daughters. |

| Frederick Temple, 5th Baron, K.P.; born June, 1826; created Baron Claneboye, in the Peerage of Great Britain, in 1850. | = | Harriet Georgina, eldest daughter of Archibald Rowan Hamilton, Esq., of Killileagh Castle, Co. Down; married 23rd Oct., 1862. | [T. O. For] |

| Archibald Temple. | | Helen Hermione. | | Terence. |

A — — — — A

B

Captain Gawin Hamilton, of Liswine and Killileagh, Co. Down, Esq.; died 27th October, 1703, aged 73.—*Ham. MSS.*, p. 118, *ante*. = Jane, daughter of Archibald Hamilton, of Co. Armagh, Esq. Mar Articles dated 1683. | William Hamilton, of Edinburgh and Killileagh, Esq.; died without issue; will dated 8th April, 1712, proved 13th August, 1716. | Robert Hamilton, Esq., died without issue.—*Ham. MSS.*, p. 73, *ante*. = Miss Meredith, daughter of Sir — Meredith.—*Ham. MSS.*, p. 73, *ante*. | Janet.—*Ham. MSS.*, p. 43, *ante*.

Archibald Hamilton, of Killileagh, Esq.; died 25th April, 1747; buried at Killileagh. = Mary, daughter of David Johnstone, Esq., of Tully, Co. Monaghan; died about 1755; buried at Killileagh. | Jane. | Mary. | Rose.

Tichborne Aston, of Beaulieu, in Co. Louth, Esq., grandson of Henry, Lord Ferrard; died 4th March, 1747; buried at Drogheda, Æt. circa 30. 1st husband. = Jane, only child of William Rowan, Esq., K.C.; born 9th Jan., 1726-7; married 28th May, 1750; died about 1793; buried at Dublin. = Gawen Hamilton, Esq., eldest son and heir; born about 1729; died 9th April, 1805; buried at St. Ann's Church, Soho, in the Co. of Middlesex. 2nd husband. | William. | Susan. | Jane. | Mary. | Rosa.

Archibald Hamilton, of the City of Dublin, Esq., took the addition of Rowan to his surname, by direction in his grandfather Rowan's will; born 12th May, 1762; died at Dublin, 1st Nov., 1834, aged 84; buried in St. Mary's Church. = Sarah Anne, daughter of Walter Dawson, Esq., of Carrickmacross, Co. Monaghan; born 14th Nov., 1794; married at Paris, 6th Oct., 1731, and subsequently at St. James's, Westminster, 13th Nov. following; died 20th February, 1834 (!) | Sidney, wife of Rev. Benjamin Beresford, Clerk.

Sydney. | Sophia.

Gawin William, Captain R.N., C.B.; born at Paris, 4th March, 1793; died 17th Aug., 1834. = Catharine, daughter of Lieut.-Gen. Sir George Cockburne; married in 1817. | Sydney Hamilton, born 19th January, 1789; died in 1847. | Ellen Jackson, mar. March, 1819; died in 1851. | Archibald, 3rd son; born 24th Nov., 1791; was a Lieut. in the 11th Regt. of Foot, and died, s.p., at Gibraltar. | Frederick, 4th son; born 26th Sept., 1793; an Officer in the R.N.; slain on the coast of Spain in 1811; died unmarried and s.p.

George = Miss Hart. | Melita = Jacob Sankey, Esq. | Archibald. | John. | Wm. | Cunningham. | Sydney. | Sarah. | Anne. | Mary. | Mildred. | Jane.

Archibald Rowan Hamilton, Captain 5th Dragoon Guards; died in May, 1859. = Catharine Anne, dau. of Rev. Geo. Caldwell and Harriett his wife, dau. of Sir Wm. Abdy, Bart.

Frederick Temple, 5th Baron Dufferin and Clandeboye, and 1st Baron Clandeboye in the Peerage of Great Britain. = Harriett Georgina. | Gawin. | George. | Sydney. | Frederick. | Gwendoline. | Catharine.

[T.8.]

b

Dawson, 5th son; born 23rd Sept., 1801; married Anne Blackwood in Nov., 1823. | Jane, born 7th Oct., 1785; died unmarried, in 1803. | Elizabeth, wife of the Rev. S. H. Beresford; married in Dec., 1819. | Mildred, wife of Sir Edward Ryan, Knt. of the Order of Maria Theresa; | Harriett, wife of Crofton Fitzgerald, Esq.; | Francesca, wife of Wm. Fletcher, Esq., son of Wm. Fletcher, Esq., one of the Judges of C.P. in Ireland.

Benjamin. Sydney. Georgina Sophia. | William V. Ryan, Esq., died in 1865. | several sons and daughters. | Wm. Frederick. Anna. Jane.

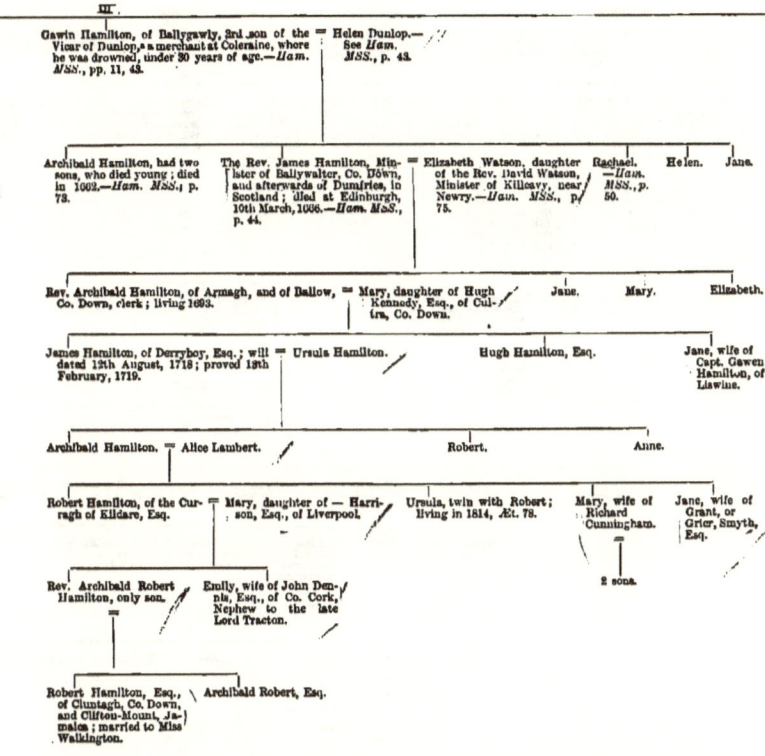

III.

Gawin Hamilton, of Ballygawly, 3rd son of the = Helen Dunlop.—
Vicar of Dunlop, a merchant at Coleraine, where   See Ham.
he was drowned, under 30 years of age.—Ham.   MSS., p. 43.
MSS., pp. 11, 43.

Archibald Hamilton, had two | The Rev. James Hamilton, Min- = Elizabeth Watson, daughter | Rachael.   Helen.   Jane.
sons, who died young ; died | ister of Ballywalter, Co. Down,   of the Rev. David Watson,   —Ham.
in 1662.—Ham. MSS., p. | and afterwards of Dumfries, in   Minister of Killeavy, near   MSS., p.
73. | Scotland ; died at Edinburgh,   Newry.—Ham. MSS., p.   50.
                            | 10th March, 1666.—Ham. MSS.,   75.
                            | p. 44.

Rev. Archibald Hamilton, of Armagh, and of Ballow, = Mary, daughter of Hugh   Jane.   Mary.   Elizabeth.
Co. Down, clerk ; living 1693.   Kennedy, Esq., of Cul-
                                                      tra, Co. Down.

James Hamilton, of Derryboy, Esq. ; will = Ursula Hamilton.   Hugh Hamilton, Esq.   Jane, wife of
dated 12th August, 1718 ; proved 13th   Capt. Gawen
February, 1719.   Hamilton, of
                                                                                              Liswine.

Archibald Hamilton. = Alice Lambert.   Robert.   Anne.

Robert Hamilton, of the Cur- = Mary, daughter of — Harri-   Ursula, twin with Robert ;   Mary, wife of   Jane, wife of
ragh of Kildare, Esq.   son, Esq., of Liverpool.   living in 1814, Æt. 78.   Richard   Grant, or
                                                                                         Cunningham.   Grier, Smyth,
                                                                                                        Esq.
                                                                                         =
Rev. Archibald Robert   Emily, wife of John Den-   2 sons.
Hamilton, only son.   nis, Esq., of Co. Cork,
                        Nephew to the late
                        Lord Tracton.

Robert Hamilton, Esq., \ Archibald Robert, Esq.
of Cluntagh, Co. Down,
and Clifton-Mount, Ja- |
maica ; married to Miss |
Walkington.

a The Christian name of the wife of the Vicar of Dunlop is correctly stated in the body of the work, at p. 3, ante, to have been
Janet ; but at p. 158, ante, it is erroneously given as Margaret, on the authority of Sir William Betham's Pedigree,—a mistake which
was overlooked until after the sheet was printed off, and which must therefore be corrected.—ED.

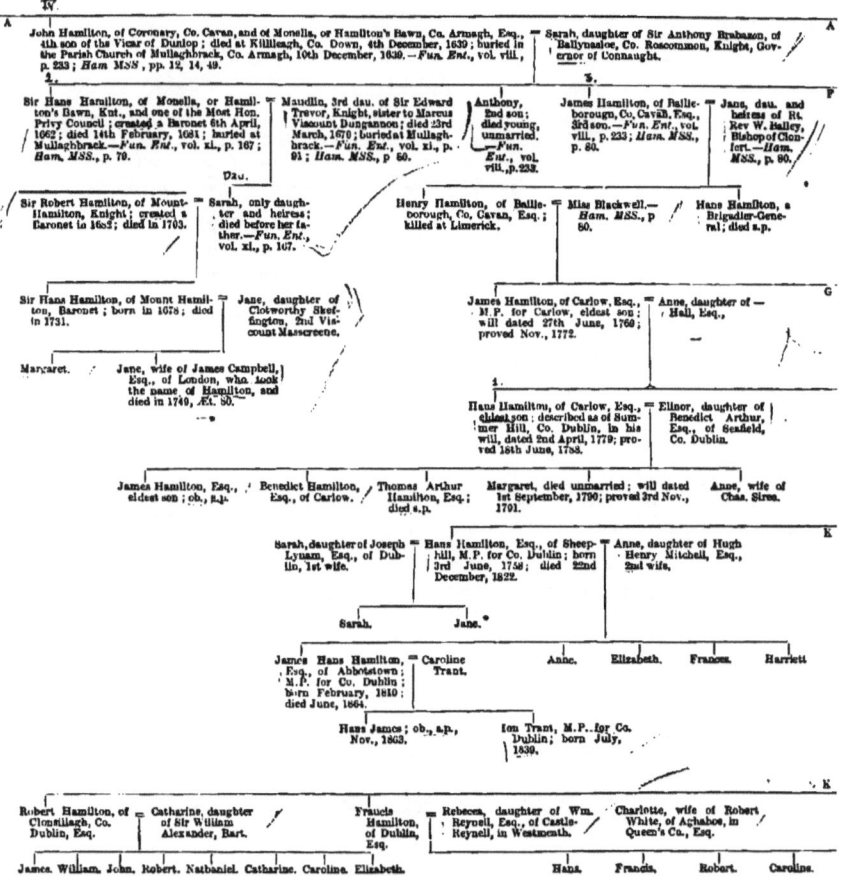

IV.

John Hamilton, of Coronary, Co. Cavan, and of Monella, or Hamilton's Bawn, Co. Armagh, Esq., 4th son of the Vicar of Dunlop ; died at Killileagh, Co. Down, 4th December, 1639 ; buried in the Parish Church of Mullaghbrack, Co. Armagh, 10th December, 1639.—*Fun. Ent.*, vol. viii., p. 233 ; *Ham MSS*, pp. 12, 14, 49.

Sarah, daughter of Sir Anthony Brabazon, of Ballynasloe, Co. Roscommon, Knight, Governor of Connaught.

Sir Hans Hamilton, of Monella, or Hamilton's Bawn, Knt., and one of the Most Hon. Privy Council ; created a Baronet 6th April, 1662 ; died 14th February, 1681 ; buried at Mullaghbrack.—*Fun. Ent.*, vol. xi., p. 167 ; *Ham. MSS.*, p. 79.

Maudlin, 3rd dau. of Sir Edward Trevor, Knight, sister to Marcus Viscount Dungannon ; died 23rd March, 1670 ; buried at Mullaghbrack.—*Fun. Ent.*, vol. xi., p. 91 ; *Ham. MSS.*, p. 60.

Anthony, 2nd son ; died young, unmarried. —*Fun. Ent.*, vol. viii.,p.233.

James Hamilton, of Bailieborough, Co. Cavan, Esq., 3rd son.—*Fun. Ent.*, vol. viii., p. 233 ; *Ham. MSS.*, p. 80.

Jane, dau. and heiress of Rt. Rev. W. Bailey, Bishop of Clonfert.—*Ham. MSS.*, p. 80.

Dau.

Sir Robert Hamilton, of Mount-Hamilton, Knight ; created a Baronet in 1682 ; died in 1703.

Sarah, only daughter and heiress ; died before her father.—*Fun. Ent.*, vol. xi., p. 167.

Henry Hamilton, of Bailieborough, Co. Cavan, Esq. ; killed at Limerick.

Miss Blackwell.—*Ham. MSS.*, p. 80.

Hans Hamilton, a Brigadier-General ; died s.p.

Sir Hans Hamilton, of Mount Hamilton, Baronet ; born in 1678 ; died in 1731.

Jane, daughter of Clotworthy Skeffington, 2nd Viscount Massereene.

James Hamilton, of Carlow, Esq., M.P. for Carlow, eldest son ; will dated 27th June, 1769 ; proved Nov., 1772.

Anne, daughter of — Hall, Esq.

Margaret.

Jane, wife of James Campbell, Esq., of London, who took the name of Hamilton, and died in 1749, Æt. 90.

Hans Hamilton, of Carlow, Esq., eldest son ; described as of Summer Hill, Co. Dublin, in his will, dated 2nd April, 1779 ; proved 18th June, 1783.

Elinor, daughter of Benedict Arthur, Esq., of Seafield, Co. Dublin.

James Hamilton, Esq., eldest son ; ob., s.p.

Benedict Hamilton, Esq., of Carlow.

Thomas Arthur Hamilton, Esq. ; died s.p.

Margaret, died unmarried ; will dated 1st September, 1790 ; proved 3rd Nov., 1791.

Anne, wife of Chas. Siree.

Sarah, daughter of Joseph Lynam, Esq., of Dublin, 1st wife.

Hans Hamilton, Esq., of Sheep-hill, M.P. for Co. Dublin ; born 3rd June, 1758 ; died 22nd December, 1822.

Anne, daughter of Hugh Henry Mitchell, Esq., 2nd wife.

Sarah.

Jane.

James Hans Hamilton, Esq., of Abbotstown ; M.P. for Co. Dublin ; born February, 1810 ; died June, 1864.

Caroline Trant.

Anne.

Elizabeth.

Frances.

Harriett.

Hans James ; ob., s.p., Nov., 1863.

Ion Trant, M.P. for Co. Dublin ; born July, 1839.

Robert Hamilton, of Clonsillagh, Co. Dublin, Esq.

Catharine, daughter of Sir William Alexander, Bart.

Francis Hamilton, of Dublin, Esq.

Rebecca, daughter of Wm. Reynell, Esq., of Castle-Reynell, in Westmeath.

Charlotte, wife of Robert White, of Aghaboe, in Queen's Co., Esq.

James. William. John. Robert. Nathaniel. Catharine. Caroline. Elizabeth.

Hans. Francis. Robert. Caroline.

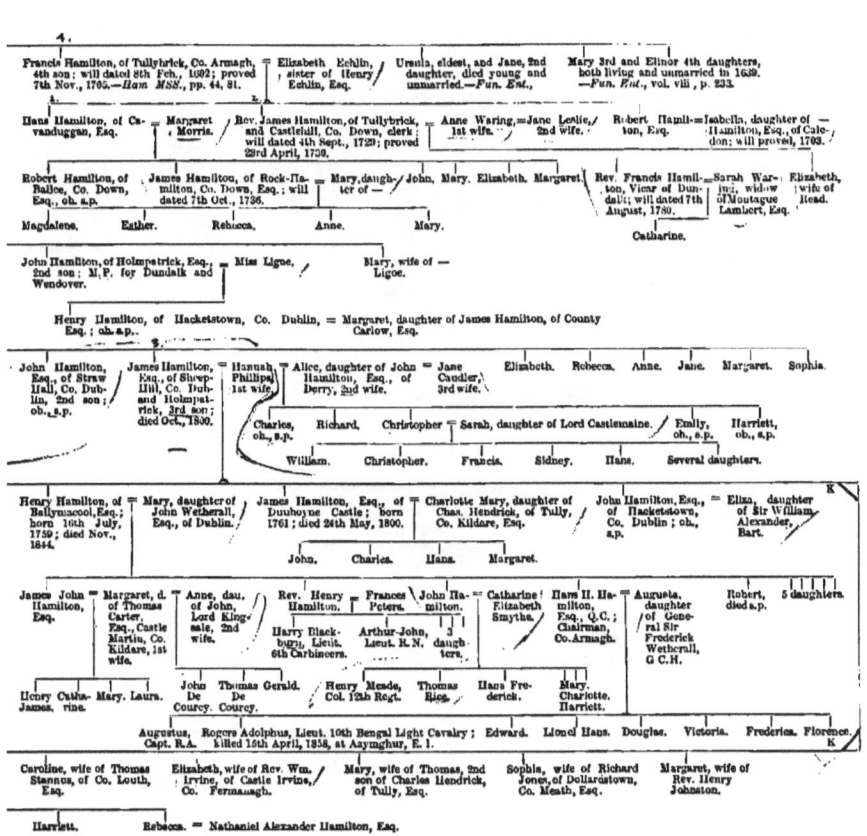

V.

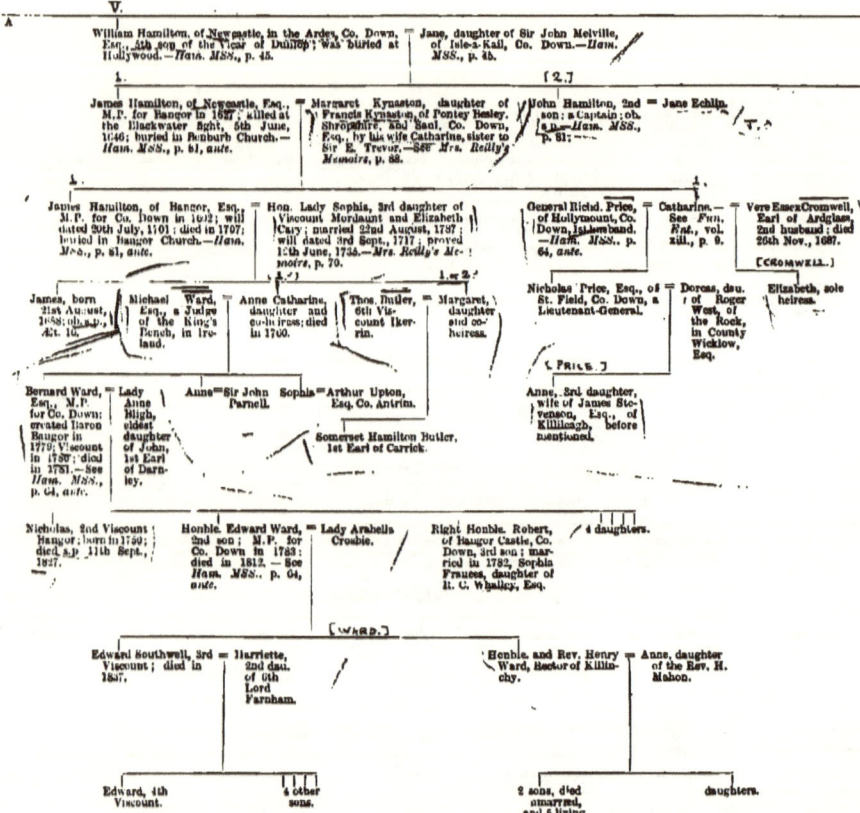

William Hamilton, of Newcastle, in the Ardes, Co. Down, Esq., 4th son of the Vicar of Dunlop; was buried at Hollywood.—*Ham. MSS.*, p. 45.
Jane, daughter of Sir John Melville, of Isle-a-Kail, Co. Down.—*Ham. MSS.*, p. 45.

[2.]

James Hamilton, of Newcastle, Esq., M.P. for Bangor in 1627; killed at the Blackwater fight, 5th June, 1646; buried in Banburb Church.—*Ham. MSS.*, p. 61, *ante.*
Margaret Kynaston, daughter of Francis Kynaston, of Ponley Besley, Shropshire, and Sacl, Co. Down, Esq., by his wife Catharine, sister to Sir E. Trevor.—*See Mrs. Reilly's Memoirs*, p. 82.
John Hamilton, 2nd son; a Captain; ob. s.p.—*Ham. MSS.*, p. 61.
Jane Echlin.

James Hamilton, of Bangor, Esq., M.P. for Co. Down in 1692; will dated 29th July, 1701; died in 1707; buried in Bangor Church.—*Ham. MSS.*, p. 61, *ante.*
Hon. Lady Sophia, 3rd daughter of Viscount Mordaunt and Elizabeth Cary; married 22nd August, 1737; will dated 3rd Sept., 1717; proved 13th June, 1755.—*Mrs. Reilly's Memoirs*, p. 70.
General Richd. Price, of Hollymount, Co. Down, 1st husband.—*Ham. MSS.*, p. 64, *ante.*
Catharine.— See *Fun. Ent.*, vol. xiii., p. 9.
Vere EsexCromwell, Earl of Ardglass, 2nd husband; died 26th Nov., 1687.

[CROMWELL.]

James, born 21st August, 1688; ob. s.p., Æt. 10.
Michael Ward, Esq., a Judge of the King's Bench, in Ireland.
Anne Catharine, daughter and co-heiress; died in 1700.
Thos. Butler, 6th Viscount Ikerrin.
Margaret, daughter and co-heiress.
Nicholas Price, Esq., of St. Field, Co. Down, a Lieutenant-General.
Dorcas, dau. of Roger West, of the Rock, in County Wicklow, Esq.
Elizabeth, sole heiress.

[PRICE.]

Bernard Ward, Esq., M.P. for Co. Down; created Baron Bangor in 1770; Viscount in 1787; died in 1781.—See *Ham. MSS.*, p. 64, *ante.*
Lady Anne Bligh, eldest daughter of John, 1st Earl of Darnley.
Anne, Sir John Parnell.
Sophia, Arthur Upton, Esq., Co. Antrim.
Anne, 3rd daughter, wife of James Stevenson, Esq., of Killileagh, before mentioned.

Somerset Hamilton Butler, 1st Earl of Carrick.

Nicholas, 2nd Viscount Bangor; born in 1750; died s.p. 11th Sept., 1827.
Honble. Edward Ward, 2nd son; M.P. for Co. Down in 1783; died in 1812.—See *Ham. MSS.*, p. 64, *ante.*
Lady Arabella Crosbie.
Right Honble. Robert, of Bangor Castle, Co. Down, 3rd son; married in 1782, Sophia Frances, daughter of R. C. Whalley, Esq.
4 daughters.

[WARD.]

Edward Southwell, 3rd Viscount; died in 1837.
Harriette, 2nd dau. of 6th Lord Farnham.
Honble. and Rev. Henry Ward, Rector of Killinchy.
Anne, daughter of the Rev. H. Mahon.

Edward, 4th Viscount.
4 other sons.
2 sons, died unmarried, and 5 living.
daughters.

A

L

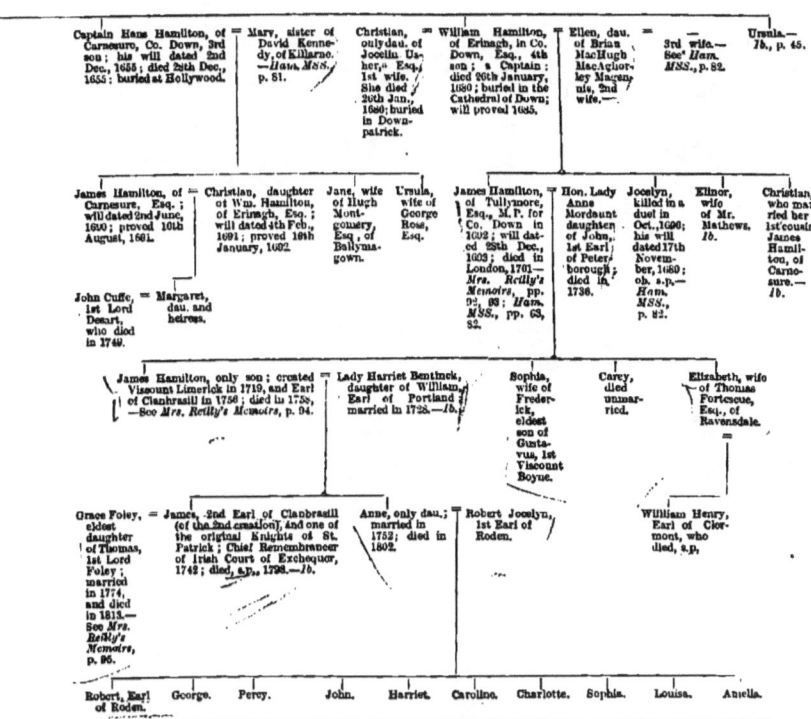

Captain Hans Hamilton, of Carnesure, Co. Down, 3rd son; his will dated 2nd Dec., 1655; died 28th Dec., 1655; buried at Hollywood.
= **Mary, sister of** David Kennedy, of Killarne. —*Ham. MSS.,* p. 81.

Christian, only dau. of Jocelin Usher,[a] Esq., 1st wife. She died 20th Jan., 1680; buried in Downpatrick.
= **William Hamilton,** of Erinagh, in Co. Down, Esq., 4th son; a Captain; died 26th January, 1680; buried in the Cathedral of Down; will proved 1685.
= **Ellen, dau.** of Brian MacHugh MacAghorley Magennis, 2nd wife.—

3rd wife.— See *Ham. MSS.,* p. 82.

Ursula. — *Ib.,* p. 45.

James Hamilton, of Carnesure, Esq.; will dated 2nd June, 1690; proved 10th August, 1691.
= **Christian, daughter** of Wm. Hamilton, of Erinagh, Esq.; will dated 4th Feb., 1691; proved 19th January, 1692.

Jane, wife of Hugh Montgomery, Esq., of Ballymagown.

Ursula, wife of George Ross, Esq.

James Hamilton, of Tullymore, Esq., M.P. for Co. Down in 1692; will dated 29th Dec., 1693; died in London, 1701.— *Mrs. Reilly's Memoirs,* pp. 92, 93; *Ham. MSS.,* pp. 63, 82.
= **Hon. Lady Anne** Mordaunt daughter of John, 1st Earl of Peterborough; died in 1736.

Jocelyn, killed in a duel in Oct., 1696; his will dated 17th November, 1680; ob. s.p.,— *Ham. MSS.,* p. 82.

Elinor, wife of Mr. Mathews.

Christian, who married her 1st cousin, James Hamilton, of Carnesure.— *Ib.*

John Cuffe, 1st Lord Desart, who died in 1749.
= **Margaret,** dau. and heiress.

James Hamilton, only son; created Viscount Limerick in 1719, and Earl of Clanbrasill in 1756; died in 1758.— See *Mrs. Reilly's Memoirs,* p. 94.
= **Lady Harriet Bentinck,** daughter of William, Earl of Portland; married in 1728.—*Ib.*

Sophia, wife of Frederick, eldest son of Gustavus, 1st Viscount Boyne.

Carey, died unmarried.

Elizabeth, wife of Thomas Fortescue, Esq., of Ravensdale.

Grace Foley, eldest daughter of Thomas, 1st Lord Foley; married in 1774, and died in 1813.— See *Mrs. Reilly's Memoirs,* p. 96.
= **James, 2nd Earl of Clanbrasill** (of the 2nd creation), and one of the original Knights of St. Patrick; Chief Remembrancer of Irish Court of Exchequer, 1742; died, s.p., 1798.—*Ib.*

Anne, only dau.; married in 1752; died in 1802.
= **Robert Jocelyn,** 1st Earl of Roden.

William Henry, Earl of Clermont, who died, s.p.

Robert, Earl of Roden. George. Percy. John. Harriet. Caroline. Charlotte. Sophia. Louisa. Amelia.

---

a At page 82, *ante*, his first wife is stated, upon the authority of Mrs. Reilly's Memoirs, p. 81, to have been a daughter of Henry Usher; but this is a mistake, as Sir William Betham's Pedigree, in which her father's name is stated to have been Jocelin, is corroborated by the Pedigree of Archbishop Usher, given in the appendix to Elrington's Life of him, in which he is also stated to have been Joslin Usher, son of Mark Usher of Balsoon.

VI.

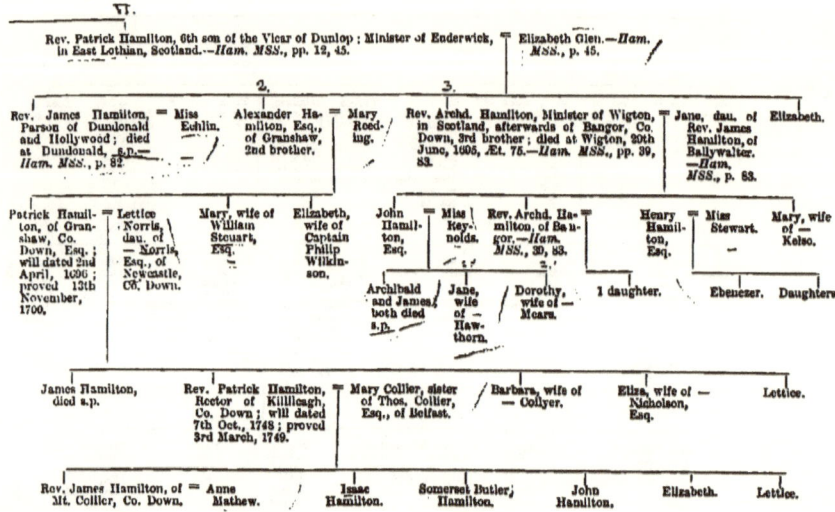

Rev. Patrick Hamilton, 6th son of the Vicar of Dunlop; Minister of Enderwick, in East Lothian, Scotland.—*Ham. MSS.*, pp. 12, 45. ⚯ Elizabeth Glen.—*Ham. MSS.*, p. 45.

2.

3.

Rev. James Hamilton, Parson of Dundonald and Hollywood; died at Dundonald, s.p.—*Ham. MSS.*, p. 82 ⚯ Miss Eshlin.

Alexander Hamilton, Esq., of Granshaw, 2nd brother. ⚯ Mary Roeding.

Rev. Archd. Hamilton, Minister of Wigton, in Scotland, afterwards of Bangor, Co. Down, 3rd brother; died at Wigton, 20th June, 1695, Æt. 75.—*Ham. MSS.*, pp. 39, 83. ⚯ Jane, dau. of Rev. James Hamilton, of Ballywalter.—*Ham. MSS.*, p. 83.

Elizabeth.

Patrick Hamilton, of Granshaw, Co. Down, Esq.; will dated 2nd April, 1696; proved 13th November, 1700. ⚯ Lettice Norris, dau. of — Norris, Esq., of Newcastle, Co. Down.

Mary, wife of William Steuart, Esq.

Elizabeth, wife of Captain Philip Wilkinson.

John Hamilton, Esq. ⚯ Miss Reynolds.

Rev. Archd. Hamilton, of Bangor.—*Ham. MSS.*, 30, 83. ⚯

Henry Hamilton, Esq. ⚯ Miss Stewart.

Mary, wife of — Kelso.

Archibald and James, both died s.p.

Jane, wife of — Hawthorn.

Dorothy, wife of — Mears.

1 daughter.

Ebenezer.

Daughters.

James Hamilton, died s.p.

Rev. Patrick Hamilton, Rector of Killileagh, Co. Down; will dated 7th Oct., 1748; proved 3rd March, 1749. ⚯ Mary Collier, sister of Thos. Collier, Esq., of Belfast.

Barbara, wife of — Collyer.

Eliza, wife of — Nicholson, Esq.

Lettice.

Rev. James Hamilton, of Mt. Collier, Co. Down. ⚯ Anne Mathew.

Isaac Hamilton.

Somerset Butler Hamilton.

John Hamilton.

Elizabeth.

Lettice.

GENERAL APPENDIX.

A

GENERAL APPENDIX.

No. I.

LETTERS PATENT OF 3RD JAMES I., 1605, TO JAMES HAMILTON, Esq.

JAMES, by the grace of God, of England, Scotland, France, and Ireland, King, Defender of the Faith, and so forth : To all to whom our present letters shall come, greeting :—Whereas, we (on the humble petition of Conat otherwise Con McBrian Fertagh O'Neile, as for and in consideration of the faithful service of our beloved Hugh Montgomery, Knight, and James Hamilton, Esq., our serjeant, rendered to us), by our certain letters, signed with our proper hand and under our seal, dated at our manor of Greenwich, the 16th day of April, in the third year of our reign of England, France, and Ireland, and of Scotland the thirty-eighth, enrolled in the rolls of our Chancery of our said kingdom of Ireland, signified our will and pleasure to be—That the aforesaid James Hamilton, his heirs and assigns, should have of our gift or grant the countries or territories of the Upper Clandeboy and Great Ards, and all castles, manors, lands, tenements, and hereditaments in the said country of the Upper Clandeboy and Great Ards, of which Neal McBrian Fertagh O'Neale, or his father, Brian Fertagh O'Neale, in their lifetimes were possessed of, and received any rents, duties, or impositions (in English, "cuttings,") with all and singular their members and appurtenances, together with a market on Thursday in every week, and one fair on the feast of St. John the Baptist, and for two days next following the said feast annually, and together with courts leet and courts baron, to be annually held at Castlereagh, parcel of the premises, and together with two other fairs, both to be held for the like time, with courts leet and courts baron, to be held within the said territories and lands, rendering to us, our heirs and successors, £100 good and lawful money of Ireland annually, at the receipt of our Exchequer there, at the two usual annual feasts, as by our said letters patent more fully and at large appears. And whereas, further, by our said letters we signified, that the aforesaid James Hamilton should promise to inhabit the said territory and lands with English or Scotchmen ; therefore, that the aforesaid James Hamilton may be the better able to inhabit the said territories, depopulated and wasted, and to pay the rent aforesaid, that the aforesaid James Hamilton, his heirs and assigns, may and can transport and convey all such grain, commodities, and benefits which grow and arise in and upon the territories and lands aforesaid, into any part of our dominions, and into all other parts in league and friendship with us (our army and military garrisons in our said province of Ulster being first, at our request and price, well provided and accommodated with grain and provisions), and to transport men, cattle, grain, and all other commodities out of our kingdoms of England and Scotland into the aforesaid territories and lands : Rendering to us, our heirs and successors, the usual customs for the same, unless it shall seem to our Deputy-General, for the time being, and our Council there, upon any special cause to prohibit the transportation of such grain and commodities ; and that it shall be lawful for the aforesaid James, his heirs and assigns, to alienate the aforesaid territories and lands, or any parcel thereof, to any person or persons, being English or Scotch, or of the blood of English or Scotchmen, and not to any of the mere Irish nation, except to the said Conat, otherwise Con O'Neile, and his heirs, to be held of the said James Hamilton, his heirs and assigns, by such rent and service as the said James Hamilton, his heirs and assigns, shall reserve, as also by our said letters, amongst other things, may more fully and at large appear.

Know ye, that We, of our special grace, certain knowledge, and, mere motion, and according to the effect of our letters above recited, with the assent of our right trusty and faithful Sir Arthur Chichester, Knt., our Deputy-General of our said kingdom of Ireland, and for the considerations aforesaid, for us our heirs and successors, Have given and granted, and by these presents, for us our heirs and successors, we do give and grant to the aforesaid James Hamilton, all those regions, countries, or territories of the Upper Clandeboy and the Great Ards in Clandeboy, in the said county of Down, in the province of Ulster, in our said kingdom of Ireland, and all other castles, manors, lands, tene-. ments, and hereditaments in the said country of Clandeboy and the Great Ards, of which Neale M‘Brien Fertagh O'Neile, or his father Brian, otherwise Brian Fertagh O'Neile, in the time of their lives was or were possessed of, or received the rents, dues, or impositions (called in English "cuttings") in the said province of Ulster : And also all and singular the towns, villages, or hamlets of Ballynagnochan, Bally-naghabricke, Ballybrinan, Ballycowan, Ballycarney, Ballyclogher, Ballycrossan, Ballycarrycroegh, Ballycreweh, Ballycargie, Ballycardganan, Ballidulloghane, Ballydrombo, Ballydulloghmuck, Balli-derrimore, Ballygrombeg, Ballyneganwyee, Ballyhollowood, Ballyhawnenewde, Ballylisnnabryne, Ballylemoghan, Ballylary, Ballyliscrean, Ballyloghany, Ballyliscowneganagh, alias Ballylisgan, Bally-liseromelaghan. Ballyloghgar, Ballyliscoodry, Ballymylagh, Ballimaltane, Ballinemony, Ballymologh, Balliomulvelagh, Ballyogheli, Ballyskean, Ballytempledrome, Ballytempleblassisse, Ballytollogh-mistikincol Ballynechallan, Ballytullowre, Ballylischackan, Ballycarrowneveigh, Ballietullogh-breckan, Ballecreignefassenagh, Ballieargeeneveigh, Ballycarrid, Ballycloinemore, Ballydromhorcke, Ballinagroven, Ballylanbeg, Ballyhalliske, Ballarecrumen, Ballideya, Ballydromveyne, Ballygoneyagh, Ballinraffooncy, Ballinlullinegwy, Ballytullaghfymean, Ballyardoman, Balliboonen, Ballivarnemagherie, Ballyclontyneglare, Ballycarnonan, Ballicarrickmanan, Ballidromehierewe, Ballidromcreagh, Ballygowan, Ballynegrosse, Ballihulle, Ballikeilogh, alias Ballykely, Ballylisnebarney, Ballimagherostowe, Bally-monastregh, Ballimertenagh, Ballimaghery, Drunnagh, Ballikegill, Ballikilleene, Ballyaghandoragh, Bally-necreeneh, Ballikillinisce, Ballitullaghmuchyvragh, Ballilogh, Balligaloglagh, Ballygraffane, Ballycar-lanevaragh, Ballecaslanbeg, Ballyhenrie, Ballilisgowan, Balliloghinkirk, Ballisbradane, Ballymoney-carvell, Ballymagreevaghan, Ballimanues, Ballioran, Ballirichard, Ballyrinhy, alias Rynerewe, Bally-rogan, Ballanliallen, Ballionerany, Ballymullidy, Ballenacultie, Balliglosedrom, Ballitullicorpane, Ballitulligarvagh, Ballinenaw, Balliloghan, the Half Town of Balliravarragh, Ballinroishe, Balliristell, Ballistockereh, Ballytullihubert, Ballytanaghnewen, Ballinacloghan, Ballyhartic, alias Agharagie, Balli-bine, Ballisline, Ballibeyne, Ballicrely, the Half Town of Dromskonell, Ballygassan, Balligrangeh, Balliglackilenagh, Ballilagygoan, Ballymoynerigh, Ballimaglafle, Ballicarewnemuck, Ballinebredagh, Ballyhackemer, Ballinafeigh, Ballygortrib, Ballihenoane, Ballyknockeolmukill, Ballislisnebroyne, Ballymackerit, Ballisorber, Ballygalvally, Ballicregie, Ballicastloreogh, Ballicreevine, Balliccarviagh, Ballinechline, Balliregin, Ballidownledy Ballidowndonell, Ballikillivagh. Ballilisniskagh, Ballicarrigo-ganedelane, Ballikelarmid, Ballinchaghan, Ballitullohenrie, Ballycrriggivaddagh, Ballydavy, Ballinegrany Ballinemoney, Ballirobert, Balliaghery, Balliawally, Balliaspragh, Ballinecrosse, Ballinecarrowreagh, Ballinecrenghy, Ballicopland, Ballicaskeragh, Ballinecallagh, Ballinerossnemucklough, Ballinemedoon, Ballinedoonever, Ballidroomeaiff, Ballidromecha, Ballydonoghdee, Ballyfranish, Ballyfarish, Ballyne-grangee, Balleneganevine, Ballygornic, Ballyneglasserie, Balligraffine, Ballenegardy, Ballyhay, Balli-hemeline, Ballykilcormock, Ballikillaghy, Ballikilbratton, Ballinekillee, Ballilisbane, Ballywilliam, Ballinemoyne, Ballycoolgrange, Ballymulter, Ballymonen, Ballymulloghmore, Ballyrowe, Ballitallogh-evevine, Ballinoregh, Ballytalbot, Ballibrallurevin, Ballymkelreene, Ballinegemurthe, Balligooneh, Ballibrekon, Ballyrinee, Ballyprushan, Ballibelare, Ballimulleragh, Ballicarroghan, Balliviacke, Balli-hullicggard, Ballimullin, Ballivackerinyloghan, Ballymuckee, Balligarvagane, Ballyupisrah, Balli-carrownesragh, Ballicarcubbine, Balliarony, Ballilimpe, Carrownescreo, Ballirowriagh, Barrecallone-callagh, the two Ballineskeaghes, Ballirogun, Ballywalter, Balliathuad, Ballynegallagh, Ballinecreagh, Ballinecabbragh Ballina, Ballimaser :—Which said towns, villages, or hamlets, are lying or being in and within the lands of the Upper Clandeboy, and the Great Ards aforesaid : And all other manors, castles, towns, townlands, hamlets, lands, tenements, and other hereditaments whatever, lying and being in or within the aforesaid regions, territories, or countries of the Upper Clandeboy, and the Great Ards, and also, all other manors, castles, towns, townlands, hamlets, lands, tenements, and hereditaments, whatsoever, lying and being in or within the limits, mears, and bounds of the said territory of the Upper Clandeboy, and the Great Ards :—That is to say, towards and adjoining the west, and northern, and western part of the territory aforesaid, the river of Lagan, which hath its course immediately into the bay of Knockfergus, is the most noted mearing of the territory aforesaid, and runs between the lands thereof, and other parcels of the territories or countries, called Maloan, Falfelogh, Kilultagh, and

M'Shane Oge's countrie in Kilultagh, in the county aforesaid, and the said river runs between the territory aforesaid, for eight miles or thereabouts, to wit, from the passage or ford of Belfast until the said river joins another river called Garricloth, and from thence towards the south and west part of the river called The Garricloth aforesaid, is the most noted mear between the lands of Upper Clandeboy and Kilwarlin, in the county aforesaid, during a course of five miles or thereabouts, until the aforesaid river falls into the lough, called Loughanny, in which Toole M'Phelim M'Ever dwells ; and the lake aforesaid is half a mile or thereabouts long, between the territories aforesaid, and from the east, and south ends of the lake near the said lake lies and is situated the marsh, (called in English "The Bog of the Dorney,") through the middle of which bog extends the boundary aforesaid, directly between the lands of the Upper Clandeboy aforesaid, and the territory called M'Cartan's country, in the county aforesaid, and during a course of about two miles and a half, unto the passage (called in English "The ford of Anaghcatt,") and from thence through the middle of the bog aforesaid, directly for half a mile by estimation, unto another passage or ford of Annagh-Dorney ; and from thence the boundary between the territories aforesaid, extends directly through the middle of a little river called Dorney, for one mile or thereabouts, until it touches the high hill called Liscoodry, situate in the Upper Clandeboy aforesaid, and there or near the said hill touches the river called Balligarry ; and from thence the boundary aforesaid, between the Upper Clandeboy and M'Cartan's country aforesaid, extends itself through the middle of the river of Ballygarry aforesaid, for the space of two miles or thereabouts, until the aforesaid river approaches the church called Killinchinickille, situate in the Upper Clandeboy aforesaid : And from thence the boundary of the Upper Clandeboy aforesaid continues itself directly between the lands of the same and the country or territory called The Dufferin in the county aforesaid, upon and by the summit of the hill called Teochrum, and from thence for a quarter of a mile or thereabouts, to the nearest end of the bog called Dorgemonye; and from thence the boundary between the territories first recited in the county aforesaid, extends for two miles by estimation, directly through the middle of the aforesaid bog, until from the said bog a river rises called Owen Mullen, which said river from thence is held to be the mete for about one mile between the territories aforesaid, until it falls into the lough, called Loughcoyne, in the county aforesaid, at or near the passage or ford of Annaghglemyniter, between the island of Maghie, in the Upper Clandeboy aforesaid, and Skatericke in The Dufferin aforesaid ; and from thence the west and northern bank of the aforesaid lough is the most noted boundary of the Upper Clandeboy aforesaid, until the river called Althanchoise falls into the lake of Loughcone aforesaid ; and from thence the northern and eastern bank of the lake of Loughcone aforesaid is the boundary of these territories, until the river of Blackstaffe falls into Loughcone aforesaid; and from thence the boundary of the territory aforesaid, between the lands thereof and the Little Ards aforesaid, continues directly through the middle of the river of Blackstaffe aforesaid, and through the middle of the passage or ford of Blackstaffe upon the same river, until the river aforesaid empties itself into a certain bog called Portaboggagh, and from thence the boundary, between the territories aforesaid, extends itself directly through the middle of the aforesaid bog, leaving the island called Island Durine, and the lough called the Lough of Kirgeston towards the south, in the Little Ards aforesaid ; and from and near the west end of the Lough of Kirgeston aforesaid, the boundary between the territories aforesaid turns itself towards the north, and issues from the bog near and under the south and east, at the foot of a certain island or hill called Island-Gorman, situate in the Great Ards, and so almost around the said hill by a certain old mearing erected on those lands, unto the little miry bog called Loughanfinn, near the north and eastern foot of the island aforesaid : And from thence the boundary between the territories aforesaid continues through the middle of a certain antient little glen or channel, extending itself towards the north, to the foot of the hill called Carnanbeanes, situate in the Little Ards, until the channel aforesaid comes to another miry wet bog called Loughanly, from which said bog passes another channel until it falls into the sea, and is the boundary between the territories aforesaid : And from thence the shore of the sea towards the east and north, is held to be the most noted mear and boundary of the territory aforesaid, unto the rock of Carnanleagh, which is situate upon the sea shore, between the Upper Clandeboy, and the Great Ards ; and from thence the sea shore aforesaid towards the east, and the bank of the bay of Knockfergus aforesaid towards the north, is held to be the most noted mear and boundary of the territory aforesaid, unto the passage otherwise the ford of Belfast above mentioned.

And also all the towns, villages, or hamlets, and lands of and in the territory or country of Kilultagh, being within the territory of Clandeboy aforesaid, in the counties of Down and Antrim aforesaid, in the province of Ulster, with their appurtenances, the names of which said towns, villages, and

lands, are as follows, viz.:—Ballihusgelane, Ballidernasire, Ballianaghwelt Ballicarnibreigh, Balli-
draughlasney, Ballimacgilcrany, Balliternane, Ballitawnyawnydonnel, Balligartchingham, Ballimag-
aberie, Ballicarloghinan, Ballinecryny, Ballinishilaghan, Ballinelermened, Ballenullaghgurten, Ballie-
donye, Grimmiselagh, Ballybrinmore, Ballynemeigh, Ballygreene, Ballifinhosseff, Ballycloghy, Balli-
madonye, Ballinahalchach, Ballintanvullag, Ballimagherstissemiske, Ballilaraghelisse, Listioghy,
Acharnan, Moybegg, Ballymacrickard, Balliaghadalan, Ballivurreolige, Ballinemore, Balliballoyen,
Ballilisnerobin, Ballialrone, Ballinskeallye, Ballicrumoygie, Ballymoneymore, Ballygortgarraffe, Balli-
cromriffe, Balliveolane, Ballibernagariff, Ballyinadorogie, Ballintennaghy, Ballinkeana, Ballinmickbrian,
Balliclonagaun, Ballishanaghill, Ballikillaghgenery, and Balliaghcarnan.   And also all other manors,
castles, villages, hamlets, lands, tenements, and other hereditaments whatsoever, lying and being in
or within the aforesaid territory or country of Kilultagh, in Clandeboy aforesaid, in the said counties
of Down and Antrim, in the said province of Ulster and the limits and circuit thereof, which said
territory or country hath the mears, circuits, bounds, and limits in form following—to wit, near and
upon the whole western part of the territory aforesaid extends part of the lough called Lougheaugh,
otherwise Loughsidney ; and on the west and northern angle of the territory aforesaid, towards the
east, the mear of the territory aforesaid extends itself through the middle of the river called Camelin,
running into the lough aforesaid, which said river runs for one mile or thereabouts between that territory and Kilmachevit, until it runs to the church called Camelin, situate in the said territory towards
the south of the said river ; and from thence the mear of the territory aforesaid extends through the
middle of the river aforesaid, extending itself towards the south, between the lands thereof and Clan-
dermet, in the lower Clandeboy, until the aforesaid river approaches a certain highway upon the
mountain lands, called Balloghmogerlye, and from thence the mear of the territory aforesaid extends
itself between the said lands and Dirrevologie, otherwise Felagh, in the Lower Clandeboy aforesaid,
about half a mile towards the Woodyvale, (in English "the Glen of Altnecalleine,") and so about a
quarter of a mile through the middle of the said glen, and further directly upon and through the top
of the hill called Mulloghneglasse, near the town aforesaid, and from thence between the territory
above recited, for about half a mile, the bound continues itself directly upon and by the top of the hill
called Castlerobin : And from thence, between the territory directly through the middle of a certain
channel or old mear, for the space of a mile by estimation, until the aforesaid mear joins the passage
or ford of Ballinacrosse, within the wood there, and from thence, for the space of half a mile or thereabouts, on the other side of the woods and plantations within the territories aforesaid, directly to the
little field called Tworibegg ; and so in and through the middle of the aforesaid field, and from thence
between the territory aforesaid, for half a mile by estimation, directly to the passage or ford upon the
River Lagan aforesaid, called Garrifinbresse, and from thence the mear of the territory aforesaid extends itself through the middle of the River Lagan aforesaid, between the lands thereof and the
Sleught O'Neales aforesaid, for the space of a mile and a half, as far as the passage or ford of Agh-
cormocke, in the Lagan aforesaid, and from thence upon and through a certain plain called Tirekillen,
through the middle of a certain fosse or old mear, for the space of a quarter of a mile, the mear
extends itself between that territory and Kilwarlin, in the County of Down aforesaid, and from thence
between the territory aforesaid for two miles, directly through the middle of another place called
Tannycarum, and from thence for half a mile, directly between the territory aforesaid, through the
middle of a certain boggy meadow called Boroughnesragh, near and upon the banks of the Lagan
aforesaid, and from thence the mear extends between that territory and Eveagh, otherwise Maginesse's
country, in the county aforesaid, for half a mile through the River Lagan, called Owenmore, unto the
passage or ford Bellainlaghan, near the old fort there situate in that territory, and from thence the
mear aforesaid extends itself between the territories aforesaid directly two miles across the woods and
plains lying on the south side of the said fort unto the passage or ford in a bog called Belaballidono-
ghan ; and from thence between the territory for half a mile unto another passage or ford in a bog
called Belagher, and from thence for half a mile upon and by the bog and plain between the territories aforesaid, directly to another passage or ford in a bog called Agheromglasney ; and from thence
for a mile upon the bog and plain between the territory aforesaid, unto another passage or ford of
Bellaghhiskilline, which said ford is the beginning of a certain river descending into Lougheaugh
aforesaid, and so through the middle of the said river, during a course of a mile, the boundary aforesaid continues itself directly between the land of the same and the Braskelagh, otherwise M'Can's
country, unto Lougheaugh aforesaid, to or near Stanford upon the banks of the said lake.

And further, of our more abundant special grace, certain knowledge, and mere motion, with the assent aforesaid, for the consideration aforesaid, for us our heirs and successors by these presents, We do give and grant to the aforesaid James Hamilton, his heirs and assigns, all and singular castles, messuages, houses, edifices, mills, buildings, barns, dovehouses, orchards, granaries, gardens, lands, tenements, meadows, pastures, feedings, commons, demesne lands, wastes, heaths, furzes, moors, marshes, woods, underwoods, advowsons of churches, tithes of grain and all other things titheable, as well great as small, and also oblations, obventions, fruits, profits, commodities, waters, watercourses, fishings, fisheries, suit, sock, mulcture, warrens, mines, quarries, rents, reversions, and services, rents of labour, rent suit, and rents and services, as well free as customary tenants, tenants' works, fee farms, annuities, escheats, reliefs, herriots, fines, amerciaments, courts leet, view of frank pledge and perquisites, and profits of courts and leets, and all things to courts leet and view of frank pledge appertaining, chattles, waifs, estrays, goods and chattles of felons and fugitives, felons of themselves outlawed and put in exigent, deodands, native men and women, villeins with their followers, estovers and commons of estover, marts, markets, tolls, customs, rights, jurisdictions, franchises, privileges, exemptions, profits, commodities, emoluments, and hereditaments of us whatsoever, with their appurtenances of whatsoever kind, nature, or species they be, or by whatsoever names they are known, deemed, called, or reputed, situate, lying and being, growing, increasing, or arising within the aforesaid regions, countries, or territories, or manors, towns, fields, places, or hamlets aforesaid, or of or in any or either of the said premises above by these presents granted, or any or either of them in any manner belonging, appertaining, incumbent, or appendant, or as member, part, or parcel of the said premises by these presents before granted, or to any or either of them ever or at any time heretofore held, known, used, accepted, occupied, or reputed : And also the reversion and reversions, remainder and remainders of us whatsoever of all and singular the premises, with the appurtenances above granted, and every parcel thereof, depending or expectant of, in, or upon any gift or gifts, grant or grants, demise or demises whatever of the premises, or any part thereof, at any time heretofore made or granted, as well being of record as not of record : Excepting, nevertheless, and out of this our grant always reserving, all castles, lands, and other hereditaments whatever of the Bishop of Down and Connor, in or within the places and territories abovementioned : And also all castles, lands, tenements, and other hereditaments whatsoever to all and singular abbeys, monasteries, priories, or other religious houses, in any manner belonging or appertaining, heretofore found by inquisition, or now remaining of record, or unjustly concealed or detained from us ; and also excepting and reserving all fisheries of every kind, and all the weirs of the River Lagan aforesaid ; and also all castles, lands, tenements, and hereditaments whatsoever, in or within the country or territory of the Lower Clandeboy, which now are or lately were in the tenure or occupation of the said Sir Arthur Chichester, Knight, or his assigns, by reason of any letters patent granted by us to the said Arthur, and also the rectories and vicarages, with their glebes and tithes whatsoever, in or within the territories aforesaid and the limits thereof ; all and singular which premises (except as before excepted) extend to the annual value of one hundred pounds : To have, hold, and enjoy all and singular the aforesaid territories, countries, lands, tenements, and hereditaments, and the rest of all and singular the premises whatsoever, with all and singular their rights, members, and appurtenances whatsoever, to the aforesaid James Hamilton, his heirs and assigns, for ever, to the sole and proper use and behoof of the said James Hamilton, his heirs and assigns, for ever : Paying thereout annually to us, our heirs and successors, at the receipt of the Exchequer of us, our heirs and successors, of our said kingdom of Ireland, to wit, to the hands of the Vice-Treasurer or General Receiver of us, our heirs and successors, for the time being, £100 current money of Ireland, at the feasts of St. Michael the Archangel, and Easter, or within forty days after such feasts, by equal portions, for all other rents and duties whatever, and to be held of us, our heirs and successors, as of our Castle of Carrickfergus in free and common soccage only, and not *in capite*, nor in soccage *in capite*, nor by knight's service.

And further, we will that the aforesaid James Hamilton, his heirs and assigns, shall find ten good and proper horsemen and twenty footmen, well instructed and armed, annually, to attend and serve for forty days our Lieutenant or Deputy-General, in our said kingdom of Ireland, when our said Lieutenant-General or Deputy-General in his proper person shall make his general journey, (or general "hostings,") in our said province of Ulster.

And further, of our more abundant special grace, certain knowledge, and mere motion, with the assent and for the considerations aforesaid, for us, our heirs and successors, We do give and grant to the aforesaid James Hamilton, his heirs and assigns, that they may have and hold, and have power and authority to have and hold one free market in and at Castlereagh, in the County of Down aforesaid, on every Thursday in every week for ever, and one fair to be held in and at Castlereagh aforesaid, on the feast of Saint John the Baptist, and for two days following the said feast in every year for ever ; and that they may have, hold, and take several courts of pye powder, and all and singular tolls, profits, perquisites commodities, and emoluments to such market and fair belonging or in any manner appertaining, without any account to us, our heirs or successors, to be rendered or paid for the same.

And further, of our more abundant special grace, certain knowledge, and mere motion, with the assent and for the considerations aforesaid, for us, our heirs and successors, We do give and grant to the aforesaid James Hamilton, his heirs and assigns, full liberty, power, and authority to have and to hold one frank pledge court leet, to be held before their seneschal or seneschals, according to the form of the statute in that case made and provided, and also a court baron, in and within the manor of Castlereagh, and the precincts and limits thereof, and in and within the mears and bounds of all the lands and tenements to the same belonging or appertaining, together with all privileges, franchises, immunities, perquisites, fines, amerciaments, profits, liberties, and commodities whatsoever, to a view of frank pledge, court leet, and court baron belonging, or in any wise appertaining, without any account to us, our heirs or successors, to be rendered thereout.

And further, of our more abundant special grace, certain knowledge, and mere motion, with the assent aforesaid, for us, our heirs and successors, We give and grant to the aforesaid James Hamilton, his heirs and assigns, that he, the aforesaid James Hamilton, his heirs and assigns, may have and hold one free market in and at Bangor, in the said county of Down, on every Monday weekly for ever, and one fair in or at Bangor aforesaid, on the feast day of St. James the Apostle, and for two days next following the said feast annually for ever ; and also one other market at Holywood, in the county aforesaid, to be held on every Wednesday weekly for ever ; and one other fair at Holywood aforesaid, to be held annually, on the twenty-fourth day of March, and for two days next following for ever : And that the aforesaid James Hamilton, his heirs and assigns, may have and hold these several courts of pye powder, and all other things to a court of pye powder or fair appertaining or in any manner belonging ; and that they may have and take all tolls, perquisites, profits, commodities, and privileges whatsoever which to fairs or markets appertain or belong, without any account to us, our heirs or successors, to be thereout rendered : And that these our letters patent shall be good and effectual in the law against us, our heirs and successors, notwithstanding that our writ of *ad quod damnum* hath not issued to inquire thereof before the making of these our letters patent, or any other act, law, usage, or ordinance to the contrary notwithstanding.

And further, of our more ample special grace, certain knowledge, and mere motion, with the assent aforesaid, We give and grant to the aforesaid James Hamilton, his heirs and assigns, that he the aforesaid James Hamilton, his heirs and assigns, may have, hold, and enjoy one market in and at Grayabbey, in the said county of Down, to be held on every Friday in every week for ever ; and one fair in or at Grayabbey aforesaid, to be held on the feast day of St. Luke, being the 18th of October, and for two days next following the said feasts annually for ever. And that the aforesaid James Hamilton, his heirs and assigns for ever, may have and hold there a court of pye powder, and all other things which to a court of pye powder or fair belong or appertain, and that they may have and take all and singular tolls, perquisites, profits, commodities, and privileges whatsoever which to any market or fair belong or appertain, without any account to be thereout rendered to us, our heirs or successors : And that these our letters patent may be valid and effectual in the law to the said James Hamilton, his heirs and assigns, against us, our heirs and successors, notwithstanding that our writ of *ad quod damnum* hath not issued to inquire thereof before the making of these our letters patent, any act, ordinance, law, or usage to the contrary notwithstanding.

And further, of our more abundant special grace, certain knowledge, and mere motion, for us, our heirs and successors, We give and grant to the aforesaid James Hamilton, his heirs and assigns, full and absolute license, power, and authority that he the said James Hamilton, his heirs and assigns, from time to time hereafter for ever, at his and their will and pleasure, may and can alienate, assign, grant, demise, enfeoff, or acknowledge by fine or fines, recovery or recoveries, or by any other manner whatsoever, all and singular the aforesaid territories, countries, lands, tenements, and hereditaments whatsoever, or any parcel thereof, to any person or persons, being English or Scotch, or of English or Scotch blood, and not being " mere Irishmen" (Con Oneale M'Brian Fertagh Oneale and his heirs only excepted) : To have and to hold to the said person or persons, their heirs and assigns, in fee simple or fee tail, to be held of the said James Hamilton, and his heirs and assigns, by such so many the like and as many services, customs, and rights as to the said James Hamilton, and his heirs and assigns, shall seem fit or pleasing : And to the said person or persons, and every or either of them, We do give, and by these presents, for us, our heirs and successors, we do grant license, authority, and power that such person or persons the premises or any parcel thereof from the said James Hamilton, his heirs or assigns, he and they may have power to receive and hold to them and their heirs, of any hereditary estate, in fee simple, or fee tail, or otherwise : And also, to hold to them, and their heirs and assigns, all manner of estates of free tenants, for term of life or lives, or otherwise, as to the said James Hamilton, his heirs and assigns, shall seem expedient, the statute of *Quia Emptores Terrarum*, or any other statute, acts, ordinance, use, law, or custom, or any other cause, matter, or thing, to the contrary thereof had, provided, used, or published, in any wise notwithstanding : Being unwilling that any or either of such persons, or any of their heirs or assigns, or the aforesaid James Hamilton, or his heirs, by reason of the premises by us, our heirs or successors, or by our justices, escheators, sheriffs, bailiffs, or other officers, or ministers of us, our heirs or successors whomsoever, therefor in any manner may be or might on any account be molested, aggrieved, vexed, or impeached.

And, further, of our more abundant and special grace, certain knowledge, and mere motion, with the assent, and for the consideration aforesaid, for us, our heirs and successors, We give and grant to the aforesaid James Hamilton, his heirs and assigns, that he, the aforesaid James Hamilton, his heirs and assigns, may have and hold, and have power to have two several views of frank pledge, or courts leet, and all things which to views of frank pledge and courts leet appertain, to be held before the seneschall, or seneschalls, according to the form of the statute in that case made and provided, and within the precinct of the territory or country of the Great Ards aforesaid : And, also, two other views of frank pledge, or courts leet, and all things to views of frank pledge and courts leet appertaining, to be held before the seneschall, or seneschalls, by the aforesaid James, his heirs or assigns, or any of them to be nominated, according to the form of the statute in that case made and provided, in or within the precincts or limits of the said territory or country of the Upper Clandeboy ; and that the aforesaid James Hamilton, his heirs and assigns, being English or Scotch, or of the blood of the English or Scotch, may further have, hold, and enjoy for ever, and every of them may have, hold, and enjoy for ever, within the several territories of the Upper Clandeboy, and the Great Ards, several courts to be held before their seneschall, or seneschalls, to enquire of all and singular such matters and things, which in courts baron, within our said kingdom of Ireland, or within our kingdom of England, ought, or are accustomed to be enquired of, and to hold pleas on every Thursday, from three weeks to three weeks, of all manner of things, debts, covenants, trespasses, accounts, detinues, and contracts, which in debt or damages do not exceed the sum of forty shillings sterling, done, or arising, in every the hundreds, baronies, manors, places, towns, villages, or boroughs, or in, or within the hundreds, baronies, manors, places, towns, townlands, or boroughs, in, or within the aforesaid territories, lands, tenements, and hereditaments, by these presents before granted, or in, or within any part or parcel thereof, or within such limits or bounds as the aforesaid James Hamilton, his heirs or assigns, within the premises by their deeds have assigned and declared, and all profits, amerciaments, issues, forfeitures, perquisites, and commodities, to those courts coming, growing, or arising, without any account to us, our heirs or successors, to be rendered or made ; and also all, and all manner of things which to a hundred appertain, in any part of the premises, and also courts and profits of the hundred aforesaid, and all things which to a court hundred appertain, or ought to appertain, without any molestation, disturbance, or inquietude of us, our heirs or successors, or of the justices, escheators, sheriffs, bailiffs, officers, or ministers of us, our heirs or successors, for ever.

And, further, of our more ample special grace, certain knowledge, and mere motion, with the assent aforesaid, for us, our heirs and successors, We do give and grant to the aforesaid James Hamilton, his heirs and assigns, that he the aforesaid James Hamilton, his heirs and assigns, and all people resident or not resident in or within the aforesaid countries, territories, lands, tenements, and hereditaments whatsoever, may be free, acquitted, released, and exonerated for ever, of and from all, and all manner of rents, exactions, and Irish customs whatsoever, called cess, bonnoght, coshery, and the like customs, and which were heretofore used, taxed, issued, imposed, or assessed, or might, or happened so to be, except the rents and services above by these presents reserved, and general hostings, for the defence or keeping of the peace in the aforesaid countries, territories, and tenements.

And, further, of our more ample special grace, certain knowledge, and mere motion, with the assent, and for the considerations aforesaid, for us, our heirs and successors, We do give and grant to the aforesaid James Hamilton, his heirs and assigns, that he, the aforesaid James Hamilton, his heirs and assigns, may have and enjoy, and every of them, for ever, may have and enjoy, within all and singular the premises, free warren, and free chase, and liberty to make several parks or chases, and free warren and chase, and have liberty in such chase warren and park, and in all woods and lands whatsoever, within the aforesaid countries and territories of Upper Clandeboy, and Great Ards, and in and within the rest of all the premises, countries, territories, and other the premises, within the mears of the forests of us, our heirs or successors, so that no other person may enter into the aforesaid territories, lands, tenements, woods, or hereditaments, nor into any part thereof to hunt therein, or to take any thing which to free warren or chase doth belong.

And, further, of our more abundant special grace, certain knowledge, and mere motion, with the assent aforesaid, for us, our heirs, and successors, We do give and grant to the aforesaid James Hamilton, his heirs and assigns, that it shall and may be lawful for the aforesaid James Hamilton, his heirs and assigns, from time to time, to export and import into the said territories or countries, or into any part thereof, men, chattels, grain, and all and all manner of commodities, as well for the use and maintenance of the said James Hamilton, his heirs and assigns, and of all men, tenants, dwellers, resident, or hereafter to reside within the aforesaid territories, countries, or regions, or within any parcel thereof, without any forfeiture, seizure, pain, penalty, or damages towards us, our heirs or successors, on account of the premises incurred, paid, or performed ; saving also to us, our heirs and successors, the imports, subsidies, and customs of wine, for the same due and accustomed, being unwilling that the aforesaid James Hamilton, his heirs or assigns, or any other or the like men, tenants, residents, or dwellers, or to dwell within the said dominions, territories, countries, lands, or hereditaments before granted, or any of them, or their heirs, or executors, or administrators, by reason of the premises, by us, our heirs or successors, or by our justices, escheators, sheriffs, bailiffs, custom or other officers or ministers of us, our heirs or successors, whatsoever, therefor upon any occasion may be molested, impeached, or in any manner aggrieved, any statute, act, ordinance, restriction, prohibition, use, law, or any other cause, matter, or thing to the contrary thereof, made, used, or provided, in any wise notwithstanding.

And, further, of our more ample grace, certain knowledge, and mere motion, with the assent, and for the consideration aforesaid, for us, our heirs and successors, We give and grant to the aforesaid James Hamilton, his heirs, and assigns, being English or Scotch, or of English or Scotch blood, and not mere Irish (except Con O'Neale aforesaid, and his heirs), for ever, full power, authority, leave, license, and power, that it shall and may be lawful for the aforesaid James Hamilton, his heirs and assigns, and every of them, being of English or Scotch extraction, to transport, export, carry, load, and unload, into all and singular countries and kingdoms, under, or in friendship with us, our heirs, or successors for the time being, all kind of grain, commodities, produce, and emoluments, and other things whatsoever, (linen yarn excepted) from henceforth coming, growing, arising, renewing, made, or to be made, in or within the aforesaid countries, territories, or any part thereof, without any pains, penalties, seizures, or forfeitures, thereout to us, our heirs or successors, to be made, rendered, paid, or incurred by us, our heirs or successors, or the officers or ministers of us, our heirs or successors, by reason of the premises to be had or levied (saving also to us, our heirs and assigns, the custom and impost of wine, and subsidies for the same due, or to grow due), unless we, or our Deputy, Justices, or Governor-general for the time being, or our Council there, upon any special cause, shall or may find it necessary to prohibit or restrain the transportation of the said grain or commodities for any reasonable time, being unwilling that the aforesaid James Hamilton, his heirs or assigns, by reason of the premises by us, our heirs or successors, or by our justices, escheators, sheriffs, bailiffs, custom or other officers, or ministers of us, or of our heirs or successors, whomsoever, by any means contrary to the tenor of these presents, may or shall be on any account molested, impeached, vexed, or in any manner aggrieved, any statute, act, ordinance, use, custom, or any other cause, matter, or thing, to the contrary thereof in any wise notwithstanding.

And, further, of our more ample special grace, certain knowledge, and mere motion, with the consent aforesaid, We do give and grant that the aforesaid James Hamilton, his heirs and assigns, being English or Scotch, or of the blood of the English or Scotch, so long as he keeps faith and allegiance towards us, our heirs and successors, may have power and authority in and within the countries, territories, lands, tenements, and hereditaments aforesaid, from time to time, to build, repair, sustain, amend, and re-edify, as often as to him the said James Hamilton, his heirs and assigns, shall seem expedient, all, every, such, and so many castles, forts, houses, edifices, defences, and bulwarks, of, in, or upon any the several parcels of the premises such, the like, and as many as to the said James Hamilton, his heirs or assigns, being English or Scotch, or of English or Scotch extraction, as aforesaid, and every of them, shall seem expedient ; and in such castles, forts, houses, defences, and bulwarks, to put, place, renew, and constitute so many such, the like, and as many arms and guns, cannon, and other ammunition whatsoever, and in the said castles, forts, houses of defence, and bulwarks, to appoint and place such and so many men, armed and unarmed, being in our faith and allegiance, for the defence and maintenance of the said castles, forts, houses of defence, and bulwarks, for ever, as to the said James Hamillon, his heirs and assigns, as aforesaid, shall seem expedient, any statute, act, ordinance, usage, law, or custom, to the contrary thereof in any wise notwithstanding.

We will also, and by these presents, for us, our heirs and successors, do grant and command, that the aforesaid James Hamilton, his heirs and assigns, being English or Scotch, or of the blood of English or Scotch, as aforesaid, may have and hold, and every of them may have and hold, all and singular gifts, grants, liberties, acquittances, franchises, and immunities, as aforesaid, and all and singular, and every of such, they may fully enjoy and use, without any impeachment, impediment, molestation, or grievance, of us, our heirs or successors, or of our justices, escheators, sheriffs, or other bailiffs, or ministers of us, our heirs or successors, whomsoever.

And, further, We will, and for us, our heirs and successors, We do grant, that upon the exhibition or showing of these our letters patent, or the enrolment thereof, as well before us in the Chancery of us, our heirs and successors, as before the Justices of both Benches, of us, our heirs and successors, within our kingdom of Ireland, and before the Treasurer and Barons of our Exchequer, of us, our heirs and successors, within our said kingdom of Ireland, and before the Treasurer and Barons of our Exchequer, of us, our heirs and successors, within our kingdom of England, and also before our Justices and Commissioners of us, our heirs and successors, as well in all and singular, the courts of us, our heirs and successors, and places of record within our said kingdom of England, or within our said kingdom of Ireland, as in all and every other the courts and places throughout our whole kingdom of England, and throughout our whole kingdom of Ireland, for anything in the said letters patent contained or specified, these our letters patent, and all grants in the same contained and specified, especially and immediately to the aforesaid James Hamilton, his heirs and assigns, being English or Scotch, or of the blood of English or Scotch, and not mere Irish (said Con O'Neale and his heirs excepted), shall be fully taken and allowed ; and that the aforesaid Treasurers, Barons, Justices, Commissioners, and other persons whomsoever, to whom it belongeth, due allowance of, and in all the premises from time to time, do make, or cause to be made, and that he, the said James Hamilton, his heirs and assigns aforesaid, may have authority, power, and liberty of nominating and giving names to all and singular the premises, and every part thereof, and that the premises and every parcel thereof, so as aforesaid nominated, shall be known, taken, and named, as well in all our courts as elsewhere, by such name or names as the said James Hamilton, his heirs or assigns, to the premises aforesaid, or any part thereof, shall have given, nominated, or attributed, any ordinance, nomination, appellation, name, or names of the premises, or any parcel thereof, in anywise notwithstanding.

And, further, of our more abundant special grace, certain knowledge, and mere motion, We will, and by these presents, for us, our heirs and successors, do grant to the aforesaid James Hamilton, his heirs and assigns, that these our letters patent, or the enrolment thereof, shall be in and by all things firm, good, valid, sufficient, and effectual in the law towards and against us, our heirs and successors, as well in all our courts as elsewhere within our said kingdom, without any other confirmation, license, or toleration from us, our heirs or successors hereafter, by the aforesaid James Hamilton, his heirs or assigns aforesaid, or either of them, to be procured or obtained : Notwithstanding the ill-naming, or ill-reciting, or not reciting the aforesaid countries, territories, lands, tenements, and hereditaments, and the rest of the premises, or any parcel thereof : And notwithstanding the not finding of any offices or inquisitions of the premises, or of any parcel thereof, by which our title, or of any or of our progenitors, ought to have been found before the making of these our letters patent : And notwithstanding the not naming, not reciting, ill-naming, or ill-reciting any demise or demises, grant or grants for the term of life, lives, or years, or in fee tail, or otherwise, of the premises, or of any parcel thereof, by us, or by any of our progenitors, or by any other person or persons, heretofore made to any person or persons, being of record or not of record, and notwithstanding the ill-naming or not naming any town, village, hamlet, parish, place, or country, in all or any of which the premises or any parcel thereof are or do lye; and notwithstanding that of the names of the farmers, or occupiers of the premises, or of the said territories, countries, lands, tenements, and hereditaments, or other the premises, or any parcel thereof, full true and certain mention be not made; and notwithstanding any defects in the certainty, computation, or declaration of the true annual value of the premises, or any parcel thereof, or the annual rents reserved of or upon the premises, or of or upon any parcel thereof, in these our letters patent expressed or contained, or not expressed; and notwithstanding any other defects whatsoever, and notwithstanding a statute in a Parliament of our Lord Henry, late King of England the Sixth, our progenitor, in the 18th year of his reign, at Westminster, made and provided, and in our kingdom of Ireland aforesaid, amongst other things, established and confirmed: And notwithstanding any other statute or statutes whatever, and notwithstanding the not rightly naming the nature, kind, species, quantity, or quality of the premises, or any parcel thereof, or any other thing, cause, or matter whatsoever, in any wise notwithstanding: Although express mention of the true yearly value, or of the certainty of the premises, or any of them, or of any other gifts or grants by us, or by any of our progenitors, to the said James Hamilton heretofore made, in these presents be in no wise made, any statute, act, ordinance, or provision, or any other thing, cause, or matter whatsoever to the contrary of the premises made, in anywise notwithstanding. In witness whereof, we have caused these our letters to be made patent: Witness our aforesaid Deputy-General, of our kingdom of Ireland, at Dublin, the fifth day of November, in the 3rd year of our reign of England, France, and Ireland, and of Scotland the 39th. By virtue of the letters of the Lord the King, sent from England, and signed by his proper hand.

No. II.

LETTERS PATENT OF 20TH APRIL, 1630, FROM CHARLES I. TO JAMES VISCOUNT CLANEBOY.

CHARLES, by the grace of God, of England, Scotland, France, and Ireland, King, Defender of the Faith, &c.: To all to whom these our present Letters shall come, greeting: Know ye that We, as well for and in consideration of the good, true, faithful, and acceptable service heretofore frequently done and performed for our father James, lately King, of happy memory, for us and our crown, by our well beloved and very faithful cousin and counsellor James Viscount Claneboy, in the county of Down, in the province of Ulster, in our kingdom of Ireland, and one of the Privy Council of our said kingdom of Ireland, as for divers other good causes and considerations, us to these presents specially moving, of our special grace, certain knowledge, and mere motion, have given, granted, confirmed, and released, and by these presents, for us our heirs and successors, do give, grant, confirm, and release to the aforesaid James Viscount Claneboy, his heirs and assigns, for ever, the entire lately dissolved Monastery or Abbey of Bangor, in the county of Down, in our said kingdom of Ireland, and the whole circuit ambit and precincts of the said late monastery, with their rights, members, and appurtenances whatsoever, and all and singular the towns, villages, hamlets, places, messuages, tenements, and hereditaments following, either known, called, or named by the names following, or lying, being, coming, or renewing in the towns, hamlets, or places following, in our said county of Down, in our kingdom of Ireland, viz.:—Bangor, Balleportavo or Balleportobo, Ballyfoderlics or Ballepheoderlie, Ballemynitragh, Ballemynultragh, Carrowreagh, Carroworlag, Ballow near the sea, Ballimulleragh or Gilgroumsport,

Ballemacormick or Ballemacosmaghs, Balle M'Connell or Balle M'Koncile, Ballecroghan, Ballyhol-viev or Ballchomie, Ballynaghie or Ballenenoghnie or Ballemenaghne, Balleonerie or Ballenriogh or Ballenyric, Ballenegrangeogh, Ballereeny or Balliocrane, Ballow near Bangor, Carrownesuire or Car-rowneser, Carrowknockanduff or Carrowslanclarkanduffe, Carrowneshroy or Collosenesaran, Balle-monecarogie or Monycaragh or Ballemonycaragh, Ballekawgeile or Ballefraghoguile, Ballelis-banc or Ballinlissclane, Ballebarne or Ballenebernen, Ballineeamanleagh or Ballecamanedeagh, Ballekillare or Ballincellor, Ballesallagh, Ballemullan or Ballemulla, Ballevernon or Ballevernocke, Ballcliddie, Ballecrott, Balleskelly or Ballyskally, and Ballygilbert, and also all and singular the towns, villages, and places following, as well spiritual as temporal, viz.:—Ballemeaghan or Ballemegh, Balle-machoris, and Ballemajor or Ballemaeer, lying in or near the plains of Belfast, with their appurtenances, and also the whole of the Grange called Earbeg in our County of Antrim, of our said kingdom of Ireland: And also all the the islands called Copeland Islands, lying and being near the bay of Carrickfergus, In said County of Antrim, with all and singular their lands, tenements, and appurtenances whatsoever ; and also the Rectory of Balleclughan or Ballcurgegan, in Lecale, with the tithes of Balleurgegan, and Corbally, belonging to same Rectory, parcel of the possession of the Abbey of Bangor aforesaid, and Ballemeghan in said County of Down, with all their rights, members, and appurtenances whatsoever : And also the whole of the Church or Chapel of Cregevada, and the tithes of the four towns fol-lowing, viz.:—Ballycregavada, Ballerobert, Balledevie, and Ballegreney, and Ballehemony, pertaining to said Monastery of Bangor : And also all the tithes of grain and hay, and all other things titheable in certain isles called the Orunglines, lying and being in the Irish Sea, near the Route in said County of Antrim, and the whole of the impropriation of the Rectory or Chapel of Holywood, with the tithes of the towns following, viz. :—Ballecultra in the Great Ards, Ballemanagh, Ballekeile, Ballinderry, and Balleknocknegony, and all the tithes of all the fish taken or imported on the south shore of the Bay of Knockfergus or Carrickfergus, from the Copeland Isles to the passage of Belfast ; and the ferry from the town of Bangor to and from Knockfergus and Antrim side ; also the advowson of all the Vicarages in all and singular the parochial towns or villages aforesaid, with their tithes, obventions; and appurtenances whatsoever.

We have given, also granted, confirmed, and released, and, by these presents, for us, our heirs and successors, do give, grant, confirm, and release to the aforesaid Viscount Claneboy, his heirs and assigns, all our towns, villages, hamlets, messuages, lands, tenements, rents, and hereditaments what-soever, either in the precincts of the Great Ards, and Upper Clandeboy, or either of them, in said County of Down, heretofore lately belonging or appertaining to the Abbey or Monastery of Bangor, being either as member, part, or parcel of said late Monastery ever heretofore had, known, received, occupied, used or enjoyed, or being ever before this parcel of the possession of said late Monastery or Abbey : Also, all and singular the tithes of grain and hay, and other things titheable whatsoever, and all other tithes whatsoever, in all and singular the towns, villages, hamlets, places, lands, and tene-ments aforesaid, and annually coming, growing, or renewing, now or heretofore belonging or apper-taining to said late Monastery or Abbey, with their appurtenances whatsoever, and all tithes what-soever belonging or appertaining to the said late Monastery or Abbey of Bangor.

We have given, also granted, confirmed, and released, and, by these presents, for us, our heirs and successors, do give, grant, confirm, and release to the aforesaid James Viscount Claneboy, his heirs and assigns, the whole of the late dissolved Priory or religious house of Holywood, in our aforesaid County of Down, in our said kingdom of Ireland, and the whole site, circuit, ambit, and precincts of the said late Priory or religious house of Holywood, with its rights, members, and appurtenances what-soever : And also all the towns, villages, hamlets, and places, with their appurtenances, viz. :—Balli-keele alias Ballkegill, Ballemacken or Ballemenagh, Ballecultrack or Ballecultra or Ballacktragath, Ballindery or Ballidory, Balliorcknegony or Balliknocknegonie, lying and being in the aforesaid County of Down, with all and singular their members and appurtenances whatsoever, and all the towns, villages, hamlets, messuages, lands, tenements, rents, and hereditaments whatsoever, ever heretofore belong-ing or appertaining to the late Priory or religious house of Holywood, in said County of Down, either as member, part, or parcel of said late Priory being at any time heretofore had, known, received, oc-cupied, used or enjoyed, or being ever before this parcel of the possession of said late Priory ; also all and singular the tithes of grain and hay, and other things titheable whatsoever, in all and singular the towns, villages, places, lands, tenements, or farms, annually coming, growing, or renewing, with their appurtenances whatsoever, formerly belonging or appertaining to the said late Priory or religious house of Holywood.

We have given, also granted, confirmed, and released, and, by these presents, for us, our heirs and successors, do give, grant, confirm, and release to the aforesaid Viscount Claneboy, his heirs and assigns, the whole of the impropriation of the Rectory of Balleoran in our aforesaid County of Down, in our said kingdom of Ireland, with all and singular the tithes in the towns, villages, hamlets, places, lands, and tenements following, with their appurtenances, viz. :—Balleoran, Neravy, Winnecarvelle, and Lisbreeden, in the territories of Hughtubrickey in our County of Down aforesaid ; and also the entire appropriation of the Rectory of Kilconby or Kircubin, with all and singular the tithes in the towns, villages, and places following, to the same appertaining, viz. :—the tithes of Kilconby or Kircubin, and Ballerunelin, in the territory of the Great Ards aforesaid.

We have given, also granted, confirmed, and released, and, by these presents, for us, our heirs and successors, do give, grant, confirm, and release to the aforesaid Viscount Claneboy, his heirs and assigns, the whole impropriation of the Rectory of Coolgrange, or Grange, in the Great Ards, near Blackstaffe ; and all and singular the tithes of all the towns, villages, hamlets, and lands of Ravarra, Carrowreagh, and Ballecloghan, lying in or near the plains of Belfast, and of Rowbane and Roureagh in the Great Ards ; and also the entire appropriation of the Rectory of Drumroan, with all and singular the tithes in the towns and villages of Drumroan, and Balleleggan, in the Great Ards, in the aforesaid County of Down, in our said kingdom of Ireland.

We have given, also granted, confirmed, and released, and, by these presents, for us, our heirs and successors, do give, grant, confirm, and release to the aforesaid Viscount Claneboy, his heirs and assigns, all the rectories, towns, villages, hamlets, places, lands, tenements, tithes, and hereditaments following, as well spiritual as temporal, parcels of the late dissolved Abbey or religious house of Comber, viz :—Ballenagratris, Corrownesuir, Ballcullentry, and Ballenicall, and all the tithes of all the towns, villages, lands, and places following, viz :—Balleristoll, Ballegrangiogh, Balbelisleyne, Ballckiell, Ballemanagh, Balletulehubert, Ballemaglagh, Ballahigill, Ballidrumcheriff, half Ballygraffin, Ballibeen, Ballemaghcriscowe or Ballemaheristowe, Ballegowne or Ballegowan : And also as much of the tithes belonging to the impropriation of the Rectory of Tanaghum as come, grow, or renew from any towns, villages, hamlets, lands, tenements, and hereditaments whatsoever, of the said Viscount Claneboy.

We have given, moreover granted, confirmed, and released, and, by these presents, for us, our heirs and successors, do give, grant, confirm, and release to the aforesaid Viscount Claneboy, his heirs and assigns, all the tithes of fish taken or imported on the southern side of the river of Comber, and as far as the lands and hereditaments of the said Viscount extend, and as much of the tithes of the impropriation of the Rectories of Killanie and Drum in the Lagan, as renew from any lands or hereditaments, of said Viscount Claneboy.

We have given, also granted, confirmed, and released, and, by these presents, for us, our heirs and successors, do give, grant, confirm, and release to the aforesaid Viscount Claneboy, his heirs and assigns, all and singular the towns, villages, places, messuages, rectories, lands, tenements, and hereditaments following, as well spiritual as temporal, viz :—The town of Balliwalter, parcel of the possession of the late dissolved Abbey or religious house of Greyabbey, in the Great Ards aforesaid, a quarter of the land called Carrowclogher, in the parish of Whitechurch, a quarter of the land called Carrownemoan, in the parish of Talbots-Town, a quarter of the land called Carow-John-Boestie, in the town of Drumroan aforesaid, and another quarter called St. John's Quarter, in Fuloghkean, and another quarter of land called Carrownilhead, or St. John's Quarter, in Kiloogin, in the Great Ards.

We have also granted, confirmed, and released, and, by these presents, for us, our heirs and successors, do give, grant, confirm, and release to the aforesaid Viscount Claneboy, his heirs and assigns, all and singular, the impropriations of the Rectories following, parcel of the possession of the dissolved Monastery, or religious house of Blackabbey, in the Great Ards, viz., the impropriation of the Rectory of Ballyhalbert, to which appertain two third parts of the tithes of the towns of Balleaspragh, Ballehalbert, Ballenchaw, Balleportovogie or Multaghmore, Ballinepinge or Negullogh, Balleglasseragh, Ballegraffan, Ballechamlin and Ballyrodeny; also the entire impropriation of the Rectory of Whitechurch or Templeffin, to which appertain two third parts of the tithes of the towns of Balleobekin, Balle M'Gown, Balleatwart, Ballcfferish, Balledownon, Templeffin or Whitechurch, Listnoganoy, and Kilbrate in the Great Ards :   Also the entire impropriation of the Rectory of Inniscargie, to which appertain two third parts of the tithes of the towns of Ballylimpt, Ballegarngan, Ballefister, Carawneskra, Carrownacalliogh, and Inniscargie or Nikellen.

We have given, moreover granted, confirmed, and released, and, by these presents, for us, our heirs and successors, do give, grant, confirm, and release to the aforesaid Viscount Claneboy, his heirs and assigns, the advowsons, donations, right of patronage, and free disposal of the several Vicarages in the several churches of Ballyhalbert or Talbotstown, Templeffin or Whitechurch, and Inniscargie, and all the tithes of every kind of fish taken or imported inland, or in the maritime places in or near the lands and hereditaments belonging to the said Viscount Claneboy, in the Great Ards, as well upon Loughcoyne side, as upon the side towards the main sea.

We have also given, granted, confirmed, and released, and, by these presents, for us, our heirs and successors, do give, grant, confirm, and release to the aforesaid Viscount Claneboy, his heirs and assigns, the impropriation of the Rectory of Ballewhillerat or Ballecollor, and Ballewhinneragh, with the advowsons, donations, and rights of patronage of the vicarage of said Rectory of Ballegalgat and Grangeowter, with their appurtenances, and all the two-third parts of the tithes of the towns and lands following, viz. :—Ballequintein, Balletullecavnan, Balledoke, Balletusselic, Balletawara, half of the towns of Quintagh, Tollemartar, and Carowmanert, with the advowson of said Rectory of Grangeowter.

We have also given, granted, confirmed, and released, and, by these presents, for us, our heirs and successors, do give, grant, confirm, and release to the aforesaid Viscount Claneboy, his heirs and assigns, the impropriation of the Rectory of Rathmullen, together with the advowsons of said Rectory, with all the tithes of the towns and lands following, viz. :—Rathmullen, Ballefunston or Luchanstown or Luckanstowne, Ballenibrit, Ballevaston, St. Johnstown, Killagh, and Blunketstown or Plunketstown : Also, the advowsons, donations, right of patronage, and free disposal of all the Rectories and Vicarages of the several churches and chapels of Dundonnell, Knockcollumkil, Bredagh, Blaris, and Tawnaghum ; and also the ferry over the river Strangford, together with the tithes of fish and fishing of said river : We have also given, granted, confirmed, and released, and by these presents, for us, our heirs and successors, do give, grant, confirm, and release to the aforesaid Viscount Claneboy, his heirs and assigns, all rectories, tithes, advowsons, hereditaments, and hereditary possessions whatsoever, lying, being, renewing, or in any manner coming in, of, or from any towns, villages, hamlets, or lands in the occupation or possession of said Viscount Claneboy, or his tenants, in the said territory of the Upper Clandeboy, or in the territory of the Great and Little Ards, or either of them, with their appurtenances whatsoever.

And, further, of our more ample special grace, certain knowledge, and mere motion, We have given, granted, confirmed, and released, and, by these presents, for us, our heirs and successors, do give, grant, confirm, and release to the aforesaid Viscount Claneboy, his heirs and assigns, all and singular the towns, villages, hamlets, places, messuages, lands, tenements, and hereditaments following, either known, called, or mentioned by the names following, or lying, being, coming, or renewing in the towns, villages, hamlets or places following, viz. :—Ballecregavadic, Ballerobert, Balledavie, Ballenegreny, Ballycloghans or Ballecloghan, Ballehacamur or Ballechakomer, Carrowmullur, Carrowcarne, Carrowtagart, Ballinechallen, Ballelisneska or Ballyhugh or Balleslionikagh, Ballercagin or Ballerigin, Balledimdonnell, Balliemalady or Balledimlady, Ballecarrowreagh or Carowreogh, Carowkilneveagh, Balleoron, Ballenarany, or Ballererain, Ballelisbraden, Ballewincawell or Ballemoneycarrel, Ballycaslanbeg, Ballebaines, Ballrestoll, Ballenegrange, Ballemarane or Ballemullare, Ballelisleyne, Ballekeyle, Ballytullyhubbart, Ballebyn, Ballegastrum or Balleglassdromon or Balleglassdornen, the half town of Ballcacrogie or Balleaghrogic, Ballclagegoan, Balledrumcheriff, Ballenegassan, Ballechigill, Ballemacheriscowe, Ballegowne, Carrickmanan or Ballecarrickmanen, the half town or part of a town of Aghinderragh, the half town of Ravarragh, Balleguntnaglare or Tulloughcaphinan, the half town of Ballenarevy or Ballenecrevagh, viz., Caroownan, and Carrowcreve, the half town of Killinchin or Killinsey, Ballysugue, a moiety or half part of Ballygraffon, Balleportovogie or Mulloghmore, Ballefringe or Negullogh, Ballehalbert, Balleuspragh, Ballyneglassnagh, Rowbane, Rowreagh, Ballefister, Ballegrangeogh or Coolegrange, Carrownesser, Ballecircubin or Kilconby, Ballemullen, Carownecalliogh, Ballecarngan or Ballegarvegan, Iniscargie or Nikellen, Balleclump, Balliehamlin, Ballerodeny, Ballengin or Ballehiggin, Balleobikin or Drumroan, Ballenigowne, Balleotwart, Balledownover, Balleferish, Balletullycarnan or Listiagnewe, Templefinn or Whitechurch, half of Balleganevy, and half of Ballekilbraten, with their appurtenances whatsoever, which same premises last mentioned are lying and being in the aforesaid territory or precinct of the Upper Clandeboy and the Great Ards, in the County of Down aforesaid.

We have also given, granted, confirmed, and released, and, by these presents, for us, our heirs and successors, do give, grant, confirm, and release to the said Viscount Claneboy, his heirs and assigns, all and singular the manors, castles, messuages, towns, villages, hamlets, lands, tenements, and hereditaments whatsoever, with their rights, members, and appurtenances whatsoever, in the aforesaid precincts of the great Ards, in the said County of Down, situate, lying, and being in the southern part or side the same territory or precincts of the Great Ards aforesaid, being divided by the mears and bounds following, viz. :—beginning at the mear or march between the Gray Abbey and the Great Ards, in or near the middle of a bog to the southern end of shrubs in the bog aforesaid, which same bog, called Carrownenowan, is also the march between the lands of Gray Abbey and the Great Ards, and from thence towards north-east, through a certain trench or dyke, in or near the middle of said bog, equally between two islands, called Island Vicar on the southern, and Horse Island on the northern part, and so from thence towards the east and north-east, through said trench or dyke in the middle of the bog aforesaid, to the forde calledAkillbroughtaine, and stops at the source of the revulet called Owenganvoy, which same rivulet is the mear or division between the two, about the middle of the aforesaid territory or precincts of the Great Ards aforesaid, until said rivulet descends into the main sea.

And, further, of our more abundant special grace, certain knowledge, and mere motion, We have given, granted, confirmed, and released, and, by these presents, for us, our heirs and successors, do give, grant, confirm, and release to the aforesaid Viscount Claneboy, his heirs and assigns, all our towns, villages, hamlets, messuages, lands, tenements, and hereditaments following, with their appurtenances whatsoever, viz. :—Ballebredagh, Balle-Knock-Collomkill, Ballemacarrett, Balleconckroy, Ballycrevyalickavrick, Balledrynan or Ballemegaymar, Balledruminclcg, Ballchesagh or Lough Hanic, Ballelesdangan or Ballelisgan, of which the parcel of land called Tannaghiren is a quarter, Ballelagegoan, Balleneglissan, Ballegalwally, Carowdorne, Levalle, Crevilloughgar, Ballenmughlagh or Ballemolaugh, Balledygginor, Balledyen, and Tollevastekynagh : We have also given, granted, confirmed, and released, and by these presents, for us, our heirs and successors, do give, grant, confirm, and release to the aforesaid Viscount Claneboy, his heirs and assigns, an half or moiety of Balledullaghan, Ballecowan, Ballenclesson, Ballenecargie or Ballclisnademan, Ballenecarne or Drumbeckly, Ballehaughliske, Balleclogher, Balledowneagh, the half of the half-town of Lisnegnol, and a moiety of all the towns and lands following, viz. :—Balledrumber, all Betullenecrosse, Balleblansh or Templeblansh, Ballenacrossan, Ballenegarrick or Balle-M'Carrick or Balle M'Garge or Ballyneganvey, Ballecarrickmadery, Carricknaveag, Ballelisdrum, Loghan or Lisbane, Balleloghgar or Balletanaghmore, Ballecaghan or Ballecaried, Levallekilleny, Ballecreviargan, Listowdric, or Ballelistowdrie, Ballenebarnes, Drumgiven or Drumvence or Drumrevan, Ballecarnganan, Carrowduffe or Thyduffe or Hughduffe, Carrowlaverogge, Carrowedenderry, Balledrumbeg or Ballegrumbeg, Levalles, Tullegowrie, Balledeniskcagh or Balleskeaghan or Balliskeagh, Lattefeaghs, Balledunkinmurick, Dologhmurick, Ballehenievc or Carrowtulliarde or Carrowlisnoad, Ballemickareveine, Ballelisneshrean, Ballekillenaire, Carrickenesassanough, Balledowncan or Lisamany or Ballekill, Balleoghiy or Fairtown or Ballenenay, Ballenelessan, quarter of Tullowre or Tullour, Ballcknockan, and Augleshin, which same premises last mentioned are situate, lying, and being in the country or precincts of Slewght O'Neill's or Slut Neales, in the territory of Upper Claneboy, in the aforesaid county of Down, in our said kingdom of Ireland: We have given, moreover, granted, confirmed, and released, and by these presents, for us, our heirs and successors, do give, grant, confirm, and release to the aforesaid Viscount Claneboy, his heirs and assigns, one moiety or equal half of all trees, woods, and underwoods, in said territory of Slewght O'Neill's or Slut Neales, in the aforesaid territory of Upper Claneboy, in the County of Down aforesaid.

And further, of our more abundant special grace, certain knowledge, and mere motion, We have given, granted, confirmed, and released, and, by these presents, for us, our heirs and successors, do give, grant, confirm, and release to the aforesaid Viscount Claneboy, his heirs and assigns, all and singular the manors, castles, towns, villages, hamlets, lands, tenements, and hereditaments whatsoever, as well spiritual as temporal, in the aforesaid territory of the Upper Clandeboy and the Great and Little Ards aforesaid, or either or any of them, in the aforesaid County of Down, with their rights, members, and appurtenances whatsoever, being in the occupation of the said Viscount or his tenants, or from which the aforesaid Viscount has received the rents or profits, by reason or pretext of any letters patent heretofore made or granted, or mentioned to be made or granted, to the said Viscount, by us, or our very dear father, late King of happy memory, and which the said Viscount has, holds, or occupies for his own portion or division, or by reason of any division of the premises above by these presents before granted, or of any parcel thereof, heretofore made, or mentioned to be made, between said Viscount Claneboy and Sir Hugh Montgomery of Newton, in the aforesaid County Down, Knight, now Viscount Ards.

And further, of our more ample special grace, certain knowledge, and mere motion, we have given, granted, confirmed, and released, and by these presents, for us, our heirs and successors, do give, grant, confirm, and release to the aforesaid Viscount Claneboy, his heirs and assigns, all and singular, the rectories, churches, chapels, vicarages, tithes great and small, oblations, obventions, fruits, and profits whatsoever, situate, lying, and being, coming, growing, renewing, arising, or happening, of, in, or within the aforesaid castles, manors, towns, villages, hamlets, and places above granted, or mentioned to be granted, of, in, or within the territory or precincts of the Upper Clandeboy and the Great and Little Ards, or either of them, with their appurtenances whatsoever, and all and singular the advowsons, donations, and free disposal of all and singular other churches and vicarages aforesaid, and all other advowsons, donations, free disposal of all and singular other chapels and vicarages aforesaid, and all other advowsons, donations, free disposal of all and singular other churches, vicarages, chapels, hospitals, and other benefices and churches whatsoever, in the aforesaid castles, manors, towns, villages, hamlets, and places above granted, or mentioned to be granted, of, in, or within the aforesaid precincts or territories of the Upper Clandeboy and Great Ards aforesaid, or either of them.

And further, of our more abundant special grace, certain knowledge, and mere motion, We have granted, confirmed, and released, and by these presents, for us, our heirs and successors, do give, grant, confirm, and release to the aforesaid Viscount Claneboy, his heirs and assigns, all the manors, castles, towns, villages, hamlets, places, lands, tenements, and hereditaments following, either known, called, or mentioned by the names following, or lying, being, coming, or renewing in the towns, villages, hamlets, or places following, viz., Ballymena, Ballehalckin or Tulleharme, Ballymuloch or Mullogh, Corbally, Ballecaslan-William or Castle-William, Ballinecarlie or Ballenecabry, Killileagh, Renechady or Rinchady, Tulfoughmore-Macmartin, Ballyrathconevan or Ballyrathconegan, Ballymacorbwell, or Ballymacromwell, Ringduffrin or Mylortin, Ballyomeron and Ballyneron or Ballymaccoran, Rathgoronan, Ballikilltenegan or Ballynegan, Carrowreagh, Carrickruske or Carrickruskie, Killinchy, Ballowe, Ballyoshen or Ballymashen, Ballemaccacrebye or Ballemmaccrelye, Ballyagullen or Carrowgullen, Ballibregagh, Balliegan or Billelisgowne or Ballegigon, Lisduffe, Balletoy or Ballycoy, Ballecley, Ballealough, Tullineagh, Callerogan, Castlenof, Ballycallegin or Ballecalogan Ballemullan, Ballehallyard, Ardegon, Ballybrowne or Tullevery, Balletrim, Ballereagh or Reaghe, Quoyle, Mamor, Rathkirron, Balliclownty or Clowntagh, Balledromore, Balletagagh or Carrickedowe, Maumore or Maghmore, Tullicowise or Tullemacknow, Killcanon or Skilltanan, Dereboy, Ballcherman, Killanreas, Rinchady, Islandmore, Islandmacshagh, Island-Davanagh or Inishdavan or Strevanan, Island-Daragh, Island-Conly, Island-Ringhady, Island-Reagh, and Innismacattarge, which same premises last mentioned are situate, lying, and being in the country or precinct called The Dufferin or Dufferins, in the aforesaid County of Down, in our said Kingdom of Ireland.

We have also given, granted, confirmed, and released, and by these presents for us, our heirs and successors, do give, grant, confirm, and release, to the aforesaid Viscount Claneboy, his heirs and assigns, the tithes of all sorts of fish taken and landed in the bays and creeks of Dufferin, in Lough Coyne, the advowsons, donations, rights of patronage, and free disposal of the rectories, vicarages, chapels, and churches of Killileagh, Killandreas, Renechedy or Killinchienamagree, in the territory of Dufferin aforesaid, in the said county Down; and all and singular the tythes of the towns following, in the Upper Clandeboy aforesaid, belonging and appertaining to the rectory of Killinchie-Nemaigrie, in the territory of The Dufferin aforesaid, viz. : the tythes of the towns of Carrickmannon, Drumcreagh, Rafry, Killinchie-Nikely, Ravarra, Ballicloughan, Leveallgown or Leveallg, Achindara or Drumcahie, with their appurtenances whatsoever ; also all other rectories, churches, vicarages, chapels, tythes great and small, oblations, obventions, fruits and profits whatsoever, situate, lying, and being, coming, growing, renewing, or arising of or within the aforesaid castles, manors, towns, hamlets, islands and places above granted, or mentioned to be granted, of, in, or within the country or precinct of Dufferin or Dufferins, with their appurtenances whatsoever, and all and singular other the churches, chapels, and vicarages aforesaid, and all other advowsons, donations, free disposal of all and singular other churches, vicarages, chapels, hospitals, and other benefices and churches in the aforesaid castles, manors, towns, villages, hamlets, islands, and places above granted, of, in, or within the aforesaid precinct or country of The Dufferin, in the aforesaid County Down, in our Kingdom of Ireland.

e

And further, of our more ample special grace, certain knowledge, and mere motion, we have given, granted, confirmed, and released, and by these presents, for us, our heirs and successors, do give, grant, confirm, and release to the said Viscount Claneboy, his heirs and assigns, all and singular our castles, messuages, houses, edifices, mills, structures, barns, stables, dovehouses, orchards, pomaries, gardens, lands, tenements, meadows, feedings, pasturages, commons-lands, demesne-lands, glebes, waters, briers, moors, marshes, woods, underwoods, and trees, and all the land, ground, and soil of said woods, underwoods, and trees, advowsons, donations, tythes of corn and grain in sheaf, and hay, wool, flax, hemp, calves, lambs, and all other tithes of all other things tytheable, great and small, also oblations, obventions, fruits, profits, commodities, waters, watercourses, fisheries, fishings, suits, liberty of jurisdiction, multures, minerals, quarries, rents, reversions, and services, rents-charge, rents-seck, and rents and services as well of free as customary tenants, works of tenants, farms, fee-farms, knight's fees, wardships, marriages, annuities, escheats, reliefs, heriots, fines, amerciaments, courts-leet, views of frankpledge, courts-leets, perquisites, and profits, and other things appertaining to courts leet and views of frankpledge, chattels, waifs, estrays, goods and chattels of felons, and fugitives, *felons-de-se*, outlaws, and put in exigent, deodands, natives, and villeins with their sequels, estovers, and commons of estover, fairs, markets, tolls, customs, rights of jurisdiction, franchises, privileges, exemptions, profits, commodities, emoluments, and hereditaments whatsoever, with their appurtenances whatsoever, of whatsoever kind, nature, or species they may be, or by whatsoever names they are ordained, considered, called, or known, situate, lying, and being, coming, growing, or arising of, in, or within the castles, manors, monasteries, abbeys, priories, rectories, granges, territories, precincts, towns, villages, hamlets, plains, places, or parishes, and other the premises aforesaid, by these presents before granted, or mentioned to be granted, of, in, or within any of them, or in any manner belonging, appertaining, happening, appending, or inclining to the aforesaid castles, manors, monasteries, abbeys, priories, granges, rectories, towns, messuages, lands, tenements, and other the premises above by these presents granted, or mentioned to be granted, or being ever heretofore had, known, received, occupied, or reputed as member, part, or parcel of said premises above by these presents granted, or any of them ; also our reversion and reversions, remainder and remainders whatsoever, of all and singular the aforesaid castles, manors, monasteries, abbeys, priories, granges, rectories, towns, messuages, lands, tenements, and other the premises above by these presents before-granted, and every parcel thereof, weighed and considered, of, in, and upon any gift or gifts, grant or grants, discharge or discharges whatsoever, or any of the premises, or any parcel thereof, ever heretofore made or granted, of record or not of record : Also all and singular rents and annual profits whatsoever reserved upon any discharge or grant of the premises by these presents above granted, or any parcel thereof howsoever made, being of record or not of record, and also all and singular rents and annual profits whatsoever recovered upon any discharge or grant of the premises by these presents above granted, or any part thereof, howsoever made, being of record or not of record, and the rents and yearly profits of all and singular the premises and every parcel thereof.

And further, of our more abundant special grace, certain knowledge, and mere motion, We have given, granted, confirmed, and released, and by these presents, for us, our heirs and successors, do give, grant, confirm, and release to the aforesaid Viscount Claneboy, his heirs and assigns, that he, the said Viscount for the rest for ever may have, hold, and enjoy, and can and may have, hold, and enjoy, within the aforesaid castles, manors, monasteries, rectories, granges, towns, villages, lands, tenements, territories, precincts, places, and hereditaments aforesaid, and within other the premises above by these presents before granted, or mentioned to be granted, and within any parcel of the same, such and such like courts leet, views of frankpledge, hundred courts, courts baron, law days, assizes, and the assay of bread, wine, and all chattels, waifs, estrays, chattels of felons, and fugitives, felons *de se*, and put in *exigent*, deodands, escheats, reliefs, heriots, free-warrens, free-parks, and freedom of warren and parks, commons of pasture, commons of turbary, commons of estover, and all rights and jurisdictions, franchises, liberties, customs, profits, privileges, commodities, annuities, advantages, emoluments, and hereditaments whatsoever, as fully, freely, and entirely, and in as ample manner and form as any Abbot of the late monastery, or late Prior of the aforesaid late Priory or religious house of Hollywood, or the aforesaid James Viscount Claneboy, by the name of Sir James Hamilton, Knight, or any other the aforesaid manors, castles, monasteries, abbeys, priories, rectories, towns, territories, places, precincts, messuages, lands, tenements, and other the premises by these presents before granted or mentioned to be granted, or any parcel thereof, ever before the having, possessing, or occupying, or being seized thereof, ever have had, held, used, or enjoyed, or ought to have, hold, use, or enjoy in the territories, precincts, towns, villages, hamlets, and places aforesaid, either in the premises by these presents before granted or mentioned to be granted, or any parcel thereof, ever before the having, possessing, or occupying, or being seized thereof, ever have had, held, used, or occupied, or ought to have, hold, use, or enjoy, in the territories, precincts, towns, villages, hamlets, and places aforesaid, either in the premises by these presents before granted, or mentioned to be granted, or in any parcel thereof, by reason or pretext of any charters or letters patent, or of any gift, grant, or confirmation by us, our very dear father, or by any other our progenitors or ancestors, heretofore made, granted, or confirmed, or by reason or pretext of any lawful prescription, use, or custom heretofore had or used, or otherwise by whatsoever legal manner, right, or title, as fully, freely, and entirely, and in as ample manner and form as we or any of our progenitors or ancestors, or the aforesaid abbott and prior, or either of them, or the aforesaid Viscount Claneboy, have had, used, and enjoyed, or ought to have, use, and enjoy, in the aforesaid manors, monasteries, castles, messuages, lands, tenements, and other singular the premises above by these presents before granted, or mentioned to be granted, or in every or any parcel thereof.

And further, of our more ample special grace, certain knowledge, and mere motion, We have given, granted, confirmed, and released, and by these presents, for us, our heirs and successors, do give, grant, confirm, and release to the aforesaid Viscount Claneboy, his heirs and assigns, in all and singular the premises above by these presents before granted, and any parcel thereof, so many and such like courts, liberties, customs, profits, privileges, or commodities, immunities, emoluments, powers, authorities, licenses, and hereditaments whatsoever, as fully, freely, and entirely, and in as ample manner and form as before mentioned to be granted by the letters patent bearing date at Westminster, the 14th day of March, in the nineteenth year of the reign of our aforesaid very dear father, Lord James, late King of England, heretofore made and granted to said Viscount, by the name of Sir James Hamilton, Knight,[a] and as many such and similar other courts, liberties, customs, profits, privileges, commodities, immunities, emoluments, powers, authorities, licenses, and hereditaments whatsoever, and as fully, freely, and entirely, and in as ample manner and form as can be found to appertain to said Viscount, by a certain inquisition taken at Downpatrick, in the County of Down aforesaid, the 13th day of October in the twenty-first year of the reign of our said late father, Lord James, late King of England,[b] and all and singular contained in same letters patent and the aforesaid inquisition, or either of them, We ratify, make stable, do approve, and confirm by these presents.

And further, by these presents for us, our heirs and successors, We do give and grant to the aforesaid Viscount Clandeboy, his heirs and assigns, the castles, manors, monasteries, abbeys, priories, territories, granges, islands, towns, messuages, lands, tenements, and all and singular other the premises above by these presents granted, or mentioned to be granted, with their rights, members, and appurtenances whatsoever, as fully, fairly, and entirely, and in as ample manner and form as all and singular said premises or any parcel thereof to our hands, or the hands of any of our progenitors or ancestors, by reason or pretext of any Act or Acts of Parliament, or by reason or pretext of any dissolution, suppression, or abandoning of any late monastery, abbey, or priory, or of any exchange or investigation, or of any gift or grant, or of any attainder, or by forfeiture, or by reason of any escheat or resumption, or by any other legal mode, right, or title have or ought to have come, or are now in our hands, or ought or should be : To have, hold, and enjoy the aforesaid territories, monasteries, abbeys, priories, rectories, granges, castles, islands, towns, villages, hamlets, lands, tenements, meadows, feedings, pastures, woods, underwoods, courts leet, views of frankpledge, liberties, rights of jurisdiction, franchises, profits, commodities, advantages, privileges, emoluments, and hereditaments, and all and singular other the premises above by these presents granted, or mentioned to be granted, with their appurtenances whatsoever, to the aforesaid James Viscount Claneboy, his heirs and assigns, to the sole and proper use and behoof of said Viscount Claneboy, his heirs and assigns for ever, the aforesaid monastery or abbey of Bangor, the aforesaid Priory or religious house of Hollywood, and all the lands, tenements, hereditaments spiritual above by these presents before granted, or mentioned to be granted, with the appurtenances, to be held of us, our heirs and successors, as of our Castle of Dublin, in our said kingdom of Ireland, by fealty only, in free and common soccage, and not *in capite*, or in soccage *in capite*, nor

---

[a] This Patent, which was never enrolled in Ireland, has been lately discovered in the Rolls Chapel in England, from which a copy of it has been obtained, and a translation of it will be given in this Appendix.

[b] A copy of this Inquisition will be also given in the Appendix.

by knights' service, nor by grand serjeanty, and the aforesaid teritories, lands, tenements, hereditaments, and the before-granted temporal premises, and the territory of the Upper Clandeboy and the
Great Ards aforesaid, in the country, precinct, or territory of the Duffren or Duffrens aforesaid, with
their appurtenances whatsoever, to be held of us, our heirs and successors, of our Castle of Knockfergus, in our said kingdom of Ireland, by fealty only, in free and common soccage, and not *in capite*,
nor in soccage *in capite*, nor by knights' service, nor by grand serjeanty; and to be rendered annually
to us, our heirs and successors, of and for the aforesaid monastery or abbey of Bangor, with its rights,
members, and appurtenances, and for all and singular the lands, tenements, hereditaments, and other the
premises formerly belonging to the said monastery or abbey of Bangor, eight pounds current money of
Ireland, in fee farm; and of and for the aforesaid priory or religious house of Hollywood, with its appur-
tenaces, and for all and singular the lands, tenements, hereditaments, and premises to said late abbey
formerly belonging, forty shillings money aforesaid, in fee farm; and of and for all other aforesaid
lands, tenements, hereditaments, and other the premises, as well spiritual as temporal, lying and being
in the territory of the Upper Clandeboy, in the Great and Little Ards aforesaid, in fee farm, seventy
pounds current money of Ireland; and of and for the aforesaid lands, tenements, hereditaments, and
other the premises lying and being in the country, precinct, or territory of Slut Neales aforesaid, in fee
farm, twenty pounds money aforesaid; and for the aforesaid lands, tenements, hereditaments, and
other the premises lying and being in the territory or precincts of Dufferin, one pair of gilt spurs, if it
shall be sought or demanded, or in place of them 10s. money aforesaid, for all other services: All and
singular which rents amount in the whole to £100 Irish money, payable at the receipt of the Treasury
of us, our heirs and successors of our said kingdom of Ireland—to wit, to the hands of the vice-treasurer or general receiver of us, our heirs and successors, of our said kingdom of Ireland, for the time
being, to be paid annually by equal portions at the feast of Saint Michael the Archangel, and Easter, and
also to find and maintain at their own proper expenses for the temporal premises above by these presents granted, lying in the aforesaid countries, territories, or precincts of the Upper Clandeboy in the
Great Ards aforesaid, six good and serviceable horsemen, and ten foot-soldiers well drilled and armed,
to attend and serve for forty days the lieutenant or deputy-general of us, our heirs and successors, of
our said kingdom of Ireland, when said lieutenant or deputy-general, in his own proper person, shall
make his general hostings in the province of Ulster.

And further, of our more special grace, certain knowledge, and mere motion, for us, our heirs and
successors, We do grant to the aforesaid Viscount Claneboy, his heirs and assigns, that neither he nor
they nor any of them, at any time hereafter, by virtue of these our letters patent, or any other letters
patent heretofore made to the aforesaid Viscount Claneboy, of the premises by these presents before
granted, or any parcel thereof, shall be burthened with the payment of any double rent, or with any
double tenure, by reason of said premises, to be paid or made to us, our heirs and successors, but
that the aforesaid Viscount, his heirs and assigns, may have, hold, and enjoy, freely and quietly, all
and singular the premises above by these presents before granted, or mentioned to be granted, and
every parcel thereof, with their appurtenances whatsoever, under the annual rent and tenure, and other
reservations and conditions above reserved and mentioned, without let or hindrance of us, our heirs
and successors, whatsoever, anything in these presents, or in any other letters patent of the premises,
or of any parcel thereof, as appears to be made, to the contrary notwithstanding.

And further, of our more abundant special grace, certain knowledge, and mere motion, We
will, and by these presents, for us, our heirs and successors, do grant to the aforesaid Viscount Claneboye, his heirs and assigns, that he, his heirs and assigns, may have and enjoy all the premises as
aforesaid, and that upon the exhibition and showing of these our letters patent, or the enrolment of the
same, as well before us in the Chancery of us, our heirs and successors, as before the Justices of either
Bench of us, our heirs and successors, of our said kingdom of Ireland, and before the treasurer and
barons of the Exchequer of us, our heirs and successors, within our said kingdom of Ireland, and also
before the justices and commissioners of us, our heirs and successors, as well in all and singular
the courts of us, our heirs and successors, and places of record within our said kingdom of Ireland,
also before the justices and commissioners of us, our heirs and successors, as well in all and singular
the courts of us, our heirs and successors, and places of record within our said kingdom, as in any
other courts and places whatsoever throughout the kingdom of Ireland, for anything in these our
letters patent contained or specified, these our letters patent, and all the grants therein contained
and specified, instantly and immediately may be in force and allowed the aforesaid Viscount Claneboy,

his heirs and assigns, and that the aforesaid treasurer, barons, justices, commissioners, and whatsoever other persons to whom it shall belong, shall make or cause to be made due allowances af all and
singular the premises from time to time ; and that these our letters patent, or the enrolment of them,
shall be in and through all things firm, valid, good, sufficient, and effectual in law, towards and against
us, our heirs and successors, as well in all our courts as anywhere else within our kingdom of Ireland,
without any confirmation, license, or toleration of us, our heirs and successors, to be procured or
obtained by the aforesaid Viscount Claneboy, his heirs and assigns, or any of them, notwithstanding
the ill meaning, or ill reciting, or not reciting, or not meaning, the aforesaid monasteries, abbeys,
priories, rectories, vicarages, granges, towns, villages, hamlets, islands, territories, places, precincts,
lands, tenements, and hereditaments, and other the premises, or any parcel thereof, and notwithstanding the not finding or ill finding the office or offices, inquisition or inquisitions of the premises, or
any parcel thereof, by which our title, or that of any of our progenitors or ancestors, ought to be found
before the making up of these our letters patent, and notwithstanding the ill meaning or not ill meaning, ill reciting or not ill reciting, any demise or grant, demises or grants for a term or terms,
for a life or lives, or years, or in fee tail, or otherwise, of the premises or any parcel thereof, by us or
any of our progenitors or predecessors, or any person or persons heretofore made to any person or
persons, being of record or not of record, and notwithstanding the ill naming or not naming any territories, towns, villages, precincts, villages, parishes, places, or countries in which the premises or any
parcel thereof are situate, lie, or exist, and notwithstanding that of the names of the tenants, farmers, or
occupiers of the premises, or any parcel thereof, full, true, and certain mention has not been made, and
notwithstanding some defects of certainty, or computation, declaration, or omission of the true yearly
value of the premises, or any parcel thereof, the annual rent reserved of, in, and upon, or for the premises, or for any parcel thereof, in these our letters patent expressed and contained, or not
expressed, and notwithstanding any other defects, and notwithstanding the statute in Parliament of
Lord Henry the 6th, late King of England, our ancestor, made and held in the 18th year of his reign at
Westminster, and in our kingdom of Ireland among other things established and confirmed, and notwithstanding the statute in Parliament of Lord Henry the 8th, late King of England, declared and
made in the 23rd year of his reign at Limerick, or anything in the statute aforesaid to the contrary in
anywise notwithstanding, and notwithstanding any other statutes whatsoever, and notwitstanding anything in any statute, and notwithstanding some defects in not rightly naming the nature, kind, species,
quantity, and quality of the premises, or any part thereof, although express mention, &c.   In witness
whereof these our letters we have caused to be made patent.   Witness myself at Dublin, the 20th day
of April, the 5th year of our reign.   By Writ of Privy Seal.

No. III.

LETTERS PATENT TO JAMES HAMILTON, DATED 14TH MARCH
(19TH JAMES I.), 1620.

The King to all to whom, &c., greeting : Whereas, in certain letters patent, sealed with our Great
Seal of Ireland, made in the 18th year of our reign of England, France, and Ireland, it is mentioned,
that we, for the considerations contained in the same, for us, our heirs and successors, by those letters
patent, have given, granted, and confirmed to our well-beloved and faithful servant, Sir James Hamilton, of Bangor, in our County of Down, in our kingdom of Ireland, Knight, one of our Privy Council
of our said kingdom, his heirs and assigns for ever, amongst other things, all that the late dissolved
Monastery or Abbey of Bangor, in the County of Down, in our said kingdom of Ireland, and the
whole scite, circuit, ambit, and precinct of the said late Monastery, with every of their rights,

f

members, and appurtenances, and all and singular the towns, villages, hamlets, places, messuages, lands, tenements, or hereditaments following, or known, called, or reputed by the names following, or lying, being, arising, or renewing in the towns, villages, hamlets, or places following, in our said County of Down, in our said kingdom of Ireland, namely : Bangor, Balliportavo *alias* Balliportabo, Ballifredor *alias* Ballipheoderly, Ballimeman *alias* Ballimenan, Ballowe, Ballivulleragh *alias* Ballimulleragh, Ballicormagh *alias* Ballimaccormick, Ballimackonnell, Ballicroghan, Ballihome *alias* Balliniminagh, Ballinenoghwe *alias* Ballinaghie *alias* Ballimagwigh, Ballonery *alias* Ballinroigh, Carrowslaneclacaduffe *alias* Carowne-Knockanduffe, Callosueron *alias* Carrownesroyane, Carrownesor *alias* Carrownesuire, Carrownereogh *alias* Carrowreogh, Ballimooney-Carrogh *alias* Ballymeoney-Carroghie, Rawgeile *alias* Ballyfragheguile, Ballinlisscbane, Ballinebarnes *alias* Ballibarnes, Ballycornedeogh *alias* Ballincarnamfeigh, Ballincelloer *alias* Ballikillar, Ballysallagh, Ballimullen, Balliorane *alias* Ballinegrene, Ballecrott, Ballyscally, Ballimeaghan, Ballimachoris, Ballimajor *alias* Ballimagher *alias* Ballimaser, with all and singular their appurtenances, and also all that Grange called Erbegg in our County of Antrim, in our said kingdom of Ireland ; and also all those islands called Copland Islands, lying and being near the Bay of Knockfergus, in the said County of Antrim, with all and singular their lands, tenements, and appurtenances ; and also the Rectory of Balliraghan *alias* Balliurgeghan, in Lecale, and Ballimeghan in the said County of Down, with all their rights and appurtenances whatsoever ; and also the advowsons of all Vicarages in all and singular the parishes, towns, or villages above mentioned, with their tithes, offerings, and appurtenances whatsoever ; and also all tithes of grain and hay, and of all other things titheable, in a certain island called Raughlins, lying or being in the Irish Sea, near the Route, in the said County of Antrim ; and that we have also given, granted, and confirmed by the same our letters patent to the aforesaid James Hamilton, Knight, his heirs and assigns, all our towns, villages, messuages, lands, tenements, rents, and hereditaments whatsoever, in the territory or precinct of the Great Ardes and Upper Clandeboy, or either of them, in our said County of Down, to the aforesaid late Monastery or Abbey of Bangor theretofore belonging or appertaining, or as member, part, or parcel of the said late Monastery ever theretofore held or known, accepted, occupied, used, or enjoyed, or ever theretofore being parcels of the possessions of the same late Monastery or Abbey; and also all and singular the tithes of grain and hay, and other titheable things whatsoever, in all and singular the towns, villages, hamlets, places, lands, and tenements aforesaid, yearly arising, growing, or renewing, with every of their appurtenances, to the said late Monastery or Abbey of Bangor then or theretofore belonging or appertaining, and all other tithes whatsoever to the said late Monastery or Abbey of Bangor belonging or appertaining : And that we have also given, granted, and confirmed by the same our letters patent, for us, our heirs and successors, to the aforesaid James Hamilton, Knight, his heirs and assigns, all that lately dissolved Priory or Religious House of Holliwood, in our County of Down aforesaid, in our said Kingdom of Ireland, and the whole scite, circuit, ambit, and precinct of the said late Priory or Religious House of Holliwood, with every of the rights, members, and appurtenances, and all those villages, hamlets, with the appurtenances, namely :—Ballikeel *alias* Ballikigill, Ballmanake *alias* Ballimanagh, Ballicultrack *alias* Ballicultra *alias* Ballactragah, Ballinderry *alias* Ballidery, and Ballierknocknegoney *alias* Ballynocknegony, lying and being in the aforesaid County of Down, with all and singular their appurtenances and members whatsoever; and all our towns, villages, hamlets, messuages, lands, tenements, rents, and hereditaments whatsoever, ever theretofore belonging, or pertaining to the late Priory or Religious House of Holliwood, in the said County of Down, or as members, parts, or parcels of the said late Priory, ever theretofore held, known, accepted, occupied, used, or enjoyed, or ever theretofore being parcels of the possessions of the same late Priory : Also all and singular the tithes of grain and hay, and of other titheable things whatsoever, in all and singular the towns, villages, places, lands, and tenements aforesaid, yearly arising, growing, or renewing, with every of their appurtenances, to the said late Priory or Religious House of Holliwood formerly belonging or pertaining : And that further, by our said letters patent, for us, our heirs and successors, we have given, granted, and confirmed to the aforesaid James Hamilton, Knight, his heirs and assigns, all and singular the towns, villages, hamlets, places, messuages, lands, tenements, and hereditaments following, or known, called, or reputed by the names following, or lying, being, arising, or renewing in the towns, villages, hamlets, or places following, viz. : Ballirobert, Balliadavic, Ballinegreene, Cregevadagh, Ballicackamer, Ballegloghans *alias* Ballicloghan *alias* Ballinacloghan, Ballybein, Ballirustell, Ballinegrauch *alias* Ballinegraugheuagh, Ballymulready *alias* Ballinallore *alias* Ballenistanere, Ballelislein, Ballikeile,

Ballitullehubbard, Ballibyn, Balligbastrum *alias* Glasdrumon, the half town of Ballidromaconnell (in English, called the half town of Ballidromachannell), the half town of Ballicregy, Ballidrumheriff, Ballichigill, Ballinacherleskowe *alias* Ballinaghereskowe, Balligowan *alias* Balliegowne, Ballicarrickmanan, the half town of Balliravarra, the half town of Balliachinderragh (in English the half town of Achinderragh), Ballitullaghfinan *alias* Ballitullachapman, Balliglontneglare, the half town of Ballinacrevie *alias* Ballinecrevegh (in English the half town of Ballincreive), the half town of Ballikillinchie *alias* Ballikillinsee (in English the half towne of Ballikillinchie), and the half town of Balligraffan ; and also the towns of Ballicarrowreigh, Ballidunlady, Ballinregin *alias* Balliregny, Ballydownedonnell, Ballinechalleine, Ballisnekah *alias* Ballisnesca, Ballicastellanbeg, Ballimonnecarvel *alias* Balliumicarvel, Ballilisbradan, Ballineraine, and Balliorane, the which last mentioned premises are situate, lying, and being in the territory or precinct called the Upper Clandeboy, in the aforesaid County of Down, in our said kingdom of Ireland : And that, further, we have given, granted, and confirmed by our said letters patent, to the aforesaid James Hamilton, Knight, his heirs and assigns, all the messuages, lands, tenements, and hereditaments, situate, lying, and being, arising, or renewing in the town of Balliwalter, in the aforesaid territory or precinct of the Great Ardes, in the aforesaid County of Down, with every of their appurtenances : And that we have also, given, granted, and confirmed by our said letters patent to the aforesaid James Hamilton, Knight, his heirs and assigns, all and singular the manors, castles, messuages, towns, villages, hamlets, lands, tenements, and hereditaments whatsoever, with every of their rights, members, and appurtenances, in the aforesaid territory or precinct of the Great Ardes, in the same County of Down, situate, lying, and being in the southern part or side of the same territory or precinct of the Great Ards aforesaid, divided by the metes and bounds following, namely, beginning at the mete or march between the Grey Abbie and the Great Ardes, in the middle, or neare the middle, of a certain moor or marsh, in English a " bogg," at the southern end of the " scrogges" or shrubbs in the moor or marsh aforesaid, the which moor or marsh is called Coronownowan, and is the division, in English " the march," between the lands of the Grey Abbie and the Great Ards, and from thence towards the north-east by a certain ditch or rivulet, in English a " trench or dike," in the middle or near the middle of said moor, equally between two islands called Island Vicar on the southern part, and Horse Island on the northern part, and so from thence towards the east and north-east, by the said ditch or rivulet, in the middle of the said moor or marsh, as far as the ford or passage called Akillburghtane, and being at the fountain or source of a certain rivulet called Ownegamure, the which rivulet is the mete or division between the two, about the middle of the aforesaid territory or precinct of the Great Ardes aforesaid, as far as where the rivulet aforesaid falls into the Irish Sea : And that we have also given, granted, and confirmed by our same letters patent, to the aforesaid James Hamilton, Knight, his heirs and assigns, all and singular the manors, castles, towns, villages, hamlets, tenements, and hereditaments whatsoever, as well spiritual as temporal, in the aforesaid territories or precincts of the Upper Clandeboye and the Great Ardes aforesaid, or in either of them, or elsewhere in the aforesaid County of Down, with every of their rights, members, and appurtenances, being in the occupation of the said James, or of his tenants, or of which the said James Hamilton then received the rents or profits, whether by reason or pretext of any our letters patent to the said James by us theretofore made or granted, or mentioned to be made or granted, and which the same James then had, held, or occupied for his portion of a division, or by any division, or by reason of any division between the said Sir James Hamilton, Knight, and Sir Hugh Montgomery, of Newton, in the aforesaid County of Down, Knight, theretofore made or mentioned to be made, as by the same letters patent (amongst other things) more fully is shown and appears.

And, whereas, the aforesaid James Hamilton, Knight, has, holds, and enjoys, or ought to have, hold, and enjoy, in the premises above recited, divers liberties, franchises, immunities, and acquittances, by virtue of other our letters patent heretofore made to him : Know ye, that we, for and in consideration of the good, true, faithful, and acceptable service to us, by the aforesaid James Hamilton, Knight, heretofore done and performed, being willing to extend our royal grace and munificence, as well in confirming the said liberties and privileges, as also in granting other things anew, as it shall seem to us best to be done, to the same James Hamilton, his heirs and assigns, of our special grace, and from our certain knowledge, and mere motion, We have given and granted, and by these presents, for us, our heirs and successors, we ordain and constitute, that henceforth for ever there may and shall be a maritime port in and upon, and near the sea, near to and at the aforesaid town of Bangor, and that the said port may and shall be named, called, and deemed the port of the town of Bangor ; and that the roadsteads or creeks of Gilgroomes, and Holliwood, may and shall be accounted members of the said port of Bangor : And that there may and shall be a maritime port in and upon and near the sea, near to and at the aforesaid town of Balliwalter, in the Great Ards aforesaid, and that the said port may and shall be called, named, and deemed the port of the town of Balliwalter : And that in like manner there may and shall be a maritime port in and upon and near the sea, near to and at the town of Killileagh, in The Dufrine, and that the said port may and shall be named, called, and deemed the port of the town of Killileagh ; and that the roadstead or creek of Carrownesuire, within the lands of Comber, may and shall be accounted a member of the said port of Killileagh : And the aforesaid maritime port in, at, or near Bangor aforesaid, and the other maritime port in, at, or near Balliwalter aforesaid, and the aforesaid other maritime port in, at, or near Killileagh aforesaid, for us, our heirs and successors, We make, ordain, erect, create, and establish, by these presents, and that the aforesaid port of Bangor, with its members aforesaid, and the aforesaid port of Ballywalter, and the aforesaid port of Killileagh, with its members aforesaid, may and shall be, and each of them, may and shall be a port, and that the ports, roadsteads, and creeks aforesaid, and each of them, may and shall be a port for the plying, arrival, and stationing of ships, boats, and other vessels, and for the loading and unloading of all and all manner of goods, wares, and merchandise, whatsoever, to be imported as well as exported, at the times therefor ordained in other ports, by the laws and statutes of our said kingdom of Ireland, with all and all manners of rights, jurisdictions, free customs and privileges, to a port or ports belonging due, or to be due : We will, however, and, firmly enjoining, We command and establish that all and singular, merchants, seamen, and all other persons whatsoever, importing or conveying any goods, wares, or merchandise to and into the ports aforesaid, or either, or any of them, or to and into any of the members or creeks of the said ports, or any or either of them, from foreign ports, for the purpose of traffic, or exporting any goods, wares, or merchandise, from or out of the ports aforesaid, or either, or any of them, or from or out of any member or creek of the aforesaid ports, or any or either of them, to foreign ports, for the purpose of traffic, in any ship, boat, or other vessel whatsoever, shall pay and satisfy to us, our heirs and successors, or the officers, deputies, or ministers of us, our heirs and successors, in that behalf to be lawfully authorised appointed, all and all manner of customs, subsidies, and impositions due and to become due for such goods, merchandise, and wares, so to be imported or exported before they shall go or depart from or out of the said ports, or any of them, or from or out of any member or creek of the same, or of any of them, or shall be there unladen or discharged, under the pain of the contempt of our royal mandate, and of the penalties due for such contempt of our royal mandate, and under the pain of the forfeiture of all such goods, merchandise, and wares, to us, our heirs and successors, anything in these presents contained to the contrary notwithstanding.

We have also given, and granted, and by these presents, for us, our heirs and successors, We give, and grant to the aforesaid James Hamilton, Knight, his heirs and assigns, that the aforesaid James Hamilton, Knight, his heirs and assigns, may, and may be able to have, enjoy, and receive all and singular plankages, anchorages, wharfages, cranages, fees, and profits, due or payable of and for all or any ships, skiffs, boats, and row boats, in the aforesaid ports, or any of them, or the members thereof, or any of them, plying, casting anchor, laden or unladen upon the wharfs, banks, or soil, of the aforesaid James Hamilton, Knight, his heir or assigns, without account or any other thing therefor, to us, our heirs or successors, in any manner to be rendered, paid or done.

And further, we will, and, by these presents, for us, our heirs and successors, we give and grant, to the aforesaid James Hamilton, Knight, his heirs and assigns, that he, his heirs and assigns, may have and hold, and may be able to have and hold, within the aforesaid town of Bangor, the liberty and precincts of the same, a court leet and view of frankpledge, and all such things which belong or may or should belong to a court leet and view of frankpledge of all the inhabitants and residents within the aforesaid lands of the aforesaid abbey of Bangor mentioned to be belonging, twice yearly, namely, once within the month next after the feast of Easter, and again within the month next after the feast of St. Michael the Archangel, before a seneschal or seneschals, by the said James Hamilton, his heirs or assigns, to be nominated and appointed :   Also a court leet, view of frankpledge, and all things which to a court leet or view of frankpledge pertain, or hereafter may or should belong, within the aforesaid town of Holliwood, the liberties and precincts thereof of all the inhabitants and residents within the aforesaid lands of the aforesaid Priory of Holliwood mentioned to be belonging, and within all other the aforesaid lands in the precinct of the Upper Clandeboy, in the said kingdom of Ireland, twice a year as is aforesaid, before a seneschal or seneschals of the said James Hamilton, Knight, his heirs or assigns, to be nominated and appointed : and all the fines, issues, and amerciaments of the said courts leet, or views of frankpledge, or in the same, or any of them, to be forfeited or assessed to the aforesaid James Hamilton, Knight, his heirs and assigns.

We have also given and granted, and by these presents, for us, our heirs and successors, We give, and grant, that the aforesaid James Hamilton, Knight, his heirs and assigns, may have and enjoy, and each of them may have and enjoy, within the aforesaid towns, villages, hamlets, lands, tenements, and hereditaments above mentioned, and by the aforesaid letters patent so as aforesaid mentioned to be granted, and every parcel thereof, a free warren, and free chase, and all that which to a free warren and free chase pertains or belongs, or hereafter may belong ; also the liberty of making several parks or chases in all his woods and lands whatsoever, or any parcel thereof, so as aforesaid mentioned to be granted to the said James Hamilton, Knight. altho' the said towns, villages, lands, tenements, and hereditaments, may or shall be, or any parcel thereof are, is, or shall be within our forest, so that no person shall enter into the said towns, villages, hamlets, lands, tenements, woods, or hereditaments, or any parcel thereof, to hunt or chase, or to take anything there which pertains to a warren, park, or chase, without the license of the said James Hamilton, his heirs or assigns.

We have also given and granted, and, by these presents, for us, our heirs and successors, we give and grant to the aforesaid James Hamilton, Knight, his heirs and assigns, that he, his heirs and assigns, henceforth for ever, may have, hold, and enjoy, and may be able to have, hold, and enjoy, all and singular goods and chattels, waifs, and estrays ; also, all and singular deodands, and goods and chattels of felons and fugitives, *felons de se*, outlawed, waived, and put in *exigent*, and of other felons whatsoever, within the aforesaid territories, towns, villages, hamlets, lands, tenements, and hereditaments aforesaid, and every parcel thereof, or the liberties or precincts of the same, or of any of them, found or to be found, and henceforth there happening to be, and all the fines, issues, and amerciaments of all the men and tenants, and other inhabitants within the said territories, lands, tenements, and hereditaments, so as aforesaid mentioned to be granted to the aforesaid James Hamilton, Knight, his heirs and assigns, so that the said James Hamilton, Knight, his heirs and assigns, themselves, or by their bailiffs or ministers, or their bailiff or minister, may levy, have, possess, and receive all the aforesaid fines, issues, amerciaments, goods, and chattels, to their proper use and behoof, without the hindrance or impediment of us, our heirs or successors, or of any of the officers or ministers of us, our heirs or successors, and without account of any other thing thereout to us, our heirs or successors, or to any other person, to be rendered.

We have also granted, and, by these presents, for us, our heirs and successors, We grant to the aforesaid James Hamilton, Knight, his heirs and assigns, that he, his heirs and assigns, henceforth for ever, may have and appoint a clerk or clerks of the market within the aforesaid territories, towns, villages, hamlets, lands, tenements, and hereditaments above in these presents mentioned, and by our aforesaid letters patent so as is aforesaid mentioned to be granted, and the liberties and precincts thereof, to do there all that which to the office of clerk of the market of the household of us, our heirs and successors, is pertaining to be done ; and that the said James Hamilton, Knight, his heirs and assigns, by the said clerk or clerks of the market, may have in the said towns, villages, lands, tenements, and hereditaments, and the liberties and precincts thereof, the assize and assay of bread, wine, and ale, and of all other victuals, measures, and weights whatsoever, and of all other things which to the office of clerk of the market of the household of us, our heirs or successors, pertains, or hereafter may pertain, with the punishment thereof, and whatsoever to that office pertains, or hereafter may pertain, to be done and executed as often as, and whensoever it shall be, needful, as fully, freely, and wholly, and in as ample manner and form as the same clerk of the household of us, our heirs or successors, should or ought to do if this our present grant had not been made ; and that the same James Hamilton, Knight, his heirs and assigns, may and shall have to their proper use, without account, all the amerciaments, fines, and other profits thereout arising, or to be assessed or placed before such clerk of the market to be received and levied by him or them, or their minister or ministers, without the hindrance, disturbance, or impediment of us, our heirs and successors, or of the clerk of the market, or other officer or minister of us, our heirs or successors, whomsoever, so that the aforesaid clerk of the market of the household of us, our heirs or successors, shall not enter the aforesaid towns, villages lands, tenements, or hereditaments, or in anything there intermeddle to do or exercise any thing there which to his office pertains, or hereafter may pertain in any manner.

g

And further, We will, and by these presents, for us, our heirs and successors, We give and grant to the aforesaid James Hamilton, Knight, his heirs and assigns, that he, the aforesaid James Hamilton, Knight, his heirs and assigns, may have, hold, and keep, and each of them may have, hold, and keep for ever, in and within the aforesaid town of Ballywalter, in the Great Ardes aforesaid, a court of record ; also another court of record in and within the aforesaid town of Bangor ; also another court of record in and within the aforesaid town of Killileagh, in the Duffrin aforesaid ; the said several courts to be held respectively every three weeks, before the seneschal or seneschals of the said James Hamilton, Knight, his heirs and assigns, by him or them, or any of them, from time to time, to be nominated and appointed, and that in every of the aforesaid courts, the aforesaid seneschal or seneschals may have full power and authority of hearing and determining, by suit to be begun in the same court, all and all manner of pleas, actions, suits, and personal demands whatsoever, of all trespasses, debts, accounts, pleas upon the case, suits, agreements, compromises, the detaining of charters, writings, muniments, and chattels, the taking and detaining of beasts and cattle, and of forbidden pledges, and other things and actions personal whatsoever, out of whatsoever causes or things within the aforesaid towns of Ballywalter, Bangor, and Killileagh, the liberties or precincts thereof respectively done, moved, had, or perpetrated, or hereafter to be done, moved, had, or perpetrated, or there respectively happening or occurring, provided the said debts, accounts, trespasses, contracts, agreements, and other actions and pleas in debt or damages do not exceed the sum of ten pounds sterling ; and that the said seneschal or seneschals, from time to time, upon such complaints, pleas, suits, and actions, may have power, authority, and faculty, to bring in the defendants against whom such suits, pleas, or actions in the courts aforesaid respectively, shall happen to be levied or moved, by summons, attachments, and distresses, to be dissected to the bailiffs or ministers of the said James Hamilton, his heirs and assigns for the time being, and by him or them or any of them, from time to time to be nominated and appointed ; and, for default of the chattels and lands of such defendants, within the aforesaid towns or any of them respectively, the liberties or precincts thereof, where or by which they cannot be summoned, attached, or distrained, by the attachment and caption of their bodies ; and to hear and determine all and singular the several actions, suits, and pleas aforesaid, and to entertain and determine them by such process, judgments, and executions of judgments, as the like pleas may be entertained and determined in any court of any city, borough, or town in the said kingdom of Ireland ; and there may be made and had execution of process, and of judgments by the aforesaid bailiffs and ministers of the aforesaid James Hamilton, his heirs and assigns ; and that the said James Hamilton, Knight, his heirs and assigns, from time to time may have all the amerciaments, fines, and other profits arising, growing, and happening from the aforesaid courts of record, and every of them, to be imposed, assessed, or forfeited in the same courts, and every or any of them, to be received and levied by the aforesaid James Hamilton, Knight, his heirs and assigns, or his or their ministers, to the sole and proper use and behoof of the said James Hamilton, Knight, his heirs and assigns for ever, without the hindrance of us, our heirs or successors, or of any of the officers or ministers of us, our heirs or successors whomsoever, and without account or any other thing therefor to us, our heirs or successors, in any manner to be rendered, paid, or made : And moreover, We will, and by these presents, for us, our heirs and successors, We grant to the aforesaid James Hamilton, Knight, his heirs and assigns, that hereafter for ever, there may and shall be within each of the aforesaid towns of Bangor, Ballywalter, and Killileagh, one or more officer or officers, minister or ministers, as the case may require, and at the discretion of the aforesaid James Hamilton, Knight, his heirs and assigns, to be limited, who may be, shall be, and shall be called a bailiff, or bail-. iffs, to serve in the courts of the said several town respectively, and to make and execute proclamations, arrests, distresses, and executions, processes, and mandates, and other business to the office of a bailiff or bailiffs pertaining, in the said several towns, or any of them respectively happening, arising, or occurring, the which said bailiffs from time to time shall be appointed, nominated, and chosen by the aforesaid James Hamilton, his heirs and assigns : We will, however, that the said bailiffs, or any of them, before they or any of them shall be admitted to the execution of the office aforesaid, shall take, and each of them shall take a corporal oath upon the holy evangelists of God, to execute, that office well and faithfully, according to the true intent of these presents ; and that, after such oath so taken, they may be able to execute and exercise that office during the pleasure of the aforesaid James Hamilton, Knight, his heirs and assigns : We will also, and by these presents, for us, our heirs and successors, ordain and constitute that the aforesaid seneschals of the courts aforesaid resectively, shall likewise take a corporal oath, upon the holy evangelists of God, well and faithfully to execute, all things to the office of seneschals pertaining ; and, that this our intention may have the better effect, for us, our heirs and successors, We give and grant to the aforesaid James Hamilton, Knight, his heirs and assigns, full power and authority to nominate, constitute, and make as well their seneschals as bailiffs aforesaid by virtue of these presents, to be made as often as it shall seem to be necessary to the said James Hamilton, Knight, his heirs and assigns : Also we give and grant to the said James Hamilton, Knight, his heirs and assigns, the like authority to administer a corporal oath to the said seneschals, and each of them, from time to time to execute their office well and faithfully in all things, and by all things to the office of seneschal pertaining, and this without any other warrant or commission therefor to be obtained or prosecuted from us, our heirs or successors : And further, by these presents, for us, our heirs and successors, We give and grant to each seneschal of a court within the aforesaid towns of Bangor, Ballywalter, and Killileagh respectively, (his oath of office of seneschal being first taken) the power and authority of giving and administering a corporal oath to the bailiff or bailiffs so as is aforesaid to be nominated to serve in the same several courts and towns, to execute his office and their offices in like manner well and faithfully, and this also without any other warrant or commission from us, our heirs or successors, to be procured or obtained : We will also, and by these presents, for us, our heirs and successors, We grant to the aforesaid James Hamilton, Knight, his heirs and assigns, that he, his heirs and assigns, hereafter for ever may have a prison within the aforesaid town of Ballywalter, the liberties or precincts of the same ; also another prison within the aforesaid town of Bangor ; and also another prison within the aforesaid town of Killileagh : for the safe custody, retention, and incarceration of all and singular the persons to be committed to the said prisons, or any of them, for debt, damage, contempt, or any action, execution, or thing whatsoever determinable in the aforesaid courts of record, or any of them respectively, or to be adjudged and determined in the same courts, or any of them, and according to the law of our said kingdom of Ireland ; and that the said James Hamilton, Knight, his heirs and assigns, may name, make, and appoint sufficient keepers of the said prisons, and each of them, from time to time for ever, any law, custom, use, or other thing to the contrary notwithstanding.

And further, of our more abundant special grace, and from our certain knowledge, and mere motion, We have given and granted to the aforesaid James Hamilton, Knight, his heirs and assigns, that it may and shall be lawful for the said James Hamilton, Knight, his heirs and assigns, from time to time to transfer and import into the aforesaid towns, villages, lands, tenements, and hereditaments, above in these presents mentioned, and by the aforesaid letters patent before granted or mentioned to be granted, or into any parts thereof, men, cattle, grain, and all and all manner of commodities, as well for defence as for the use and maintenance of the said James Hamilton, Knight, his heirs and assigns, and of the men, tenants, dwellers, and residents, and of those hereafter dwelling within the said towns, villages, lands, tenements, and hereditaments, or any parcel thereof, without any forfeiture, seizure, pain, penalty, or damage to be incurred, paid, or made towards us, our heirs or successors, on account of the premises, saving to us, our heirs and successors, the imposts of wine, and of other merchandise, and the subsidies and customs due and accustomed for the same, We not being willing that the aforesaid James Hamilton, his heirs or assigns, or any other persons, or any of the men, tenants, residents, or dwellers, or those who may dwell within the said towns, villages, lands, tenements, and hereditaments, or any part or parcel thereof, their heirs, executors, or administrators, by reason of the premises, should be hindered, molested, impeded, or in any manner aggrieved by us, our heirs or successors, or by the justices, escheators, sheriffs, bailiffs, customers, or other officers or ministers of us, our heirs or successors whomsoever, therefor in any manner, any statute, act, ordinance, restriction, prohibition, use, law, or any other thing, cause, or matter, to the contrary thereof made, done, ordained, used, or provided in any manner notwithstanding.

And further, of our more ample and special grace, certain knowledge, and mere motion, for us, our heirs and successors, We give and grant to the aforesaid James Hamilton, Knight, his heirs and assigns, being English or Scotch, or of English or Scotch blood, and not mere Irish, full authority, faculty, license, and power, that it may and shall be lawful for the aforesaid James Hamilton, his heirs and assigns, and each of them, being English or Scotch, or of English or Scotch blood, to transport, export, ship, carry, load, and unload from any part of our said kingdom of Ireland, to all and singular regions and kingdoms under or in the friendship of us, our heirs or successors, for the time being, all and all manner of grain, commodities, profits, emoluments, and things whatever (lynnen

yarne excepted) hereafter arising, growing, emerging, imported, or to be made in or within the aforesaid towns, villages, lands, tenements, and premises, so as aforesaid mentioned to be granted by the
aforesaid letters patent, or any parcel thereof, without any punishment, penalty, seizure, or forfeiture
thereof to be made, rendered, paid, or incurred to us, our heirs or successors, or to be had or levied
by us, our heirs or successors, or the officers or ministers of us, our heirs or successors whomsoever,
by reason of the premises ; saving also always to us, our heirs and successors, the customs and imposts
of wine, and of other merchandise and subsidies, due or to become due for the same, unless we, our
heirs or successors, or the Deputy, Justiciary, or Governor-General of our said Kingdom of Ireland for
the time being, or the Council of us, our heirs or successors, there upon any special cause shall esteem
it to be fit and necessary to prohibit or restrict the transportation of the said grain or commodities to
any reasonable time, We being unwilling that the aforesaid James Hamilton, Knight, his heirs or
assigns, or any of them, by reason of the same premises should be therefor hindered, molested, impeded,
vexed, or in any manner aggrieved by us, our heirs or successors, or by the justices, escheators,
sheriffs, bailiffs, customers, or other officers of us, our heirs or successors whomsoever, any statute,
ordinance, use, or custom heretofore had, made, published, ordained, or provided, or any other thing,
cause, or matter whatsoever to the contrary thereof in any manner notwithstanding.

And further, of our more abundant and special grace, and from our certain knowledge, and mere
motion, we have given, granted, and confirmed, and by these presents, for us, our heirs and successors,
We give, grant, and confirm, to the aforesaid James Hamilton, Knight, his heirs and assigns, full and
absolute license, power, and authority, that he, the aforesaid James Hamilton, Knight, his heirs and
assigns, from time to time hereafter for ever, at his or their will and pleasure, may and may be able to
assign, alien, grant, demise, enfeoff, and acknowledge by fine or fines, recovery or recoveries, or in
any other manner whatsoever, all and singular the aforesaid territories, towns, hamlets, rectories,
messuages, lands, tenements, and hereditaments whatsoever, or any parcel thereof, to any person or
persons, being English or Scotch, or of the English or Scotch blood, not being mere Irish, willing to
take or receive them, and to hold to the same person or persons willing to take or receive them, their
heirs and assigns, in fee simple, or fee tail, to be held of the aforesaid James Hamilton, Knight, his
heirs and assigns, by so many such and the like services, customs, and rents, as to the said James
Hamilton, Knight, his heirs and assigns, shall seem fitting ; and to the same person and persons, and
each and every of them, We give, and by these presents, for us, our heirs and successors, We grant,
license, authority, and power, that such person or persons may receive the premises, or any parcel
thereof, of the aforesaid James Hamilton, Knight, his heirs and assigns, and hold them to him and
them, and to his heirs and assigns, of any hereditary estate, in fee simple, or fee tail, also to hold them
to them, their heirs and assigns, of any estate of freehold, for a term of life, lives, or years, or otherwise,
as to the same James Hamilton, his heirs or assigns, shall seem expedient, the statute in the Parliament of our Lord Edward the First, late King of England, our ancestor, published, commonly called
the statute of "*Quia emptores terrarum*," or any other statute, act, ordinance, use, law, or custom,
or any other thing, cause, or matter, to the contrary thereof in anywise notwithstanding, We being
unwilling that such or such like persons, or any of them, or their heirs or assigns, or the aforesaid
James Hamilton, or his heirs or assigns, either by reason of the premises, or of any of them, should
be hindered, molested, impeded, vexed, or in any manner aggrieved, by us, our heirs or successors, or
by the justices, sheriffs, escheators, bailiffs, officers, or ministers of us, our heirs or successors, whomsoever, in any manner.

And further, of our more ample special grace, and from our certain knowledge, and mere motion, We
have given and granted, and by these presents, for us, our heirs and successors, We give and grant to the
aforesaid James Hamilton, Knight, his heirs and assigns, being the English or Scotch, or of English or
Scotch blood, whilst they shall remain in their allegiance and fealty towards us, our heirs and successors,
the faculty, power, and authority, from time to time, to build, repair, sustain, and find, and to rebuild, in
and within the aforesaid territories, lands, tenements, and hereditaments aforesaid, so often as it shall
seem expedient to them the aforesaid James Hamilton, Knight, his heirs and assigns, so many, such,
and such like castles, forts, houses, edifices, defences, and bulwarks, of, in, or upon any of the several
parcels of the said premises, and to embattle and fortify the same, as and in such manner as to the aforesaid James Hamilton, his heirs and assigns aforesaid, being English or Scotch, or of the English or
Scotch blood, as is aforesaid, or to any of them shall seem expedient, and in such castles, forts,
houses, defences, and bulwarks, to place, put, renew, remove, and constitute so many such and such

like arms, guns, weapons, and other munitions whatsoever, and in the same castles, forts, houses, defences, and bulwarks, to constitute and place such and so many armed and unarmed men being in our faith and obedience, for the defence or protection of the said castles, forts, houses, defences, and bulwarks, for ever, as to the aforesaid James Hamilton, Knight, his heirs and assigns, as is aforesaid, shall seem expedient, any statute, act, ordinance, use, law, or custom to the contrary thereof, in anywise notwithstanding : We also will, and by these presents, for us, our heirs and successors, we firmly grant and command that the aforesaid James Hamilton, Knight, his heirs and assigns, being English or Scotch, or of the English or Scotch blood, as aforesaid, may have and hold, and each of them have and hold, all and singular the gifts, grants, liberties, acquittances, franchises, and immunities aforesaid, without the hindrance, impediment, disturbance, molestation, or grievance of us, our heirs or successors, the justices, escheators, sheriffs, or other bailiffs or ministers of us, our heirs or successors, whomsoever.

And further, of our more abundant special grace, and from our certain knowledge and mere motion, We will, and by these presents, for us, our heirs and successors, We grant to the aforesaid James Hamilton, Knight, his heirs and assigns, that he, his heirs and assigns, may have and enjoy all the premises as is aforesaid, and upon the showing and demonstration of these our letters patent, or the enrolment thereof, as well before us in the Chancery of us, our heirs and successors, as before the Justices of either Bench of us, our heirs and successors, of our kingdom of Ireland, and before the Treasurer and Barons of the Exchequer of us, our heirs and successors, within our said kingdom of Ireland, also before the Justices and Commissioners of us, our heirs and successors, as well in all and singular the courts of us, our heirs and successors, and the places of record within our said kingdom of Ireland, as in any other courts and places whatsoever throughout the whole kingdom of Ireland, for any thing or things contained or specified in these our letters patent, that these letters patent, and all the grants in the same contained, at once and immediately may be allowed to the aforesaid James Hamilton, Knight, his heirs and assigns : And that the aforesaid treasurer, barons, justices, commissioners, and others whomsoever to whom it shall pertain, may make, or shall cause to be made, due allowance of all and singular the premises from time to time, and that he, the aforesaid James Hamilton, Knight, his heirs and assigns, may have liberty of naming, and of giving names to all and singular the castles, towns, hamlets, places, and lands aforesaid, and each of them, and that the same premises, and every parcel thereof, so as aforesaid named, shall be called, named, accepted, and deemed as well in all the courts and places aforesaid as elsewhere, by such name and names as the aforesaid James Hamilton, his heirs or assigns, shall give or attribute to the said castles or premises, or any of them, any ordinance, nomination, appellation, name or names of the premises, or any parcel thereof, to the contrary thereof in anywise notwithstanding.

And further, of our more abundant special grace, and from our certain knowledge and mere motion, We will, and by these presents, for us, our heirs and successors, We grant to the aforesaid James Hamilton, Knight, his heirs and assigns, that the aforesaid James Hamilton, his heirs and assigns, may have and enjoy all the premises as is aforesaid, and that these our letters patent, or the enrolment thereof, shall be in all things firm, valid, good, sufficient, and effectual in the law against us, our heirs and successors, as well in all our courts as elsewhere within our kingdom aforesaid, without any confirmation, license, or toleration of us, our heirs or successors, by the aforesaid James Hamilton, Knight, his heirs and assigns, or any of them, to be procured or obtained, notwithstanding the ill naming, or ill reciting, or not reciting, or not naming, the aforesaid monasteries, abbeys, priories, rectories, granges, towns, villages, hamlets, territories, places, precincts, lands, tenements, and hereditaments, and other the premises, or any parcel thereof, and notwithstanding the not finding, or ill finding of the office or offices, or inquisition or inquisitions, of the premises, or of any parcel thereof, by which the title of us, or of any of our progenitors or ancestors, should have been found before the making of these our letters patent, and notwithstanding the ill naming, ill reciting, or not reciting any demise or demises, grant or grants, for a term or terms of life, lives, or years, or in fee tail, or otherwise of the premises, or of any parcel thereof, by us or by any of our progenitors or ancestors, or by any other person or persons heretofore made to any other person or persons, being of record or not of record, and notwithstanding the ill naming or not naming any town, hamlet, parish, place, or county, in which the premises or any parcel thereof are situate, lying, or being, and notwithstanding that of the names of the tenants, farmers, or occupiers of the premises, or of any parcel thereof, full, true, and certain mention be not made, and notwithstanding any defects

h

of the certainty or computation, or declaration, or omission of the true yearly value of the premises, or of any parcel thereof, or of the yearly rents reserved of, in, and upon the premises, or for any parcel thereof, in these our letters patent expressed and contained, or not expressed, and notwithstanding any other defects whatsoever, and notwithstanding the statute in the Parliament of Lord Henry the Sixth, late King of England, our ancestor, in the 18th year of his reign, made and published at Westminster, and in our said kingdom of Ireland, amongst others, established and confirmed ; and notwithstanding any other statute, or any other statutes whatsoever, and notwithstanding any defects in the not certainly naming the nature, kind, species, quantity, or quality of the premises, or any parcel thereof.

And further, We will, and, by these presents, for us, our heirs and successors, grant, that he, the aforesaid James Hamilton, Knight, his heirs and assigns, hereafter for ever, may have, hold, and keep, and may be able to have, hold, and keep yearly within the aforesaid town of Carrownesuire, within the lands of Cumber aforesaid, in the aforesaid territory or precinct of the Upper Clandeboy, and the libertie or precincts of the same town, two fairs or markets, the first of the said fairs or markets yearly to begin on the 17th day of March, and for all that day and two other days immediately following to be continued and to last ; and the second fair or market, of the aforesaid two fairs or markets, to begin on the feast or day of St. Bartholomew, the Apostle, yearly, and to be continued and to last for the entire of that day or feast, and for the two other days immediately following ; together with courts of piepowder there to be held at the time of the aforesaid fairs or markets, and with all the liberties and free customs, tolls, stallages, pickages, fines, amerciaments, and all other profits, commodities, and emoluments whatsoever to such fairs or markets, and courts of piepowder pertaining, happening, incident, or belonging : Wherefore we will, and, by these presents, for us, our heirs and successors, firmly We command and direct, that the aforesaid James Hamilton, Knight, his heirs and assigns hereafter for ever, yearly and every year, may have, hold, and keep, and may be and be able to have, hold, and keep, in or within the aforesaid town of Carrownesuire, and the liberties or precincts thereof aforesaid, two markets, the first of the said fairs or markets yearly to begin on the aforesaid 17th day of March, and to be continued and to last for the entire of that day and the two other days immediately following ; and the other fair of the aforesaid two fairs or markets, to be begun on the aforesaid feast or day of St. Bartholomew, the Apostle, and to be continued and to last for the whole of that day or feast and the two days immediately following, together with the court of piepowder there to be held at the time of the said fairs or markets, and with all the liberties and tree customs, tolls, stallages, pickages, fines, amerciaments, and all other profits, commodities, and emoluments whatsoever, to such fairs or markets and courts of piepowder belonging or pertaining, and this without any writ of *Ad quod damnum*, or any other writ, commission, or inquisition in that behalf to be obtained, prosecuted, or returned, and without any molestation, grievance, impediment, or contradiction of us, our heirs or successors, or of any of the officers or ministers of us, our heirs or successors whomsoever, although express mention, &c. In testimony of which, &c. Witness the King at Westminster, minster, the 14th day of March, in the 19th year of our Reign, &c. By Writ of Privy Seal, &c.

No. IV.

COPY INQUISITION, DATED 13TH OCTOBER, 1623.

AN INQUISITION taken at Downepatrick, within the Countie of Downe aforesaid, upon the 13th day of October, Anno Domini, 1623, and in the year of the raigne of our Sovereign Lord James, by the grace of God, of England, France, and Ireland, King, defender of the faith, &c., the one and twentieth, and of Scotland the seven and fiftieth, before Sir John Blencrhasset, Knt., Lord Chief Baron of his Majesty's Court of Exchequer, in this his said realm of Ireland, Sir Christopher Sibthorpe, Knt., Second Justice of his Majesty's Court of Chiefe Place within the said realme, Richard West, Walter Ivers, Esquires, and Stephen Allen, Esq., Deputie Escheator of the said province of Ulster, Commissioners of our said Sovereign Lord the King, by virtue of His Highness's Commission under the Great Seal of His Highness's said realm of Ireland, bearing date at Dublin, the 27th day of June, in the said one and twentieth year of His Majesty's said raigne of England, France, and Ireland, to them the said Commissioners and others, or anie foure or more of them, in that behalf directed, and to this Inquisition annexed, by the oathes of good and lawful men of the said countie, whose names are underwritten, viz., Nicholas Ward, of Castleward, Esq., George Russell, of Rathmullen, Gent., Richard Russell, of Rossglass, Gent., Simon Jordan, of Dansford, Gent., Owen M'Rowry, of Clogher, jun., Gent., Robert Sword, of Rathcolp, Gent., Patrick M'Cartan, of B. Keene, Gent., Patrick M'Cormick, of Killescolban, Gent., George Russell, of Quoniamstown, Gent., Ferdorogh Magines, of Clonvaraghan, junior, Gent., Owen M'Cartan, of Lisenguy, Gent., John Russell, of Killogh, Gent., James Audley, of Audleystown, Gent., Bryan M'Ever Magines, of Shanker, Gent., Shane M'Bryan, of Ballintegart, Gent., whoe being duly sworne upon theire oathes doe saie as followeth, viz. : That the territorie or countrie of Clandeboy, in the said Countie of Downe, hath her metes, bounds, and lymitts in form following, viz., towards and nigh to the north-west part of the territorie aforesaid the river of Laggan, which hath his course immediately into the baye of Knockfergus, is the most knowne bound of the territory aforesaid, and runneth betweene the lands of the same and other parcells of lands or countrie called Maloane, and Fullfeloagh, Kilultagh, and M'Shane Oge's country in Kilultagh, in the county aforesaid ; and the same river is the mete betweene the said territory for eight miles or thereabouts, that is to say, from the foord of Belfast until the same cometh into another river called the Garricklogh ; and from thence, towards the south and south-west part of the river of Garricklogh aforesaid, is the most knowne mete between the lands of the Upper Clandeboy aforesaid and Kilwarlin, in the countrie aforesaid, contynuing his course five myles or thereabouts, until the said river falleth into the loghe called Loghanny, in which Towell M'Pheland M'Ever dwelleth, and the said logh hath half a mile or thereabouts in length in the territory aforesaid ; and from the west and south parts of the said logh neare unto the said logh, lyeth the bog of Dorney, through the middlest of which bog or moor the mete aforesaid extendeth directly betwene the lands of the Upper Clandeboy aforesaid, and the territory called M'Carten's country, in the county aforesaid, contynuing his course about two myles and a halfe unto the foord of Anagheat ; and from thence through the middlest of the bog aforesaid, for halfe a myle or thereabouts, unto another foord called the foord of Annaghdoney, and from thence the mete between the territories aforesaid extendeth itself directly through the middlest of the little river called Dorney, for one myle or thereabouts, untill it cometh unto the foot of the hill called Liscoodry, in the Upper Clandeboy aforesaid ; and there or neare to the said hill, the river of Dorney aforesaid cometh into the river called Ballygany, and from thence the mete aforesaid betweene the Upper Clandeboy aforesaid, and M'Carten's countrie aforesaid, extendeth itself through the middlest of the river of Ballyganny by the space of two myles or thereabouts, until the said river cometh neare the church called Killinchie-Ne-Kelly, situate in the Upper Clandeboy aforesaid ; and from thence the mete of the Upper Clandeboy aforesaid holdeth out directly betwene the lands of the said territorie and the countrie or territory called the Dufferin, in the county aforesaid, and over and through the top or hight of the hill called Teochrum, and from thence for a quarter of a mile or thereabouts unto the nearer end of the moor called Dargmeny ; and from thence the mete between the territory last recyted in the county aforesaid, extendeth itself for two myles or thereabouts, directly through the middlest of the said bog untill that out of the said bog there ariseth a river called Owen-Mullen, which river from thence by the extent of one myle or thereabouts is held to be the bound betweene the territorie aforesaid untill it falleth into the logh called Loghcoyne, in the countie aforesaid, unto or near the foorde of Annaghgleny, between the island Maghy in the Upper Clandeboy, and Satterick in the Du'ferin aforesaid ; and from thence, west and by north, the bank of the logh aforesaid is the most knowne mete of the Upper Clandeboy aforesaid, untyll the river called Alchancoiss descendeth into the lough called Loughcoyne aforesaid ; and from thence the mete of the territory aforesaid between the lands of the same and the Great Ardes aforesaid, in the county aforesaid extendeth itself for one mile and a halfe through the middlest of the river aforesaid, until the said river falleth into the bog of Lisbany ; and from thence the mete between the territory aforesaid extendeth directlie about one mile through the middlest of the bog aforesaid, unto the hill of Lisbany, and so over and through the top of the hill aforesaid, and from thence between the territories aforesaid, directly over and through the top of the hill aforesaid, and from thence between the territories aforesaid, directly over and through the top of the hill called Barnanmore, and so directly over and through the top of the hill called Carnabeg, and from thence between the territories aforesaid directly over and through the top of the hill called Creeghmuldooy, and so directly over and through the top of the Rockie Hill, alias the Rock of Carnanleagh upon the sea shoare ; and from the sea shoare aforesaid towards the east and the bank of the bay of Knockfergus, towards the west, is held the most knowne mete and bound of the territory aforesaid, unto the foord of Belfast above mentioned : We find further, that the territory of the Great Ardes in the said countie of Downe hath his metes, bounds, lymitts, and circuits in form following, that is to say, towards the north-west part of the territories aforesaid the mete of the same extendeth between the lands of the same territorie of the Great Ardes and the Upper Clandeboy aforesaid, in the said countie as is above particularly specified, and towards the west part of the same territorie, the mete aforesaid itselfe by the north-easte, upon the banck of the logh called Loghcoyne aforesaid, from the river of Alchancoiss aforesaid until the river of Blackstaffe falleth into Loughcoyne ; and from thence the mete of the territorie aforesaid, between the lands of the same and the Little Ardes holdeth itself directly through the middlest of the river of Blackstaffe, and through the middle of the foord of Blackstaffe until the said river, until the said river cometh out of a certaine bog called Portabogagh, and from thence the mete between the territories aforesaid, extendeth itselfe directly through the middlest of the said bog, leaving the island Island-Wine and the logh of Kirgestowne towards the south in the Little Ardes aforesaid, and from and next the west part of the logh of Kirgestowne aforesaid, the mete between the territories aforesaid turneth itselfe towards the north and goeth out of the bog aforesaid, near and under the south-east foot of a certain island or hill called Island-Gorman, situate in the Great Ardes, and so near to the circumference of said hill through certain old moors erected and made of the earth, unto the bog called the little myery bog towards the north-west foot of the island aforesaid towards Loughanfinn, and from thence the mete between the territories aforesaid holdeth itselfe through the middle of a certain little old ditch or channell extending itself towards the north foot of the hill called Carnanebeanes in the Little Ards, untyll the said ditch cometh into another mycrie wett bog called Loghawlie, through which bog passeth another little channell until it descendeth unto the sea, and is the mete between the territorie aforesaid, and from thence the sea shoare aforesaid towards the east and south is held the most knowne mete and bound of the territories aforesaid, unto the rock called Carnanleagh in or nigh the Upper Clandeboy aforesaid, in the said County of Downe.

And wee doe further find, that within the severall territories before mentioned are situated the severall abbays, monasteries, pryories, or religious houses followinge, viz., Bangor, Gray-Abbay, Movilla, Black-Abbay, Cumber, Newton, and Hollywood, and the rectories impropriate of Ballymonastry, Ballyorane, Coolgrange, Bally-Richard, Kilcoby alias Kircubin, Kilcolmac, and the advowson of the Church or Rectorie of Ballytrosnon.   And wee further finde, that at the time of the dissolution of the said Abbay of Bangor there was and yett is belonging to the same these towns, lands, rectories, impropriate, and other hereditaments following, viz., the scite, circuit, and precincts of the said abbay, and also all these townes and lands following, as well in spiritualities as in temporalities, viz., the town and lands of Bangor, Bally-Portavo alias Ballyportabo, Ballyffoderlie alias Ballypheoderlie, Ballymyn-Itragh, Ballymyn-Ultragh, Carrowreagh, Caroworlog, Ballowe-juxta-mare, Ballymulleragh, alias Gilgrooms-Port, Bally-M'Cormick, alias Ballymacormugh, Ballymaconnell, alias Bally-M'Conyle, Ballycroghen, Ballyholmie, Bally-Naghie, alias Bally-Nenoghne, alias Ballymenaghne, Ballyionery, alias Bally-Nyrie *alias* Ballinroigh, Ballynegrangeogh, Ballyreeny *alias* Ballyocrane, Ballowe-*juxta-Bangor*, Carrowne-suire *alias* Canowneser, Camowknokanduff *alias* Carouslanclarckanduff, Carowneshroyan *alias* Callose-neseron, Ballymoneycarogie *alias* Money-Caragh *alias* Ballymony-Carogh, Ballykawgeile *alias* Bally-fraghoguile, Ballylisbane *alias* Ballinlisselane, Ballybarne *alias* Ballynebarnen, Ballynecamanleagh *alias* Bally-Camandeagh, Bally-Killare *alias* Ballincellor, Ballysallogh, Ballymullen *alias* Ballymulla, Ballyvernon *alias* Ballyvernock, Bally-Liddy, Bally-Crott, Bally-Skelly *alias* Bally-Skally, and Bally-Gilbert : And we find also these townes followinge, lying in or neare the Plaines of Belfast, to be parcells of the possessions of the said abbay, as well in spiritualities as in temporalities, viz., Ballymeaghan *alias* Ballymegh, Ballymachoris, and Ballymajor *alias* Ballemacer : And wee find also the church or chapell of Cregavada to be a chapell of ease belonging to the said Abbay of Bangor, whereunto the tithes of the five towns followinge are belonginge, viz., Cregavada, Bally-Robert, Bally-Davie, Bally-greny, and Ballynemony : Wee find further, that the church or chapell of Hollywood, together with the tithes of the five townes followinge, doe belonge to the said abbay, viz., Ballycultra as parcell of the said pryorie in the Great Ardes, Ballmanagh, Ballykeile, Ballinderry, and Ballyknocknegony : We find also the church or rectorie impropriate of Bally-Lioghan *alias* Ballyurkegan in Lecale, in the said Countie of Downe, whereunto the tithes of the townes followinge doe belonge unto the said Abbay of Bangor, viz., Ballyurkegan and Corbally, and also the advowsons of the vicaradages in all the churches and lands aforesaid : And also the tithes of all sorts of fish taken and landed upon the south side of the bay of Knockfergus, from the Copeland Isles to the foord of Belfast, together with the ferry over the said bay of Knockfergus, from the towne of Bangor to and from Knockfergus and Antrim side : And we find also, that, at the tyme of the said dissolution, there was and yet is these townes, lands, rectories impropriate, and other hereditaments following, belonging to the said Graie-Abbey, viz., the scite, circuit, and precinct of the said abbay, and also all these towns and lands following, as well in spiritualities as in temporalities, viz., the towns and lands of Ballymonestragh *alias* Corvalee, in the Great Ardes, Ballybrene, Ballynestore, Ballywalter *alias* Ballywaltra, Ballywanell *alias* Ballynellan, Ballymencok, Balleneboyle, the Cardie, Ballynegrange *alias* Kilmanagh, Ballenicholl, Ballemuckley, *alias* Tullymucklie, Ballycaslen, Ballyblack *alias* Balliprepiscragh, Carrowtullikevin *alias* Tundon, Carrowdorne, and Carrownesker: And we doe further fynd, that the grange and rectorie of Tullum-grange, with the tithes of these towns followinge, in the territorie of Lecale, doe belong unto the said abbay, viz., the tithes of the two Tullumgranges, Ballebeg, the two townes of Bally-Edocks, and Sheep-landbeg, and also the tithes of all the fish taken between the mere of Iniscargie to the river of the Cumber.

We find also, that, at the tyme of the said dissolution, there was and yet is these townes, lands, rectories impropriate, and other hereditaments following, belonging to the late dissolved Abbay or Monasterie of Movilla in the Great Ardes, viz., the scite, circuit, and precinct of the said abbay or monastery, and also all these towns and lands following, as well in spiritualities as in temporalities, that is to say, the towns and lands of Ballinreagh *alias* Movilla, Ballyhary, Ballydrumhurke *alias* Ballygunnhirk, in the Great Ardes, Ballyallicocke *alias* Drumchynne *alias* Ballyalgo, Ballyloghiescowe, Ballywatticock, Ballehamlie, Ballyhest *alias* Raghone *alias* Ballinhalta, and all the tithes of these towns following, viz., Ballyhenry *alias* Drumhany, and Ballymagrevegan *alias* Ballegin, lying in the Upper Clandeboy : And we find also that these several granges and rectories following, doe belong unto the said Abacie or Rectorie of Movilla, viz., the Grange or Rectorie of Derry, whereunto belongeth the tithes of these two townes following, being in the Little Ardes, viz., Ballyderry, and Ballecam ; the Grange or Rectorie of Rowbane, whereunto belongeth the tithes of these three townes following, viz., Ballerobane, Balleroreagh, in the Great Ardes, and Ballebranemore in the Little Ardes, and the grange or rectorie of Ballydrumroan, *alias* Drumfin, whereunto belongeth the tithes of these two townes follow-ing, lying in the Great Ardes, viz., Ballegin, *alias* Ballyhiggen, and Ballydrumroan, and the Granges or Rectorie of Anaghalon, *alias* Killenie, whereunto belongeth the tithes of these townlands following, lying in the Sleught-Neiles, viz., the half towne of Killenie, Ballycarricknefeigh, *alias* Ballycarrickveagh, Ballynebresagh, Ballycarrickvadory, and Ballydrumneleg, *alias* Ballydrumleg : And we also further fynd, that the tithes of Carigogantelon are a mensall belonging to the said abbay or monasterie, together with the whole tithes whatsoever of the lands of the Newton, except the tithes of Lisneavan which be-longeth to the priorie of the Newtown, all lying within the Great Ardes, in the Upper Clandeboy ; and also all the tithes whatsoever, with the appurtenances, belonging to a chapel called Kiltuga, which hath the tithes of Killeman, and Ballerogan: And we find also that the rectorie impropriate of Drum, in the Lagan, belongeth to Movilla, whereunto belongeth the tithes of these townes and lands following, viz., Ballerdrum, *alias* Ballydrumbeg, and Levalletulligoan, and the tythes of the two towns following, and the tithes of divers other townes and lands in the Countie of Antrim, with the advowson and right viz., Ballenehaghliske and Ballydunkinmuck, in the territories of Sleught-Neiles in the Countie of Downe, of patronadge of the Vicaradges of Drum and Killenie, and of all other the several vicaradges of the said rectories.

And we find also, that at the time of the said dissolution there was and yet is these townes, lands, rectories impropriate, and other hereditaments following, belonging to the late dissolved Abbay or Religious House of Black-Abbay, viz., the scite, circuit, and precinct of the said abbay or religious house, and also all these townes and lands following, as well in spiritualities as in temporalities, viz., the towns and lands of Ballymonestraduffe, *alias* Ballylisbrane, Ballykiloolgan, *alias* Ballykerok, Ballinemanagh, and there is also belonging unto the Black-Abbay aforesaid, the impropriate rectories of these four churches following, viz., Balle-Halbert, Iniscargie, White Church, and Donoghdie, with the advowsons of the vicaradges of the said several churches, and also two third parts of the tythes of these towns following, lying within the parish of Ballyhalbert, viz., Balleaspragh, Ballyhalbert, Bally-Richard, Portovogie, Ballyfringe *alias* Ballenegallogh, Balleglasserogh, Ballygraffan, Ballehamlin, and Balle-Rodine, as also of the two third parts of the tithes of these towns following, lying in the parish of Iniscargie, viz., Ballesumpt, Ballegrangan, Ballefister, Carrownesker, Iniscargie, *alias* M'Killen, and Ballyggin *alias* Ballyhigan : Likewise, we find belonging to the said abbay the two third part of the tithes of the towns and lands following, lying within the parish of Whitechurch, viz., Balleneganoy, Ballyferish, Balle-downover, Balle-Templefin, *alias* Whitechurch, Balle-Lisciagnewe, Ballyatwart, Ballygowne, and Ballyobekin : We further find belonging to the said abbay the rectorie impropriate of Donaghdee, with the two third parts of the tithes of the townes and lands following, viz., Balle-M'William, Balle-nova, Ballenecrosse, Ballenemonie, Balle-Carowreagh, *alias* Ballycreasie, Ballevacter, Ballenecreboy, *alias* Balle-M'Cabry, Ballycopland, Balle-Killaghie, Balle-Kilcolmuck, Balle-Drumchaie, and the half townland of Donaghdie.

We find further, that at the time of the dissolution, there was and yet is these townes, lands, rectories impropriate, and other hereditaments belonging to the said late dissolved Abbay or Religious House of Cumber, viz., the scite, circuit, and precincts of the said abbay, or religious house, and also all these townes and lands following, as well in spiritualties as in temporalities, viz., Ballenemanagh, *alias* Balle-nevanie, Ballealtechillegon, *alias* Balleganonie, Ballegarduffe, Ballecumber, Ballymonester, Carrowne-suir, Ballenicoll, Ballenegatugg, and Ballenecullentric ; and also that the tithes of these towns following were and are belonging to the said Abbay of Cumber, viz., Ballestoker, Balleristoll, Balle-M'Glaffe, Gran-giah, Lisleyn, Ballekeile, Ballymanagh, Bally-Tullchubbert, Tulligarvan, Moylogh, and the half towne-land of Colintinakellic ; and the said abbay hath also thereunto belonging the Rectorie of Kilmood-managh, together with the land and tithes of the quarter of Kilmood aforesaid, with the tithes of these townlands following, viz., Ballclisnebarnes, Ballechogle, Balletullenegarie, *alias* Ballyhullenegie, Balle-drumheriffe, and Ballygraffan : And we find likewise the Rectorie of Balle-M'Keoghan belongs unto the said abbay, which hath the tithes of these towns following, viz., Bally-M'Keoghan, Ballemeledie, Ballealoghlie, Balle-Tuarnenelege, *alias* Tullycopan, Ballycrely, Balle-Rusth, Balle-Byn, Balle-magheris-cowe, and the half towne of Balle-M'Gowne : And we also find belonging to the said abbay, the Rectorie of Tonaghwyn, whereunto the townland of Tonaghwyn aforesaid doth belong, with the tithes thereof, and that it hath likewise the tithes of these towns following, viz., Ballclagegoan, Ballenegassan, Ballenghargie, Ballcliswyne, Balleglasdromon, and Balle-Dromaconell ; and also the advowsons and right of patronadge of all the several vicaradges belonging to the said rectories ; and the possession of Tonaghwyn we find in the Bishope these thirtie years : And we find likewise, that at the time of the said dissolution, there was and yet is these townes, lands, and other hereditaments following, belonging to the said late dissolved Pryorie, or Religious House of the Newton, in the Great Ardes, viz., the scite, circuit, and precinct of the said late dissolved Pryorie or Religious House of Newtown, and also of the towneland of Balle-Lisnevan, *alias* Ballenoc, as well in spiritualities as temporalities, and also these towns and lands following, viz., Levalle-Tullenroigh, Carrow-Cam-Choise, Carow-M'Croghan, Carow-Crosnemuckley, Bucaghmore, Balle-Kilcunan, *alias* Balle-Kilcowman, Ballebernes, *alias* Barnes, and Carrowtullichaggart.

We find likewise that at the time of the said dissolution there was, and yet is, these towns and lands, and other hereditaments following belonging to the late dissolved Priory or Religious House of

Holliwood, the scite, circuit, and precinct of the same, and also all these towns and lands following, viz :—Ballykeile *alias* Ballycreel, Ballymanock *alias* Ballymanogh, Balle-Cultrack *alias* Ballycultragh, *alias* Ballactragothe, Ballaendeny, *alias* Balledone, and Ballaerknocknegonie, *alias* Balleknocknegonie, in the Great Ardes.

We find likewise that there is belonging unto the said Impropriate Rectory of Ballyorane the tithes of these townes following, viz :—the tithes of Balleorane-Nerany, Wynick-arwell, and Lisbraden, in the said territorie of Sleught-Hubrick : Wee find also, that there is belonging unto the said Rectorie of Coolgrange, the tithes of the said townes and lands of Coolegrange, *alias* Grange, in the Great Ardes, neare Blackstaffe : Wee find further, that there is belonging unto the said Rectoric of Balle Richard, *alias* Ballegard, Ballerencreavie, Balle-Ganvic, *alias* Balleganeny, and Balle-Castlencvaric : Wee find that there is belonging to the said Rectorie of Kilcooby, *alias* Kircubbin, the tithes of these towns following, viz :—the tithes of Kilcooby, *alias* Kircubin, and Ballymullen, in the territorie of the Great Ardes ; Wee find likewise, that there is belonging to the said Rectorie of Kilcolmuck, these lands and hereditaments following, viz :—one quarter of land called Carrow-Calliduffe, as well in spiritualities as in temporalities, and the tithes of these townes following, viz :—of the townes and lands of Bally-grangeogh, Ballybutler, Ballyfrainys, and Balleuttagic, in the Great Ardes aforesaid : Wee further find also, that there are lying and being within the said territories of Upper Clandeboye and Great Ardes, these townes, lands, and hereditaments following, viz :—one quarter of land in Canvie, lying in the Great Ardes aforesaid, as well in spiritualities as in temporalities, one other quarter of land called Carrowneclogher, lying in the parish of Whitechurch, in the territorie of the Great Ardes aforesaid, as well in spiritualities as in temporalities, and two townelands called Ballyhayes, lying in the parish of Donoghdie, in the Great Ardes, in the county aforesaid, as well in spiritualities as in temporalities, one Carrow of land, called Carrownemoan, *alias* Carrownenoan, lying in the parish of Talbotstown, in the Great Ardes aforesaid, as well in spiritualities as in temporalities, one other quarter of land called Carrow-John-Boyestie, lying in the town of Drumoan, *alias* Drumfin, in the Great Ardes aforesaid, as well in spiritualities as in temporalities, one other quarter of land called St. John's quarter, lying in Fullokeis, and another quarter of land called St. John's Quarter, *alias* Carownechegle, in Kilnolgan, in the Great Ardes aforesaid, as well in spiritualities as in temporalities, and one quarter of land called Carrownemurchie, lying near the island Slesne, in Loghcoyne, in the Upper Clandeboye, another quarter of land called Carrownemuck, lying neare Knockcollumkill, in the Upper Clandeboye aforesaid, as well in spiritualities as in temporalities, all which last recyted premises are parcell of the late dissolved Priory or Religious House of St. John's of Jerusalem, one other quarter of land called Carrownathan, in the Great Ardes aforesaid, as well in spiritualities as in temporalities, being parcell of the Abbey of Muckmore, in the countie of Antrim, and the advowson or right of patronage of the Parsonadge of Ballyrolly, in the Great Ardes, the tithes of the townes and lands of Mavara, Cameragh *alias* Carow, in the Upper Clandeboy parcel of the late dissolved Pryorie of the Inch, in Lecale, the advowson and right of patronadge of the Rectories and Churches of Dundonell, Knockcollumkill, Bredagh, and Templeblairis, in the Upper Clandeboy aforesaid : We likewise find, that within the said territory of the Upper Clandeboye, there are contained these lesser territories following, viz :—Castlereagh, and Gallowgh, Slewght-Neiles, Slewght-Henrikies, Slewght-Kellies, Slewght-Durnings, Slewghtowen-M'Quinn, and Plaines of Belfast, Slewght-Hubricks, and Slewght-Bryan-Boy : We find also, that within the lesser territory of Castlereagh and Gallowgh, there are contained of temporal lands belonging unto the said last recyted territorie, these townes and lands following, viz :—Bally-Castlerogh, Ballyleronnell, Ballelisnebren, Ballecrosnecraven, Balle-M'Conoghie, the half towne of Monilohoge, being parcell of Rosboie, Ballegregogie, Ballenefeigh, Ballebredagh, Balleknock-Collumb-kill, Ballenegalwally, Balle-M'Caritt, Ballerosboie, Ballehenoad, Balledengilnehir, [   ] Gorterib, and Balletullecarnan : Wee find likewise, that within the said lesser territorie of the Slewght-Neiles, there are contained of temporall lands belonging unto the said lesser territorie of Slewght-Neiles, these townes and lands following, viz :—Ballebaines, *alias* Listroudie, Ballenecreven-Ergan, Ballydrum-given, *alias* Ballydrumvena, *alias* Ballydrumgevan, Ballindin *alias* Balledyan, *alias* Ballindiggon, Balle-Caryed *alias* Ballechaghard, Balle-M'Craven *alias* Bally-M'Crevan, *alias* Ballevickcravenie, Ballytullyvostokinagh, *alias* Ballytulloghmistikinagh, Balletanaghmore, Ballcloghgar, *alias* Levale-crevieloghgar, Carownedome, Ballelisdromlaghan, *alias* Lisbane, Ballelisdalgan, *alias* Taunaghwyn, Ballecaricknesassanagh, Balleoghly, *alias* Fairetoune, *alias* Bally-Lenny, Ballelisdownean *alias* Balle-keall, Balie-Lisdynan *alias* Downean, *alias* Ballyganear, Ballenelessan three quarters, and Tullowre the fourth quarter, Balleneknockan, Ballemillagh, *alias* Ballemoughlogh, Ballelclontonikelly, Ballekillenure, Ballecarvick, *alias* Ballyganvie, Ballekillmanaghcom *alias* Kaira, *alias* Balle-M'Car, Ballebarneganan, Ballendrynan, *alias* Balle-M'Grynan, Canwenebravie, *alias* Carowdrumrane, Ballenecrevie, Alickwick, Ballencrossan, Carow-Lagecory, Ballelisneshrean, Balle-M'Brenan, Ballecloghan, Balleomalten, *alias* Downemulchany, *alias* Ballemaltin, *alias* Tircronagh, *alias* Trecuimen, Tallyard, *alias* Hymenude, *alias* Lisnoad, Balledrumboe, Carowelaneroge, Ballycane, *alias* Dumbrackley, Ballechreggie, *alias* Listrademan, *alias* Ballenclessan, Baliemylagh, Carowhuduffe, *alias* Carrow-Iduffe, *alias* Carouty-Duffe, Ballyknockbrekan, *alias* Tulloghbreckan, Ballelenoghan, *alias* Dunreagin, *alias* Ballydeymore, Ballendulloghan, Balle-Ivullvaly, *alias* Balleomulvally, Ballinlay, *alias* Ballene-hatti-M'Evely, Carowchonte, *alias* Edendera, Half towne of Dankinmuck, Ballinhaughliske, Balletullegoan, *alias* Balledrum, *alias* Balledrumbeg, *alias* Ballytemple-Drum, Balleneskeagh, *alias* Balleskeaghan, *alias* Balledowneskeagh, *alias* Skeagh-Lattefeagh, Balletullenecross, Ballene-Croawbie, Balletulliconnell, *alias* Liskieghan, Ballenonellan, Balle-Largmore, Ballenagharick, *alias* Ballyminy, *alias* Ballehawick, *alias* Lisbany, *alias* Ballebroghintham, Balletynan, *alias* Down-Cumber, Balleblarish, *alias* Ballytemple, Blarish-Levalle, Lisnegnoe, Balledowneogh, *alias* Ballegunnemagh, Ballecarigaghcroy, Ballecaricneveagh, Levallenay, *alias* Killanie, Ballybresagh, *alias* Loghanie, Ballecarickmaderoy, Ballydumbeg, *alias* Balledrumneleck, Balle-Cowan, Balleholliwood.

Wee find, likewise, that within the said lesser territorie of Slut-Henrickies, there are contained of temporal lands belonging to the said territorie, these townes and lands following, viz :—Balle-Carickmanan, Levalle-Ravara, Levalle-Drumchaie, *alias* Achanderagh, *alias* Levalle-Drumchaie, Balle-Liswyne, Balle-Clontonoglare, *alias* Clunitineclare, Ballenecrevie, Lavalle-Barnemacher or Ballimapher Balle-Drumcreagh, Balleobunden, Ballegraffan, Ballehullengie, Balle-Lisnebarnes, Levalle-Killinchie, *alias* Levale-Kyllinche, Tulloghaphynan, Balle-M'Gowen, Ballemagheriscowe, Ballechegle, Balledrumheriffe.

Wee also find, that within the said lesser territorie of Slut-Kellies, there are contained of temporal lands belonginge to the said territorie these townes and lands following, viz :—Ballebeine, Balle-M'Graffe, Ballestoker, Ballerustell, Ballenegrange, Balle-Lisbane, Ballekeile, Ballemanare, Balletullehubbert, Balletulligarvan, Balle-Cloghan, Balleahergie, Balleneglasdromon, Ballelagegowan, Ballenegassan, Levalle-Dromachonell, Levalle-Revara, Ballegalloughie, Ballemeledie, Balletullecoppan, Towernenelegg, Balleurush, *alias* Enrasse and Ballycrealy, Balle-M'Caghan, and Carow-Edenslatt.

We further find, that within the lesser territory of Sleught-Durnings, Sleught-Owen-M'Quin, and the Plaines of Belfast, there are contained of temporal lands belonging unto the said territories these towns and lands following : Ballechackamore, Ballecarigogautelen, two Balleneskeaghs, Carowne-Calleduffe, Balle-Killemed, Balle-Kerowreagh, Balledamlady, Ballereagin, Ballyhugh, *alias* Ballylisnisca, Balledundonnell, Ballecloghan, Ballenechallen, Carrow-Kilneveagh, Carrownecarne, and Carrownemullen : We find likewise, that within the lesser territorie of Sleught-Hubricks, there are contained of temporall lands belonging to the said territorie, these townes and lands following, viz., Ballenngereve, Balleneganvie, Ballyhenrie, Ballecaslanevery, Ballelissegowan, Ballerogan, Balle-M'Grevaghan, Balleorane, Ballinrany, Balle-Lisewaden, Ballewynnycarvell, Ballyloghan, Balleregard, Ballecastlanbeg, and Island Slesney : We likewise find, that within the lesser territorie of Sleught-Bryan-Boy, there are contained of temporal lands belonging to the said territorie these towns and lands following : Ballycregavada, Ballenegreeney, Halle-Robert, Halle-Davie, and Ballynemonie : We find that within the said territorie of the Great Ardes there are contained of temporal lands these townes and lands following, viz. : Balle-M'William, Ballenova, Ballenecrosse, Ballenemoynie, Balle-Carrowreagh, *alias* Ballenecreaghie, Ballevaster, Ballecreboy, *alias* Ballenecrevy, Ballycopland, Halle-Killaghie, Ballekilcormick, Balle-Drumchaie, the half towne of Donaghodie, Ballenegrange, Ballybutler, Ballyfrenish, Balle-Cottagie, Carrow-Calledowe, parcel of Ballecotagie, Balle-Rolloy, Balle-M'Crevil, Ballycosker, Ballenemonic, Balleaghrea, Ballinrea, Balliganvie, Ballekibratten, Balletullicanvan, *alias* Listeagnewe, Templeffiin, *alias* Whitechurch, Ballefirish, Ballydownover, Balleatwart, Balle-M'Goure, Ballcobiken, Ballegin, *alias* Ballehiggen, Ballendome, Balle-Lumpt, Balle-Iniscargie, *alias* Neckgellen, Ballegaman, Carrow-Calliogh, Ballymullen, Ballekircubin, Balle-Hamlin, Carrow-Nesteragh, Grangeogh, *alias* Coolgrange, Ballefister, Ballerowreogh, Halle-Robane, Hallegraffan, Balleglasserogh, Balleaspragh, Ballehalbert, Balleffringe, *alias* Ballenegallogh, and Balleportevogie, *alias* Mulloghmore : Wee find that all the temporall lands within the said territorie, came into the hands of the late Queen Elizabeth, by virtue of an Act of Parliament, made in the eleventh yeare of her raigne, intituled " An Act for the attainder of Shane O'Neale :" Wee find that all the said abbayes, monasteries, pryories, rectories impropriate, and other religious houses, with all the said lands, tenements, and hereditaments unto them belonging, came into the handes of the said late Qucene Elizabeth by the several dissolution of the said several religious houses : We find that the said late Queene Elizabeth was seized of all and singular the premises, with the appurtenances, of and in the manors, lands, tenements, rectories, tithes, hereditaments following, viz. : the Manor or Preceptorie of St. Johnstowne *alias* Castleboic, Dromarden, Ballyadams *alias* Adamstowne, Balle-Nicholas *alias* Tullycaman, the half town of Cloghie, the half town of Tollytomen ; and also the Rectorie of Rathmullen, together with the two-third part of the tithes of Rathmullen, Ballyfunston and Luchanston, Ballenebirt, St. Johnstowne, Killiough, Cawinullen, Plunkettstowne, and also of and in the advowson and right of patronage of the Vicaradge of Rathmullen aforesaid in Lecale ; and of and the Rectorie or Church of Ballytrossnon *alias* Ballytrustan, in the Little Ardes, to which belongeth two third parts of the tithes of Ballytullyboord, Ballefenor, Grannagh, Ballebranigan, Ballicame, Ballecarrough, Ballcfenoragh, the half town of Cloghargie, and the half town of Dumtayle *alias* Loughduff ; and of and in the Rectorie of Ballegalgat *alias* Ballegnegh, together with two third parts of the tithes of Ballegalgat, Ballwhincragh, and Ballewhillerat, lying in the Little Ardes ; the Rectorie of Grange-Owter, together with two third parts of the tithes of Ballygruntein, Tullycaman, Balle-Hocke, Tussellhauragh, the half towne of Quintagh, the half towne of Carrictressil, Tollemart, and Camemaller, with the advowson and right of patronage of the Vicarage or Church of Grange-Owter, within the said Little Ardes, and the tithes of the fishing of the river of Strongford, in right of her said Crowne : and, being thereof so seized, did make certain letters patent, bearing date at Westminster, in England, the 16th day of November, in the 13th yeare of Her Majesty's said raigne, to Sir Thomas Smith, the father, and Thomas Smith, the sonne, according to the intent, effect, and covenants of certain indentures made between the said late Queen Elizabeth on the one part, bearing date the 1st of October, in the said 16th yeare of the said raigne, which said letters patent and indentures we find *in hæc verba:* "ELIZABETH *Dei gratia,*" &*c.,* "THIS INDENTURE," &c. : We find also, that the said Thomas, the sonne, with a few Englishmen, the 12th day of October, *Anno* 1572, upon lycence had and obtained of the said late Queene Elizabeth, by the said Thomas, the sonne, in that behalfe, did enter into the said Earldome of Ulster, at which tyme, and for the space of twentie years next after, there were many rebels residing in open and actual rebellion within the said Great and Little Ardes, and that neither Sir Thomas Smith, the father, Knight, nor Thomas Smith, the son, nor either of them, nor their heires or assigns, nor their nor any of their friendes, followers, or adherents, then nor at any tyme did subdue, represse, expel, or bring into Her Majesty's mercie any rebel, or naytive : We find also that neither the said Sir Thomas Smith, the father, nor Thomas Smith, the sonne, nor either of them, nor the heires of either of them, did settle, plant, or inhabit, the said landes, territories, or countries mentioned in the letters patent, or any part thereof, with true and faithful subjects, as is in the said indenture contayned, although they have had convenyent tyme to have done the same since the making of the said letters patent and indentures : We find also, that neither the said Sir Thomas Smith, the father, nor the said Thomas Smith, the sonne, nor their heires or assignes, nor the heires or assignee of either of them, after the 28th daie of March, 1579, had at any tyme in a readiness within the said landes, territories, and countries mentioned in the said letters patent, or any part thereof, for every plowland, or 120 acres of arable land, of the said territorie, one English footman souldier, armed and furnished for the warres, after the manner of England, nor for every two plowlands, or 240 acres of arable land, of the said territorie, of such measure as is expressed in the said indenture, one English light horseman souldier, armed and furnished for the wars, to serve in defence of the same, although that since the said 28th daie of March, 1579, there were great wars and rebellyon, and great occasion of service within the said territorie mentioned in the said letters patent, and other the parts of Ulster thereunto next adjacent : We find also that neither Sir Thomas Smith, the father, nor Thomas Smith, the sonne, nor their heires or assignes, nor the heires or assignes of either of them, before the said 28th daie of March, which was in the yeare of our Lord, 1579, did win, possess, inhabit, or divide any of the castles, manors, lordships, pryories, landes, tenements, and other hereditaments lying and being within the precinct of the countries mentioned in the said letters patente, or in any of them, in manner and forme covenanted in the said indenture or otherwise ; and also the said Jurors doe find further, that after the said letters patente as aforesaid, and after the said 20th day of March, 1579, there were great wars and rebellions in the said Earldome of Ulster, and that several and many general hostinges were there proclaymed after the

k

said letters patente, and àfter the said 28th daie of March, 1579, and fifteen dayes' warning thereof was given in and upon the said landes mentioned in the said letters patente, within the said Earldom of Ulster, and that, on the 25th day of August, 1581, by command from Arthur Lord Gray, then Lord Deputie General to our said late Soveraigne Lady Queene Elizabeth, of this realme of Ireland, there was one general hosting summoned and proclaymed by publique proclamation, within the said Countie of Downe, fifteen daies before the beginning thereof, and that the said Lord Deputie was then personally present at the said general hosting by the space of fortie dayes and upwards, and that neither the said Sir Thomas Smith, the father, nor Thomas Smith, the sonne, nor their assigns, nor any for them, had any horsemen or footmen in a readiness to attend the said Lord Deputie, according to their said covenants in that behalf; and that neither Sir Thomas Smith, the father, nor Thomas Smith, the sonne, nor their heires nor assignes, nor the heires nor assignes of either of them, had at any such general hosting in a readiness to attend the Lord Deputie of Ireland for the time being, any leaders or captaines, nor any horsemen or footmen souldiers, as by their covenant in their said indentures they were bound to fynd within the countries and lands aforesaid to serve the late Queen, her heirs and successors, under the Deputie, or any other Chiefe Governor for the tyme being, for the space of fortie dayes, in any place of the said Earldome of Ulster, according to the effect and meaning of the said covenants and agreements contained in the said indentures : We find also, that neither the said Sir Thomas Smith, the father, nor Thomas Smith, the sonne, nor either of them, nor their nor either of their heires or assignes, nor any other person or persons in their names, or in the names or behalf of them or any of them, since the Feast of Saint Michael the Archangel, which was in *Anno* 1576, did pay or cause to be paid to our late Sovereign Lady the Queen Elizabeth, or her successors, nor to any sheriffe of the Countie of Down for the time being, for every plowland of 120 acres arable land as aforesaid, 20 shillings current money of Ireland, yearly, or any part thereof, neither did any sheriffe for the said Countie of Downe for the time being, collect or levie the said yearlie rent, or any part thereof, according to the tenor of the said letters patent and indentures, and the covenants and agreements in the same : We likewise fynd that the said 20 shillings per annum, mentioned by the said indentures to be paid out of every plowland of the premises, is altogether behind, in arrear, and unpaid from the said Feast of St. Michael, in *Anno* 1576, until the daie and tyme of taking of this inquisition : We find further, that our Soveraigne Lord, King James that now is, was seized in his demeasne as of fee in the right of the Crowne of England, of and in all and singular the said lands, tenements, and premises, with the appurtenances : We find further, that covenants and agreements were made by deeds indented tripartite between Con Oneale M'Bryan Fertagh Oneale, of Clanboies, in the province of Ulster, in the realme of Ireland, Esq., on the first part, the Lord Vicecount Mountgomerie of the Ardes, by the name of Hugh Mountgomery of London, Esq., of the second part, and the Lord Vicecount Claneboy, by the name of James Hamilton of London, Esq., one of His Majesty's Serjeants, on the third part, bearing date the last day of April, in the 3rd yeare of His Majesty's raigne of England, France, and Ireland, and of Scotland the 38th, as by the said deed appeareth, which we find *in hæc verba :* "THIS INDENTURE," &c. : We find that our said Soveraigne Lord, King James that now is, being so seized of all and singular the premises, did make certayne letters patent, bearing date 5th November, 3*d Jac. Reg.*, purporting a grant of all the temporal lands and territories of the Upper Clandeboyes and Great Ardes to the Lord Vicecount Claneboy, by the name of James Hamilton, Esq., and his heirs, *prout* in the said letters patent, which we find *in hæc verba,* viz. : "*Jacobus Dei gratia,*" &*c.* : We find that our said Soveraigne Lord, King James that now is, made other letters patent, bearing date the 14th day of February, and 3*d Jac. Reg.*, purporting a grant (*inter alia*) unto the Lord Vicecount Claneboy, by the name of James Hamilton, Esq., of the Abbay of Cumber, and all the towne lands and hereditaments belonging to the same, and also the Rectories impropriate of Ballemoneshey, Balleorane, Cool-Grange, and the tithes of the fishings of the river of Strangford, Balle-Richard, Kilcooby, Kilcolmuck, with all the Glebe landes and hereditaments belonging to the same, and also the Rectorie of Ballygalgat, in the Little Ardes, the Rectorie of Grange-Owter, and the advowson of the Vicaradge of the same, and also the advowson of the Vicaradge of the Church of Balletrosnon, in the Little Ardes, and the Manor or Preceptorie of St. Johnston, in the Little Ardes, with the appurtenances : And the said quarter of lande in Carroye, in the Great Ardes, and the said other quarter of land called Carrowclogher, and the said other two townes and landes called Baile-Heayes, and Carrownemoan *alias* Carrownenoan aforesaid, and also the quarter of land called Carrow-John-Beistie, and the said quarter of land called St. John's Quarter, in Culloghkevin, and the said quarter of land called St. John's Quarter, in Kilvolgan, and the said quarter called Carnemuck, neare the Island of Slesney, in Loghcoyne, and the said quarter of land called Carnemuck, neare Knock-Columkill, and the tithes of the townes and lands of Ravarra, Carrowreagh *alias* Carnereagh, and Ballenecloghan, *prout* in the said letters patent appeareth, which letters patent, for so much as concerne the said recyted premises, we fynd *in hæc verba:* " *Jac. Dei gratia,*" &*c.*

We find that the said Lord Vicecount Claneboy, being seized of all and singular the premises as aforesaid, did make a deed indented, purporting a feoffment to the said Lord Vicecount Mountgomerie, of the Abbaie of Movilla, and divers other landes and hereditaments mentioned in the said deed, bearing date the first day of October, the 3rd yeare of His Majesty's raigne, *prout* the said deed, which we find *in hæc verba:* "THIS INDENTURE," &c. ; and we find the execution of the said deed by livery and seizen to be the 11th daie of January then next after the date of the said deed : We find that the said Lord Vicecount Claneboy, being seized, as aforesaid, of all and singular the premises aforesaid, did make a deed indented, purporting a feoffment, dated the 6th day of November, 3d *Jac. Reg.*, to the said Con Oneale, of the townes and lands of Ballyknockan, and divers other townes and lands mentioned in the said deed, which we fynd *in hæc verba:* "THIS INDENTURE," &c. ; and wee fynd the execution of said deed by livery and seizen to be the 14th day of January then next ensuing after the date of the said deed : We fynd that the said Lord Vicecount Claneboy, being seized of all and singular the premises aforesaid, did make a deed indented, purporting a feoffment to the said Lord Vicecount Ardes, by the name of Sir Hugh Montgomerie, Knight, bearing date the 7th of November, 3d *Jac. Reg.*, of the townes and landes of Ballekenoad, and divers other towns and lands mentioned in the said deed, *prout* in the said deed, which we find *in hæc verba:* "THIS INDENTURE," &c. ; and wee fynd the execution of the said deed by livery and seizen to be the 15th day of January next ensuing after the date of the said deed : We find further, that the said Lord Vicecount Claneboy, by the name of Sir James Hamilton, Knight, being seized as aforesaid, did make a deed indented, bearing 23rd day of Maie, 1618, to the said Lord Vicecount Ardes, by the name of Sir Hugh Montgomerie, Knight, amongst other things, of the late Monastery or Religious House of the Black-Abbay, with the appurtenances, and also of four townes or towne landes, parcel of the late Monastery or Religious House of the Cumber, viz. : BalleneCumber, &c., *prout* in the said deed, which deed we find *in hæc verba:* "THIS INDENTURE," &c. ; and we find the execution of the said deed to be made by livery and seizen accordingly : We fynd likewise, that the said Lord Vicecount Mountgomerie, by the name of Sir Hugh Mountgomerie, Knight, did make a deed indented, bearing date the said 23d daie of Maie, 1618, to the said Lord Vicecount Claneboy, by the name of Sir James Hamilton, Knight, of the moytie of all the woodes and underwoodes in the territories of Castlereogh and Slewght-Neiles, and the moytie of all these townes, viz. : Balledouneagh, &c., *prout* in the said deed, which deed we fynd *in hæc verba:* "THIS INDENTURE," &c. ; and we find the execution of the said deed to be made by livery and seizen accordingly : We further find, that certaine articles of agreement were made between the said Lord Vicecount Mountgomery, of the Ardes, and the said Con Oneale, bearing date the 24th day of December, and the 3rd yeare of His Majesty's said raigne of England, France, and Ireland, &c., *prout* in the said articles, which we find *in hæc verba:* "ARTICLES, covenants, grants, and agreements indented," &c. : We fynd, also that the said Con Oneale, on the 14th daie of March, and 3d *Jac. Reg.*, made a deed purporting a feoffment of the townes and landes of Balleneknockan, and other landes mentioned in the said deed, unto the said Lord Vicecount of the Ardes, by the name of Sir Hugh Mountgomerie, of Bradstone, Knight, *prout* the said deed, which deed we find *in hæc verba:*—"BE IT KNOWN to all men," &c. ; and we find that on the 5th day of September, 1607, the said deed was duly perfected by livery and seizen as is endorsed, *prout* the said deed, which endorsement we find *in hæc verba prout* the indorsement : We find likewise, that the said Con Oneale, by his deed indented, bearing date the last daie of April, in *Anno Domino* 1606, did demise unto Michael White the townes and landes of Ballybredagh and Ballygallwally above mentioned, as by the same deed doth more at large appear, which we find *in hæc verba*, &c. : "THIS INDENTURE made," &c. : And We find that John M'Dowell, Lord of Garthland, and the Lord Vicecount Mountgomerie were witnesses to the said deed, and that the said Michael White entered into the premises the 10th daie of Jime, and he and his assigns have enjoyed the same accordingly : We find also, that after the time of the making of the said deed poll, purporting a feoffment to the said Lord Vicecount Mountgomerie by the said Con Oneale, of the landes in the said deed contayned, and after livery and seizin thereupon, the said Con

Oneale did continually hold possession, enjoie, and retain the profits of all the said landes contained in the said deed, and did make leases for yeares and other conveyances of several parcels of the premises : We find further, that the said deed of feoffment was made upon confidence and trust, that the said Lord Vicecount Mountgomerie should reconvey the said landes and premises unto the said Con Oneale, and the heires maile of his bodie, according to his said articles, bearing date the 24th day of December, *Anno 3d Jac. Reg.* : We further fynd, that the said Con Oneale, by his deed dated the 22nd August, *Anno 4, Jac. Reg.*, duly perfected by liverie and seizin, for the consideration of the sum of £317, expressed in the said deed, and £250 more, in the said deed not expressed, did grant and convey unto the said Lord Vicecount Mountgomerie, by the name of Sir Hugh Mountgomerie, Knight, the said towns and lands of Ballenedulloghan *alias* Ballinedullaghan, Ballinelessan, Balleconoghan *alias* Balleleloghan, Ballebaine *alias* Ballenecarne *alias* Drumbrackly, with their appurtenances, and the woodes and underwoodes, *prout* in the said deed, which we find *in hæc verba:* "THIS INDENTURE," &c. : We fynd further, that Sir Foulke Conway, Knight, being in the possession of the townes and lands of Ballilargemore, Ballenenellan, Balle-Toolconell, and Balle-O'Maltan, with their appurtenances, by virtue and force of an interest of foure scoure and nyneteen yeares, formerlie by him bought from Hugh Mergagh Oneale, that the said Con Oneale, by his deed indented, bearing date the 23rd of Januarie, 1608, did give, grante, bargaine, sell, and confirme unto the said Sir Foulke Conway, Knight, and his heires, the said townes and landes, with all other his landes, tenements, and hereditaments mentioned in the said deed, *prout* in the said deed, which we fynd *in hæe verba :—* "THIS INDENTURE," &c. ; and we fynd the execution of the said deed to be made by livery and seizin, according to the indorsement of said deed : We fynd that the said Con Oneale, with the express consent and advice of the said Lord Vicecount Mountgomerie of the Ardes, did grant unto Colonel David Boyd and his heirs the town and landes of Bally-M'Carritt, and one parcel of land called Stonemore, with their appurtenances, as by his deede, dated the second daie of August, 1609, appeareth, which deed we find *in hæc verba:* "THIS INDENTURE made," &c.; and we fynd the execution of the said deed to be made and executed by livery and seizin, according to the said deed, *prout* the indorsement of the same, which estate of the said Colonel David Boyd came by meane conveyance from the said David Boyd unto James Cathcart, and from him by like meane conveyance is come unto the said Lord Vicecount Claneboy and his heirs : We find also that the said Con Oneale, by his indenture bearing date the 29th daie of December, 1609, did demise and to farme let unto the said Sir Foulke Conway, Knight, the townes and landes of Balledowneconner, Balletyan, and Ballemoney, with the appurtenances, for the term of twenty-one years then next ensuing, and under the yearlie rent of 20s. sterling for each towne, *prout* in the said deed appeareth, which we find *in hæc verba :—* "THIS INDENTURE," &c. : We further fynd, that the said Con Oneale, by his deed bearing date the 13th daie of January (*Anno 7mo, Jac. Reg.*), 1609, did release unto the said Sir Foulke Conway the said yearlie rent reserved upon the said last recyted lease, *prout* in the said release, which we fynd *in hæc verba*, &c. : We further find that the said Con Oneale, by his indenture bearing date the 17th of November, 1615, did give, grant, bargain, sell, and confirme unto the said Sir Foulke Conway, and his heires, the said townes and landes of Ballymony *alias* Lisbary, and Ballydounconor *alias* Ballymytyan, with the rents and reversion of the same put in the said deed, which we find *in hæc verba* : "THIS INDENTURE made," &c; and we find the execution of the said deed by livery and seisin according to the indorsements of the said deed, the said Sir Foulke Conway being then, and at the making of the said deed, in quiet and actual possession of the said premises :   Wee find that the said Lo: Vicecount Mountgomerie, by the name of Sir Hugh Montgomerie, Knt., and the said Con O'Neale, by their Indenture bearing date the 30th of July, *in anno*, 1607, did give, grant, bargaine, sell and enfeoffe Sir George Sexton, Knt., by the name of George Sexton, Esq., the townes and lands of Ballenhattie, *alias* Lary, and Ballemulvally, with the appurtenances in the Sleught-Neiles, in the saide Countie of Downe, *prout* in the said deed, which we find *in hæc verba* : "THIS INDENTURE," &c.; and we fynd that livery and seizin was executed thereupon, the 9th daie of August, *in anno*, 1607, *prout*, the indorcement of the said deed, which we likewise find, &c :   Wee further find that the said Con O'Neale made an Indenture purporting a deed of feoffment, bearing date the 25th day of October, 1608, of the townes and landes of Ballenefeogh, with the appurtenances, to Sir Tho : Hibbots, and his heires, *prout* the said deed, which we find *in hæc verba :—* "THIS INDENTURE," &c., and the execution of the said deed by livery, seisin to be made according to the indorsement of the said deed, *prout*, the said indorsements, which we likewise find : Wee further find, that the said Sir Thomas Hibbots, by his

Indenture, bearing date the 4th day of December, in the eighth yeare of His Majesty's raigne, did lett to farme to Walter Kilman, and Jo : Spenser, the said towne and land of Ballenefeogh, with the appurtenances, for the term of 41 yeares, under certaine rent and covenants in the said Indenture expressed, *prout* the said Indenture, which we find *in hæc verba* : " THIS INDENTURE made," &c. ; and we further find, that the said Kilman and Spenser did assigne over their whole interest and estate unto the said Sir Moyses Hill, Knt., whoe by force thereof did enter into the premises, and the possession thereof continued unto this day : Wee find also, that the said Sir Moyses Hill, after his entry in the premises, did paie the rents reserved upon the said demise, unto the said Sir Tho : Hibbots, until and at the feast of the Annuntiation of our Ladie, one thousand six hundred and twenty : Wee further find, that the said Sir Thomas Hibbots, the 7th day of April, 1619, (*anno, 17mo. Jac. Reg.*), did make an Indenture purportinge a grant of said towne and lands of Ballenefeogh, to him the said Sir Foulke Conway, and his heires, *prout* the said deed, which we find *in hæc verba* : " THIS INDENTURE made," & c : And wee find the execution of the deed *prout* the indorcements of the said deed, &c. ; and wee find that the said Sir Moyses Hill, was at the time of the making of the said deed, and the execution of the same, in possession of the said premises by virtue of the said lease : Wee further find, that the said Lord Vicecount Montgomerie, by the name of Sir Hugh Montgomerie, Knt., in performance of the intent of the said articles of 24th December, 3rd *Jac.*, and the trust of the said deed of feoffment, dated the 14th day of March, in the 3rd year of His Majesty's raigne, made a certaine Indenture, bearing date the 15th day of March, 1601, purporting a gift in tail unto the said Con Oneale, of the towns, lands, and hereditaments, herein specified, excepting the town lands in the exception of the said deed expressed, and under the provisoes of the said deed, which deed we find *in hæc verba* : " THIS INDENTURE," &c. : And we find the execution of the said deed, *prout* the indorsement of the same : And wee further fynd, that the reason of the excepting of eight of the said ten townes in the deed mentioned, was because foure of the said townes excepted were by the former deed of the 22nd of August, *Anno* 4 *Jac. Reg.*, conveyed by the said Con Oneale unto the said Vicecount Montgomerie, discharged of the said trust, and the rest of the said eight townes were either formerlie conveyed by the said Con unto others, or not passed by the Lord Vicecount Claneboye unto Con Oneale : And we further fynd, that the said deed of entayle, made by the said Vicecount Montgomerie unto the said Con Oneale, was made in performance of the trust of the said intended articles of the 24th December, 3*d Jac.*, to the use of the said Con Oneale, and the heires maile of his bodye ; and we doe also find the said Con Oneale accepted of the said deed of entayle, *prout* in the said deed is expressed, and, by his deed bearing date the 15th of Maie, 1616, for the considerations therein expressed, did release unto the said Lord Vicecount Montgomerie, and his heires, all former articles, covenants, and demands whatsoever, *prout* in the said release may appear, which we fynd *in hæc verba* : " Be it known," &c. : Wee further fynd that the said Con Oneale made a lease by deed indented, dated 3rd February, 1611, of Bally-Dunkinmuck, Balle-Tullegoan, and Balle-Crossan aforesaid, unto the Lord Vicecount Mountgomerie for three years, as appeareth by the said lease, which lease we find *in hæc verba* : " THIS INDENTURE," &c., which lease the said Lord Vicecount Mountgomerie obtained from the said Con Oneale, to the intent that Sir Robert M'Clelland, Knight, should have the same : Wee further find, that the said Sir Robert M'Clelland is now in possession of the said landes, but by what tytle we know not : Wee further find, that the said Con Oneale by his deed duly perfected, bearing date the 26th of March, 1612, for the considerations therein expressed, did release to the said Lord Vicecount Mountgomerie, his heires and assignes, all duties, actions, covenants, conditions, and demands whatsoever, *prout* in the same deed, which we find *in hæc verba* : " To all Christian people," &c. : We further finde, that the said Con Oneale, by his like deed of release, duly perfected, bearing date the 20th day of December, 13*th Jac. Reg.*, for the considerations therein expressed, did also release unto the said Lord Vicecount Mountgomerie, his heires and assignes, all duties, actions, covenants, conditions, and demands whatsoever *prout* the said deed, which wee find *in hæc verba* : " To all Christian people," &c. : We further find that the said Con Oneale did make a deed indented, tripartite, between himself on the first part, the Lord Vicecount Claneboie, by the name of Sir James Hamilton, Knight, on the second part, and Sir Moyses Hill, Knight, on the third part, bearing date the 2nd daie of December, 1616, purportinge a grant, bargaine, sale, feoffment, release, and confirmation to the said Lord Vicecount Claneboye and his heires, of the townes and landes of Balle-Carrickroy, and other landes, and also purporting a grant, bargaine, sale, feoffment, release, and confirmation unto the said Sir Moyses Hill, and his heires, of the castle, townes,

l

and landes of Castlereogh, and other landes, and also purportinge a grant, bargaine, and sale, &c., unto the Lord Vicecount Claneboye, and his heirs, of the moytie of the townes, and landes of Balle-Listowdrie, and of divers other landes, and purporting a grant, bargaine, and sale, &c., unto the said Sir Moyses Hill, and his heirs, of the other moytie of the said Balle-Listowdrie, and of the other landes, *prout* in the said deed, which we fynd *in hæc verba*, &c. : We further fynd, that in Michaelmas Tearme in the 15th yeare of the King's Majestie's raigne that now is, the said Sir Moyses Hyll, Knt., by a common recovery by writ of entry *sur desseisin en le post*, did recover against the said Con O'Neall and his heirs, the lands in the said recovery, which we fynd *in hæc verba :* "JAMES," &c. : We fynd that the said Con O'Neale, in the said Michaelmas Term, in the 15th yeare of the King's raigne, did levie a fyne into the said Sir Moyes Hill, and his heirs, of the lands and herditaments in the said fyne mentioned, *prout* in the said fyne, which we find *in hæc verba*, viz. :—"Final's Concordia," &c. : We further fynd, that the said Lo. Vicecount Claneboy, by the name of Sir James Hamilton, Knt., in Trinitie Tearme, 15mo *Jac. Reg.*, did by a common recovery, by writ of entry *sur disseisin in le post*, recover against the said Con O'Neale and his heirs, the landes in the said common recovery mentioned, *prout* in the said recovery, which we fynd *in hæc verba* : We fynd that livery and seizin was executed unto the said Sir Moyses Hill upon the said tripartite Indenture, after the suffering of the said several recoveries, and levying of the said fyne ; We further fynd, that, at the time of the making the said tripartite Indenture betwen the said Con O'Neale, the Lord Vicecount Claneboy, and Sir Moyses Hill, they, the said Con, Lord Vicecount, and Sir Moyses, had notice of the aforesaid estate in tayle conveyed by said Lord Vicécount Mountgomerie unto the said Con aforesaid : And we further find, that the said grant, bargaine, sale, feoffment, release, and confirmation were made without the consent of the said Lord Vicecount Mountgomerie : And we further find, that before the said fyne levyed, and the said severall recoveries suffered, the said Lord Vicecount Mountgomerie delivered unto the Right Honorable Sir Oliver St. John, Knt., then Lord Deputie-General of this realme of Ireland, his Majesty's letters of inhibition or caveat, bearing date at Westminster, the 20th of July, 14th *Jac. Reg.*, (as by the same appeareth, which we find *in hæc verba*, viz. : "Right trusty," &c.,) concerning the Lord Vicecount Mountgomerie's lands and hereditaments, and desired his Lordship to be pleased to make staie of the said fyne and recoveries, untill his Majesty's pleasure were further knowen concerning the premises, and that there was a stay of the said fyne and recoveries unto Sir Moyses Hill, from Trinitie till Michaelmas Tearme then next following : Wee further fynd, that the said Lord Vicecount Claneboye, and Sir Moyses Hill were in possession of the said lands, in the Sleught-Neiles, excepting all such landes as we find by this office to be formerly conveyed away by Con O'Neale, at the time of the said fyne levied and the said recovery suffered, untill which time they were as tenants at will to the said Con O'Neile : Wee further fynd, that the said Lord Vicecount Mountgomerie, within five years next after the said fine levyed, on the 15th daie of Januarie, A.D., 1621, entered into all the landes, tenements, and hereditaments following, viz., Balletullecaman, Edengilnehirk, Balle-Cronell, Ballcromecrevin, Balle-Castlereogh, Balle-M'Conoghie, Balle-Lenoghan, Carrow-Augduff, Carrow-Laveroge, Balletullenecrose, Ballebrawlie, Ballenellan, Ballytulleconell, Ballytyan, Bally-Largimore, Balle-Loughavick, Carrow-Laghchory, Ballycarrickray, Ballecrossan, Ballecrevie, Alickevick, Ballydynan, Carrow-Drumreogh, Ballynebressagh, Ballecarrickmaderoy, Bally-Drumnebeg, Balle-Carnefeagh, Balle-Caricknessassanagh, Ballenelessan, *alias* Tullore, Ballelisdalgan, Levalle, Crevie-Loghgar, Balle-Taunaghwin, *alias* Loghgan, Balle-Tullevestikinagh, Carrow-Dome, Balle-M'Cravinie, Balledrumgivin, Balledyan, Balle-Listowdry, Balle-Lisdownean, and Balleknockan, and made his claime unto the said landes, as well in the name of those landes, as also unto all the rest of the townes and landes whereunto he the said Lo : Vicecount of the Ardes had right unto, in the said Countie of Downe : Wee further find, that the said Lord Vicecount Claneboy, by the name of James Hamilton, Esq., and Con O'Neale, for valuable consideration by their deed, bearing date the 20th of December, 1605, did give, grant, bargaine, and sell unto the said Sir George Sexton, Knt., by the name of George Sexton, Esq., the towne and landes of Balle-Lenoghan and Balle-Tullore, with their appurtenances in the Sleught-Neiles aforesaid, *prout* in the said deed, which we find *in hæc verba :* "THIS INDENTURE made," &c. ; and that the said was sealed and delivered accordingly, and wee find, that the said Sir George Sexton, by his Indenture bearing date the last of July, 1607, did give, grant, bargaine, sell, and enfeoffe the said Lord Vicecount Mountgomerie, and his heires, by the name of Sir Hugh Mountgomerie, and his heires, Knt., the said townes and townelands of Ballelenoghan and Balletulloore, with the appurtenances, *prout* in the said deed, which we find *in hæc verba :*

"This Indenture made," &c.; wee further find, that livery and seisin was made according to the said deed the 28th of August, 1608, *prout* the said indorsement, which we likewise find: Wee finde that the only consideration for the making feoffment of the said town and landes was the said townes and landes of Ballemulvalle, and Balle-Lary, conveyed to the said Sir George as aforesaid, and wee find further, that the said townes of Ballenehaughle, *alias* Balle-Lary, and Ballemilvale, at the time of the conveyance of them unto the said Sir George Sexton, and even before, were in the possession and seisin of the said Con O'Neile, and he was ever reputed the owner and proprietor thereof, and wee find further, that after the making of the said feoffment of Ballelenoghan and Ballytulloore, the said Con O'Neile received the proffits of the same for three yeares, until he conveyed Balle-Lenoghan unto John Hamilton, and his heires: and wee further find, that the said feoffment made to the said Lord Vicecount Mountgomerie, was made upon confidence and trust, and by the appointment of the said Con O'Neale, to be to the use and behoof of the said Con and his heires: and wee further find that the said Con Oneale, on the 3rd day of October, A.D., 1609, did, for valuable consideration, by his deed indented, convey and assure the said lands of Balle-Lenoghan unto the said John Hamilton and his heires, *prout* in the said deed, which we find *in hæc verba*: "This Indenture made," &c.; wee find the execution of the said deed to be made by livery and seisin according to the indorsement of the said deed, and that the said John by virtue thereof, did enter and hath been ever since in possession thereof: Wee further find, that upon a submission of all controversies between the Lord Vicecount Mountgomerie, and the said Lord Vicecount Claneboie, unto the decision and arbitrament of the Right Honble. the Earle of Abercorne, the said Earle, amongst other things, by his arbitrament, dated the 2nd daie of August, 1615, did order for the same towne and landes of Balle-Lenoghan, as followeth, viz.: "Likewise I descerned the said Sir Hugh Mountgomerie to make to the said Sir James, his heires and assignes, sufficient hereditable right and conveyance as the said Sir James his learned councell can devise, of all and whole the equall half or moytie of all and sondrie the landes of Castlereogh and Sleught-Neiles, and of the townes of Ballenegassan and Balle-Lagegoan, in the Sleught-Kellics, and of the equal halfe and moytie of all other landes whatsoever conveyed by the said Sir James to Con Oneale, and by the said Con to the said Sir Hugh and his tenants, lying within the boundes and territory of Castlereogh and Sleught-Neiles, with all immunities and priviledges whatsoever thereto belonging, so that the said Sir James Hamilton must possess the same equal halfe of the said landes of Castlereogh and Sleught-Neiles, and other lands disposed by the said Con to the said Sir Hugh, or presentlie possessed by him or his sub-tenants within the said bounds, in as ample manner as the said Sir Hugh may brooke, and possess the same himselfe by vertue of the conveyance made to him by the said Con, or otherwise howsoever, to be holden by the said Sir James and his aforesaids, of our Sovereign Lord and his successors, as freelie as the said Sir Hugh holdeth the same himselfe, providing alwaies that Sir Hugh shall no waies be oblig [ ] in warrantize of the propertie, but only of the superioritie of the landes conveyed back by t [ ] said Sir Hugh to the said Con Oneale, according to the last conveyance, which is dated the [ ] day of [ ] in the yeare of God [ ] and of [ ] excepted alwaies out of the right and conveyance afforesaid, to be made by the said Sir Hugh to the said Sir James, the townes and townelands underwritten, viz., of Ballyhenoad, Ballegortcrib, Ballebinghon, Ballemylagh past to the said Sir Hugh, Balle-Lenoghan, and Balletulloore, conveyed to Mr. Sexton, Ballehackmoye, Balle-Davie, and Ballegeny excepted to Sir James Hamilton out of the conveyance made by him to Con Oneale, and appertaining to the said Sir James hereditably, BalleKoshoy, conveyed by Con to Thomas Mountgomerie, and the townelands of [ ], disposed of by the late Bishop of Downe to William Dundas, and by him to Sir Hugh, provided the same be found to be Bishoppe's landes, and that the said William had power and right to dispose of the same:" We further find, that Lord Vicecount Claneboy, in performance of the said order and arbitrament made by the said Earle of Abercorne, did make unto the said Lord Vicecount Mountgomerie a deed indented, dated the 3rd of Maie, 1618, purporting, a grant feoffment, and confirmation of the lands, tenements, and hereditaments therein mentioned unto the said Lord Vicecount Montgomerie and his heires, in which deed is, amongst other things, excepted the moietie of all the townes, landes, and hereditaments in Slewght-Neiles, and the townes and landes of Ballyhenoad, Ballebrackan, Ballyncelagh, Ballclenoghan, Balletulloore, Ballerosboy, as by the said deed appeareth, which deed is formerlie found *in hæc verba*: Wee further finde, that of the temporall landes above mentioned, these parcels following, on the 8th daie of December last, were and yet are in the possession of the Lord Vicecount Mountgomerie and his assigns, viz.:

Ballchenoad, Ballegortcrib, Balletulloghbrackan *alias* Ballcknockbrackan, Ballemylagh, Ballyne-money, lying neare Cregevada, BalleM'Glaff, Ballestoker, Balleomeledy, Ballegalloughly, Balletully-copan, Balle-Tuarnenealegie, Balle-Emash, *alias* Enrasse, Ballemackachan, Bally-brealy, Balletulle-garvan, Ballecloghan, Levalle-Aghragie, Levalle-Aghrogie, Levalle-Ravarra, Carow-Edenslatt, Balle-Lisnebarnes, Ballehollencguie, Ballebarnemagher, Balle-Papher, and Balle-Drumreagh, two quar-ters of Ballenecrely, viz., Carow-Lissara one quarter, and Carow-Castlekamy, another quarter of Ballebunden, that part of Balleaghinderagh *alias* Balle-Drumchaie, which is in the possession of the Lord Viccount Mountgomerie's, and Ballemonestragh, the equal halfe of Ballegraffan, Balle-nicrevye, Balle-Richard *alias* Balleregard, Balleganvic *alias* Ncencnie, Balle-Henvie, Balle-Cashlane-vanye, Ballcrogan, Balle-Lisegowne, Balle-M'Grevaghan *alias* Ballemegrevagan, Island-Slesney, Balle-Carigogantelon, Balle-Loghan, the two Balleneskeaghes, Ballekillerned, Carow-Calleduffe, Balle-M'Urllen, Ballecona, Ballenecrosse, Ballenemony, Balle-Carowreogh *alias* Ballenecreaghce, Ballene-creboy *alias* Ballencecrevey, Ballekilcormick, Ballewaster, Ballecopland, Ballekillaghy, Balle-Drum-chey, the halfe towne of Donoghdie, Ballenegrange, Balle-Butler, Ballefrenish, Balleuttagie, Balle-rolly, Balle-M'Creavey, Balle-Cosker, Ballenemony, Balleghrea, Balle-Errea, the half towne of Balle-neganvic, the halfe towne of Ballekilbratten ; and also of and in the moitie or one halfe of all these townes and landes following, viz. :—Ballecowan, Balle-Carne *alias* Drumbrackley, Balleclogher, Balle-nedulloghan, and Ballenehaughlisk, Balle-Downeagh *alias* Ballegonemagh, Ballenelessan, and Levalle-Lisnegnoe, and of the moitie of all the woods and underwoods : And wee further find, that of the temporal landes above mentioned, these townes, villages, and parcels following, on the 8th daie of December last were and yett are in possession of the said Lord Vicecount Claneboy and his assignes, viz. :—Balle-Cregavadie, Balle-Robert, Balle-Davie, Ballengreny, Ballocloghans, Ballechackamus, Carowmullen, Carowneccaine, Carowtagart, Ballenechallen, Ballelisnescra *alias* Ballehugh, Balle-Reaynie, Balle-Dundouell, and Balle-Dunlady, Balle-Carrowreagh *alias* Carowreagh, Carow-Kilne-vagh, Ballcorane, Ballencrany, Balle-Lisbraden, Ballewynnicarwell *alias* Ballemonycarwell, Balle-easlanbeg, Ballebeene, Balleristool, Ballenegrange, Ballenranare *alias* Ballemullere, Balle-Lisleyne, Ballekeile, Ballytullyhulbert, Ballebyn, Ballyglastrum *alias* Balleglasdromen, the halfe towne of Balle-drumaconell, the half towne of Balleaghrogie, Ballelagegoan, Balle-Drumheriff, Balleneglassan, Balle-chigill, Ballemagheicscowe, Ballegowne, Carickmanon, that part of the halfe towne of Aghinderagh, now in the possession of the Lord Vicecount Claneboy, the halfe towne of Ravarra, Ballegiuntneglare *alias* Tulloughcaphynan, the half towne of Ballenecreavey, viz., Carownan and Carowcrevic, the half towne of Killinchie, Balle-Liswyne, the equal moytie or halfe of Ballegrafian, Balleportevogie *alias* Mullogmore, Balleffringe *alias* Megallogh, Ballchalbert, Balle-Aspragh, Balleneglasserogh, Balle-graffan, Rowbane, Rowreagh, Ballefister, Ballegrangegeogh *alias* Coolgrange, Carowaneler, Ballekir-cubin *alias* Kilcooby, Ballemullen, Carownecalliogh, Balle-Carugan *alias* Ballecarvegan, Enniscargie, *alias* Neckellen, Balle-Sumpt, Ballchamlin, Ballekodony, Ballegin *alias* Ballchiggin, Balleobkin *alias* Drumroan, Balle-M'Gowne, Balle-Atwart, Balle-Doune, [   ] Balleferish, Ballytullycarnan *alias* Listyagnew, Templefin *alias* Whitechurch, halfe of Balleganvie, halfe of Ballekibbratten, Ballebredagh, Ballcknockcolumkill, Balle-M'Carrick, Balle-Carickoye, Balle-Crevy-Abickawicke, Balle-Drynan *alias* Balle M'Grynan, Balledrumoieleg, Ballebresagh, *alias* Loghanie, Ballelisdalgan, *alias* Balle-Lisgan, whereof the parcel of land called Taunagh [   ] is a quarter, Ballegalwally, Carowdome, Levalle-Crevie-Loglıgar, Ballemoghlaugh, Balle-Dygen, *alias* Balle-Dyan, Tollevostikinagh, *alias* Tollivastikinoll, and also of and in the one moytie or half of all and singular these townes and lands following, viz., Balle-Dul-loghan, Balle-Icowan, Ballenelassan, Ballenecargie, *alias* Balle-Lisrademan, Ballenecame, *alias* Drum-bccklie, Ballchaughlike, Balle-Clogher, Ball-Downeagh, *alias* Cunnemagh, the halfe of the halfe towne of Lisnegnoe ; and that also, the said Lord Vicecount Claneboy was and is possessed of one moytie of all these townes and landes following, viz., Balle-Drumboe, Balletullenecrosse, Balleblarish, *alias* Temple-Blarish, Ballenecrossan, Ballenegarick, *alias* Ballenecarick, Ballenecarge, *alias* Ballenenoganvie, Ballecarrickmaderoy, Carrickneveagh, Balle-Lisdromloghan, *alias* Lisbane, Ballelogher, *alias* Taun-aghmore, Balle-Caghare, Balle-Caryed, Levalle-Killeny, Ballecrevicorgan, [   ] Listowdrie, Balle-Listowdrie, *alias* Ballenebaine, Drumgivin, *alias* Drumvena, *alias* Drumgevan, [   ] Carnganan, [   ] *alias* Toyduffe, *alias* Hughduffe, Carow-Laverogge, Carow-Edenderry, Balle-Drumbeg, *alias* Ballegrumbeg, Levalle-Tullegowne, Balle-Drumskeagh, *alias* Balleskeaghan, *alias* Balle-Skeaghlatti-fagh, Balledunkinmuck, *alias* Dulloghmucke, Ballchimmeude, *alias* Carow-Tulliard, *alias* Carow-Lis-noad, Ballemuckcravenie, Ballelisnesheran, Balle-Killenure, Carricknesassanagh, Balledownian, *alias*

Balle-Lisdownean, *alias* Lisdoonan, Ballikill, Ballcoghley, *alias* Fairetowne, *alias* Balleneny, Ballenelessan, quarter of Tulloore, Ballencknockan, and Angleshire : and we also find that the Lord Vicecount Claneboy, to be in the like possession of the one moitie or equal halfe of all the woods and underwoods in the territory of the Sleught-Neiles : Wee further find that of the temporall lands above mentioned, these parcells followinge, on the 8th daie of December last, were and yet are in the possession of Sir Foulke Conwaie, Knt., and his assigns, viz., Balle-Largemore, Balleninellan, Balletoolcconnell, *alias* Lissecheckan, Ballemaltan, *alias* Downem-ultrain, *alias* Trecrenan, *alias* Ballecroalie, Balle-Mary, *alias* Lisbany, *alias* Punchoise, *alias* Ballenehawick, *alias* Broghin-Shedran, Balleduncomore, *alias* Ballyan, and Ballenefengh, *alias* Ballenefeigh : wee find likewise, that of the temporall lands above mentioned, these parcels followinge, on the 8th day of December last, were and yet are in the possession of Sir Moyses Hill, Knt., and his assigns, viz., Balle-Castlereogh, Balle-Cronell, Balle-Lisnebrenie, Ballecrosnecrevin, *alias* Ballecrevin, Balle-M'Conkey, the halfe towne of Monyloghy, the quarter towne of Carnemuck, *alias* Crumreagh, Ballecregagie, Balle-M'Carr, *alias* Kilmaneckum, *alias* Cana, *alias* Balle-M'Caher, Balle-M'Crenan, Balle-Clontonkely, Carownecraire, *alias* Carowdrumra, and Carow-Lagecurry : and wee further find, that the said Sir Moyses Hill was likewise possessed of the said moytie or one halfe of all these townes and landes followinge, viz., Balle-Listowdrie, *alias* Ballebanns, Ballenecrevie-Ergan, near Listowdrie, Balledrumgivin, *alias* Drumvena, *alias* Drumnevan, Ballebaryed, *alias* Ballechagard, Balle-Loghar, *alias* Taunaghmore, Balle-Lisdrum-Laghan, *alias* Lisbane, Balle-Carickneveagh, Ballecargavan, Ballecarickmaderoy, Balledrumbo, Balle-Lisnoad, *alias* Tullyard, Balletrymnewd, Carow-Edendery, *alias* Carow-Choine, Balletullenecrosse, Ball-Clarish, *alias* Templeblaris, Ballebrossan, Balle-Lisneshean, Carow-Eduffe, *alias* Carow-Hugh-Duffe, *alias* Tyduffe, Balle-leargie, *alias* Ballyleanick, Carow-Laveroge, Ballehillame, *alias* Levallcanie, Ball-dormiskeagh, *alias* Balleneskeaghan, *alias* Skeagh, late Feagh, Ballydrumbeg, *alias* Ballydrum, *alias* Ballygrumbeg, *alias* Templedrum, Balletullegoan, Balledumkinmuck, *alias* Balledulloghmock, Ballekillenure, Ballemicavin, *alias* Balle-M'Grevan, Caricknessassanagh, Ballewdownean, *alias* Balle-Lisdownean, Balleoghly, Ballenelessan, the quarter of Tulloore, and Balleknockan : and wee find also, that of the temporall lands above mentioned, these parcells following, on the 8th daie of December last, were and yett are in the possession of Sir George Sexton, Knt., and his assignes, viz., Ballenehayte, *alias* Lary, *alias* Hattie-M'Evlevy, and Ballemulvallic, *alias* O'Mullvally : Wee find further, that of the temporall lands abovenamed, these parcells followinge, on the 8th day of December last, were and yett are in the possession of John Hamilton, Esq., and his assignes, viz., Balle-Lenoghan, *alias* Balle-Denimore, and Dowregan, and quarters M'Inespicke, and,Downespicke, parcell of the said lands of Ballelenoghan : Wee find also, that of the temporall landes above mentioned, these parcells followinge, on the 8th daie of December last, were and yet are in the possession of Donell O'Neale, Esq., and his assignes, viz., Balle-Tullecarnan, and Edengilncherick : Wee find further, that of the temporall landes above mentioned, these parcells followinge, on the 8th daie of December last, were and yett are in the possession of Sir Robert M'Clelland, Knt., and his assignes, viz., Balledrumbeg, Balledowneskeagh, Balledunkinmuck, and Balltullegoan : wee find further, that of the temporall lands above mentioned, these parcells followinge, on the 8th daie of December last, were and yet are in the possession of James Cathcart and his'assignes, viz., Bally-M'Carritt, with the ferrie there, Ballerogan, the quarter of Lough-Neromy, Balletullyalton, *alias* Balle-M'Greveigan, Ballealter, and five score acres of land lying on the west side of Scrabo, as tenant at will to the Lord Vicecount of the Ardes : Wee likewise find, that of the temporall lands above mentioned, these parcells followinge, on the 8th daie of December last, were and yett are in the possession of Michael White, Gent., and his assignes : viz., Ballebredagh, and Ballygalwally : Wee also find, that of the said temporall lands above mentioned, these parcells followinge, on the 8th day of December last, were and yett are in the possession of Thomas Mountgomerie, Esq., and his assignes, viz., Ballerosboy : Wee do likewise further find, that of the abbaies, landes, and hereditaments belonging unto the religious house above mentioned, these parcels following, on the 8th daie of December last, were and yett are in the possession of the Lord Vicecount Mountgomerie of the Ardes, and his assignes, viz., the scite, circuit, and precinct of the Gray Abbey, [   ] and all these townes and landes following, as well in spiritualities as in temporalities : viz., the towne and landes of Ballemonestragh, *alias* Cavalle, in the Great Ardes, Balebronie, Ballenestore, Balle [   ] *alias* Ballenellan, Ballennucock, Balleneboyle, The Cardie, Ballenegrange, *alias* Killemanagh, Ballenecholl, Ballemucklie, *alias* Tullemuckley, Ballecaslen, Balleblack, *alias* Ballenepistrough, Carow-tullykeavin, *alias* Tuardon, Carow-Downe, and Carownesker, and the Grange

m

and Rectorie of Tullumgrange, with the tithes of these townes followinge in the territorie of Lecale, belonging to the said abaie, viz., the tithes of the two Tullumgranges, Ballebegg, the two townes of Balle-Edockes, and of Sheeplandbeg, with all and singular the rectories, lands, tithes, and hereditaments and hereditarie profitts whatsoever above mentioned, or belonging to the said abbay, except 1000 acres of land, as they are meared and bounded out by indenture, bearing date the 7th day of September, A.D. 1607, made between the said Lord Vicecount Mountgomerie of the one part, and Colonell David Boyd of the other part ; except also two old towne landes called B.Brely, and part of Ballemonestragh, as the same is bounded by a Scottish contract, bearing date at Cumber, the 15th of August, A.D. 1607, and now in the possession of William Edmonston, Esquire, according to an order of councell table, bearing date 20th of February, 1616 ; except also the townland of Ballymenock [   ] of Hugh Mackessan, heire to John Mackessan, by virtue of a writinge purportinge [   ] from the said Lord Vicecount Mountgomerie to the said Mackessan, bearing date the last [   ] 1607 : Wee likewise further find that the Abbay of Movilla, with the lands and hereditaments belonging to the said Abbay or Religious House of Movilla, on the 8th day of December last, were and yett are in the possession of the Lord Vicecount Mountgomerie of the Ardes, and his assignes, viz., the scite, circuit, and precinct of the said Abbay of Movilla, and all the Rectories, lands, tithes, and hereditaments, as well spiritual as temporal, viz., the townes and landes of Ballinieagh *alias* Movilla, Ballcheine, Balledrumhurke, *alias* Ballegreinhirke, in the Great Ardes, Balle-Allicocke, *alias* Drumchyne, *alias* Ballyalgo, Ballcloghniscowe, Ballewattecock, Ballchawlie, and Ballehest, *alias* Ragherie, *alias* Ballinhalta, and all the tithes of these townes following, viz. : Ballchenrie, *alias* Drumhary, and Balle-M'Grevagan, *alias* Ballegin, lying in the Upper Clandeboy, and also the said several Granges and Rectories following, belonging to the said Abbaie of Movilla, viz. : the Grange or Rectorie of Derry, whereunto belongeth the tithes of these townes following, lying in Little Ardes, viz. : Balledery and Ballecam ; and also the tithes of Ballycranemore, in the Little Ardes, parcel of the said Grange or Rectorie of Rowbane aforesaid ; and also the severall Granges or Rectories of Anaghala, *alias* Killeny, and Drum, in the Lagan, with all the tithes unto them or either of them belonging, except such of the said tithes as are renewing or accruing upon the landes of the said Lord Vicecount Claneboies, and the tithes of Carrickgagantelon, as a mensall belonging to the said Abbaie, together with the whole tithes of the landes of Newton, except the tithes of Lisnevan, which doe belong unto the Pryorie of Newton, all of them in the Great Ardes aforesaid ; and also the tithes belonging to the Chapell of Kiltego, which hath thereunto belonging the tithes of Killemed and Ballerogan, with the advowson and right of patronage of the said Vicaradges of the Rectories of Drum and Killeney : Wee likewise further find, that the said Pryorie of Newton, with these landes and hereditaments belonging to the said Pryorie or Religious House of the Newton, on the said 8th daie of December last, were and yett are in the possession of the Lord Vicecount Montgomerie of the Ardes, and his assignes, viz. : the scite, circuit, and precinct of the said Pryorie of Newton, and the towne and landes of Lisnevan, *alias* Ballenoe, as well in spiritualities as in temporalities, and also these townes and landes following, viz. : Levalle-Tullencrough, Carowcamcoyse, Karow-M'Cloghan, Carow-Crossenemucklie, Binaghmore, Balle-Kilcolman, Ballenebearnes, *alias* Barnes, and Carow-Tullehaggart : Wee likewise find, that of the Black-Abbay these landes and hereditaments following belonging to the said Religious House of Black-Abbay, on the said 8th day of December last, were and yett are in the possession of the Lord Vicecount Mountgomerie of the Ardes, and his assignes, viz.: the scite, circuit, and precinct of the said Abbay, and these townes following, as well in spiritualities as in temporalities, viz.: Ballemonestraduffe, *alias* Ballylisclrane, Ballekilvoigan, *alias* Balleknocke and Ballemanagh ; the impropriate Parsonadge of Donoghdie, and the two third parts of the tithes of the townes and landes following, lying within the parish of Donoghdie, viz. : Balle-M'William, Ballenona, Ballenecrosse, Ballemoyne, Balle-Carowreogh, *alias* Balle-M'Creaghie, Ballevaster, Ballenecreboy, Balle-M'Ceuly, Balle-Copland, Balle-Killaghee, Balle-Kilcormuck, Balledrumchai, and the halfe towne of Donoghdie, : Wee likewise further find, that of the said Abbay these landes and hereditaments following, belonging to the said Abbay of Cumber, on the said 8th day of December, were and yett are in the possession of the Lord Vicecount Mountgomerie and his assignes, viz., the scite, circuit, and precinct of the said Abbay, and the townes following, as well in spiritualities as in temporalities, viz., Ballenemanie, *alias* Ballenevanie, Balle-Altekillegan, Ballegarduffe, *alias* Ballegariff, and Balle-Cumber, *alias* Ballemonestra, and also the tithes of these townes following—Ballestoker, Ballemaglaff, Ballehenood, and Carow-Edenslatt, the impropriate Rectory of Kilimoodmanagh, with the quarter of land called Kilmood, as well in spiritualitie as in temporalitie, and the tithes of Ballelisnebarnes, Balletullnegu, and half of Ballegraffan, and the advowson of the vicarage of the said Rectory of Kilmoodmanagh, the Impropriate Rectory of Balle-M'Kearchim, with the tithes of these townes and landes followinge, viz.: Balle-M'Keaghan, Ballemaledy, Balleolloghlee, Ballecrealie, Ballerush, Balletullecoppan, *alias* Balletumenelaggy : And wee find also, that the said Lord Vicecount Mountgomerie and his assignes, on the said 8th day of December last past, were and yett are in the possession of these severall rectories, impropriate lands, tenements, and hereditaments following, viz., the impropriate Rectory of Ballerichard *alias* Balleregard, with the tithes of these towns following, viz., Ballerichard, Ballerincreame, Balleganvie, Balle-Castlnevarry : And wee find that the said Lord Vicecount of the Ardes now possesseth the said Rectory and tithes of Ballerichard, by demise from Lieftenant Richard West, under a yearly rent, which Lieftenant West is lessee thereof, by demise from the Lady Frances, Countess of Kildare, but what title the said Countess hath wee know not ; and the Rectory of Ballemonestra, together with the town of Ballemonestra, both in spiritualities and temporalities with the appurtenances ; the Rectory of Kilcomucke, with a quarter of land called Carrow-Calliduffe, and the tithes of these towns and lands following, viz., Ballegranegeogh, Ballebutler, Bellefinie, and Balleuttagee in the Great Ardes, and of the two towne lands called Ballehaies, both in spiritualities and temporalities, parcell of the lands of St. John's of Jerusalem, and a quarter of Carrow-Nathan, both in spiritualities and temporallities, and likewise a quarter of land, called Carrownemucke, both in spiritualities and temporalities, and the advowson of the Rectory of Ballekelly, and also so much of the tithes of the Rectorie of Tanaughwine as is not acrewing out of the lands of the said Lord Vicecount Claneboye, which is excepted reserved unto him : and also the tithes of all the fish taken and landed between the meire of Iniscargie, and the river of the Cumber [   ] [   ] impropriate Rectorie of Ballclaghan *alias* Balleurkegan in Lecale, parcell of the possession of the said Abbaie of Bangor, whereunto the tithes of these towns following doe belong, viz. :—Balleurkegan, and Corballie, and also of the advowsons of the severall vicaradges in all the churches aforesaid|: Wee likewise find the said Lord Vicecount Claneboy, and his assigns, to be in like possession of the said late dissolved Pryorie or Religious House of Holliwood ; and of the scite, circuit, and precinct of the same, and also of all these towns and lands following :—Ballekeile, *alias* Ballekegill, Ballemanack, *alias* Ballemanagh, Ballecultrack, *alias* Ballecultra, *alias* Ballacktraghagh, Ballinderry, *alias* Balliderry, and Baller-Knocknegony, *alias* Balleknocknegony : We likewise find the said Lord Vicecount Claneboy, and his assigns, to be in like possession of the said impropriate Rectorie of Balleorane, Nerany, Winnecarwell, and Lisbraden, in the territory of Slewht-Hubricks : Wee find likewise the said Lord Vicecount Claneboy, and his assignes, on the said 8th day of December last past, to be in like possession of the Rectorie of Kilcooby, *alias* Kircubin, and the tithes of these towns following, thereunto belonging, viz. :— the tithes of Kilcooby, *alias* Kircubin, and Ballemullen, in the territory of the Great Ardes : Wee likewise find the said Lord Vicecount Claneboy, and his assignes, on the said 8th day of December last past, to be in like possession of said Rectory of Coolgrange, and the tithes of the said towne and lands of Coolgrange, *alias* Grange, in the Great Ardes neare Blackstaffe, and also of a d in the tithes of the towne and lands of Ravarra, Carrowreogh, and Ballecloghan, lying in or neare t e plaines of Belfast, and of Rowbane, Rowreagh in the Great Ardes, and of the impropriate Rectorie of Drumroan, which hath the tithes of the townes of Drumroan and Ballyhiggin, in the Great Ardes : Wee likewise further find, that the said Lord Vicecount Claneboy, and his assignes, on the said 8th daie of December last past, were and yet are in like possession of these rectories, towns, lands, tithes, and hereditaments, parcell of the said late dissolved Abbay or Religious House of the Cumber following : viz., Ballenegatug, Carrownesuir, Ballecullentry, and Ballenicile, as well in spiritualities as temporalities, and of the tithes of these towns and landes following, viz., Balleristoll, Ballegrangeogh, Balle-Lisneyne, Ballekeil, Ballemenere, Balletullehulbert, Ballemoughlagh, Ballechigill, Balledrumsheriffe, half Ballegraffan, Ballebein, Ballemagheriscowe, and Ballegowne, and of so much of the tithes belonging to the said impropriate Rectorie of Taunaghwin as doe or shall acrewe or grow out of anie of the townes, lands, and other hereditaments of the said Lord Vicecount Claneboy ; and also all the tithes of the fish taken and landed upon the south side of the river of Cumber, so far as the said Lord Vicecount Claneboye his lands extend, and of so much of the tithes of Kilanie and Drum, in the Laggan, as shall acrewe out of any the townes lands, and other hereditaments of the said Lord Vicecount Claneboy : Wee also find the said Lord Vicecount Claneboy, and his assigns, to be in the like possession of the towns and lands following, in the Great Ardes, as well in spiritualities as in temporalites, viz. :—the town of Ballewalter, parcell of the possession of the Gray Abbie aforesaid, the quarter land called St. John's Quarter, in Canvie, one other quarter of land called Carow-Cloghgor, in the Parish of Whitechurch, a quarter of land called Carownemoan, in the Parish of Talbotstown, one other quarter of land called Carow-John-Boistie, in the town of Drumroan aforesaid, one other quarter of land called St. John's Quarter, in Killyvolgan, in the Great Ardes: And we also find, that the said Lord Vicecount Claneboy, and his assigns, on the said 8th day of December last past, were and yett are in the possession of all and singular the said Rectories impropriate following, parcell of the possession of Black Abbay, in the Great Ardes, and of and in the impropriate Rectory of Ballehalbert, to which belongeth two-thirdes partes of the tithes of the towns of Balleuspragh, Ballehalbert, Balle-Richard, Balleportevogie, *alias* Mulloghmore, Balleneffringe, *alias* Negallogh, Balleglasserogh, Ballegraffan, Ballehamlin, and Ballerodony, and of and in the impropriate Rectory of Whitechurch, *alias* Templefin, to which belongeth two third partes of the tithes of the two townes of Ballecobikin, Balle-M'Gowne, Balleatwart, Balle-Terish, Balledownen, Templefin, *alias* Whitechurch, Listiagnen, Balle-Canvy, and Kilbratan in the Great Ardes, and also of and in the impropriate Rectory of Iniscargie, to which belongeth two third partes of the tithes of the towns of Ballelimpt, Ballegarngan, Ballefister, Carrow-neskra, and Carrownecalliogh, Iniscargie, *alias* Nikillen: And wee find alsoe, the said Lord Viscount Claneboy to be in the like possession of the advowson and right of patronage of the severall vicaradges in the said severall Churches of Ballehalbert, *alias* Talbotstowne, Templefin, *alias* Whitechurch, and Inniscargie, and also of and in the tithes of all sorts of fish whatsoever taken and landed upon all the coastes along the lands of the said Lord Vicecount Claneboy in the Great Ardes, as well upon Loghcoyne side as upon the main sea: And wee [   ] in the like possession of and in the [   ]: And wee likewise find, that the said Sir Henrie Peirse, Knt., and his assignes, on the said 8th day of December last past, were and yett are possessed of the said Manor or Preceptorie of St.-John's-towne, in the Ardes, with the appurtenances, and of and in the townes and lands followinge, as well in spiritualities as in temporalities, viz., Castleboy, *alias* Johns-towne, Dromarden, Ballecaddany, Ballenicoll, *alias* Tullecarnan, *alias* Loughduffe, the halfe towne of Clogher, and the halfe towne of Tullecreman, and of and in the Rectory of Balletrosnon, as well in spiritualities as in temporalities, with the two third partes of the tithes of these towns following, viz. :—Ballytulleboord, Ballefenore, Ballebrand, Ballegrangan, Ballecarne, Balleanough, Ballyfoneragh, the half-town of Cloghargie, the half-towne of Drumtayle, *alias* Loughduffe, free and exempted from all exactions, cesse, and all other charges, as the same is found by an office taken at Ballehacamur, on the last daie of September, in A.D. 1512, and of one weekly market, to be holden every Saturdaie at Castleboy, *alias* St. Johnstowne, and one faire every year upon the feast of St. John Baptist, commonly called Midsomer daie, and two daies then next following, with a court of pie-powder, and the tolls, proffits, customs, and perquisites of the same, and court baron, and court leet, and view of frankpledge, with felons' goodes, waifes, strays, &c., as the same is found by the said office taken at Ballehackamur aforesaid, all which last recited manors and premises with the appurtenances are now held and enjoyed by William Hamilton, Esq., as lessee for yeares to the said Sir Henry Peirse.

Wee further find, that Rowland White, sonne to Sir Patrick White, late of Flemyngton, in the County of Meath, Knt., Second Baron of his Majesty's Exchequer of Ireland, was seized in his demeasne as of fee, of and in the Manor and Castle of Renchaddy, *alias* Renogaddy, and Killileagh, with the appurtenances, and of and in all the manors, castles, townes, villadges, messuadges, lands, tenements, rents, reversions, and services, waters, loghs, pooles, ilands, fishings, and advowson of the churches, and of all homadges and services of free tenants, and all royalties, with other hereditaments whatsoever, with all and singular their rights, members, and appurtenances, within the territorie or countrie called the Duffrin, *alias* Duffrins, or the lordship of the same, within the said Countie of Down, in the province of Ulster, which said territorie doth contain these towns and hamlets following, viz.; Ballinemona, Balleholleken, Ballemullagh, Corbally, the castle and towne of Ballecaslan-William, Ballenecabry, the towne and castle of Killileagh, Tulloghin-Martin, Balle-Rathconevan, Ballemacorboll, the castle and towne of Rinduffrin, otherwise called Meylerton, Balleomerran, Ballynecarran, the castle and town of Rathgorman, Ballckiltinegan, Carrickrouske, Ballinchey, Ballowe, Ballemacoshen, Ballemackirelly, Balleogullone, Ballebregagh, Ballyleggan, Bally-Lisduffe, Ballecoye, Ballycley, *alias* Clegh, Balledromore, Ballecoskrigan, Castlegaly, Lisonagh, Balletoagh, *alias* Toy, Ballygavan, Balleroyan, the castle and town of Casclannegayse, Ballyleggan, Ballemullin, Ballyholliard, Ardagone, Ballyboynemery, *alias* Tollymery, Balletrim, Ballircogh, Ballecoolly, Rathkirin, Balleconety, *alias* Cloney, Ballecargagh, Tullyconysh *alias* Knoise, Ballykillchannan, and Ballcherman, with the appurtenances ; and also of and in divers ilands in Loghcoyne, viz.: the Iland of Renechady, and Ranny's, Polle Iland, Red-Isle, Conlegh-Island, Much-Isle, otherwise called Ilandmore, Dunshagh-Iland, Inis-M'Tegart, Inish-Dowran, and Iland-Darragh, with the appurtenances ; and of and in certain advowsons, nominations, presentations, and rights of patronage of the Churches or Rectories, viz., of the Rectorie of Killinchene-Maghery, of the Rectorie of Renchaddy, of the Rectory of Killaureys, of the Rectory of Killileagh, with all and singular the rights, members, and appurtenances ; and the said Rowland White, being thereof so seized, and in actuall possession, Patrick White, late of Flemington, in the Countie of Meath, Gent., sonne and heire of Nicholas White deceased, son and heire of the said Sir Patrick White, by his deed in writing, in due form of law executed, and in evidence produced, bearing date the 23rd daie of Maie, in the 8th year of the raigne of our said late Soveraigne Ladie Elizabeth, did remise and release unto the said Rowland White, all his whole right, title, and interest of and in all and singular the said premises, and every parcell thereof ; and that, likewise, John White, late of Ballergin, within the Countie of Louth, Gent., by his deed in writing, in due form of law executed, and in evidence likewise produced, bearing date the 23rd daie of April, in the said 8th year of the raigne of the late Queen Elizabeth, did remise and release unto the said Rowland White, being [　　　　　　　] of April, 1603, enfeoffe [

　　　　　　　　　　　　　　　　　　　　　　　　　　] Magh-

more, by force whereof the said Patrick M'Nabb was seized [

　　　　　　　　　　　　　　　] Cressecan, of and in the said half towne of Maghmore, and that they, the said Patrick M'Cressecan and Patrick M'Nabb, being so seized of the said half town of Maghmore as aforesaid, they the said Patrick and Patrick, by their deed, bearing date the 12th daie of November, in the 20th year of His Majesty's raigne that now is, for valuable consideration, did enfeoffe the said Lord Viscount Claneboy of and in the said halfe townland of Maghmore *alias* Craigdowe, to hold to him and his heirs for ever, by force whereof the said Lord Viscount Claneboy did enter, and was and yet is seized of the said halfe towneland of Maghmore to him and his heirs for ever : We find further, that the said John White, at the Courts in Dublin, before Sir William Weston, Knight, and William Bath, Esq., then Justices of our said late Soveraigne Ladie Elizabeth, of Her Highness's Court of Common Pleas in this realme of Ireland, and others Her Majesty's good and faithfull subjects, did levie and acknowledge a fyne of all and singular the said premises, with the appurtenances, unto one Walter Dalton, and his heirs for ever, by the name of 7 castles, 200 messuages, 200 tofts, 3 water-mylls, 100 gardens, 7,040 acres of land, 200 acres of meadowe, 1,500 acres of pasture, 1,000 acres of underwood, 1,000 acres of moor, and 12 weires and fishing places, with the appurtenances, in Ballenemona, Ballehollcken, Ballemullagh, Corbally, Ballecaslanwilliam, Ballenecabry, Killaleagh, Tolloghmore-Martin, Balle-Rathconevan, Balle-Maccorbel, Rindoffrin, *alias* Meylerton, Balleomeran, Balleneccarran, Rathgorman, Ballekiltinegan, Carrickruske, Ballinchey, Balow, Ballimecoshen, Ballemackirrelly, Ballcogullone, *alias* Balle-Augullen, Ballebregagh, Balle-Leggen, Balle-Lishduffe, Ballecoy, Ballecley, *alias* Balleclegh, Balledrommore, Ballecosskrigan, Castlegaley, Lissonagh, Balletoagh *alias* Balletoy, Ballegavan *alias* Scatterick, Ballcroyen, Casselannegayse, Ballcleggan, Ballemullin, Balleholliard, Ardagone, Balleboynemery *alias* Tollymery, Ballitrim, Ballerogh, Ballecoolly, Rathkirin, Balleconety *alias* Cloney, Ballecaragagh, Tollyconysh *alias* Knoise, Ballekilchanan, Balleherman, Renechaddy, Kilaureas, Killinchie, Inis-M'Tegart, I————, Iland-More, Iland-Dunshagh, Inish-Dowran, Iland-Darragh, Iland-Conlie, Iland-Rinhaddie, and the advowson of the Churches of Killileagh, Killaureas, Renechadie, and Killinchie, in the said County of Down ; and that the said Walter Dalton, by the same fyne, did grant and render the premises to the said John White and his heirs ; and we likewise find, that the said John White, of all and singular the rest of the said manors, lordshipps, and premisses of the Duffrius, not conveyed to the said John M'Cressecan as aforesaid, was seized in his demesne as of fee, and thereof being so seized as aforesaid, he the said John White, and Nicholas White his sonne and heire, together with John Allen, of St. Woolston's, in the Countie of Killdare, Esq,, and James White, of Drogheda, Alderman, surviving feoffees of the said John White, for a good valuable consideration, by their deed of seoffment, in due form of law executed, bearing date the 1st daie of July, in the 8th yeare of His Majesty's raigne, of all and singular the said premises did enfeoffe the said Lord Viscount Claneboy and his heirs for ever, to the use of the said Lord Vicecount and his heirs for ever, by vertue of which said feoffment the said Lord Vicecount into all and singular the said premises did enter, and on the said 8th daie of December last, was and yett is in possession of all and singular the said premises, with the appurtenances, and then and yett taketh and receiveth the rents, issues, and proffitts thereof : We find further, that said John White died, and that in the tearme of St. Michaell, on the Octave of St. Martin of the said tearme, in the 20th year of His Majesty's said raigne that now is, of England, France, and Ireland, the said Nicholas White, at the King's Courts in Dublin, before Sir Dominick Sarcefield, Knight and Bart., Gerald Lowther, and John Philpott, Esqrs., and others, His Majesty's good and faithful subjects, did levie and acknowledge a fyne of all and singular the said premises, with the appurtenances, unto the said Lord Vicecount Claneboy and his heirs for ever, by the name of the manors of Killileagh and Ringhaddy, with the appurtenances, and of 10 castles, 1,000 messuages, 1,600 cottages, 200 tofts, 10 watermills, 1,000 gardens, 15,000 acres of arable land, 1,000 acres of meadow, 4,000 acres of pasture, 10,000 acres of wood, 1,000 acres of moor, 1,000 acres of heath and furze, three [   ] with the appurtenance in Ballemona [

                                                    ] and his heires remysed and [   ]
and his heires for ever ; and further, the said Nicholas White covenanted for him and for his heires, that they should warrant the manors, castles, tenements, fishings, and advowsons, with the appurtenances, to the aforesaid James Lord Vicecount Claneboy, his heires and assigns, against the said Nicholas, his heirs and assigns, for ever, by virtue whereof the said James Lord Vicecount Claneboy is seized in his demesne as of fee, of all and singular the said premises, with the appurtenances as aforesaid : And we further find, that all and singular the said manors, castles, landes, tenements, and hereditaments of the said territory or countrie of the Duffrin, then were and are holden of our Soveraigne the King's Majesty, in free and common soccage, as of His Highness's Castle of Carrickfergus, and by the rent of 6s. 8d. sterling, for all other services : And further, we find that there doth belong to the Rectorie of the parish of Killinchie-Nemaghrie, in the said Duffrin, the tithes of the townes following, in the Upper Clanneboy, viz., Carickman, Drumcreagh, Raffry, Killinchie-Nekelly, Ravarra, Ballencloghan, Levalle-Gowne, and Levalle-Achinderra *alias* Drumchaie : And wee further find that the Lord Cromwell claimeth the town and land of Balle-Clontogh, as supposed to be passed unto him from His Majesty, and that his right, if any he hath, may be saved unto him : And wee further find, that the said Frances, Countesse of Kildare, claimeth the Rectorie and tithes of Clontogh, in the Duffrin, and that her right, if anie she hath, maie be saved unto her.

Wee find further that Robert Hemstowe, late Lord Bishop of Down and Conor, was seized in his demeasne as of fee, in the right of his Bushoprick of Down, of and in all that territorie, precinct, scope or extent of land comonlie called the Lordship or Manor of Ballindrin *alias* Iland Maghee, and of and in the towne and land following, viz., Ballecaslanespick, Balleliddell *alias* Balleglegony, Ballelisbane, Ballemartin *alias* Ballemartinagh, Ballegavegan, Ballekeneneile, situate lying and being in the Upper Clandeboy, in the County of Downe, with all the rights, members, and appurtenances to the same belonging or appertaining, together with the Ilands called the Castle Iland, Iland Reagh, Iland Rawlie, Iland-Magneish, in the county of Downe aforesaid, and all and singular the manors, castles, lands, messuages, buildings, orchards, gardens, townes, villages, hamlets, lands, tenements, meadows, pastures, feedings, commons, demeasnes, heathes, furzes, moors, marshes, woods, underwoods, tithes of corne, graine, hay, wool, slyie, hempe, flax, lambes, and all other tithes whatsoever, as well great as small, and also all offerings, obventions, fruites, profitts, fishings, suites-court, warrens, myneralls, quarries, rents, reversions, and services, rents-charge, rents-seck, and the rents and services as well of the free and customerie tenants, work of tenants farmes, wards, marriages, goods of felons, and outlaws, escheates, releises, courts-leet, courts-baron, view of frankpledge, and the profitts, perquisites, and commodoties thereof, faires and markets, customs, rights, jurisdictions, authorities, presentments, advantages, emoluments, and hereditaments whatsoever, as well spirituall as temporall, to the said Iland-Maghee, or to any of the premises before recited, or to any part or parcell thereof any waies belonging, appertaining,

───────────────────────────

b See an earlier Inquisition relating to the Dufferin, taken on the 4th of July, 1605, at p. 58, *ante.*

incident, or appendant, or which hath been at anie time heretofore accepted, reputed, or knowne, held, occupied, used, or enjoyed as part, member, or parcell of the said Iland-Maghee, or of any of the premises, or of anie part or parcell thereof, being parcell of the lands and possessions belonging to the said Bishop of Downe and Conor : We further find, that the aforesaid Robert, Bishop of Downe and Conor, being so seized, and in actual possession of all and singular the premises, and every part and parcell thereof, of such an estate as aforesaid, by his deed indented, duelie perfected, and executed by liverie and seizen, and to us the jurie shewed in evidence, bearing date the 9th daie of July, 1606, and in the 4th yeare of the raigne of our Soveraigne Lord, King James that now is, of England, France, and Ireland, and of Scotland the nyne and thirtieth, for and in the consideration of the sume of £100 sterling, curant monie of and in England, in hand paid to him the said Lord Bishope, before the en-sealing thereof by Sir Henrie Peirse, and Francis Annesley, by the name of Henrie Peirse, and Francis Annesley, of Dublin, Gent., all and singular the premises with the appurtenances, to have and to hold unto the said Sir Henrie Peirse, and Francis Annesley, their heirs and assigns for evermore, yielding and paying yearlie for the same, unto the said Robert, Lord Bishope of Downe and Conor, and to his successors, Bishops of Downe aforesaid, the sum of £6 16s. 4d., at the feast of St. Michaell the Archangell, or within six weeks after the said feast, yearlie, by vertue whereof the said Sir Henrie Peirse, and Sir Francis Annesley, were of the said premises seized in their demeasne as of fee : We find further, that the said premises are holden of our Soveraigne Lord the King, in soccage *in capite*, and by what rent we know not : And we further find, that the said Sir Henrie Peirse, and Sir Francis Annesley, being by vertue of the said Indenture seized jointly to them and their heirs, John Christain, Archdeacon of the Cathedrall Church of Downe, Robert Maxwell, Archdeacon of Conore, and the clergie of both the [   ] deed sealed with their seales perfected in [

                     ] woods, underwoods, tithes of corne, [   ] as well great as small, as all offerings, oblations, obventions, fruites, profitts, [   ] mineralls, quarries, rents, reversions, and services, rents-charge, rents-seck, and the rents and services as well of the free as customarie tenants' farmes, wardes, marriages, goods of felons, and outlaws, escheates, reliefs, courts-leet, courts-baron, view of frankpledge, and the profitts, perquisites, and commodoties thereof, faires, markets, customs, rights, jurisdictione, authorities, prcheminences, advantages, emoluments, and hereditaments whatsoever, the spirituall jurisdiction only reserved to the said Bishop, and his successors and officers, to the said Iland-Maghee, or to any of the premises before recyted, or to any part or parcell thereof in anie wise belonging or appertaining, or incedent, or appendant, or which hath at anie time heretofore been accepted, reputed, or knowne as part, parcell, or member of the said Iland of Maghee, and of anie of the premises before mentioned, or of anie part or anie parcell thereof, beinge parcell of the lands and possessions belonging to the Bishop of Downe : To have, hold, occupie, possesse, and enjoy all and singular the said Iland, manors castles, messuages, tenements, and hereditaments, and all other the premises and every part and parcell thereof, with their appurtenances, by what other name or additions of names these or anie of them have beene theretofore reputed, called, knowne, or taken, unto the said Hugh Collane, and Anthonie Peirse, their executors, administrators, and assigns, for and during the full tearme and tyme of 3 score yeares, and immediatlie ensuing the date of these presents, fullie to be complete and ended : yielding and paying, therefore, yearlie unto the said Robert, now Lord Bishop of Downe and Conor, and his successors, Bishops of Downe, the yearlie rent of £30 sterling, good and lawful monie of and in England, at the feast of All Saints, being the first daie of November, and of Phillip and Jacob, commonlie called Maie Daie, by even and equall portions, by virtue and form of which Indenture the said Hugh Collane, and Anthonie Peirse, were possessed of all and singular the premises with their appurtenances to the use of the said Sir Henrie Peirse, Bart., the said Hugh Collane, and Anthonie Peirse at his request, by Indenture bearing date, the 20th daie of December, 1622, and in the 12th year of his Majestie's raigne of England, France, and Ireland, did give, grant, assigne, sett over, and confirme unto William Hamilton, of Ballemcaghan, in the Countie of Downe, Esq., and John Keneday, of the Citie of Dublin, Esq., all and singular the premises, and everie part and parcell thereof, with the appurtenances : To have, and to hold unto him the said William Hamilton, and John Keneday, theire and every of theire executors, administrators, and assigns, for and during all the residue of the tearme of 3 score years yet to come and unexpired, upon confidence and trust to the use and behoofe of the said Lord Vicecount Claneboy, by vertue of which deed they the said William

Hamilton, and John Keneday, are now possessed of all and singular the premises with the appurtenances accordinglie.[e]

And we find further, that all the abbaies, priories, and other the spirituall landes, tenements, and hereditaments above mentioned, were and are holden of our said Soveraigne Lord, King James that now is, by such rents, tenures, and services, as are specified and expressed in the said severall letters patent, bearing date the 20th of July, 3 *Jac. Reg.;* yet, neverthelesse, we find that by agreement between the said Viscecount Mountgomerie, and the Lord Viscecount Claneboy and others, the said rents and services are now answered and paid unto his Majesty by particular parties as followeth, viz. : Out of the said Abbaie of Movilla, with the lands, tenements, and hereditaments thereto belonging, now in the possession of the said Lord Viscecount of the Ardes as aforesaid, there is now answered and paid by him to His Majesty, the yearlic rent of £3 3s. 4d. sterling, to be paid as in the said letters patente of the 14th February, 3d *Jac.,* is reserved : Out of the Monasterie or Religious House of the Black Abbay aforesaid, with the lands, tenements, and hereditaments thereunto belonging : There is likewise answered and paid by the said Lord Viscecount Montgomerie the yearly rent of £1 3s. 4d. sterling, to be paid, *ut supra,* out of the said late Religious House of Gray Abbay, with the lands, tenements, and hereditaments thereunto belonging, and now in the possession of the said Lord Viscecount of the Ardes : There is by him answered and paid to His Majestie the yearlie rent of 40s. sterling, to be paid, *ut supra,* out of the said late dissolved Priorie of the Newton aforesaid, now in possession of the said Lord Viscecount of the Ardes : Wee find there is answered and paid by him to His Majesty the yearly rent of 13s. 4d. sterling, to be paid *ut supra,* out of so much of the lands, tenements, and hereditaments of the late dissolved Abbey or Religious House of the Cumber aforesaid, before mentioned and expressed to be in the possession of the said Lord Viscecount of the Ardes : We find there is answered and by him paid unto His Majestie, the yearly rent of 21s., to be paid as aforesaid, which is the one moyetie of the whole rent reserved to be paid for the said Abbay of the Cumber, of those parcells of the lands, tenements, and hereditaments of the before mentioned premises, belonging unto the said late Religious House of St. John's of Jerusalem, granted at the rent of 11s. sterling as aforesaid, and formerlie found to be in the possession of the said Lord Viscecount of the Ardes : We find there is answered and paid unto his Majesty by the said Lord Viscecount of the Ardes, for so much as is in his possession as aforesaid, the yearly rent of 5s. 6d. sterling, being likewise the one moiety of the said rent, and out of the Rectorie of Kilcolmuck aforesaid, possessed by the said [   ] by him unto his Majestie for the same, [   ]
deed indented, dated 17th [
                                                                  ] sterling, at Michaelmas and Easter, or within fortie days after, and two able horsemen [   ] and six footmen, armed and furnished for the wars, to be found to attend, *ut supra :* Out of the said landes, conveyed by the said Lord Viscecount Clane-

---

[e] The following Inquisition respecting the townland of Ballymartin, parcel of the manor of Ballydreene, or Islandmaghie, was taken in the year 1617 :—" COUNTY OF DOWN.—*Tullonikill, 18th October, 15th year, James 1st.*—The townland of Ballymartin, *alias* Ballymartynagh, is, and anciently hath been, parcell of the manor of Ballydreene, *alias* Islandmaghie, and the said manor is the ancient inheritance of the Bishop of Downe.—[   ] Merryman, late Bishop of Downe, was seised of the said manor of Ballydreene, in right of his said Bishoprick, and was also seised, as of fee, of the towneland of Ballymartyn, as part of the said manor.—The sept or family called Slut M'Henry Keyes, did lately expulse and disseize the late bishop out of the whole manor aforesaid, in tyme of warre and rehellion.—One Rowland Savage, of Ballygalgett, some tyme entered upon and possessed the said manor of Ballydreene, *alias* Islandmaghie, as tenant or farmer to the then Bishop of Downe, and did also hold the towneland of Ballymartin, *alias* Ballymartynagh, and did pay for the said lands, yearly, the rent of £4, for the space of three years together, to one Rob. Humston, late Bishop of Downe, and did also give to the said Bishop a horse valued at £20, for and in the name of a fine or income for a lease of the said lands, for three years.—The tenants and farmers of the now or late Bishop of Downe, were and did contynue in the quiet possession of the said towneland of Ballymartyn, *alias* Ballymartynagh, as parcell of the said manor, untill Sir Hugh Montgomery, Knt., did, about nine yeares now past, disseize them from and out of the same.—There are no rents, duties, customs, or services due to the King out of the said manor of Ballidreene, or out of any lands thereunto belonging.—The river or brooke called the Mill-water, in the said county, is the knowne meare or bounds between the said towneland of Ballymartyn, and the towne or lands of Ballycargaherusky, parcell of the territorie of the Duffrens, and the saide river extendeth to the townland of Ballymonastragh, parcell of the land of said Sir Hugh Montgomery. The meare and bounds aforesaid beginn at the said river within the woods, by a knowne ould ditch which extendeth to a plain hill called Dromseagh, leaving most of the said hill within the towneland of Ballymartyn,[   ], and extendeth through the said playne hill by an ancient stone ditch, and thence goeth along the said ditch through the wood westward, into a deep valley, leading the said meare or bounds to the south end of a lough called Lough-nacargabaso, leaving the hill called Mullaghgibbagh, within the aforesaid Ballymartyn and Ballymonastragh. The meares between the town of Ballyglegory, parcell of the manor of Ballindreene, appertaining to the said bishop, and of Lisbarnan, being the lands of the said Sir Hugh Montgomery, have bene troden, beginning on the side of the lands of Lisnefynene, along a hedge to a little house wherein Donell M'Phidian, a Scotishman, dwelleth, leaving the house of the said Donell in Ballyglegory, and the haggard of the said Donell in Lisbarnan, and so goeth to a gray high stone, and from thence to an ould staked hedge, which meareth along to a little rock or hill called the Hill of Controversy."—*Inq. of Ulster, Rec. Com.*

boie unto the said Sir Foulk Conway, by deed indented, dated the 7th daie of November, *Anno 3d Jac. Reg.*, there is answered to His Majesty the rent of £8 18s. sterling at Michaelmas and Easter, or within fortie days after, and 2 able horsemen and 4 footmen, armed and furnished for the wars, yearlie to be bound to attend and serve *ut supra:* Out of the landes conveyed by the said Lord Viccount Montgomerie and Con O'Neale unto Sir George Sexton, Knight, by indenture dated the 30th of Julie, A.D. 1607, *anno, 5mo. Jac. Reg.*, there is answered to His Majesry the rent of 18s. 8d. sterling, at Michaelmas and Easter, or within thirty days after : Out of the foure townes, viz., Ballegartgarie, Ballincomrise, Balleviolan, and Balleshangill, conveyed to Sir Hercules Langford, by deed indented, bearing date [   ] there is answered by the said Sir Hercules to His Majestie the rent of 16s. 8d. sterling : And that all the rest of the lands, tenements, and hereditaments aforesaid, mentioned and expressed to be in the possession of the said Lord Viccount Claneboye and his assigns, as well spirituall as temporall (excepted the temporall landes in the Slewght-Neiles, the Abbay of Bangor, and Rectories of Ballegalget and Grange-Owter, and Priorie) are held by the said Lord Viccount Claneboy, of His Majesty as of his Castle of Carrickfergus, in free and common soccage, and by the yearlie rent of £70 sterling, by him to be paid at Michaelmas and Easter as aforesaid, and further to find and maintain at his own costs and charges, out of his part of the said countrie or territorie of the Upper Clandeboye and Grent Ardes, foure good and able horsemen, and seven footmen, well instructed and armed, yearlie to attend and serve the Lord Lieftenant or Deputie General of Ireland, by the space of fortie daies, when the said Lord Lieftenant or Deputie General shall make a general journey or hosting, in his owne person, in the province of Ulster, as appeareth by the said letters patente, dated the 2nd daie of Maie, in the 18th year of His Majestie's said raigne : And we find further, that the Abbay of Bangor, and all the landes, tenements, and hereditaments thereunto belonging, are holden by the said Lord Viccount Claneboie of our said Soveraigne Lord the Kinge, as of his Castle of Dublin, in free and common soccage, and by the yearly rent of £8 sterling, to be by him paid at Easter and Michaelmas, by equall portions as aforesaid : And we further fynd, that the said Priorie of Holliwood, with all the lands, tenements, and hereditaments thereunto, are likewise holden by the said Lord Viccount Claneboy of our said Soveraigne the King's Majestie, as of his said Castle of Dublin, in free and common soccage, at the yearly rent of £10 6s. 8d. sterling, to be paid by him *ut supra:* And wee further find, that the said Preceptorie or Manor of St. Johnston, with the appurtenances, and all the lands, tenements, and hereditaments thereunto belonging, in the possession of the said Sir Henry Peirse, and his assignes, are holden of His Majestie, as of His Highness's Castle of Dublin, in free and common soccage, and by the yearlie rent of £3 6s. 8d. sterling, to be paid by him *ut supra:* And we further find, that the said Rectorie of Ballegalgat, with the appurtenances, in the Little Ardes, now in the possession of the Lord Viceccount Claneboy, are held of His Majestie, as of His Highness's Castle of Dublin, in free and common soccage, and by the yearly rent of 5s. sterling, to be paid *ut supra;* and that the Rectorie of Grange-Owter aforesaid, now in the possession of the said Lord Viceccount Claneboy, is likewise held by him to be paid *ut supra:* Wee further find, that the said Lord Viceccount Montgomerie of the Ardes, on the said 8th daie of December last, did and yett doth receive and take to his own use, within all the territories, landes, tenements, and hereditaments in his possession, all the whole benefitt and profits of the severall fishings in the severall loghs, rivers, bayes, ports, creeks, and arms of the sea following, viz. : the river of Owen Mullen, as it is bounded with his own lands ; the baie and river of the Cumber, so far forth as it lies or is bounded by the Lord Viccount Ardes' lands ; the baie of the Newton, betwixt the river of the Cumber and the Cunneburne, with all the creeks and little rivers falling into the said baie ; and from the brook of the Cunneburne, all along the whole baies, creeks, and little brooks lying and adjoining to the landes and liberties of the Gray Abbay, till the meire of Iniscargie ; the river of the Canevey, so far forth as the said Lord Viceccount Ardes' landes lye, and to the bay of Ballecasker ; the bay of Ballemulcrevy ; the bay of Ballerolly ; the bay of Donoghdie ; the baie of Ballewillin ; so much of the fishing of the river of [   ] that falls into Strangford, as lies joined to the said Lord Viceccount Ardes' land ; and of all other creekes, rivers, and brookes lying and adjoining to the said Lord Viceccount Montgomerie's landes, within the County of Down and Upper Clandeboy : Wee further find, that the said Lord Viceccount Montgomerie of the Ardes, on the said 8th day of December last, did and yett doth hold, possesse, and enjoye within all and singular the said territories, landes, tenements, and hereditaments, these liberties, privileges, franchises, and immunities following, viz. : courts leet and view of frankpledge, courts baron, hundred courts, and other courts of record, with power to

o

hold plea of all actions [   ] covenants, trespasses, accompts, and [
                                                                          ] and
all tolls, proffitts, and perquisites thereunto belonginge [   ] Satterdaie weekly for ever, and
two faires yearlie for ever, with like courts of pie-powder during the said faires, and the tolls, profitts,
and perquisites thereto belonging, viz. : the one faire to be held yearlie on the 3rd of March, and two
daies then next following ; the other yearly on the 20th of September, and for two days then next
following ; likewise one markett to be holden at the Cumber everie Thursdaie weeklie, and also one
fair there on the 8th of October, and for two daies then next following, yearly, with like courts of piepowder, tolls, profits, and perquisites as aforesaid ; and also another market to be holden weeklie
everie Wedensdaie for ever at Donoghdie, together with a faire there, on the [   ] daie of [   ]
and for two daies after next ensuing, with the courts of pie-powder, tolls, profitts, and perquisites as
aforesaid.

 Wee further find, that the said Lord Vicecount Claneboie, on the said 8th daie of December last,
did and yet doth receive and take to his own use within all the territories, landes, tenements, and
hereditaments in his possession as aforesaid, all the whole benefitt, tythes, and profits of the severall
fishings of salmons, and all other kindes of fish in the loghes, rivers, baies, ports, roades, soundes, and
creekes of the sea following, viz : in the bay of Killileagh ; in the river of Owen-Mullen, so far as it
is bounded with his own landes ; in the baie of Iland-Maghee ; in the river or water of the Cumber,
so far forth as it is bounded with his own landes ; in the baie of Ballewalter ; in the baie of Canvie, so
far as his own landes ; in the river and baie of Balleholme ; the river and baie of Ballywillen *alias*
Ballemullen ; in the river and baie of Owen O'Corke ; and in the baies and point of Balle-M'Caritt :
Wee further find likewise, that the said Lord Vicecount Claneboy, on the said 8th daie of December
last, did and yett doth hold, possesse, and enjoy within all and singular the territories, lands, tenements, and hereditaments in his possession as aforesaid, these liberties, priviledges, franchises, and
immunityes following, viz. : two courts leet and view of frankpledge yearly to be kept, with all fines,
issues, amerciaments, proffits, and perquisites thereunto belonging or appertaining, within the
Barony of Great Ardes, in such place as the said Lord Vicecount Claneboy shall appoint ; two courts
leet and view of frankpledge in the Upper Clandeboy, with all profits as aforesaid ; and a court leet
and view of frankpledge, in the territory of the Duffrin, with the proffits as aforesaid, in such place
as shall be appointed by him the said Lord Vicecount Claneboy : And that he hath also unto him and
his heires, the grant of all and singular waifes, straies, deodands, goods, and chattels of felons, *felons
de se*, and fugitives, outlaws, and put *in exigent*, and of all other felons whatsoever within his lands,
and all fines, issues, and amerciaments whatsoever, of all person and persons, tenants, and inhabitants within his said landes, with power to take and receive the said goods, chattels, deodands, &c.,
by himself, his officers, and servants, to his proper use and behoofte, without any account to His
Majesty for the same ; and that he hath also chases, parkes, and free warrens, within his landes, &c. :
And further, that the said Lord Vicecount Claneboy hath power to make and appoint, within his
said lands, the Clark and Clarkes of the Markett, with full power to do all and whatsoever belongeth
to the Clarke of the Markett to do, together with all fynes, issues, amerciaments, and profits
whatsoever, thereby arising or imposed, to be receaved by him the said Lord Vicecount Claneboie,
and his officers, to his own use, without accompt as aforesaid, so as no other Clarke of the Markett
may exercise anie thinge belonging to the office of the Clarke of the Markett within his said landes :
And further, wee find that the said Lord Vicecount Claneboie hath a court of record at Bangor, and
another court of record at Killeleagh, and another court of record at Ballewalter, which said courts
of record are to be held before the steward or seneseall of the said Vicecount Claneboy, from three
weekes to three weekes, severally at the said towns of Bangor for the Upper Claneboy, Ballewalter
for the Great Ardes, and Killeleagh for the Duffrin, for hearing and determining of all actions, pleas,
suites, and demands, trespasses, debts, accompts, contracts, and other actions personall, not exceed-
inge in debt or damage the sum of £10 sterling, with power to attach and arrest by his bailiffs the
goods or bodies of the defendants, as need shall require, and to use all other processes, proceedinges,
judgments, and executions as are used in anie other court in anie other town in the Kingdom of Ireland, together with fines, issues, amerciaments, and profits of the courts aforesaid ; and with libertie
to appoint for that end within the severall townes of Bangor, Ballewalter, and Killileagh aforesaid, and
the liberties there, one or more sergeant or sergeants for the service of the said courts, with power to
the steward to minister an oath to the sergeant or sergeants for the true execution of his and their

place and places, and with power to the said Lord Claneboie to minister an oath to his said steward for the due execution of his place ; and also power of having several prisons in the said several towns of Bangor, Ballewalter, and Killeleagh, for the comitment of such persons as for anie cause are to be comitted to the same, with power also to appoint sufficient jailors for the keeping of the same : And also at Bangor two mercatts every week, weeklie for ever, viz. : the first on Mondaie, and the second on Thursdaie ; and three faires yearly, the first on the feast day of Philip and Jacob, and for two days after ; the second on St. James's Daie, and for two days after ; and the third on the 11th of November, and two days after, together with all courts of piepowder, and all liberties, customs, tolls, powers, perquisites, and proffits to the said courts-markett and faires belonging, with picadge, stallage, tolladge, weights, and measures, within said town and liberties : And also at Holliwood, one markett on Wedensdaie every week, weeklie for ever ; and two faires, the first on the 24th [

　　　　　　　　　　　　　　　　　　　　　　　　　　　　　　　] And that the said Lord Vicecount Claneboie is entitled to [　　　　　　　] anchoradge, wharfage, cranadge, and other duties upon [　　　　　] and other vessels arriving, casting anchor, loading, or unloading upon anie the wharfs, keys, bancks, and soyle of him the said Lord Vicecount Claneboie, without any accompt to His Majestie for the same, and also power of exportation and importation of all manner of commodities, goods, and things whatsoever (lynen yarn excepted), in and out of any port in the kingdome, paying His Majestie's customs and subsidies for the same, with sondrie other liberties and priviledges, *prout* in the letters pattent, dated 5th November, 3d *Jac.*, as by the same letters pattent, whereunto relacion being had more at large it doth and maie apere : We further find, that the Abbot of the late abbaie or religious house of monks of the order of St. Benedict, called Black Abbaie, in the Great Ardes aforesaid, in the said Countie of Down, at the time of the dissolution thereof, was seized of the said abbaie, with the appurtenances, in his demeasne as of fee in right of his said abbaie, and that by vertue of the said dissolucion, and of the statute of 33d King Henry the 8th, entitled the Act for the Suppression of Kilmaynhan and other Religious Houses, our Soveraigne Lord, the King that now is, was seized of the said abbaie, with the appurtenances, in his demeasne as of fee in right of his crowne, as hath been formerlie found by two severall offices taken in this countie, viz. : the one at Ardwhyn, the 4th of July, 1605,[4] and the other at Ballechachamur, the last day daie of September, 1612 :[a] And wee further find, that our Soveraigne Lord the King that now is, being seized as aforesaid in the said abbaie, with the appurtenances, did by his letters patente, dated at Dublin, the 20th daie of July, in the third yeare of His Highness's raigne, grant the said abbaie, with the appurtenances, unto the said Lord Vicecount Claneboy, by the name of James Hamilton, Esq., his heirs and assignes for ever, by vertue whereof the said Lord Vicecount Claneboy did enter into the same, and was and is thereof seized accordingly, and that the said Lord Vicecount Claneboy and his assignes have been ever since the date of the said letters pattente and yett are in possession thereof, and have received and yett doe receive the rents, issues, and proffitts thereof : And we further find, that the said Black Abbay, with the appurtenances, have ever since the said dissolution been taken, known, and reputed by the name of the Black Abbey, and not by any other name : And wee further find, that Richard, sometime Archbishop of Ardmagh, purchased, in augmentacion of his Bishoprick, the Black Priorie of St. Andrewe's, in the Ardes in Ulster, to hold to him and his successors in right of his said Bishoprick, as by a record produced before us in evidence, exemplified under the Great Scale of England, which exemplification wee find *in hæc verba :*—" *Jacobus Dei Gra.*," &c. : And wee likewise find, that several of the Archbishops of Ardmagh have in ancient tyme receaved rents out of the said Black Abbay, and that the said Black Abbay and the said Black Priorie are one and the same thing : Wee find further, that the said Con O'Neale, by his deed indented, dated the 25th of April, 1606, did make a writing purporting a feoffment unto Tho : Montgomerie of the townes and landes of B. Rosboy, in Gallough, with the appurtenances, which deed we find was sealed and delivered by the said Con O'Neale with a blanck for the atturnies' names, and which deed we fine *in hæc verba :* " THIS INDENTURE," &c. ; and we find further, that after the deliverie and sealing thereof, the atturnies' names, viz., Thom : Leake, and Dermud Hud, were incerted in the said deed, and that thereupon

---

a The following mention of this Inquisition of Office is made in the Inquisitions of Ulster, published by the Record Commission :—
" Co. Down.—*Ballykacann ult. die Sept.*, 1612. *Hæc Inquisitio valde obliterata est, præpue in initio et fine.*

afterwardes the said named atturnies, on the 28th of August, 1606, did make livery and seizen, *prout* the indorsement of the said deed, which we likewise find : We find further, that the said Con O'Neale did make a deed or writing, bearing date the 1st of June, 1606, purporting a lease unto Elice M'Neall his wife, and to Hugh Boy O'Neall his sonne, of the town and landes of B.Carganan, Bresagh, and Crcive, *prout* the said writing, which writinge we find *in hæc verba :* "THIS INDENTURE," &c. ; and we find the said Con delivered the same writinge unto Elice his wife, to the use of the said Hugh, being then a child about foure or five yeares of age, and then present in the house : And we further find, that the said Con O'Neall did, by a tripartite Indenture, dated the 2nd of December, 1616, make conveyance of the said landes above mentioned unto the said Lord Vicecount Claneboy and Sir Moyses Hill as aforesaid, which landes wee find to be in the possession of the said Lord Vicecount Claneboy and Sir Moyses Hill, as aforesaid, ever since the conveyance made unto them : We find that the said Con O'Neale did, by a writing under his hand and scale, demise, among other things, unto his brother, Hugh Mergagh O'Neale, the townes and landes of Ballenelessan, whereof Tulloore is a quarter, B.Oghley, Killenura, Ballecaricknesassanagh, B.Lisdownean, and the mill of B.Knockan, with the appurtenances, for the terme of foure score and nyncteen yeares, to begin the 1st May, 1606, the said Hugh Mergagh, his heires and assignes, yielding and paieing for and out of the premises the yearlie rent of 11s. sterling, English monie, out of every of the said townes ; and yielding and paying the yearlie rents proportionablie due out of the same unto His Majestie, which lease or writing cannot be had, but hath been proved by severall witnesses before us to be dulie perfected, which wee find to have beene perfected accordinglie, by vertue whereof the said Hugh Mergagh did enter into the premises, and was possessed thereof accordinglie, and conveyed and assigned all his interest in all the said last recyted townes and premises unto the said Foulke Conwaie, Knight, on the said last daie of December last, who was and yett is in the possession thereof, and so has beene for the space of these 17 years last past, or thereabouts ; and wee find that the said Con O'Neall, by the same demyse last before recyted, did likewise thereby demise to the said Hugh Mergagh the towne and landes of Clontenekelly, with the appurtenances, for the terme and under the like rent as aforesaid, who entered and was possessed accordinglie, and did by his Indenture, bearing date the [   ] daie of [
         ] demise and sett the same to Sir Moyses Hill, Knight, for the terme of [   ]
and under the yearly rent of.[   ], and wee find that the said Sir Moyses Hill was and is in the possession thereof, by vertue of the said lease ; and wee find that the said Hugh Mergagh did, by his Indenture, bearing date 27th of June, 1614, grant, assigne, and sett over unto the said Sir Foulke Conwaie, Knight, all his whole right, title, and [
         ] Clontanekelly, [
for the terme of nyncteene [
for the same yearlie £10 sterling, as appeareth by the said articles of agreement, [
and wee find the said William Hamilton in like possession of the parcell of land called Ballecloghan, bounded and meired as appeareth by a deed bearing date 29th of September, 1611, which deed wee find *in hæc verba*, &c. : Wee find the said William Hamilton to be in like possession of a quarter of Ballcknockan, by virtue of a lease from Hugh Mergagh, for four score and 19 years, and in the like possession of Crevie-Loghar, by lease from the said Hugh Mergagh, the said William paieing therefor yearly 10s sterling : Wee find that the said Con did, by his deed bearing date 23d June, 1610, demise unto Towell O'Neale his brother, the three townes lands and a half known by the name of B.Taughmore, B.Cahard, and B.Digen, with the appurtenances, for 28 yeares, and under the rent of 21s. sterling, and the King's rent, *prout* the deed : Wee find that Balle-Loughan Balle-stoker, aud B.M'Claffe are in the possession of Sir Jo : M'Dowell, by an estate from the Lord Vicecount of Ardes, but what the estate is wee knowe not : Wee find that Con O'Neale, together with the Lord Vicecount Ardes, by their deed dated 9th June, 13*th Jac. Reg.*, did demise unto William Smith the towne and landes of Balle-Listowdrie, together with other landes in the said deed mentioned for 21 yeares, and at the yearly rent of 50s., *prout* in the deed, which wee find *in hæc verba :* Wee further find that the said Con, by his deed, dated 2d of July, 1616, did demise to Owen M'Levertie the towne and landes of Ballenegarick, with the appurtenances, for 60 yeares, and under the rent of 10s. yearly, *prout* the deed, which wee find : We further find, that the said Con, by his deed dated the last daie of March, 1616, did demise unto William Moore, the towne and lande of Ballincrossan, with the appurtenances, for 21 yeares, at and under the rent of 20s. sterling, *prout* the deed : We find that the Lord Vicecount Montgomerie, by deed dated [   ] day of [   ] and [   ] did enfeoff John Cunigher,

of 11 score acres of the lands of Balle-Rincreivie and Carnamuck, *prout* the said deed : Wee find that
the said Lord Viccount of Ardes, by deed dated *ult.* December, 1607, did enfeoff Jo : M'Cassan, of
B.Murchoie, *prout* the said deed : We find that the said Lord Viccount Ardes, by deed dated
19th July, 1616, did enfeoffe Pat. Montgomerie, of B.Stenood and other landes in the said deed mentioned, *prout* the said deed : We find that the Lord Viccount Ardes, by deed dated 7th September, 1607, did enfeoffe Collonell David Boide of the towne of Ballincrevie, with other landes in the
said deed mentioned, *prout* the said deed : Wee find likewise, that the Lord Viccount of Ardes, by
deed dated 16th of May, 1623, did enfeoffe Jo : Peacocke, and his heires, of Tullekevin, with other
landes in the said deed mentioned, *prout* the said deed : We find that the said Lord Viccount Ardes,
by deed dated 19th July, 1616, did enfeoff Jo : Shawe and his heires of 120 acres of land in the said
deed mentioned, *prout* the said deed : We find that Con O'Neale, by indenture dated 1st November,
1615, demised to Toole M'Cormick M'Donnell M'Cormick O'Neale, a quarter of Thyduffe, in the
Sleught-Neiles, to hold for 11 years, under the rent of 20s. sterling *per annum, prout* the said deed :
Wee find that the said Lord Viccount Ardes, by deed dated 28th July, 16*th Jac.*, did enfeoffe David
Anderson of a townland called Scrabo, with the appurtenances, *prout* the said deed : We find that
Con O'Neale, by his writing, dated the last daie of Aprill, 1611, did demise unto Edward Barry the
towne and lands of Knockcolumkill for 21 years, under the rent of 20s. sterling *per annum, prout* the
said deed : Wee find that the said Con, by deed dated 18th April, 1614, did demise unto the said
Edmond Barry the towne and landes of Carrickneveagh, for 23 yeares, under the rent of 40s sterling
per annum, prout the said deed : Wee find that Edmond Barry is in like possession of a quarter of
the towne and lands of B.Knockan, by vertue of an assignment to him thereof made by Hugh Mergagh O'Neale, who held the same by vertue of a demise alledged to be made thereof, among other
lands, unto the said Hugh Mergagh from the said Con for 99 years, and that the said Hugh Mergagh,
by his deed in writing, dated 12th Aprill, 1622, did assign over the said quarter of B.Knockan, rent
free, for four score and three years, as by the said writing may appear : We find that B.Brenan and
B.M'Brynan are one and the same, and not divers : We find that the B.Dulloghmuck and B.Dunkin-
muck are one and the same and not divers :   We find that B.Crevan and B.Crosnecrevan are one and
the same and not divers :   Wee find Ballecrosan and Ballenecrosan to be one and the same and not
divers :   Wee find B.Carne and Ballynecarne and Downe-Bracklie to be one and the same and not
divers :   Wee find B.Dulloghan and B.Nedulloghan to be one and the same and not divers :   Wee find
B.Drum, B.Drumbeg, and B.Crumbeg, and Templedrum, to be one and the same and not divers :
Wee find B.Canvy, B.Caridge, B.Negarick, and B.Necargie to be one and the same and not divers :
Wee find B.Caryed and B.Cahard to be one and the same and not divers :   Wee find B.Blaris and
B.Temple-Blaris one and the same and not divers :   Wee find that B.Vicaravene is the true name of
the towne, and for the other names following, viz., B.M'Greven, B.Vicaravenie and B.M'Grevan, wee
knowe no such townes :   Wee find that Drumvena, Drumzevan, and B.Drumgiven, are one and the same
and not divers :   Wee find that B.Downeagh and B.Gownemagh are one and the same and not divers ;
Wee find Carrow-Lisnoad, Tullyard, and B.Hemynude to be one and the same and not divers : Wee find
B.Lenoghan, Downrogan, Carrow-Enespicke, and B.Derrymore to be one and the same and not divers:
Wee find B.Drumburk, Tullycarnan, and Tullyhirk, are one and the same and not divers :   Wee find
B.Broghinshdram, B.Havrick, B.Mony, B.Broghorge, B.Lisbany, and Purchaise, to be one and not
divers ;   Wee find B.Mullagh and B.Moghlagh are one and the same and not divers :   Wee find Tulle-
esticknagh and Tullenestickincoll are one and the same and not divers :   Wee find Ballydrynan and
B.Grenan to be one and not divers :   We find B.Tulle [   ] B.Lessechekan, B.Scheh [
                                                                                                                                    ]
Wee find Caricknesassanagh and Agleshin are one and not divers :   Wee find that Skeagh-Lottiefeagh
is the right name, and the other names, viz., Balleneskeagh, Balleskeaghan, B-Downskeagh, and B-
Neskeaghan, wee knowe not :   Wee find that B.Taunaghmore and Loghgar are one and not divers,
and Crevy-Loghgar to be halfe a towne belonging to Loghgar :   Wee find B.Necrosse and Tullencrosse
are one and the same :   Wee find Levalle-Tullegoan is half a towneland itself :   Wee find B.Lessan
and Balletulloore to be one and not divers :   Wee find Drumneleg, and the Loghnagh, and the Leg-
gan, are one and not divers ;   and as for B.Nechallon wee knowe nott ;   Wee find that B.Bronnell is
parcell of Castlereagh, and do further find it hath been alwaies occupied and enjoied with the same,
saving a little parcell belonging to Edengilneherick :   And wee find B.Bronnell, B.M'Clonghee,
Tullecarnan, Edengilneherick, and part of Clentonekelly, to be within two myles of Castlereagh :   Wee

p

find that the townes and landes not expressly named in the said conveyance made by the said Lord Vicecount Claneboy unto the said Con O'Neale, bearing date the 6th of November, 3rd *Jac. Reg.*, the moytie whereof is claimed by the said Lord Vict. Montgomerie, are these following, viz., Edengilne-hericke, Balle-M'Care, B.M'Haw, *alias* Kilmanchome, B.Clontonkellie, Carrownebracer, *alias* Carow-drum, Carrow-Legacory, B.Croawly, B.Carrickmaderie, B.Vicaraveny, Carrownedome, B.Drum-nelegge, B.Lisdownean, B.Killenure, B.Nelessan, B.Crevicalickviricke, Carrow-Leverog, Carrow-Iduffe, *alias* Carrow-Hughduffe, *alias* Carrow-Tyduffe. Carrowcombe, *alias* Carrow-Edenderry, B.Tullenecrosse, Ballenellan, B.Largmore, Ballentyan, *alias* Downe-Cumber, *alias* Purchoise, Levalle-Tullegoan, and Killany : Wee find that the said Lord Vicecount Claneboy, by virtue of the said Letters Pattente, made of the possession of St. Johns, dated the 14th February, *Anno*, 3rd *Jac. Reg.*, was seized in his demeasne as of fee of Carrownemucke, near Castle-Reogh, and that he gave the same in exchange to Con O'Neale and his heires, for other lands in the said countie given in ex-change by the said Con to him and his heires for ever, and that the said exchange was executed on both parts by entrie and possession, and the said Con O'Neale afterwards conveyed the said Carrow-nemucke, amonge other landes, unto Sir Moyses Hill and his heires for ever : And wee further find, that these townes are the demeasne landes belonging to Castlereagh, viz., Castlereagh, B.Bronell, B.-Lisnebranic, B.Crevan, *alias* Ballecrossnecreavin, B.M'Comagh, halfe Mono-Loghoge, B.Cregogie, and B.Nefeagh : Wee further find, that these townes following, viz., B.Bronell, B.M'Cenoghie, Tulle-carnan, Edengilneherick, B.Clontonkelly, B.Tullenecrosse, Carrow-Edenderie, Carrow-Laverog, Car-row-Iduffe, Killany, B.Nelessan, B.Crevic, Alickavrick, Drumilegge, Cerrownecravir, B.M'Card, B.-Killenure, B.Lisdownean, B.Largmore, B.Nynellan, B.Dunconnor, Carrow-Legacorry, Croawlie, B.Carickmaderoie, Levalletullegoan, Carrowdome, Tullyord, and B.M'Cravene, are within the halfe teritorie of the Upper Clandeboy, which is next unto Castlereagh, and farthest from the Great Ardes : Wee find also, that the above specified towns have been enjoied by the said Con O'Neale, and his as-signs, ever since the grant made by the Lord Vicecount Claneboy unto the said Con O'Neale ; and for the questions whether the townes above named, and the rest of the townes mentioned in the convey-ance to the said Con O'Neale doe not exceed the one halfe or moytie of the said teritorie of the Upper Clandeboys wee knowe not, in regard we are strangers in these parts.

STEPHEN ALLENE, *Deputy Escheator.*

I find this to be a true copy of the original Inquisition of the above date, at present in the Usher's Office of His Majesty's High Court of Chancery of Ireland.   Dated this 29th day of March, 1834.

SIMON MADDOCK, *Deputy Usher.*

No. V.

COPY INQUISITION, DATED 14TH JANUARY, 1644.

COUNTY OF DOWN—*Killileagh*, 14*th January*, 1644.—James, late Viscount Claneboy, in his lifetime was seised of the manors, demesnes, castles, monasteries, and abbeys following, viz. :—the Monastery of Bangor, in the County of Down, and of the towns and lands following, viz. : Bangor, Portavo, Ballefodderlie or Ballephcoderlie, Ballemenen-itragh, Ballemenen-outragh, Carrowreagh, Carrowoorloge, Ballow near the sea, Ballemulleragh or Gilgroomsporte, Ballenacormuck or Ballema-cormagh, Ballemaconell or Ballemackonill, Ballecroghan, Ballehelme or Ballehomie, Ballynayue or Ballynehue or Balleneaghugh, Balleonerie or Ballenreagh or Ballenrie, Balleneyrange, Ballynegreme or Balleocrane, Balow near Bangor, Carrownesure or Carrowneser, Carrowknockanduff or Carrow-slanclackanduff, Carrowneshroyan or Collosenesseran, Ballemonycorrogie or Ballemonycorregy, Ballerangeile or Ballefyanghoguile, Ballelisbane or Ballelissebane, Ballebarnes or Ballebrennan, Ballecarnanleaghy or Ballecarnedeagh, Ballekillare or Ballecollar, Ballef [   ] Ballemullen or Ballmulle, Ballevernan or Ballevernock, Balledie, Ballecrott, Balleskellie or Balleskady, and Ballegilbert ; and of the towns as well temporal as spiritual following, viz. : Ballemeghan or Ballemeaghie, Ballemachoris, Ballemachor or Ballemacer, lying near Belfast, with the appurtenances ; and also of tue Rectory of Balleclughan or Balleurgegan, in Lecale, with the tithes of Balleurgegan, parcel of the possessions of the said Abbey of Bangor, and of Ballemeghan, in the County aforesaid ; also of the Rectory of Clonuff, with the two-fifth parts of the tithes of Clonuff, Balleaghen, and Ballelatrin ; of the Church of Cragyvadda, and the tithes of grain of the towns following, viz. : Ballecragyvadda, Ballenobert, Balledavid, and Ballegene or Ballegreine, to the said late Monastery of Bangor belonging ; of the Rectory of Hollywood, with the tithes of the towns following, viz. : Ballenultra, Ballecinanagh, Ballekeele, Ballenderrie, and Ballekurcknagonie ; and also of the tithes of all fish taken or landed on the southern side of the Bay of Knockfergus, from Copeland Isles to the ford or passage of Belfast ; and also of the passage or ferry from Bangor across the said Bay of Knockfergus ; also, of the advowson of all vicarages in all the parishes in the towns aforesaid, with their tithes. He was also seized of the late dissolved Priory or Religious House of Hollywood, in the county aforesaid, with the appurtenances, and of all the towns following, viz. : Ballekeele or Ballekeigle, Ballemanack or Ballemanagh, Ballecultragh or Ballecultra or Balleaghtraghagh, Ballenderric or Ballendearie, and Ballyerknocknegony or Balleknocknegome, lying in the county aforesaid, with the appurtenances ; of the Rectory of Balleorane, with the tithes in the towns following, viz. : Ballcorane, Nerany, Wynnecarvell, and Lisbraden, in the territory of Slught-Hubricks, in the county aforesaid ; of the Rectory of Kilcouby or Kircubin, with the tithes of Kilcouby or Kircubin, and Ballemullen, in the territory of the Great Ardes ; of the Rectory of Coolgrange, with the tithes of the town of Coolgrange or Grange, in the Great Ardes, near Blackstaff, and of the tithes of the town of Ravarra, Carrowreagh, and Ballecloyhan, lying in or near Belfast, and Rowbane and Rowreagh, in the Great Ardes ; of the Rectory of Drumroan, with the tithes in the towns of Drumroan and Ballchiggin ; and also of all the rectories and towns following, parcell of the late aforesaid dissolved Abbey of Cumber, viz. : Ballenegatnyc, Carrownesurc, Ballecullentry, Ballenicoll, and the tithes of all the towns following, viz. : Balbristoll, Ballegrangy, Ballelisleene, Ballekeele, Ballemanerie, Balletullehubbarte, Ballemoughlagh, Balleheyle, Balledrumheriffe, half of Ballegraffan, Ballebein, Ballemagheriscowe or Ballevagheriescowe, and Ballegowne or Ballegowan ; the tithes of the Rectory of Tawnaghwin, with the appurtenances ; and all the tithes of fish taken on the southern side of the river of Cumber ; and of the tithes of the Rectory of Killeine, and the tithes in the Laggan ; and of the following towns, viz. : Ballewalter, parcell of the possession of the late Monastery of Grey Abbey, in the Great Ardes, the quarter of land called St. John's Quarter, in the Banwie, and the quarter of land called Carrowclogher, in the parish of Whytchurch ; the quarter of land called Carrownemoen, in the parish of Talbotstowne ; the quarter of land called Carrowjohnboston, in the town of Drumroan ; the quarter of land called St. John's Quarter, in Fulloghkeavan ; and the quarter of land called Carrownneychigle St. John's Quarter, in Kilvogan, in the Great Ardes ; and of all the rectories impropriate following, parcell of the possessions of the late dissolved Monastery of Black Abbey, viz. : the Rectory of Ballchalbert, with the appurtenances ; and two-thirds of the towns of Ballyeasperagh, Ballehalbert, Ballerickard, Balleportavogie or Mullaghmore, Ballenefringe or Negalley, Balleglasseragh, Ballygraffin, Ballyhamlin, Ballerodony ; also the Rectory of Whytchurch or Templefin, with the appurtenances ; two-third parts of the tithes of the townes of Balleobikin, Ballemagowne, Balleatward, Balleferish, Balledownan or Balledownour, Templefin or Whytchurch, Listiagnery, Balleganny, and Ballekilbrattan, in the Great Ardes ; of the whole of the Rectory of Iniscrgie, with the appurtennces ; two-third parts of the tithes of the townes of Ballylimpt, Ballegarugan, Ballefister, Carrownesera, Carrownetalbragh, and Inniscrogie or Nekillen ; of the advowsons of the several vicarages in the churches of Ballehalbert or Talbotstowne, Templefin or Whytchurch, and the tithes of fish of whatever kind taken or landed on the lands, or maritime places in or near the lands or hereditaments of the aforesaid late Viscount Claneboy, in the Great Ardes, as well on the Loghcoyne side as on that towards the deep sea ; and also of the Rectory impropriate of Ballygalgat, in the Little Ardes, with the tithes in the following towns, viz. : Ballegalgett, Ballewhilterate or Balleciller, and Ballewhitneragh, with the advowsons of Ballegalgett and Grangeouter ; two-thirds of the tithes of the following towns, viz. : Ballequinteene, Balletullecarnan, Balleedock, Balletussellie, Balletaura, half of the town of Quintagh, and Carrowdressagh, Tullemarter and

Carrowmallert, with the advowson of the Vicarage of Grangeowter; of the Rectory impropriate of Rathmullen, together with the advowson of the said rectory, with the tithes of the towns following, viz.: Rathmullen, Ballefunstowne or Luckhanston or Lenkanstowne, Ballenebirte, Ballevaston, St. Johnstowne, Killogh, and Blunketistowne or Plunketstowne; also of the advowsons of all the rectories and vicarages, separate churches and chapels of Dundonell, Knockcolmkill, Bredagh, and Tawnaghwin; and also of the passages or ferries across the river of Strangford, together with the tithes of fish and fisheries of the river; and the tithes of the towns following, viz.; Ballycragyvadie, Ballerobart, Balledavid, Ballegreine, Ballecloghans or Ballecloghan, Ballechachanur or Ballechakamer, Carrowmullen, Carrownecarne, Carrowtagarte, Ballenechallen, Ballelisnefca or Ballelisnekagh, Ballerergan or Balleregin, Balledundonell, Balledunlady, Ballecarowreagh or Carowreagh, Carrowkelneveagh, Ballearne, Ballenerany or Balleneran, Ballelisdrumbraden, Ballenynnecarvell or Ballemonycarvell, Ballecaslanbege, Ballebein, Ballcrestoll, Ballenegrange, Ballemanere or Ballenullere, Ballelisleene, Ballekeele, Balletullchubbarte, Ballebyn, Balleglastrum or Balleglasdromem or Balleglasdromen, half the town of Balledrumaconell, half the town of Balleacrogie or Balleaghrogie, Ballelaghgoan, Balledrumheriff, Ballenegassen, Ballethigle, Ballemagheriscowc, Ballegowne, Carrickmaran or Ballecarrickmanen, half the town of Aughindarragh, lately in the possession of the aforesaid late Viscount Claneboy, deceased; half the town of Ravara, Ballegluntneglare or Tullecaphinan, half the town of Ballenecrevy or Ballenecrevegy, Carnownan, and Carrowcrevy, half the town of Killinchy or Killinse, and Ballcliswoyn, half of Ballerraffan, Balleportivogie or Mulloghmore, Ballenefringe or Negallogh, Ballehalbert, Ballcasragy, Balleneglasseragh, Ballegraffan, Rowbane, Rowreagh, Ballefister, Ballegrangeogh or Coolgrange, Carrowneser, Ballekircubbin or Kilcouby, Ballemullen, Carrownecaliagh, Ballegaruggan, Ballenegargavan, Iniscargie or Nekillen, Ballclumpt, Ballehamlin, Ballerodony, Ballenggin or Ballchiggin, Ballcobekin or Drumroan, Ballemagowne, Balleattwarte, Balledonouer, Ballcferish, Balletullecarnan or Listiagnewe, Templefyn or Whytechurch, half of Ballyganwy, and half of Ballekilbratten, with the appurtenances, which same premises lie in the territories of the Upper Clandeboye and the Great Ardes, in the county aforesaid. He was also seized of all the following towns, viz. Ballebredagh, Ballcknockcolmekill, Ballemaccaritt, Ballecrevicalickavrick, Balledriman, or Ballemacgoryman, Balledromnelege, Ballclisdalgan, or Ballelisgan, and of a certain parcel of land called Tawnagh in West Quarter, Ballelagegom, Ballenegassan, Ballegalwallie, Carrowdirue, the town of Creevicloughgur, and Ballemullagh, or Ballemoughlagh, (saving however to the executors or assigns of William Hamilton, deceased, all the interest which he had of and in the town of Creevicloughgar and the quarter of Ballemullagh, as appears by the Inquisition taken at Downpatrick, in the county aforesaid, on the 13th of October, 1623,) Balledoggan, or Balledyan, Tullevasackenagh, or Tullevostikinell, and of all the towns following, viz., Balledulloghan, Ballcowane, and Balleles, [   ] and also of all the towns and lands following, viz., Drumboe, Ballenegarrick or Ballcnccargie or Ballenegamvie, Balleloghgare or Ballctawnaghmore, Ballecahard, or Ballecaryed, Ballecreeve-ergan near Liscowdrie, Ballclistowdrie, or Ballenebarnes, Drumgiven, or Drumvena, or Drumzevan, Carrow-Edenderre, Balledrumbege, or Ballegrumbege, Levalle-Tullegowne, Ballchemenudc, or Carrowtulleard, Ballemaceravenie, Ballekillemore, Carricknessassanagh, Balledownean or Ballelisdruncan or Lisdinan or Ballekeile, Balleoghly, or Faintowne, or Ballenencny, Ballenelassan, the quarter of Tullore or Tulloure, Balleknockan, and Angelshin; and also of all the chief rents and services reserved upon the lands and tenements of Ballenchattie, or Ballelavrie, Ballemulvalle or Ballcomulvalle, Ballelencghan, and the quarter of M'Enespick; and also of all the young oaks under six inches square upon the premises, and of all the woods and underwoods of whatsoever kind upon all the towns and lands of Ballyknockan, Killinora, Lisdownane, Drumnelege, Carrowneveagh, Carrickmadcroy, Carruganan, Bressagh, Creevicalickavrick, Crossan Carrowlagycorrie, Carrickcroye, Carrowdrumbraire, Killaine, Lisdrumlaughane, Carricknessanagh, Lassan, Tulloure-Lisdalgan, Tawnaghmore, Tullevostikinagh, M'Eravaine, Carrowdurne, Cachard, Creevicloughgare, Creevicergan, Drumgiven, Balledyan, Listouder, and Ballemullagh (except as is excepted); and also of all the castles, manors, lands, and tenements following, viz., the town and land of Ballemona, Ballehollckin, or Tullechene, Ballemullagh or Mullogh, Corbally, Ballecaslanwilliam or Castlewilliam, Ballenacabrie or Ballenecabby, Killileagh, Renechady or Ringhaddy, Tulloghmoremacmaritt, Ballerathconevan or Ballevathconegan, Ballemaccorvibill or Ballemaccromwell or Cromwell, Ringduffrin or Mylertone, Ballcomeran or Ballencran, Ballemacoran, Rathgorman, Ballykiltinegan, or Ballykilmegan, Carrowreagh, Carrickruske, or Carrickruskie, Killinchie, Balowe, Ballemoshen or Ballemacashen, Ballemaccacrelie or Ballemac-Crelie, Balleagullen or Carrowgullen, Balle-bregagh, Ballileggan or Ballelissowne or Balleyegon, Lisduffe, Balletoye or Ballecoye, Ballcclaye or Ballecleigh, Balleossgreyhan or Ballecoskregan, Castlegalle, Lissoncagh, Ballegavin, Tullenoagh, Callerogen, Caslancaise, Balleallegan or Ballullegan, Ballemullen, Bulleholyard, Ardigoan, Ballebro-merie or Tulleviric, Balletrim, Ballereagh or Reaghie, Queoylie, Mamore, Rathkirron, Ballecontic or Cluntogh or Clontogh, Balledromore, Balletagagh, or Currickdowe, Munmore or Maghmore, Tulli-cowise or Tullimacknowe, Kilcanan or Skiltanan, Derreboye, Ballehernan, Kilanreas, Rinchaddy, Islandmore, Islanddunshagh, Islanddaviagh or Inishdavan or Strevana, Islandarragh, Island-conlen, Island-Rinchady, Islandreagh, and Inishmacattaggarte, lying in the territory of Duffrin, in the County of Down ; and of the tithes of all fish of whatsoever kind taken in the bays and ports of the Duffrin near Loghcoyne, also of the advowsons and donations, rectories, vicarages, chapels and churches of Killileagh, Kilandreas, Renechady, and Killinchieniemachric, in the territory of Duffrin afore-said, and the tithes in the towns following in the Upper Clandeboy, belonging to the aforesaid Rectory of Killinchieniemachric, viz., the tithes of the towns of Carrickmanan, Drumcreagh, Rafry, Killinchiene-kille, Ravarra, Ballenecloghan, Levallegowne, and Levalle-Achindeeragh, or Drumchic, with the ap-purtenances, and also of all the castles, demesnes, houses, edifices, mills, lands, tenements, meadows, advowsons, donations, tithes of grass, grain and hay, wool, flax, &c., as by the letters patent of the now King, bearing date the 20th April, in the 5th year of his reign, granted to James, late Viscount Claneboye, his heirs and assigns, of all the aforesaid premises, (except as excepted) and as mentioned in the letters patent of the late King James, bearing date at Westminster, 14th March, in the 19th year of his reign, made to the late Viscount Claneboye, by the name of James Hamilton, Knight, his heirs and assigns, appeared. The aforesaid Hugh, late Viscount Mountgomerie of Ardes, and James Mountgomerie, Knight, brother of the aforesaid late Viscount, (in fulfilment of the articles of agree-ment concluded and agreed on between the aforesaid Hugh, late Viscount Montgomerie, deceased, father of the late Viscount Montgomerie, and the said late Viscount, and James Montgomery, Knight, the second son of the aforesaid Hugh, on the one part, and James, late Viscount Claneboye, on the other part, bearing date 17th December, 1633,) by their writing, bearing date 7th October, 1636, granted to James, late Viscount Claneboye, deceased, his heirs and assigns, all right, &c., which the aforesaid late Viscount Montgomerie, and James Montgomerie, or either of them, had to all the manors, lands, tenements, &c., aforesaid, the tenor of which writing follows in the original. A cer-tain deed of exchange bearing date 13th July, 1637, was made between Viscount Claneboy and Fran-cis Hill, for exchange of certain lands and tenements, the tenor of which writing follows in the origi-nal, by virtue of which certain writing the aforesaid late Viscount Claneboye was seised of the towns and lands following, viz., Tullenecrosse, Dunskeagh, and Blarish, which certain towns and lands in the lifetime of the aforesaid Viscount Claneboye he granted in exchange for certain other lands and tene-ments, to Edward, Viscount Conway and Kilultagh, his heirs and assigns, and so being seised, he died. He was also seised of the towns and lands following, viz., Drumboge, or Drumboe, Tulliard, Ballenegarrick, Balleloghgar, and Balleknockan, (saving to the executors and assigns of William Ha-milton, deceased, such interest as they had in the quarter of the aforesaid town of Balleknockan, as appeareth from the Inquisition taken at Downepatrick, 13th of October, 1623,) and also of all the chief rents and services issuing out of the lands and lands of Drumboe and Tulliard, Ballenchattie, or Ballelarie, Ballemulvalie or Balleomullvally, Balleleloughan, and the quarter of M'Enespicke. There was a cer-tain deed or writing dividing lands, dearing date, 19th August, 1635, made between the aforesaid late Viscount Claneboye, and the late Viscount Montgomerie, the tenor of which deed follows in the original. The aforesaid late Viscount Claneboye, being thus seised of all the premises, died 24th January, 1643, and James, the present Viscount Claneboye, his son and heir, was then of full age, and married. The aforesaid Monastery of Bangor, the Priory of Hollywood and all the lands and tene-ments aforesaid, belonging to them as above, are held of the King by fealty only, in free and common soccage. The aforesaid territory of the Upper Claneboye and the Great Ardes, and the country or ter-ritory of the Duffrin or Dufferin, with the appurtenances, are also held of the King by fealty only, in free and common soccage. Jane, Dowager of Claneboye, widow, is dowable of the said premises. The aforesaid late Viscount Claneboye, being seised of the premises, by his Indenture bearing date 9th May, 1626, granted to Archibald Hamilton, late of Ballerott, in the County Down aforesaid, and to his heirs and assigns, all that town in the parish of Bangor, called Ballekelly, or Balleskally, in perpe-tuity, the tenor of which Indenture follows in the original. By another Indenture, bearing date 20th

q

November, 1639, he granted to John Hamilton, his heirs and assigns, all the town called Ballerobert, in the county aforesaid, in perpetuity, the tenor of which Indenture also follows in the original.   By another Indenture, bearing date 13th January, 1639, he granted to James Hamilton all that aforesaid town and lands of Ballecloghan, in Westhollywood, in the barony of Castlereagh, in the aforesaid county, the tenor of which Indenture also follows in the original.   By another Indenture, bearing date 17th May, 1628, he granted to William Moore, and Jane his wife, all that town and land in the Duffrins, called Ballebregagh, the tenor of which Indenture also follows in the original.   By another Indenture, bearing date 23rd November, 1636, he granted to Rowland Savage the town and lands of Magherascowe, in the Sluthenderkies, the tenor of which indenture follows in the original.   The aforesaid late Viscount Claneboye, Francis Lord Mountnoris, William Parsons, Knight and Baronet, Adam Loftus, of Rasarnam, in County Dublin, Knight, Edward Bolton, Knight, and John Hamilton, by another writing, bearing date 7th October, 1636, granted to Hugh, late Viscount Montgomerie, of Ardes, and James Montgomerie, Knight, the whole of their interest of and in all the houses, demesnes, and manors, towns, lands, tenements, and tithes specified in the aforesaid deed, the tenor of which writing also follows in the original   The aforesaid late Viscount by another deed, bearing date 26th July, 1637, remised and released the aforesaid late Viscount Montgomerie, and James Montgomerie, Knight, of all and every kind of error and cause of error in the premises, the tenor of which deed also follows in the original.   The aforesaid late Viscount Claneboye, by his Indenture, bearing date 22nd August, 1623, granted to John Maxwell all that town with the appurtenances called Ballespragh, in the county aforesaid, the tenor of which Indenture also follows in the original.—*Inq. of Ulster, Rec. Com.*, DOWN, No. 104.‡

---

‡ The following Inquisition (No. 105 in the same volume), which was taken on the 29th of August, 1644, appears to be intimately connected with the foregoing Inquisitions:—"There are so many trees now standing in Slutt-M'Neale's country, of the size of 6 inches square at the butt, at least, as amount to the number 8,883 ;—that is to say, upon the lands of Ballylenaghan, 119 ; Ballyvullvally, 75 ; Ballydulloghan, 101 ; Ballykoan, 160 ; Carewedenderry, 151 ; Ballylary, 21 ; Ballynelassan, 407 ; Ballykarney, 203 ; upon Drumboe, 27 ; Donkynmuck, 1,130 ; Ballyaghaliske, 461 ; Drombegge, 37 ; Skeaghlatifeagh, 75 ; Tullagherosse, 452 ; Ballylean, 14 ; Ballhaverick, 845 ; Lisnagnow, 15 ; upon Blaryes, 52 ; Lisdalgan, 342 ; Carricknesassanagh, 534 ; Tawnaghmore, 290 ; Lisdromlaghan, 475 ; Killany, 162 ; Tullywastekentia, 56 ; Crevylogbqarre, 221 ; upon Sir Foulke Conway's 5 townes, viz. : Ballymaltoan, Croall, Tullyconell *alias* Liskechall, Ballynenelan, and Largamore, 2,336 ; Listoodrie, 39 ; and Carnehughduffe, 93. Since the 22nd August, in the 4th year of the late King's reign, there have been cutt on the said lands, of oaks of the aforesaid size (under which there are not accompted any as oakes), the number of 11,631, appearing by the stocks, whereof there hath beene cutt for the use of the Lord Chichester, towards the building of his houses at Knockfergus and Belfast, upon the lands of Ballynelassan, Ballykoan, Ballykarney, and the rest of the townes adjoining, the number of 500 oakes. One Adam Montgomery did cutt and fell trees, parte of 2 sumers, with 3 or 4 men in his company, on Lisdalgan and other inland townes, not less than 40 trees. Mr. Dallaway cutt upon Donkynmucke, and other towns adjoining, 60 trees. One Antony Coslett, beinge tennant to Sir Moyses Hill, on the lands of Blaryes, hath cutt 127 trees, all which amount to the number of 727, which have been cutt without lycence, either from the Lord Viscount Claneboyes, the Lord of Ardes, Sir Foulke Conway, his lady, or any their agents, and are fit to be deducted out of the gross some of 11,631 trees, and not to be charged upon the Lord Viscount Montgomery and Lady Montgomery. There hath been cutt to the Lord Claneboye's use, by one Robert Rely, 26 oakes, and by one Kennedy 40 oakes, by warrant from Mr. William Hamilton ; and by one William Dunlapp, by like warrant, 20 oakes, which being in chardge of the Lord Viscount Claneboye, are to be deducted out of the remaining number of 10,904. There was cutt on Ballynelassan, by the Lord of Ardes' warrant, 20 oakes. John King did cutt upon Lisdalgan, and other inland tymber townes, with sundry workmen with him for a year and a half, great store of timber trees, converting the same to pipe-staves, hogsheade-staves, barrell-staves, keeve-staves, and spoakes for carts, of which wares there was transported 5 barque loads from Owen O'Mullyn, 3 of the said barques bearing the burden of 30 tunne apiece, and the other two 16 tunne apiece ; and although a tree will make a tunne or two of timber, yet there are such wastes in making those wares, that they tooke up at least 200 trees. One John Makinlas, with others in his company, were sett on worke in the said woods of Lisdalgan, and the rest of the towns adjoining, by the Lord of Ardes, where he made roases for the Church of Gray Abbey and Old Cumber, and some other store of tymber for building at Newtown and Donaghdee, converting some 6 trees to his own use, by his Lordship's allowance, for which he had about 30s., all which could not be less than 100 trees. One Mr. Hillenan, of Knockfergus, did cutt 300 oake trees, by agreement with Sir Thomas Hibbots, Knight, grounded on a warrant of the Lord of Ardes, on the townes of Ballynelassan and other adjoining townes, for which the sayd Sir Thomas payed £40 to the Lord of Ardes. One Gilbert Kennedy did cutt by the Lord of Ardes' warrant, some trees upon the lands of Lisdalgan and the adjoining towns, estimated at 20 trees. There were cutt at Aghalisk 323 trees by the tenants of Drumbeg, being tenants of the Lord of Ardes, and by Sir Foulke Conway's agents."

No. VI.

COPY INQUISITION, DATED 9TH APRIL, 1662.

COUNTY OF DOWN.—An Inquisition indented, taken at Downpatrick, in the County of Down aforesaid, on the 9th day of April, in the year of our Lord 1662, and in the fourteenth year of the reign of the most illustrious Prince and Lord, our Lord Charles the Second, by the grace of God, King of England, Scotland, France, and Ireland, before James Leslie and Robert Ward, Esqrs., Deputy Escheators of the province of Ulster, and Robert Graydon, Esq., Deputy Feudary of the said province, by virtue of a commission of the said Lord the King, under the Great Seal of his Kingdom of Ireland, bearing date, at Dublin, the 28th day of January, in the thirteenth year of his reign, and directed to them, or any two or more of them, whereof the said Escheator of our said Lord the King, of his province of Ulster, or his Deputy, or the Feudary of the said Lord the King of the same province of Ulster, or his Deputy, to be one, to enquire after the death of all and singular the tenants of our said Lord the King in the county aforesaid ; likewise to enquire concerning all wards, liveries, intrusions, alienations, made without license of the said Lord the King, or of any [   ] idiots, lunatics, widows, [   ] without license of our said Lord the King [   ] heriots, and of all other things, profits, commodities, emoluments whatsoever, touching our said Lord the King, by reason of any [   ] as by the said commission more fully appears : By the oath of good and lawful men of the county aforesaid, whose names ensue, to wit : Colin Maxwell, Gent. ; John Blackwood, Gent. ; James M'Dowell, Gent. ; Thomas Dixon, Gent. ; Robert Hamilton, Gent. ; William Barkley, Gent. ; William Johnston, Gent. ; Thomas M'Crew, Gent. ; John Speir, Gent. ; and John Gordon, Gent. ; William [   ], Gent. ; Jenkyn Fitz Sh. [   ], Gent. ; John Lofty, Gent. ; Leonard Drake, Gent. ; James Pattowne, Gent., Jurors, which Jurors on their oath aforesaid say that James, late Earl of Clanbrazill and Viscount Claneboy, deceased, in his life was seized in his demesne as of fee of and in all the monasteries, abbeys, priories, rectories, tithes, islands, messuages, edifices, and lands following, viz. : of all that dissolved Monastery or Abbey of Bangor, in the County of Down aforesaid, and the scite, circuit, ambit, and precinct of the said late dissolved monastery, with the appurtenances, and of the towns and hamlets following, viz. : Bangor, containing 120 acres ; Portavo, 120 acres ; Ballyfoddyglan or Ballyfadderly, 120 acres ; Ballymenenitragh, containing 120 acres ; Ballymenenutragh, 120 acres ; Carrowreagh, 120 acres ; Carroworloge, 120 acres ; Ballow near the sea, 120 acres ; Ballymulleragh, otherwise Gillgroomsporte, 120 acres ; Bally-Maccormick, otherwise Ballymacormagh, 120 acres ; Ballymaconnell, otherwise Ballymakonill, 120 acres ; Ballycroghan, 120 acres ; Ballyholince, 120 acres ; Ballenagud, or Ballynathud, or Ballynahugh, 120 acres ; Ballyonered, or Ballycureagh, or Ballyred, 120 acres ; Ballynegragen, 120 acres ; Ballenegreind, or Bullyocrand, 120 acres ; Ballow near Bangor, 120 acres ; Carrownesurd, or Carrowneser, 120 acres ; Carrowknockanduffe, or Carrowflenclackonduffe, 120 acres ; Carrowneshewyan, or Colloseneseleran, 120 acres ; Ballymonycarrogie, or Ballymoneycarragh, 120 acres ; Ballyrangcile, or Ballyfrangaghguile, 120 acres ; Ballelisbane, or Ballelisebane, 120 acres (saving the interest of James Hamilton, Gent., of a parcel of the said Ballefrangahguile and the townland of Ballegilbert, in the parish of Bangor) ; the town and lands of Ballebarne, or Ballebrenan, containing 120 acres ; the town and lands of Ballecarnanleagh, or Ballenecarnedeagh, 120 acres ; Ballykillare, or Ballecoller, 120 acres ; Ballesallagh, 120 acres ; Ballemullen, or Ballemule, 120 acres ; Ballyvernon, or Ballyvernocke, 120 acres ; Ballylidie, containing 120 acres ; Ballycrott, 120 acres ; Balleskelly, or Ballyskeally, 120 acres ; aud Ballygilbert, 120 acres : And that he was seised of the towns and lands of Ballymeaghan, or Ballymeigh, containing 120 acres ; Ballymachoris, 120 acres ; Ballynemajor, or Ballymair, 120 acres ; lying in or near the plains of Belfast, with the appurtenances : And also of the Rectory of Ballelughan, or Balleurgegan, in Lecale, with the tithes to the said Rectory pertaining, parcell of the possession of the aforesaid Abbey of Bangor ; and of the Rectory of Clonuffe, with two-third parts of the tithes ; and of the church or chapel of Creggavadda, and the tithes of the towns following, viz. Ballegregyvadda, Ballyrobert, Ballydavid, and Ballygreine, or Ballygenie, pertaining to the said late

Monastery of Bangor ; and of the impropriate Rectory or Chapel of Holywood, with the tithes of the towns following, to wit : Ballecultra, Ballemanagh, Ballekcille, Ballenderrie, and Balleknocknegonie ; and also of and in all tithes of fish taken or landed in the south of the Bay of Carrickfergus, from the Copeland Islands to the way or passage of Belfast ; and also of and in the whole passage or ferry from the town of Bangor to and from Knockfergus and Antrim side ; and also of and in the advowson of all vicarages in the parishes, towns, or townlands aforesaid, with all their tithes, obventions, and appurtenances whatsoever ; and also of and in the lately dissolved Priory or Religious House of Holywood, in the county aforesaid, and the scite, circuit, ambit, and precinct of the said lately dissolved Priory, with the appurtenances ; also of and in the towns, townlands, hamlets, and places following, with the appurtenances, viz. : the town and lands of Ballykelle or Ballekigill, containing 120 acres ; Ballymanack, or Ballemanagh, containing 120 acres ; Ballycultrack, or Ballycultra, or Ballycultraghagh, containing 120 acres ; Ballenderrie, or Ballederrie, containing 120 acres ; Ballygreknocknegonie, or Balleknocknegonie, containing 120 acres ; which said premises are lying and being in the aforesaid County of Down ; and also of and in the impropriate Rectory of Balleorane, in the County of Down aforesaid, with the tithes of the towns following, viz. : Balleorane, Nerany, Wynnecarvall, and Lisbraden, in the territory of Slught-Hubrick, in the county aforesaid ; and of the Rectory impropriate of Kilcouby, or Kirkcubin, with the tithes in the towns and places following, viz. :— the tithes of Killcuby, or Kircuby, and Ballemulen, in the territory of the Great Ards ; and of the Rectory impropriate of Coolegrange, with the tithes in the town of Coolegrange, or Grange, in Great Ardes, near Blackstaffe ; and the towns and lands of Ravarra, Carrowreagh, and Ballecloghan, lying in or near the Plains of Belfast, and the tithes of Rowbane and Rowreagh, in the Great Ards ; and also of the Rectory impropriate of Drumroan, with the tithes in the towns of Drumroan and Ballyhiggin, in the Great Ards ; and also of the rectories, towns, villages, places, lands, tenements, tithes, and hereditaments following, parcel of the late dissolved Abbey of Cumber, viz. : of and in the town and lands of Ballenegatuge, containing 120 acres ; Carrower, 120 acres ; Ballecullentry, 120 acres ; Ballenicoll, 120 acres ; and all the tithes of the towns and places following, viz. : Ballerestoll, Ballegrangeogh, Ballelisbeene, Ballekeele, Ballemanare, Balletullehubbert, Ballemouglagh, Ballechegle, Ballydrumheriffe, half the town of Ballegraffan, Ballebein, Ballemaghcriscue or Ballevagherlescowe, and Ballegowne or Ballegowan ; and of and in so much of the Rectorial tithes of Taunaghain, coming, growing, or increasing in any of the towns, townlands, hamlets, lands, tenements, and hereditaments whatsoever of the said Earl of Clanbrazill ; and of and in all tithes of fish caught or landed in the southern side of the river of Cumber, and to the lands and hereditaments of the said Earl of Clanbrazill thereto extending ; and also of and in so much of the tithes of the impropriate Rectory of Killane and Drum, in the Lagan, or increasing from any of the lands and hereditaments belonging to the aforesaid Earl, and also of and in all and singular the towns, places, messuages, rectories, and lands following, as well spiritual as temporal, viz. : Ballewalter, parcel of the possession of the late dissolved Monastery of Gray Abbey, in the Great Ardes aforesaid, containing 120 acres ; the quarter of land called St. John's Quarter, in the Ganwie, containing 30 acres ; the quarter of land called Carrowclogher, in the parish of Whittchurch, containing 30 acres ; the quarter of land called Carrownemoan, in the parish of Talbotstowne, containing 30 acres ; the quarter of land called Carrow-John-Bostie, in the town of Drumroan, containing 30 acres ; another quarter of land called St. John's Quarter, in Fulleaghkeavan, containing 30 acres ; that quarter of land called Carrowknechigle, or St. John's Quarter, in Kilrolgan, in the Great Ardes, containing 30 acres ; and also in all the impropriate rectories following, parcel of the possession of the late dissolved Monastery of Black Abbey, in the Great Ardes, viz. : the Rectory impropriate of Ballyhalbert, two-third parts of the tithes of the towns of Ballesperagh, Ballyhalbert, Ballyrichard, Ballyeportavogie or Mullaghmore, Ballenefringe or Negallogh, Balleglastragh, [   ] ; and of the Rectory of Whittchurch or Templefin, with the appurtenances, and of two-third parts of the tithes of the towns of Balleobeckan, Ballemagan, [   ] Balledownever [   ] Templefin or Whittchurch, Listiagners, Ballyganway, and Ballekilleraten, in the Great Ardes ; and of and in the rectory impropriate of Iniscargie, with the appurtenances, two-third parts of the the tithes of the town and lands of Ballelimpt ; Ballegarrugan, containing [   ] acres ; Ballefister, containing 120 acres ; Carrownesca, containing 120 acres ; [containing 120 acres ; Iniscavan [   ] ; Ballchollekin, or Tullochene, 120 acres ; Ballemullagh, or Mullagh, 120 acres ; Corball, 120 acres ; Ballecastlanwilliam, or Castlewilliam, 120 acres ; Ballenecarie, or Ballenecabbrie, 120 acres ; Killileagh, 120 acres ; Rinchady, or Renechady,

120 acres; Tulloghmoremacmartin, 120 acres; Ballyrathconeva, or Ballerathconegan, 120 acres; Ballemaccorberell, or Ballymacromwell, or Cromwell, 120 acres; Rindufferin, or Mylerton, 120 acres; Ballyomeran and Balleneran, 120 acres; Ballemaccoran, 120 acres; Rathgoronan, 120 acres; Ballekiltenegan, or Ballenegan, 120 acres; Carrowreagh, 120 acres; Carrickruske, or Carrickruskie, 120 acres; Killnichie, 120 acres; Ballow, 120 acres; Balleoshen, or Ballemashen, 120 acres; Ballemaccacrebye, or Ballemaccrelye, 120 acres; Balleagullen, or Carrowgullen, 120 acres; Ballebregagh, 120 acres; Ballegan, or Ballelisgowne, or Ballegigon, 120 acres; Lisduffe, 120 acres; Balletoge, or Ballecoge, 120 acres; Balleleye, or Ballecleighe, 120 acres; Ballecosgrehan, or Ballecoskeran, 120 acres; Castlegallie, 120 acres; Liscreagh, 120 acres; Ballygarvin, 120 acres; Tullenoagh, 120 acres; Calleragan, 120 acres; Castlanroise, 120 acres; Ballealogan, or Balleologan, 120 acres; Ballemullin, 120 acres; Ballehollyard, 120 acres; Ardygon, 120 acres; Ballebrown, or Tulleviric, 120 acres; Balletrim, 120 acres; Ballereagh, or Reaghe, 120 acres, Quoile, 120 acres; Rathkirren, 120 acres; Ballyconty, 120 acres; Balledrumore, 120 acres; Balletagath, or Carrickdowe, 120 acres; Maumore, or Maghmore, 120 acres; Tullecowise, or Tullymachnowe, 120 acres; Kilcanon, or Skiltanan, 120 acres; Derrebaye, 120 acres; Balleherman, 120 acres; Killanreas, 120 acres; Rinchady, 120 acres; Islandmore, 120 acres; Islandmacshagh, 120 acres; Islandavanagh, or Inishdavan, or Streranan, 120 acres; Islandarragh, 120 acres; Islandconily, 120 acres; Island-Rinchady, 120 acres; Islandreagh, 120 acres; and in the Island of Inishmacattarge, 120 acres, lying in the territory of the Dufferin, in the county aforesaid; and also of all the tithes of fish taken or landed into the Dufferin upon Loghcoine, and of the advowsons, donations, rights of patronage and disposition of the Rectories, Vicarages, churches, chapels, &c., of Killileagh, Killandreas, Renechady, and Killinchienemagherrie, in the territorie aforesaid, and the tithes, towns, and lands of Killinchinnikillye, wheresoever they be; and of all castles, messuages, houses, edifices, lands, tenements, pastures, and glebe lands, and of all other tithes, as well great as small, as oblations and obventions, courts leet, and view of frankpledge whatsoever, with the appurtenances, lying within the castles, manors, monasteries, abbeys, priories, and other the premises aforesaid (except as is excepted and appears by letters patent of the late King Charles, bearing date 20th April, in the 5th year of his reign, granted to James Viscount Claneboy, his heirs and assigns); and that being so seised, the aforesaid late Earl died on the 20th of June, 1659; and that Henry, now Earl of Clanbrassil, his son and heir, was then twelve years of age, and not married. The aforesaid James Earl of Clanbrasill, by the name of James Viscount Claneboy, by his deed granted to Henry Earl of Monmouth and another, certain lands, being part of the premises, the tenor of which deed follows in the original.—*Ulst. Inq. No. 23, Co. Down.*⁸

No. VII.

CHARTER OF THE BOROUGH OF KILLYLEAGH, DATED 10TH MARCH, 1612.

JAMES, by the grace of God, of England, Scotland, France, and Ireland, King, Defender of the Faith, &c. To all people to whom our present letters shall come, greeting: Know ye, that we, as well at the humble petition of the inhaitants of the village of Killyleagh, in the Dufferin, within our County of Down, in our Province of Ulster, within our Kingdom of Ireland, as for the inhabiting and planting

⁸ The following Inquisition relating to the chief rent of the Dufferin, appears to have been taken on the same day, and is numbered 8 in the same volume:—"Downpatrick, 9th April, 1662.—Christopher Whyte, of Karringston, in County Lowth, was seised as of fee of a certain chief rent of £40 from the territory of the Dufferin, in County Down; also of a certain debt of £40 sterling, which both were due to the aforesaid Christopher Whyte by the late Viscount Claneboy, for which the aforesaid Christopher was to receive £60 yearly for his interest: And being so seised, the aforesaid Christ. Whyte, 30 [   ] 1642, at Killileagh, in the County aforesaid, and at divers other places in the aforesaid County, was in actual rebellion, and continued in the same rebellion till the 10th September, 1648, and afterwards died; by reason whereof the premises have devolved upon King Charles that now is. The aforesaid King, by his letters patent under the Great Seal of Ireland, granted all the premises to Henry, now Earl of Clanbrazill, and his heirs."

r

the Northern parts of our said Kingdom, which are waste and uninhabited, according to the laudable form of government established in our Kingdom of England, and for the better progress and perfection of that new plantation happily begun there, of our special grace, certain knowledge, and proper motion, by the advice of our trusty and well-beloved Councillor Sir Arthur Chichester, Knight, our Deputy General of the said Kingdom of Ireland, as also according to the intent and purport of certain letters signed with our hand and under our signet, dated at our Court at Hampton Court, the 26th day of September, in the 10th year of our reign of England, France, and Ireland, and in the 46th of Scotland, and now enrolled in the records of our Chancery of our said Kingdom of Ireland : Have by these presents appointed, ordained, and declared, that the said village or town of Killyleagh, and all and singular castles, messuages, tofts, mills, houses, edifices, buildings, curtilages, yards, orchards, gardens, waste-grounds, lands, tenements, and hereditaments whatsoever, lying or being in or within the said village or town of Killyleagh, or within the precincts of the said village or town, from henceforth are, and for ever hereafter shall be one entire and free Borough of itself, by the name of the Borough, and be nominated and called from henceforth the Borough of Killyleagh ; and We have by these presents erected, appointed, and ordained, all those in one entire and free Borough of itself, by the name of the Borough of Killyleagh.   And further, We do by these presents will, ordain, and appoint, that there be within the said Borough, one body corporate and politic, consisting of one Provost, twelve free Burgesses, and of a Community, and that all the inhabitants within the said village and lands aforesaid, are and for ever hereafter by force of these presents shall be one body corporate and politic really in deed and by name, by the name of the Provost, free Burgesses, and Community of the Borough of Killyleagh : and We do by these presents for us our heirs and successors, erect, make, ordain, and appoint them by the name of the Provost, free Burgesses, and Community of the Borough of Killyleagh aforesaid, one body corporate and politic in reality, deed, and name, really and to the full, and that by the same name they may have a perpetual succession, and that by the name of the Provost, free Burgesses, and Community of the Borough of Killyleagh, they are and for ever hereafter shall be persons qualified and capable in law to have, purchase, receive and possess lands, tenements, liberties, privileges, jurisdictions, franchises, and hereditaments whatsoever, of whatever kind, nature, or sort they be, to them and their successors, in fee and perpetuity ; and likewise goods and chattels, and other things of whatsoever kind, nature, or sort they be ; and also to give, grant, set and assign lands, tenements and hereditaments, and all and singular other deeds and things to do and execute by the said name, and that they by the name of the Provost, free Burgesses, and Community of the Borough of Killyleagh aforesaid, may sue and be impleaded, answer and be answered, defend and be defended, before us, our heirs and successors, and before whatsoever the justices and judges of us, or our heirs and successors, and others whatsoever, in whatever Courts of us, our heirs and successors, and in any other place whatsoever, in and concerning all and all manner of actions, suits, pleas, plaints, and demands whatsoever, to be prosecuted or brought by or against them, in any manner or way : And that they, the said Provost and free Burgesses of the Borough aforesaid, and their successors, may for ever have full power and authority to choose, send, and return two understanding and fit men, for serving and attending in any Parliament, hereafter to be held in our Kingdom of Ireland, and that such men so chosen, sent, and returned, may have full power and authority to treat and consult upon those matters and things which to them and others there shall be exhibited or declared, and to give freely their votes and suffrages thereupon, and to do or execute other things whatsoever, as fully and freely as any other Burgesses, of any other ancient Borough, in our said Kingdom of Ireland, or within our said Kingdom of England, in our Parliament there used to do or execute : Wherefore we will, and by these presents for us, our heirs and successors, do give and grant unto the said Provost and free Burgesses of the said Borough, and their successors, and also we charge, and for us, our heirs and successors, strictly command all the sheriffs, officers, and ministers of us, our heirs and successors whatsoever, of our said County of Down, for the time being, to whom any of our writ or writs for choosing Parliament Burgesses within our County of Down shall at any time be directed, that every such sheriffs, officers, or ministers, to whom any of our writ or writs of this nature shall so be directed as aforesaid, shall make his command to the Provost and free Burgesses of the said Borough of Killyleagh, for the time being, for the election and return of the said two Burgesses, according to the form or effect of the same writ or writs.   And these our letters patent or the enrolment thereof shall be a sufficient warrant and discharge in that part, as well unto the said Provost and free Burgesses of the Borough aforesaid, and their successors, as unto all and singular the sheriffs, officers, and ministers of us, our heirs and successors whatsoever.[b] And to the intent it may unto after ages appear that this new Corporation was (at first) composed of circumspect and honest men, we make, constitute, and nominate William Hamilton to be and become the first and present Provost of the said Borough, to be continued in the same office until the feast of St. Michael the Archangel, next ensuing the date of these presents; and in like manner we make, constitute, and nominate William Dunbar, James Williamson, Alexander Cunningham, John Moore, Thomas Baily, Thomas Danby, Peter Hamilton, James Hamilton, John Montgomery, Walter O'Lynn, Richard Oher, and Hugh Hamilton, to be and become the first and present twelve free Burgesses of the said Borough, to be continued in the same office of the free Burgesses of the same Borough, during their several lives, unless in the meantime they or some of them, for their misbehaviour or some other reasonable cause, shall be removed from their

---

[b] The following list of Members returned to the Irish Parliament for the Borough of Killileagh, in pursuance of their Charter, from 1613 till the union with Great Britain in 1801, has been extracted from the Journals of the Irish House of Commons:—

1613, April.—EDWARD TREVOR, Esq. (Knight), Rose-Trevor.
    JOHN HAMILTON, Esq., Corronery.[a]
1634, June.—PAUL REYNOLDS, Esq.
    JOHN HAMILTON, Esq., Corronery.

1639, March 5.—PAUL REYNOLDS, Esq.
    GEORGE NETTLETON, Gent.
1661, April 18.—COLYN MAXWELL, Esq.[b]
    JOHN SWADLYN, Esq.[c]
1692, Sept. 29.—JAMES SLOAN, Esq., Killileagh.[d]
1695, Aug. 8.—HANS HAMILTON, Esq., Frankfort.
    JAMES SLOANE, Esq., Killileagh.
    PATRICK DUN, M.D. (Knight), Dublin.[e]

---

[a] This John Hamilton was the third brother of Sir James Hamilton.—See page 12 of MSS., ante. The following extract respecting him has also been obtained from the Funeral Entries in Ulster's Office:—"John Hamilton, of Corronemie, in the County of Cavan, Esq., fourth sonne of Hans Hamilton, of Dunlopp, in Scotland, and fourth brother to the Right Honourable James, Viscount Clane- boy. The said first-mentioned John took to wife Sarah, daughter of Anthony Brabazon, of Benllanasloe, in the County of Roscommon, Esq., by whome he had issue, four sonnes, and four daughters, viz., Hans, eldest sonne; Anthony, second sonne, died young, and unmarried; James, third sonne, and Francis, fourth sonne, all as yett unmarried; Ursula, eldest daughter, died young, and unmarried; Jane, second daughter, died alsoe; Mary, third daughter, Ellinor, fourth daughter, both as yett unmarried. The said first-mentioned John departed this mortall life at Killileagh, in the County of Downe, the 4th of December, 1639, and was interred in the Parish Church of Mullaghbreack, in the County of Armagh, about the 10th of the same monneth. The truth of the premises is testified by the subscription of the said Hans Hamilton, eldest sonne and heire of the said defunct, whoe hath returned this certificat into my office to be there recorded. Taken by me, Thomas Preston, Esq., Ulaester King of Armes, the 26th of January, 1639."—Fun. Ent., vol. 8, p. 233.

[b] Captain Collin Maxwell is named in the will of James, 1st Earl of Clanbrassil, ante, at p. 84, as one of the persons to be aiding in assisting to his executors therein named in setting, letting, leasing out, and bettering the rents of such lands as were to be set, the leases whereof were already determined, or might run out before his eldest son came to age, as therein mentioned. Colin Maxwell is also named as one of the jurors who took the Inquisition of 9th April, 1662, on the death of James Earl of Clanbrassill, which is printed at page lxi, ante, of the Appendix. On the 28th of Nov., 1664, a writ of salary issued to Colyn Maxwell from the Hanaper Office as Burgess for the Borough of Killileagh.—Com. Jour.

[c] At p. 91, ante, a Mr. Swadlin is mentioned as the Steward of Henry, 2nd Earl of Clanbrassil, to whom the custody of Earl James's will was entrusted, who is probably the John Swadlyn above named.

[d] Alexander Sloan, who is also named, at p. 84, ante, in the will of James Earl of Clanbrassil, as one of the persons to aid and assist his executors, was the father of this James Sloan, and of his younger brother, Sir Hans Sloan, the founder of the British Museum, who was born at Killileagh, in 1660. Alexander Sloan, who was of Scotch descent, was Receiver-General of Taxes in the County of Down, during the Civil War, and one of the Commissioners of Array after the Restoration. He married Sarah, daughter of Dr. Hicks, who was one of the Chaplains of Archbishop Laud, and one of the Prebends of Winchester. He had by her seven sons,

of whom Sir Hans was the youngest. James Sloan is mentioned at p. 102, ante, as one of Countess Alice's great agents and confidants; and again, at p. 122, as one of the persons set on to ask from the five uncles "gratifications for their kindness and good services;" and his name appears in the rental of the estate for 1689, at p. 126, ante, as tenant of Lisan, and again, at p. 131, as claiming a lease of it in reversion. On the 24th of October, 1692, James Sloan was also returned for the Borough of Roscommon, but elected to serve for Killileagh.—Irish Com. Jour.

[e] Sir Patrick Dun, Knight, was a native of Aberdeen, born, in 1642, of a family long settled in that city, and a branch, it is stated, of the ancient family of Dun of Dun. The medical career of Sir Patrick Dun is involved in total obscurity, till we find him, in 1693, settled as a Physician in Dublin, being in that year President of the College of Physicians, founded by Charter of Charles II. He appears to have taken an active part in procuring the Charter of William and Mary, constituting the present King and Queen's College of Physicians, and was appointed the first President of that body in the same year (1693). He evidently occupied a high rank in his profession, and filled the office of State Physician for several years previous to his death. He married Miss Jephson, of the County Cork, and dying in 1714, left no issue. Lady Dun who survived him, died in 1748. His will, dated 16th November, 1711, endowing the College of Physicians with lands in County Waterford, is printed at length in the introduction to the Annals of Sir Patrick Dun's Hospital, Dublin, for the year ending 5th January, 1831, from which the above facts are extracted. In a memoir of Sir Patrick Dun, since published by Dr. Belcher of Dublin, he says, at p. 18—"I have searched in vain for any particulars of Sir Patrick's early career; and the first notice of him, so far as I know, occurs in a letter written from Dublin Castle by Sir John Hill to John Forbes, then of Culloden, near Inverness. Hill writes, under date 14th February, 1696—'Here is one Dr. Dun, an Aberdeensman, who is Physician to the State and to my Lord Lieutenant, desires to have his service remembered to your son Duncan, with whom he had acquaintance in Paris.'" This memoir, at p. 29, also contains the following notice of Sir Patrick's Parliamentary career:—"Having succeeded in his profession, and feeling ambitious of public honours, Dr. Dun decided on entering Parliament; and, accordingly, he became a member of the Irish House of Commons in 1692. On the 29th of September in that year he was returned member for the Manor of Mullingar, and on the 29th of the same month, he was also returned for the Borough of Killileagh, Co. Down. He elected to sit for the latter." Dr. Belcher, in a note to this passage, says—"The Borough of Killileagh was very much under the influence of Dun's friends, the Hamiltons."

office aforesaid ; and we will, appoint, and ordain all the inhabitants of the said village, and all and such other men as the Provost and free Burgesses of the same Borough for the time being shall admit into the freedom of the Borough aforesaid, to be and become members of the community of the

---

1703, Sept. 21.—HANS STEVENSON, Esq., Killileagh.*f*
　　JOHN HALTRIDGE, Esq., Dromore.*g*
1713, Nov. 11.—JOHN HALTRIDGE, Esq., Dromore.
　　JAMES STEVENSON, Merchant, Dublin.*h*
1715, Oct. 20.—JOHN HALTRIDGE, Esq., Dromore.
　　ROBERT ROSS, Esq., Rosetrevor.
1725, Sept. 18.—JAMES STEVENSON, Esq., Killileagh, *vice* Haltridge, deceased.*i*
1727, Sept. 29.—JAMES STEVENSON, Esq., Killileagh.
　　JAMES STEVENSON, Esq., Dublin.

1739, Oct. 18.—ALEXANDER HAMILTON, Esq., The Fues, Armagh ; The Knock, Dublin, *vice* James Stevenson, sen., deceased.*k*
1761, April 30.—BERNARD WARD, Esq., Castleward.*l*
　　JOHN CONGREVE, Esq., Mount Congreve, Co. Waterford.
1761, Oct. 31.—JOHN BLACKWOOD, Esq., Ballyliddy, *vice* Ward, who made his election to serve for County Down.*m*

---

f Hans Stevenson, of Ballygrott, was the eldest son of John Stevenson, Esq., of Ballywooly, by Rachel Hamilton his wife, one of the three daughters of John Hamilton, eldest son of Archibald Hamilton, of Halcraig, and nephew of the first Viscount Claneboye. He married his cousin, Anne Hamilton, one of the daughters and co-heiresses of James Hamilton of Neilsbrook, who eventually became his sole heiress, as stated at p. 145, *ante*. In one of his letters to Mr. William Hamilton, referred to at p. 146, *ante*, dated from London, on the 26th of April, 1694, he states having, with much difficulty, got a company in the Lord Charlemont's regiment ; and some of his subsequent letters in 1696, are dated from Waterford, and Duncannon Fort, where his regiment was quartered. It does not appear from them how long he continued in the army ; but he eventually obtained the rank of colonel, his commission for which is in Lord Dufferin's possession. Judging from these letters, he was evidently a good man of business, and, with his wife's uncle, William Hamilton, seems to have ably, though unsuccessfully, fought the battle of the Killileagh section of the family as to the division of the Claneboye estates, with James Hamilton of Bangor, and James Hamilton of Tollymore, and more particularly with Sir Robert, and his son, Sir Hans Hamilton, of Hamilton's-Bawn, Co. Armagh. During the whole of this correspondence from 1694 to 1705, the greatest kindness seems to have prevailed between him and his "Dear Unkell," as he styled William Hamilton, concluding as his "dutiful nevoy," though he was only such by marriage with his niece, Anne Hamilton, whom he often writes of as his "dear Nan," to whom, as well as his children, he seems to have been greatly attached. He died in 1713, leaving James Stevenson, Esq., of Killileagh, his eldest son and heir.

g One of his daughters, Grace, married Isaac Macartney, Esq., of Belfast, whose daughter Grace was second wife to Sir Robert Blackwood, of Ballyleidy, who married 5th November, 1694 ; created a baronet, 1st July, 1763 ; and died in 1774.

h This James Stevenson, described as James, senior, of Dublin, was second son of John Stevenson, Esq., of Ballywooly, and younger brother of Colonel Hans Stevenson, who had sat for this borough in the previous Parliament. James had previously been returned, on 15th October, 1715, for the Borough of Randalstown, probably in consequence of his elder brother Hans's connexion with it through his marriage with a daughter of James Hamilton, of Neilsbrook, which must have been situate in the immediate vicinity of it, as in some of Colonel Stevenson's letters to Mr. William Hamilton, before referred to, he asks after "the good family at the Main Water." The following announcement of his death is taken from the *Belfast News-Letter* of Tuesday, Nov. 21, 1738 :—"Dublin, Nov. 18.— Last Wednesday morning died James Stevenson, Esq., Member of Parliament for the Borough of Killileagh, a most eminent merchant, and formerly one of the greatest dealers in the kingdom. This worthy gentleman, by endeavouring to relieve the poor of the nation, imported a vast quantity of corn into this country in the year 1729, by which he lost £9,000. He was a fair and honourable dealer, which makes his death universally lamented, as it is a great loss to the public." On the 9th of October, 1739, a new writ for the Borough of Killileagh issued in the room of James Stevenson, Esq., sen., deceased.—4 *Ir. Com. Jour.*, p. 295.

i James Stevenson, Esq., of Killileagh, known as James Stevenson, jun., was eldest son of Colonel Hans Stevenson, of Ballygrott,

and Anne Hamilton, his wife. He married Anne, third daughter of Nicholas Price, Esq., of Saintfield, by whom he had an only child, Dorcas, who married Sir John Blackwood, and was created Baroness Dufferin and Claneboye, at p. 1800.

k Alexander Hamilton, Esq., of Knock, Co. Dublin, and Newtownhamilton, Co. Armagh, married Isabella, daughter of Robert Maxwell, Esq., of Finnebrogue, and had by her four sons, and three daughters. He represented Killileagh in the Irish Parliament, from 1739 to 1761, and died in 1768. He was one of the 124 members who successfully opposed the pretensions of the English Crown, in 1753, for commemoration of which a large gold medal was struck and presented to each of the patriotic members. Mr. Hamilton's medal is stated, in *Burke's Landed Gentry*, to be still preserved as an heirloom in the family. His third son, the Honorable George Hamilton, of Hampton-Hall, Co. Dublin, was M.P. for Belfast, in the Irish Parliament, for many years, and was raised to the Irish Bench, in 1776, as a Baron of the Court of Exchequer. Baron Hamilton was eminently distinguished for his public spirit, and was the first person who introduced the manufacture of cotton hosiery into Ireland, at Balbriggan, for which it has since become so celebrated. He died in 1793, and was succeeded by his son Alexander Hamilton, Esq., who represented Belfast in the Irish Parliament when the Union was proposed, but vacated his seat in Parliament, and the lucrative post of Cursitor of the Irish Exchequer, rather than support the measure. His nephew, George Alex. Hamilton, Esq., of Hampton-Hall, Co. Dublin, succeeded to his estates ; and, after representing Trinity College for several years in the British Parliament, is now Under-Secretary to the Treasury.

l Bernard Ward was returned for the County of Down, on the 29th day of April, 1761, for which he made his election to serve.—See Memoir of him at p. 64, *ante*.

m John Blackwood, Esq., who was so returned in the place of Bernard Ward, Esq., was the eldest son of Sir Robert Blackwood, of Ballyleidy, Co. Down, who was created a Baronet of Ireland, 1st July, 1763, Sir Robert married first Joyce, sister of Joseph Leeson, Esq., first Earl of Miltown, by whom he had two sons, John, his heir, born in 1721, and Leeson, who died unmarried, in 1773. Sir John, who succeeded on his father's death, in 1774, to the Baronetcy, married Dorcas, only daughter and heiress of James Stevenson, Esq., of Killileagh, who, after his death, was created, on 3rd July, 1800, Baroness Dufferin and Claneboye, of Ballyleidy and Killileagh, Co. Down. Sir John was in politics a Whig, and was opposed to the Union with Great Britain ; and, during the intrigues for its accomplishment, the following anecdote is related of him :—On one occasion an emissary from the Castle was dining with him, and after dinner, taking up one of the spoons, observed, "Sir John, I greatly admire your crest, don't you think it would be a great improvement if it were surmounted with balls?" "Perhaps it might," replied Sir John, "but do me the favour to bestow part of your admiration on the motto, *per vias rectas*."

The following spirited letter from him to Lord Castlereagh, on the same subject, is printed in the "Castlereagh Memoirs and Correspondence," Vol. ii., p. 213 :—

"January 15, 1798, [1799.]

" MY LORD,—I received, in a letter yesterday, from your office of the 7th instant, an unusual summons to me, by the direction of the Lord Lieutenant, to attend in Parliament on 22nd instant, on

Borough aforesaid. And further, We will that the said William Hamilton, whom we by these presents have made Provost aforesaid of the said Borough, shall come before our Justices at the Assizes or the General Sessions to be holden within the said County of Down, next after the date of these presents,

---

1768, July 15.—HENRY THOMAS BUTLER, Viscount IKERRIN, Ballylinch, Kilkenny.*u*

Sir ARCHIBALD ACHESON, Bart., Markethill, Armagh.

1769, Nov. 2.—ARTHUR JOHNSTON, Esq., Redemon,*o vice* Acheson, for Co. Armagh.

1776, June 11.—Sir JOHN BLACKWOOD, Bart.

ROBERT BLACKWOOD, Esq.*p*

1788, Jan. 17.—Sir JOHN BLACKWOOD, Bart.

1789, Feb. 17.—JAMES STEVENSON BLACKWOOD, Esq.*q*

1790, July 2.—Hon. ROBERT WARD.

JAMES STEVENSON BLACKWOOD, Esq.

1798, Jan. 9.—Sir JOHN BLACKWOOD, Bart.

JAMES STEVENSON BLACKWOOD, Esq.

1799, April 3.—HANS BLACKWOOD, Esq.,*r vice* Sir John Blackwood, deceased.

1800, Jan. 15.—Sir JAMES STEVENSON BLACKWOOD, Bart.

HANS BLACKWOOD, Esq.

—— March 14.—DANIEL MUSSENDEN, Esq., *vice* Hans Blackwood, Esq.

---

business of the greatest importance which will be submitted to Parliament on that day, &c.   I have been a member forty years : by many of the Lord Lieutenants I have been honoured even with social intercourse ; none, however, have presumed to call for my attendance on any Parliamentary subject. This is the first, without any previous knowledge of me, who has condescended to summon me in the style as to one of the vassals of administration. The only authority I acknowledge is that of our Speaker, as directed by the call of our House. I wish to inform the Lord Lieutenant that I have the pride of feeling my own independence, —*nullius addictus in verba jurare magistri*—a pride I would not barter for any honour, station, place, or pension in his power to grant ; and while I can maintain my own opinion and judgment on all public questions, I will not part with the approbation of my own mind, nor permit the interposition of any Lord Lieutenant, without expressing my indignation at such treatment. Your Lordship knows I had intended to have attended my duty ; let it not be said I attend by the persuasion of His Excellency's summons. *Entre nous*, as to the momentous question, I shall not be finally determined till I have heard and digested the best information on the subject in the House. I am now consulting old as well as late constitutional authorities, as I never take assertions for historical truths. I have the honour to be, &c.

"JOHN BLACKWOOD.

"P.S.—If you can foresee that the business of the Union may not come on the 5th of February, as your last information suggests, I will be obliged by the earliest intelligence, as my health will be benefited by the delay, the length of the day, and the warmth of the weather increasing. The filling up the vacancies will require more time than you mention, and it will be decent to have the fullest House possible."

The foregoing letter, though purporting to be dated in 1798, was in fact written in 1799, as appears by the editor's correction in the Castlereagh Memoirs and Correspondence ; and it would seem that Sir John's declining health, to which he refers in the postscript, did not enable him again to take his seat in the House, or to give his vote on the then "momentous question," as he terms it in the foregoing letter, of the Union of Great Britain and Ireland ; for he died on the 27th of February, 1799, and was succeeded in his Baronetcy and estates by his eldest son, Sir James Stevenson Blackwood. On the 9th of March, 1799, a new writ was ordered to be issued for the Borough of Killileagh, in the room of Sir John Blackwood, Bart., deceased.—*18 Ir. Com. Jour.*, 64.

n On 21st April, 1774, a new writ issued for Killileagh, in room of the Hon. Henry Thomas Butler, commonly called Lord Ikerrin, on his succeeding to the Earldom of Carrick.—*9 Irish Com. Jour.*, 133.

o This gentleman was a member of the Irish Bar, and is believed to have been the maternal ancestor of his namesake, the present Arthur Sharman Crawford, Esq. ; but the editor regrets not having been able to obtain more particulars respecting him before these members went to press.

p Robert Blackwood, Esq., was the eldest son of Sir John Blackwood, but died before his father, having on the 29th of January, 1786, been killed by a fall from his horse, on the high road between

Ballyleidy and Killyleagh. On the 17th of January, 1788, a new writ was issued for Killileagh, in the room of Robert Blackwood, Esq., deceased.—*12 Irish Com. Jour.*, 301.

q James Stevenson Blackwood, Esq., the second son of Sir John Blackwood, succeeded, in consequence of his eldest brother Robert's death in his father's lifetime, to his father's Baronetcy and estates, on his death, in 1799 ; and to his mother's title at her death, on 18th February, 1808, as second Baron Dufferin and Claneboye. He married Anne Dorothea, only daughter of John, first Lord Oriel, on 15th November, 1801, and died *s.p.* 8th August, 1836. His widow long survived him, but died in 1865. See copy of the inscription on his monument in Killileagh Church, given in the note at p. 35, *ante*. The following letter from Sir James S. Blackwood to Lord Castlereagh, on the subject of the Irish Union, is taken from the third volume of the "Castlereagh Memoirs and Correspondence," p. 20 :—

"Ballyleidy, December 21, 1799.

"I have received your Lordship's letters of the 14th, on my return home this day. As a well-wisher to the general concerns of my country, and of the great question you mention to come forward early in the Session, I shall certainly attend on the 15th, and am obliged for the intimation. With respect to my brother [Hans Blackwood, Esq.], I cannot saything. I have not heard his opinion lately, and cannot pretend to lead his judgment, any more than I could bear to have my own directed : feeling as I do, I hope he will not vote against the Union. When we last conversed, he wished to retire : I believe it is still his desire. This must, however, come entirely from himself, as I cannot speak to him upon the business, nor can it be done in any other shape than what has been already mentioned. He is now in Dublin ; perhaps it may suit your Lordship's leisure to converse with him upon it. I have much satisfaction at hearing from your authority that the terms to be now offered have the appearance of giving general satisfaction ; much as I wish a support for the Government, and much as I approve of the principle, so much do I hope the terms may be such as to enable me to vote for them with a conviction of reciprocal advantages to both countries.—Yours very truly,

"J. S. BLACKWOOD."

r This Hans Blackwood, Esq., who afterwards became third Baron Dufferin and Claneboye, on the death of his elder brother James, the second Baron, without issue, in 1834, was born in 1758, and married, 1st, Mehetabel Hester, second daughter and co-heiress of Sir Robert Temple, Bart. ; and, 2ndly, Elizabeth Finlay, 8th July 1801. Of the issue of his first marriage, his eldest son Price, born 6th May, 1794, succeeded on his father's death, in 1839, as fourth Baron Dufferin and Claneboye. He married, 4th July, 1825, Helen Selina, eldest daughter of the late Thos. Sheridan, Esq., by whom he had an only son, Frederick Temple, who, on his father's death in 1841, became fifth Baron Dufferin and Clandeboye in the Peerage of Ireland, and was created Baron Clandeboye in the Peerage of Great Britain, in 1850. On 10th February, 1800, the Speaker's warrant issued for a new writ for Killileagh, in the room of Hans Blackwood, Esq., who had accepted the office of Escheator of Munster.—*19 Irish Com. Jour.*, p. 37.

s

and in due manner give, as well the oath, commonly called in English the Oath of Supremacy, as his own corporal oath for well and truly executing the office of Provost of the Borough aforesaid, until the Feast of Saint Michael the Archangel, next ensuing as is aforesaid, and that the Provost of the said Borough be yearly and elective. And, therefore, we will, and by these presents for us, our heirs and successors, grant unto the said Provost, free Burgesses, and Community of the Borough aforesaid, and their successors, that the said Provost and free Burgesses of the Borough aforesaid for the time being, may and can for ever, yearly at the Feast of the Nativity of Saint John the Baptist, assemble themselves within the Borough aforesaid, and that the said Provost and free Burgesses so met together, or the major part of them, may, before they depart there, choose one of the more understanding Burgesses of the said Borough, to execute the office of the Provost of the Borough aforesaid, for one year from the Feast of Saint Michael the Archangel, then next ensuing, and until which time another of the Burgesses of the same Borough was in due manner elected, sworn, and preferred to that office; and that every Provost so chosen, shall, before he be admitted to execute the office aforesaid, or be esteemed, as well give the said oath, commonly called (in English) the Oath of Supremacy, as his own corporal oath, for well and truly executing the office of Provost of the Borough aforesaid, until the Feast of Saint Michael the Archangel next ensuing such Election, before the Provost of the said Borough, who presided in the office the foregoing year; and we give full power and authority to every such last predecessor of whatever Provost of the Borough aforesaid for the time being, to take the aforesaid oaths of every such Provost to be of the new elected.

And, moreover, We of our special grace, and from our certain knowledge and mere motion, will, and by these presents for us, our heirs and successors, grant unto the said Provost, free Burgesses, and Community of the said Borough, and their successors, that if and how often as it shall happen the Provost of the said Borough for the time being to die, or the aforesaid office any way to become vacant within one year after he is elected and sworn to the office of the Provost of the said Borough, as is aforesaid, that then, and so often the free Burgesses and Community of the said Borough, and their successors, may and can, within fifteen days next after such vacation, choose a fit person out of the number of the free Burgesses to be Provost of the Borough aforesaid, to rule and govern the same Borough during the remainder of that year, and that every person or persons so chosen and elected unto the office of Provost of the said Borough as aforesaid, may and can execute that office of Provost of the said Borough until the feast of Saint Michael the Archangel, next ensuing such election, having first taken the aforesaid oath, called (in English) the Oath of Supremacy, and also the said oath for the due execution of his office of Provost of the said Borough in manner aforesaid ; and further, We, of our special grace, and from our certain knowledge and proper motion, will, and by these presents for us, our heirs and successors, do grant unto the said Provost, free Burgesses, and Community of the said Borough, and their successors, that, if one or any of the said free Burgesses of said Borough named in as aforesaid, or any one or more to be hereafter chosen free Burgesses of the same Borough, shall die or be removed from that office (which said free Burgesses and any one or more of them We will to be removed for misbehaviour in that office at the pleasure of the Provost, free Burgesses, or greatest part of them, of the said Borough for the time being), that then the Provost and the rest of the free Burgesses of the said Borough for the time being, may and can, within seven days next after the death or removal of such free Burgesses, assemble themselves in some convenient place within the said Borough, and that the said Provost and free Burgesses so assembled, or the greater part of them, may and can, before they dismiss, choose one or as many as shall be wanting of the said number of twelve free Burgesses out of the better and more circumspect inhabitants of the said Borough, into the place or places of the free Burgess or Burgesses so deceased, or removed from that or those office or offices, to be continued in the same office during their natural lives, unless in the meantime they or any of them shall, for their mal-administration and ill-behaviour in that post, be removed ; and that every person so chosen, unto the office of a free Burgess of the said Borough, shall, before he be suffered to execute that office, within seven days from election, give his corporal oath for his exercising well and truly the office of a free Burgess of the said Borough, before the Provost thereof for the time being, or before the rest of the free Burgesses of the said Borough then surviving and remaining in that office, or the greater part of them ; to which said Provost for the time being, or the free Burgesses or greater part of them for the time being, We do by these presents give and grant full power and authority to take the aforesaid oath of every of such said free Burgesses to be of new elected ; and that as often as the case shall so happen. And further, We, of our special grace, certain knowledge, and mere motion, will, and by these presents for us, our heirs and successors, do grant unto the said Provost, free Burgesses, and Community of the Borough aforesaid, and their successors, that they and their successors may for ever have and hold, and may and can for ever have and hold, one Court in some fit and convenient place in the said Borough, to be held before the Provost of the same Borough for the time being ; and in the same Court to hold suits on every Tuesday, from week to week, concerning all and every personal action, debt, covenant, trespass, deteanor, contract, and demand whatsoever, not exceeding the sum of five marks sterling, that shall happen or fall out within the said Borough of Killyleagh, or the liberties of the same ; and that such Court be reputed and esteemed a Court of Record for ever : We also will, and for our abundant special grace, certain knowledge, and mere motion, do by these presents, for us, our heirs and successors, grant unto the said Provost, free Burgesses, and Community, of the said Borough, and their successors, that they and their successors may and can from time, as often as they shall think fit, convene and assemble themselves in some convenient place within the said Borough, and in their assemblies there, may statute, ordain, and establish such and such like acts, ordinances, and statutes (in English by law) for the good rule and wholesome government of the said Borough, and the inhabitants thereof, in such sort as to them or the greater part of them shall seem necessary ; and that they may have power and authority to punish, chastise, and correct by fines and pecuniary mulcts all persons trespassing against such acts, ordinances, and statutes ; provided the acts, ordinances, and statutes, fines and mulcts be reasonable, and be not contrary or repugnant to the laws and statutes of our Kingdom of Ireland.   And further, We will, and by these presents for us, our heirs and successors, and do grant unto the aforesaid Provost, free Burgesses, and Community of the Borough aforesaid, and their successors for ever, that they may have a Merchant Guild within the said Borough, and one common seal of such form, and with such arms engraven therein, as to them shall seem best for serving the affairs of the said Borough for ever, and that they can and may for ever, from time to time, as often as it shall be needful, of themselves, there appoint and ordain two constables and other inferior officers or ministers necessary for the better government of the said Borough and the inhabitants thereof ; and every person from time to time so chosen, appointed, and ordained, we make, appoint, and ordain to be and become constables, and other officers and ministers of the said Borough respectively, and to continue in their offices during their good behaviour, or at the will and pleasure of the said Provost, free Burgesses, and Community of the said Borough ; and that every such constable, officer, and minister shall, before he be admitted to exercise his office, give his corporal oath, before the Provost of the said Borough for the time being, that he shall well and truly execute his said office.   And moreover, we, with a special regard to advice, of our certain knowledge and mere motion, do will, and by these presents for us, our heirs and successors, give and grant unto the said Provost, free Burgesses, and Community of the said Borough, and their successors for ever, that they and their successors from henceforth and for ever, may have and hold, and may and can have and hold, one free market in or near the village or Borough aforesaid, to be held on every Monday of each week, for ever, and also two fairs to be held there yearly ; that is to say, one fair in or near the village or Borough every Monday of Holy Trinity, called in English Trinity Monday, to be held yearly for ever, and to continue for the day immediately following ; and another fair more near the village or Borough aforesaid, every feast day of Saint Andrew, to be held yearly for ever, and continue during the next following Tuesday, unless the said feast day of Saint Andrew happens to be a Sabbath or Lord's Day, in which case we will and grant that such fair shall be begun and held upon the Monday from thence next ensuing, and be continued the next following day, to be held yearly for ever, as often as it shall so happen ; and that the Provost of the said Borough for the time being shall be Clerk of the Market within the said Borough, and the liberties thereof, and may from time to time have full power and authority to make and execute all and every things belonging and appertaining to the office of Clerk of the Market within the said Borough, so as no other Clerk of the Market of us, our heirs and successors, may enter the said Borough, or the franchises thereof, there to do and execute the office of Clerk of the Market, or anything unto the said office belonging or appertaining, nor any way intermeddle himself in any office of Clerk of the Market within the said Borough, or any thing interfering with the liberties thereof.

And further, We, of our more abundant special grace, certain knowledge, and mere motion, do grant unto the aforesaid Provost, free Burgesses, and Community of the said Borough, and their successors for ever, and that these our letters patents, and every article and clause in the same or in the enrolment thereof contained, shall be construed and adjudged to the best advantage, benefit, and

favour of the said Provost, free Burgesses, and Community of the Borough aforesaid, and their successors, towards and against us, our heirs and successors, as well in all our Courts as in any other
place within our Kingdom of Ireland, or elsewhere whatsoever, without any confirmations to be hereafter procured or obtained. Notwithstanding that our writ of *ad quod damnum* did not issue for enquiring into the premises before the making of these our letters patents, and notwithstanding any
other defect, or any other thing, cause, or matter whatsoever, to the contrary notwithstanding, so as
express mention do not appear to be made in these presents of the true yearly value or certainty of
the premises, or of any of them, or of any other gifts or grants heretofore made by us or any of our
progenitors unto the said Provost, free Burgesses, and Community of the Borough aforesaid ; any
statute, act, ordinance, or proviso, or any other thing, cause, or matter whatsoever made to the contrary of these premises, or any of them, anyways notwithstanding. In testimony of which We have
made these our letters patent. Witness our said Deputy General of our Kingdom of Ireland, at Dublin, the tenth day of March, in the tenth year of our reign of England, France, and Ireland, and forty-
sixth of Scotland.

ENDORSED THUS :—

In the Rolls of Patents of the Chancery of Ireland, in the Year of the Reign of King James of Eng-
     land, France, and Ireland, the Tenth, and of Scotland the Forty-sixth. Examined by me
     James Newman, Clerk in the Office of the Master of the Rolls.

No. VIII.

REPORT OF THE IRISH CORPORATION COMMISSIONERS ON THE BOROUGH OF KILLILEAGH.

---

1. This borough is situate in the County of Down, upon an arm of Lough Strangford, and within
five miles of Downpatrick, the assize town of the county. The charter describes it as "Vill. de Killileagh in le Duffrine." It is in the parish of Killileagh and barony of Dufferin.
    The limits of the borough extend about one mile by half a mile over the town lands of "Castle-
william," " Corbally," and " the corporation," and contain about 1,173 acres.
    2. The Charter bears date the 10th March, 10 James I. (A.D. 1612), and is stated to have been
made at the petition of the inhabitants of the town. It is enrolled (Rot. Pat. 10 Jac. I. p. 4, m. 50.)
    A Book of Proceedings of the Corporation, commencing in 1761, was produced to us. Some ac-
count was given to us, in evidence, of the mutilation and loss of the older corporation books and other
documents.
    The title of the Corporation is " The Provost, Free Burgesses, and Commonalty of the Borough
of Killileagh."
    The Provost is, by the charter, eligible annually by and from amongst the free burgesses on the
Feast of Saint John, and holds for one year from the ensuing Michaelmas, and until another free burgess be sworn into the office. The provost is, in general, annually elected, but occasionally holds
over until a new provost is sworn in.
    He is constituted by the charter judge of a Borough Court of Record, with jurisdiction in per-
sonal actions to the extent of five marks ; but this court has long been disused. He is also clerk of
the market within the borough ; and, before the Union, was the returning officer upon elections for
members to serve in Parliament. He has no salary or official emolument.
    The number of free burgesses is limited by the charter to 12. They hold during good behaviour.
The charter directed that they should be elected from the inhabitants, but that qualification was dis-

pensed with by the 21 Geo. II. c. 10, s. 8. The power of filling vacancies is vested in the provost and remaining free burgesses, or the greater part of them. The provost and free burgesses, before the Union, returned two members to the Parliament of Ireland.

None of the Acts conferring local powers on the provost and free burgesses (as to appointing a weighmaster of butter, supplying pipe-water, &c.) appear to have been called into action in this corporation. The free burgesses do not now perform any duties except those of occasionally attending meetings for the election of officers, &c. There are no emoluments of any kind attached to the office. Seven of them are non-resident.

The present number of Freemen is supposed not to exceed 12. They do not attend any of the meetings of the corporation. The charter went to incorporate all the inhabitants in the usual form of the charters of the same date, but the right of admission has not been insisted upon, at least in modern times. All admissions into the corporation appear to have taken place by special favour, and usually without the application of the person elected.

We are disposed to infer here, from the existence of such an institution as the " Corporation Jury," which we shall presently notice, that the right of freedom by inhabitancy formerly prevailed.

The appointment of a Town Clerk has lately been entered on the corporation proceedings, but no duties appear to be attached to the office, nor are any emoluments derived from it.

Two Sergeants-at-Mace are named in the charter, but none are now appointed. The appointment of these and of other inferior officers is vested in the whole body of the corporation.

The Provost, from the earliest period (1761) to which the books produced to us refer, has been, almost without exception, either the land agent or a member of the Blackwood family ; the head of which (Lord Dufferin) received the compensation of £15,000 for the extinction of the elective franchise at the time of the Union. He continues to exercise a predominant control over all the acts of the corporation, and admissions to freedom are in fact made at his nomination, though, in form, the act of the provost and free burgesses.

The election of members of the corporation appears to take place without having a legal number present. This appears a natural result from the election of free burgesses and freemen being made without reference to residence as a necessary qualification, and from the inutility of the corporation as at present constituted.

No Roman Catholics have been admitted in this corporation since 1793, when they were rendered eligible. One Protestant Dissenter has been elected a free burgess.

The Borough Court of Record has long been disused.

The corporation district is comprised within the manor of Killileagh and Killinchy. Archibald Hamilton Rowan, Esq., as lord of the manor, appoints the seneschal, who holds a Court Leet once in the year, at which a market jury, petty constables to collect the county cess within the manor, and appraisers, are appointed. The seneschal also holds a Court of Record from three weeks to three weeks, with jurisdiction to the amount of £10 Irish. Upon goods being attached the debt is usually settled. Bail is taken before the bailiff of the court, as well as before the seneschal. The court has been usually held in a room in a public house in the town.

The only place of confinement in the town is called "the Black Hole," which is said to be under the care of the provost for the time being.

The county magistrates commit to this prison, but only as a place of temporary confinement, and not for a longer period than one night. It is stated to be a "wretched and unwholesome place."

A party of the county constabulary stationed in the town form the only Police force within the district.

The streets and roads are repaired by presentment of the County of Down grand juries at assizes. There is no provision made for lighting or watching the town.

The "Corporation Jury" which we have mentioned, is constituted of a foreman and 12 other jurors, who are named by the provost, and, when once sworn, are jurors for life, unless removed for misbehaviour by the provost, who considers that his power of removal is discretionary. They are selected from the householders who have been resident seven years within the borough. The present foreman (who is Lord Dufferin's steward), is a freeman. This jury appoints annually the following officers :—Two Prizers and a Thirdsman ; Constable ; Pound keeper and Town Sergeant ; Cranemaster ; also, the Herdsman of the Commons. The principal business of the jurors consists in the regulation of weights and measures, and of grazing of the Commons.

By deed dated the 8th of March, 1652, Lord Claneboy recited, "that his father, in his lifetime, had purposely laid off the Commons belonging to Killileagh for the only benefit of those which had not town acres, either for corn or grass ; which good intention of his towards them they had been deprived of, since the breaking out of the rebellion, by the richer and abler sort," and he required and authorised the provost "to appoint and agree with a herd for the cattle belonging to them in the town which want land, charging him to preserve the said commons for their only use."

According to one statement, the ground so allocated contained about 100 acres. The commons, as at present enclosed, contain only about 57 acres, They have been taken under the control of the Corporation Jury, by whom a regulation has been made, that the inhabitants must be resident seven years before they are eligible to derive any advantage from the commons. They (the jury) collect about £14 annually from the owners of cattle grazing, and expend it in various necessary outlays on the commons.

Well-grounded complaints have been made to us of the original intentions not being fulfilled, by means of a partial distribution of the right of commonage to members of the jury, and others, who possess land, and do not come within the meaning of the grant.[1]

---

[1] It will be seen by the following documents, that these complaints have been since effectually redressed at the instance of the present Lord Dufferin and the late lamented Captain Hamilton, who joined in petitioning for, and procuring the appointment of, new Trustees, and the settlement of a scheme for the management of these Commons, which when fully carried out will confer upon the inhabitants of Killileagh advantages that few towns in Ireland of the same size possess :—

"IN CHANCERY.

" To the Right Honble. Maziere Brady, Lord High Chancellor of Ireland.

"In the Matter of the COM-
MONS OF KILLILEAGH, and the
Act of the 3rd and 4th Victoria,
chap. 108.

"THE Petition of the Right Honourable Frederick Temple, Baron Dufferin and Claneboye, and of Archibald Rowan Hamilton, Esq., of Killyleagh Castle, in the County of Down, Lord of the Manor of Killileagh, Humbly Showeth, that the Manor of Killileagh, together with other large tracts of land, in the County of Down, being then the estate of Sir James Hamilton, Knight (afterwards created Viscount Claneboye', he, in the 20th year of the reign of King James the First, procured a Charter of Incorporation for the village of Killileagh, and a small district of the surrounding lands, formerly part of the said Manor, which has ever since been called and known as the Corporation of Killileagh, whereby all the inhabitants within said village and lands were erected into a Corporation, by the name of the Provost, Free Burgesses, and Communality of the Borough of Killileagh, and, among other powers and privileges, were rendered capable in law to have, purchase, receive, and possess lands, tenements, and hereditaments, to them or their successors, in perpetuity.

"That, after the grant of such letters patent, the said Sir James Hamilton laid off a portion of his said manor, within the precincts of said Corporation, as Commons for the use and benefit of such poor inhabitants of said village and Corporation as had no lands of their own.

"That, upon his death, the said manor of Killileagh, having, with his other estates, descended to, and become legally vested in his son James, the second Lord Claneboye (afterwards created Earl Clanbrassil', the said James, Lord Claneboye, on or about the 8th day of March, 1652, executed a Deed Poll declaring the uses and purposes for which said Commons were granted in the words and figures following :—

" Whereas, great and manifold clamours and complaints have frequently risen and do daily increase by the abuse of the Commons belonging to Killileagh, which were purposely laid off by my father in his lifetime, for the only benefit of those who had not town acres either for corn or grass, which good intention of his towards them they have been deprived of since the breaking out of the rebellion, by reason that the richer and abler sort of indwellers within the said town, have, through avarice, altogether made use of the acres in their own holdings under corn and grain, and reserving none for grass, have fostered on the Commons, to the prejudice of the poor people, by exacting from them extraordinary rates for the feeding of their cows in the summer season, casting them loose all the year over, to graze and trespass on the neighbouring grounds belonging to the leaseholders, and on the parks, grounds, and demesne belonging to the castle : for preventing which disorders and abuses for time coming; I do require and authorise the Provost of the said town to appoint and agree with a herd for the cattle belonging to them in the town which want lands, charging him to preserve the said commons for their only use, and to suffer no beast else to graze thereupon, but such as belongs to the parties undernamed, or to others in the same condition : and to warn the rest of the inhabitants to put their cattle on their own grass, or provide themselves elsewhere, without grazing on the Commons at all : hereby commanding the said herd to drive, and impound all such horses, cows, sheep, goats, or other kind of cattle which shall be found on said Commons from this day forth : for doing of all which this shall be a sufficient warrant in that behalf. Given under my hand and seal, this 8th day of March, 1652.

"'CLANEBOY.'

"As by the original thereof among the papers of such Corporation, or by a copy thereof in the possession of Petitioners, printed by the late Archibald Rowan, Esq., the then Lord of said Manor of Killyleagh, to which petitioners crave leave to refer, may appear. That, from the date of such Deed Poll, down to the dissolution of said Corporation, which took place on the 25th day of October, 1841, in consequence of the provisions of the 13th section of the Act in the title of this matter mentioned, the said Corporation, under and by virtue of said Deed Poll, claimed and exercised the power of deciding on the right of all persons claiming the benefit of such Commons under the charitable trusts therein contained, but which they only granted to such native or resident inhabitants as, within the meaning of said charter, they considered entitled to the freedom of said Corporation, and not to strangers or persons taking up a temporary residence within said town and Corporation. That, for a considerable time after the date of said Deed Poll of 8th March, 1652, the Provost of said Corporation for the time being was in the habit of himself appointing a herd for said Commons, and that articles of agreement were entered into between such Provost and the herd so appointed by him, as appears by a copy of one of such articles, bearing date the first of May, 1730, found among the family papers of petitioner, A. R. Hamilton, Esq. ; but that subsequently, and for many years previous to the dissolution of said Corporation, the authority given by said Deed to the Provost for the time being, was delegated by said Corporation to a committee or body appointed by them from time to time, called " The Commons Jury," who decided upon all claims as to the admission of cattle to said Commons, and appointed a herd, and took upon themselves the entire management thereof, down to the time of the dissolution of said Corporation. That, since such dissolution, there has been nobody or person legally autho-

There is not now any Public School connected with the corporation ; a school is supported by Lord Dufferin.

It appears that James, the first Lord Clanbrassil, devised £20 a-year to "the school at Killileagh," to be duly paid for the masters enabling of them to educate poor scholars. On the same will the present Lord Dufferin rests his title to the property. We have mentioned in our report upon the town of Bangor, a similar bequest made by this will for the school of that town.

Payment of this bequest has not been made for many years. "The school of Killileagh" seems to have belonged to the corporation, for, the only ancient school, of which there is any trace, is that

rised to execute the charitable trusts of said Deed Poll of the 8th day of March, 1652, and, in consequence thereof, the same cannot be carried into execution, there being no person competent to decide on the rights of parties claiming the benefit, or to prevent an infringement of the provisions of said deed. That said Commons, which consist of nearly 100 acres of excellent land, have become almost entirely covered with furze or whins ; and, being left badly fenced and undrained, are by no means fit to graze the number of cattle which they would otherwise do, if proper measures were taken for their reclamation and preservation ; and that said Commons would, if proper directions were given for their management, be a source of great advantage and benefit to the poor inhabitants of said town and Corporation for whom the same were originally granted, and whose rights and interests therein are preserved and perpetuated by the 2nd section of the Act, in the title to this matter mentioned. That Petitioners, being the owners of said town and Corporation lands, are desirous, on behalf of the poor inhabitants of said town and Corporation entitled to the benefit of said Commons, to effectuate the charitable intentions of said donor, and that the instructions of said donor should be carried into execution, and proper trustees forthwith appointed by your Lordship, pursuant to the provisions of said Act. May it therefore please your Lordship, pursuant to the provisions of the 112th section of the said Act of the 3 & 4 Vict., c. 108, to order that one or more fit and proper person or persons may be appointed trustee or trustees for the administration of such charitable trust estate as aforesaid, and that all proper and necessary directions may be given to such trustee or trustees for the management of said Common lands, in such manner as may most effectually carry out the charitable intentions of the original donor and the provisions of said Act, and, if necessary, to approve of a scheme for the management thereof. And Petitioners will pray."

" LORD CHANCELLOR.

" Saturday, the 2nd of June, 1849.

"In the Matter of the COM-   "WHEREAS, the Right Honor-
MONS OF KILLILEAGH, and the able Frederick, Baron Dufferin
Act of the 3rd and 4th Victoria, and Claneboy, and Archibald Ha-
chap. 108.   milton Rowan Hamilton, of Killi-
leagh Castle, County of Down, Esquire, Lord of the Manor of Killileagh, did on the 30th day of May last, prefer their Petition to the Right Honorable the Lord High Chancellor of Ireland, setting forth as therein is set forth, and praying that pursuant to the provisions of the 112th section of the said Act of the 3rd and 4th Victoria, chapter 108, one or more fit and proper person or persons might be appointed trustee or trustees for the administration of such Charitable Trust Estate as in the petition stated, and that all proper and necessary directions might be given to such trustee or trustees for the management of such Common lands, in such manner as might most effectuate and carry out the charitable intentions of the original donor, and the provisions of the said Act, and, if necessary, to approve of a scheme for the regulation and management thereof : WHEREUPON, all parties concerned were ordered to attend before his Lordship on the matter of the said petition : And Mr. LOWRY of Counsel with the Petitioners on this day attending accordingly, upon reading the said petition and order for hearing, and hearing what was alleged by said Counsel, HIS LORDSHIP DOTH ORDER that it be referred to William Brooke, Esq., the Master of this Court in rotation, to enquire and report whether at the time of the passing of the statute of the 3rd and 4th Victoria, chapter 108, the Corporation of the

Provost, Burgesses, and Commonality of Killileagh, or any member or members of said Corporation as such, were or was seized of any Commons or other land under or by virtue of the Deed Poll of the 8th of March, 1652, in the petition mentioned, or exercised any power or authority over any such lands, and if so, for what purpose or purposes, and how such lands are now possessed or enjoyed? and under whose authority or control? AND IT IS FURTHER ORDERED, that the said Master, if he shall consider it necessary, and if the said lands shall be held on charitable trusts, do settle a scheme for the future care and management thereof, and appoint such number of trustees for that purpose as he shall think necessary : And it is further Ordered, that Her Majesty's Attorney General, and all persons in occupation of the said lands or of any part thereof, and all such other persons as the Master shall think fit, do have notice of all proceedings under this order : And it is further Ordered, that the said Master be at liberty to direct such notices to be given by advertisement, or otherwise, to all parties who may be interested in the matter of this reference, as he may think proper : And his Lordship doth reserve further Order until the said Master shall have made his report.

"YELVERTON O'KEEFFE, Registrar."

" To the Right Honble. Maziere Brady, Lord High Chancellor
of Ireland.

" In the Matter of the COM-   "MAY IT PLEASE YOUR LORD-
MONS of KILLYLEAGH, and the SHIP—Pursuant to your Lord-
Act of the 3rd and 4th Victoria, ship's order made it this matter,
chap. 108.   and bearing date the 2nd day of
June, 1849, whereby it was referred to me. I have examined into the matter so to me referred, in presence of the counsel and solicitor concerned for the Petitioners in this matter, no other persons having attended before me, although I caused a copy of said order and of a summons for the purpose to be served on Her Majesty's Attorney General, and printed handbills to be circulated and posted in and about the town of Killyleagh, and an advertisement to be inserted in the Downpatrick Recorder newspaper ; and I find that at the time of the passing of the Statute of the 3rd and 4th of Victoria, chap. 108, the Corporation of the Provost, Burgesses, and Commonality of Killileagh were seized of certain lands, commonly called "The Commons of Killyleagh," under and by virtue of the Deed Poll, dated the 8th day of March, 1652, in the petition mentioned.

" I further find, that said Commons are situate within one mile of the town of Killyleagh, and contain by the Ordnance Survey 74½ statute acres ; and that about one-fourth thereof is good arable ; one-fourth thereof shallow, moory arable ; one-fourth low, swampy, boggy arable ; and one-fourth rocky pasture ; but that the whole extent thereof is more or less covered with furze.

" I further find, that the management of the said Commons was originally entrusted to the Provost of the said Corporation of Killyleagh, as appears by the said grant of the 8th of March, 1652, in the petition in this matter mentioned ; but was by him delegated to the Jury of said Corporation ; and that a herd was by them appointed, whose duties were to attend to the care of the cattle when on the Commons, and to drive them into and out of the town of Killyleagh, every morning and evening.

" I further find, that this herd was paid one shilling per head for all cattle grazing on the commons (usually from 30 to 50), and had the privilege of grazing two cows, a horse, and a few goats of his own, and that he had a residence upon the Commons, and had laid

which was held on premises belonging to the corporation, which they gave up to Mr. Stevenson in 1725, as hereinafter mentioned ; and we have it in evidence that in the then newly-acquired premises a school was afterwards held, at which the present Lord Dufferin, and others of the inhabitants, were educated. The premises (the market-house) have long become ruinous.

By an Act (5 Geo. III. c. 1, s. 7) of 1765, a grant was made of "the sum of £1,200 to John Blackwood, Esq., to erect a pier at Killileagh, in the barony of Dufferin, in the County of Down, the said John Blackwood giving security by recognizance before one of the Barons of the Exchequer for the execution of the said work, and that no further sum shall be requested from Parliament for completing the same." There is a pier, or quay, for vessels to unload at, which, it appears, was built originally from the funds arising from the above grant. The road-way upon the pier has been repaired by

---

off to him a few acres of ground adjoining to his house for tillage purposes, for which he paid a merely nominal rent to said Corporation jury ; and that the site of the house and lands which he was required to keep in tillage was periodically changed, so that as great an extent as possible might be kept free of the furze which covered the surface of the said Commons.

"I further find, that the persons considered properly entitled to the privilege of pasture on said Commons, were persons not having any lands of their own, living within the boundary of the said Corporation : but that frequently persons having such lands were admitted to a like enjoyment, and that a residence of seven years was considered necessary to constitute them inhabitants and freemen of the Corporation ; and although I do not find that any freeman's roll has been made out since the extinction of said Corporation by said recited Act, yet as by the provisions thereof, there is not only a power reserved for making out such roll, but as by the warrant of the Lord Lieutenant a person has been appointed for such Borough to make out and revise such roll, there can be no difficulty, under the provisions of said Act, in ascertaining the persons so entitled. I find that the Jury of said Corporation, who were in office at the time of the dissolution of said Corporation, have since continued to manage the same, and more in accordance with the original trusts than before ; and that any departure from the strict rule of admitting none but poor persons, labourers, or mechanics, not having other lands, has been made from the necessity of raising funds sufficient to meet the liabilities of said common lands, and that in any such instance the next best entitled was chosen.

"I further find the entire income derived from said Commons consisted of grazing money, collected on the 12th of May in each year from those persons whose cattle were admitted to said Commons, and that 3s. per head was the sum usually paid until the said Commons became subject to tithe-rent charge, when the admission was raised to 5s. 6d. ; and that subsequently, when County Cess and Poor-rates were levied, the sum became 7s. 6d., at which it remains at present, and that the average annual receipts for the last twenty years amount to about £13, of which I find that from £5 to £9 is expended in paying the tithe rent charge, county-rates, and Poor-rates, and that the herd received 1s. per head on all cattle admitted, and that the remainder of said sum has been generally expended in stubbing the furze on said Commons, building and repairing fences and gates and that latterly some small patches of draining have been executed : but that on one occasion a small sum, being the accumulated annual savings of said income, was lost by the death of the foreman of the Jury, who acted as treasurer, and on another occasion by the inability or insolvency of the foreman.

"I further find, that from a considerable part of said Commons being much injured by water, and from deep gravel pits remaining unfilled, and also from many high knolls upon the surface composed of large loose stones, but more particularly from the eatage being almost entirely covered with furze, the said Commons are at present of comparatively little benefit to the poor of the Corporation ; and I therefore find, that the following improvements should be made, and that for this purpose a sum of money should be either borrowed from the Board of Works (if procurable,) or from some private party ; but, as the payment of a large sum for interest, in addition to the present liabilities, could not be made from the Commons in their present state, I am of opinion that the sum should

be, at present, limited to £150, and that the draining, levelling, stubbing, clearing from stones, fencing, and other improvements, should be done in small divisions, so that, if from the Board of Works not more than £50, or, if from a private party not more than £30 should be borrowed in one year, and that so soon as one division be completed, it should be then put through a judicious course of cropping, before its being laid permanently down in pasture ; but that such course of cropping should always be conducive to the benefit of the parties entitled to grazing, or as much so as circumstances would permit, and should be as follows :—1st, potatoes, or other root crop, planted by the parties entitled to grazing ; 2nd, vetches for feeding their cattle ; 3rd, potatoes, or other roots, as before ; 4th, corn or flax, to be sown with permanent pasture seeds, the proceeds of such crop of corn or flax to assist in carrying on the improvements ; and that by these means the ground would be perfectly tilled, and freed from the overgrowing furze, and at a very trifling cost, leaving a surplus to aid improvements, and thereby diminish the sum which would otherwise require to be borrowed

"I further find, that after the said Commons are permanently laid down in grazing in the manner aforesaid, it will be occasionally necessary, in order totally to eradicate the furze, to repeat the course of labour mentioned, or some other course equally conducive to the interest of the parties.

"I find that the few acres of scanty rocky pasture, on said Commons, which are quite irreclaimable, might with advantage be planted with timber trees, which would be serviceable for making paleing for said Commons ; and that a belt of planting, and a walk, should be made round the entire of the said Commons, which are at present an eye-sore on the face of the country, and that their appearance would not only be greatly improved thereby, but they would furnish an agreeable and wholesome place of recreation for the poorer inhabitants of the village, to whose use, and for whose benefit the said Commons were by said original grant dedicated.

"I further find, it will be unnecessary and improper to permit the herd in future to break up any portion of said Commons for tillage, but that he should have a stated amount of wages sufficient to remunerate him for his services, and that the benefits of tillage and turbary now afforded him should be wholly withdrawn, and that, instead of residing in the centre of said Commons, a small gate-house or lodge should be built for him, adjoining some of the entrance-gates to said Commons, at the discretion of the trustees hereafter appointed

"I further find, that such trustees and their successors should have the power of rating the cattle admitted to the said Commons, and changing such rates when circumstances render such changes necessary, and of appointing and removing the herd at their discretion ; and I further find, that said trustees should be empowered to straighten the boundaries of said Commons with the owners of the adjoining lands, and generally to carry into effect the foregoing schemes for the management of said charity.

"I further find, having by this my report submitted to your Lordship a scheme for the future care and management of said Commons, that the following persons should be, and I accordingly do hereby appoint them trustees for that purpose, pursuant to your Lordship's said order, viz., the Right Honble. Lord Dufferin and Claneboy, Archd. Rowan Hamilton, Esq., of Killileagh Castle ; James Bailie, Esq., of Ringdufferin ; John Martin, Esq., of Shrig-

county presentment, and appears to have been considered public property. However, Lord Dufferin has of late claimed the ownership of it, and exercised the right of preventing vessels from making use of it without paying the fees demanded by his agent.

The inhabitants allege that the pier has been built on ground which lay between the high and low sea-mark. That soil, *primâ facie*, belongs to the Crown ; and, even if it belonged to Lord Dufferin, the exaction of quayage, where the pier has been founded by such a grant as the above, appears unreasonable.k

The charter granted to the corporation a free market on every Monday, and two fairs annnally, viz., on every Trinity Monday, and the day following, and on the Feast of St. Andrew, and the day following, except the feast happened on Saturday or Sunday, and then on the Monday and day following. No grant of toll is contained in the charter.

No tolls or customs have been for many years collected in the town, but formerly it seems the corporation did assume a right of levying toll.

The cranemaster appointed by the " Corporation Jury" claims fees as weighmaster. He charges one halfpenny for each cwt. of corn, meal, &c., weighed at his crane. For the weighing of meat his charges are—Beef, each carcass, 4d. ; pigs and sheep, ditto, 2d. ; each hide, 1d. ; cake of fat, 1d. In these respects, the fees charged by the cranemaster exceed the sums allowed by the statutes regulating the amount of the weighmaster's fees, 4 Ann. c. 14, 25 Geo. II. c. 15.

The Commons, above described, form the only available property of the corporation.

In 1725, it appears, the corporation were in possession of a tenement then commonly known by the name of " The Court and School-House," and conveyed it to James Stevenson, Esq., one of the proprietors of the estate of Killileagh, and in consideration of that assignment, Mr. Stevenson demised, to the sovereign, burgesses, &c., in trust for the corporation, premises, described as follows :—" All that part of the old house or walls of Killileagh, formerly possessed by John Campbell, containing in length 38 feet, and in breadth 38 feet, bounded on the east with the Bridge-street, and on the west with Thomas Clarke's holding," to hold for lives renewable for ever, at the yearly rent of a peppercorn at Michaelmas, if demanded, and a pepper-corn for renewal. Upon this ground the market-house was built.

It is alleged, apparently with truth, that Lord Dufferin has lately taken possession of a small portion of the ground belonging to the corporation market-house, and assumed the power of leasing it, with other property of his Lordship's immediately adjoining.

The corporation had an ancient pound in Killileagh ; but this having become ruinous, and not being conformable to the Act 6 Geo. IV. c. 43, it was given up by order of the provost and corpora-

---

ley ; John H. Howe, Esq., of Killileagh ; and Robert Heron, Esq., of Ardigon : and Messrs. Mortimer Thompson, Andrew Ringland. James M'Kee, of Killileagh ; and Messrs. Adam Kenning and Hugh Hay, of Corporation. All which I certify and submit to your Lordship as my report, this 10th day of February, 1852.

" WILLIAM BROOKE.

" Schedule of Evidence on which the foregoing Report is founded :—
" Copy Deed Poll of 8th March, 1652.
" Copy of the Charter of the Borough of Killileagh, dated 10th March, 1612.
" Printed Report of Enquiry held the 10th of October, 1833, by the Irish Corporation Commissioners, and presented to both Houses of Parliament by command of His Majesty King William the Fourth.
" Advertisement in *Downpatrick Recorder* of 14th July, 1849."

" LORD CHANCELLOR.

" *Friday, the 23rd day of April,* 1852.

" In the Matter of the COM-
MONS OF KILLYLEAGH, and the
Act of the 3rd and 4th Victoria,
chap. 108.
" WHEREAS, the Right Honorable Frederick Baron Dufferin and Claneboy, and Archibald R. Hamilton, of Killyleagh Castle, in the County of Down, Esq., did, on the 15th day of April, 1852, prefer their petition to the Right Honorable the Lord High Chancellor of Ireland, setting forth as therein is set forth, and praying that

the Report filed the 10th day of February, 1852, might stand confirmed, &c. WHEREUPON, and on reading the said petition and prayer, as also the Report filed the 10th day of February, 1852, His LORDSHIP DOTH ORDER, that the said Report do stand confirmed, and accordingly that the said scheme so settled by William Brooke, Esq., the Master in this matter, for the future care and management of the said charity be adopted ; and it is further ordered that the trustees therein named do carry the same into execution ; and it is further ordered that the petitioners be declared entitled to their costs incurred in this matter in the necessary preparation for and of obtaining said order of and June, 1849, and said report thereunder, and of confirming same, and of the necessary proceedings to carry the scheme therein contained into effect ; and it is further ordered that said trustees be at liberty to pay out of said charitable estate said costs, when taxed and ascertained : and it is further ordered that it be referred to one of the taxing masters of this Court to tax and ascertain the same.

" ROBERT LONG, *Registrar.*"

k The present Lord Dufferin has since expended upon this quay, which has been considerably extended, a much larger sum than was originally granted by the Irish Parliament ; and at the time this report was made, the Letters Patent of 19 James I., which were only enrolled in England, had not been discovered ; on reference to which, at p. xxii of the Appendix, it will be seen that Killileagh was thereby made a port, and that port and harbour dues were thereby granted to Sir James Hamilton, his heirs and assigns, without which they were not legally payable.

u

tion jury to Lord Dufferin, in 1828, Lord Dufferin granting to the corporation in lieu of it "ground in an eligible situation below James Shaw's garden, adjoining the river, and near the bridge of Killi-leagh," on which he had caused a pound to be built, conformably to law, at his own expense.

The population of this borough, as returned in the census of 1831, was as follows :—

Males, 536 ; Females, 611. Total - - - - -		1,147
Families employed chiefly in agriculture - - - - -	39	
„ in trade, manufactures, or handicraft - - - - -	78	
„ not comprised in those two classes - - - - - -	100	
Total - - - -		—— 217
Houses inhabited - - - - -	189	
„ uninhabited - - - - - -	8	
„ building - - - - - -	10	
Total - - - -		—— 207

The town is stated to be improving, but is still extremely limited in extent and population.
We send with this report copies of the following documents :—

1. Extracts from Corporation Proceedings.
2. Oaths.
3. Extracts of Proceedings of Corporation Jury, 1828—1833.
4. Lord Claneboy's Confirmation of Grant of Commons, 1652 ; case respecting the Commons.
5. Extract from Lord Clanbrassill's Will.
6. Memorial respecting Compensation in 1800.

WILLIAM ELLIOT HUDSON, } Commissioners.
MATTHEW RICHARD SAUSSE, }

Inquiry held the 16th day of October, 1833.

No. IX.

CHARTER OF THE BOROUGH OF BANGOR, DATED 18TH MARCH, 1612.

JAMES, by the grace of God, of England, Scotland, France, and Ireland, King, Defender of the Faith, &c.   To all people to whom our present letters shall come, greeting : Know ye, that We, as well at the humble petition of the inhabitants of the village or town of Bangor, within our County of Down, in our Province of Ulster, within our Kingdom of Ireland, as for the inhabiting and planting the Northern parts of our said Kingdom, which are waste and uninhabited, according to the laudable form of government established in our Kingdom of England, and for the better progress and perfection of that new plantation happily begun there, of our special grace, certain knowledge, and mere motion, by the advice of our trusty and well-beloved Councillor Sir Arthur Chichester, Knight, our Deputy General of the said Kingdom of Ireland, as also according to the intent and purport of certain letters signed with our hand and under our signet, dated at our Court at Hampton Court, the 26th day of September, in the 10th year of our reign of England, France, and Ireland, and in the 46th of Scotland, and now enrolled in the records of our Chancery of our said Kingdom of Ireland : Have by these presents appointed, ordained, and declared, that the said village or town of Bangor, and all and singular castles, messuages, tofts, mills, houses, edifices, buildings, curtilages, yards, orchards, gardens, waste-grounds, lands, tenements, and hereditaments whatsoever, lying or being in or within the said village or town of Bangor, or within the precincts of the said village or town, from henceforth are, and for ever hereafter shall be one entire and free Borough of itself, by the name of the Borough, and be nominated and called from henceforth the Borough of Bangor ; and We have by these presents erected, appointed, and ordained, all those in one entire and free Borough of itself, by the name of the Borough of Bangor.   And further, We do by these presents will, ordain, and appoint, that there be within the said Borough, one body corporate and politic, consisting of one Provost, twelve free Burgesses, and of a Commonalty, and that all the inhabitants within the said village and lands aforesaid, are and for ever hereafter by force of these presents shall be one body corporate and politic really in deed and by name, by the name of the Provost, free Burgesses, and Commonalty of the Borough of Bangor : and We do by these presents for us our heirs and successors, erect, make, ordain, and appoint them by the name of the Provost, free Burgesses, and Commonality of the Borough of Bangor aforesaid, one body corporate and politic in reality, deed, and name, really and to the full, and that by the same name they may have a perpetual succession, and that by the name of the Provost, free Burgesses, and Commonalty of the Borough of Bangor, they are and for ever hereafter shall be persons qualified and capable in law to have, purchase, receive and possess lands, tenements, liberties, privileges, jurisdictions, franchises, and hereditaments whatsoever, of whatever kind, nature, or sort they be, to them and their successors, in fee and perpetuity ; and likewise goods and chattels, and other things of whatsoever kind, nature, or sort they be ; and also to give, grant, set and assign lands, tenements and hereditaments, and all and singular other deeds and things to do and execute by the said name, and that they, by the name of the Provost, free Burgesses, and Commonalty of the Borough of Bangor aforesaid, may sue and be impleaded, answer and be answered, defend and be defended, before us, our heirs and successors, and before whatsoever the justices and judges of us, or our heirs and successors, and others whatsoever, in whatever Courts of us, our heirs and successors, and in any other place whatsoever, in and concerning all and all manner of actions, suits, pleas, plaints, and demands whatsoever, to be prosecuted or brought by or against them, in any manner or way : And that they, the said Provost and free Burgesses of the Borough aforesaid, and their successors, may for ever have full power and authority to choose, send, and return two understanding and fit men, for serving and attending in any Parliament, hereafter to be held in our Kingdom of Ireland, and that such men so chosen, sent, and returned, may have full power and authority to treat and consult upon those matters and things which to them and others there shall be exhibited or declared, and to give freely their votes and suffrages thereupon, and to do or execute other things whatsoever, as fully and freely as any other Burgesses, of any other ancient Borough in our said Kingdom of Ireland, or within our said Kingdom of England, in our Parliament there used to do or execute : Wherefore, we will, and by these presents for us, our heirs and successors, do give and grant unto the said Provost and free Burgesses of the said Borough, and their successors, and also we charge, and for us, our heirs and successors, strictly command all the sheriffs, officers, and ministers of us, our heirs and successors whatsoever, of our said County of Down, for the time being, to whom any of our writ or writs for choosing Parliament Burgesses within our County of Down shall at any time be directed, that every such sheriffs, officers, or ministers, to whom any of our writ or writs of this nature shall so be directed as aforesaid, shall make his command to the Provost and free Burgesses of the said Borough of Bangor, for the time being, for the election and return of the said two Burgesses, according to the form or effect of the same writ or writs: And these our letters patent, or the enrolment thereof, shall be a sufficient warrant and discharge in that behalf, as well unto the said Provost and free Burgesses of the Borough aforesaid, and their successors, as unto all and singular the sheriffs, officers, and ministers of us, our heirs and successors whatsoever.[1]   And to the intent it may unto after ages appear that this new Cor-

---

1 The following list of Members returned to the Irish Parliament for the Borough of Bangor, has been extracted from the Journals of the Irish House of Commons :—

1613, April.— Sir EDWARD BRABAZON, Knight, Thomas-Court, Dublin.a
JOHN DALWAY, Esq., Brayde-Island, Antrim.b

---

a Sir Edward Brabazon was father-in-law of Sir James Hamilton (afterwards created Viscount Claneboye), being the father of his second wife, Ursula Brabazon. He was elevated to the Peerage of Ireland, 19th July, 1566, as Baron Brabazon of Ardee, and was the lineal ancestor of the present Earl of Meath.
b John Dalway was the first of that family who settled in Ireland. He came over from Devonshire in 1573, a cornet in the army of Queen Elizabeth, under the command of Walter Devereux, Earl of Essex. He married Jane O'Bryne, grand-daughter of Hugh O'Neill, Earl of Tyrone, and related by her mother to Shane M'Bryan Mac Phelim O'Neile, Chief of the O'Neills, of North or Lower Clandeboy, from whom he obtained a grant of the

greater part of the Tuogh of Braidenisland, or Braidisland, and the lands of Kilroot. On the 8th of October, 1603, John Dallwaye, then Constable of Carrickfergue Castle, obtained from King James I., a grant of the Barony of Braidisland to hold for ever, in free and common soccage, as of the Castle of Carrickfergus. These lands, together with others purchased from Sir James Hamilton, were, on the 8th of July, 1608, erected by letters patent into the Manor of Dallwaye. John Daliwaye was Mayor of Carrickfergus in 1592; and, in 1600, by his marriage with Jane O'Bryne, he had an only child, Margaret, who was married, about the year 1603, to John, lineal ancestor of the present Conway Richard Dobbs, Esq., of Castle Dobbs. This John Dallwaye

poration was (at first) composed of circumspect and honest men, we make, constitute, and nominate John Hamilton to be and become the first and present Provost of the said Borough, to be continued

---

| 1634, June | .—Sir ARTHUR BASSETT, Knight, Mountjoy, Tyrone.c |
| | MALBY BRABAZON, Esq., Ballynasloe, Roscommon.d |
| 1639, Mar. 5.—JOHN HAMILTON, Esq., Ballygrot.e |
| | JAMES HAMILTON, Esq., Ballycloghan.f |
| 1651, April 22—WILLIAM CONYNGHAM, Esq. |
| | THOMAS BOYD, Merchant, Dublin.g |

| 1655, Nov. —WILLIAM HAMILTON, Esq., vice Boyd, expelled |
| | 14th November, 1655, for the plot in 1663. |
| 1692, Sept. 30—FRANCIS ANNESLEY. Magirnock.h |
| | DAVID CAMPBELL, Esq.,, Cumber.i |
| 1695, Aug. 13.—JAMES HAMILTON, Esq., Bangor. |
| | DAVID CAMPBELL, Esq., Cumber. |

died about the year 1618; and the present Marriott Dalway, Esq., of Bella-Hill, is lineally descended from his brother Giles.

c On 9th December, 1634. it was ordered by the House, that "Whereas Sir Arthur Bassett, Knight, returned a burgess for the Borough of Bangor, in the County of Down, having especial occasion to go into England, hath made his humble suit unto this House for his license for England, and that a new election might be made for another in his place; it therefore ordered, that the said Sir Arthur Bassett is licensed to go into England, and that a writ de novo to that purpose shall issue to the sheriff of the said County of Downe as is desired.—Irish Com. Jour. This Sir A. Bassett was nephew of Sir Arthur Chichester, and died at Belfast, on the 30th of June, 1640. as appears by the following funeral entry in Sir Bernard Burke's (Ulster's) office:—"Sir Arthur Bassett, of Belfast, in the County of Antrim, Knight, second sonne of Sir Arthur Basset, of Umberley, in the County of Devon, in the Kingdome of England, Knight, departed this mortall life (being never married), at Belfast, the last day of June, 1640, and was interred the end day of July, 1640, in the church of Carrickfergus, in the vault there belonginge to the late Right Honble. Arthur Viscount Chichester of Carrickfergus, and Baron of Belfast, deceased, his coffin being placed in the said vaulte next unto the coffin of the said Viscount; which first mentioned Sir Arthur Bassett was nephew unto the said Viscount. The truth of the premisses is testified by the subscription of John Lyde, Gent., sole executor to the said defunct, who hath returned this certificat to be recorded in the office of Uluester King of Armes.—Taken by me Thomas Preston, Esq., Uluester King of Armes, the 24th of July, 1640."—Fun. Ent., Vol. ix. p. 79.

d Malby Brabazon was only surviving son of Sir Anthony Brabazon, of Ballynasloe, Knight, Governor of Connaught ‑brother of Sir Edward Brabazon, afterwards Lord Brabazon of Ardee', and his wife Ursula, daughter of Sir Nicholas Malby, Knight, Governor of Connaught and Thomond. Malby Brabazon's second sister, Sarah, married John Hamilton, Esq., of Coronery, County Cavan, third brother of Sir James Hamilton.

e John Hamilton, of Ballygrott, was the nephew of Lord Claneboy, being the eldest son of his next brother, Archibald Hamilton, by his wife, Rachel Carmichael. John Hamilton married a lady named West, by whom he had two daughters—Jane, wife of Wm. Hogg, of Rathgael; and Rachel, wife of John Stevenson, of Ballywooly, both in the parish of Bangor. On the 27th day of May, 1641, it was ordered by the House of Commons, that a warrant should be granted for the issuing of a writ for the electing of a burgess in the room of John Hamilton, Esq., of Bangor; and on the 17th June following, it was further ordered, "that John Hamilton, Esq., shall be admitted into this House, and be forthwith settled and established a member thereof, and that the former order conceived in the House, for the electing and returning of another burgess in his stead from Bangor, in the County of Down is now made void, and of no effect, there being none returned according to the contents of the said order.—Irish Com. Jour.

f This James Hamilton, of Ballycloghan, was also a nephew of Viscount Claneboy, being the eldest son of his fourth brother, William Hamilton. In Mrs. Reilly's "Memoirs of the Hamilton Family," (quoted at page 81, ante, n.l.,) it is stated that John Hamilton, his younger brother, was his colleague; but this is a mistake, as it was his cousin, John Hamilton, of Ballygrott, mentioned in the preceding note. Ballicrott, or Ballygrott, was devised by Sir James Hamilton's will (which see at page 56, ante) to

his eldest brother, Archibald of Halcraig, the father of John Hamilton, from whom it has descended in direct succession to the present Lord Dufferin, as the representative of the eldest of the five uncles of Viscount Claneboy, and now forms part of his large estates.

g Thomas Boyd was a member of the Kilmarnock family. He married, in 1653, Mary, fourth daughter of Sir Adam Loftus, of Rathfarnham, and died in October, 1696, having had issue by her three sons and three daughters, who all died young and without issue, except the youngest, Letitia, who married first, in July, 1682, William Lord Boyd, son and successor to William Boyd, first Earl of Kilmarnock, who by him had a son, William, the third Earl, who died 22nd November, 1717, and who was father of William, the fourth Earl of Kilmarnock, whose unfortunate engagement in the rebellion of 1745, brought him to the scaffold. Thomas Boyd was, on account of his having been concerned in the plot of 1663, expelled from the House of Commons, on the 14th November, 1665, and a writ was ordered to issue for the election of a burgess in his stead, when William Hamilton, Esq., of Erynah, the father of James of Tullymore, was elected, and appears to have sat for the Borough till his death, in 1680.

h Francis Annesley was born in 1663. He was son of Francis Annesley, of Castlewellan, and was educated at the Inner Temple, from which several of his letters to Sir Arthur Rawdon, given in the "Rawdon Papers," are dated. By an Act of 11th and 12th of William III., he was appointed one of the Trustees for the sale of the forfeited estates; and, in the reign of Queen Anne, constituted one of the Commissioners for stating the public accounts of Ireland. He served in several Parliaments, both in England and Ireland, and married Elizabeth, daughter of Sir Joseph Martin, —See Rawdon Pap. 364. The present Lord Annesley is their descendant.

i See the Rawdon Papers for several letters from this David Campbell who was in King William's Army to Sir Arthur Rawdon, written after the Battle of the Boyne. The first, dated 24th July, 1690, " from the King's Camp at Carick-on-Suir, near Waterford," gives an account of the summoning Waterford, and the terms on which the garrison, after some hesitation, surrendered. In a postscript to it he adds· "I have some design, whenever the campaign is over, to part with my employment; for I confess it is a life as Prince Rupert said of it of honor, but a dog would not lead it.· Rawdon Pap, p. 329. The other letters are written "from the Camp before Limbrick," between 11th August and 6th December, 1690, and give an account of the siege of that city. In one of them, dated 12th August, he says—"I have not had for myself and servant a bit of bread these three days, but of barley cakes: for we are supplied out of the stores, though they have no reason to brag. I offered half-a-crown for a sixpenny loaf, and could not prevail: abominable ill drink, and that at 8d. per quart; brandy, 4s, 6d., claret, 2s. 6d., a quart. I have got two guineas' worth of that which shall serve for meat, and drink, and bread, and all. I pray God things may not prove scarce."—Ib. 333. In a note to this letter, it is stated that the following orders were issued about ascertaining the rates of provisions:—"White bread to be be sold at 3d. a pound; all ale from Dublin or Wicklow at 6d. a quart; brandy at 12s. a gallon; and claret at 2s 6d. a quart." On the 27th September, 1698, it was ordered that Mr. Speaker do issue his warrant to the Clerk of the Crown to make out a writ to the Sheriff of the County of Down for electing a burgess for the Borough of Bangor, in the room of David Campbell, Esq., deceased.—Irish Com. Jour.

in the same office until the feast of St. Michael the Archangel, next ensuing the date of these presents ; and in like manner we make, constitute, and nominate James Hamilton, Knight, William Bailie, Patrick M'Dougall, William Cunningham, Cothered M'Dougall, Robert Hamilton, John Ralston, John Hamilton, William Stephenson, Alexander Blaire, James Blaire, and Francis Austin, to be and become the first and present twelve free Burgesses of the said Borough, to be continued in the same office of the free Burgesses of the same Borough, during their several lives, unless in the meantime they or some of them, for their misbehaviour or some other reasonable cause, shall be removed from their office aforesaid ; and we will, appoint, and ordain all the inhabitants of the said village, and all and

---

1698, Oct. 7.—Sir RICHARD LEVINGE, Knt., Mullalea, West-
    meath, *vice* Campbell, deceased.*k*
  Oct. 25.—HENRY MAXWELL, Esq., Finebroge, *vice* Levinge,
    for Longford.*l*

1703, Sep. 21,—JAMES HAMILTON, Esq., Bangor.*m*
    HENRY MAXWELL, Esq., Finebroge.
1707, July 10.—CHARLES O'NEILL, Esq., Shane's Castle, Antrim,*n*
    vice Hamilton, deceased.

---

k Sir Richard Levinge, who was returned in the place of David Campbell, Esq., deceased, was also returned to serve in this Parliament as a burgess for the Borough of Longford, for which, by leave of the House, he made his election to serve, whereupon a writ was ordered for the election of a burgess of Bangor, and Henry Maxwell, of Finebroge, was returned in his place. This Sir Richard Levinge was Recorder of, and member for, Chester ; and, having been, in 1690, appointed Solicitor-General for Ireland, was, on the 20th October, 1692 (being then member for Blessington, Co. Wicklow), chosen Speaker of the House of Commons ; and was created a Baronet of that kingdom, on the 26th October, 1704. He was lineal ancestor of the present Sir Richard Levinge, Bart., of Knockdrin Castle, Co. Westmeath.

l Henry Maxwell, Esq., of Finnebrogue, who was returned for Bangor in 1698 and 1703, was again returned to the next Parliament of 1713 for the Borough of Killybegs, and in November, 1715, for the Borough of Donegal, for which he was re-elected in September, 1727. He was created a Privy Councillor for his public services, but declined accepting office of any kind. He died at Dublin on 12th February, 1729—30, and was buried in Mary's Church in that city. He was twice married—1st, to June, daughter of the Rev. Henry Maxwell, of Armagh, sister to John, first Lord Farnham ; and 2dly, to Dorothy, daughter of Edward Brice, of Kilroot, County Antrim, Esq.

m This James Hamilton, so often mentioned in these pages as "James of Bangor," was the only son of James Hamilton, Esq., of Newcastle, in the Ardes, Co. Down (by his wife Margaret Kynaston), who was the eldest son of William Hamilton, Esq., of Newcastle (by his wife Jane, daughter of Sir John Melville), fourth brother of Lord Claneboye, and one of the five uncles of James Earl of Clanbrassill. He married the Honble. Sophia, second daughter of John Viscount Mordaunt, of Avalon, in Somersetshire, and had by her one son, James, who died unmarried, and two daughters—Anna Catherina, born in 1692, and married in 1709, to Michael Ward, Esq., barrister, afterwards a Judge of the Court of King's Bench in Ireland, by whom she was mother of Bernard Ward, created Baron, and subsequently Viscount Bangor, of Castleward, in Co. Down ; and Margaret, born in 1696, who was married 6th June, 1713, to the Rev. Thomas Butler, sixth Viscount Ikerrin, lineal ancestor of Somerset Arthur Butler, the present Earl of Carrick. "James of Bangor" died in January, 1706 ; and, by his will, dated 25th July, 1701, and proved 26th February, 1706, bequeathed £100 to the poor of the parish of Bangor ; £10 to the poor of the parish of Downpatrick ; £5 to the poor of the parish of Saul ; £5 to the poor of the parish of Tonaghnieve ; £8 to the poor of the parishes of Holywood, Knock, and Bredagh ; and £400 to the poor of Slanes : which several sums he directed to be raised, and put out upon security, or in the purchase of lands, and the yearly interest, produce, or profit thereof to be payable for ever to the several and respective ministers and churchwardens of the parishes aforesaid, for the time being, for the use of the poor of those parishes, who were thereby desired to distribute the same accordingly. Sophia, his widow, by her will, dated 5th September, 1717, and proved 12th June, 1735, also left £100 to the parish of Bangor. The following MS. letter from Dr. Dunn

to this James Hamilton, gives an interesting account of the landing of Duke Schomberg's army at Bangor :—

     "Chester, Tuesday, 20th August, 1689.
"DEAR SIR—Seaventy saile of the ships that went with the Duke of Shomberg's army returned last night, being Munday. They bring the news, that the Duke of Shomberg landed all his men on Teusday was seaven night, before sun-set at Bangor ; att their landing the Irish fled, but the Protestants came flocking in to him ; that his Grace lodged that night in your house in Bangor, he went from thence to Newtown, and there he keepeth his headquarters ; that Colonell Wharton's regiment and another regiment are in Belfast ; that it was not burnt, nor Carrickfergus, as was reported ; that they found provision very plentifull, a sheep for two shillings, a good cow for 16 or twenty shillings, butter att twopence the pound, and that there never was a better appearance of a good crop of corn. For this reason, 'tis said that the ships have brought back a great part of the provision of beef, cheese, and bear they caryed over with them, to serve the remaining part of the army for which the ships were sent back, while they are transporting. The Duke caryed with him but 13 regiments of foot ; there is a regiment of horse and another of dragoons already shipt, but it is not certaine whether they are sayled or not. Ships came from Lough Foyle and Lough Swilly reports that the Enniskillon men fell upon the Irish army, in their retreat from Derry, committed on them a great slaughter, took their baggage and artillery, and that Parson Walker is landed in Scotland, and is going to London. If you please to write to me, I might stay here about a week, direct it to the Post and Anchor, Alderman Anderson's house, in Chester. Remember your promise to me att parting, that so soon as you could with safety, you would make haste down and goe to Bangor. If your brother Tulleymore did not leave London on Munday last, as he expected, you may come down with him. Present my most humble duty to his lady and your son. Let her not, for all this news, stir till she hath gott good advice, and done something for her health. I beg the favor of you to communicate this letter to the Bishop of Drummore ; he lodgeth in Berry Street, att the Barber's pole, at Mr. Ilot's house.
    "To James Hamilton, of Bangor, Esq.
    "To be left at the Right Honble. the Countess of Arglass's house, in St. James' Street, within two doors of the Golden Head, London."

n Charles O'Neill, Esq., of Shane's Castle, was son of Captain John O'Neill, son of Arthur O'Neill, second son of Shane M'Brian Mac Phelim O'Neill, Chief of North Clandeboy, and ancestor of the present Rev. William Chichester O'Neill, of Shane's Castle, who is descended from Phelim Duff O'Neill, third and youngest son of Shane Mac Brian Mac Phelim. He married Lady Mary Poulet, sister of Lady Frances Poulet, who was the wife of Lord Mordaunt, the brother of Henrietta Mordaunt, Marchioness of Huntley, and afterwards second Duchess of Gordon, at whose instance, it is stated (in Mrs. Reilly's Memoirs, p. 64', that Charles O'Neill was returned for the Borough of Bangor, in consequence of a letter written by her to her aunt, Sophia Mordaunt, wife of James Hamilton of Bangor, asking her to get him to return Mr. O'Neill for Bangor. He was afterwards returned, as Col. Chas. O'Neill, to the Irish Parliament, for the Borough of Randalstown, in 1713.

v

such other men as the Provost and free Burgesses of the same Borough for the time being shall admit into the freedom of the Borough aforesaid, to be and become members of the Commonalty of the Borough aforesaid. And further, We will that the said John Hamilton, whom we by these presents have made Provost aforesaid of the said Borough, shall come before our Justices at the Assizes or at the

---

1713, Nov. 13—Hon. CAPEL MOORE.
ROBERT WARD, Esq.o
1715, Nov. 8.—MICHAEL WARD, Esq., Castle-Ward.p
HANS HAMILTON, Esq., Frankfort, Armagh.q
Jan. 24.—EDWARD RIGGS, Esq., Riggsdale, Cork, vice Hamilton, for Newry.
ACHESON MOORE, Esq., Aghnecloy, Tyrone, or Moorestown, vice Ward, for County Down.r
1727, Nov. 3.—ACHESON MOORE, Esq., Aghnecloy, Tyrone.
MICHAEL WARD, Esq., Castle-Ward.
Dec. 8.—Sir ROBERT MAUDE, Bart.,s Dundrum, Tipperary, vice Ward, J.K.B.
1751, Nov. 7.—MATTHEW FORDE, the elder, Esq., Seaford,t vice Maude, deceased.
1761, April 18—ROBERT WARD, Esq.
ROBERT HAMILTON, Esq., Frankfort, Armagh.
1767, Dec. 18.—JOHN PARNELL, Esq., Rathleague, Queen's Co.,u vice Ward, deceased.

1768, July 14.—BERNARD WARD, Esq., Castle-Ward.v
JOHN BLACKWOOD, Esq., Ballyliddy.w
1771, Oct. 8.—JOHN BLACKWOOD, Esq,
Hon. NICHOLAS WARD.x
1776, June 11.—Hon. PIERCE BUTLER.
Hon. EDWARD WARD.y
1779, Oct. 12.—EDWARD HUNT, Esq.z
1783. Oct. 14.—Hon. EDWARD WARD.a
EDWARD HUNT, Esq.
RICHARD MAGENNIS, Esq., vice Ward, returned for County Down.
1790, July 2.—Sir JOHN BLACKWOOD, Bart.
Right Honble. Sir JOHN PARNELL, Bart.
1791, Jan, 20.—JOHN KEANE, Esq., vice Sir John Parnell, returned for Queen's County.b
1798, Jan, 9.—Honble. ROBERT WARD.c
JOHN STEWART, Esq., Dublin.

---

o Robert Ward, Esq., was third and youngest son of Bernard Ward and his wife, Mary, sister of Michael Ward, provost of Trinity College, Dublin, who died Bishop of Derry. Robert Ward was collector of the port of Strangford ; he was born in 1684, and by his wife, Elizabeth Bayley, had one son, Michael, born in 1730, and two daughters, Elizabeth, married 30th June, 1748, to William Percival, Esq., barrister-at-law, of the family of Temple-House, County Sligo ; and Anne, married to Robert Maxwell, Esq., of Finnibrogue, grandfather of the present John Waring Maxwell, Esq.

p Michael Ward, Esq., having been also returned to serve in this Parliament, as Knight of the Shire for the County of Down, by leave of the House, made his election to serve for the County of Down, and it was accordingly—"Ordered, that Mr. Speaker do issue his warrant to the Clerk of the Crown to make out a writ to the Sheriff of the County of Down for electing a burgess to serve in this Parliament for the said Borough of Bangor, in the room of the said Mr. Ward."—Irish Com. Jour. On the 24th January, 1715, Acheson Moore, Esq., of Aughnacloy, County Tyrone, was returned in the room of Michael Ward, Esq., for the Borough of Bangor. See memoir of Michael Ward, as M.P. for County Down, at page 64, ante.

q Hans Hamilton, Esq., being returned to serve as burgess for the Borough of Newry, and also for the Borough of Bangor, in the County of Down, having by leave of the House made his election to serve for the Borough of Newry, it was, on the 22d December, 1715—"Ordered, that Mr. Speaker do issue his warrant to the Clerk of the Crown, for electing a burgess to serve in this Parliament for the Borough of Bangor, in the room of the said Mr. Hamilton," and Edmund Riggs, Esq., of Riggsdale, County Cork, was, on the 24th of January, 1715, returned in the room of Hans Hamilton, Esq., to serve for the Borough of Bangor.

r Acheson Moore, Esq., who was so returned in the room of Michael Ward, Esq., was son of James Moore, Esq., of Aughnacloy, County Tyrone, and his wife, Mary, daughter of Sir George Acheson, Bart. (by his second wife, Margaret, third daughter of Sir William Caulfield, second Baron Charlemont), lineal ancestor of Archibald Acheson, the present Earl of Gosford. He married, 26th April, 1793, Sidney, daughter of Edward Wingfield, Esq., barrister (and sister of Richard Wingfield, created Viscount Powerscourt), and by her (who died 10th December, 1797) had issue one son, James, and three daughters, Eleanor, and Mary, who married 26th June, 1753, Roger Palmer, of Palmerstown, County Mayo, Esq., and Sidney (born on the day of her mother's death), who married, on 25th April, 1751, Hodgson Gage, Esq., of Magilligan, County Derry.

s Sir Robert Maude, of Dundrum, Co. Tipperary, Bart., who was returned in the room of Michael Ward, Esq., on his being made a Justice of the King's Bench, in 1727, was the lineal ancestor of Cornwallis Maude, the present Viscount Hawarden ; and died 4th August, 1750.

t Matthew Forde, the elder, Esq., of Seaforde, Co. Down, who took the oaths and his seat for Bangor, vice Maude, deceased, on the 10th December, 1757, was lineal ancestor of the present William Brownlow Forde, Esq., M.P. for Co. Down.

u John Parnell, Esq., was only son of Sir John Parnell, and his wife Anne, who was a daughter of Mr. Justice Ward. He was returned again for Bangor in 1790, as Sir John Parnell ; but, having been also returned for the Queen's County, he elected to serve for it.

v Bernard Ward was also returned to this Parliament, in 1768, as member for the County of Down, for which he elected to serve. —See memoir of him at p. 64, ante.

w John Blackwood, Esq., Ballyliddy, afterwards Sir John Blackwood, Bart.—See memoir of him as M.P. for Killileagh, at p. lxv, ante.

x The Hon. Nicholas Ward was the eldest son and heir of Bernard Viscount Bangor, by his wife, the Lady Anne Bligh, eldest daughter of John, first Earl of Darnley, and widow of Robert Hawkins Magill, Esq., of Gill Hall, Co. Down. He was born in 1750 ; succeeded his father as second Viscount Bangor, in 1781, and died without issue, on 11th September, 1827.

y The Honble. Pierce Butler was second son of Somerset Hamilton Butler, eighth Viscount Ikerrin, and grandson of Margaret Hamilton, daughter of "James of Bangor."

z Edward Hunt, Esq., of Stafford Street, Dublin, and of Jerpoint, Thomastown, Kilkenny, was the son of Christopher Hunt, Esq., of Jerpoint, whose will was proved 19th May, 1763.

a The Honble Edward Ward was third son of Bernard, first Viscount Bangor, and grandson of Anna Catharina·Hamilton, eldest daughter of "James of Bangor." He was born in 1753 ; married to Lady Arabella, daughter of William Crosbie, Earl of Glandore. He was also returned as M.P. for Co. Down, in 1783, for which he elected to serve ; and died in 1812.—See p. 64, ante.

b The Honble. Robert Ward was third and youngest son of Bernard, first Viscount Bangor, and was born 14th July, 1764. He married in 1782—1st, Sophia Frances, third daughter of Richard Chapel Whaley, Esq., of Whaley Abbey, Co. Wicklow, and was by her grandfather of the present Robert Edward Ward, Esq., of Bangor Castle, Co. Down, who married Harriette, daughter of the Hon. and Rev. Henry Ward, Rector of Killinchy.

c John Keane, Esq., of Belmont, Co. Waterford, created a Baronet, 1st August, 1801. He was father of John Lord Keane, created a Baron for distinguished military services in India.

General Sessions to be holden within the said County of Down next after the date of these presents, and in due manner give, as well the oath, commonly called in English the Oath of Supremacy, as his own corporal oath, for well and truly executing the office of Provost of the Borough aforesaid, until the Feast of Saint Michael the Archangel, next ensuing as is aforesaid, and that the Provost of the said Borough be yearly and elective. And, therefore, we will, and by these presents for us, our heirs and successors, grant unto the said Provost, free Burgesses, and Commonalty of the Borough aforesaid, and their successors, that the said Provost and free Burgesses of the Borough aforesaid for the time being, may and can for ever, yearly at the Feast of the Nativity of Saint John the Baptist, assemble themselves within the Borough aforesaid, and that the said Provost and free Burgesses so met together, or the major part of them, may, before they depart thence, choose one of the more understanding Burgesses of the said Borough, to execute the office of the Provost of the Borough aforesaid, for one year from the Feast of Saint Michael the Archangel, then next ensuing, and until which time another of the Burgesses of the same Borough was in due manner elected, sworn, and preferred to that office; and that every Provost so chosen, shall, before he be admitted to execute the office aforesaid, or be esteemed, as well give the said oath, commonly called (in English) the Oath of Supremacy, as his own corporal oath, for well and truly executing the office of Provost of the Borough aforesaid, until the Feast of Saint Michael the Archangel next ensuing such Election, before the Provost of the said Borough, who presided in the office the foregoing year; and we give full power and authority to every such last predecessor of whatever Provost of the Borough aforesaid for the time being, to take the aforesaid oaths of every such Provost to be of the new elected.

And, moreover, We of our special grace, and from our certain knowledge and mere motion, will, and by these presents for us, our heirs and successors, grant unto the said Provost, free Burgesses, and Commonalty of the said Borough, and their successors, that if and how often as it shall happen the Provost of the said Borough for the time being to die, or the aforesaid office any way to become vacant within one year after he is elected and sworn to the office of the Provost of the said Borough, as is aforesaid, that then, and so often as the free Burgesses and Commonalty of the said Borough, and their successors, may and can, within fifteen days next after such vacation, choose a fit person out of the number of the free Burgesses to be Provost of the Borough aforesaid, to rule and govern the same Borough during the remainder of that year, and that every person or persons so chosen and elected unto the office of Provost of the said Borough as aforesaid, may and can execute that office of Provost of the said Borough until the feast of Saint Michael the Archangel, next ensuing such election, having first taken the aforesaid oath, called (in English) the Oath of Supremacy, and also the said oath for the due execution of his office of Provost of the said Borough in manner aforesaid : And further, We, of our special grace, and from our certain knowledge and proper motion, will, and by these presents for us, our heirs and successors, do grant unto the said Provost, free Burgesses, and Commonalty of the said Borough, and their successors, that, if one or any of the said free Burgesses of said Borough so nominated as aforesaid, or any one or more to be hereafter chosen free Burgesses of the same Borough, shall die or be removed from that office (which said free Burgesses, and any one or more of them, We will to be removed for misbehaviour in that office at the pleasure of the Provost, free Burgesses, or greatest part of them, of the said Borough for the time being), that then the Provost and the rest of the free Burgesses of the said Borough for the time being, may and can, within seven days next after the death or removal of such free Burgesses, assemble themselves in some convenient place within the said Borough, and that the said Provost and free Burgesses so assembled, or the greater part of them, may and can, before they dismiss, choose one or as many as shall be wanting of the said number of twelve free Burgesses out of the better and more circumspect inhabitants of the said Borough, into the place or places of the free Burgess or Burgesses so deceased, or removed from that or those office or offices, to be continued in the same office during their natural lives, unless in the meantime they or any of them shall, for their mal-administration and ill-behaviour in that behalf be removed ; and that every person so elected into the office of a free Burgess of the said Borough, shall, before he be suffered to execute that office, within seven days from election, give his corporal oath for his exercising well and truly the office of a free Burgess of the said Borough, before the Provost thereof for the time being, or before the rest of the free Burgesses of the said Borough then surviving and remaining in that office, or the greater part of them ; to which said Provost for the time being, or the free Burgesses or greater part of them for the time being, We do, by these presents, give and grant full power and authority to take the aforesaid oath of every of such said free Burgesses to be of new elected ; and that as often as the case shall so happen. And further, We, of our special grace, certain knowledge, and mere motion, will, and by these presents for us, our heirs and successors, do grant unto the said Provost, free Burgesses, and Commonalty of the Borough aforesaid, and their successors, that they and their successors may for ever have and hold, and may and can for ever have and hold, one Court in some fit and convenient place in the said Borough, to be held before the Provost of the same Borough for the time being; and in the same Court to hold suits on every Saturday, from week to week, concerning all and every personal action, debt, covenant, trespass, deteanor, contract, and demand whatsoever, not exceeding the sum of five marks sterling, that shall happen or fall out within the said Borough of Bangor, or the liberties of the same; and that such Court be reputed and esteemed a Court of Record for ever : We also will, and of our abundant special grace, certain knowledge, and mere motion, do by these presents, for us, our heirs and successors, grant unto the said Provost, free Burgesses, and Commonalty of the said Borough, and their successors, that they and their successors may and can from time, as often as they shall think fit, convene and assemble themselves in some convenient place within the said Borough, and in their assemblies there, may statute, ordain, and establish such and such like acts, ordinances, and statutes (in English by law) for the good rule and wholesome government of the said Borough, and the inhabitants thereof, in such sort as to them or the greater part of them shall seem necessary ; and that they may have power and authority to punish, chastise, and correct by fines and pecuniary mulcts all persons trespassing against such acts, ordinances, and statutes ; provided the acts, ordinances, and statutes, fines and mulcts be reasonable, and be not contrary or repugnant to the laws and statutes of our Kingdom of Ireland. And further, We will, and by these presents for us, our heirs and successors, and do grant unto the aforesaid Provost, free Burgesses, and Commonalty of the Borough aforesaid, and their successors for ever, that they may have a Merchant Guild within the said Borough, and one common seal of such form, and with such arms engraven therein, as to them shall seem best for serving the affairs of the said Borough for ever, and that they can and may for ever, from time to time, as often as it shall be needful, of themselves, there appoint and ordain two Sergeants at Mace and other inferior officers or ministers necessary for the better government of the said Borough and the inhabitants thereof ; and every person from time to time so chosen, appointed, and ordained, we make, appoint, and ordain to be and become sergeants and other officers and ministers of the said Borough respectively, and to continue in their offices during their good behaviour, or at the will and pleasure of the said Provost, free Burgesses, and Commonalty of the said Borough ; and that every such serjeant, officer, and minister shall, before he be admitted to exercise his office, give his corporal oath, before the Provost of the said Borough for the time being, that he shall well and truly execute his said office. And moreover, We, of our special grace, certain knowledge, and mere motion, do will, and by these presents for us, our heirs and successors, give and grant unto the said Provost, free Burgesses, and Commonalty of the said Borough, and their successors for ever, that they and their successors from henceforth and for ever, may have and hold, and may and can have and hold, one free market in or near the town or Borough aforesaid, to be held on every Thursday of each week, for ever, and also two fairs to be held there yearly ; that is to say, one fair in or near the said town or Borough on every 11th day of November, to be held yearly for ever, and to continue for the day immediately following ; and another fair in or near the village or Borough aforesaid, on every first day of May, to be held yearly for ever, and continue during the next following day, unless the said 11th day of November, or first day of May shall happen to be a Saturday or Sunday, in which case we will and grant that such fair shall be begun and held upon the Monday then next following, and be continued the next following day, to be held yearly for ever, as often as it shall so happen ; and that the Provost of the said Borough for the time being shall be Clerk of the Market within the said Borough, and the liberties thereof, and may from time to time have full power and authority to make and execute all and every things belonging and appertaining to the office of Clerk of the Market within the said Borough, so as no other Clerk of the Market of us, our heirs and successors, may enter the said Borough, or the franchises thereof, there to do and execute the office of Clerk of the Market, or anything unto the said office belonging or appertaining, nor any way intermeddle himself in any office of Clerk of the Market within the said Borough, or any thing interfering with the liberties thereof.

And further, We, of our more abundant special grace, certain knowledge, and mere motion, do grant unto the aforesaid Provost, free Burgesses, and Commonalty of the said Borough, and their successors for ever, and that these our letters patents, and every article and clause·in the same or in the enrolment thereof contained, shall be construed and adjudged to the best advantage, benefit, and favour of the said Provost, free Burgesses, and Commonalty of the Borough aforesaid, and their successors, towards and against us, our heirs and successors, as well in all our Courts as in any other place within our Kingdom of Ireland, or elsewhere whatsoever, without any confirmation to be hereafter procured or obtained : Notwithstanding that our writ of *ad quod damnum* did not issue for enquiring into the premises before the making of these our letters patents, and notwithstanding any other defect, or any other thing, cause, or matter whatsoever to the contrary notwithstanding, so as express mention do not appear to be made in these presents of the true yearly value or certainty of the premises, or of any of them, or of any other gifts or grants heretofore made by us or any of our progenitors unto the said Provost, free Burgesses, and Commonalty of the Borough aforesaid ; any statute, act, ordinance, or proviso, or any other thing, cause, or matter whatsoever made to the contrary of these premises, or any of them, anyways notwithstanding. In testimony of which We have made these our letters patent. Witness our said Deputy General of our Kingdom of Ireland, at Dublin, the eighteenth day of March, in the tenth year of our reign of England, France, and Ireland, and forty-sixth of Scotland. By virtue of letters of our Lord the King, sent from England, and signed with his own hand.

No. X.

REPORT OF THE IRISH CORPORATION COMMISSIONERS ON THE BOROUGH OF BANGOR.

---

1. The Borough of Bangor is situate in the County of Down, upon the southern shore, and near the entrance of the Lough of Belfast, and is distant from the town of Belfast about ten miles. It is in the parish of Bangor, and barony of Ardes. The limits of the borough include the town and a small surrounding district, locally termed "The Corporation," the exact boundaries of which we were unable to ascertain.

2. This borough was incorporated by Charter of the 18th March, 10 James I. (A.D. 1612), which is enrolled in Chancery. (Rot. Pat. 10 Jac. I. p. 4, m. 48.) The Corporation are not now in possession of any original of the grant. We do not find any other charter relating to the Corporation.

3. The present Book of Corporation Proceedings, commencing 24th June, 1776, was produced to us by the Provost ; no other is forthcoming. Some of the muniments of the Corporation property we found in the possession of the provost ; others were in the hands of Mr. Thomas Brownrigg, who had formerly held the office.

4. The corporate name is "The Provost, Free Burgesses, and Commonalty of the Borough of Bangor."

5. By the charter, the constituent parts of the body are—
> One Provost,
> Twelve (other) Free Burgesses, and
> Freemen without limit to the number.

But no freemen, as a separate class, existed at the time of our Inquiry.
There is no select body.

6. The only inferior officer appointed is a town sergeant. Two sergeants-at-mace are named in the charter.

7. The Provost is eligible annually from the free burgesses, by the major part of the free burgesses assembled on the feast of St. John, and holds for one year from the ensuing Michaelmas, and

until another of the free burgesses is duly elected, and sworn to the office. No qualification but that of being a free burgess is required, and no fee is paid on the election.

8. Vacancies in the nmber of free burgesses are to be filled up by the provost and remaining free burgesses, or the greater part of the body. They hold during good behaviour. The charter directed that they should be selected from the better and more honest inhabitants of the borough ; but this qualification was dispensed with by the 21 Geo. II. c. 10, s. 8, and has been little attended to in practice. It has been usual to admit the party as a freeman, and then to elect him a free burgess. No fees are paid on admission, and, it seems, not even the stamp duty.

9. The terms of the charter proceed, in the form usual at the period of its being granted, to incorporate all the inhabitants. From the want of all records of the early proceedings of the corporation, we had no means of investigating the former practice of the body in respect to admissions to freedom. Of late years, few have been admitted ; and those have, in general, been immediately after elected free burgesses. The existence of any class of freemen, distinct from the free burgesses, in practice, is wholly disregarded.

10. The town sergeant ought to be appointed by the whole body, to hold either during good behaviour, or at the will of the Corporation. What the tenure of the present officer is, does not appear from the resolution of the provost and free burgesses appointing him.

11. The provost was returning officer of the borough when it returned Members to the Irish Parliament. He is constituted, by the charter, Judge of a Borough Court of Record, to be held on every Saturday, with jurisdiction in personal actions for demands not exceeding five marks ; but we have not found that such a court has ever been held here. He is also constituted clerk of the market within the borough and its liberty, in which certain fairs and markets are granted by the same charter to the Corporation. He has no salary ; formerly he claimed, as tolls, the tongues of beasts slaughtered in the markets.

12. Before the Union, this borough returned two Members to the Parliament of Ireland ; the charter placed the franchise in the provost and free burgesses alone, and it was exercised accordingly. The free burgesses still possess the right of electing to the offices of provost and free burgesses ; they have no other peculiar functions, and no emoluments.

13. The power of making bye-laws, with fines for the breach of them, is vested in the whole body of the Corporation ; so, also, the power of electing from themselves the two sergeants-at-mace and other inferior officers necessary for the government of the borough. No separate class of admitted freemen existing, a doubt occurs as to the legality of those acts of the Corporation, to which the concurrence of the freemen is requisite.

14 The duties performed by the town sergeant appear to be merely those of a constable assisting in the preservation of order in the town.

A salary of eight guineas a-year is now paid him out of the Corporation funds. The amount has often been varied. In 1809, 2s. 8¼d. a day each, was allowed for one sergeant, or two, while employed ; in 1826, £20 per annum ; in 1830, four guineas per annum.

15. The entire Corporation is, as it has been for many years, composed of members of the Ward family, their friends and dependents. A more than usual number, 10 out of the 12 persons, of whom the Corporation was composed at the time of our Inquiry, were stated to be resident. Two of the 12 are Protestant Dissenters ; the rest, of the Established Church. No Roman Catholic has been a member. Indeed, the provost (Colonel Ward) laboured under an impression that the charter, which purports to be granted on petition of the inhabitants, and for the better progress and perfection of the new plantation lately begun in Ulster, requires that the Corporators should be Protestants, and had never heard of the alterations in the law by the Acts of 1793, &c., (33 Geo. III. c. 21, &c.,) dispensing with the oaths and declarations to which Roman Catholics could not subscribe.

16. The Compensation (£15,000) for the extinction of the elective franchise at the time of the Union, was ordered to be paid,—£7,500 to Henry Thomas Earl of Carrick, and £7,500 to the Hon. Edward Ward, and Sir John Parnell, Bart., committees of the estate of Nicholas Viscount Bangor, a lunatic, upon trust to be applied to the payment of incumbrances affecting the lands comprised in a settlement, dated 2d January, 1773, and the overplus of this £7,500 to be invested to the uses of the settlement. No trust was declared for the inhabitants or the Corporation.

17. The jurisdiction of the Corporation, in its Borough Court, has not, as already mentioned, been exercised ; but a local court is held here before a seneschal, for the Manor of Bangor, from three weeks to three weeks, on Thursdays, with jurisdiction to the amount of £20 Irish.   The proceedings are either according to the course of the common law, commencing by attachment of goods, or by civil bill, under the statutes permitting that form of proceeding in Manor Courts.   The costs of attachment amount to about 15s. ; of the whole proceedings, to execution on judgment by default, 21s. 6d. ; and not much more upon a verdict on issue joined.   In the last three years, but seven attachments were issued, on only one of which were further proceedings had.

18. A Court Leet is held by the seneschal once a year, at which constables for the several town-lands in the manor are appointed, but no other business is transacted.

19. The functions of the provost and town sergeant for preserving order and preventing nuisances, seem to be principally enforced under the powers of the Road Acts, before the justices of the peace for the County of Down, who hold their Petty Sessions in the town, and of those the present provost happens to be one ; but he is not constituted a justice of the peace by charter.

20. There is a place of confinement in the town, called "The Black Hole," to which the provost claims the power of committing disturbers of the peace, and, if detained for the night, of compelling them to pay a fine of 1s. for straw supplied.   We were glad to find that the provost could only recollect a single instance in which he had exercised this authority.

21. A part of the county constabulary are stationed here ; there is no corporate police, unless the sergeant-at-mace can be so considered.

22. There is no lighting or watching.   Some of the corporate income is devoted to the repair of the streets and footways.

23. The small pier, which forms the Harbour of Bangor, seems to have been originally built, about the year 1757, by means of a Parliamentary grant of £500 to "the Corporation for promoting and carrying on the inland navigation of Ireland, to be by them applied in completing and erecting a pier in the bay of Bangor, in the county of Down, and to be by them accounted for to Parliament ;" 31 Geo. II. c. 1, s. 14.

In the bye-laws of 29th September, 1809, it is directed "that it be the duty of the provost, for the time being, to preserve the quay and harbour in good order and regulation." We find by the Corporation proceedings, that a sum of £50 was directed (29th September, 1814,) to be applied to the harbour ; and subsequent grants and orders have been made connected with it : as, 24th June, 1816, a place to be prepared for bathing ; 25th June, 1827, complaints were heard against the harbour master ; and in 1830, 1831, we find, cash paid for oars for boat.

24. Small harbour dues are collected here, varying from 1s. to 2s. 6d. on each vessel, according to the tonnage ; also for ballast.   The total receipts for five years have been £115 16s. 9d., being, on the average, about £20 a year for harbour dues, and £3 a year for ballast.   In the same years the whole disbursements have been, £11 in salary to the harbour master, and £21 18s. 9½d. in repairs to the harbour ; leaving a surplus of £82 17s. 11½d.   It is said that the Corporation have nothing to do with the harbour, and that the right is in the lords of the manor, as owners of the soil of the harbour.   This may be the case ; but if the harbour dues be private property, the expenditure of the corporate income upon that property seems, under the circumstances, not to have been very warrantable.   The harbour master was appointed by the late Right Hon. Colonel Ward ; but, according to the above statement, not as provost.

25. The charter grants to the Corporation a free market in the borough on every Thursday, and two fairs annually (viz. on the 11th of November and the day following, and the 1st of May and day following, or if the 1st of May be Saturday or Sunday, then on the Monday following); but it contains no grant of tolls ; and we do not find that any claim in the nature of toll or custom has ever been made here, except that for the "tongues" of cattle slaughtered in the market.   The present provost finding the shambles not fit for use, has very properly relinquished the claim.

26. We found the practice in respect to " Cranage" here, as usual, to be in violation of the Acts of Parliament (4 Ann, c. 14; 25 Geo. II. c. 15; 27 Geo. III. c. 41); but the provost, upon being apprized of the provisions of the statutes, immediately announced his determination no longer to permit the infraction.

The prevailing charges were, in no case, under 1d., and for any draught weighing over 3 cwt. 1½d., and the weighing of potatoes was charged for, and at the same rate.

In 1830, 1831, a sum of £20 was paid out of the Corporation funds for a weighing engine ; and it was considered that this improvement in the machinery gave a right to increase the charge, but we conceive without foundation.

27. No regular appointment of a weighmaster is made. The lords of the manor had lately built a market-house, and it was supposed that the fees for weighing were therefore enjoyed under them as private property. But the right of appointment appears to be in the provost, no other person being entitled to toll.

In September, 1813, an order of the Corporation was made that the provost should provide a proper place for building a market ; but we do not find anything done upon it.

28. As clerk of the market, the provost, assisted by the town sergeant, performs the duty of seeing the weights and measures within the borough adjusted to the standard weights and measures which he himself keeps.

29. This Corporation presents a rare instance of a property preserved with care, and an income, generally speaking, usefully expended, and satisfactorily accounted for. The property consists of several plots of ground lying in various directions about the town, and containing in the whole 59a. 1r. 18p. statute measure, now occupied in very small lots, and at small rents, by 43 tenants, some holding from year to year, and others under leases (for terms not exceeding three lives), the rents forming a gross amount of £52 13s. 2d. per annum. A recent and careful survey was made, and the surveyor's map was produced to us by the provost.

30. These grounds appear to have been anciently " Commons," to the use of which, under the control of the Corporation, the inhabitants were entitled ; we examined several very old witnesses, and, although it appears that there were formerly other unenclosed plots about the town, we do not think there is reason to suppose that the grounds in which the inhabitants exercised a right of common ever were more extensive than the property above mentioned. On the contrary, the witnesses who recollect the enclosing of the commons, have described the entire to us precisely as it is found in the possession of the Corporation and its tenants at the present moment.

It appeared that on one occasion of an encroachment on the commons, two of the freemen threw down the enclosure, whether claiming any exclusive right as freemen, or as inhabitants generally, was not ascertained.

The title of the Corporation to these premises is disputed by Lord Bangor, in whom one moiety of the manor of Bangor is vested, the other being in Mr. Ward (still under age), representative of Lord Carrick, the former proprietor ; and we are told that one of the Masters in Chancery, in the matter of the late Lord Bangor (a lunatic), made a report, about the year 1810, against the title of the Corporation. However, there are strong grounds for considering the title of the Corporation as valid. One of the witnesses recollects the lands having been used by the inhabitants as commons so long as 70 years ago.

The claim of the Corporation, too, appears by their own proceedings, to have been much older than the enclosing in 1792 ; for, on the 24th of June, 1787 (and both the Earl Carrick and Viscount Bangor wore at that time free burgesses), it was resolved " that a survey of the commons of this Corporation be made out," &c. ; and further, " that A. Hamilton be directed to attend more particularly to the privileges of this Corporation, and to the commons and rights of commonage."

Again, on the 6th of October, 1787, the Rev. J. H. Clewlow was appointed "to enclose and ditch-in the common of this Corporation, and set them to tenants ; rents to be disposed of in wheels, or looms, for the poor, or otherwise, as Corporation may direct."

The actual enclosing and setting to tenants was stated to us to have taken place about the year 1792, and the right of commonage appears to have been willingly relinquished by the inhabitants, the advantages which resulted from that right having probably been inconsiderable.

The Corporation have ever since been in receipt of the rents, and leases have been made.

It is true, no doubt, those leases (some of which were produced before us) are informal documents, not being under the Corporation seal, and the grantor being " The Right Honourable Robert Ward, of Bangor Castle, County of Down ;" but it is added, " provost, in the name of provost, free burgesses, and of the commons of Bangor ;" and such an instrument, coupled with the regular payment of rent to, and receipt by the sovereign on behalf of the Corporation, seems very sufficient evidence of their title, as was held in a similar case (Wood v. Tate, 2 Bos. and Pull. N. R. 247).

RENTAL.

Original Lessee.	Present Tenant.	Premises.		A.	R.	P.	Tenure.	Yearly Rent.		£	s.	D.
	John Campbell ..	Land	..	1	3	10	At will			3	12	6
	Edw. Mitchell ..	Do.	..	0	3	8	Do.			0	19	8
	Ramsay Hughan..	Do.	..	2	1	15	Do.			3	17	6
	Thomas Brownrigg	Do.	..	2	1	15	Do.			3	17	6
	Widow of G. Neill	Do.	..	1	3	25	Do.			3	17	6
	Do. of H. Ferguson	Do.	..	0	2	5	Do.			0	19	4
	James Pollock ..	Do.	..	0	1	25	Do.			0	19	4
	Wm. Campbell ..	Do.	..	2	0	2	Do.			0	19	4
	Clerk Pollock ..	Do.	..	1	3	22	A lease for his own life			3	17	6
	Mrs. Adair ..	Do.	..	0	3	19	At will			1	18	8
	Henry Brown ..	Do.	..	1	3	37	A lease for three lives, date 1795 ..			2	0	0
A. M'Cartney.	Alex. Barron ..	Do.	..	1	2	1	At will			1	18	8
	John Campbell ..	Do.	.	1	3	30	Lease expired, now at will			3	3	0
	John M'Dowell ..	Do.	..	2	0	5	At will			1	9	2
	James Keenan ..	Do.	..	3	0	20	A lease for his own life			1	18	8
	Jas. Witherspoon..	Do.	..	1	2	36	At will			1	9	0
W. Fulton .	Thos. Brownrigg..	Do.	..	1	3	33	Lease for life of lessee			1	18	8
	Patrick Campbell	Do.	..	2	0	11	At will			1	18	8
	Hamilton Stewart	Do.	..	1	1	31	Do.			2	4	0
	Alex. M'Coubrey	Tenement and Garden.					Do.			1	1	0
	Magnus Sibbison..	Garden.					Do.			0	10	6
	James Murphy ..	Land	..	0	1	8	Agreement for a lease			0	4	0
	Richard Seay ..	Tenement.					A lease for three lives, dated 1824 ..			0	15	0
	James M'Kerrall..	Do.					At will			0	9	8
	James Mawhinny	Do.					A lease for one life			0	8	8
	David Stewart ..	Do.					At will			0	7	2
J. Kearns .	Robert Gallie ..	Do.					A lease			0	11	0
	H. M'Cutcheon ..	Do.					A lease			0	11	6
	Alex. Campbell ..	Do.					A lease for three lives			0	10	2
	James Baird ..	Do.					A lease for three lives			0	9	8
	James Kennedy ..	Do. and land		1	1	15	At will			0	10	4
	Hugh M'Shane ..	Do.					A lease dated 1824, for three lives, one dead			0	10	8
	Wm. Harnan ..	Do.					A lease, 1824, for three lives ..			0	10	0
	A. M'Coubrey ..	Do.					Promise of lease			0	10	8
	James M'Cartney	Do.					A lease, dated 1824, for three lives			0	10	8
	A. Mawhinny ..	Do.					At will			0	10	6
	A. Barron ..	Do. and land		1	0	13	Do.			0	10	8
	H. M'Sheane ..	Tenement.					Do.			0	10	8
	W. Bryan ..	Do.					Promise for a lease			0	10	8
	James Ferguson ..	Land	..	1	0	20	At will			0	5	0
— Hassan .	Geo. Ferguson ..	Tenement.					Promise for a lease			0	10	8
	James Baird ..	Do.					A lease for three lives, two dead ..			0	10	4
	Richard Seay ..	Do.					Promise for a lease			0	4	0
									£52	13	2

31. The disbursements have been generally for public and useful objects, including the salaries of the town sergeant, and of the person taking care of the town clock, the cleansing and repairing of the streets and footways, subscriptions of £60 for the fitting up, and £10 annually to the maintaining of an infant school, &c.

In the last year there was a subscription of £20 to the parish church, but we do not find any ever made to places of worship of dissenters from the Establishment; a circumstance not to be wondered at, considering the constitution of the Corporation.

We have already noticed the grants by the Corporation of money for the harbour and markets.

The accounts for the last two years are as follows—

PROVOST in ACCOUNT CURRENT with the CORPORATION of BANGOR, for the Year ending June 24th, 1832.

	£	s.	d.		£	s.	d.	£	s.	d.
1831.				**1832.**						
June 24.—To balance from old account	104	9	6½	June 24.—By cash paid street labourers ..	10	7	4			
To interest from savings' bank	3	6	5	By do. repairing footpaths ..	35	1	0			
To manure sold	3	9	6	By do. to Mrs. Hawley, on account of the late Town Sergeant Hawley, as per vote of Corporation	4	0	0			
1832.				By S. M'Knight's salary	5	0	0			
May 1.—To rents received to this date	62	19	4½	By Serjeant Buchannan, 1½ year's salary	12	12	0			
1833.				By cash manure depôt..	1	2	10			
Jan. 1.—To balance to new account	92	17	4					68	3	2
June 24.—To rents received	7	1	3	By agent's fees and stamps ..	3	4	4			
To manure sold	2	11	8	By subscription to infant school	10	0	0			
				By balance in savings' bank ..	89	10	7			
				Ditto in agent's hands ..	3	6	9			
								92	17	4
				1833.						
				June 24.—By making manure cart ..				2	14	6
				By survey and map of Corporation ..				4	9	4
				By town sergeant's salary, half-a-year				4	4	0
				By Samuel M'Knight's do, one year				5	0	0
				By repair of streets ..				4	6	8
				By subscription to church ..				20	0	0
				By balance				61	16	3
	£276	15	1					£276	15	1
To balance new account .. £61 16 3										

32. There is a further property in lands, called "Charity Lands," adjoining the town, vested in some one (but we could not ascertain in whom) in trust for charitable purposes. It was alleged that there were 70 acres subject to this trust; but we were unable to ascertain more than about 20, which are let in five small divisions, and are in the hands of the tenants from year to year, paying rents amounting annually to £42 11s. 1d. One of the receipts passed in 1820, was for rent due "to the Right Honorable Robert Ward, provost of Bangor;" but we cannot determine whether the payment was to him in his corporate capacity.

The trust, however, is fully acknowledged by the members of the Ward Family, and the funds are applied to charitable uses.

The following is the rental :—

Tenants' Names.	Premises. A. R.	Tenure.	Yearly Rental. £ s. d.
John Henry	4 0	At Will.	9 2 2
George Carlisle	2 2	"	6 3 0
Widow Kyle ..	4 0	"	5 14 3
Hugh Moore ..	5 0	"	11 11 8
James Graham	4 0	"	10 10 0
	19 2		£42 11 1

The following is a copy of the latest account furnished of the disbursements of this charity :

ROBERT RICHARD TIGHE in ACCOUNT CURRENT with the TRUSTEE from June 24th, 1831, to May 1st, 1833.

1831.		£	s.	d.	1832.		£	s.	d.
June 24.—To balance from old account ..	..	17	18	7	Dec. 24.—By two years' subscription to mendicity ..	..	20	0	0
1833.					By two years to schoolmistress ..	..	36	18	8
May 1.—To rents received to this date	..	85	2	2	By two years to infant school ..	..	30	0	0
					By balance handed Rev. H. G. Johnson ..	..	16	2	1
		£103	0	9			£103	0	9

33. A plot of ground in the town, on which the old shambles and two or three houses were built, has been alleged to be corporate property ; and there seems to be some colour for the claim. The tenants of two of the houses, we are told, are not now paying rent. The Corporation certainly exercised an ownership over the shambles, the provost having for a length of time, and until the shambles became ruinous, claimed and taken the tongues of all beasts slaughtered and sold there ; a claim only referrible here to "stallage," and consequently to an exercise of ownership of the soil. In 1830, 1831, it appears by the Corporation accounts, a sum of £5 was expended upon "butchers' stalls."

34. There is also a school-house here and premises adjoining. It is said to have been called the old Corporation school-house ; and we found it occupied in part by the school supported by the Corporation funds, and in part by the town sergeant. But we were unable to find how he got the possession, not having had an opportunity of examining him.

35. A tract of land called the Bangor, or Common Moss, was said to have belonged to the Corporation ; but no evidence of the title was adduced.

36. We are also referred to the will of James Hamilton, first Earl of Clanbrassil, dated 18th June, 1659, (under which the Ward Family now possess the Manor of Bangor ;) among other donations he charged on his estate £20 a year "to the school of Bangor, to be paid for the masters, enabling of them to educate poor scholars." No such payment is now made.

There is an annuity, amounting, according to one statement, to £5 yearly in the whole, but according to other evidence to £5 from each moiety of the estate, payable towards the support of a school.

We have not had the means of properly investigating the nature of these payments.

Another charitable bequest mentioned to us is one of £1,000, bequeathed by the late Right Honorable Robert Ward, "for the use of the provost and burgesses of the Corporation of Bangor, to be expended by them in building and endowing a school-house for the education of boys in mathematics, astronomy, and navigation, so as to qualify the students to navigate and take charge of merchant vessels as masters on foreign voyages," &c.

The provost stated that he apprehended a deficiency of assets, and that little benefit was likely to arise from the bequest. We have had no opportunity of gaining other information on this subject.

37. A portion of the Corporation income, and the available charitable funds, are applied, in part to the maintenance of the schools, and in part to the support of a poor-house and mendicity institution.

Another useful application of the small income of this Corporation deserves notice—the establishment of a bank for savings, mentioned in the proceedings of the 29th of October, 1814 ; it appears by the accounts for 1828 and 1829, that the bank had defrayed the expenses of management, and placed a sum of £78 9s. 3d. of its surplus funds at the disposal of the Corporation.

The population of the town of Bangor, as returned by the census of 1831, was as follows :—

Males, 1,104 ; Females, 1,637. Total	-	-	-	-	-	-		2,741
Families chiefly employed in agriculture	-	-	-	-	-	-	63	
„ in trade, manufactures, or handicraft	-	-	-	-	-	-	250	
„ not comprised in those two classes	-	-	-	-	-	-	258	
Total	-	-	-	-				—— 571
Houses inhabited	-	-	-	-	-	-	507	
" uninhabited	-	-	-	-	-	-	54	
" building	-	-	-	-	-	-	2	
Total	-	-	-	-	-			—— 563

There are two cotton factories established here, and the town is stated to be improving considerably in its trade and circumstances.

The harbour is said to have great capabilities, and no doubt is advantageously situated as an out-port ; but a large outlay of money would be requisite to render it as available for trade and the protection of shipping in distress as its position on the lough of Belfast admits.

39. We send with this report the following documents :—

1. List of Free Burgesses, April, 1833.
2. Extracts from Corporation Proceedings.
3. Corporation Receipt and Expenditure for Five Years.
4. Corporation Rental.
5. Charity Lands, Rental, Receipt, and Expenditure for Three Years.
6. Bangor Harbour, Receipts and Disbursements for Five Years.
7. Manor Court, Returns and Forms of Proceedings.

WILLIAM ELLIOT HUDSON, } *Commissioners.*
MATTHEW RICHARD SAUSSE, }

Inquiry held 15th October, 1833, and 6th January, 1834

INDEX.

in 1640, but never sat for it, 63; his death and burial at Mullabrack, Co. Armagh, 45, 63; findings as to lands in his possession, xviii.

Sir Hans, of Hamilton's Bawn, his eldest son, educated at Glasgow College, 79; goes to Ireland on his father's death, *ib.*; joins in the Irish War, 80; made Captain of Horse by Viscount Claneboy, *ib.*; promoted to be Lieut.-Colonel, *ib.*; Knighted and made a Baronet, and of the Privy Council, by Charles II., 80; married Miss Trevor, 80; their only daughter Sarah married Sir Robert Hamilton, 107; his parentage, education, and character, 105—107; Sir Hans at first joins in the suit against Countess Alice for establishing Earl James's will, 98, 99; but joins with James of Newcastle in purchasing up Lord Bargany's and the Moore's titles to the Clanbrassil estates, 102—109; which they divide between them, 115; except the jointure lands, which are partitioned amongst the descendants of the five uncles of Earl James, 147; Sir Hans's death and character, 80; Sir Robert, his son-in-law, and James of Newcastle keep the rest of the estates, 144; decree made against them by Lord Chancellor Methuen, 155; appeal to the English House of Lords against, 154; decree partly affirmed and partly reversed, but suit never revived, 146; part of Sir Hans Hamilton's (jun.) estates sold under a private Act of Parliament for payment of his debts, 156.

Anthony, second son of John of Monella, died young and unmarried, 162.

James, his third son, served as Cornet in Irish Wars, 80; married Jane Baily, daughter of Bishop of Clonfert, *ib.*; had issue two sons and a daughter, *ib.*; his character, and death, *ib.*

Francis, of Tullybrick, third son of John of Monella, 81, 156, 163.

Hamilton, William, of Newcastle, fifth son of the Vicar of Dunlop, 12, 164; called into Ireland, 12; purchases estate in Co. Down, *ib.*; letters to, from Sir James Hamilton, *ib.*; married Miss Melville, 45; had issue six children, *ib.*; his death and burial at Hollywood, *ib.*

James, of Newcastle, his eldest son, married Margaret Kynaston, by whom he had two children, 81, 164; bred a soldier, and killed at Blackwater

fight, *ib.*; his epitaph on tablet in Benburb Church, *ib.*

James, of Bangor, his only son, repaired Bangor Church, 42; married Hon. Sophia Mordaunt, 81; tablet to his memory in, and inscription on, 43; joins first with his cousins in law-suit, 98; but purchases up the Bargany and Moore's title, to estates with Sir Hans Hamilton, *ib.* to 115; was M.P. for Bangor in 1703, lxxix.

Catherine, his only daughter, married General Richard Price, 81.

Hamilton, John, second son of William of Newcastle, 81, 164; was a Captain, and died without issue, 81.

Hamilton, Captain Hans, of Carnysure, third son of William of Newcastle, 165; married Mary Kennedy, 81; had issue three children, 82; his death and burial at Hollywood, *ib.*

Hamilton, William, of Erinagh, fourth son of William of Newcastle, 82, 165; married first a daughter of Jocelin Ussher, 83; secondly, a daughter of Brian MacHugh Agherley Magennis, *ib.*; his character and death, 82; left two sons and two daughters.

James, of Tullymore, his eldest son, 165; M.P. for Co. Down, in 1692, 63; Memoir of him *ib.*; died in London, 1701, *ib.*

Jocelyn, his second son, killed in a duel with Bernard Ward, 82.

Hamilton, Patrick, sixth son of the Vicar of Dunlop, 12, 166; studies Divinity, 12; becomes Minister of Enderwick, in East Lothian. *ib.*; marries Miss Glenn, 45; had issue four children, *ib.*; his death, *ib.*

The Rev. James, his eldest son, 166; married Miss Echlin, 82; was Parson of Dundonald and Hollywood, *ib.*; his character and death, 83.

Alexander, of Granshaw, Co. Down, his second son, 166; was a Captain of Foot, 83; married Mary Reeding, by whom he had issue one son and two daughters, 83.

Archibald, the Rev., his third son, was first Minister of a Parish in Galloway, Scotland, and afterwards at Bangor, Co. Down, 39, 83; married Jane Hamilton, by whom he had several children, 83; removed to Wigtown, where he died, 39; his son Archibald, succeeded him as Minister at Bangor, 39, 83.

Hamilton, Rev. Archibald, of Armagh, 161.

ERRATA.

At p. 21, in note f, for "curry," read "carry."

For Mr. Hamilton, "grandson" of Archibald Hamilton, at p. 39, read "son"—and see p. 83.

For "1716," in note p at p. 72, read "1712."

At p. 81, in note h, for "16 ," read "1646"; and see note f, at p. lxxvii, for correction of Mrs. Reilly's Memoirs of John Hamilton, in note l in this page.

For "Henry," read "Jocelin" Usher, at p. 82.

For "investing," at p. 114, read "investigating."

For "Margaret," at p. 158, read "Janet Denham."

At p. xci, under title "Great Ardes," for Charles II., read Charles I.

At p. xcv, under title "Echlin, Bishop of Down, for "sentenced," read "silenced Livingston."

Re=Publication

OF

THE MONTGOMERY MANUSCRIPTS.

R EADERS already acquainted with the compilation known as THE MONT-GOMERY MANUSCRIPTS are able to appreciate its undoubted value as an historical and genealogical record. In a letter of Sir WALTER SCOTT to the late HENRY JOY, Esq., acknowledging a copy of the First Edition, the writer says :—" I am honoured with a copy of your edition of the MONTGOMERYS, which " interests me in the highest degree, and is one of those works which carry us back to " the times of our ancestors, and give us the most correct ideas of their sentiments " and manners." Such a distinct expression of approval, coming from so high an authority, is the best recommendation that any book of this class could possess. A compilation of Family Papers which interested the great novelist in the *highest degree*, ought to have rare attractions for readers of every class and rank in the community.

Although THE MONTGOMERY MANUSCRIPTS are to be regarded mainly as a Family record, they contain much curious and reliable information on the political and social condition of Ulster in the seventeenth century. Indeed, as the MONT-GOMERYS occupied so prominent a place in the civil affairs of this province, their family history necessarily includes the history also of many leading events connected with the Plantation of 1608, the Rebellion of 1641, and the Revolution of 1688-9. The Memoirs of the first Viscount MONTGOMERY present a graphic account of the Scottish Settlement in the Ards, under the superintendence of that distinguished and most energetic man. The Memoirs of his second son, Sir JAMES MONTGOMERY of Rosemount, and of his grandson, who became first Earl of MOUNT-ALEXANDER, contain certain curious records, nowhere else to be found, of military operations in Ulster, at the commencement of the Rebellion, and during the dreary years of internecine strife that succeeded. The Memoirs of the second Earl of MOUNT-

ALEXANDER reach to the year 1706, affording vivid glimpses at the state of society here, before and after the great revolutionary struggle. With these chronicles of important public events, numerous notices of family matters are quaintly interspersed, thus relieving the narrative, and rendering it, in most instances, thoroughly attractive.

THE MONTGOMERY MANUSCRIPTS were first printed in the columns of the *Belfast News-Letter*, from which they were published, in a duodecimo volume, under the superintendence, principally, of the late HENRY JOY, Esq., in the year 1830. As this First Edition has been long out of print, and as, of late, a desire has been pretty generally expressed for a new Edition, it is our intention to re-print the whole Collection, in a quarto form, exactly similar in size to the *Ulster Journal of Archæology*. Our Edition will contain a curious fragment of the original work which has been recovered by the Rev. WILLIAM MACILWAINE, Incumbent of St. George's, Belfast, and printed in Vol. IX. of the *Journal* above named. Several original letters, and other highly-interesting documents, which throw considerable light on these Manuscripts, through the instrumentality of the same gentleman, after search made in rare family archives, have been procured for the use of the Editor; and the information supplied by them will be found embodied in the Notes and Appendix. The new Edition will also be accompanied by carefully-prepared Notes, derived from the most reliable sources, and embracing a large amount of genealogical and topographical history. These Notes will necessarily contain full references to certain Irish leaders and chiefs,—to several English and Scottish families of the Plantation,—to the numerous connexions of the MONT-GOMERYS throughout the County of Ayr, in the seventeenth century,—and to such other topics as have been specially introduced by the Author in the text.

It is expected that the Work, including Appendix, will contain from 450 to 500 pages; and the annexed two pages are given as a specimen of the type with which it will be printed, and the quality of the paper to be used. It will be handsomely bound in cloth, with red edges.

The price to Subscribers, who pay on delivery, will be 15s., and to the Public, 18s.; and so soon as 200 Subscribers offer, the Work will be put to press.

The Montgomery Manuscripts.

HE said Sir Hugh had (no doubt) further troubles between the said year 1618 and 1623, because, at his own instance and request, and for his greater security, the King granted a commission and order, directed unto Henry Lord Viscount Faulkland, Lord Deputy of Ireland, for holding an Inquisition concerning the lands, spiritual and temporal, therein mentioned, which began to be held before Sir John Blennerhassett, Lord Chief Baron, at Downpatrick, the 13th October, 1623. This inquest is often cited, and is commonly called the Grand Office.[a] Again, Sir Hugh (that he might be the more complete by sufferings) is assailed by Sir Wm. Smith, who strove to hinder the passing of the King's patent to him; on notice whereof, Sir Hugh writes

[a] This Grand Office or Inquisition was held, in consequence of "divers causes and controversies, which had long depended, or been stirred, or moved, between Lord Viscount Montgomery, Lord Viscount Claneboy, Sir Henry Piers, Sir Robert M'Clelland, Sir Moses Hill, Donald O'Neale, John Hamilton, James Cathcart, William Edmunson, Michael White, and others, as competitors for or concerning the said Con O'Neale's late estate and possessions, or some parts of them, in the said County of Down, wherein each of them did severally pretend to have several interests or rights." The Commission for holding this investigation was granted, as the author states, principally at the urgent request, and for the security, of the first Viscount Montgomery of the Ards, who appears to have had the greatest interest at stake. The inquisition was held at Downpatrick, commencing on the 13th of October, 1623, and the report of the Commission was delivered into Chancery on the 22nd of June, 1624. The Commissioners, five of whom acted, were Sir John Blennerhasset, Sir Wm. Parsons, Sir Thos. Hibbotts, Sir Christopher Sibthorpe, Sir Wm. Sparke, Sir Wm. Rives, Nathaniel Catelyne, Richard West, Walter Ivers, Peter Clinton, and Stephen Allen. The jurors, thirteen of whom served, were Nicholas Ward, of Castleward, Esq.; George Russell, of Rathmullen, gent.; Richard Russell, of Rossglass, gent.; Simon Joran (Jordan), of Dunsford, gent.; Owen M'Rory, of Clogher, gent.; Robert Swords, of Rathcolp, gent.; Patrick M'Cartane, of Ballykin, gent.; Patrick M'Cormick, of Killescolban, gent.; George Russell, of Quoniamstown, gent; Ferdoragh Maginnis, of Clonvoraghan, gent.; Owen M'Cartane, of Lissenguy, gent.; John Russell, of Killoregan, gent.; James Audley, of Audleyston, gent.; Bryan M'Ever Maginnis, of Shanko, gent.; and Shem (Shane) M'Bryan, of Ballenteggard, gent. The task imposed on these gentlemen—commissioners and jurors alike—was such as needed the exercise of more than ordinary patience and discretion. It required the examination of many witnesses, and of innumerable papers. It implied a thorough in-

vestigation respecting—*first*, the titles and boundaries of the lands claimed by the several disputants above-mentioned; *secondly*, the castles, lands, tenements, rectories, tithes, advowsons, glebes, fisheries, and other hereditaments, belonging to the monasteries of Bangor, Greyabbey, Movilla, Black Abbey, Comber, and the priories of Newton and Holiwood; *thirdly*, the spiritual lands, tithes, and advowsons, in the territories of Upper Clannaboy and the Great Ards, previously granted to James Hamilton, with all other in the same territories; *fourthly*, the bishop's lands, the glebe lands, and the several incumbents' and vicars' maintenances, allotted to them for their cures from the temporal lands; *fifthly*, the impropriate tithes and impropriate rectories in the Upper Clannaboy and the Great Ards; *sixthly*, the bounds of every parish, as far as they could be discovered; and, *seventhly*, what castles, lordships, manors, lands, religious houses, rectories, tithes, fishings, and other hereditaments, as well spiritual as temporal, belonged to the Lord Viscount Montgomery, Lord Viscount Clannaboy, Sir Foulke Conway, and the several other claimants above-named.—*MS. Inquisition of 1623*, pp. 1—10. In Dr. Erck's *Account of the Ecclesiastical Establishments of Ireland*, p. 30, the author has the following reference to this Inquisition:—"It may be observed, however, that the Commission contains very little information relative to the property of the bishop and clergy of Down; for the Commissioners themselves, being claimants of the possessions, under patent from King James, not only concealed, as it would seem, but usurped upon the spiritual lands, glebes, tithes, and advowsons of the greater part of the livings in those districts, which of right belonged to the bishops and clergy." The possessions of the religious houses above-named belonged, with slight exceptions, to the Viscounts Ards and Clannaboy, so that the Commissioner, could not have been influenced by the motives here ascribed to them by Dr. Erck.

The King had forgiven all persons but the regicides, whom the Lord Earle (to vindicate the kingdom's honour) would not forgive, but capitally punished them as paracides,[c] according to the law. And then the affairs of Ireland falling soon under consideration, there issued a commission for putting in execution his Majesty's gracious declaration at Breda, and our Viscount was named among the chiefs of the commissioners. I saw him and them sit in court at the inns of law in Dublin, where were determined many claims of adventurers soldiers (who shared in the benefit thereof) and many innocent Papists and also Protestants returned to their estates. At the issuing the first commission for justices of peace, I was named one for the County of Downe, and his Lordship was Custos Rotulorum Pacis, and he (unrequested) made me his deputy in that office. His

---

b The enmity, if any, existed between them when Monk was the Parliamentary leader in Ulster, and drove Viscount Montgomery into an alliance with the Covenanters which proved so disagreeable to both parties in the end. Although Monk had been a traitor, first to the King, and finally to the people, his cunning enabled him to seize the lion's share in the end. Charles II., on landing at Dover, embraced him, and kissed him, and the country loaded him with wealth and honours. He became forthwith a Knight of the Garter, a Privy Councillor, Master of the Horse, a Gentleman of the Bed-Chamber, First Lord of the Treasury, Baron Monk of Potheridge, Beauchamp, and Tees, Earl of Torrington, and Duke of Albemarle. He was voted £20,000 in hand, together with an estate worth, at that time, the enormous sum of £7,000 per annum.—*Chalmers's Biographical Dictionary*, vol. xxii., p. 239.

c The term *parricide* is not exclusively applied to the murderer of a father or mother. It was often used to denote one who destroys any person whom he ought to reverence, such as his patron, or king. Sir James Ware speaks (*Works*, Vol. i., p. 209) of the execution of Charles I. as "the horrid parricide of that excellent monarch." Of the persons actually concerned in the trial and execution of Charles I., twenty-five had died, sixteen had escaped to various places on the Continent, and three to New England, in America. Besides these, there remained twenty-nine in England, all of whom were tried and sentenced to death; but the execution of such as had surrendered themselves was postponed for future consideration. The regicides selected for execution were Harrison,

Scot, Carew, Jones, Clements, and Scroop, who had signed the warrant for the King's death; Coke, who acted as solicitor on the trial; Axtele and Hacker, who guarded the prisoner; and Hugh Peters, an eloquent but intemperate preacher. These men, with the exceptions of Harrison and Peters, belonged to families of the old English gentry, were educated generally at the Universities, owned landed estates, and served in Parliament—the majority being members of the Council of State. One, Axtele, was governor of Kilkenny for a time; and another, Jones, served as one of the five Commissioner appointed for the government of Ireland. Harrison had risen from the ranks to be a major-general. During his trial, the executioner, bearing a halter, was placed beside him; and so barbarously was his sentence inflicted, that he was cut down while alive, and actually saw his entrails flung into the fire.—*Ludlow's Memoirs*, vol. iii., pp. 33—103; *Pepys' Diary*, edited by Lord Braybrooke, vol. i., pp. 113—115, 129, 146, 251, 271; vol. ii., p. 23; vol. iv., p. 330. Other executions followed in due course; but until they could be arranged, royalist revenge was gratified by the strange and revolting spectacle of inflicting the last penalties of the law on the remains of dead regicides. By an order of the two Houses of Parliament, approved by the King, the bodies of Cromwell, Bradshaw, and Ireton were raised from their graves, drawn on hurdles to Tyburn, hung and decapitated, the heads being fixed on the front of Westminster Hall, and the trunks flung into a pit at the place of execution.—*Lingard's Hist. of England*, vol. ix., p. 8; *Pepys*, vol. i., pp. 129, 148—9.

www.ingramcontent.com/pod-product-compliance
Lightning Source LLC
Chambersburg PA
CBHW020902020726
47497CB00005B/1519